P. G. Wodehouse was born in Guildford in 1881 and educated at Dulwich College. After working for the Hong Kong and Shanghai Bank for two years, he left to earn his living as a journalist and storywriter, writing the 'By the Way' column in the old *Globe*. He also contributed a series of school stories to a magazine for boys, the *Captain*, in one of which Psmith made his first appearance. Going to America before the First World War, he sold a serial to the *Saturday Evening Post*, and for the next twenty-five years almost all his books appeared first in this magazine. He was part author and writer of the lyrics of eighteen musical comedies, including *Kissing Time*. He married in 1914 and in 1955 took American citizenship. He wrote over ninety books, most of which are published by Penguin, and his work has won worldwide acclaim, having been translated into many languages. *The Times* hailed him as a 'comic genius recognized in his lifetime as a classic and an old master of farce'.

P. G. Wodehouse said, 'I believe there are two ways of writing novels. One is mine, making a sort of musical comedy without music and ignoring real life altogether; the other is going right deep down into life and not caring a damn . . .' He was created a Knight of the British Empire in the New Year's Honours List in 1975. In a BBC interview he said that he had no ambition left now that he had been knighted and there was a waxwork of him in Madame Tussaud's. He died on St Valentine's Day in 1975 at the age of ninety-three.

P. G. WODEHOUSE IN PENGUIN

*The Uncle Fred Books:*

Uncle Fred in the Springtime
Uncle Dynamite
Cocktail Time
Service with a Smile

*and:*

Uncle Fred: An Omnibus

P. G. Wodehouse

# UNCLE FRED:

## AN OMNIBUS

*Uncle Fred in the Springtime*

*Uncle Dynamite*

*Cocktail Time*

PENGUIN BOOKS

PENGUIN BOOKS

Published by the Penguin Group
Penguin Books Ltd, 27 Wrights Lane, London w8 5tz, England
Penguin Books USA Inc., 375 Hudson Street, New York, New York 10014, USA
Penguin Books Australia Ltd, Ringwood, Victoria, Australia
Penguin Books Canada Ltd, 10 Alcorn Avenue, Toronto, Ontario, Canada M4V 3B2
Penguin Books (NZ) Ltd, 182–190 Wairau Road, Auckland 10, New Zealand

Penguin Books Ltd, Registered Offices: Harmondsworth, Middlesex, England

*Uncle Fred in the Springtime* first published by Herbert Jenkins 1939
Published in Penguin Books 1954
Copyright 1939 by P. G. Wodehouse

*Uncle Dynamite* first published by Herbert Jenkins 1948
Published in Penguin Books 1966
Copyright 1948 by P. G. Wodehouse

*Cocktail Time* first published by Herbert Jenkins 1958
Published in Penguin Books 1987
Copyright © P. G. Wodehouse, 1958

This omnibus edition published in Penguin Books 1992
5  7  9  10  8  6  4

Typeset by DatIX International Limited, Bungay, Suffolk
Printed in England by Clays Ltd, St Ives plc

# Contents

# UNCLE FRED
# IN THE SPRINGTIME

# Chapter 1

The door of the Drones Club swung open, and a young man in form-fitting tweeds came down the steps and started to walk westwards. An observant passer-by, scanning his face, would have fancied that he discerned on it a keen, tense look, like that of an African hunter stalking a hippopotamus. And he would have been right. Pongo Twistleton – for it was he – was on his way to try to touch Horace Pendlebury-Davenport for two hundred pounds.

To touch Horace Pendlebury-Davenport, if you are coming from the Drones, you go down Hay Hill, through Berkeley Square, along Mount Street and up Park Lane to the new block of luxury flats which they have built where Bloxham House used to be: and it did not take Pongo long to reach journey's end. It was perhaps ten minutes later that Webster, Horace's man, opened the door in answer to his ring.

'What ho, Webster. Mr Davenport in?'

'No, sir. He has stepped out to take a dancing lesson.'

'Well, he won't be long, I suppose, what? I'll come in, shall I?'

'Very good, sir. Perhaps you would not mind waiting in the library. The sitting-room is in some little disorder at the moment.'

'Spring cleaning?'

'No, sir. Mr Davenport has been entertaining his uncle, the Duke of Dunstable, to luncheon, and over the coffee His Grace broke most of the sitting-room furniture with the poker.'

To say that this information surprised Pongo would be correct. To say that he was astounded, however, would be going too far. His Uncle Alaric's eccentricities were a favourite theme of conversation with Horace Davenport, and in Pongo he had always found a sympathetic confidant, for Pongo had an eccentric uncle himself. Though hearing Horace speak of his Uncle Alaric and thinking of his own Uncle Fred, he felt like Noah listening to someone making a fuss about a drizzle.

3

'What made him do that?'

'I am inclined to think, sir, that something may have occurred to annoy His Grace.'

This seemed plausible, and in the absence of further data Pongo left it at that. He made his way to the small apartment dignified by the name of library, and wandering to the window stood looking out on Park Lane.

It was a cheerless prospect that met his eyes. Like all English springs, the one which had just come to London seemed totally unable to make up its fat-headed mind whether it was supposed to be that ethereal mildness of which the poet sings or something suitable for ski-ers left over from the winter. A few moments before, the sun had been shining with extraordinary brilliance, but now a sort of young blizzard was raging, and the spectacle had the effect of plunging Pongo into despondency.

Horace was engaged to marry his sister Valerie, but was it conceivable, he asked himself, that any man, even to oblige a future brother-in-law, would cough up the colossal sum of two hundred potatoes? The answer, he felt, was in the negative, and with a mournful sigh he turned away and began to pace the room.

If you pace the library of Number 52 Bloxham Mansions, starting at the window and going straight across country, your outward journey takes you past the writing-table. And as Pongo reached this writing-table, something there attracted his eye. From beneath the blotter the end of a paper was protruding, and on it were written the intriguing words:

*Signed*

CLAUDE POTT

(*Private Investigator*)

They brought him up with as round a turn as if he had seen a baronet lying on the floor with an Oriental paper-knife of antique design in his back. An overwhelming desire came upon him to see what all this was about. He was not in the habit of reading other people's letters, but here was one which a man of the nicest scruples could scarcely be expected to pass up.

The thing was cast in narrative form, being, he found on examination, a sort of saga in which the leading character – a star part, if

4

ever there was one – was somebody referred to as The Subject.
From the activities of this individual Claude Pott seemed unable to
tear himself away.

The Subject, who appeared to be abroad somewhere, for there
was frequent mention of a Casino, was evidently one of those
people who live for pleasure alone. You didn't catch The Subject
doing good to the poor or making a thoughtful study of local
political conditions. When he – or she – was not entering Casino in
comp. of friends (two male, one female) at 11.17 p.m., he – or she,
for there was no clue as to whether this was a story with a hero or
a heroine – was playing tenn., riding h.'s, out on the golf links,
lunching with three f.'s, driving to Montreuil with one m., or
dancing with party consisting of four m.'s, ditto f.'s, and in this
latter case keeping it up into the small hours. Pongo was familiar
with the expression 'living the life of Riley', and that it was a life of
this nature that The Subject had been leading was manifest in the
document's every sentence.

But what the idea behind the narrative could be he found himself
unable to divine. Claude Pott had a nice, crisp style, but his work
was marred by the same obscurity which has caused complaint in
the case of the poet Browning.

He had begun to read it for the third time, hoping for enlighten-
ment, when the click of a latchkey came to his ears, and as he hastily
restored the paper to its place the door opened and there entered a
young man of great height but lacking the width of shoulder and
ruggedness of limb which make height impressive. Nature, stretch-
ing Horace Davenport out, had forgotten to stretch him sideways,
and one could have pictured Euclid, had they met, nudging a friend
and saying: 'Don't look now, but this chap coming along illustrates
exactly what I was telling you about a straight line having length
without breadth.'

Farthest north of this great expanse there appeared a
tortoiseshell-rimmed-spectacled face of so much amiability of expression that Pongo, sighting it, found himself once again hoping for
the best.

'What ho, Horace,' he said, almost exuberantly.

'Hullo, Pongo. You here? Has Webster told you about my
uncle's latest?'

'He did just touch on it. His theory is that the old boy was annoyed about something. Does that seem to fit the facts?'

'Absolutely. He was annoyed about quite a number of things. In the first place, he was going off to the country to-day and he had been counting on that fellow Baxter, his secretary, to go with him. He always likes to have someone with him on a railway journey.'

'To dance before him, no doubt, and generally entertain him?'

'And at the last moment Baxter said he would have to stay on in London to do some work at the British Museum in connexion with that Family History Uncle Alaric has been messing about with for years. This made him shirty, for a start. He seemed to think it came under the head of being thwarted.'

'A touch of thwarting about it, perhaps.'

'And before coming to me he had been to see my cousin Ricky, and Ricky had managed to put his back up about something. So he was in dangerous mood when he got here. And we had scarcely sat down to lunch, when up popped a *soufflé* looking like a diseased custard. This did not help to ease the strain. And when we had had our coffee, and the time came for him to catch his train and he told me to go to the station with him and I said I couldn't, that seemed to touch him off. He reached for the poker and started in.'

'Why wouldn't you go to the station with him?'

'I couldn't. I was late for my dancing lesson.'

'I was going to ask you about that. What's this idea of your suddenly taking dancing lessons?'

'Valerie insisted on it. She said I danced like a dromedary with the staggers.'

Pongo did not blame his sister. Indeed, in comparing her loved one to a dromedary with the staggers she had been, he thought, rather complimentary.

'How are you coming along?'

'I think I'm making progress. Polly assures me so. Polly says I shall be able to go to the Ball to-morrow night. The Bohemian Ball at the Albert Hall. I'm going as a Boy Scout. I want to take Valerie to it and surprise her. Polly thinks I can get by all right.'

'But isn't Val at Le Touquet?'

'She's flying back to-day.'

'Oh, I see. Tell me, who is this Polly who has crept into your conversation?'

'She's the girl who's teaching me. I met her through Ricky. She's a friend of his. Polly Pott. A nice, sympathetic sort of girl I'd always found her, so when this business of staggering dromedaries came up, I asked her if she would give me a few lessons.'

A pang of pity for this heroine shot through Pongo. He himself was reading for the Bar and had sometimes felt like cracking under the strain of it all, but he saw that compared with Polly Pott he was on velvet. Between trying to extract some meaning from the rambling writings of the Messrs Coke and Littleton and teaching dancing to Horace Davenport there was a substantial difference, and it was the person on whom life had thrust the latter task who must be considered to have drawn the short straw. The trouble was, he reflected, that Horace was so tall. A chap of that length didn't really get on to what his feet were doing till some minutes after it had happened. What you wanted, of course, was to slice him in half and have two Horaces.

'Polly Pott, eh? Any relation to Claude Pott, private investigator?'

'His daughter. What do you know about Claude Pott, private investigator?'

Pongo stirred uneasily. Too late, he saw that he had rather invited the question.

'Well, the fact is, old man, happening to pass the writing-table just now, and chancing inadvertently to catch sight of that document –'

'I wish you wouldn't read my letters.'

'Oh, I wouldn't. But I could see that this wasn't a letter. Just a document. So I ran my eye over it. I thought it might possibly be something with reference to which you were going to seek my advice, knowing me to be a bit of a nib in legal matters, and I felt that a lot of time would be saved if I had the *res* at my fingers' ends.'

'And now I suppose you'll go racing off to Valerie to tell her I had her watched by detectives while she was at Le Touquet.'

A blinding light flashed upon Pongo.

'Great Scott! Was that what the thing was about?'

He pursed his lips – not too tightly, for he was still hoping to float that loan, but tightly enough to indicate that the Twistletons had their pride and resented their sisters being tailed up by detectives. Horace read his thoughts correctly.

'Yes, I know, but you don't realize the position, Pongo. It was the Drones Club week-end at Le Touquet. The thought of the girl I loved surrounded by about eighty-seven members of the Drones in the lax atmosphere of a foreign pleasure resort while I was far away was like a knife in my heart. Polly happened to mention that her father was a private investigator, never happier than when putting on a false nose and shadowing people, and the temptation was more than I could resist. Pongo, for Heaven's sake don't breathe a word about this to Valerie. If she has a fault, it is that she's touchy. The sweetest of her sex, but a bit apt to go in off the deep end, when stirred. I can trust you?'

Pongo unpursed his lips. He understood all and pardoned all.

'Of course, old man. She shall never learn from me. You don't suppose I would wreck the happiness of my best friend . . . my oldest friend . . . my dearest friend . . . Horace, old top,' said Pongo, for it was a Twistleton trait to recognize when the iron was hot, 'I wonder if . . . I wonder whether . . . I wonder if you could possibly . . .'

'Mr Claude Pott,' announced Webster at the door.

To Pongo Twistleton, whose idea of a private investigator was a hawk-faced man with keen, piercing eyes and the general deportment of a leopard, Claude Pott came as a complete surprise. Hawks have no chins. Claude Pott had two. Leopards pad. Pott waddled. And his eyes, so far from being keen and piercing, were dull and expressionless, seeming, as is so often the case with those who go through life endeavouring to conceal their thoughts from the world, to be covered with a sort of film or glaze.

He was a stout, round, bald, pursy little man of about fifty, who might have been taken for a Silver Ring bookie or a minor Shakespearian actor – and, oddly enough, in the course of a life in which he had played many parts, he had actually been both.

'Good afternoon, Mr D.,' said this gargoyle.

'Hullo, Mr Pott. When did you get back?'

'Last night, sir. And thinking it over in bed this morning it occurred to me that it might be best if I were to deliver the concluding portion of my report verbally, thus saving time.'

'Oh, there's some more?'

'Yes, sir. I will apprise you of the facts,' said Claude Pott, giving Pongo a rather hard stare, 'when you are at liberty.'

'Oh, that's all right. You may speak freely before Mr Twistleton. He knows all. This is Mr Twistleton, The Subject's brother.'

'Pongo to pals,' murmured that young man weakly. He was finding the hard stare trying.

The austerity of the investigator's manner relaxed.

'Mr Pongo Twistleton? Then you must be the nephew of the Earl of Ickenham that he used to talk about.'

'Yes, he's my uncle.'

'A splendid gentleman. One of the real old school. A sportsman to his fingertips.'

Pongo, though fond of his uncle, could not quite bring himself to share this wholehearted enthusiasm.

'Yes, Uncle Fred's all right, I suppose,' he said. 'Apart from being loopy to the tonsils. You know him, do you?'

'I do indeed, sir. It was he who most kindly advanced me the money to start in business as a private investigator. So The Subject is Lord I.'s niece, is she? How odd! That his lordship should have financed me in my venture, I mean, and before I know where I am, I'm following his niece and taking notes of her movements. Strange!' said Mr Pott. 'Queer!'

'Curious,' assented Pongo.

'Unusual,' said Claude Pott.

'Bizarre,' suggested Pongo.

'Most. Shows what a small world it is.'

'Dashed small.'

Horace, who had been listening to these philosophical exchanges with some impatience, intervened.

'You were going to make your report, Mr Pott.'

'Coo!' said Claude Pott, called to order. 'That's right, isn't it? Well then, Mr D., to put the thing in a nutshell, I regret to have to inform you that there's been what you might call a bit of an unfortunate occurrence. On the nineteenth Ap., which was yesterday, The Subject, having lunched at Hotel Picardy with party consisting of two females, three males, proceeded to the golf club, where she took out her hockey-knockers and started playing round with one associate, the junior professional, self following at a cautious distance. For some time nothing noteworthy transpired, but at the fourteenth hole ... I don't know if you happen to be familiar with the golf links at Le Touquet, sir?'

'Oh, rather.'

'Then you will be aware that as you pass from the fourteenth tee along the fairway you come opposite a house with a hedge in front of it. And just as The Subject came opposite this house, there appeared behind the hedge two males, one with cocktail shaker. They started yodelling to The Subject, evidently inviting her to step along and have one, and The Subject, dismissing her associate, went through the gate in the hedge and by the time I came up was lost to sight in the house.'

A soft groan broke from Horace Davenport. He had the air of a man who was contemplating burying his face in his hands.

'Acting in your interests, I, too, passed through the gate and crept to the window from behind which I could hear chat and revelry in progress. And I was just stooping down to investigate further, when a hand fell on my shoulder and, turning, I perceived one male. And at the same moment The Subject, poking her head out of the window, observed "Nice work, Barmy. That's the blighter that's been following me about all the week. You be knocking his head off, while Catsmeat phones for the police. We'll have him sent to the guillotine for ingrowing molestation." And I saw that there was only one course for me to pursue.'

'I wouldn't have thought even that,' said Pongo, who had been following the narrative with close attention.

'Yes, sir – one. I could clear myself by issuing a full statement.'

A sharp, agonized cry escaped Horace Davenport.

'Yes, sir. I'm sorry, but there was no alternative. I had no desire to get embroiled with French rozzers. I issued my statement. While the male, Barmy, was calling me a trailing arbutus and the male, Catsmeat, was saying did anyone know the French for "police" and The Subject was talking about horsewhips, I explained the situation fully. It took me some time to get the facts into their heads, but I

managed it finally and was permitted to depart, The Subject saying
that if she ever set eyes on me again –'

'Miss Twistleton,' announced Webster.

'Well, good-bye, all,' said Claude Pott.

A critic who had been disappointed by the absence of the leopard
note in Mr Pott's demeanour would have found nothing to complain
of in that of Pongo's sister Valerie. She was a tall, handsome girl,
who seemed to be running a temperature, and her whole aspect, as
she came into the room, was that of some jungle creature advancing
on its prey.

'Worm!' she said, opening the conversation.

'Valerie, darling, let me explain!'

'Let *me* explain,' said Pongo.

His sister directed at him a stare of a hardness far exceeding that
of Mr Pott.

'Could you possibly keep your fat head out of this?'

'No, I couldn't keep my fat head out of it,' said Pongo. 'You
don't think I'm going to stand supinely by and see a good man
wronged, do you? Why should you barge in here, gnashing your
bally teeth, just because Horace sicked Claude Pott, private investigator, on to you? If you had any sense, you would see that it was a
compliment, really. Shows how much he loves you.'

'Oh, does it? Well –'

'Valerie, darling!'

The girl turned to Pongo.

'Would you,' she said formally, 'be good enough to ask your
friend not to address me as "Valerie, darling." My name is Miss
Twistleton.'

'Your name,' said Pongo, with brotherly sternness, 'will be mud
if you pass up an excellent bet like good old Horace Davenport –
the whitest man I know – simply because his great love made him
want to keep an eye on you during Drones Club week-end.'

'I did not –'

'And as events have proved he was thoroughly justified in the
course he took. You appear to have been cutting up like a glamour
girl at a Hollywood party. What about those two males, one with
cocktail shaker?'

'I did not –'

'And the m. you drove to Montreuil with?'

'Yes,' said Horace, for the first time perking up and showing a little of the Pendlebury-Davenport fire. 'What about the m. you drove to Montreuil with?'

Valerie Twistleton's face was cold and hard.

'If you will allow me to speak for a moment and not keep interrupting every time I open my mouth, I was about to say that I did not come here to argue. I merely came to inform you that our engagement is at an end, and that a notice to that effect will appear in *The Times* to-morrow morning. The only explanation I can think of that offers a particle of excuse for your conduct is that you have finally gone off your rocker. I've been expecting it for months. Look at your Uncle Alaric. Barmy to the back teeth.'

Horace Davenport was in the depths, but he could not let this pass.

'That's all right about my Uncle Alaric. What price your Uncle Fred?'

'What about him?'

'Loopy to the tonsils.'

'My Uncle Fred is not loopy to the tonsils.'

'Yes, he is. Pongo says so.'

'Pongo's an ass.'

Pongo raised his eyebrows.

'Cannot we,' he suggested coldly, 'preserve the decencies of debate?'

'This isn't a debate. As I told you before, I came here simply to inform Mr Davenport that our engagement is jolly well terminated.'

There was a set look on Horace's face. He took off his spectacles, and polished them with an ominous calm.

'So you're handing me the mitten?'

'Yes, I am.'

'You'll be sorry.'

'No, I shan't.'

'I shall go straight to the devil.'

'All right, trot along.'

'I shall plunge into a riot of reckless living.'

'Go ahead.'

'And my first step, I may mention, will be to take Polly Pott to that Bohemian Ball at the Albert Hall.'

'Poor soul! I hope you will do the square thing by her.'

'I fail to understand you.'

'Well, she'll need a pair of crutches next day. In common fairness you ought to pay for them.'

There was a silence. Only the sound of tense breathing could be heard – the breathing of a man with whom a woman has gone just too far.

'If you will be kind enough to buzz off,' said Horace icily, 'I will be ringing her up now.'

The door slammed. He went to the telephone.

Pongo cleared his throat. It was not precisely the moment he would have chosen for putting his fortune to the test, had he been free to choose, but his needs were immediate, the day was already well advanced and no business done, and he had gathered that Horace's time in the near future was likely to be rather fully occupied. So now he cleared his throat and, shooting his cuffs, called upon the splendid Twistleton courage to nerve him for his task.

'Horace, old man.'

'Hullo?'

'Horace, old chap.'

'Hullo? Polly?'

'Horace, old egg.'

'Half a minute. There's somebody talking. Well?'

'Horace, old top, you remember what we were starting to chat about when the recent Pott blew in. What I was going to say, when we were interrupted, was that owing to circumstances over which I had no – or very little – control . . .'

'Buck up. Don't take all day over it.'

Pongo saw that preambles would have to be dispensed with.

'Can you lend me two hundred quid?'

'No.'

'Oh? Right ho. Well, in that case,' said Pongo stiffly, 'tinkerty-tonk.'

He left the room and walked round to the garage where he kept his Buffy-Porson two-seater, and instructed the proprietor to have it in readiness for him on the morrow.

'Going far, sir?'

'To Ickenham, in Hampshire,' said Pongo.

He spoke moodily. He had not planned to reveal his financial difficulties to his Uncle Fred, but he could think of no other source of revenue.

# Chapter 2

Having put the finishing touches to his nephew's sitting-room and removed himself from Bloxham Mansions in a cab, the Duke of Dunstable, feeling much better after his little bit of exercise, had driven to Paddington Station and caught the 2.45 train to Market Blandings in the county of Shropshire. For he had invited himself – he was a man of too impatient spirit to hang about waiting for other people to invite him – to spend an indefinite period as the guest of Clarence, ninth Earl of Emsworth, and his sister, Lady Constance Keeble, at that haunt of ancient peace, Blandings Castle.

The postcard which he had dispatched some days previously announcing his impending arrival and ordering an airy ground-floor bedroom with a southern exposure and a quiet sitting-room in which he could work with his secretary, Rupert Baxter, on his history of the family had had a mixed reception at the Blandings breakfast-table.

Lord Emsworth, frankly appalled, had received the bad news with a sharp 'Eh, what? Oh, I say, dash it!' He had disliked the Duke in a dreamy way for forty-seven years, and as for Rupert Baxter he had hoped never to be obliged to meet him again either in this world or the next. Until fairly recently that efficient young man had been his own secretary, and his attitude towards him was a little like that of some miraculously cured convalescent towards the hideous disease which has come within an ace of laying him low. It was true, of course, that this time the frightful fellow would be infesting the castle in the capacity of somebody else's employee, but he drew small comfort from that. The mere thought of being under the same roof with Rupert Baxter was revolting to him.

Lady Constance, on the other hand, was pleased. She was a devoted admirer of the efficient Baxter, and there had been a time, when the world was young, when she and the Duke of Dunstable had whispered together in dim conservatories and been the last couple to straggle home from picnics. And though nothing had come of it – it was long before he succeeded to the title, and they shipped him abroad at about that time to allow an England which he had made too hot for him to cool off a little – the memory lingered.

Lord Emsworth lodged a protest, though realizing as he did so that it was purely formal. He was, and always had been, a cipher in the home.

'It's only about a week since he was here last.'

'It is nearly seven months.'

'Can't you tell him we're full up?'

'Of course I can't.'

'The last time he was here,' said Lord Emsworth broodingly, 'he poked the Empress in the ribs with an umbrella.'

'Well, I am certainly not going to offend one of my oldest friends just because he poked your pig with an umbrella,' said Lady Constance. 'I shall write to Alaric and tell him that we shall be delighted to have him for as long as he cares to stay. I see that he says he must be on the ground floor, because he is nervous of fire. He had better have the Garden Suite.'

And so it was in that luxurious set of apartments that the Duke awoke on the morning following his luncheon-party at Bloxham Mansions. For some time he lay gazing at the sunlight that filtered through the curtains which covered the french windows opening on the lawn: then, ringing the bell, he instructed the footman to bring him toast, marmalade, a pot of China tea, two lightly boiled eggs and *The Times*. And it was perhaps twenty minutes later that Lady Constance, sunning herself on the terrace, was informed by Beach, her butler, that His Grace would be glad if she would step to his room for a moment.

Her immediate sensation, on receiving this summons, was one of apprehension and alarm. The story which the Duke had told at dinner on the previous night, at great length and with a ghoulish relish, of the lesson which he had taught his nephew Horace had made a deep impression on her, and she fully expected on reaching the Blue Room to find it – possibly owing to some lapse from the required standard in His Grace's breakfast – a devastated area. It was with profound relief that she saw that all was well. The ducal poker remained a potential threat in the background, but it had not been brought into operation as yet, and she looked at the mauve-pyjamaed occupant of the bed with that quiet affection which hostesses feel towards guests who have not smashed their furniture – blended with the tenderness which a woman never quite loses for the man who has once breathed words of love down the back of her neck.

'Good morning, Alaric.'

''Morning, Connie. I say, who the devil's that whistling feller?'

'What do you mean?'

'I mean the whistling feller. A feller who whistles. There's been a blighter outside my window ever since I woke up, whistling the "Bonny Bonny Banks of Loch Lomond".'

'One of the gardeners, I expect.'

'Ah!' said the Duke quietly.

Pongo Twistleton had been surprised that a private investigator could look like Claude Pott, and he would have been equally surprised if he had been introduced to the Duke of Dunstable and informed that this was the notorious sitting-room-wrecker of whom he had heard so much. The Duke did not look a killer. Except for the Dunstable nose, always a little startling at first sight, there was nothing obviously formidable and intimidating about Horace's Uncle Alaric. A bald head ... A cascade of white moustache ... Prominent blue eyes ... A rather nice old bird, you would have said.

'Was that what you wanted to see me about?'

'No. Have the car ready to take me to the station directly after lunch. I've got to go to London.'

'But you only came last night.'

'It doesn't matter what happened last night. It's what has happened this morning. I glance through my *Times*, and what do I see? My nephew Horace has gone and got his engagement broken off.'

'What!'

'You heard.'

'But why?'

'How the dickens should I know why? It's just because I don't know why that I've got to go and find out. When an engagement has been broken off *The Times* doesn't print long reports from its special correspondent. It simply says "The marriage arranged between George Tiddlypush and Amelia Stick-in-the-mud will not take place."'

'The girl was Lord Ickenham's niece, wasn't she?'

'Still is.'

'I know Lady Ickenham, but I have never met Lord Ickenham.'

'Nor have I. But she's his niece, just the same.'

'They say he is very eccentric.'

'He's potty. Everybody's potty nowadays, except a few people like myself. It's the spirit of the age. Look at Clarence. Ought to have been certified years ago.'

'Don't you think that it's simply that he is dreamy and absent-minded?'

'Absent-minded be blowed. He's potty. So's Horace. So's my other nephew, Ricky. You take my advice, Connie. Never have nephews.'

Lady Constance's sigh seemed to say that he spoke too late.

'I've got dozens, Alaric.'

'Potty?'

'I sometimes think so. They seem to do the most extraordinary things.'

'I'll bet they don't do such extraordinary things as mine.'

'My nephew Ronald married a chorus girl.'

'My nephew Ricky writes poetry.'

'My nephew Bosham once bought a gold brick from a man in the street.'

'And now he wants to sell soup.'

'Bosham?'

'Ricky. He wants to sell soup.'

'Sell soup?'

'Good God, Connie, don't repeat everything I say, as if you were an echo in the Swiss mountains. I tell you he wants to sell soup. I go and see him yesterday, and he has the impertinence, if you please, to ask me to give him five hundred pounds to buy an onion soup bar. I refused to give him a penny, of course. He was as sick as mud. Not so sick as Horace will be, though, when he's finished with me. I shall start by disembowelling him. Go and order that car.'

'Well, it does seem a shame that you should have to go to London on a lovely day like this.'

'You don't think I want to go, do you? I've got to go.'

'Couldn't you tell Mr Baxter to go and see Horace? He is still in London, isn't he?'

'Yes, he is, the shirking, scrimshanking, four-eyed young son of a what-not, and I'm quite convinced that he stayed there because he was planning to go on a toot the moment my back was turned. If I can bring it home to him, by George, I'll sack him as soon as he shows his ugly face here. No, I couldn't tell Baxter to go and see Horace. I'm not going to have my nephew, half-witted though he is, subjected to the inquisition of a dashed underling.'

There were several points in this speech, which, if it had not been for the thought of that poker which hung over Blandings Castle like a sword of Damocles, Lady Constance would have liked to criticize. She resented the suggestion that Rupert Baxter was a man capable of going on toots. She did not consider his face ugly. And it pained her to hear him described as a dashed underling. But there are times when the tongue must be curbed. She maintained a discreet silence, from which she emerged a few moments later with a suggestion.

'I know! Bosham is going to London this morning. Why couldn't Horace drive him back in his car? Then you could have your talk with him without any trouble or inconvenience.'

'The first sensible word you've spoken since you came into this room,' said the Duke approvingly. 'Yes, tell Bosham to rout him out and bring him back alive or dead. Well, I can't stay here talking to you all day, Connie. Got to get up, got to get up. Where's Clarence?'

'Down at the pig-sty, I suppose.'

'Don't tell me he's still mooning over that pig of his.'

'He's quite absurd about it.'

'Quite crazy, you mean. If you want to know what I think, Connie, it's that pig that's at the root of his whole trouble. It's a very bad influence in his life, and if something isn't done soon to remove it you'll find him suddenly sticking straws in his hair and saying he's a poached egg. Talking of eggs, send me up a dozen.'

'Eggs? But haven't you had your breakfast?'

'Of course I've had my breakfast.'

'I see. But you want some more,' said Lady Constance pacifically. 'How would you like them done?'

'I don't want them done at all. I don't want eating eggs. I want throwing eggs. I intend to give that whistling feller a sharp lesson. Hark! There he is again. Singing now.'

'Alaric,' said Lady Constance, a pleading note in her voice, 'must you throw eggs at the gardeners?'

'Yes.'

'Very well,' said Lady Constance resignedly, and went off to avert the threatened horror by removing the vocalist from the danger zone.

Her thoughts, as she went, were long, long thoughts.

Lord Emsworth, meanwhile, unaware of the solicitude which he was causing, was down in the meadow by the kitchen garden, drooping over the comfortable sty which housed his pre-eminent sow, Empress of Blandings, twice in successive years silver medallist in the Fat Pigs' class at the Shropshire Agricultural Show. The noble animal, under his adoring eyes, was finishing a late breakfast.

The ninth Earl of Emsworth was a resilient man. It had not taken him long to get over the first sharp agony of the discovery that Rupert Baxter was about to re-enter his life. This morning, Baxter was forgotten, and he was experiencing that perfect happiness which comes from a clear conscience, absence of loved ones, congenial society and fine weather. For once in a way there was nothing which he was trying to conceal from his sister Constance, no disrupting influences had come to mar his communion with the Empress, and the weather, as almost always in this favoured spot, was wonderful. We have seen spring being whimsical and capricious in London, but it knew enough not to try anything of that sort on Blandings Castle.

The only concern Lord Emsworth had was a fear that this golden solitude could not last, and the apprehension was well founded. A raucous cry shattered the drowsy stillness and, turning, he perceived, as Claude Pott would have said, one male. His guest, the Duke, was crossing the meadow towards him.

''Morning, Clarence.'

'Good morning, Alaric.'

Lord Emsworth forced a welcoming smile to his lips. His breeding — and about fifteen thousand words from Lady Constance from time to time — had taught him that a host must wear the mask. He tried his hardest not to feel like a stag at bay.

'Seen Bosham anywhere?'

'No. No, I have not.'

'I want a word with him before he leaves. I'll wait here and intercept him on his way out. He's going to London to-day, to bring Horace here. His engagement has been broken off.'

This puzzled Lord Emsworth. His son and heir, Lord Bosham, who was visiting the castle for the Bridgeford races, had been, he felt pretty sure, for some years a married man. He mentioned this.

'Not Bosham's engagement. Horace's.'

Again Lord Emsworth was at a loss.

'Who is Horace?'

'My nephew.'

'And he is engaged?'

'He was. Ickenham's niece.'

'Who is?'

'The girl he was engaged to.'

'Who is Ickenham?'

'Her uncle.'

'Oh,' said Lord Emsworth, brightening. The name had struck a chord in his memory. 'Oh, Ickenham? Of course. Ickenham, to be sure. I know Ickenham. He is a friend of my brother Galahad. I think they used to be thrown out of night clubs together. I am glad Ickenham is coming here.'

'He isn't.'

'You said he was.'

'I didn't say he was. I said Horace was.'

The name was new to Lord Emsworth.

'Who,' he asked, 'is Horace?'

'I told you two seconds ago,' said the Duke, with the asperity which never left him for long, 'that he was my nephew. I have no reason to believe that conditions have altered since.'

'Oh?' said Lord Emsworth. 'Ah? Yes. Yes, to be sure. Your nephew. Well, we must try to make his stay pleasant. Perhaps he is interested in pigs. Are you interested in pigs, Alaric? You know my sow, Empress of Blandings, I think. I believe you met when you were here in the summer.'

He moved aside to allow his guest an uninterrupted view of the superb animal. The Duke advanced to the rail, and there followed a brief silence – on Lord Emsworth's side reverent, on that of the Duke austere. He had produced a large pair of spectacles from his breast pocket and through them was scrutinizing the silver medallist in a spirit only too plainly captious and disrespectful.

'Disgusting!' he said at length.

Lord Emsworth started violently. He could scarcely believe that he had heard aright.

'What!'

'That pig is too fat.'

'Too fat?'

'Much too fat. Look at her. Bulging.'

'But my dear Alaric, she is supposed to be fat.'

'Not as fat as that.'

'Yes, I assure you. She has already been given two medals for being fat.'

'Don't be silly, Clarence. What would a pig do with medals? It's no good trying to shirk the issue. There is only one word for that pig – gross. She reminds me of my Aunt Horatia, who died of apoplexy during Christmas dinner. Keeled over half-way through her second helping of plum pudding and never spoke again. This animal might be her double. And what do you expect? You stuff her and stuff her and stuff her, and I don't suppose she gets a lick of exercise from one week's end to another. What she wants is a cracking good gallop every morning, and no starchy foods. That would get her into shape.'

Lord Emsworth had recovered the pince-nez which emotion had caused, as it always did, to leap from his nose. He replaced them insecurely.

'Are you under the impression,' he said, for when deeply moved he could be terribly sarcastic, 'that I want to enter my pig for the Derby?'

The Duke had been musing. He had not liked that nonsense about pigs being given medals and he was thinking how sad all this was for poor Connie. But at these words he looked up sharply. An involuntary shudder shook him, and his manner took on a sort of bedside tenderness.

'I wouldn't, Clarence.'

'Wouldn't what?'

'Enter this pig for the Derby. She might not win, and then you would have had all your trouble for nothing. What you want is to get her out of your life. And I'll tell you what I'll do. Listen, my dear Clarence,' said the Duke, patting his host's shoulder, 'I'll take this pig over – lock, stock and barrel. Yes, I mean it. Have her sent to my place – I'll wire them to expect her – and in a few weeks' time she will be a different creature. Keen, alert, eyes sparkling. And you'll be different, too. Brighter. Less potty. Improved out of all knowledge . . . Ah, there's Bosham. Hi, Bosham! Half a minute, Bosham, I want a word with you.'

For some moments after his companion had left him, Lord Emsworth remained leaning limply against the rail of the sty. The sun was bright. The sky was blue. A gentle breeze caressed the Empress's tail, as it wiggled over the trough. But to him the heavens seemed darkened by a murky mist, and there appeared to be an east wind blowing through the world. It was not for some time that he became aware that a voice was speaking his name, but he heard it at last and pulling himself together with a powerful effort, saw his sister Constance.

She was asking him if he was getting deaf. He said No, he was not getting deaf.

'Well, I've been shouting at you for ever so long. I wish you would listen to me sometimes. Clarence, I have come to have a talk about Alaric. I am very worried about him. He seems to have got so odd.'

'Odd? I should say he was odd. Do you know what, Connie? He came to me just now –'

'He was asking me to give him eggs to throw at the gardeners.'

At a less tense moment, her words would have shocked Lord Emsworth. An English landed proprietor of the better type comes to regard himself as *in loco parentis* to those in his employment, and if visitors start throwing eggs at them he resents it. But now he did not even lose his pince-nez.

'And do you know what he said to me?'

'He can't be sane, if he wants to throw eggs at gardeners.'

'He can't be sane, if he wants me to give him the Empress.'

'Does he?'

'Yes.'

'Then, of course,' said Lady Constance, 'you will have to.'

This time Lord Emsworth did lose his pince-nez, and lose them thoroughly. They flew at the end of their string like leaves in a storm. He stared incredulously.

'What!'

'You *are* getting deaf.'

'I am not getting deaf. When I said "What!" I didn't mean "What?" I meant "What!!"'

'What on earth are you talking about?'

'I'm talking about this extraordinary remark of yours. I tell you this frightful Duke wants me to give him the Empress, and instead of being appalled and horrified and – er – appalled you say "Of course you will have to!" Without turning an eyelash! God bless my soul, do you imagine for an instant –'

'And do you imagine for an instant that I am going to run the risk of having Alaric career through the castle with a poker? If he destroyed all the furniture in his nephew Horace's sitting-room just because Horace wouldn't go to the station and see him off, what do you think he would do in a case like this? I do not intend to have my home wrecked for the sake of a pig. Personally, I think it's a blessing that we are going to get rid of the miserable animal.'

'Did you say "miserable animal"?'

'Yes, I did say "miserable animal". Alaric was telling me that he thought it a very bad influence in your life.'

'Dash his impertinence!'

'And I quite agree with him. In any case, there is no use arguing about it. If he wants the pig, he must have it.'

'Oh, very well, very well, very well, very well,' said Lord Emsworth. 'I suppose the next thing he'll want will be the castle, and you'll give him that. Be sure to tell him not to be afraid to ask for it, if he takes a fancy to it. I think I will go and read a little in the library, before Alaric decides to have all my books packed up and shipped off.'

It was a good exit speech – mordant – bitter, satirical – but it brought no glow of satisfaction to Lord Emsworth as he uttered it. His heart was bowed down with weight of woe. The experience gained from a hundred battles had taught him that his sister Constance always got her way. One might bluster and one might struggle, one might raise hands to heaven and clench fists and shake them, but in the end the result was always the same – Connie got what she wanted.

As he sat some ten minutes later in the cloistered coolness of the library, vainly trying to concentrate his attention on *Whiffle On The Care Of The Pig*, a feeling of being alone and helpless in a hostile world came upon Lord Emsworth. What he needed above all else in this crisis which had come to blast his life was a friend . . . an ally . . . a sympathetic adviser. But who was there to whom he could turn? Bosham was useless. Beach, his butler, was sympathetic, but not a constructive thinker. And his brother Galahad, the only male member of the family capable of coping with that family's females, was away . . .

Lord Emsworth started. A thought had struck him. Musing on Galahad, he had suddenly remembered that friend of his, that redoubtable Lord Ickenham of whom the Duke had been talking just now.

The Hon. Galahad Threepwood was a man of high standards. He weighed people before stamping them with the seal of his approval, and picked his words before he spoke. If Galahad Threepwood said a man was hot stuff, he used the phrase not carelessly but in its deepest sense. And not once but many times had Lord Emsworth heard him bestow this accolade on Frederick, Earl of Ickenham.

His eyes gleamed behind their pince-nez with a new light. He was planning and scheming. Debrett's Peerage, standing over there on its shelf, would inform him of this wonder-man's address, and what more simple than to ring him up on the telephone and arrange a meeting and then pop up to London and place the facts before him and seek his advice. A man like that would have a hundred ideas for the saving of the Empress . . .

The gleam died away. In classing the act of popping up to London as simple, he saw that he had erred. While this ghastly Duke remained on the premises, there was not the slightest hope of

Connie allowing him to get away, even for a night. Boys who stood on burning decks had a better chance of leaving their post than the master of Blandings Castle when there were visitors.

He was just reaching feebly for his *Whiffle*, which he had dropped in his anguish, hoping that its magic pages would act as an opiate, when Lady Constance burst into the room.

'Clarence!'

'Eh?'

'Clarence, did you tell Alaric you wanted to enter your pig for the Derby?'

'No, I told him I didn't.'

'Then he misunderstood you. He said you did. And he wants me to get a brain specialist down to observe you.'

'I like his dashed cheek!'

'So you must go to London immediately.'

Once more *Whiffle* fell from Lord Emsworth's limp hand.

'Go to London?'

'Now, please, Clarence, don't be difficult. There is no need for you to tell me how you dislike going to London. But this is vitally important. Ever since Alaric arrived, I have been feeling that he ought to be under the observation of some good brain specialist, but I couldn't think how it was to be managed without offending him. This has solved everything. Do you know Sir Roderick Glossop?'

'Never heard of him.'

'He is supposed to be quite the best man in that line. Lady Gimblett told me he had done wonders for her sister's problem child. I want you to go to London this afternoon and bring him back with you. Give him lunch at your club to-morrow and explain the whole situation to him. Assure him that expense is no object, and that he must come back with you. He will tell us what is the best thing to be done about poor Alaric. I am hopeful that some quite simple form of treatment may be all that is required. You must catch the two o'clock train.'

'Very well, Connie. If you say so.'

There was a strange look on Lord Emsworth's face as the door closed. It was the look of a man who has just found himself on the receiving end of a miracle. His knees were trembling a little as he rose and walked to the book-case, where the red and gold of *Debrett's Peerage* gleamed like the ray of a light-house guiding a storm-tossed mariner.

Beach, the butler, hearing the bell, presented himself at the library.

'M'lord?'

'Oh, Beach, I want you to put in a trunk telephone call for me. I don't know the number, but the address is Ickenham Hall, Ickenham, Hampshire. I want a personal call to Lord Ickenham.'

'Very good, m'lord.'

'And when you get it,' said Lord Emsworth, glancing nervously over his shoulder, 'have it put through to my bedroom.'

## Chapter 3

If your Buffy-Porson is running well, the journey from London to Hampshire does not take long. Pongo Twistleton, making good time, arrived at Ickenham Hall a few minutes before noon – at about the moment, in fact, when Lord Emsworth in far-off Shropshire was sitting down in the library of Blandings Castle to his *Whiffle On The Care Of The Pig.*

Half-way up the drive, where the rhododendrons masked a sharp turning, he nearly collided with the Hall Rolls, proceeding in the opposite direction, and a glimpse of luggage on its grid caused him to fear that he might just have missed his uncle. But all was well. Reaching the house, he found him standing on the front steps.

Frederick Altamont Cornwallis Twistleton, fifth Earl of Ickenham, was a tall, slim, distinguished-looking man with a jaunty moustache and an alert and enterprising eye. In actual count of time, he was no longer in his first youth. The spring now enlivening England with its alternate sunshine and blizzards was one of many that had passed over his head, leaving it a becoming iron-grey. But just as the years had failed to deprive him of his slender figure, so had they been impotent to quench his indomitable spirit. Together with a juvenile waist-line, he still retained the bright enthusiasms and the fresh, unspoiled outlook of a slightly inebriated undergraduate – though to catch him at his best, as he would have been the first to admit, you had to catch him in London.

It was for this reason that Jane, Countess of Ickenham, had prudently decided that the evening of her husband's life should be spent exclusively at his rural seat, going so far as to inform him that if he ever tried to sneak up to London she would skin him with a blunt knife. And if, as he now stood on the steps, his agreeable face seemed to be alight with some inner glow, this was due to the reflection that she had just left for a distant spot where she proposed to remain for some considerable time. He was devoted to his helpmeet, never wavering in the opinion that she was the sweetest thing that had ever replied 'Yes' to a clergyman's 'Wilt thou?', but there was no gainsaying the fact that her absence would render it easier for him to get that breath of London air which keeps a man from growing rusty and puts him in touch with the latest developments of modern thought.

At the sight of his nephew, his cheerfulness increased. He was very fond of Pongo, in whose society many of his happiest and most instructive hours had been passed. A day which they had spent together at the Dog Races some months before still haunted the young man's dreams.

'Why, hullo, my boy,' he cried. 'Delighted to see you. Park the scooter and come in. What a morning! Warm, fragrant, balmy, yet with just that nip in the air that puts a fellow on his toes. I saw one of those Western pictures at our local cinema last night, in which a character described himself as being all spooked up with zip and vinegar. That is precisely how I feel. The yeast of spring is fermenting in my veins, and I am ready for anything. You've just missed the boss.'

'Was that Aunt Jane I saw going off in the car?'

'That was the Big White Chief.'

The information relieved Pongo. He respected and admired his aunt, but from boyhood days she had always inspired him with a certain fear, and he was glad that he had not got to meet her while he was passing through his present financial crisis. Like so many aunts, she was gifted with a sort of second sight and one glance at his face would almost certainly have told her that he was two hundred in the red. From that to the confession that his difficulties were due to unsuccessful speculations on the turf would have been the shortest of steps. He did not like to think what would happen if she discovered his recent activities.

'She's motoring to Dover to catch the afternoon boat. She is off to the South of France to nurse her mother, who is having one of her spells.'

'Then you're all alone?'

'Except for your sister Valerie.'

29

'Oh, my gosh. Is she here?'

'She arrived last night, breathing flame through her nostrils. You've heard about her broken engagement? Perhaps you have come here with the idea of comforting her in her distress?'

'Well, not absolutely. In fact, between you and me, I'm not any too keen on meeting her at the moment. I rather took Horace's side in the recent brawl, and our relations are distant.'

Lord Ickenham nodded.

'Yes, now that you mention it, I recollect her saying something about your being some offensive breed of insect. An emotional girl.'

'Yes.'

'But I can't understand her making such heavy weather over the thing. Everybody knows a broken engagement doesn't amount to anything. Your aunt, I remember, broke ours six times in all before making me the happiest man in the world. Bless her! The sweetest, truest wife man ever had. I hope her mother responds to treatment and that she will be back with me soon. But not too soon. You know, Pongo, it's an odd thing that the detective Horace commissioned to chase Valerie across the ice with bloodhounds should have been old Pott. Mustard Pott, we used to call him. I've known him for years.'

'Yes, he was telling me. You started him as a sleuth.'

'That's right. A versatile chap, Mustard. There aren't many things he hasn't done in his time. He was on the stage once, I believe. Then he took to Silver Ring bookeying. Then he ran a club. And I rather suspect him of being a defrocked butler. Though what Nature really intended him to be, I have always felt, was a confidence-trick man. Which, by the way, is a thing I've wanted to have a shot at all my life, but never seemed able to get round to somehow.'

'What rot.'

'It isn't rot. You shouldn't mock at an old man's day-dreams. Every time I read one of those bits in the paper about Another Victim Of The Confidence Trick, I yearn to try it for myself, because I simply cannot bring myself to believe that there are people in the world mugs enough to fall for it. Well, young Pongo, how much?'

'Eh?'

'I can see in your eye that you've come to make a touch. What's the figure?'

Such ready intelligence on the part of an uncle should have pleased a nephew, but Pongo remained sombre. Now that the moment had come, his natural pessimism had asserted itself again.

'Well, it's rather a lot.'

'A fiver?'

'A bit more than that.'

'Ten?'

'Two hundred.'

'Two – *what*? How in the world did you manage to get in the hole for a sum like that?'

'I came a bit of a mucker at Lincoln, being led astray by my advisers, and when I tried to get it back at Hurst Park things came unstuck again, and the outcome and upshot is that I owe a bookie named George Budd two hundred quid. Do you know George Budd?'

'Since my time. When I was a prominent figure on the turf, George Budd was probably in his cradle, sucking his pink toes.'

'Well, he isn't sucking any pink toes now. He's a tough egg. Bingo Little had a bit on the slate with him last winter, and when he started trying to break it gently to him that he might not be able to pay up, this Budd said he did hope he would –'

'So the modern bookie feels like that, does he? The ones in my time always used to.'

'– because he said he knew it was silly to be superstitious but he had noticed that every time anyone did him down for money some nasty accident happened to them. He said it was like some sort of fate. And he summoned a great beefy brute called Erb and dangled him before Bingo's eyes. Erb called on me yesterday.'

'What did he say?'

'He didn't say anything. He seemed to be one of those strong, silent men. He just looked at me and nodded. So if you could possibly see your way, Uncle Fred, to advancing –'

Lord Ickenham shook his head regretfully.

'Alas, my boy, the ear which you are trying to bite, though not unresponsive, is helpless to assist. There has been a shake-up in the

Treasury department here. Some little time ago, your aunt unfortunately decided to take over the family finances and administer them herself, leaving me with just that bit of spending money which a man requires for tobacco, self-respect, golf-balls and what not. My limit is a tenner.'

'Oh, my gosh! And Erb's going to call again on Wednesday.'

There was a wealth of sympathy and understanding in Lord Ickenham's eye, as he patted his nephew's shoulder. He was gazing back across the years and seeing himself, an ardent lad in the twenties, thoughtfully gluing a large black moustache above his lips, his motive being to deceive and frustrate a bygone turf commissioner doing business under the name of Jimmy Timms, the Safe Man.

'I know just how you must be feeling, my boy. We have all gone through it, from the Archbishop of Canterbury, I imagine, downwards. Thirty-six years ago, almost to this very day, I was climbing out of a window and shinning down a waterspout to avoid a muscular individual named Syd, employed by a bookie who was my creditor at the moment in very much the same executive capacity as this Erb of yours. I got away all right, I remember, though what I have always thought must have been an ormolu clock missed me by inches. There is only one thing to be done. You must touch Horace Davenport.'

A bitter smile wreathed Pongo's lips.

'Ha!' he said briefly.

'You mean you have already tried? And failed? Too bad. Still, I wouldn't despair. No doubt you went the wrong way to work. I fancy that we shall find that when tactfully approached by a man of my presence and dignity he will prove far more plastic. Leave it to me. I will get into his ribs for you. There are no limits, literally none, to what I can accomplish in the springtime.'

'But you can't come to London.'

'Can't come to London? I don't understand you.'

'Didn't Aunt Jane say she would skin you if you did?'

'In her whimsical way she did say something to that effect, true. But you appear to have forgotten that she is on her way to the South of France.'

'Yes – leaving Valerie here to keep an eye on you.'

'I see what you mean. Yes, now that you mention it, there may possibly have been some idea in her mind that Valerie would maintain an affectionate watch over my movements during her absence. But be of good cheer. Valerie is not making a long stay. She will be returning to London with you in your car.'

'What?'

'Yes. She does not know it yet – in fact, I understood her to say that she was proposing to remain some weeks – but I think you will find her at your side.'

'What do you mean? You can't chuck her out.'

'My dear boy!' said Lord Ickenham, shocked. 'Of course not. But one has one's methods. Ah, there she is,' he went on, as a girlish figure came round the corner of the house. 'Valerie, my dear, here's Pongo.'

Valerie Twistleton had paused to stare at a passing snail – coldly and forbiddingly, as if it had been Horace Davenport. Looking up, she transferred this cold stare to her brother.

'So I see,' she said distantly. 'What's he doing here?'

'He has come to take you back to London.'

'I have no intention whatsoever –'

'Nothing,' proceeded Lord Ickenham, 'could be more delightful than to have you with me to cheer my loneliness, but Pongo feels – and I must say I agree with him – that you are making a great mistake in running away like this.'

'Doing *what*?'

'I'm afraid that is the construction people will place on the fact of your leaving London after what has happened. You know what people are. They sneer. They jibe. They laugh behind the back. It will be different, of course, with your real friends. They will merely feel a tender pity. They will look on you as the wounded animal crawling to its lair, and will understand and sympathize. But I repeat that in my opinion you are making a mistake. We Twistletons have always rather prided ourselves on keeping the stiff upper lip in times of trouble, and I confess that if I were in your place my impulse would be to show myself in my usual haunts – gay, smiling, debonair . . . Yes, Coggs?'

The butler had appeared from the hall.

'A trunk call for you, m'lord.'

'I will come at once. Be thinking it over, my dear.'

For some moments there had been proceeding from Valerie Twistleton a soft noise like the escape of steam. It now ceased, and her teeth came together with a sharp, unpleasant click.

'Can you wait ten minutes while I pack, Pongo?' she said. 'I will try not to keep you longer.'

She passed into the house, and Pongo lit a reverent cigarette. He did not approve of his Uncle Fred, but he could not but admire his work.

Lord Ickenham returned, looking about him.

'Where's Valerie?'

'Upstairs, packing.'

'Ah, she decided to leave, then? I think she was wise. That was old Emsworth on the phone. I don't think you've met him, have you? Lives at Blandings Castle in Shropshire. I hardly know him myself, but he is the brother of a very old pal of mine. He wants me to lunch with him at his club tomorrow. It will fit in quite nicely. We'll get this business of Horace over with in the morning. I'll meet you at the Drones at about twelve. And now come in and have a quick one. Bless my soul, it's wonderful to think that to-morrow I shall be in London. I feel like a child about to be taken to the circus.'

Pongo's feelings, as he followed his uncle to the smoking-room, were more mixed. It was stimulating, of course, to think that by his arts the other might succeed in inducing Horace Davenport to join the Share-The-Wealth movement, but the picture of him loose in London was one that tended definitely to knit the brow. As always when Lord Ickenham proposed to share with him the bracing atmosphere of the metropolis, he found himself regarding with apprehension the shape of things to come.

A thoughtful member of the Drones had once put the thing in a nutshell.

'The trouble with Pongo's Uncle Fred,' he had said, and the Drones is about the only place nowadays where you hear sound, penetrating stuff like this, 'is that, though sixty if a day, he becomes on arriving in London as young as he feels – which is, apparently, a youngish twenty-two. He has a nasty way of lugging Pongo out into the open and there, right in the public eye, proceeding to step high, wide and plentiful. I don't know if you happen to know what the word "excesses" means, but those are what Pongo's Uncle Fred, when in London, invariably commits.'

The young man's face, as he sipped his cocktail, was a little drawn and anxious.

# *Chapter 4*

His Uncle Fred's theory that Horace Davenport, scientifically worked, would develop pay gold had impressed Pongo Twistleton a good deal both when he heard it and during the remainder of the day. Throughout the drive back to London it kept him in optimistic mood. But when he woke on the following morning the idea struck him as unsound and impractical.

It was hopeless, he felt, to expect to mace any one given person for a sum like two hundred pounds. The only possible solution of his financial worries was to open a subscription list and let the general public in on the thing. He decided to look in at the Drones immediately and test the sentiment of the investors. And having arrived there, he was gratified to note that all the indications seemed to point to a successful flotation.

The atmosphere in the smoking-room of the Drones Club on the return of its members from their annual week-end at Le Touquet was not always one of cheerfulness and gaiety – there had been years when you might have mistaken the place for the Wailing Wall of Jerusalem – but to-day a delightful spirit of happiness prevailed. The dingy gods who preside over the *chemin-de-fer* tables at Continental Casinos had, it appeared, been extraordinarily kind to many of the Eggs, Beans and Crumpets revelling at the bar. And Pongo, drinking in the tales of their exploits, had just decided to raise the assessment of several of those present another ten pounds, when through the haze of cigarette smoke he caught sight of a familiar face. On a chair at the far end of the room sat Claude Pott.

It was not merely curiosity as to what Mr Pott was doing there or a fear lest he might be feeling lonely in these unaccustomed surroundings that caused Pongo to go and engage him in conversation. At the sight of the private investigator, there had floated into his mind like drifting thistledown the thought that it might be possible to start the ball rolling by obtaining a small donation from him. He crossed the room with outstretched hand.

'Why, hullo, Mr Pott. What brings you here?'

'Good morning, sir. I came with Mr Davenport. He is at the moment in the telephone booth, telephoning.'

'I didn't know old Horace ever got up as early as this.'

'He has not retired to bed yet. He went to a dance last night.'

'Of course, yes. The Bohemian Ball at the Albert Hall. I remember. Well, it's nice seeing you again, Mr Pott. You left a bit hurriedly that time we met.'

'Yes,' said Claude Pott meditatively. 'How did you come out with The Subject?'

'Not too well. She threw her weight about a bit.'

'I had an idea she would.'

'You were better away.'

'That's what I thought.'

'Still,' said Pongo heartily, 'I was very sorry you had to go, very. I could see that we were a couple of chaps who were going to get along together. Will you have a drink or something?'

'No, thank you, Mr T.'

'A cigarette or something?'

'No, thank you.'

'A chair or something? Oh, you've got one. I say, Mr Pott,' said Pongo, 'I was wondering –'

The babble at the bar had risen to a sudden crescendo. Oofy Prosser, the club's tame millionaire, was repeating for the benefit of some new arrivals the story of how he had rung his bank seven times, and there had come into Mr Pott's eyes a dull glow, like the phosphorescent gleam on the stomach of a dead fish.

'Coo!' he said, directing at Oofy the sort of look a thoughtful vulture in the Sahara casts at a dying camel. 'Seems to be a lot of money in here this morning.'

'Yes. And talking of money –'

'Now would be just the time to run the old Hat Stakes.'

'Hat Stakes?'

'Haven't you ever heard of the Hat Stakes? It sometimes seems to me they don't teach you boys nothing at your public schools. Here's the way it works. You take somebody, as it might be me, and he opens a book on the Hat Race, the finish to be wherever you like – call it that door over there. See what I mean? The punters would bet on what sort of hat the first bloke coming in through that door would be wearing. You, for instance, might feel like having a tenner –'

Pongo flicked a speck of dust from his companion's sleeve.

'Ah, but I haven't got a tenner,' he said. 'And that's precisely why I was saying that I wondered –'

'– on Top Hat. Then if a feller wearing a top hat was the first to come in, you'd cop.'

'Yes, I see the idea. Amusing. Ingenious.'

'But you can't play the Hat Stakes nowadays, with everybody wearing these Homburgs. There wouldn't be enough starters. Cor!'

'Cor!' agreed Pongo sympathetically. 'You'd have to make it clothes or something, what? But you were speaking of tenners, and while on that subject . . . Stop me if you've heard this before . . .'

Claude Pott, who had seemed about to sink into a brooding reverie, came out of his meditations with a start.

'What's that you said?'

'I was saying that while on the subject of tenners –'

'Clothes!' Mr Pott rose from his chair with a spasmodic leap, as if he had seen The Subject entering the room. 'Well, strike me pink!'

He shot for the door at a speed quite remarkable in a man of his build. A few moments later, he shot back again, and suddenly the Eggs, Beans and Crumpets assembled at the bar were shocked to discover that some bounder, contrary to all club etiquette, was making a speech.

'Gentlemen!'

The babble died away, to be succeeded by a stunned silence, through which there came the voice of Claude Pott, speaking with all the fervour and *brio* of his Silver Ring days.

'Gentlemen and sportsmen, if I may claim your kind indulgence for one instant! Gentlemen and sportsmen, I know gentlemen and sportsmen when I see them, and what I have been privileged to overhear of your conversation since entering this room has shown me that you are all gentlemen and sportsmen who are ready at all times to take part in a little sporting flutter.'

The words 'sporting flutter' were words which never failed to touch a chord in the members of the Drones Club. Something resembling warmth and sympathy began to creep into the atmosphere of cold disapproval. How this little blister had managed to worm his way into their smoking-room they were still at a loss to understand, but the initial impulse of those present to bung him out on his ear had softened into a more friendly desire to hear what he had to say.

'Pott is my name, gentlemen – a name at one time, I venture to assert, not unfamiliar to patrons of the sport of kings, and though I have retired from active business as a turf commission agent I am still willing to make a little book from time to time to entertain sportsmen and gentlemen, and there's no time like the present. Here we all are – you with the money, me with the book – so I say again, gentlemen, let's have a little flutter. Gentlemen all, the Clothes Stakes are about to be run.'

Few members of the Drones are at their brightest and alertest in the morning. There was a puzzled murmur. A Bean said, 'What did he say?' and a Crumpet whispered, 'The what Stakes?'

'I was explaining the how-you-do-it of the Hat Stakes to my friend Mr Twistleton over there, and the Clothes Stakes are run on precisely the same principle. There is at the present moment a gentleman in the telephone booth along the corridor, and I have just taken the precaution to instruct a pageboy to shove a wedge under the door, thus ensuring that he will remain there and so accord you all ample leisure in which to place your wagers. Coo!' said Claude Pott, struck by an unpleasant idea. 'Nobody's going to come along and let him out, are they?'

'Of course not!' cried his audience indignantly. The thought of anybody wantonly releasing a fellow member who had got stuck in the telephone booth, a thing that only happened once in a blue moon, was revolting to them.

'Then that's all right. Now then, gentlemen, the simple question you have to ask yourselves is – What is the gentleman in the telephone booth wearing? Or putting it another way – What's he got on? Hence the term Clothes Stakes. It might be one thing, or it might be another. He might be in his Sunday-go-to-meetings, or he might have been taking a dip in the Serpentine and be in his little bathing suit. Or he may have joined the Salvation Army. To give you a lead, I am offering nine to four against Blue Serge, four to one Pin Striped Grey Tweed, ten to one Golf Coat and Plus Fours, a hundred to six Gymnasium Vest and Running Shorts, twenty to one Court Dress as worn at Buckingham Palace, nine to four the field. And perhaps you, sir,' said Mr Pott, addressing an adjacent Egg, 'would be good enough to officiate as my clerk.'

'That doesn't mean I can't have a bit on?'

'By no means, sir. Follow the dictates of your heart and fear nothing.'

'What are you giving Herringbone Cheviot Lounge?'

'Six to one Herringbone Cheviot Lounge, sir.'

'I'll have ten bob.'

'Right, sir. Six halves Herringbone Cheviot Lounge. Ready money, if you please, sir. It's not that I don't trust you, but I'm not allowed by law. Thank you, sir. Walk up, walk up, my noble sportsmen. Nine to four the field.'

The lead thus given them removed the last inhibitions of the company. Business became brisk, and it was not long before Mr Pott had vanished completely behind a mass of eager punters.

Among the first to invest had been Pongo Twistleton. Hastening to the hall porter's desk, he had written a cheque for his last ten pounds in the world, and he was now leaning against the bar, filled with the quiet satisfaction of the man who has spotted the winner and got his money down in good time.

For from the very inception of these proceedings it had been clear to Pongo that Fortune, hitherto capricious, had at last decided that it was no use trying to keep a good man down and had handed him something on a plate. To be a successful punter, what you need is information, and this he possessed in abundant measure. Alone of those present, he was aware of the identity of the gentleman in the telephone booth, and he had the additional advantage of knowing the inside facts about the latter's wardrobe.

You take a chap like – say – Catsmeat Potter-Pirbright, that modern Brummel, and you might guess for hours without hitting on the precise suit he would be wearing on any given morning. But with Horace Pendlebury-Davenport it was different. Horace had never been a vivacious dresser. He liked to stick to the old and tried till they came apart on him, and it was this idiosyncrasy of his which had caused his recent *fiancée*, just before her departure for Le Touquet, to take a drastic step.

Swooping down on Horace's flat, at a moment when Pongo was there chatting with its proprietor, and ignoring her loved one's protesting cries, Valerie Twistleton had scooped up virtually his entire outfit and borne it away in a cab, to be given to the deserving poor. She could not actually leave the unhappy man in the nude, so she had allowed him to retain the shabby grey flannel suit he stood up in and also the morning clothes which he was reserving for the wedding day. But she had got away with all the rest, and as no tailor could have delivered a fresh supply at this early date, Pongo had felt justified in plunging to the uttermost. The bulk of his fortune on Grey Flannel at ten to one and a small covering bet on Morning Suit, and there he was, sitting pretty.

And he was just sipping his cocktail and reflecting that while his winnings must necessarily fall far short of the stupendous sum which he owed to George Budd, they would at least constitute something on account and remove the dark shadow of Erb at any rate temporarily from his life, when like a blow on the base of the skull there came to him the realization that he had overlooked a vital point.

The opening words of his conversation with Claude Pott came back to him, and he remembered that Mr Pott, in addition to informing him that Horace was in the telephone booth, had stated that the latter had attended the Bohemian Ball at the Albert Hall and had not been to bed yet. And like the knell of a tolling bell there rang in his ears Horace's words: 'I am going as a Boy Scout.'

The smoking-room reeled before Pongo's eyes. He saw now why Claude Pott had leaped so enthusiastically at the idea of starting these Clothes Stakes. The man had known it would be a skinner for the book. The shrewdest and most imaginative Drone would never think of Boy Scouts in telephone booths at this hour of the morning.

He uttered a stricken cry. At the eleventh hour the road to wealth had been indicated to him, and owing to that ready-money clause he was not in a position to take advantage of the fact. And then he caught sight of Oofy Prosser at the other end of the bar, and saw how by swift, decisive action he might save his fortunes from the wreck.

The attitude of Oofy Prosser towards the Clothes Stakes had been from the first contemptuous and supercilious, like that of a Wolf of Wall Street watching small boys scrambling for pennies. This Silver Ring stuff did not interest Oofy. He held himself aloof from it, and as the latter slid down the bar and accosted him he tried to hold himself aloof from Pongo. It was only by clutching his coat sleeve and holding on to it with a fevered grip that Pongo was able to keep him rooted to the spot.

'I say, Oofy –'

'No,' replied Oofy Prosser curtly. 'Not a penny!'

Pongo danced a few frantic dance steps. Already there was a lull over by the table where Mr Pott was conducting his business, and the closing of the book seemed imminent.

'But I want to put you on to a good thing!'

'Oh?'

'A cert.'

'Ah?'

'An absolute dashed cast-iron cert.'

Oofy Prosser sneered visibly.

'I'm not betting. What's the use of winning a couple of quid? Why, last Sunday at the big table at Le Touquet –'

Pongo sped towards Claude Pott, scattering Eggs, Beans and Crumpets from his path.

'Mr Pott!'

'Sir?'

'Any limit?'

'No, sir.'

'I've a friend here who wants to put on something big.'

'Ready money only, Mr T., may I remind you? It's the law.'

'Nonsense. This is Mr Prosser. You can take his cheque. You must have heard of Mr Prosser.'

'Oh, Mr Prosser? Yes, that's different. I don't mind breaking the law to oblige Mr Prosser.'

Pongo, bounding back to the bar, found there an Oofy no longer aloof and supercilious.

'Do you really know something, Pongo?'

'You bet I know something. Will you cut me in for fifty?'

'All right.'

'Then put your shirt on Boy Scout,' hissed Pongo. 'I have first-hand stable information that the bloke in the telephone booth is Horace Davenport, and I happen to know that he went to a fancy-dress dance last night as a Boy Scout and hasn't been home to change yet.'

'What! Is that right?'

'Absolutely official.'

'Then it's money for jam!'

'Money for pickles,' asserted Pongo enthusiastically. 'Follow me and fear nothing. And don't forget I'm in for the sum I mentioned.'

With a kindling eye he watched his financial backer force his way into the local Tattersall's, and it was at this tense moment that a page-boy came up and informed him that Lord Ickenham was waiting for him in the hall. He went floating out to meet him, his feet scarcely touching the carpet.

Lord Ickenham watched his approach with interest.

'Aha!' he said.

'Aha!' said Pongo, but absently, as one who has no time for formal greetings. 'Listen, Uncle Fred, slip me every bally cent you've got on you. I may just be able to get it down before the book closes. Your pal, Claude Pott, came here with Horace Davenport –'

'I wonder what Horace was doing, bringing Mustard to the Drones. Capital chap, of course, but quite the wrong person to let loose in a gathering of impressionable young men.'

Pongo's manner betrayed impatience.

'We haven't time to go into the ethics of the thing. Suffice it that Horace did bring him, and he shut Horace up in the telephone booth and started a book on what sort of clothes he had on. How much can you raise?'

'To wager against Mustard Pott?' Lord Ickenham smiled gently. 'Nothing, my dear boy, nothing. One of the hard lessons Life will teach you, as you grow to know him better, is that you can't make money out of Mustard. Hundreds have tried it, and hundreds have failed.'

Pongo shrugged his shoulders. He had done his best.

'Well, you're missing the chance of a lifetime. I happen to know that Horace went to a dance last night as a Boy Scout, and I have it from Pott's own lips that he hasn't been home to change. Oofy Prosser is carrying me for fifty.'

It was evident from his expression that Lord Ickenham was genuinely shocked.

'Horace Davenport went to a dance as a Boy Scout? What a ghastly sight he must have looked. I can't believe this. I must verify it. Bates,' said Lord Ickenham, walking over to the hall-porter's desk, 'were you here when Mr Davenport came in?'

'Yes, m'lord.'

'How did he look?'

'Terrible, m'lord.'

It seemed to Pongo that his uncle had wandered from the point.

'I concede,' he said, 'that a chap of Horace's height and skinniness ought to have been shrewder than to flaunt himself at a public dance in the costume of a Boy Scout. Involving as it does, knicker-bockers and bare knees –'

'But he didn't, sir.'

'What!'

The hall-porter was polite, but firm.

'Mr Davenport didn't go to no dance as no Boy ruddy Scout, if you'll pardon me contradicting you, sir. More like some sort of negroid character, it seemed to me. His face was all blacked up, and he had a spear with him. Gave me a nasty turn when he come through.'

Pongo clutched the desk. The hall-porter's seventeen stone seemed to be swaying before his eyes.

'Blacked up?'

A movement along the passage attracted their attention. Claude Pott, accompanied by a small committee, was proceeding to the telephone booth. He removed the wedge from beneath the door, and as he opened it there emerged a figure.

Nature hath framed strange fellows in her time, but few stranger than the one that now whizzed out of the telephone booth, whizzed down the corridor, whizzed past the little group at the desk and, bursting through the door of the club, whizzed down the steps and into a passing cab.

The face of this individual, as the hall-porter had foreshadowed, was a rich black in colour. Its long body was draped in tights of the same sombre hue, surmounted by a leopard's skin. Towering above his head was a head-dress of ostrich feathers, and in its right hand it grasped an assegai. It was wearing tortoiseshell-rimmed spectacles.

Pongo, sliding back against the desk, found his arm gripped by a kindly hand.

'Shift ho, my boy, I think, eh?' said Lord Ickenham. 'There would appear to be nothing to keep you here, and a meeting with Oofy Prosser at this moment might be fraught with pain and embarrassment. Let us follow Horace – he seemed to be homing – and hold an enquiry into this in-and-out running of his. Tell me, how much did you say Oofy Prosser was carrying you for? Fifty pounds?'

Pongo nodded bleakly.

'Then let us assemble the facts. Your assets are nil. You owe George Budd two hundred. You now owe Oofy fifty. If you don't pay Oofy, he will presumably report you to the committee and have you thrown into the street, where you will doubtless find Erb waiting for you with a knuckleduster. Well,' said Lord Ickenham, impressed, 'nobody can say you don't lead a full life. To a yokel like myself all this is very stimulating. One has the sense of being right at the pulsing heart of things.'

They came to Bloxham Mansions, and were informed by Webster that Mr Davenport was in his bath.

## Chapter 5

The Horace who entered the library some ten minutes later in
pyjamas and a dressing-gown was a far more prepossessing spectacle
than the ghastly figure which had popped out of the Drones Club
telephone booth, but he was still patently a man who had suffered.
His face, scrubbed with butter and rinsed with soap and water,
shone rosily, but it was a haggard face, and the eyes were dark with
anguish.

Into these eyes, as he beheld the senior of his two visitors, there
crept a look of alarm. Horace Davenport was not unfamiliar with
stories in which the male relatives of injured girls called on young
men with horsewhips.

Lord Ickenham's manner, however, was reassuring. Though considering him weak in the head, he had always liked Horace, and he
was touched by the forlornness of his aspect.

'How are you, my dear fellow? I looked in earlier in the day, but
you were out.'

'Yes, Webster told me.'

'And when I saw you at the Drones just now, you seemed
pressed for time and not in the mood for conversation. I wanted to
have a talk with you about this unfortunate rift between yourself
and Valerie. She has given me a fairly comprehensive eyewitness's
report of the facts.'

Horace seemed to swallow something jagged.

'Oh, has she?'

'Yes. I was chatting with her last night, and your name happened
to come up.'

'Oh, did it?'

'Yes. In fact, she rather dwelt on you. Valerie – we must face it –
is piqued.'

'Yes.'

'But don't let that worry you,' said Lord Ickenham cheerily. 'She'll come round. I'm convinced of it. When you reach my age, you will know that it is an excellent sign when a girl speaks of a man as a goggle-eyed nit-wit and says that her dearest wish is to dip him in boiling oil and watch him wriggle.'

'Did she say that?'

'Yes, she was most definite about it – showing, I feel, that love still lingers. My advice is – give her a day or two to cool off, and then start sending her flowers. She will tear them to shreds. Send some more. She will rend them to ribbons. Shoot in a further supply. And very soon, if you persevere, you will find that the little daily dose is having its effect. I anticipate a complete reconciliation somewhere about the first week in May.'

'I see,' said Horace moodily. 'Well, that's fine.'

Lord Ickenham felt a trifle ruffled.

'You don't seem pleased.'

'Oh, I am. Oh yes, rather.'

'Then why do you continue to look like a dead fish on a slab?'

'Well, the fact is, there's something else worrying me a bit at the moment.'

Pongo broke a silence which had lasted for some twenty minutes. Since entering the apartment he had been sitting with folded arms, as if hewn from the living rock.

'Oh, is there?' he cried. 'And there's something that's jolly well worrying me at the moment. Did you or did you not, you blighted Pendlebury-Davenport, definitely and specifically state to me that you were going to that Ball as a Boy Scout? Come on now. Did you or didn't you?'

'Yes, I did. I remember. But I changed my mind.'

'Changed your mind! Coo!' said Pongo, speaking through tightly clenched teeth and borrowing from the powerful vocabulary of Claude Pott to give emphasis to his words. 'He changed his mind! He changed his bally mind! Ha! Coo! Cor!'

'Why, what's up?'

'Oh, nothing. You have merely utterly and completely ruined me, that's all.'

'Yes, my dear Horace,' said Lord Ickenham, 'I'm afraid you have

47

let Pongo down rather badly. When Pongo joins the Foreign Legion, the responsibility will be yours. You give him your solemn assurance that you are going to the Ball in one costume and actually attend it in another. Not very British.'

'But why does it matter?'

'There was some betting in the club smoking-room on what you were wearing, and Pongo, unhappy lad, plunging in the light of what he thought was inside knowledge on Boy Scout, took the knock.'

'Oh, I say! I'm frightfully sorry.'

'Too late to be sorry now.'

'The thing was, you see, that Polly thought it would be fun if I went as a Zulu warrior.'

'Evidently a girl of exotic and rather unwholesome tastes. The word "morbid" is one that springs to the lips. Who is this Polly?'

'Pott's daughter. She went to the Ball with me.'

Lord Ickenham uttered an exclamation.

'Not little Polly Pott? Good heavens, how time flies. Fancy Polly being old enough to go to dances. I knew her when she was a kid. She used to come and spend her holidays at Ickenham. A very jolly child she was, too, beloved by all. Quite grown up now, eh? Well, well, we're none of us getting younger. I was a boy in the early fifties when I saw her last. So you took Polly to the Ball, did you?'

'Yes. You see, the original idea was that Valerie was to have gone. But when she gave me the bird, I told her I would take Polly instead.'

'Your view being, of course, that that would learn her? A fine, defiant gesture. Did Pott go along?'

'No, he wasn't there.'

'Then what was he doing at the Drones with you?'

'Well, you see, he had come to Marlborough Street to pay my fine, and we sort of drifted on there afterwards. I suppose I had some idea of buying him a drink or something.'

A faint stir of interest ruffled the stone of Pongo's face.

'What do you mean, your fine? Were you pinched last night?'

'Yes. There was a bit of unpleasantness at the Ball, and they scooped me in. It was Ricky's fault.'

'Who,' asked Lord Ickenham, 'is Ricky?'

'My cousin. Alaric Gilpin.'

'Poet. Beefy chap with red hair. It was he who introduced this girl Polly to Horace,' interpolated Pongo, supplying additional footnotes. 'She was giving him dancing lessons.'

'And how did he come to mix you up in unpleasantness?'

'Well, it was like this. Ricky, though I didn't know it, is engaged to Polly. And another thing I didn't know was that he hadn't much liked the idea of her giving me dancing lessons and, when she told him I was taking her to the Ball, expressly forbade her to go. So when he found us together there . . . I say, he wasn't hanging about outside when you arrived, was he?'

'I saw no lurking figure.'

'He said he was going to look in to-day and break my neck.'

'I didn't know poets broke people's necks.'

'Ricky does. He once took on three simultaneous costermongers in Covent Garden and cleaned them up in five minutes. He had gone there to get inspiration for a pastoral, and they started chi-iking him, and he sailed in and knocked them base over apex into a pile of Brussels sprouts.'

'How different from the home life of the late Lord Tennyson. But you were telling us about this trouble at the Ball.'

Horace mused for a moment, his thoughts in the stormy past.

'Well, it was after the proceedings had been in progress for about a couple of hours that it started. Polly was off somewhere, hobnobbing with pals, and I was having a smoke and resting the ankles, when Ricky appeared and came up and joined me. He said a friend of his had given him a ticket at the last moment and he thought he might as well look in for a bit, so he hired a Little Lord Fauntleroy suit and came along. He was perfectly all right then – in fact, exceptionally affable. He sat down and tried to borrow five hundred pounds from me to buy an onion soup bar.'

Lord Ickenham shook his head.

'You are taking me out of my depth. We rustics who don't get up to London much are not in touch with the latest developments of modern civilization. What is an onion soup bar?'

'Place where you sell onion soup,' explained Pongo. 'There are lots of them round Piccadilly Circus way these days. You stay open all night and sell onion soup to the multitude as they reel out of the bottle-party places. Pots of money in it, I believe.'

'So Ricky said. A pal of his, an American, started one a couple of years ago in Coventry Street and, according to him, worked the profits up to about two thousand quid a year. But apparently he has got homesick and wants to sell out and go back to New York, and he's willing to let Ricky have the thing for five hundred. And Ricky wanted me to lend it to him. And he was just getting rather eloquent and convincing, when he suddenly broke off and I saw that he was glaring at something over my shoulder.'

'Don't tell me,' said Lord Ickenham. 'Let me guess. Polly?'

'In person. And then the whole aspect of affairs changed. He had just been stroking my arm and saying what pals we had always been and asking me if I remembered the days when we used to go ratting together at my father's place, and he cheesed it like a flash. He turned vermilion, and the next moment he had started kicking up a frightful row ... cursing me ... cursing Polly ... showing quite a different side to his nature, I mean to say. Well, you know how it is when you do that sort of thing at a place like the Albert Hall. People began to cluster round, asking questions. And what with one thing and another, I got a bit rattled, and I suppose it was because I was rattled that I did it. It was a mistake, of course. I see that now.'

'Did what?'

'Jabbed him with my assegai. Mind you,' said Horace, 'I didn't mean to. It wasn't as if I had had any settled plans. I was just trying to hold him off. But I misjudged the distance, and the next thing I knew he was rubbing his stomach and coming for me with a nasty glint in his eyes. So I jabbed him again, and then things hotted up still further. And what really led to my getting arrested was that he managed to edge past the assegai and land me a juicy one on the jaw.'

Lord Ickenham found himself unable to reconcile cause and effect.

'But surely no policeman, however flat-footed, would take a man into custody for being landed a juicy one on the jaw. You have probably got your facts twisted. I expect we shall find, when we look into it, that it was Ricky who was taken to Marlborough Street.'

'No, you see what happened was this juicy one on the jaw made me a bit dizzy, and I didn't quite know what I was doing. Everything was a sort of blur, and I just jabbed wildly in the general direction of what I thought was the seat of the trouble. And after a while I discovered that I was jabbing a female dressed as Marie Antoinette. It came as a great surprise to me. As a matter of fact, I had been rather puzzled for some moments. You see, I could feel the assegai going into some yielding substance, and I was surprised that Ricky was so squashy and had such a high voice. And then, as I say, I found it wasn't Ricky, but this woman.'

'Embarrassing.'

'It was a bit. The man who was with the woman summoned the cops. And what made it still more awkward was that by that time Ricky was nowhere near. Almost at the start of the proceedings, it appeared, people had gripped him and bustled him off. So that when the policeman arrived and found me running amuck with an assegai apparently without provocation, it was rather difficult to convince him that I wasn't tight. In fact, I didn't convince him. The magistrate was a bit terse about it all this morning. I say, are you sure Ricky wasn't hanging about outside?'

'We saw no signs of him.'

'Then I'll get dressed and go round and see Polly.'

'With what motive?'

'Well, dash it, I want to tell her to go and explain to Ricky that my behaviour towards her throughout was scrupulously correct. At present, he's got the idea that I'm a kind of . . . Who was the chap who was such a devil with the other sex? . . . Donald something.'

'Donald Duck?'

'Don Juan. That's the fellow I mean. Unless I can convince Ricky immediately that I'm not a Don Juan and was not up to any funny business with Polly, the worst will happen. You've no notion what he was like last night. Absolutely frothing at the mouth. I must go and see her at once.'

'And if he comes in while you are there?'

Horace, half-way to the door, halted.

'I never thought of that.'

'No.'

'You think it would be better to telephone her?'

'I don't think anything of the sort. You can't conduct a delicate negotiation like this over the telephone. You need the language of the eye . . . those little appealing gestures of the hand . . . Obviously you must entrust the thing to an ambassador. And what better ambassador could you have than Pongo here?'

'Pongo?'

'A silver-tongued orator, if ever there was one. Oh, I know what you are thinking,' said Lord Ickenham. 'You feel that there may be a coolness on his side, due to the fact that you recently refused to lend him a bit of money. My dear boy, Pongo is too big and fine to be unwilling to help you out because of that. Besides, in return for his services you will of course naturally slip him the trifle he requires.'

'But he said he wanted two hundred pounds.'

'Two hundred and fifty. He doesn't always speak distinctly.'

'But that's a frightful lot.'

'To a man of your wealth as the price of your safety? You show a cheeseparing spirit which I do not like to see. Fight against it.'

'But, dash it, why does everybody come trying to touch *me*?'

'Because you've got the stuff, my boy. It is the penalty you pay for having an ancestress who couldn't say No to Charles the Second.'

Horace chewed a dubious lip.

'I don't see how I can manage –'

'Well, please yourself, of course. Tell me about this fellow Ricky, Pongo. A rather formidable chap, is he? Robust? Well-developed? Muscular? His strength is as the strength of ten?'

'Definitely, Uncle Fred.'

'And in addition to that he appears to be both jealous and quick-tempered. An unpleasant combination. One of those men, I imagine, who if he inflicted some serious injury on anyone, would be the first to regret it after he had calmed down, but would calm down about ten minutes too late. I've met the type. There was a chap named Bricky Bostock in my young days who laid a fellow out for weeks over some misunderstanding about a girl, and it was pitiful to see his remorse when he realized what he had done. Used to hang about outside the hospital all the time the man was in danger, trembling like a leaf. But, as I said to him, "What's the use of trembling like a leaf now? The time to have trembled like a leaf was when you had your hands on his throat and were starting to squeeze the juice out of him.'"'

'It'll be all right about that two-fifty, Pongo,' said Horace.

'Thanks, old man.'

'When can you go and see Polly?'

'The instant I've had a bite of lunch.'

'I'll give you her address. You will find her a most intelligent girl, quick to understand. But pitch it strong.'

'Leave it to me.'

'And impress upon her particularly that there is no time to waste. Full explanations should be made to Ricky by this evening at the latest. And now,' said Horace, 'I suppose I'd better go and dress.'

The door closed. Lord Ickenham glanced at his watch.

'Hullo,' he said. 'I must be off. I have to go to the Senior Conservative Club to meet old Emsworth. So good-bye, my dear boy, for the present. I am delighted that everything has come out so smoothly. We shall probably meet at Pott's. I am going to slip round there after lunch and see Polly. Give her my love, and don't let Mustard lure you into any card game. A dear, good chap, one of the best, but rather apt to try to get people to play something he calls Persian Monarchs. When he was running that club of his, I've known him to go through the place like a devouring flame, leaving ruin and desolation behind him on every side.'

# Chapter 6

The method of Lord Emsworth, when telling a story, being to repeat all the unimportant parts several times and to diverge from the main stream of narrative at intervals in order to supply lengthy character studies of the various persons involved in it, luncheon was almost over before he was able to place his guest in full possession of the facts relating to the Empress of Blandings. When eventually he had succeeded in doing so, he adjusted his pince-nez and looked hopefully across the table.

'What do you advise, my dear Ickenham?'

Lord Ickenham ate a thoughtful cheese straw.

'Well, it is obvious that immediate steps must be taken through the proper channels, but the question that presents itself is "What steps?"'

'Exactly.'

'We have here,' said Lord Ickenham, illustrating by means of a knife, a radish and a piece of bread, 'one pig, one sister, one Duke.'

'Yes.'

'The Duke wants the pig.'

'Quite.'

'The sister says he's got to have it.'

'Precisely.'

'The pig, no doubt, would prefer to be dissociated from the affair altogether. Very well, then. To what conclusion do we come?'

'I don't know,' said Lord Emsworth.

'We come to the conclusion that the whole situation pivots on the pig. Eliminate the pig, and we see daylight. "What, no pig?" says the Duke, and after a little natural disappointment turns his thoughts to other things – I don't know what, but whatever things

Dukes do turn their thoughts to. There must be dozens. This leaves us with the simple problem – How is the existing state of what I might call "plus pig" to be converted into a state of "minus pig"? There can be only one answer, my dear Emsworth. The pig must be smuggled away to a place of safety and kept under cover till the Duke has blown over.'

Lord Emsworth, as always when confronted with a problem, had allowed his lower jaw to sag restfully.

'How?' he asked.

Lord Ickenham regarded him with approval.

'I was expecting you to say that. I knew your razor-like brain would cut cleanly to the heart of the thing. Well, it ought not to be difficult. You creep out by night with an accomplice and – one shoving and one pulling – you load the animal into some vehicle and ship her off to my family seat, where she will be looked after like a favourite child till you are ready to receive her again. It is a long journey from Shropshire to Hampshire, of course, but she can stop off from time to time for a strengthening bran-mash or a quick acorn. The only point to be decided is who draws the job of accomplice. Who is there at Blandings that you can trust?'

'Nobody,' said Lord Emsworth promptly.

'Ah? That seems to constitute an obstacle.'

'I suppose you would not care to come down yourself?'

'I should love it, and it is what I would have suggested. But unfortunately I am under strict orders from my wife to remain at Ickenham. My wife, I should mention, is a woman who believes in a strong centralized government.'

'But you aren't at Ickenham.'

'No. The Boss being away, I am playing hookey at the moment. But I have often heard her mention her friend Lady Constance Keeble, and were I to come to Blandings Lady Constance would inevitably reveal the fact to her sooner or later. Some casual remark in a letter, perhaps, saying how delightful it had been to meet her old bit of trouble at last and how my visit had brightened up the place. You see what I mean?'

'Oh, quite. Yes, quite, dash it.'

'My prestige in the home is already low, and a substantiated charge of being AWOL would put a further crimp in it, from which it might never recover.'

'I see.'

'But I think,' said Lord Ickenham, helping himself to the radish which had been doing duty as Lady Constance, 'that I have got the solution. There is always a way. We must place the thing in the hands of Mustard Pott.'

'Who is Mustard Pott?'

'A very dear and valued friend of mine. I feel pretty sure that, if we stress the fact that there is a bit in it for him, he would be delighted to smuggle pigs. Mustard is always ready and anxious to add to his bank balance. I was intending to call upon him after lunch, to renew our old acquaintance. Would you care to come along and sound him?'

'It is a most admirable idea. Does he live far from here?'

'No, quite close. Down in the Sloane Square neighbourhood.'

'I ask because I have an appointment with Sir Roderick Glossop at three o'clock. Connie told me to ask him to lunch, but I was dashed if I was going to do that. Do you know Sir Roderick Glossop, the brain specialist?'

'Only to the extent of having sat next to him at a public dinner not long ago.'

'A talented man, I believe.'

'So he told me. He spoke very highly of himself.'

'Connie wants me to bring him to Blandings, to observe the Duke, and he made an appointment with me for three o'clock. But I am all anxiety to see this man Pott. Would there be time?'

'Oh, certainly. And I think we have found the right way out of the impasse. If it had been a question of introducing Mustard into the home, I might have hesitated. But in this case he will put up at the local inn and confine himself entirely to outside work. You won't even have to ask him to dinner. The only danger I can see is that he may get this pig of yours into a friendly game and take her last bit of potato peel off her. Still, that is a risk that must be faced.'

'Of course.'

'Nothing venture, nothing have, eh?'

'Precisely.'

'Then suppose we dispense with coffee and go round and see

him. We shall probably find my nephew Pongo there. A nice boy. You will like him.'

Pongo Twistleton had arrived at Claude Pott's residence at about the time when Lord Emsworth and his guest were leaving the Senior Conservative Club, and had almost immediately tried to borrow ten pounds from him. For even though Horace Davenport had guaranteed in the event of his soothing Ricky Gilpin to underwrite his gambling losses, he could not forget that he was still fiscally crippled, and he felt that he owed it to himself to omit no word or act which might lead to the acquisition of a bit of the needful.

In the sleuth hound of 6, Wilbraham Place, Sloane Square, however, he speedily discovered that he had come up against one of the Untouchables, a man to whom even Oofy Prosser, that outstanding non-parter, would have felt compelled to raise his hat. Beginning by quoting from Polonius' speech to Laertes, which a surprising number of people whom you would not have suspected of familiarity with the writings of Shakespeare seem to know, Mr Pott had gone on to say that lending money always made him feel as if he were rubbing velvet the wrong way, and that in any case he would not lend it to Pongo, because he valued his friendship too highly. The surest method of creating a rift between two pals, explained Mr Pott, was for one pal to place the other pal under a financial obligation.

It was, in consequence, into an atmosphere of some slight strain that the Lords Emsworth and Ickenham entered a few moments later. And though the mutual courtesies of the latter and Claude Pott, getting together again after long separation, lightened the gloom temporarily, the clouds gathered once more when Mr Pott, having listened to Lord Emsworth's proposal, regretfully declined to have anything to do with removing the Empress from her sty and wafting her away to Ickenham Hall.

'I couldn't do it, Lord E.'

'Eh? Why not?'

'It wouldn't be in accordance with the dignity of the profession.'

Lord Ickenham resented this superior attitude.

'Don't stick on such beastly side, Mustard. You and your bally dignity! I never heard such swank.'

'One has one's self-respect.'

'What's self-respect got to do with it? There's nothing *infra dig* about snitching pigs. If I were differently situated, I'd do it like a shot. And I'm one of the haughtiest men in Hampshire.'

'Well, between you and me, Lord I.,' said Claude Pott, discarding loftiness and coming clean, 'there's another reason. I was once bitten by a pig.'

'Not really?'

'Yes, sir. And ever since then I've had a horror of the animals.'

Lord Emsworth hastened to point out that the present was a special case.

'You can't be bitten by the Empress.'

'Oh, no? Who made that rule?'

'She's as gentle as a lamb.'

'I was once bitten by a lamb.'

Lord Ickenham was surprised.

'What an extraordinary past you seem to have had, Mustard. One whirl of excitement. One of these days you must look me up and tell me some of the things you haven't been bitten by. Well, if you won't take the job on, you won't, of course. But I'm disappointed in you.'

Mr Pott sighed slightly, but it was plain that he did not intend to recede from his attitude of civil disobedience.

'I suppose I shall now have to approach the matter from another angle. If you're seeing Glossop at three, Emsworth, you'd better be starting.'

'Eh? Oh, ah, yes. True.'

'You leaving us, Lord E.?' said Mr Pott. 'Which way are you going?'

'I have an appointment in Harley Street.'

'I'll come with you,' said Mr Pott, who had marked down the dreamy peer as almost an ideal person with whom to play Persian Monarchs and wished to cement their acquaintanceship. 'I've got to see a man up in that direction. We could share a cab.'

He escorted Lord Emsworth lovingly to the door, and Lord Ickenham stood brooding.

'A set-back,' he said. 'An unquestionable set-back. I had been relying on Mustard. Still, if a fellow's been bitten by pigs I suppose his views on associating with them do get coloured. But how the devil does a man *get* bitten by a pig? I wouldn't have thought they would ever meet on that footing. Ah, well, there it is. And now what about Polly? There seem to be no signs of her. Is she out?'

Pongo roused himself from a brown study.

'She's in her room, Pott told me. Dressing or something, I take it.'

Lord Ickenham went to the door.

'Ahoy!' he shouted. 'Polly!'

There came in reply from somewhere in the distance a voice which even in his gloom Pongo was able to recognize as silvery.

'Hullo?'

'Come here. I want to see you.'

'Who's there?'

'Frederick Altamont Cornwallis Twistleton, fifth Earl of good old Ickenham. Have you forgotten your honorary uncle Fred?'

'Oo!' cried the silvery voice. There was a patter of feet in the passage, and a kimono-clad figure burst into the room.

'Uncle Fur-RED! Well, it is nice seeing you again!'

'Dashed mutual, I assure you, my dear. I say, you've grown.'

'Well, it's six years.'

'So it is, by Jove.'

'You're just as handsome as ever.'

'Handsomer, I should have said. And you're prettier than ever. But what's become of your legs?'

'They're still there.'

'Yes, but when I saw you last they were about eight feet long, like a colt's.'

'I was at the awkward age.'

'You aren't now, by George. How old are you, Polly?'

'Twenty-one.'

'Gol durn yuh, l'il gal, as my spooked-up-with-vinegar friend would say, you're a peach!'

Lord Ickenham patted her hand, put his arm about her waist and kissed her tenderly. Pongo wished he had thought of that himself. He reflected moodily that this was always the way. In the course of their previous adventures together, if there had ever been any kissing or hand-patting or waist-encircling to be done, it had always been his nimbler uncle who had nipped in ahead of him and attended to it. He coughed austerely.

'Oh, hullo! I'd forgotten you were there,' said Lord Ickenham, apologetically. 'Miss Polly Pott . . . My nephew – such as he is – Pongo Twistleton.'

'How do you do?'

'How do you do?' said Pongo.

He spoke a little huskily, for he had once more fallen in love at first sight. The heart of Pongo Twistleton had always been an open door with 'Welcome' clearly inscribed on the mat, and you never knew what would walk in next. At brief intervals during the past few years he had fallen in love at first sight with a mixed gaggle or assortment of females to the number of about twenty, but as he gazed at this girl like an ostrich goggling at a brass door-knob it seemed to him that here was the best yet. There was something about her that differentiated her from the other lodgers.

It was not the fact that she was small, though the troupe hitherto had tended to be on the tall and willowy side. It was not that her eyes were grey and soft, while his tastes previously had rather lain in the direction of the dark and bold and flashing. It was something about her personality – a mateyness, a simplicity, an absence of that lipsticky sophistication to which the others had been so addicted. This was a cosy girl. A girl you could tell your troubles to. You could lay your head in her lap and ask her to stroke it.

Not that he did, of course. He merely lit a cigarette.

'Won't you . . . sit down?' he said.

'What I'd really like to do,' said Polly Pott, 'is to lie down – and go to sleep. I'm a wreck, Uncle Fred. I was up nearly all last night at a dance.'

'We know all about your last night's goings-on, my child,' said Lord Ickenham. 'That is why we are here. We have come on behalf of Horace Davenport, who is in a state of alarm and despondency on account of the unfriendly attitude of your young man.'

The girl laughed – the gay, wholehearted laugh of youth. Pongo remembered that he had laughed like that in the days before he had begun to see so much of his Uncle Fred.

'Ricky was marvellous last night. You ought to have seen him jumping about, trying to dodge Horace's spear.'

'He speaks of breaking Horace's neck.'

'Yes, I remember he said something about that. Ricky's got rather a way of wanting to break people's necks.'

'And we would like you to get in touch with him immediately and assure him that this will not be necessary, because Horace's behaviour towards you has always been gentlemanly, respectful – in short, *preux* to the last drop. I don't know if this public menace you're engaged to has ever heard of Sir Galahad but, if so, convey the idea that the heart of that stainless knight might have been even purer if he had taken a tip or two from Horace.'

'Oh, but everything is quite all right now. I've calmed Ricky down, and he has forgiven Horace. Has Horace been worrying?'

'That is not overstating it. Horace *has* been worrying.'

'I'll ring him up and tell him there's no need to, shall I?'

'On no account,' said Lord Ickenham. 'Pongo will handle the whole affair, acting as your agent. It would be tedious to go into the reasons for this, but you can take it from me that it is essential. You had better be toddling off, Pongo, and bringing the roses back to Horace's cheeks.'

'I will.'

'The sooner you get that cheque, the better. Run along. I will remain and pick up the threads with Polly. I feel that she owes me an explanation. The moment my back is turned, she appears to have gone and got engaged to a young plug-ugly who seems to possess all the less engaging qualities of a Borneo head-hunter. Tell me about this lad of yours, Polly,' said Lord Ickenham, as the door closed. 'You seem to like them tough. Where did you find him? On Devil's Island?'

'He brought Father home one night.'

'You mean Father brought him home.'

'No, I don't. Father couldn't walk very well, and Ricky was practically carrying him. Apparently Father had been set upon in the street by some men who had a grudge against him – I don't know why.'

Lord Ickenham thought he could guess. He was well aware that, given a pack of cards, Claude Pott could offend the mildest lamb. Indeed, it was a tenable theory that this might have been the cause of his once having been bitten by one.

'And Ricky happened to be passing, and he jumped in and rescued him.'

'How many men were there?'

'Thousands, I believe.'

'But he wouldn't mind that?'

'Oh, no.'

'He just broke their necks.'

'I expect so. He had a black eye. I put steak on it.'

'Romantic. Did you fall in love at first sight?'

'Oh, yes.'

'My nephew Pongo always does. Perhaps it's the best way. Saves time. Did he fall in love with you at first sight?'

'Oh, yes.'

'I begin to think better of this Borstal exhibit. He will probably wind up in Broadmoor, but he has taste.'

'You would never have thought so, though; he just sat and glared at me with his good eye, and growled when I spoke to him.'

'Uncouth young wart-hog.'

'He's nothing of the kind. He was shy. Later on, he got better.'

'And when he was better, was he good?'

'Yes.'

'I wish I could have heard him propose. The sort of chap who would be likely to think up something new.'

'He did, rather. He grabbed me by the wrist and nearly broke it and told me to marry him. I said I would.'

'Well, you know your own business best, of course. What does your father think of it?'

'He doesn't approve. He says Ricky isn't worthy of me.'

'What a judge!'

'And he's got an extraordinary idea into his head that if I'm encouraged I may marry Horace. He was encouraging me all this morning. It's just because Ricky hasn't any money, of course. But I don't care. He's sweet.'

'Would you call that the *mot juste*?'

'Yes, I would. Most of the time he's an absolute darling. He can't help being jealous.'

'Well, all right. I suppose I shall have to give my consent. Bless you, my children. And here is a piece of advice which you will find useful in your married life. Don't watch his eyes. Watch his knees. They will tell you when he is setting himself for a swing. And when he swings, roll with the punch.'

'But when am I going to get any married life? He makes practically nothing with his poetry.'

'Still, he may have a flair for selling onion soup.'

'But how are we going to find the money to buy the bar? And his friend won't hold the offer open for ever.'

'I see what you mean, and I wish I could help you, my dear. But I can't raise anything like the sum you need. Hasn't he any money at all?'

'There's a little bit his mother left him, but he can't get at the capital. He tried to borrow some from his uncle. Do you know the Duke of Dunstable?'

'Only from hearing Horace speak of him.'

'He seems an awful old man. When Ricky told him he wanted five hundred pounds to buy an onion soup bar, he was furious.'

'Did he say he wanted to get married?'

'No. He thought it would be better not to.'

'I don't agree with him. He should have told Dunstable all about it and shown him your photograph.'

'He didn't dare risk it.'

'Well, I think he missed a trick. The ideal thing, of course, would be if you could meet Dunstable without him knowing who you are and play upon him like a stringed instrument. Because you could, you know. You've no notion what a pretty, charming girl you are, Polly. You'd be surprised. When you came in just now, I was stunned. I would have given you anything you asked, even unto half my kingdom. And I see no reason why Dunstable's reactions should not be the same. Dukes are not above the softer emotions. If somehow we could work it so that you slid imperceptibly into his life . . .'

He looked up, annoyed. The door-bell had rung.

'Callers? Just when we need to be alone in order to concentrate. I'll tell them to go to blazes.'

He went down the passage. His nephew Pongo was standing on the mat.

## Chapter 7

Pongo's manner was marked by the extreme of agitation. His eyes were bulging, and he began to pour out his troubles almost before the door was open. There was nothing in his bearing of a young man who has just concluded a satisfactory financial deal.

'I say, Uncle Fred, he's not there! Horace, I mean. At his flat, I mean. He's gone, I mean.'

'Gone?'

'Webster told me he had just left in his car with a gentleman.'

Lord Ickenham, while appreciating his nephew's natural chagrin, was disposed to make light of the matter.

'A little after-luncheon spin through the park with a crony, no doubt. He will return.'

'But he won't, dash it!' cried Pongo, performing the opening steps of a sort of tarantella. 'That's the whole point. He took a lot of luggage with him. He may be away for weeks. And George Budd planning to unleash Erb on me if I don't pay up by Wednesday!'

Lord Ickenham perceived that the situation was more serious than he had supposed.

'Did Webster say where he was off to?'

'No. He didn't know.'

'Tell me the whole story in your own words, my boy, omitting no detail, however slight.'

Pongo marshalled his facts.

'Well, apparently the first thing that happened was that Horace, having lunched frugally off some tinned stuff, sent Webster out to take a look round and see if Ricky was hanging about, telling him — if he wasn't — to go round to the garage and get his car, as he thought he would take a drive in order to correct a slight headache.

He said it caught him just above the eyebrows,' added Pongo, mindful of the injunction not to omit details.

'I see. And then?'

'Webster came back and reported that the car was outside but Ricky wasn't, and Horace said "Thanks." And Horace went to the front door and opened it, as a preliminary to making his get-away, and there on the mat, his hand just raised to press the bell, was this bloke.'

'What sort of bloke?'

'Webster describes him as a pink chap.'

'Park Lane seems to have been very much congested with pink chaps to-day. I had a chat there with one this morning. Some convention up in town, perhaps. What was his name?'

'No names were exchanged. Horace said "Oh, hullo!" and the chap said "Hullo!" and Horace said "Did you come to see me?" and the chap said "Yes," and Horace said "Step this way," or words to that effect, and they went into the library. Webster states that they were closeted there for some ten minutes, and then Horace rang for Webster and told him to pack his things and put them in the car. And Webster packed his things and put them in the car and came back to Horace and said "I have packed your things and put them in the car, sir," and Horace said "Right ho" and shot out, followed by the pink chap. Webster describes him as pale and anxious-looking, as if he were going to meet some doom.'

Lord Ickenham pondered. The story, admirably clear in its construction and delivery, left no room for doubt concerning the probability of an extended absence on the part of the young seigneur of 52, Bloxham Mansions.

'H'm!' he said. 'Well, it's a little awkward that this should have arisen just now, my boy, because I am not really at liberty to weigh the thing and decide what is to be done for the best. Just at the moment my brain is bespoke. I am immersed in a discussion of ways and means with Polly. She is in trouble, poor child.'

All that was fine and chivalrous in Pongo Twistleton rose to the surface. He had been expecting to reel for some time beneath the stunning blow of Horace's disappearance, but now he forgot self.

'Trouble?'

He was deeply concerned. As a rule, when he fell in love at first sight, his primary impulse was a desire to reach out for the adored object and start handling her like a sack of coals, but the love with which this girl inspired him was a tender, chivalrous love. Her appeal was to his finer side, not to the caveman who lurked in all the Twistletons. He wanted to shield her from a harsh world. He wanted to perform knightly services for her. She was the sort of girl he could see himself kissing gently on the forehead and then going out into the sunset. And the thought of her being in trouble gashed him like a knife.

'Trouble? Oh, I say! Why, what's the matter?'

'The old, old story. Like so many of us, she is in sore need of the ready, and does not see where she is going to get it. Her young man has this glittering opportunity of buying a lucrative onion-soupery, which would enable them to get married, but he seeks in vain for someone to come across with the purchase price. Owing to that unfortunate affair at the Ball, he failed to enlist Horace's sympathy. The Duke of Dunstable, whom he also approached, proved equally unresponsive. I was starting to tell Polly, when you arrived, that the only solution is for her to meet Dunstable and fascinate him, and we were wondering how this was to be contrived. Step along and join us. Your fresh young intelligence may be just what we require. Here is Pongo, Polly,' he said, rejoining the girl. 'It is possible that he may have an idea. He nearly had one about three years ago. At any rate, he wishes to espouse your cause. Eh, Pongo?'

'Oh, rather.'

'Well, then, as I was saying, Polly, the solution is for you to meet the Duke, but it must not be as Ricky's *fiancée* –'

'Why not?' asked Pongo, starting to display the fresh young intelligence.

'Because he wouldn't think me good enough,' said Polly.

'My dear,' Lord Ickenham assured her, patting her hand, 'if you are good enough for me, you are good enough for a blasted, pop-eyed Duke. But the trouble is that he is the one who has to be conciliated, and it would be fatal to make a bad start. You must meet him as a stranger. You must glide imperceptibly into his life and fascinate him before he knows who you are. We want to get him saying to himself "A charming girl, egad! Just the sort I could wish my nephew Ricky to marry." And then along comes the anthropoid ape to whom you have given your heart and says he thinks so, too. All that is quite straight. But how the dickens are you to glide imperceptibly into his life? How do you establish contact?'

Pongo bent himself frowningly to the problem. He was aware of a keen agony at the reflection that the cream of his brain was being given to thinking up ways of getting this girl married to another man, but together with the agony there was a comfortable glow, as he felt that the opportunity of helping her had been accorded him. He reminded himself of Cyrano de Bergerac.

'Difficult,' he said. 'For one thing, the Duke's away somewhere. I remember Horace telling me that it was because he wouldn't go to the station and see him off that he broke up the sitting-room with the poker. Of course, he may just have been going home. He has a lair in Wiltshire, I believe.'

'No, I know where he's gone. He is at Blandings Castle.'

'Isn't that your pal Emsworth's place?'

'It is.'

'Well, then, there you are,' said Pongo, feeling how lucky it was that there was a trained legal mind present to solve all perplexities. 'You get Emsworth to invite Miss Pott down there.'

Lord Ickenham shook his head.

'It is not quite so simple as that, I fear. You have a rather inaccurate idea of Emsworth's position at Blandings. He was telling me about it at lunch and, broadly, what it amounts to is this. There may be men who are able to invite unattached and unexplained girls of great personal charm to their homes, but Emsworth is not one of them. He has a sister, Lady Constance Keeble, who holds revisionary powers over his visiting list.'

Pongo caught his drift. He remembered having heard his friend Ronnie Fish speak of Lady Constance Keeble in a critical spirit, and Ronnie's views had been endorsed by others of his circle who had encountered the lady.

'If Emsworth invited Polly to stay, Lady Constance would have her out of the place within five minutes of her arrival.'

'Yes, I understand she's more or less of a fiend in human shape,' assented Pongo. 'Never met her myself, but I have it from three separate sources – Ronnie Fish, Hugo Carmody and Monty Bodkin – that strong men run like rabbits to avoid meeting her.'

'Precisely. And so . . . Oh, my Lord, that bell again!'

'I'll go,' said Polly, and vanished in the direction of the front door.

Lord Ickenham took advantage of her absence to point out the fundamental difficulty of the position.

'You see, Pongo, the real trouble is old Mustard. If Polly had a presentable father, everything would be simple. Emsworth may not be able to issue invitations to unattached girls, but even he, I imagine, would be allowed to bring a friend and his daughter to stay. But with a father like hers this is not practicable. I wouldn't for the world say a word against Mustard – one of Nature's gentlemen – but his greatest admirer couldn't call him a social asset to a girl. Mustard – there is no getting away from it – looks just what he is – a retired Silver Ring bookie who for years has been doing himself too well on the starchy foods. And even if he were an Adonis, I would still be disinclined to let him loose in a refined English home. I say this in no derogatory sense, of course. One of my oldest pals. Still, there it is.'

Pongo felt that the moment had come to clear up a mystery. Voices could be heard in the passage, but there was just time to put the question which had been perplexing him ever since Polly Pott had glided imperceptibly into his life.

'I say, how does a chap like that come to be her father?'

'He married her mother. You understand the facts of life, don't you?'

'You mean she's his stepdaughter?'

'I was too elliptical. What I should have said was that he married the woman who subsequently became her mother. A delightful creature she was, too.'

'But why did a delightful creature marry Pott?'

'Why does anyone marry anybody? Why does Polly want to marry a modern poet of apparently homicidal tendencies? Why have you wanted to marry the last forty-six frightful girls you've met? . . . But hist!'

'Eh?'

'I said "Hist!"'

'Oh, hist?' said Pongo, once more catching his drift. The door had opened, and Polly was with them again.

She was accompanied by Lord Emsworth, not looking his best.

The ninth Earl of Emsworth was a man who in times of stress always tended to resemble the Aged Parent in an old-fashioned melodrama when informed that the villain intended to foreclose the mortgage. He wore now a disintegrated air, as if somebody had removed most of his interior organs. You see the same sort of thing in stuffed parrots when the sawdust has leaked out of them. His pince-nez were askew, and his collar had come off its stud.

'Could I have a glass of water?' he asked feebly, like a hart heated in the chase.

Polly hurried off solicitously, and Lord Ickenham regarded his brother Peer with growing interest.

'Something the matter?'

'My dear Ickenham, a disastrous thing has happened.'

'Tell me all.'

'What I am to say to Connie, I really do not know.'

'What about?'

'She will be furious.'

'Why?'

'And she is a woman who can make things so confoundedly uncomfortable about the place when she is annoyed. Ah, thank you, my dear.'

Lord Emsworth drained the contents of the glass gratefully, and became more lucid.

'You remember, my dear Ickenham, that I left you to keep an appointment with Sir Roderick Glossop, the brain specialist. My sister Constance, I think I told you, had given me the strictest instructions to bring him back to Blandings, to observe Dunstable. Dunstable's behaviour has been worrying her. He breaks furniture with pokers and throws eggs at gardeners. So Connie sent me to bring Glossop.'

'And –?'

'My dear fellow, he won't come!'

'But why should that upset you so much? Lady Constance surely can't blame you for not producing brain specialists, if they're too busy to leave London.'

Lord Emsworth moaned softly.

'He is not too busy to leave London. He refuses to come because he says I insulted him.'

'Did you?'

'Yes.'

'How?'

'Well, it started with my calling him "Pimples". He didn't like it.'

'I don't quite follow you.'

'Who do you think this Sir Roderick Glossop turned out to be, Ickenham? A boy whom I had known at school. A most unpleasant boy with a nasty, superior manner and an extraordinary number of spots on his face. I was shown in, and he said: "Well, it's a long time since we met, eh?" And I said: "Eh?" And he said: "You don't remember me, eh?" And I said: "Eh?" And then I took a good look at him, and I said: "God bless my soul! Why, it's Pimples!"'

'An affecting reunion.'

'I recall now that he seemed to flush, and his manner lost its cordiality. It took on that supercilious superiority which I had always so much resented, and he asked me brusquely to state my business. I told him all about Dunstable wanting the Empress, and he became most offensive. He said something about being a busy man and having no time to waste, and he sneered openly at what he called "this absurd fuss" that was being made about what he described as "a mere pig".'

Lord Emsworth's face darkened. It was plain that the wound still throbbed.

'Well, I wasn't going to stand that sort of thing from young Pimples. I told him not to be a conceited ass. And he, I think, called me a doddering old fool. Something of that general nature, at any rate. And one word led to another, and in the end I confess that I did become perhaps a little more outspoken than was prudent. I remembered that there had been a scandal connected with his name – something to do with overeating himself and being sick at the house supper – and rather injudiciously I brought this up. And shortly afterwards he was ringing the bell for me to be shown out and telling me that nothing would induce him to come to Blandings after what had occurred. And now I am wondering how I am to explain to Constance.'

Lord Ickenham nodded brightly. There had come into his eyes a gleam which Pongo had no difficulty in recognizing. He had observed it on several previous occasions, notably during that visit to the Dog Races just before his uncle's behaviour had attracted the attention of the police. He could read its message. It meant that some pleasing inspiration had floated into Lord Ickenham's mind, and it caused a strong shudder to pass through his frame, together with a wish that he were far away. When pleasing inspirations floated into Lord Ickenham's mind, the prudent man made for the nearest bombproof shelter.

'This is all most interesting.'

'It is a terrible state of affairs.'

'On the contrary, nothing more fortunate could have happened. I now see daylight.'

'Eh?'

'You were not here when we were holding our conference just now, my dear Emsworth, or your lightning mind would long ere this have leaped at my meaning. Briefly, the position is as follows. It is essential that young Polly . . . By the way, you don't know each other, do you? Miss Polly Pott, only daughter of Claude ("Mustard") Pott – Lord Emsworth.'

'How do you do?'

'It is essential, I was saying, that Polly goes to Blandings and there meets and fascinates Dunstable.'

'Why?'

'She desires his approval of her projected union with his nephew, a young thug named Ricky Gilpin.'

'Ah?'

'And the snag against which we had come up, when you arrived, was the problem of how to get her to Blandings. You, we felt, were scarcely in a position to invite her by herself and there are various reasons, into which I need not go, why old Mustard should not trail along. Everything is now simple. You are in urgent need of a Sir Roderick Glossop. She is in urgent need of an impressive father. I am prepared to play both roles. To-morrow, by a suitable train, Sir Roderick Glossop will set out with you for Blandings Castle, accompanied by his daughter and secretary –'

'Hey!' said Pongo, speaking abruptly.

Lord Ickenham surveyed him with mild surprise.

'You are surely not proposing to remain in London, my dear boy? Didn't you tell me that you were expecting a visit from Erb on Wednesday?'

'Oh!'

'Exactly. You must obviously get away and lie low somewhere. And what better haven could you find than Blandings Castle? But perhaps you were thinking that you would rather go there as my valet?'

'No, I'm dashed if I was.'

'Very well, then. Secretary it shall be. You follow what I am driving at, Emsworth?'

'No,' said Lord Emsworth, who seldom followed what people were driving at.

'I will run through the agenda again.'

He did so, and this time a faint light of intelligence seemed to brighten Lord Emsworth's eye.

'Oh, ah, yes. Yes, I think I see what you mean. But can you –'

'Get away with it? My dear fellow! Pongo here will tell you that on one occasion last year, in the course of a single afternoon in the suburb of Valley Fields, I impersonated with complete success not only an official from the bird shop, come to clip the claws of the parrot at The Cedars, Mafeking Road, but Mr Roddis, owner of The Cedars, and a Mr J. G. Bulstrode, a resident of the same neighbourhood. And I have no doubt that, if called upon to do so, I could have done them a very good parrot, too. The present task will be a childishly simple one to a man of my gifts. When were you thinking of returning to Blandings?'

'I should like to catch the five o'clock train this afternoon.'

'That will fit in admirably with our plans. You will go down to-day on the five o'clock train and announce that Sir Roderick Glossop will be arriving to-morrow with his secretary, and that you have invited him to bring his charming daughter. What good trains have you? The two-forty-five? Excellent. We will catch that, and there we shall be. I don't think that even you, Pongo, can pick any holes in that scenario.'

' 'I can tell you this, if you care to hear it, that you're definitely cuckoo and that everything is jolly well bound to go wrong and land us in the soup.'

'Nothing of the kind. I hope he isn't frightening you, Polly.'

'He is.'

'Don't let him. When you get to know Pongo better,' said Lord Ickenham, 'you will realize that he is always like this – moody, sombre, full of doubts and misgivings. Shakespeare drew Hamlet from him. You will feel better, my boy, when you have had a drink. Let us nip round to my club and get a swift one.'

## Chapter 8

The two-forty-five express – Paddington to Market Blandings, first stop Oxford – stood at its platform with that air of well-bred reserve which is characteristic of Paddington trains, and Pongo Twistleton and Lord Ickenham stood beside it, waiting for Polly Pott. The clock over the bookstall pointed to thirty-eight minutes after the hour.

Anyone ignorant of the difference between a pessimist and an optimist would have been able to pick up a useful pointer or two by scanning the faces of this nephew and this uncle. The passage of time had done nothing to relieve Pongo's apprehensions regarding the expedition on which he was about to embark, and his mobile features indicated clearly the concern with which he was viewing the future. As always when fate had linked his movements with those of the head of the family, he was feeling like a man floating over Niagara Falls in a barrel.

Lord Ickenham, on the other hand, was all that was jovial and debonair. Tilting his hat at a jaunty angle, he gazed about him with approval at the decorous station which has for so many years echoed to the tread of county families.

'To one like myself,' he said, 'who, living in Hampshire, gets out of the metropolis, when he is fortunate enough to get into it, *via* Waterloo, there is something very soothing in the note of refined calm which Paddington strikes. At Waterloo, all is hustle and bustle, and the society tends to be mixed. Here a leisured peace prevails, and you get only the best people – cultured men accustomed to mingling with basset hounds and women in tailored suits who look like horses. Note the chap next door. No doubt some son of the ruling classes, returning after a quiet jaunt in London to his huntin', shootin' and fishin'.'

The individual to whom he alluded was a swarthy young man

74

who was leaning out of the window of the adjoining compartment, surveying the Paddington scene through a pair of steel-rimmed spectacles. Pongo, who thought he looked a bit of a blister, said so, and the rancour of his tone caused Lord Ickenham to shoot a quick, reproachful glance at him. Feeling himself like a schoolboy going home for Christmas, he wanted happy, smiling faces about him.

'I don't believe you're enjoying this, Pongo. I wish you would try to get the holiday spirit. That day down at Valley Fields you were the life and soul of the party. Don't you like spreading sweetness and light?'

'If by spreading sweetness and light, you mean gatecrashing a strange house and –'

'Not so loud,' said Lord Ickenham warningly, 'stations have ears.'

He led his nephew away down the platform apologizing with a charming affability to the various travellers with whom the latter collided from time to time in his preoccupation. One of these, a portly man of imposing aspect, paused for an instant on seeing Lord Ickenham, as if wavering on the verge of recognition. Lord Ickenham passed on with a genial nod.

'Who was that?' asked Pongo dully.

'I haven't an idea,' said Lord Ickenham. 'I seem to have a vague recollection of having met him somewhere, but I can't place him and do not propose to institute enquiries. He would probably turn out to be someone who was at school with me, though some years my junior. When you reach my age, you learn to avoid these reunions. The last man I met who was at school with me, though some years my junior, had a long white beard and no teeth. It blurred the picture I had formed of myself as a sprightly young fellow on the threshold of life. Ah, here's Polly.'

He moved forward with elastic step and folded the girl in a warm embrace. It seemed to Pongo, not for the first time, that this man went out of his way to kiss girls. On the present occasion, a fatherly nod would amply have met the case.

'Well, my dear, so here you are. Did you have any trouble getting away?'

'Trouble?'

'I should have supposed that your father would have been

curious as to where you were off to. But no doubt you told him some frank, straightforward story about visiting a school friend.'

'I told him I was going to stay with you for a few days. Of course, he may have thought I meant that I was going to Ickenham.'

'True. He may. But it wouldn't have done to have revealed the actual facts to him. He might have disapproved. There is an odd, Puritan streak in old Mustard. Well, everything seems to be working out capitally. You're looking wonderful, Polly. If this Duke has a spark of human feeling in him, he cannot fail to fall for you like a ton of bricks. You remind me of some radiant spirit of the Spring. Pongo, on the other hand, does not. There is something worrying Pongo, and I can't make out what it is.'

'Ha!'

'Don't say "Ha!", my boy. You ought to be jumping with joy at the thought of going to a delightful place like Blandings Castle.'

'I ought, ought I? How about Lady Constance?'

'What about her?'

'She's waiting for us at the other end, isn't she? And what a pal! Ronnie Fish says she has to be seen to be believed. Hugo Carmody paled beneath his tan as he spoke of her. Monty Bodkin strongly suspects that she conducts human sacrifices at the time of the full moon.'

'Nonsense. These boys exaggerate so. Probably a gentle, sweet-faced lady of the old school, with mittens. You must fight against this tendency of yours to take the sombre view. Where you get your streak of pessimism from, I can't imagine. Not from my side of the family. Nothing will go wrong. I feel it in my bones. I am convinced that this is going to be one of my major triumphs.'

'Like that day at the Dog Races.'

'I wish you would not keep harping on that day at the Dog Races. I have always maintained that the constable acted far too precipitately on that occasion. They are letting a rather neurotic type of man into the Force nowadays. Well, if we are going to Blandings Castle for a restful little holiday, I suppose we ought to be taking our seats. I notice an official down the platform fidgeting with a green flag.'

They entered their compartment. The young man in spectacles

was still leaning out of the window. As they passed him, he eyed them keenly – so keenly, indeed, that one might have supposed that he had found in these three fellow-travellers something to view with suspicion. This, however, was not the case. Rupert Baxter, formerly secretary to Lord Emsworth and now secretary to the Duke of Dunstable, always eyed people keenly. It was pure routine.

All that he was actually feeling at the moment was that the elder of the two men looked a pleasant old buffer, that the younger seemed to have something on his mind, and that the girl was a pretty girl. He also had a nebulous idea that he had seen her before somewhere. But he did not follow up this train of thought. Substituting a travelling-cap for the rather forbidding black hat which he was wearing, he took his seat and leaned back with closed eyes. And presently Rupert Baxter slept.

In the next compartment, Lord Ickenham was attending to some minor details.

'A thing we have got to get settled before our arrival,' he said, 'is the question of names. Nothing is more difficult than to think of a good name on the spur of the moment. That day at the Dog Races, I remember, we were well on our way to the police station before I was able to select "George Robinson" for myself and to lean over to Pongo and whisper that he was Edwin Smith. And I felt all the while that, as names, they were poor stuff. They did not satisfy the artist in me. This time we must do much better. I, of course, automatically become Sir Roderick Glossop. You, Polly, had better be Gwendoline. "Polly" seems to me not quite dignified enough for one in your position. But what of Pongo?'

Pongo bared his teeth in a bitter smile.

'I wouldn't worry about me. What I am going to be called is "this man". "Ptarmigan," Lady Constance will say, addressing the butler –'

'Ptarmigan isn't a bad name.'

'"Ptarmigan, send for Charles and Herbert and throw this man out. And see that he lands on something sharp."'

'That pessimistic streak again! Think of some movie stars, Polly.'

'Fred Astaire?'

'No.'

'Warner Baxter?'

'Baxter would be excellent, but we can't use it. It is the name of the Duke's secretary. Emsworth was telling me about him. It would be confusing to have two Baxters about the place. Why, of course, I've got it. Glossop. Sir Roderick Glossop, as I see it, was one of two brothers and, as so often happens, the younger brother did not equal the elder's success in life. He became a curate, dreaming away the years in a country parish, and when he died, leaving only a copy of Hymns Ancient and Modern and a son called Basil, Sir Roderick found himself stuck with the latter. So with the idea of saving something out of the wreck he made him his secretary. That's what I call a nice, well-rounded story. Telling it will give you something to talk about to Lady Constance over the pipes and whisky in her boudoir. If you get to her boudoir, that is to say. I am not quite clear as to the social standing of secretaries. Do they mingle with the nobs or squash in with the domestic staff?'

A flicker of animation lit up Pongo's sombre eyes.

'I'll be dashed if I squash in with any domestic staff.'

'Well, we'll try you on the nobs,' said Lord Ickenham doubtfully. 'But don't blame me if it turns out that that's the wrong thing and Lady Constance takes her lorgnette to you. God bless my soul, though, you can't compare the lorgnettes of to-day with the ones I used to know as a boy. I remember walking one day in Grosvenor Square with my aunt Brenda and her pug dog Jabberwocky, and a policeman came up and said that the latter ought to be wearing a muzzle. My aunt made no verbal reply. She merely whipped her lorgnette from its holster and looked at the man, who gave one choking gasp and fell back against the railings, without a mark on him but with an awful look of horror in his staring eyes, as if he had seen some dreadful sight. A doctor was sent for, and they managed to bring him round, but he was never the same again. He had to leave the Force, and eventually drifted into the grocery business. And that is how Sir Thomas Lipton got his start.'

He broke off. During his remarks, a face had been peering in through the glass door of the compartment, and now entered a portly man of imposing aspect with a large, round head like the dome of St Paul's. He stood framed in the doorway, his manner majestic but benevolent.

'Ah,' he said. 'So it was you, Ickenham. I thought I recognized you on the platform just now. You remember me?'

Now that he was seeing him without his hat, Lord Ickenham did, and seemed delighted at the happy chance that had brought them together again.

'Of course.'

'May I come in, or am I interrupting a private conversation?'

'Of course come in, my dear fellow. We were only talking about lorgnettes. I was saying that in the deepest and fullest sense of the word there are none nowadays. Where are you off to?'

'My immediate objective is an obscure station in Shropshire of the name of Market Blandings. One alights there, I understand, for Blandings Castle.'

'Blandings Castle?'

'The residence of Lord Emsworth. That is my ultimate destination. You know the place?'

'I have heard of it. By the way, you have not met my daughter and nephew. My daughter Gwendoline and my nephew Basil – Sir Roderick Glossop.'

Sir Roderick Glossop seated himself, shooting a keen glance at Polly and Pongo as he did so. Their demeanour had aroused his professional interest. From the young man, as Lord Ickenham performed the ceremony of introduction, there had proceeded a bubbling grunt like that of some strong swimmer in his agony, while the girl's eyes had become like saucers. She was now breathing in an odd, gasping sort of way. It was not Sir Roderick's place to drum up trade by suggesting it, but he found himself strongly of the opinion that these young folks would do well to place themselves in the care of a good nerve specialist.

Lord Ickenham, apparently oblivious to the seismic upheaval which had left his nephew a mere pile of ruins, had begun to prattle genially.

'Well, Glossop, it's extraordinary nice, seeing you again. We haven't met since that dinner of the Loyal Sons of Hampshire, where you got so tight. How are all the loonies? It must be amazingly interesting work, sitting on people's heads and yelling to somebody to hurry up with the strait waistcoat.'

Sir Roderick Glossop, who had stiffened, relaxed. The monstrous suggestion that he had been intemperate at the annual banquet of the Loyal Sons of Hampshire had offended him deeply, nor had he liked that reference to sitting on people's heads. But he was a man who pined without conversation, and in order to carry on this particular conversation it appeared to be necessary to accept his companion's peculiar way of expressing himself.

'Yes,' he said, 'the work, though sometimes distressing, is as you say, full of interest.'

'And you're always at it, I suppose? You are going to Blandings Castle now, no doubt, to inspect some well-connected screwball?'

Sir Roderick pursed his lips.

'You are asking me to betray confidences, I fear, my dear Ickenham. However, I may perhaps gratify your curiosity to the extent of saying that my visit is a professional one. A friend of the family has been giving evidence of an over-excited nervous condition.'

'There is no need to be coy with me, Glossop. You are going to Blandings to put ice on the head of the chap with the egg-throwing urge.'

Sir Roderick started.

'You appear singularly well-informed.'

'I had that one straight from the stable. Emsworth told me.'

'Oh, you know Emsworth?'

'Intimately. I was lunching with him yesterday, and he went off to see you. But when I ran into him later in the day, he rather hinted that things had not gone too well between you, with the result that you had refused to interest yourself in this unbalanced egg-jerker.'

Sir Roderick flushed.

'You are perfectly correct. Emsworth's manner left me no alternative but to decline the commission. But this morning I received a letter from his sister, Lady Constance Keeble, so charming in its tone that I was constrained to change my mind. You know Lady Constance?'

'What, dear old Connie? I should say so! A lifelong friend. My nephew Basil there looks on her as a second mother.'

'Indeed? I have not yet met her myself.'

'You haven't? Capital!'

'I beg your pardon?'

'You still have that treat in store,' explained Lord Ickenham.

'Lady Constance expressed so strong a desire that I should go to Blandings that I decided to overlook Emsworth's discourtesy. The summons comes at a singularly inopportune time, unfortunately, for I have an important conference in London to-morrow afternoon. However, I have been looking up the trains, and I see that there is one that leaves Market Blandings at eight-twenty in the morning, arriving at Paddington shortly before noon, so I shall be able to make my examination and return in time.'

'Surely a single examination won't work the trick?'

'Oh, I think so.'

'I wish I had a brain like yours,' said Lord Ickenham. 'What an amazing thing. I suppose you could walk down a line of people, giving each of them a quick glance, and separate the sheep from the goats like shelling peas ... "Loony ... not loony ... This one wants watching ... This one's all right ... Keep an eye on this chap. Don't let him get near the bread-knife ..." Extraordinary. What do you do exactly? Ask questions? Start topics and observe reactions?'

'Yes, I suppose you might say – broadly – that that is the method I employ.'

'I see. You bring the conversation round to the subject of birds, for instance, and if the fellow says he's a canary and hops on to the mantelpiece and starts singing, you sense that there is something wrong. Yes, I understand. Well, it seems to me that, if it's as simple as that, you could save yourself a lot of trouble by making your examination now.'

'I do not understand you.'

'You're in luck, Glossop. The man Emsworth wants you to run the rule over is on the train. You'll find him in the compartment next door. A dark chap with spectacles. Emsworth asked me to keep an eye on him during the journey, but if you want my opinion – there's nothing wrong with the fellow at all. Connie was always such a nervous little soul, bless her. I suppose some chance remark of his about eggs gave her the idea that he had said he wanted to throw them, and she went all of a twitter. Why don't you go in and engage him in conversation and note the results? If there's anything wrong with him, that sixth sense of yours will enable you to spot it in a second. If he's all right, on the other hand, you could leave the train at Oxford and return to London in comfort.'

'It is a most admirable idea.'

'Don't mention my name, of course.'

'My dear Ickenham, you may trust me to exercise perfect discretion. The whole thing will be perfectly casual. I shall embark on our little talk quite simply and naturally by asking him if he can oblige me with a match.'

'Genius!' said Lord Ickenham.

The silence which followed Sir Roderick's departure was broken by a groan from Pongo.

'I knew something like this would happen,' he said.

'But my dear boy,' protested Lord Ickenham, 'what has happened, except that I have been refreshed by an intelligent chat with a fine mind, and have picked up some hints on deportment for brain specialists which should prove invaluable? The old Gawd-help-us will alight at Oxford –'

'So will I jolly well alight at Oxford!'

'And return to your flat? I wonder if you will find Erb waiting for you on the doorstep?'

'Oh, gosh!'

'Yes, I thought you had overlooked that point. Pull yourself together, my dear Pongo. Stiffen the sinews, summon up the blood. Everything is going to be all right. You seem thoughtful, Polly.'

'I was only wondering why Lord Emsworth called him Pimples.'

'You mean he hasn't any now? No, I noticed that,' said Lord Ickenham. 'It is so often the way. We start out in life with more pimples than we know what to do with, and in the careless arrogance of youth think they are going to last for ever. But comes a day when we suddenly find that we are down to our last half-dozen. And then those go. There is a lesson in this for all of us. Ah, Glossop, what news from the front?'

Sir Roderick Glossop radiated satisfaction.

'You were perfectly correct, my dear Ickenham. Absolutely nothing wrong. No indication whatsoever of any egg-fixation. There was no basis at all for Lady Constance's alarm. I should describe the man as exceptionally intelligent. But I was surprised to find him so young.'

'We all were once.'

'True. But I had imagined from Lady Constance's letter that he

82

was far older. Whether she said so or not, I cannot recall, but the impression I gathered was that he was a contemporary of Emsworth's.'

'Probably looks younger than he is. The country air. Or as a child he may have been fed on Bevo.'

'Ah,' said Sir Roderick non-committally. 'Well, if I am to leave the train at Oxford, I must be getting back to my compartment and collecting my things. It has been a great pleasure meeting you again, Ickenham, and I am exceedingly obliged for that very thoughtful suggestion of yours. I confess that I was not looking forward to an early morning journey. Good-bye.'

'Good-bye.'

'Good-bye,' said Polly.

'Good-bye,' said Pongo, speaking last and speaking with difficulty. He had been sitting for some moments in a deep silence, broken only by an occasional sharp, whistling intake of breath. Sir Roderick carried away with him an impression of a sombre and introspective young man. He mentioned him later in a lecture to the Mothers of West Kensington as an example of the tendency of post-war youth towards a brooding melancholia.

Lord Ickenham, too, seemed to feel that he needed cheering up, and for the remainder of the journey spared no effort to amuse and entertain. All through the afternoon he maintained a high level of sprightliness and gaiety, and it was only when they had alighted at Market Blandings station that he found himself compelled to strike a jarring note.

Market Blandings station, never a congested area, was this evening more than usually somnolent and deserted. Its only occupants were a porter and a cat. The swarthy young man got out and walked to the end of the train, where the porter was extracting luggage from the van. Polly wandered off to fraternize with the cat. And Lord Ickenham, having bought Pongo a pennyworth of butterscotch from the slot machine, was just commenting on the remissness of his host and hostess in not sending anyone down to meet so distinguished a guest, when there came on to the platform a solid man in the middle thirties. The afterglow of the sunset lit up his face, and it was at this point that Lord Ickenham struck the jarring note.

'I wonder if you remember, Pongo,' he said, 'that when you looked in on me at Ickenham the day before yesterday I mentioned that it had always been the ambition of my life to play the confidence trick on someone? Owing to all the rush and bustle of this Emsworth business, I quite forgot to tell you that yesterday morning the opportunity arose.'

'What!'

'Yes. Before coming to the Drones, I went to call on Horace Davenport, and finding him not at home, waited for a while in the street outside his flat. And while I was doing so a pink chap came along, and it seemed to me that if ever I was going to make the experiment, now was the time. There was something about this fellow that told me that I could never hope for a better subject. And so it proved. He handed me over his wallet, and I walked off with it. The whole affair was a triumph of mind over matter, and I am modestly proud of it.'

It had always been an axiom with Pongo Twistleton that his Uncle Fred was one of those people who ought not to be allowed at large, but he had never suspected that the reasons for not allowing him at large were so solidly based as this. He clutched his brow.

As had happened that day at the Dog Races, this man seemed to have taken him into a strange nightmare world.

'I sent the wallet back, of course. My interest in the experiment was purely scientific. I had no thought of vulgar gain. The chap's card was inside, and I shipped it off by registered post. And the reason why I mention it now ... Do you see the fellow coming along the platform?'

Pongo turned an ashen face.

'You don't mean —?'

'Yes,' said Lord Ickenham, with a breezy insouciance which cut his nephew like a knife, 'that's the chap.'

## Chapter 9

'His name,' said Lord Ickenham, 'is Bosham. It was on the card I found in his wallet. But I distinctly remember that the address on the card was some place down in Hampshire, not far from my own little dosshouse, so it seems extremely odd that he should be here. It looks to me like one of those strained coincidences which are so inartistic. Unless he's a ghost.'

Pongo, who might have been taken for one himself by a short-sighted man, found speech. For some moments he had been squeaking and gibbering like the sheeted dead in the Roman streets a little ere the mightiest Julius fell.

'Bosham is Lord Emsworth's son,' he said hollowly.

'Is he, indeed? I am not very well up in the Peerage. I seldom read it except to get a laugh out of the names. Then that explains it,' said Lord Ickenham heartily. 'He must have been on a visit to Blandings, and when he ran up to London for the day to get his hair cut the Duke told him on no account to fail, while there, to go and slap his nephew Horace on the back and give him his best. It was perfectly natural that his pilgrimage to Bloxham Mansions should chance to synchronize with mine. How simple these apparently extraordinary things are, when you go into them.'

'He's coming this way.'

'He would be. I presume he is here to escort us to the castle.'

'But, dash it, what are you going to do?'

'Do? Why, nothing.'

'Well, I'll bet he will. Do you mean to tell me that if a chap has the confidence trick played on him by a chap, and meets the chap again, he isn't going to set about the chap?'

'My dear boy, for a young man who has enjoyed the advantage of having a refined uncle constantly at his elbow, you seem singularly ignorant of the manners and customs of good society. We bloods do not make scenes in public places.'

'You think he will wait till later before having you pinched?'

Lord Ickenham clicked his tongue.

'My dear Pongo, you have a gift for taking the dark view that amounts almost to genius. I should imagine that the prophet Isaiah as a young man must have been very like you. Tell me – I don't want to turn till I can see the whites of his eyes – where is our friend? Does he approach?'

'He's sort of backing and filling at the moment.'

'I quite understand. It is the decent diffidence of the English upper classes. All his life he has been brought up in the creed that there is nothing that is more beastly bad form than accosting a stranger, and he is wondering if I am indeed the Sir Glossop of whom he has heard so much. He shrinks from taking a chance. I think it must be your presence that is bothering him. No doubt Emsworth completely forgot to mention that I should be accompanied by my secretary, and this has made him confused. "It may be Glossop," he is saying to himself. "I wouldn't be prepared to bet it isn't Glossop. But if it is Glossop, who's the chap with him? There was nothing in my instructions about chaps-with-Glossop." And so he backs and fills. Well, this gives us time to go further into the matter we were discussing. What on earth leads you to suppose that this Bosham will denounce me for having played the confidence trick on him? The moment I say that I am Sir Roderick Glossop, the eagerly awaited guest, he will naturally assume that he was deceived by a chance resemblance. Where is he now?'

'Just abaft the try-your-weight machine.'

'Then watch me turn and nonplus him,' said Lord Ickenham, and pivoted gracefully. 'Excuse me, sir,' he said. 'I wonder if you could inform me if there is any possibility of my obtaining a vehicle of some sort here, to take me to Blandings Castle?'

He had not overestimated the effect of his manoeuvre. Lord Bosham halted as if he had walked into a lamp-post, and stood gaping.

The heir to the Earldom of Emsworth was a slow thinker, but he was not incapable of inductive reasoning. He had been told to meet an elderly gentleman who would arrive on the two-forty-five train en route for Blandings Castle. The only elderly gentleman who had arrived on the two-forty-five train en route for Blandings Castle was the elderly gentleman before him. This elderly gentleman, therefore, must be that elderly gentleman. In which case, he was Sir Roderick Glossop, the eminent brain-specialist, and so could not be, as in that first instant of seeing his face he had been prepared to swear he was, the pleasant stranger who had relieved him of his wallet in Park Lane.

For Lord Bosham, though he lived a secluded life in a remote corner of Hampshire, was sufficiently in touch with things to know that eminent brain-specialists do not go about playing the confidence trick on people. Every young man starting out in the world, he was aware, has his choice. He can become an eminent brain-specialist, or he can become a confidence trickster. But not both.

'Are you Sir Roderick Glossop?' he asked, his round eyes drinking in those features that had seemed so familiar.

'That is my name.'

'Oh? Ah? Mine's Bosham. We – er – we haven't met before, by any chance?'

'Unfortunately, no. The loss,' said Lord Ickenham, courteously but inaccurately, 'was mine. But I have heard of you. When I saw him yesterday, Lord Emsworth spoke with a fatherly warmth of your many gifts.'

'Ah? Well, I tooled down in the car to meet you.'

'Vastly civil of you, my dear Bosham.'

'You've got some luggage in the van, I take it, what? I'll slide along and see to it.'

'Thank you, thank you.'

'Then we can tool up to the castle.'

'Precisely what I would have suggested myself. Is there a large party there?'

'Eh? Oh, no. Only my father and my aunt and the Duke and Horace Davenport.'

'Horace Davenport?'

'The Duke's nephew. Well, I'll be sliding along and seeing about that luggage.'

He slid, and Pongo resumed his imitation of the sheeted dead.

'Well?' he said, at length becoming coherent. 'Now what? On

arrival at this ghastly castle, we shall immediately find ourselves cheek by jowl with a chap who knows you, knows Miss Pott and has been a close pal of mine for years. "Hullo, Pongo!" he will say, bounding up, as we stand chatting with Lady Constance. "Hullo, Lord Ickenham! Golly, Polly, isn't this jolly, here we all are, what?" If you have nothing else to do at the moment, you might be trying that one over on your bazooka.'

Lord Ickenham did not reply. He was looking down the platform. At the far end, a reunion seemed to be taking place between Lord Bosham and the swarthy young man who had occupied the adjoining compartment on the train. They had just shaken hands, and were now engaged in conversation.

'You were saying, my boy?' he asked, coming out of his thoughts.

Pongo repeated the substance of his remarks.

'Yes, I see what you mean,' agreed Lord Ickenham. 'You must always remember, however, that there is nothing either good or bad, but thinking makes it so. Still, in feeling that a problem has arisen I am not saying that you are not right. I confess that I had not anticipated Horace. Fate seems to have arranged that this shall be Old Home Week at Blandings Castle. We only need Mustard Pott and my dear wife to have what you might call a full hand.'

'Could we get hold of him before he spills the beans, and explain things to him and ask him to sit in?'

Lord Ickenham shook his head.

'I think not. Horace is a nice boy, but he would be a total loss as a conspirator.'

'Then what are we going to do?'

'Keep cool.'

'A fat lot of help keeping cool will be.'

'This is the pessimist in you speaking again. What I was about to say was that we must keep cool and level heads and deny our identity.'

'And you think he will swallow that? Ha!'

'I wish you wouldn't say "Ha!" Why shouldn't he swallow it? Who can say what limits, if any, there are to what Horace Davenport will swallow? With an uncle like his, if he is anything of a student of heredity, he must frequently have speculated on the possibility of his little grey cells suddenly turning blue on him. I imagine that he will think that it is this disaster that has happened. Still, I feel that we would do well to separate, so that we steal upon him little by little, as it were, instead of confronting him in a solid bunch. If the distance is not too great, I shall walk to the castle, allowing you and Polly to go on ahead in the car and pave the way.'

'Or we might all walk back to London.'

'My dear boy, do try to rid yourself of this horrible defeatist attitude. You have seen for yourself how stout denial of identity affected our friend Bosham. All you have to do, when you meet Horace, is to give him a cold stare and say that your name is Basil. That in itself should carry conviction, for who would say his name was Basil if he did not know that it could be proved against him? As for Polly, I have no misgivings. She will hold her end up. She is Mustard's daughter and must have been taught to tell the tale as soon as her infant lips could lisp. And if you don't think it's difficult to say "lips could lisp", try it yourself. You might step over and explain the situation to her. And now,' said Lord Ickenham, with relish, 'we come to another small difficulty.'

A sound like the dying gurgle of a siphon of soda water proceeded from Pongo.

'Oh, golly! Don't tell me there's something else?'

A happy smile was playing over Lord Ickenham's handsome face.

'Things are certainly being made somewhat intricate for us on this little expedition of ours,' he said contentedly. 'I had anticipated strolling in over the red carpet and being accepted without demur at my face value, but apparently this is not to be.'

'What the dickens has happened?'

'It is not so much what has happened as what is going to happen. If you glance along the platform, you will note that Bosham is returning, accompanied not only by a porter in a uniform much too tight for him but by our dark friend in the spectacles. Does it not occur to you that when Bosham introduces me to him, he may feel that Sir Roderick Glossop has changed a bit since he saw him last?'

'Oh, my aunt!'

'Yes, stimulating, isn't it?'

'Perhaps Glossop didn't tell him he was Glossop.'

'If you suppose that Glossop could be alone with anyone for two minutes without telling him he was Glossop, you are a very in-different reader of character.'

'We must clear out of here at once!'

Lord Ickenham was shocked.

'Clear out? That is no way for a member of a proud family to talk. Did Twistletons clear out at Agincourt and Crecy? At Mal-plaquet and Blenheim? When the Old Guard made their last desper-ate charge up the blood-soaked slopes of Waterloo, do you suppose that Wellington, glancing over his shoulder, saw a Twistleton sneaking off with ill-assumed carelessness in the direction of Brus-sels? We Twistletons do not clear out, my boy. We stick around, generally long after we have outstayed our welcome. I feel sure that I shall be able to find some way of dealing with the matter. All it needs is a little thought, and my brain is at its brightest this evening. Run along and explain things to Polly, and I will have everything comfortably adjusted by the time you return ... Ah, Bosham, my dear fellow, I see that you have collected our impedi-menta. Very good of you to have bothered.'

'Eh? Oh no, not a bit.'

'Tell me, Bosham, is it far to the castle?'

'About a couple of miles.'

'Then I think, if you don't mind, that I will walk. It would be pleasant to stretch my legs.'

Lord Bosham seemed relieved.

'Well, that's fine, if you'd like to. Might have been a bit of a squash in the car. I didn't know Baxter was turning up. This is Mr Baxter, the Duke's secretary – Sir Roderick Glossop.'

'How do you do? I am very glad you did turn up, Mr Baxter,' said Lord Ickenham, beaming upon the dark young man, who was eyeing him with silent intentness. 'It gives me the opportunity of discussing that poor fellow on the train. I saw him go into your compartment, but I hesitated to intrude upon you and ask you what you made of him. One of my patients,' explained Lord Ickenham. 'He suffers from delusions – or did. I am hopeful that my treatment may have been effective. Certainly he seemed normal enough while he was talking to me. But in these cases a relapse often comes like a flash, and I know the presence of strangers excites him. Did he by any chance tell you he was Mussolini?'

'He did not.'

'Or Shirley Temple?'

'He told me that he was Sir Roderick Glossop.'

'Then I am in distinguished company. Not that it is anything to joke about, of course. The whole thing is terribly sad and disheartening. Evidently all my work has gone for nothing. It almost makes one lose confidence in oneself.'

'I should not have thought that you were a man who easily lost his self-confidence.'

'Kind of you to say so, my dear fellow. No, as a rule, I do not. But absolute failure like this . . . Ah, well, one must keep one's flag flying, must one not? You humoured him, I hope? It is always the best and safest plan. Well, here are my daughter and my nephew Basil, who acts as my secretary. This is Lord Bosham, my dear, Lord Emsworth's son. And Mr Baxter. I was telling them that I thought I would walk to the castle. I am feeling a little cramped after the journey. We shall meet at Philippi.'

## Chapter 10

To reach Blandings Castle from Market Blandings, you leave the latter, if you can bear to tear yourself away from one of the most picturesque little towns in England, by way of the High Street. This, ending in a flurry of old-world cottages, takes you to a broad highway, running between leafy hedges that border pasture land and barley fields, and you come eventually to the great stone gates by the main lodge and through these to a drive which winds uphill for some three-quarters of a mile. A testing bit, this last, for the indifferent pedestrian. Beach, the butler, who sometimes walked to Market Blandings and back to discipline his figure, always felt a sinking feeling as he approached it.

Lord Ickenham took it in his stride. The recent happenings on the station platform had left him pleasantly exhilarated, and he was all eagerness to get to his destination and see what further entertainment awaited him in the shape of obstacles and problems. Breasting the slope with a song on his lips, he had reached the last of the bends in the drive and was pausing to admire the grey bulk of the castle as it stood out against the saffron sky, when he observed coming towards him a man of his own age but much fatter and not half as beautiful.

'Hoy!' cried this person.

'Hoy!' responded Lord Ickenham civilly.

The fact that he had heard Horace Davenport speak of his uncle Alaric as a baldheaded old coot with a walrus moustache had enabled him to identify the newcomer without difficulty. Few coots could have had less hair than this man, and any walrus would have been proud to possess the moustache at which he was puffing.

'You the brain chap?'

Rightly concluding that this was a crisper and neater way of saying 'psychiatrist', Lord Ickenham replied that he was.

'The others are in the hall, having drinks and things. When I heard you were walking up, I thought I'd come along and meet you. Dunstable's my name. The Duke of Dunstable.'

They fell into step together. The Duke produced a bandanna handkerchief and mopped his forehead with it. The evening was warm, and he was not in the best of condition.

'I wanted a quiet talk –' he began.

'Speaking of Dukes,' said Lord Ickenham, 'did you ever hear the one about the Duke and the lady snake-charmer?'

It was a jocund little tale, slightly blue in spots, and he told it well. But though his companion was plainly amused, his chief emotion appeared to be perplexity.

'Are you really Sir Roderick Glossop?'

'Why do you ask?'

'Man at the club told me he was a pompous old ass. But you're not a pompous old ass.'

'Your friend probably met me in my professional capacity. You know how it is. One puts on a bit of dog in office hours, to impress the customers. I dare say you have done the same thing yourself in the House of Lords.'

'That's true.'

'But you were saying something about wanting a quiet talk.'

'Exactly. Before Connie could get hold of you and stuff you up with a lot of nonsense. Emsworth's sister, Lady Constance Keeble. She's like all women – won't face facts. The first thing she's going to do when she meets you is to try to pull the wool over your eyes and persuade you that he's as sane as I am. Quite understandable, no doubt. Her brother, and all that.'

'You are speaking of Lord Emsworth?'

'Yes. What did you make of him?'

'He seemed clean and sober.'

Again the Duke appeared a little puzzled.

'Why shouldn't he be sober?'

'Don't think I am complaining,' Lord Ickenham hastened to assure him. 'I was pleased.'

'Oh? Well, as I was saying, Connie will try to make you think that the whole thing has been much exaggerated and that he's simply dreamy and absent-minded. Don't let her fool you. The man's potty.'

'Indeed?'

'No question about it. The whole family's potty. You saw Bosham at the station. There's a loony for you. Goes up to London and lets a chap play the confidence trick on him. "Give me your wallet to show you trust me," says the chap. "Right ho," says Bosham. Just like that. Ever meet the other boy – Freddie Threepwood? Worse than Bosham. Sells dog-biscuits. So you can get a rough idea what Emsworth must be like. Man can't have two sons like that and be sane himself, I mean to say. You've got to start with that idea well in your head, or you'll never get anywhere. Shall I tell you about Emsworth?'

'Do.'

'Here are the facts. He's got a pig, and he's crazy about it.'

'The good man loves his pig.'

'Yes, but he doesn't want to run it in the Derby.'

'Does Emsworth?'

'Told me so himself.'

Lord Ickenham looked dubious.

'I doubt if the Stewards would accept a pig. You might starch its ears and enter it as a greyhound for the Waterloo Cup, but not the Derby.'

'Exactly. Well, that shows you.'

'It does, indeed.'

The Duke puffed at his moustache approvingly, so that it flew before him like a banner. It pleased him to find this expert in such complete agreement with his views. The man, he could see, knew his business, and he decided to abandon reserve and lay bare the skeleton in his own cupboard. He had not intended to draw attention to the dark shadow which had fallen on the house of Dunstable, but he saw now that it would be best to tell all. In the hall which he had just left, strange and disconcerting things had been happening, and he wanted a skilled opinion on them.

'A nice little place Emsworth has here,' said Lord Ickenham, as they reached the broad gravel sweep that flanked the terrace.

'Not so bad. Makes it all the sadder that he'll probably end his days in Colney Hatch. Unless you can cure him.'

'I seldom fail.'

'Then I wish,' said the Duke, coming out with it, 'that while you're here you would take a look at my nephew Horace.'

'Is he giving you cause for anxiety?'

'Acute anxiety.'

The Duke, about to unveil the Dunstable skeleton, checked himself abruptly and blew furiously at his moustache. From some spot hidden from them by thick shrubberies there had come the sound of a pleasant tenor voice. It was rendering the 'Bonny Bonny Banks of Loch Lomond', and putting a good deal of feeling into it.

'Gah! That whistling feller again!'

'I beg your pardon?'

'Chap who comes whistling and singing outside my window,' said the Duke, like the heroine of an old-fashioned novelette speaking of her lover. 'I've been trying to get to grips with him ever since I arrived, but he eludes me. Well I can wait. I've got a dozen best new-laid eggs in my room, and sooner or later . . . But I was telling you about Horace.'

'Yes, I want to hear all about Horace. Your nephew, you say?'

'One of them. My late brother's son. He's potty. The other's my late sister's son. He's potty, too. My late brother was potty. So was my late sister.'

'And where would you rank Horace in this galaxy of goofiness? Is he, in your opinion, above or below the family average?'

The Duke considered.

'Above. Decidedly above. After what happened in the hall just now, most emphatically above. Do you know what happened in the hall just now?'

'I'm sorry, no. I'm a stranger in these parts myself.'

'It shocked me profoundly.'

'What happened in the hall?'

'And always the "Bonny Bonny Banks of Loch Lomond",' said the Duke peevishly. 'A song I've hated all my life. Who wrote the beastly thing?'

'Burns, I believe. But you were going to tell me what happened in the hall.'

'Yes. So I was. It showed me that I had wronged that chap Baxter. I expect you met Baxter at the station. My secretary. He was on your train. He should have come down with me, but he insisted on remaining in London on the plea that he had work to do in connexion with a history of my family that I'm writing. I didn't believe him. It seemed to me that he had a furtive look in his eye. My feeling all along was that he was planning to go on some toot. And when Horace told me this morning that he had seen him at some dance or other a couple of nights ago, leaping about all over the place in the costume of a Corsican brigand, I was all ready for him. The moment his foot crossed the threshold, I sacked him. And then this thing happened in the hall.'

'You were going to tell me about that, weren't you?'

'I am telling you about it. It was when we were in the hall. Connie had taken your daughter out to show her the portraits in the gallery, though why any girl should be supposed to be anxious to look at that collection of gargoyles is more than I can imagine. I should be vastly surprised to learn that there was an uglier lot of devils in the whole of England than Emsworth's ancestors. However, be that as it may, Connie had taken your daughter to see them, leaving Bosham and your nephew and myself in the hall. And in comes Horace. And no sooner had I directed his attention to your nephew than he gives a jump and says "Pongo!" See? "Pongo!" Like that. Your nephew looked taken aback, and said in a low voice that his name was Basil.'

'Brave lad!'

'What?'

'I said "Brave lad!"'

'Why?'

'Why not?' argued Lord Ickenham.

The Duke turned this over for a moment, and seemed to see justice in it.

'What had happened, you see, was that Horace had mistaken him for a friend of his. Well, all right. Nothing so very remarkable about that, you are saying. Sort of thing that might happen to anyone. Quite. But mark the sequel. If Burns thought "Loch Lomond" rhymes with "before ye",' said the Duke, with a return of his peevishness, 'he must have been a borderline case.'

'And the sequel, you were about to say?'

'Eh? Oh, the sequel. I'm coming to that. Not that there are many rhymes to "Loch Lomond". Got to be fair to the chap, I suppose. Yes, the sequel. Well, right on top of this, Connie comes back with your daughter. She's charming.'

'I have not met Lady Constance.'

'Your daughter, I mean.'

'Oh, very. Her name is Gwendoline.'

'So she told us. But that didn't stop Horace from going up to her and calling her Polly.'

'Polly?'

'Polly. "Why, hullo, Polly!" were his exact words.'

Lord Ickenham reflected.

'The conclusion that suggests itself is that he had mistaken her for a girl called Polly.'

'Exactly. The very thought that flashed on me. Well, you can imagine that that made me realize that matters were grave. One bloomer of that sort – yes. But when it happens twice in two minutes, you begin to fear the worst. I've always been uneasy about Horace's mental condition, ever since he had measles as a boy and suddenly shot up to the height of about eight foot six. It stands to reason a chap's brain can't be all that way from his heart and still function normally. Look at the distance the blood's got to travel. Well, here we are,' said the Duke, as they passed through the great front door that stood hospitably open. 'Hullo, where's everybody? Dressing, I suppose. You'll be wanting to go to your room. I'll take you there. You're in the Red Room. The bathroom's at the end of the passage. What was I saying? Oh, yes. I said I began to fear the worst. I reasoned the whole thing out. A chap can't be eight foot six and the son of my late brother and expect to carry on as if nothing had happened. Something's bound to give. I remembered what he had told me about thinking he had seen Baxter at the Ball, and it suddenly struck me like a blow that he must have developed – I don't know what you call it, but I suppose there's some scientific term for it when a feller starts seeing things.'

'You mean a sublunary medulla oblongata diathesis.'

'Very possibly. I can see now why that girl broke off the engagement. She must have realized that he had got this – whatever it was you said – and decided it wasn't good enough. No girl wants a potty husband, though it's dashed hard not to get one nowadays. Here's your room. I wish you would see what you can do for the boy. Can't you examine him or something?'

'I shall be delighted to examine him. Just give me time to have a bath, and I will be at his disposal.'

'Then I'll send him to you. If there's anything to be done for him, I'd be glad if you would do it. What with him and Bosham and Emsworth and that whistling feller, I feel as if I were living in a private asylum, and I don't like it.'

The Duke stumped off, and Lord Ickenham, armed with his great sponge Joyeuse, made his way to the bathroom. He had just got back from a refreshing dip, when there was a knock at the door and Horace entered. And, having done so, he stood staring dumbly.

Horace Davenport's face had two features that called for attention. From his father he had inherited the spacious Dunstable nose; from his mother, a Hilsbury-Hepworth, the large, fawnlike eyes which distinguish that family. This nose, as he gazed at Lord Ickenham, was twitching like a rabbit's, and in the eyes behind their tortoiseshell-rimmed spectacles there was dawning slowly a look of incredulous horror. It was as if he had been cast for the part of Macbeth and was starting to run through the Banquo's ghost scene.

The events of the evening had come as a great shock to Horace. Firmly convinced for some time past that his Uncle Alaric was one of England's outstanding schizophrenetic cases, a naturally nervous disposition had led him to look on the latter's mental condition as something which might at any moment spread to himself, like a cold in the head. The double hallucination which he had so recently experienced, coming on top of the delusion he had had about seeing Baxter at the Ball, had rendered him apprehensive in the last degree, and he had welcomed the suggestion that he should get together with Sir Roderick Glossop for a quiet talk.

And now, so all his senses told him, he was suffering yet another hallucination. In the bathrobed figure before him, he could have sworn that he was gazing at his late *fiancée*'s uncle, the Earl of Ickenham.

Yet this was the Red Room, and in the Red Room, he had been specifically informed, Sir Roderick Glossop was to be found. More-over, in the other's demeanour there was no suggestion of recognition, merely a courteous air of mild enquiry.

After what seemed an age-long pause, he managed to speak.

'Sir Roderick Glossop?'

'Yes.'

'Er – my name's Davenport.'

'Of course, yes. Come in, my dear fellow. You won't mind if I dress while we are talking? I haven't left myself too much time.'

Horace watched him with a dazed eye as he dived with boyish animation into a studded shirt. The grey head, popping out a moment later at shirt's end, gave him a renewed sense of shock, so intensely Ickenhamian was it in every respect.

A sudden feeble hope came to him that this time there might be a simple explanation. It might prove to be one of those cases of extraordinary physical resemblance of which you read in the papers.

'I – er – I say,' he asked, 'do you by any chance know a man named Lord Ickenham?'

'Lord Ickenham?' said Lord Ickenham, springing into dress trousers like a trained acrobat. 'Yes. I've met him.'

'You're amazingly like him, aren't you?'

Lord Ickenham did not reply for a moment. He was tying his tie, and on these occasions the conscientious man anxious to give of his best at the dinner-table rivets his attention on the task in hand. Presently the frown passed from his face, and he was his genial self again.

'I'm afraid I missed that. You were saying –'

'You and Lord Ickenham look exactly alike, don't you?'

His companion seemed surprised.

'Well, that's a thing nobody has ever said to me before. Considering that Lord Ickenham is tall and slender – while I am short and stout . . .'

'Short?'

'Quite short.'

'And stout?'

'Extremely stout.'

A low gulp escaped Horace Davenport. It might have been the expiring gurgle of that feeble hope. The sound caused his companion to look at him sharply, and as he did so his manner changed.

'You really must forgive me,' he said. 'I fear I missed the point of what you have been saying. Inexcusable of me, for your uncle gave me your case history. He told me how in the hall this evening you mistook my daughter and nephew for old acquaintances, and there was something about thinking that a man you saw at some Ball in

London was his secretary Mr Baxter. Was that the first time this sort of thing happened?'

'Yes.'

'I see. The delusion metabolis came on quite suddenly, as it so often does. Can you suggest anything that might account for it?'

Horace hesitated. He shrank from putting his secret fears into words.

'Well, I was wondering . . .'

'Yes?'

'Is loopiness hereditary?'

'It can be, no doubt.'

'Noses are.'

'True.'

'This beezer of mine has come down through the ages.'

'Indeed?'

'So what I was wondering was, if a chap's got a dotty uncle, is he bound to catch it?'

'I would not say it was inevitable. Still . . . How dotty is your uncle?'

'Quite fairly dotty.'

'I see. Had your father any such structural weakness?'

'No. No, he was all right. He collected Japanese prints,' said Horace, with an afterthought.

'He didn't think he *was* a Japanese print?'

'Oh, no. Rather not.'

'Then that is all right. I feel sure that there need be no real anxiety. I am convinced that all that we are suffering from is some minor nervous lesion, brought about possibly by worry. Have we been worried lately?'

The question seemed to affect Horace Davenport much as it might have affected Job. He stared at his companion as at one who does not know the half of it.

'Have we!'

'We have?'

'You bet we have.'

'Then what we need is a long sea voyage.'

'But, dash it, we're a rotten sailor. Would you mind awfully if we got a second opinion?'

'By all means.'

'The other chap might simply tell us to go to Bournemouth or somewhere.'

'Bournemouth would be just as good. We came here in our car, did we not? Then directly after dinner I advise that we steal quietly off, without going through the strain of saying good-bye to anyone, and drive to London. Having reached London, we can pack anything that may be necessary and go to Bournemouth and stay there.'

'And you think that that will put us right?'

'Unquestionably.'

'And one other point. Would there be any medical objection to just one good, stiff, energetic binge in London? You see,' said Horace, with a touch of apology, 'we do rather feel, what with one thing and another, as if we wanted taking out of ourself at the moment.'

Lord Ickenham patted his shoulder.

'My dear boy, it is what any member of my profession would advise. Do we by any chance know a beverage called May Queen? Its full name is "To-morrow'll be of all the year the maddest, merriest day, for I'm to be Queen of the May, mother, I'm to be Queen of the May". A clumsy title, generally shortened for purposes of ordinary conversation. Its foundation is any good, dry champagne, to which is added liqueur brandy, armagnac, kummel, yellow chartreuse and old stout, to taste. It is a good many years since I tried it myself, but I can thoroughly recommend it to alleviate the deepest despondency. Ah!' said Lord Ickenham, as a mellow booming rose from below. 'Dinner. Let us be going down. We do not want to be late for the trough our first night at a house, do we? Creates a bad impression.'

# Chapter 11

It had been Lord Ickenham's intention, directly dinner was over, to seek out his nephew Pongo with a view to giving him a bracing pep talk. But a lengthy conference with his hostess delayed him in the drawing-room, and it was only after the subject of the Duke had been thoroughly threshed out between them that he was able to tear himself away. He found the young man eventually in the billiard-room, practising solitary cannons.

Pongo's demeanour at dinner had been such as to cause concern to an uncle and a fellow-conspirator. Solomon in all his glory, arrayed for the banquet, could not have surpassed him in splendour, but there is no question that he would have looked happier. Pongo's tie was right, and his shirt was right, and his socks were right, and the crease in his trousers was a genuine feast for the eye, but his resemblance to a fox with a pack of hounds and a bevy of the best people on its trail, which had been so noticeable all through the day, had become more pronounced than ever.

It was the cheerful, stimulating note, accordingly, that Lord Ickenham now set himself to strike. This wilting object before him was patently in need of all the cheer and stimulation he could get.

'Well, my young ray of sunshine,' he said, 'I can see by our expression that we are feeling that everything is going like a breeze. I hear you put it across Horace properly.'

Pongo brightened momentarily, as a veteran of Agincourt might have done at the mention of the name of Crispian.

'Yes, I put it across old H. all right.'

'You did indeed. You appear to have conducted yourself with admirable *sang-froid*. I am proud of you.'

'But what's the use?' said Pongo, subsiding into gloom once more. 'It can't last. Even a goop like Horace, though nonplussed for the moment, is bound to start figuring things out and arriving at the nub. Directly he sees you –'

'He has seen me.'

'Oh, my gosh! What happened?'

'We had a long and interesting conversation, and I am happy to be able to report that he is leaving immediately for Bournemouth, merely pausing in London on his way, like some butterfly alighting on a flower, in order to get pickled to the tonsils.'

Pongo, listening attentively to the *précis* of recent events, seemed grudgingly pleased.

'Well, that's something, I suppose,' he said. 'Getting Horace out of the place is better than nothing.'

His tone pained Lord Ickenham.

'You appear still moody,' he said reproachfully. 'I had supposed that my narrative would have had you dancing about the room, clapping your little hands. Is it possible that you are still finding Lady Constance a source of anxiety?'

'And that man Baxter.'

Lord Ickenham waved a cue in airy scorn of his hostess and the spectacled secretary.

'Why do you bother about Connie and Baxter? A gorilla could lick them both. What has she been doing to you?'

'She hasn't been doing anything, exactly. She's been quite matey, as a matter of fact. But my informants were right. She is the sort of woman who makes you feel that, no matter how suave her manner for the nonce, she is at heart a twenty-minute egg and may start functioning at any moment.'

Lord Ickenham nodded.

'I know what you mean. I have noticed the same thing in volcanoes, and the head mistress of my first kindergarten was just like that. It is several years, of course, since I graduated from the old place, but I can remember her vividly. The sweet, placid face . . . the cooing voice . . . but always, like some haunting strain in a piece of music, that underlying suggestion of the sudden whack over the knuckles with a ruler. Why did Baxter jar upon you?'

'He kept asking me questions about my methods of work.'

'Ah, the two secs getting together and swapping shop. I thought that might happen.'

'Then I wish you had warned me. That bird gives me the creeps.'

'He struck you as sinister, did he? I have felt the same thing myself. Our conversation on the platform left me not altogether satisfied in my mind about that young man. It seemed to me that during my explanations with reference to the poor fellow on the train who thought he was Sir Roderick Glossop I detected a certain dryness in his manner, a subtle something that suggested that, lacking our friend Bosham's Norman blood, he was equally deficient in that simple faith which the poet ranks even more highly. If you ask me, my dear Pongo, Baxter suspects.'

'Then I'm jolly well going to get out of this!'

'Impossible. Have you forgotten that Polly has to fascinate the Duke and will be lost without you beside her to stimulate and encourage? Where's your chivalry? A nice figure you would have cut at King Arthur's Round Table.'

He had found the talking point. Pongo said Yes, there was something in that. Lord Ickenham said he had known that Pongo would arrive at that conclusion, once he had really given his keen brain to the thing.

'Yes,' he said, 'we have set our hands to the plough, and we cannot sheathe the sword. Besides, I shall require your help in snitching the pig. But I was forgetting. You are not abreast of that side of our activities, are you? Emsworth has a pig. The Duke wants it. Emsworth would like to defy him, but dare not, owing to that twist in the other's character which leads him, when defied on any premises, to give those premises the works with a poker. So, on my advice, he is resorting to strategy. I have promised him that we will remove the animal from its sty, and you will then drive it across country to Ickenham, where it can lie low till the danger is past.'

It was not often that Pongo Twistleton disarranged his hair, once he had brushed it for the evening, but he did so now. Such was his emotion that he plunged both hands through those perfect waves.

'Ha!'

'I keep asking you not to say "Ha!" my boy.'

'So that's the latest, is it? I'm to become a blasted pig's chauffeur, am I?'

'A brilliant summing-up of the situation. Flaubert could not have put it better.'

'I absolutely and definitely refuse to have anything to do with the bally scheme.'

'That is your last word?'

'Specifically.'

'I see. Well, it's a pity, for Emsworth would undoubtedly have rewarded you with a purse of gold. Noblesse would have obliged. He has the stuff in sackfuls, and this pig is the apple of his eye. And you could do with a purse of gold just now, could you not?'

Pongo started. He had missed this angle of the situation.

'Oh! I didn't think of that.'

'Start pondering on it now. And while you are doing so,' said Lord Ickenham, 'I will show you how billiards should be played. Watch this shot.'

He had begun to bend over the table, a bright eye fixed on the object ball, when he glanced round. The door had opened, and he was aware of something like a death ray playing about his person.

Rupert Baxter was there, staring at him through his spectacles.

To most people at whom the efficient Baxter directed that silent, steely, spectacled stare of his there was wont to come a sudden malaise, a disposition to shuffle the feet and explore the conscience guiltily: and even those whose consciences were clear generally quailed a little. Lord Ickenham, however, continued undisturbed.

'Ah, my dear Baxter. Looking for me?'

'I should be glad if you could spare me a moment.'

'Something you want to talk to me about?'

'If you have no objection.'

'You have not come to consult me in my professional capacity, I trust? We have not been suffering from delusions, have we?'

'I never suffer from delusions.'

'No, I should imagine not. Well, come on in. Push off, Basil.'

'He can remain,' said Baxter sombrely. 'What I have to say will interest him also.'

It seemed to Pongo, as he withdrew into the farthest corner of the room and ran a finger round the inside of his collar, that if ever he had heard the voice of doom speak, he had heard it then. To him there was something so menacing in the secretary's manner that he marvelled at his uncle's lack of emotion. Lord Ickenham, having scattered the red and spot balls carelessly about the table, was now preparing to execute a tricky shot.

'Lovely evening,' he said.

'Very. You had a pleasant walk, I hope?'

'That is understating it. Ecstatic,' said Lord Ickenham, making a dextrous cannon, 'would be a better word. What with the pure air, the majestic scenery, the old gypsy feeling of tramping along the high road and the Duke's conversation, I don't know when I have enjoyed a walk more. By the way, the Duke was telling me that there had been a little friction on your arrival. He said he had handed you the two weeks' notice because Horace Davenport told him that he had seen you at a Ball in London.'

'Yes.'

'Everything satisfactory now, I hope?'

'Quite. He discovered that he had been misinformed, and apologized. I am continuing in his employment.'

'I'm glad. You wouldn't want to lose a job like that. A man can stick on a lot of side about being secretary to a Duke. Practically as good as being a Duke himself. I am afraid Basil here has no such excuse for spiritual uplift. Just an ordinary secretary – Basil.'

'A very peculiar one, I should have said.'

'Peculiar? In what respect? In the words of the bridegroom of Antigua, is it manners you mean or do you refer to his figuah?'

'He seems ignorant of the very rudiments of his work.'

'Yes, I fear poor Basil would strike a man like you as something of an amateur. He has not had your wide experience. You were Lord Emsworth's secretary once, were you not?'

'I was.'

A flush deepened the swarthiness of Rupert Baxter's cheek. He had been Lord Emsworth's secretary several times, and on each occasion his employer, aided by the breaks, had succeeded in throwing him out. He did not care to be reminded of these flaws in a successful career.

'And before that?'

'I was with Sir Ralph Dillingworth, a Yorkshire baronet.'

'Yours has been a very steady rise in the social scale,' said Lord Ickenham admiringly. 'Starting at the bottom with a humble baronet – slumming, you might almost call it – you go on to an earl and then to a duke. It does you credit.'

'Thank you.'

'Not at all. I think I've heard of Dillingworth. Odd sort of fellow, isn't he?'

'Very.'

'There was some story about him shooting mice in the drawing-room with an elephant gun.'

'Yes.'

'Painful for the family. For the mice, too, of course.'

'Most.'

'They should have called me in.'

'They did.'

'I beg your pardon?'

'I say they did.'

'I don't remember it.'

'I am not surprised.'

Rupert Baxter was sitting back in his chair, tapping the tips of his fingers together. It seemed to Pongo, watching him pallidly from afar, that if he had had a different-shaped face and had not worn spectacles he would have looked like Sherlock Holmes.

'It was unfortunate for you that I should have met the real Sir Roderick. When I saw him on the train, he had forgotten me, of course, but I knew him immediately. He has altered very little!'

Lord Ickenham raised his eyebrows.

'Are you insinuating that I am not Sir Roderick Glossop?'

'I am.'

'I see. You accuse me of assuming another man's identity, do you, of abusing Lady Constance's hospitality by entering her house under false pretences? You deliberately assert that I am a fraud and an impostor?'

'I do.'

'And how right you are, my dear fellow!' said Lord Ickenham. 'How right you are.'

Rupert Baxter continued to tap his fingertips together and to project through his spectacles as stern a glare as they had ever been called upon to filter, but he was conscious as he did so of a certain sense of flatness. Unmasked Guilt, in his opinion, should have taken it rather bigger than this man before him appeared to be doing. Lord Ickenham was now peering at himself in the mirror and fiddling with his moustache. He may have been feeling as if the bottom of his world had dropped out, but he did not look it.

'I don't know who you are –'

'Call me Uncle Fred.'

'I will not call you Uncle Fred!' said Rupert Baxter violently.

He restored his composure with a glance at Pongo. There, he felt, was Unmasked Guilt looking as Unmasked Guilt should look.

'Well, there you are,' he resumed, becoming calmer. 'The risk you run, when you impersonate another man, is that you are apt to come up against somebody to whom his appearance is familiar.'

'Trite, but true. Do you like me with my moustache like that? Or like this?'

Rupert Baxter's impatient gesture seemed to say that he was Nemesis, not a judge in a male beauty contest.

'Perhaps it would interest you now,' he said, 'to hear about the local train service.'

'Is there a milk train?' asked Pongo, speaking for the first time.

'I expect so,' said Baxter, giving him a cold look, 'but probably you would prefer to take the eight-twenty in the morning.'

Lord Ickenham seemed puzzled.

'You speak as if you were under the impression that we were leaving.'

'That is my impression.'

'You are not going to respect our little secret, then?'

'I intend to expose you immediately.'

'Even if I assure you that we did not come here after the spoons, but rather to do two loving hearts a bit of good?'

'Your motives do not interest me.'

Lord Ickenham gave his moustache a thoughtful twirl.

'I see. You are a hard man, Baxter.'

'I do my duty.'

'Not always, surely? How about the toot in London?'

'I don't understand you.'

'So you won't talk? Still, you know you went to that Ball at the Albert Hall. Horace Davenport saw you there.'

'Horace!'

'Yes, I admit that at the moment what Horace says is not evidence. But why is it not evidence, Baxter? Simply because the

Duke, after seeing him make what appeared to be two bad shots at identifying people this evening, assumes that he must also have been mistaken in thinking that he saw you at the Ball. He supposes that his young relative is suffering from hallucinations. But if you denounce me, my daughter and nephew will testify that they really are the persons he supposed them to be, and it will become clear to the Duke that Horace is not suffering from hallucinations and that when he says he saw you at the Ball he did see you at the Ball. Then where will you be?'

He paused, and in the background Pongo revived like a watered flower. During this admirably lucid exposition of the state of affairs, there had come into his eyes a look of worshipping admiration which was not always there when he gazed at his uncle.

'At-a-boy!' he said reverently. 'It's a dead stymie.'

'I think so.'

Rupert Baxter's was one of those strong, square jaws which do not readily fall, but it had undeniably wavered, as if its steely muscles were about to relax. And though he hitched it up, there was dismay in the eyes behind the spectacles.

'It doesn't follow at all!'

'Baxter, it must follow as the night the day.'

'I shall deny —'

'What's the use? I have not known the Duke long, but I have known him long enough to be able to recognize him as one of those sturdy, tenacious souls, the backbone of England, who when they have once got an idea into their fat heads are not to be induced to relinquish it by any denials. No, if you do not wish to imperil the cordial relations existing between your employer and yourself, I would reflect, Baxter.'

'Definitely,' said Pongo.

'I would consider.'

'Like billy-o.'

'If you do, you will perceive that we stand or fall together. You cannot unmask us without unmasking yourself. But whereas we, unmasked, merely suffer the passing embarrassment of being thrown out by strong-armed domestics, you lose that splendid post of yours and have to go back to mixing with baronets. And how do you know,' said Lord Ickenham, 'that next time it would even be a baronet? It might be some bounder of a knight.'

He placed a kindly hand on the secretary's arm, and led him to the door.

'I really think, my dear fellow,' he said, 'that we had better pursue a mutual policy of Live and Let Live. Let our motto be that of the great Roi Pausole – *Ne nuis pas à ton voisin*. It is the only way to get comfortably through life.'

He closed the door. Pongo drew a deep breath.

'Uncle Fred,' he said, 'there have been times, I don't mind admitting, when I have viewed you with concern –'

'You mean that afternoon down at Valley Fields?'

'I was thinking more of our day at the Dog Races.'

'Ah, yes. We did slip up a little there.'

'But this time you have saved my life.'

'My dear boy, you embarrass me. A mere nothing. It is always my aim to try to spread sweetness and light.'

'I should describe that bird as baffled, wouldn't you?'

'Baffled as few secretaries have ever been, I think. We can look upon him, I fancy, as a spent force. And now, my boy, if you will excuse me, I must leave you. I promised the Duke to drop in on him for a chat round about ten o'clock.'

## Chapter 12

In supposing that their heart-to-heart talk would cause Rupert Baxter to abandon his intention of making a public exposure of his machinations, Lord Ickenham had been correct. In his assumption that he had rendered the man behind the steel-rimmed spectacles a spent force, however, he had erred. Baxter's hat was still in the ring. At Blandings Castle he had a staunch ally in whom he could always confide, and it was to her boudoir that he made his way within five minutes of leaving the billiard-room.

'Could I speak to you for a moment, Lady Constance?'

'Certainly, Mr Baxter.'

'Thank you,' said the secretary, and took a seat.

He had found Lady Constance in a mood of serene contentment. In the drawing-room over the coffee she had had an extended interview with that eminent brain-specialist, Sir Roderick Glossop, and his views regarding the Duke, she was pleased to find, were in complete accord with her own. He endorsed her opinion that steps must be taken immediately, but assured her that only the simplest form of treatment was required to render His Grace a man who, if you put an egg into his hand, would not know what to do with it.

And she had been running over in her mind a few of his most soothing pronouncements and thinking what a delightful man he was, when in came Baxter. And within a minute, for he was never a man to beat about the bush and break things gently, he had wrecked her peace of mind as thoroughly as if it had been a sitting-room and he her old friend with a whippy-shafted poker in his hand.

'Mr Baxter!' she cried.

From anyone else she would have received the extraordinary statement which he had just made with raised eyebrows and a shrivelling stare. But her faith in this man was the faith of a little child. The strength of his personality, though she had a strong personality herself, had always dominated her completely.

'Mr BAX-ter!'

The secretary had anticipated some such reaction on her part. This spasm of emotion was what is known in the motion-picture world as 'the quick take 'um', and in the circumstances he supposed that it was inevitable. He waited in stern silence for it to expend itself.

'Are you sure?'

A flash of steel-rimmed spectacles told her that Rupert Baxter was not a man who made statements without being sure.

'He admitted it to me personally.'

'But he is such a charming man.'

'Naturally. Charm is the chief stock-in-trade of persons of that type.'

Lady Constance's mind was beginning to adjust itself to the position of affairs. After all, she reflected, this was not the first time that impostors had insinuated themselves into Blandings Castle. Her nephew Ronald's chorus-girl, to name one instance, had arrived in the guise of an American heiress. And there had been other cases. Indeed, she might have felt justified in moments of depression in yielding to the gloomy view that her visiting list consisted almost exclusively of impostors. There appeared to be something about Blandings Castle that attracted impostors as cat-nip attracts cats.

'You say he admitted it?'

'He had no alternative.'

'Then I suppose he has left the house?'

Something of embarrassment crept into Rupert Baxter's manner. His spectacles seemed to flicker.

'Well, no,' he said.

'No?' cried Lady Constance, amazed. Impostors were tougher stuff than she had supposed.

'A difficulty has arisen.'

It is never pleasant for a proud man to have to confess that scoundrels have got him in cleft sticks, and in Rupert Baxter's manner as he told his tale there was nothing of relish. But painful though it was, he told it clearly.

'To make anything in the nature of an overt move is impossible. It would result in my losing my post, and my post is all important to me. It is my intention ultimately to become the Duke's man of affairs, in charge of all his interests. I hope I can rely on you to do nothing that will jeopardize my career.'

'Of course,' said Lady Constance. Not for an instant did she contemplate the idea of hindering this man's rise to the heights. Nevertheless, she chafed. 'But is there nothing to be done? Are we to allow this person to remain and loot the house at his leisure?'

On this point, Rupert Baxter felt that he was in a position to reassure her.

'He is not here with any motive of robbery. He has come in the hope of trapping Horace Davenport into marriage with that girl.'

'What!'

'He virtually said as much. When I told him that I knew him to be an impostor, he said something flippant about not having come after the spoons but because he was trying to do what he described as "a bit of good to two loving hearts". His meaning escaped me at the time, but I have now remembered something which had been hovering on the edge of my mind ever since I saw these people at Paddington. I had had one of those vague ideas one gets that I had seen this girl before somewhere. It has now come back to me. She was at that Ball with Horace Davenport. One sees the whole thing quite clearly. In London, presumably, she was unable to make him commit himself definitely, so she has followed him here in the hope of creating some situation which will compel him to marry her.'

The fiendish cunning of the scheme appalled Lady Constance.

'But what can we do?'

'I myself, as I have explained, can do nothing. But surely a hint from you to the Duke that his nephew is in danger of being lured into a disastrous marriage –'

'But he does not know it is a disastrous marriage.'

'You mean that he is under the impression that the girl is the daughter of Sir Roderick Glossop, the brain specialist? But even so. The Duke is a man acutely alive to the existence of class distinctions, and I think that as a wife for his nephew he would consider the daughter of a brain specialist hardly –'

'Oh, yes,' said Lady Constance, brightening. 'I see what you mean. Yes, Alaric is and always has been a perfect snob.'

'Quite,' said Baxter, glad to find his point taken. 'I feel sure that it will not be difficult for you to influence him. Then I will leave the matter in your hands.'

The initial emotion of Lady Constance, when she found herself alone, was relief, and for a while nothing came to weaken this relief. Rupert Baxter, as always, seemed in his efficient way to have put everything right and pointed out with masterly clearness the solution of the problem. There was, she felt, as she had so often felt, nobody like him.

But gradually, now that his magnetic personality was no longer there to sway her mind, there began to steal over her a growing uneasiness. Specious though the theory was which he had put forward, that the current instalment of impostors at Blandings Castle had no designs on the castle's many valuable contents but were bent simply on the task of getting Horace Davenport into a morning coat and sponge-bag trousers and leading him up the aisle, she found herself less and less able to credit it.

To Lady Constance's mind, impostors were not like that. Practical rather than romantic, as she saw it, they preferred jewellery to wedding bells. They might not actually disdain the 'Voice That Breathed O'er Eden', but in their scale of values it ran a very poor second to diamond necklaces.

She rose from her chair in agitation. She felt that something must be done, and done immediately. Even in her alarm, of course, she did not consider the idea of finding Rupert Baxter and trying to argue him out of his opinions. One did not argue with Rupert Baxter. What he said, he said, and you had to accept it. Her desire was to buttonhole some soothingly solid person who would listen to her and either allay her fears or suggest some way of staving off disaster. And it so happened that Blandings Castle housed at that moment perhaps the most solid person who had ever said 'Yoicks' to a fox-hound.

In the hope that he would also prove soothing, she hurried from the room in quest of her nephew, Lord Bosham.

*

Rupert Baxter, meanwhile, feeling in need of fresh air after the mental strain to which he had been subjected, had left the house and was strolling under the stars. His wandering feet had taken him to that velvet lawn which lay outside the Garden Suite. There, pacing up and down, brow knitted and hands clasped behind back, he gave himself up to thought.

His admission to Lady Constance that there was nothing which he himself could do in this situation which called so imperiously for decisive action, had irked Rupert Baxter and wounded his self-esteem. That remark of Pongo's, moreover, about a dead stymie still rankled in his bosom like a poisoned dart. He was not accustomed to being laid dead stymies by the dregs of the underworld. Was there, he asked himself, no method by which he could express his personality, no means whereby he could make his presence felt? He concentrated on the problem, exercising his brain vigorously.

It often happens that great brains, when vigorously exercised, find a musical accompaniment of assistance to their activities. Or, putting it another way, thinkers, while thinking, frequently whistle. Rupert Baxter did, selecting for his purpose a melody which had always been a favourite of his – the 'Bonny Bonny Banks of Loch Lomond'.

If he had been less preoccupied, he would have observed that at about the fourth bar a certain liveliness had begun to manifest itself behind the french window which he was passing. It opened softly, and a white-moustached head peered furtively out. But he was preoccupied, and consequently did not observe it. He reached the end of the lawn, ground a heel into the immemorial turf and turned. Starting his measured walk anew, he once more approached the window.

He was now singing. He had a pleasant tenor voice.

> 'You take the high road
> And I'll take the low road,
> And I'll be in Scotland a-FORE ye.
> For I and my true love
> Will never meet again –'

The starlight gleamed on a white-moustached figure.

'On the bonny bonny BANKS of Loch LO –'

Something whizzed through the night air . . . crashed on Rupert Baxter's cheek . . . spread itself in sticky ruin . . .

And simultaneously there came from the Garden Suite the sudden, sharp cry of a strong man in pain.

It was perhaps half an hour after he had left it that Lord Ickenham returned to the billiard-room. He found Pongo still there, but no longer alone. He had been joined by Lord Bosham, who had suggested a hundred up, and Lord Ickenham found the game nearing its conclusion, with Pongo, exhilarated by recent happenings, performing prodigies with the cue. He took a seat, and with a decent respect for the amenities waited in silence until the struggle was over.

Lord Bosham resumed his coat.

'Jolly well played, sir,' he said handsomely, a gallant loser. 'Jolly good game. Very jolly, the whole thing.' He paused, and looked at Lord Ickenham enquiringly. The latter had clicked his tongue and was shaking his head with an air of rebuke. 'Eh?' he said.

'It was simply that the irony of the thing struck me,' explained Lord Ickenham. 'Tragedy has been stalking through this house: doctors have been telephoned for, sick rooms made ready, cool compresses prepared: and here are you two young men carelessly playing billiards. Fiddling while Rome burns is about what it amounts to.'

'Eh?' said Lord Bosham again, this time adding a 'What?' to lend the word greater weight. He found him cryptic.

'Somebody ill?' asked Pongo. 'Not Baxter?' he went on, a note of hope in his voice.

'I would not say that Baxter was actually ill,' said Lord Ickenham, 'though no doubt much bruised in spirit. He got an egg on the left cheek-bone. But soap and water will by now have put this right. Far more serious is the case of the Duke. It was he who threw the egg, and overestimating the limberness of what is known in America, I believe, as the old soupbone, he put his shoulder out. I left him drinking barley-water with his arm in a sling.'

'I say!' said Lord Bosham. 'How dashed unpleasant for him.'

'Yes, he didn't seem too elated about it.'

'Still,' argued Pongo, pointing out the bright side, 'he got Baxter all right?'

'Oh, he got him squarely. I must confess that my respect for the Duke has become considerably enhanced by to-night's exhibition of marksmanship. Say what you will, there is something fine about our old aristocracy. I'll bet Trotsky couldn't hit a moving secretary with an egg on a dark night.'

A point occurred to Lord Bosham. His was rather a slow mind, but he had a way of getting down to essentials.

'Why did old Dunstable bung an egg at Baxter?'

'I thought you might want to know that. Events moved towards the big moment with the inevitability of Greek tragedy. There appears to be a member of the gardening staff of Blandings Castle who has a partiality for the "Bonny Bonny Banks of Loch Lomond", and he whistles and sings it outside the Duke's window, with the result that the latter has for some time been lying in wait for him with a basket of eggs. To-night, for some reason which I am unable to explain, Baxter put himself on as an understudy. The Duke and I were in the Garden Suite, chatting of this and that, when he suddenly came on the air and the Duke, diving into a cupboard like a performing seal, emerged with laden hands and started to say it with eggs. I should have explained that he has a rooted distaste for that particular song. I gather that his sensitive ear is offended by that rather daring rhyme – "Loch Lomond" and "afore ye". Still, if I had given the matter more thought, I would have warned him. You can't throw eggs at his age without –'

The opening of the door caused him to suspend his remarks. Lady Constance came in. Her sigh of relief as she saw Lord Bosham died away as she perceived the low company he was keeping.

'Oh!' she said, surveying his foul associates with unconcealed dislike, and Pongo, on whom the first full force of her gaze had been turned, shook like a jelly and fell backwards against the billiard-table.

Lord Ickenham, as usual, remained suave and debonair.

'Ah, Lady Constance. I have just been telling the boys about the Duke's unfortunate accident.'

'Yes,' said Lord Bosham. 'It's true, is it, that the old bird has bust a flipper?'

'He has wrenched his shoulder most painfully,' assented Lady Constance, with a happier choice of phrase. 'Have you finished your game, Bosham? Then I would like to speak to you.'

She led her nephew out, and Lord Ickenham looked after her thoughtfully.

'Odd,' he said. 'Surely her manner was frigid? Did you notice a frigidity in her manner, Pongo?'

'I don't know about her manner. Her eye was piping hot,' said Pongo, who was still quivering.

'Warm eye, cold manner ... This must mean something. Can Baxter have been blowing the gaff, after all? But no, he wouldn't dare. I suppose it was just a hostess's natural reaction to having her guests wrench themselves asunder and involve her in a lot of fuss with doctors. Let us dismiss her from our thoughts, for we have plenty of other things to talk about. To begin with, that pig-snitching scheme is off.'

'Eh?'

'You remember I outlined it to you? It was to have started with you driving Emsworth's pig to Ickenham and ended with him gratefully pressing purses of gold into your hand, but I'm afraid it is not to be. The Duke's stranglehold on Emsworth, you will recall, was the fact that if the latter did not obey his lightest word he would wreck the home with a poker. This accident, of course, has rendered him incapable of any serious poker-work for some time to come, and Emsworth, seizing his advantage like a master-strategist, has notified him that he cannot have the pig. So he no longer wishes it snitched.'

Pongo had listened to this exposition with mixed feelings. On the whole, relief prevailed. A purse of gold would undoubtedly have come in uncommonly handy, but better, he felt, to give it a miss than to pass a night of terror in a car with a pig. Like so many sensitive young men, he shrank from making himself conspicuous, and only a person wilfully blind to the realities of life could deny that you made yourself dashed conspicuous, driving pigs across England in cars.

'Well,' he said, having considered, 'I could have used a purse of gold, but I don't know that I'm sorry.'

'You may be.'

'What do you mean?'

'Another complication has arisen, which is going to make it a little difficult for us to linger here and look about at our leisure for ways of collecting cash.'

'Oh, my gosh, what's wrong now?'

'I would not say that there was anything *wrong*. This is just an additional obstacle, and one welcomes obstacles. They put one on one's mettle and bring out the best in one.'

Pongo danced a step or two.

'Can't you tell me what has happened?'

'I will tell you in a word. You know Polly's minstrel boy. The poet with a punch.'

'What about him?'

'He will shortly be with us.'

'What?'

'Yes, he's joining the troupe. When we were alone together, after the tumult and the shouting had died and the captains and kings – I allude to Emsworth, Connie and the doctor – had departed, the Duke confided in me that he was going to show Emsworth what was what. That pig, he said, had been definitely promised to him, and if Emsworth thought he could double-cross him, he was dashed well mistaken. He intends to steal the pig, and has sent for Ricky Gilpin to come and do it. In my presence, he dictated a long telegram to the young man, commanding his instant presence.'

'But if Ricky comes here and meets Miss Pott, we shall be dished. You can't fool a hardheaded bird like that the way we did Horace.'

'No. That is why I called it an obstacle. Still, he will not actually be in residence at the castle. The Duke's instructions to him were to take a room at the Emsworth Arms. He may not meet Polly.'

'A fat chance!'

'Pretty obese, I admit. Still, we must hope for the best. Pull yourself together, my dear Pongo. Square the shoulders and chuck out the chest. Sing like the birdies sing – Tweet, tweet-tweet, tweet-tweet.'

'If you're interested in my plans, I'm going to bed.'

'Yes, do, and get a nice rest.'

'Rest!'

'You think you may have some difficulty in dropping off? Count sheep.'

'Sheep! I shall count Baxters and Lady Constances and loony uncles. Ha!' said Pongo, withdrawing.

Lord Ickenham took up a cue and gave the white ball a pensive tap. He was a little perplexed. The reference to Baxter and Lady Constance he could understand. It was the allusion to loony uncles that puzzled him.

Lady Constance Keeble was a gifted *raconteuse*. She had the knack of telling a story in a way that left her audience, even when it consisted of a nephew who had to have the He-and-She jokes in the comic papers explained to him, with a clear grasp of what she was talking about. After a shaky start, Lord Bosham followed her like a bloodhound. Long before she had finished speaking, he had gathered that what Blandings Castle was overrun with was impostors, not mice.

His first words indicated this.

'What ho!' he said. 'Impostors!'

'Impostors!' said Lady Constance, driving it home.

'What ho, what ho!' said Lord Bosham, giving additional proof that he was alive to the gravity of the situation.

A silence followed. Furrows across his forehead and a tense look on his pink face showed that Lord Bosham was thinking.

'Then, by Jove,' he said, 'this bird is the bird, after all! I thought for a while,' he explained, 'that he couldn't be the bird, but now you've told me this it's quite clear he must be the bird. The bird in the flesh, by Jingo! Well, I'm dashed!'

Lady Constance was very seldom in the mood for this sort of thing, and to-night after the nervous strain to which she had been subjected she was less in the mood for it than ever.

'What *are* you talking about, George?'

'This bird,' said Lord Bosham, seeing that he had not made himself clear. 'It turns out he was the bird, after all.'

'Oh, George!' Lady Constance paused for an instant. It was a hard thing that she was going to say, but she felt she must say it. 'Really, there are times when you are exactly like your father!'

'The confidence-trick bird,' said Lord Bosham, annoyed at her slowness of comprehension. 'Dash it, you can't have forgotten me telling you about the suave bimbo who got away with my wallet in Park Lane.'

Lady Constance's fine eyes widened.

'You don't mean –?'

'Yes, I do. That's just what I do mean. Absolutely. When I met him at the station, the first thing I said to myself was "What ho, the bird!" Then I said to myself: "What ho, no, not the bird." Because you had told me he was a big bug in the medical world. But now you tell me he isn't a big bug in the medical world –'

Lady Constance brought her hand sharply down on the arm of her chair.

'This settles it! Mr Baxter was wrong.'

'Eh?'

'Mr Baxter thinks that the reason these people have come here is that they are trying to trap Horace Davenport into marrying the girl. I don't believe it. They are after my diamond necklace. George, we must act immediately!'

'How?' asked Lord Bosham, and for the second time since their conference had begun Lady Constance was struck by the resemblance of his thought-processes to those of a brother whom she had often wanted to hit over the head with a blunt instrument.

'There is only one thing to do. We must –'

'But half a jiffy. Aren't you missing the nub? If you know these bounders are wrong 'uns, why don't we just whistle up the local police force?'

'We can't. Do you suppose I did not think of that? It would mean that Mr Baxter would lose his position with Alaric.'

'Eh? Why? What? Which? Wherefore? Why would Baxter lose his posish?'

It irked Lady Constance to be obliged to waste valuable time in order to explain the position of affairs, but she did it.

'Oh, ah?' said Lord Bosham, enlightened. 'Yes, I see. But couldn't he get another job?'

'Of course he could. But he was emphatic about wishing to continue in Alaric's employment, so what you suggest is out of the question. We must –'

'I'll tell you one thing. I don't intend to be far away from my gun these next few days. This is official.'

Lady Constance stamped her foot. It was not an easy thing for a sitting woman to do impressively, but she did it in a way that effectually silenced a nephew who in his boyhood had frequently been spanked by her with the back of a hairbrush. Lord Bosham, who had intended to speak further of his gun, of which he was very fond, desisted.

'Will you please not keep interrupting me, George! I say there is only one thing to do. We must send for a detective to watch these people.'

'Why, of course!' Like his younger brother, Frederick Threepwood, now over in the United States of America selling the dog-biscuits manufactured by the father of his charming wife, Lord Bosham was a great reader of thrillers, and anything about detectives touched a ready chord in him. 'That's the stuff! And you know just the man, don't you?'

'I?'

'Wasn't there a detective here last summer?'

Lady Constance shuddered. The visit of the person to whom he alluded had not passed from her memory. Sometimes she thought it never would. Occasionally in the late afternoon, when the vitality is low and one tends to fall a prey to strange, morbid fancies, she had the illusion that she was still seeing that waxed moustache of his.

'Pilbeam!' she cried. 'I would rather be murdered in my bed than have that man Pilbeam in the house again. Don't you know any detectives?'

'Me? No. Why should I know any ... By Jove, yes, I do, though,' said Lord Bosham, inspired. 'By Jingo, now I come to think of it, of course I do. That man of Horace's.'

'What man of Horace's?'

Lord Bosham dissembled. Belatedly, he had realized that he was on the verge of betraying confidences. Horace, he recalled, when unburdening his soul during their drive from London, had sworn him to the strictest secrecy on the subject of his activities as an employer of private investigators.

'Well, when I say he was a man of Horace's, of course I'm sort of speaking loosely. He was a fellow Horace told me about that a friend of his engaged to – to – er – do something or other.'

'And did he do it?'

'Oh, yes, he did it.'

'He is competent, then?'

'Oh, most competent.'

'What is his name?'

'Pott. Claude Pott.'

'Do you know his address?'

'I expect it would be in the book.'

'Then go and speak to him now. Tell him to come down here immediately.'

'Right ho,' said Lord Bosham.

## Chapter 13

The Duke's decision, on receiving Lord Emsworth's ultimatum regarding the Empress of Blandings, to mobilize his nephew Ricky and plunge immediately into power politics was one which would have occasioned no surprise to anybody acquainted with the militant traditions of his proud family. It was this man's father who had twice cut down the barbed wire fence separating the garden of his villa in the South of France from the local golf links. His grandfather, lunching at his club, had once rubbed the nose of a member of the committee in an unsatisfactory omelette. The Dukes of Dunstable had always been men of a high and haughty spirit, swift to resent affronts and institute reprisals – the last persons in the world, in short, from whom you could hope to withhold pigs with impunity.

His shoulder, thanks to the prompt treatment it had received, had soon ceased to pain him. Waking next morning, he found himself troubled physically by nothing worse than an uncomfortable stiffness. But there was no corresponding improvement in his spiritual condition. Far into the night he had lain brooding on Lord Emsworth's chicanery, and a new day brought no relief. The bitterness still persisted, and with it the grim determination to fight for his rights.

At lunch-time a telegram came from his nephew saying that he was catching the five o'clock train, and at ten o'clock on the following morning, after another wakeful night, he summoned his secretary, Rupert Baxter, and bade him commandeer a car from the castle garage and drive him to the Emsworth Arms. He arrived there at half-past ten precisely, and a red-haired, thick-set, freckled young man came bounding across the lounge to greet him.

Between Horace Davenport and his cousin Alaric Gilpin there was nothing in the nature of a family resemblance. Each had inherited his physique from his father, and the father of Ricky Gilpin had been an outsize gentleman with a chest like an all-in wrestler's. This chest he had handed down to his son, together with enough muscle to have fitted out two sons. Looking at Ricky, you might be a little surprised that he wrote poetry, but you had no difficulty in understanding how he was able to clean up costermongers in Covent Garden.

But though externally as intimidating as ever and continuing to give the impression of being a young man with whom no prudent person would walk down a dark alley, Ricky Gilpin on this April morning was feeling a sort of universal benevolence towards all created things. A child could have played with him, and the cat attached to the Emsworth Arms had actually done so. Outwardly tough, inwardly he was a Cheeryble Brother.

There is nothing that so braces a young man in love as a statement on the part of the girl of his dreams, after events have occurred which have made him think her ardour has begun to cool, that he is the only man for her, and that though she may have attended dances in the company of Zulu warriors the latter are to be looked on as the mere playthings of an idle hour. Polly Pott's assurance after that scene at the Bohemian Ball that Horace Davenport was a purely negligible factor in her life had affected Ricky profoundly. And on top of that had come his uncle's telegram.

That telegram, he considered, could mean only one thing. He was about to be afforded the opportunity of placing him under an obligation – of putting him in a position, in short, where he could scarcely fail to do the decent thing in return. The Duke's attitude in the matter of sympathy and support for that onion soup project would, he felt, be very different after he had been helped out of whatever difficulty it was that had caused him to start dispatching SOSs.

It was a buoyant and optimistic Ricky Gilpin who had caught the five o'clock train to Market Blandings on the previous afternoon, and it was a gay and effervescent Ricky Gilpin who now bounded forward with a hamlike hand outstretched. Only then did he observe that his relative's right arm was in a sling.

'Good Lord, Uncle Alaric,' he cried, in a voice vibrant with dismay and concern, 'have you hurt yourself? I'm so sorry. What a shame! How absolutely rotten! How did it happen?'

The Duke snorted.

'I put my shoulder out, throwing an egg at my secretary.'

Many young men, on receipt of this information, would have said the wrong thing. Ricky's manner, however, was perfect. He placed the blame in the right quarter.

'What the dickens was he doing, making you throw eggs at him?' he demanded indignantly. 'The man must be an ass. You ought to sack him.'

'I'm going to, directly we've had our talk. It was only this morning that I found out he was the feller. Ever since I came here,' explained the Duke, 'there's been a mystery man whistling the "Bonny Bonny Banks of Loch Lomond" day in and day out on the lawn outside my room. Got on my nerves. Beastly song.'

'Foul.'

'I wasn't going to stand it.'

'Quite right.'

'I laid in eggs.'

'Very sensible.'

'To throw at him.'

'Of course.'

'Last night, there he was again with his "You take the high road" and all the rest of it, and I loosed off. And this morning Connie comes to me and says I ought to be ashamed of myself for behaving like that to poor Mr Baxter.'

'What an absolutely imbecile thing to say! Who is this fathead?'

'Emsworth's sister. Lord Emsworth. Blandings Castle. I'm staying there. She's potty, of course.'

'Must be. Any balanced woman would have seen in a second that you had right on your side. It seems to me, Uncle Alaric,' said Ricky, with warmth, 'that you have been subjected to a campaign of deliberate and systematic persecution, and I'm not surprised that you decided to send for me. What do you want me to do? Throw some more eggs at this man Baxter? Say the word, and I start to-day.'

If his arm had not been in a sling, the Duke would have patted his nephew on the back. He was conscious of a keen remorse for having so misjudged him all these years. Ricky Gilpin might have his faults – one looked askance at that habit of his of writing poetry – but his heart was sound.

'No,' he said. 'After to-night there won't be any Baxter to throw eggs at. I sacked him a couple of days ago, and with foolish kindheartedness took him back, but this time it's final. What I've come to talk to you about is this pig.'

'What pig would that be?'

'Emsworth's. And there's another high-handed outrage!'

Ricky was not quite able to follow the trend of his uncle's remarks.

'They've been setting the pig on you?' he asked, groping.

'Emsworth promised to give it to me.'

'Oh, I see.'

'Nothing down in writing, of course, but a gentleman's agreement, thoroughly understood on both sides. And now he says he won't.'

'What!' Ricky had not thought that human nature could sink so low. 'You mean he intends to go back on his sacred word? The man must be a louse of the first water.'

The Duke was now quite certain that he had been all wrong about this splendid young man.

'That's how it strikes you, eh?'

'It is how it would strike any right-thinking person. After all, one has a certain code.'

'Exactly.'

'And one expects other people to live up to it.'

'Quite.'

'So I suppose you want me to pinch this pig for you?' said Ricky.

The Duke gasped. His admiration for his nephew had now reached boiling point. He had been expecting to have to spend long minutes in tedious explanation. It was not often, he felt, that you found in the youth of to-day such lightning intelligence combined with so fine a moral outlook.

'Precisely,' he said. 'When you're dealing with men like Emsworth, you can't be too nice in your methods.'

'I should say not. Anything goes. Well, how do I set about it? I shall require some pointers, you know.'

'Of course, of course, of course. You shall have them. I have been giving this matter a great deal of thought. I lay awake most of last night –'

'What a shame!'

'– and before I went to sleep I had my plan of campaign mapped out to the last detail. I examined it this morning, and it seems to me flawless. Have you a pencil and a piece of paper?'

'Here you are. I'll tear off the top page. It has a few rough notes for a ballade on it.'

'Thanks. Now then,' said the Duke, puffing at his moustache under the strain of artistic composition, 'I'll draw a map for you. Here's the castle. Here's my room. It's got a lawn outside it. Lawn,' he announced, having drawn something that looked like a clumsily-fried egg.

'Lawn,' said Ricky, looking over his shoulder. 'I see.'

'Now along here, round the end of the lawn, curves the drive. It curves past a thick shrubbery – that's at the farther side of the lawn – and then curves past a meadow which adjoins the kitchen garden. In this meadow,' said the Duke, marking the spot with a cross, 'is the sty where the pig resides. You see the strategic significance of this?'

'No,' said Ricky.

'Nor did I,' admitted the Duke handsomely, 'till I was brushing my teeth this morning. Then it suddenly flashed on me.'

'You have an extraordinarily fine brain, Uncle Alaric. I've sometimes thought you would have made a great general.'

'Look at it for yourself. Anybody removing that pig from its sty could dive into the shrubbery with it, thus securing excellent cover, and the only time he would be in danger of being observed would be when he was crossing the lawn to my room. And I propose to select a moment for the operation when there will be no eye-witnesses.'

Ricky blinked.

'I don't quite follow that, Uncle Alaric. You aren't going to keep the animal in your room?'

'That is exactly what I am going to do. It's on the ground floor, with serviceable french windows. What simpler than to bring the pig in through these windows and lodge it in the bathroom?'

'What, and keep it there all night?'

'Who said anything about night? It enters the bathroom at two o'clock in the afternoon. Use your intelligence. At two o'clock in the afternoon everyone's at lunch. Butler, footmen and so forth, all in the dining-room. Maids of all descriptions, their work in the bedrooms completed during the morning, in the kitchen or the housekeeper's room or wherever they go. And the pig-man, I happen to know, off having his dinner. The coast is clear. A thousand men could steal a thousand pigs from the piggeries of Blandings Castle at two o'clock in the afternoon, and defy detection.'

Ricky was impressed. This was unquestionably GHQ stuff.

'Throughout the afternoon,' continued the Duke, 'the pig remains in the bathroom, and continues to do so till nightfall. Then —'

'But, Uncle Alaric, somebody's sure to go into the bathroom before that. Housemaids with clean towels . . .'

The Duke swelled belligerently.

'I'd like to see anybody go into my bathroom, after I've issued orders that they're not to. I shall stay in my room all through the day, refusing admittance to one and all. I shall have my dinner there on a tray. And if any dashed housemaid thinks she's going to muscle in with clean towels, she'll soon find herself sent off with a flea in her ear. And during dinner you will return. You will have a car waiting here' — he prodded the sketch map with a large thumb — 'where the road curves along the bushes at the end of the lawn. You will remove the pig, place it in the car and drive it to my house in Wiltshire. That is the plan I have evolved. Is there anything about it you don't understand?'

'Not a thing, Uncle Alaric!'

'And you think you can do it?'

'On my head, Uncle Alaric. It's in the bag. And may I say, Uncle Alaric, that I don't believe there's another man in England who could have thought all that out as you have done. It's genius.'

'Would you call it that?'

'I certainly would.'

'Perhaps you're right.'

'I know I'm right. It's the most extraordinary exhibition of sheer ice-cold brainwork that I've ever encountered. What did you do in the Great War, Uncle Alaric?'

'Oh, this and that. Work of national importance, you know.'

'I mean, they didn't put you on the Staff?'

'Oh, no. Nothing of that sort.'

'What waste! What criminal waste! Thank God we had a Navy.'

The most delightful atmosphere now prevailed in the lounge of the Emsworth Arms. The Duke said it was extremely kind of Ricky to be so flattering. Ricky said that 'flattering' was surely hardly the word, for he had merely given a frank opinion which would have been the opinion of anybody who recognized genius when they came across it. The Duke said would Ricky have a drink? Ricky, thanking him profusely, said it was a bit early. The Duke asked Ricky if he had been writing anything lately. Ricky said not just lately, but he had a sonnet coming out in the *Poetry Review* next month. Dashed interesting things, sonnets, said the Duke, and asked if Ricky had regular hours for sitting at his desk or did he wait for an inspiration. Ricky said he found the policy that suited him best was to lurk quietly till an idea came along and then jump out and land on the back of its neck with both feet. The Duke said that if somebody offered him a million pounds he himself would be incapable of writing a sonnet. Ricky said Oh, it was just a knack – not to be compared with work that took real, hard thinking, and gave as an instance of such work the planning out of campaigns for stealing pigs. To do that, said Ricky, a fellow really had to have something.

There was, in fact, only one word to describe what was in progress in that dim lounge – the word 'Love-feast'. And it was a thousand pities, therefore, that Ricky should have proceeded, as he now did, to destroy the harmony.

Poets, as a class, are business men. Shakespeare describes the poet's eye as rolling in a fine frenzy from heaven to earth, from earth to heaven, and giving to airy nothing a local habitation and a name, but in practice you will find that one corner of that eye is generally glued on the royalty returns. Ricky was no exception. Like all poets, he had his times of dreaminess, but an editor who sent him a cheque for a pound instead of the guinea which had been agreed upon as the price of his latest *morceau* was very little older before he found a sharp letter on his desk or felt his ear burning at what was coming over the telephone wire. And now, having accepted this commission and discussed it in broad outline, he was anxious to get the terms settled.

'By the way, Uncle Alaric,' he said.

'Hey?' said the Duke, who had been interrupted in what promised to be rather a long story about a man he had known in South Africa who had once written a limerick.

Ricky, though feeling that this sort of negotiation would have been better placed in the hands of one's agent, was resolute.

'There's just one small point,' he said. 'Would you rather give me your cheque before I do the job, or after?'

The cosy glow which had been enveloping the Duke became shot through by a sudden chill. It was as if he had been luxuriating in a warm shower-bath, and some hidden hand had turned on the cold tap.

'My cheque? What do you mean, my cheque?'

'For two hundred and fifty pounds.'

The Duke shot back in his chair, and his moustache, foaming upwards as if a gale had struck it, broke like a wave on the stern and rockbound coast of the Dunstable nose. A lesser moustache, under the impact of that quick, agonized expulsion of breath, would have worked loose at the roots. His recent high opinion of his nephew had undergone a sharp revision. Though there were many points on which their souls would not have touched, he was at one with Mr Pott in his dislike of parting with money. Only a man of very exceptional charm could have retained his esteem after asking him for two hundred and fifty pounds.

'What the devil are you talking about?' he cried.

Ricky was looking anxious, like one *vis-à-vis* with a tiger and not any too sure that the bars of the cage are to be depended on, but he continued resolute.

'I am taking it for granted that you will now let me have the money to buy that onion soup bar. You remember we discussed it in London a few days ago. At that time five hundred was the price, but the man has since come down to two hundred and fifty, provided the cash is in his hands by the end of the week. The most convenient thing for me, of course, would be if you would write out a cheque now. Then I could mail it to him this morning and he would get it first thing to-morrow. Still, suit yourself about that. Just so long as I get the money by Friday –'

'I never heard anything so dashed absurd in my life!'

'You mean you won't give me two hundred and fifty pounds?'

'Of course I mean I won't give you two hundred and fifty pounds,' said the Duke, recovering his moustache and starting to chew it. 'Gah!' he said, summing up.

The love-feast was over.

A tense silence fell upon the lounge of the Emsworth Arms.

'I thought I had heard the last of that silly nonsense,' said the Duke, breaking it. 'What on earth do you want with an onion soup bar?'

It was perhaps the memory of how close they had been to one another only a few brief minutes back – two of the boys kidding back and forth about the Sonnet question, as you might say – that decided Ricky to be frank with his uncle. He was conscious as he spoke that frankness is a quality that can be overdone and one which in the present case might lead to disagreeable consequences, but some powerful argument had to be produced if there was to be a change for the better in the other's attitude. And there was just a chance – Mr Pott in his Silver Ring days would probably have estimated it at 100–8 – that what he was about to say would touch the man's heart. After all, the toughest specimens were sometimes melted by a tale of true love.

'I want to get married,' he said.

If the Duke's heart was touched, his rugged exterior showed no sign of it. His eyes came out of his head like a prawn's, and once more his moustache foamed up against his breakwater of a nose.

'Married?' he cried. 'What do you mean, married? Don't be an ass.'

Ricky had started the day with a tenderness towards all created things, and this attitude he had hoped to be able to maintain. But he could not help feeling that Providence, in creating his Uncle Alaric, was trying him a little high.

'I never heard such nonsense in my life. How the devil can you afford to get married? You've got about twopence a year which your mother left you, and I don't suppose you make enough out of those sonnets of yours to keep you in cigarettes.'

'That's why I want to buy this onion soup bar.'

'And a nice fool you would look, selling onion soup.'

With a strong effort, Ricky succeeded in making no comment on this. It seemed to him that silence was best. Galling though it was to allow his companion to score debating points, it was better than to close all avenues leading to an appeasement with a blistering repartee. At the moment, moreover, he could not think of a blistering repartee.

The Duke's moustache was rising and falling like seaweed on an ebb tide.

'And a nice fool I'd look, going about trying to explain away a nephew who dished soup out of a tureen. It's been bad enough having to tell my friends you write poetry. "What's that nephew of yours doing these days?"' the Duke proceeded, giving an imitation of an enquiring friend with – for some reason – a falsetto voice. '"The Guards? Diplomatic Service? Reading for the Bar?" "No," I tell them. "He's writing poetry," and there's an awkward silence. And now you want me to have to spread it about that you've become a blasted soup-dispenser. Gah!'

A deep flush had spread itself over Ricky's face. His temper, always a little inclined to be up and doing, had begun to flex its muscles like an acrobat about to do a trick.

'As for this idea of yours of getting married ... Why do you want to get married? Hey? Why?'

'Oh, just to score off the girl. I dislike her.'

'What!'

'Why do you think I want to get married? Why do people usually want to get married? I want to get married because I've found the most wonderful girl in the world, and I love her.'

'You said you disliked her.'

'I was merely trying to be funny.'

The Duke took in a mouthful of moustache, chewed it for a moment, seemed dissatisfied with the flavour and expelled it again with another forceful puff.

'Who is she?'

'Nobody you know.'

'Well, who's her father?'

'Oh, nobody special.'

A sudden, sinister calm fell upon the Duke, causing his manner to resemble that of a volcano which is holding itself in by sheer will-power.

'You don't need to tell me any more. I see it all. The wench is a dashed outsider.'

'She is not!'

'Don't argue with me. Well, that settles it. Not a penny do you get from me.'

'All right. And not a pig do you get from me.'

'Hey?'

The Duke was taken aback. It was seldom that he found himself in the position of having to deal with open mutiny in the ranks. Indeed, the experience had never happened to him before, and for an instant he was at a loss. Then he recovered himself, and the old imperious glare returned to his bulging eyes.

'Don't take that tone with me, young man.'

'Not one single, solitary porker do you set your hands on,' said Ricky. 'My price for stealing pigs is two hundred and fifty pounds per pig per person, and if you don't wish to meet my terms, the deal is off. If, on the other hand, you consent to pay this absurdly moderate fee for a very difficult and exacting piece of work, I on my side am willing to overlook the offensive things you have said about a girl you ought to think yourself honoured to have the chance of welcoming into the family.'

'Stop talking like a damned fool. She's obviously the scum of the earth. The way a man's nephews get entangled with the dregs of the human species is enough to give one apoplexy. I absolutely forbid you to marry this female crossing-sweeper.'

Ricky drew a deep breath. His face was like a stormy sky, and his eyes bored into his uncle like bradawls.

'Uncle Alaric,' he said, 'your white hairs protect you. You are an old man on the brink of the tomb –'

The Duke started.

'What do you mean, on the brink of the tomb?'

'On the brink of the tomb,' repeated Ricky firmly. 'And I am not going to shove you into it by giving you the slosh on the jaw which you have been asking for with every word you have uttered. But I would just like to say this. You are without exception the worst tick and bounder that ever got fatty degeneration of the heart through half a century of gorging food and swilling wine wrenched from the lips of a starving proletariat. You make me sick. You poison the air.

Good-bye, Uncle Alaric,' said Ricky, drawing away rather ostentatiously. 'I think that we had better terminate this interview, or I may become brusque.'

With a parting look of a kind which no nephew should have cast at an uncle, Ricky Gilpin strode to the door and was gone. The Duke remained where he sat. He felt himself for the moment incapable of rising.

It is bad enough for a man of imperious soul to be defied by a beardless boy, and his nephew's determination, in face of his opposition, to cling to the ballet girl or whatever she might be with whom he had become entangled would have been in itself enough to cause a temporary coma. But far more paralysing was the reflection that in alienating Ricky Gilpin he had alienated the one man who could secure the person of the Empress for him. Pig-kidnappers do not grow on every bush.

The Duke of Dunstable's mind was one of those which readily fall into the grip of obsessions, and though reason now strove to convince him that there were prizes in life worth striving for beside the acquisition of a pig, he still felt that only that way lay happiness and contentment. He was a man who wanted what he wanted when he wanted it, and what he wanted now was the Empress of Blandings.

A cold voice, speaking at his side, roused him from his reverie.

'Pardon me, your Grace.'

'Hey? What's the matter?'

Rupert Baxter continued to speak coldly. He was feeling bleakly hostile towards this old image. He disliked people who threw eggs at him. Nor was he the man to allow himself to be softened by any sportsmanlike admiration for a shot which had unquestionably been a very creditable one, showing great accuracy of aim under testing conditions.

'A policeman has just informed me that I must move the car from the inn door.'

'He has, has he? Well, tell him from me that he's a blasted officious jack-in-office.'

'With your Grace's permission, I propose to drive it round the corner.'

The Duke did not speak. A sudden, flaming inspiration had come to him.

'Hey, you,' he said. 'Sit down.'

Rupert Baxter sat down. The Duke eyed him closely, and felt that his inspiration had been sound. The secretary, he observed, had a strong, well-knit frame, admirably suited for the performance of such feats as the removal of pigs from their sties. A moment before, he had been feeling that, Ricky having failed him, he would seek in vain for an assistant to do the rough work. And now, it seemed, he had found him. From this quarter he anticipated no defiance. He was well aware of the high value which Rupert Baxter placed upon his job.

'Ever done any pig-stealing?' he asked.

'I have not,' said Rupert Baxter coldly.

'Well, you start to-day,' said the Duke.

# Chapter 14

It was at about three o'clock that afternoon that the Market Blandings station cab (Ed. Robinson, propr.) turned in at the gates of Blandings Castle and started creakily up the long drive. And presently Mr Pott, seated in its smelly interior, was setting eyes for the first time on the historic home of the Earls of Emsworth.

His emotions, as he did so, differed a good deal from those of the ordinary visitor in such circumstances. Claude Pott was a realist, and this tended to colour his outlook. Where others, getting their initial glimpse of this last stronghold of an old order, usually admired the rolling parkland and the noble trees or thrilled with romantic awe as they thought of what sights those grey walls must have seen in the days when knights were bold, he merely felt that the owner of a place like this must unquestionably have what it takes to play Persian Monarchs.

Mr Pott, like Ricky, had arrived at Market Blandings in good spirits. Lord Bosham's telephone call, coming through just as he was dropping off to sleep, had at first inclined him to peevishness. But when he discovered that he was talking to a client, and not only to a client but a client who was inviting him to Blandings Castle, he had become sunny to a degree. And this sunniness still lingered.

Ever since he had made Lord Emsworth's acquaintance, Claude Pott had been sighing for a closer intimacy with one whom his experienced eye had classified immediately as the king of the mugs. There, he had felt, went one literally designed by Nature to be a good man's opponent at Persian Monarchs, and the thought that they had met and parted like ships that pass in the night was very bitter to him. And now he was being asked to come to Lord Emsworth's home and, what was more, was being paid for coming.

Little wonder that life looked rosy to Claude Pott. And he was still suffused with an optimistic glow, when the cab drew up at the front door and he was conducted by Beach, the butler, to the smoking-room, where he found a substantial, pink young man warming a solid trouser-seat in front of a cheerful fire.

'Mr Claude Pott, m'lord,' announced Beach, and withdrew with just that touch of aloofness in his manner which butlers exhibit when they would prefer not to be held responsible for peculiar visitors.

The pink young man, on the other hand, was cordiality itself.

'Hullo, Pott. So here you are, Pott, what? Fine. Splendid. Excellent. Capital. Take a seat, dear old clue-collector. My name's Bosham. I'm by way of being Lord Emsworth's son. To refresh your memory, I'm the bird who rang you up.'

Mr Pott found himself unable to speak. The sight of his employer had stirred him to his depths.

Up till now, he had regarded Lord Emsworth as the most promising claim that any prospector for ore could hope to stake out, but one glance at the latter's son told him that he had been mistaken. This was the mug of a good man's dreams. For a long instant he stood staring silently at Lord Bosham with the same undisguised interest which stout Cortez had once displayed when inspecting the Pacific. It is scarcely exaggerating to say that Mr Pott was feeling as if a new planet had swum into his ken.

Lord Bosham, too, after that opening speech of welcome, had fallen into a thoughtful silence. Like so many men who have done their business on the mail-order system, he was reflecting, now that the parcel had been unwrapped, that it would have been more prudent to have inspected the goods before purchasing. It seemed to him, as it had seemed to Pongo Twistleton on a former occasion, that if this rummy object before him was a detective, his whole ideas about detectives would have to be revised from the bottom up.

'You *are* the right Pott?' he said.

Mr Pott seemed to find a difficulty in helping him out. The question of the rightness or wrongness of Potts appeared to be one on which he was loth to set himself up as an authority.

'The private investigator, I mean. The bloodstain-and-magnifying-glass bloke.'

'My card,' said Pott, who had been through this sort of thing before.

Lord Bosham examined the card, and was convinced.

'Ah,' he said. 'Fine. Well, going back to what I was saying, here you are, what?'

'Yes, sir.'

'I was expecting you yesterday.'

'I'm sorry, Lord B. I'd have come if I could. But the boys at the Yard just wouldn't let me.'

'What yard would that be?'

'Scotland Yard.'

'Oh, ah, of course. You work for them, do you?' said Lord Bosham, feeling that this was more the stuff.

'When they get stuck, they generally call me in,' said Pott nonchalantly. 'This was a particularly tough job.'

'What was it?'

'I can't tell you that,' said Mr Pott, 'my lips being sealed by the Official Secrets Act, of which you have doubtless heard.'

Lord Bosham felt that his misgivings had been unworthy. He remembered now that quite a number of the hottest detectives on his library list had been handicapped – or possibly assisted – by a misleading appearance. Buxton Black in *Three Dead at Mistleigh Court* and Drake Denver in *The Blue Ribbon Murders* were instances that sprang to the mind. The former had looked like a prosperous solicitor, the latter like a pleasure-loving young man about town. What Mr Pott looked like he could not have said on the spur of the moment, but the point was that it didn't matter.

'Well, let's get down to it, shall we?'

'I should be glad to have a brief outline of the position of affairs.'

'Brief?' Lord Bosham looked dubious. 'I'm not so sure about that. As a matter of fact, bloodhound, it's rather a long and intricate story. But I'll cut it as short as I can. Do you know what impostors are?'

'Yes, sir.'

'Well, we've got them in the house. That's the nub of the thing. Three of them – count 'em! Three! – all imposting away like the dickens.'

'H'm.'

'You may well say "H'm". It's a most exasperating state of affairs, and I don't wonder my aunt's upset. Not nice for a woman, feeling that every time she goes to her room to fetch a handkerchief or what not she may find the place littered with bounders rifling her jewel-case.'

'Are these impostors male?'

'Two of them are. The third, in sharp contradistinction, is female. And speaking of her brings us to what you will probably find it convenient to register in your mind as the Baxter Theory. Do you register things in your mind, or do you use a notebook?'

'Is Baxter an impostor?'

'No,' said Lord Bosham, with the air of one being fair. 'He's a gosh-awful tick with steel-rimmed spectacles, but he's not an impostor. He's the Duke's secretary, and his theory is that these blighters are here not for what they can pouch, but in order to lure the Duke into allowing his nephew to marry the girl. Ingenious, of course, but in my opinion there is nothing to it and you may dismiss it absolutely. They are after the swag. Well, when I tell you that one of them played the confidence trick on me a couple of days ago, you will be able to estimate the sort of hell-hounds they are. Write them down in your notebook, if you use a notebook, as men who will stick at nothing.'

Mr Pott was beginning to feel fogged. If anything emerged clearly from this narrative, it seemed to him that it was the fact that the entire household was fully aware of the moral character of these miscreants. And yet they were apparently being given the run of the house and encouraged to make themselves at home.

'But if you know that these individuals are here with criminal intent –'

'Why don't we have them led off with gyves upon their wrists? My dear old cigar-ash inspector, it's what I'd give my eye-teeth to do, but it can't be done. You wouldn't understand, if I explained for an hour, so just take it at this, that no – what's that word beginning with "o"?'

'What word beginning with "o"?'

'That's what I'm asking you. Opal? Oval? Ha! Got it! Overt. You must just accept the fact that no overt act can be contemplated, because it would lead to consequences which we don't want led to. When I say "we", I speak principally for my aunt. Personally, I don't care if Baxter loses his job to-morrow.'

Mr Pott gave it up.

'I don't follow you, Lord B.'

'I thought you wouldn't. Still, you've grasped the salient fact that the place is crawling with impostors?'

Mr Pott said he had.

'Then that's all right. That's all you really need to know. Your job is to keep an eye on them. See what I mean? You follow them about watchfully, and if you see them dipping into the till, you shout "Hoy!" and they cheese it. That's simple enough? Fine,' said Lord Bosham. 'Capital. Excellent. Splendid. Then you can start in at once. And, by the way, you'd like something in the nature of a retaining fee, what?'

Mr Pott said he would, and his employer suddenly began to spray bank-notes like a fountain. It was Lord Bosham's prudent practice, when he attended a rural meeting, as he proposed to do on the morrow, to have plenty of ready cash on his person.

'Call it a tenner?'

'Thank you, Lord B.'

'Here you are, then.'

Mr Pott's eyes were glistening a little, as he trousered the note.

'You've got a lot of money there, Lord B.'

'And I may need it before to-morrow's sun has set. It's the first day of the Bridgeford races, where I usually get skinned to the bone. Very hard to estimate form at these country meetings. You interested in racing?'

'I was at one time a turf commissioner, operating in the Silver Ring.'

'Good Lord! Were you really? My young brother Freddie was a partner in a bookie's firm once. His father-in-law made him give it up and go over to America and peddle dog-biscuits. Absorbing work.'

'Most.'

'I expect you miss it, don't you?'

'I do at times, Lord B.'

'What do you do for amusement these days?'

'I like a quiet little game of cards.'

'So do I.' Lord Bosham regarded this twin soul with a kindly eye. Deep had spoken to deep. 'Only the trouble is, it's a dashed difficult thing for a married man to get. You a married man?'

'A widower, Lord B.'

'I wish you wouldn't keep saying "Lord B." It sounds as if you had been starting to call me something improper and changed your mind. Where was I? Oh, yes. When I'm at home, I don't get a chance of little games of cards. My wife objects.'

'Some wives are like that.'

'All wives are like that. You start out in life a willing, eager sportsman, ready to take anybody on at anything, and then you meet a girl and fall in love, and when you come out of the ether you find not only that you are married but that you have signed on for a lifetime of bridge at threepence a hundred.'

'Too true,' sighed Mr Pott.

'No more friendly little games with nothing barred except biting and bottles.'

'Ah!' said Mr Pott.

'We could do far worse,' said Lord Bosham, 'while we're waiting for these impostors to get up steam, than have a friendly little game now.'

'As your lordship pleases.'

Lord Bosham winced.

'I wish you wouldn't use that expression. It was what counsel for the defence kept saying to the judge at my breach-of-promise case, every time the latter ticked him off for talking out of his turn. So don't do it, if you don't mind.'

'Very good, your lordship.'

'And don't call me "your lordship", either. I hate all this formality. I like your face . . . well, no, that's overstating it a bit . . . put it this way, I like your personality, bloodhound, and feel that we shall be friends. Call me Bosham.'

'Right ho, Bosham.'

'I'll ring for some cards, shall I?'

'Don't bother to do that, Bosham. I have some.'

The sudden appearance of a well-thumbed pack from the recesses of Mr Pott's costume seemed to interest Lord Bosham.

'Do you always go about with a pack of cards on you?'

'When I travel. I like to play solitaire in the train.'

'Do you play anything else?'

'I am fond of Snap.'

'Yes, Snap's a good game.'

'And Animal Grab.'

'That's not bad, either. But I can tell you something that's better than both.'

'Have –' said Mr Pott.

'Have you –' said Lord Bosham.

'Have you ever –' said Mr Pott.

'Have you ever,' concluded Lord Bosham, 'heard of a game called Persian Monarchs?'

Mr Pott's eyes rolled up to the ceiling, and for an instant he could not speak. His lips moved silently. He may have been praying.

'No,' he said, at length. 'What is it?'

'It's a thing I used to play a good deal at one time,' said Lord Bosham, 'though in recent years I've dropped it a bit. As I say, a married man of the right sort defers to his wife's wishes. If she's around. But now she isn't around, and it would be interesting to see if the old skill still lingers.'

'It's a pretty name,' said Mr Pott, still experiencing some trouble with his vocal chords. 'Is it difficult to learn?'

'I could teach it you in a minute. In its essentials it is not unlike Blind Hooky. Here's the way it goes. You cut a card, if you see what I mean, and the other fellow cuts a card, if you follow me. Then if the card you've cut is higher than the card the other fellow has cut, you win. While, conversely, if the card the other fellow's cut is higher than the card you've cut, he wins.'

He shot an anxious glance at Mr Pott, as if wondering if he had been too abstruse. But Mr Pott appeared to have followed him perfectly.

'I think I see the idea,' he said. 'Anyway, I'll pick it up as I go along. Come on, my noble sportsman. Follow the dictates of your heart and fear nothing. Roll, bowl or pitch! Ladies half-way and all bad nuts returned! If you don't speculate, you can't accumulate.'

'You have a rummy way of expressing yourself,' said Lord Bosham, 'but no doubt your heart is in the right place. Start ho, Pott?'

'Start ho, Bosham!'

*

Twilight had begun to fall, the soft mysterious twilight of an English spring evening, when a rotund figure came out of the front door of Blandings Castle and began to walk down the drive. It was Claude Pott, private investigator, on his way to the Emsworth Arms to have a couple. The beer, he knew, was admirable there. And if it should seem strange that one so recently arrived in Market Blandings was in possession of this local knowledge, it may be explained that his first act on alighting from the station cab had been to canvass Ed. Robinson's views on the matter. Like some canny explorer in the wilds, Mr Pott, on coming to a strange place, always made sure of his drink supply before doing anything else.

Ed. Robinson, a perfect encyclopaedia on the subject in hand, had been fluent and informative. But while he had spoken with a generous warmth of the Wheatsheaf, the Waggoner's Rest, the Beetle and Wedge, the Stitch in Time, the Blue Cow, the Blue Boar, the Blue Dragon and the Jolly Cricketers, for he was always a man to give credit where credit was due, he had made it quite clear where his heart lay, and it was thither that Mr Pott was now proceeding.

He walked slowly, with bowed head, for he was counting ten-pound notes. And it was because his head was bowed that he did not immediately observe the approach of his old friend Lord Ickenham, who was coming with springy steps along the drive towards him. It was only when he heard a surprised voice utter his name that he looked up.

Lord Ickenham had been for an afternoon ramble, in the course of which he had seen many interesting objects of the countryside, but here was one which he had not expected to see, and in his eyes as he saw it there was no welcoming glow. Claude Pott's advent, he could not but feel, added another complication to an already complicated situation. And even a man who holds that complications lend spice to life may legitimately consider that enough is enough.

'Mustard!'

'Coo! Lord I.!'

'What on earth are you doing in the middle of Shropshire, Mustard?'

Mr Pott hesitated. For a moment, it seemed that professional caution was about to cause him to be evasive. Then he decided that so ancient a crony as his companion deserved to enjoy his confidence.

'Well, it's a secret, Lord I., but I know you won't let it go any further. I was sent for.'

'Sent for? By Polly?'

'Polly? She's not here?'

'Yes, she is.'

'I thought she was at your country seat.'

'No, she's at this country seat. Who sent for you?'

'A member of the aristocracy residing at Blandings Castle. Name of Bosham. He rang me up night before last, engaging my professional services. Seems there's impostors in the place, and he wants an eye kept on them.'

For the first time since George, Viscount Bosham, had come into his life, Lord Ickenham began to feel a grudging respect for that young man's intelligence stealing over him. It was clear that he had formed too low an estimate of this adversary. In lulling suspicion as he had done on the station platform by looking pink and letting his mouth hang open, while all the time he was planning to send for detectives, the other had acted, he was forced to confess, with a shrewdness amounting to the snaky.

'Does he, by Jove?' he said, giving his moustache a thoughtful twirl.

'Yes, I'm to take up my residence as an unsuspected guest and keep my eyes skinned to see that they don't walk off with the *objets d'art*.'

'I see. What did he tell you about these impostors? Did he go into details?'

'Not what you would call details. But he told me there was three of them – two *m*., one *f*.'

'Myself, my nephew Pongo and your daughter Polly.'

'Eh?'

'The impostors to whom Bosham refers are – reading from right to left – your daughter Polly, my nephew Pongo and myself.'

'You're pulling my leg, Lord I.'

'No.'

'Well, this beats me.'

'I thought it might. Perhaps I had better explain.'

Before starting to do so, however, Lord Ickenham paused for a moment in thought. He had just remembered that Mr Pott was not an admirer of Ricky Gilpin and did not approve of his daughter's desire to marry that ineligible young man. He also recalled that Polly had said that it was her father's hope that she would succumb to the charms of Horace Davenport. It seemed to him, therefore, that if Mr Pott's sympathy for and co-operation in their little venture was to be secured, it would be necessary to deviate slightly from the actual facts. So he deviated from them. He was a man who was always ready to deviate from facts when the cause was good.

'Polly,' he began, 'is in love with Horace Davenport.'

Mr Pott's eyes widened to saucerlike dimensions, and such was his emotion that he dropped a ten-pound note. Lord Ickenham picked it up, and looked at it with interest.

'Hullo! Somebody been leaving you a fortune, Mustard?'

Mr Pott smirked.

'Tantamount to that, Lord I. Young Bosham – and a nice young fellow he is – was teaching me to play Persian Monarchs.'

'You seem to have cleaned up.'

'I had beginner's luck,' said Mr Pott modestly.

'How much did you get away with?'

'Two hundred and fifty I make it. He had a system which involved doubling up when he lost.'

'That will make a nice little dowry for Polly. Help her to buy her trousseau.'

'Eh?'

'But I shall be coming back to that later. For the moment, I will be putting you *au courant* with the position of affairs at Blandings Castle. The key to the whole business, the thing you have to grasp at the outset, is that Polly is in love with Horace Davenport.'

'When you told me that, you could have knocked me down with a feather. I thought the one she was in love with was young Gilpin.'

'Oh, that? A mere passing flirtation. And even if it had been anything deeper, his behaviour at that Ball would have quenched love's spark.'

'Love's what?'

'Spark.'

'Oh, spark? Yes, that's right, too,' said Mr Pott, beginning to get the whole thing into perspective. 'Cursing and swearing and calling her names, all because she went to a dance with somebody, such as is happening in our midst every day. Seems he'd told her not to go. A nice way to carry on with a girl of spirit. What right has he to get bossy and tell my dear daughter what she can do and what she can't do? Who does he think he is? Ben Bolt?'

'Ben who?'

'Bolt. Bloke with the girl called Sweet-Alice-With-Hair-So-Brown who laughed with delight at his smile and trembled with fear at his frown. Does he expect my dear daughter to do that? Coo! Whoever heard of such a thing? Is this Greece?'

Lord Ickenham weighed the question.

'Not that I know of. Why?'

'I didn't mean Greece,' said Mr Pott, correcting himself with some annoyance. 'I meant Turkey, where women are kept in subjection and daren't call their souls their own. If Polly hadn't got a sweet nature, she'd have hit him with a bottle. But she's her mother's daughter.'

'Whose daughter did you expect her to be?'

'You don't apprehend my meaning, Lord I.,' said Mr Pott patiently. 'I meant that she takes after her dear mother in having a sweet nature. Her dear mother had the loving kindness of an angel or something, and so has Polly. That's what I meant. Her dear mother wouldn't hurt a fly, nor would Polly hurt a fly. I've seen her dear mother take a fly tenderly in her hand –'

Lord Ickenham interrupted. He would have liked to hear all about the late Mrs Pott and the insect kingdom, but time was getting on.

'Suppose we shelve the subject of flies for the moment, shall we, Mustard? Let us get back to Horace Davenport. As I was saying, he is the man Polly has got her eye on. And he loves her just as she loves him. He came down here the day after that dance, and we came the day after, following him.'

'Why?'

'It's quite simple. You know who Horace is, Mustard. The nephew and heir of the Duke of Dunstable.'

'Ah!' said Mr Pott, and seemed about to bare his head.

'And we have come here in the humble capacity of impostors

because it is essential, if there is to be a happy ending, that Polly shall fascinate the Duke and set him thinking that she is the ideal girl to marry his nephew and heir. This Duke is tough, Mustard. He nails his collar to the back of his neck to save buying studs. Horace has been scared to death of him since infancy, and would never have the nerve to marry unless the first put up the All Right sign. Before Polly can walk up the aisle with Horace Davenport, the Duke has got to be worked on lovingly and patiently. And I cannot impress it upon you too emphatically that you must keep yourself in the background, Mustard. Polly is supposed to be my daughter.'

In a few well-chosen words Lord Ickenham sketched out the position of affairs. Mr Pott, when he had finished, seemed inclined to be critical.

'Seems a roundabout way of doing things,' he complained. 'Why couldn't she have come here as my daughter?'

'Well, it just happened to work out the other way,' said Lord Ickenham tactfully. 'Too late to do anything about it now. But you understand?'

'Oh, I understand.'

'I knew you would. Nobody has ever disparaged your intelligence, though I have known people to be a bit captious about that habit of yours of always cutting the ace. And that brings me back to what I was saying just now. This money you've taken off Bosham. Kiss it good-bye, Mustard.'

'I don't follow you, Lord I.'

'I want you to give me that money, my dear old friend –'

'What!'

'– and I will hand it over to Polly as her wedding portion. I know, I know,' said Lord Ickenham sympathetically. 'You've no need to tell me that it will be agony. I can see the thought searing your soul. But there comes a time in every man's life, Mustard, when he has to decide whether to do the fine, generous thing or be as the beasts that perish. Put yourself in Polly's place. The child must have her little bit of stuff, to make her feel that she is not going empty-handed to the man she loves. Her pride demands it.'

'Yes, but hoy –!'

'And think how you have always watched over her with a father's tender care. Did she have measles as a child?'

'Yes, she had measles, but that's not the point –'

'It is the point, Mustard. Throw your mind back to the picture of her lying there, flushed and feverish. You would have given all you possessed to help her then. I see your eyes are wet with tears.'

'No, they aren't.'

'Well, they ought to be.'

'I don't approve of a young girl having a lot of money. I wouldn't mind giving her a tenner.'

'Pah!'

'Yes, but two hundred and fifty –'

'A trifle compared with your peace of mind. If you fail her now, you will never have another happy moment. It would be criminal to allow a sensitive girl like Polly to get married without a penny in her pocket. You're a man of the world, Mustard. You know what buying a trousseau means. She will need two of everything. And can you subject her to the degradation of going and touching her future husband for those intimate articles of underclothing which a nice girl shrinks from naming when there are gentlemen present? Compel her to do so, and you leave a scar on her pure soul which the years may hide but which will always be there.'

Mr Pott shuffled his feet.

'She needn't tell him what she wants the money for.'

'For Heaven's sake, Mustard, don't try to evade the issue. Of course, she would have to tell him what she wanted the money for. A girl can't be whispering in the twilight with the man she loves and suddenly introduce a demand for two hundred and fifty pounds as a sort of side issue. She will have to get right down to it and speak of camisoles and slips. Are you going to force her to do that? It will not make very pleasant reading in your Biography, my dear chap. As I see it,' said Lord Ickenham gravely, 'you are standing at the crossroads, Mustard. This way lies happiness for Polly, peace of mind for you ... that way, self-scorn for you, misery for her. Which road will you take? I seem to picture your late wife asking herself the same question. I can see her up there now ... watching ... waiting ... all agog ... wondering if you are going to do the square thing. Don't disappoint her, Mustard.'

Mr Pott continued to shuffle his feet. It was plain that in one sense he was touched, but not so certain that he intended to be in another.

'How about a nice twenty?'

'All or nothing, Mustard, all or nothing. Dash it, it's not as if the money would be lost. You can always take it off Horace at Persian Monarchs after the honeymoon.'

Mr Pott's face lit up with a sudden glow that made it for a moment almost beautiful.

'Coo! That's right, isn't it?'

'It seems to me to solve the whole difficulty.'

'Of course I can. Here you are, Lord I.'

'Thank you, Mustard. I knew you would not fail. And now, if you will excuse me, I will be going and taking a bath. In the course of my rambles I seem to have got quite a lot of Shropshire on my person. The moment I have removed it, I will find Polly and tell her the good news. You will never regret this, my dear fellow.'

In this prediction, Lord Ickenham was wrong. Mr Pott was regretting it rather keenly. He was not the man to see two hundred and fifty pounds pass from his possession without a pang, and already a doubt had begun to creep over him as to whether the transaction could, as his companion had so jauntily suggested, be looked on as merely a temporary loan. Long before he reached Market Blandings he had begun to wonder if he could really rely on Horace Davenport. It takes two to play Persian Monarchs, and it might be that Horace would prove to be one of those odd, unpleasant people who have no fondness for the game. He had sometimes met them on race trains.

However, there is always something stimulating in the doing of a good deed, and Claude Pott, as he entered the private bar of the Emsworth Arms, could have been written down as on the whole a reasonably happy man. He was at any rate sufficiently uplifted to be in a mood for conversation, and it was with the idea of initiating a feast of reason and a flow of soul that he addressed the only other occupant of the bar, a thick-set young man seated at its shadowy end.

'Nice day,' he said.

His fellow-customer turned, revealing himself as Ricky Gilpin.

# Chapter 15

Ricky had come to the private bar in search of relief for his bruised soul, and he could have made no wiser move. Nothing can ever render the shattering of his hopes and the bringing of his dream castles to ruin about his ears really agreeable to a young man, but the beer purveyed by G. Ovens, proprietor of the Emsworth Arms, unquestionably does its best. The Ovens home-brewed is a liquid Pollyanna, for ever pointing out the bright side and indicating silver linings. It slips its little hand in yours, and whispers 'Cheer up!' If King Lear had had a tankard of it handy, we should have had far less of that 'Blow, winds, and crack your cheeks!' stuff.

On Ricky it acted like magic. Hours of brooding over that interview with his Uncle Alaric had brought him into the bar a broken man. At the moment of Mr Pott's entry, he was once more facing the future with something like fortitude.

Money, the beer pointed out, was not everything. 'Look at it this way,' it argued. 'It's absurd to say there aren't a hundred ways by which a smart and enterprising young fellow can get enough money to marry on. The essential thing about this marrying business is not money, but the girl. If the girl's all right, everything's all right. It's true that at the moment you're down among the wines and spirits a bit financially, but what of it? Polly's still there, loving you just as much as ever. And something is sure to turn up.'

And now Mr Pott had turned up. And at the sight of him it was as if the scales had suddenly fallen from Ricky Gilpin's eyes.

Until this moment, the idea of trying to secure the purchase price of the onion soup bar from Claude Pott had never occurred to him. But when you examined it, what an obvious solution it seemed. Mr Pott was Polly's father. He had once rescued Mr Pott from an infuriated mob. That Mr Pott should supply the money to ensure

Polly's happiness and repay that old debt was one of the things that one recognizes as dramatically right.

'Why, hullo, Mr Pott!' he said.

The affection in his voice was quite untinged with surprise. A ready explanation of the other's presence here had presented itself. He assumed he had come for the Bridgeford races, of which he had been hearing so much since his arrival in Market Blandings. But if he was not surprised to see Mr Pott, Mr Pott was extremely surprised to see him.

'Young Gilpin! What are you doing here?'

'My uncle sent for me. He's staying at Blandings Castle, a couple of miles down the road. He wanted to see me on a business matter.'

Mr Pott was aghast.

'You mean you're going to the castle?'

'No. My uncle came down here this morning to discuss the thing, but it fell through. I'm leaving for London this evening.'

Mr Pott breathed again. The thought of this young man coming blundering into the delicate web of intrigue at Blandings Castle had appalled him.

'You're here for the races, of course?'

'That's right,' said Mr Pott, grateful for the suggestion.

'Where are you staying?'

'In the vicinity.'

'Have some of this beer. It's good.'

'Thanks,' said Mr Pott. 'Thanks.'

Until his guest had been supplied with the refreshment, Ricky did not speak again. All his life he had been sturdy and independent, and it embarrassed him to have to ask a comparative stranger for money. This diffidence, with an effort, he overcame. Stranger or no stranger, he reminded himself, Claude Pott would most certainly have spent several weeks in hospital but for the prowess of Alaric Gilpin.

'Mr Pott.'

'Sir?'

'There's something I would like a word with you about, Mr Pott.'

'Oh?'

'Are you fond of onion soup?'

'No.'

'Well, lots of people are. And in this connexion I want to put a business proposition up to you.'

'Ah?'

Ricky took a sip of G. Ovens's home-brewed. It had not escaped him that his companion's manner was reserved. Mr Pott's eyes seemed always to be covered by a protective layer of film. Now, it was as if another layer had been superimposed.

'I don't know if Polly has happened to mention to you, Mr Pott, that I have the opportunity of buying one of these onion soup bars? You've probably noticed them round Piccadilly Circus way.'

'I seem to remember her talking about it.'

'Enthusiastically, I expect. They coin money. Gold mines, every one of them. The one I'm speaking of belongs to an American friend of mine. He has offered to let me have it for two hundred and fifty pounds.'

The mention of that exact sum caused Mr Pott to wince a little, as if an exposed nerve had been touched. He was still unable to make up his mind about Horace Davenport as a sportsman with a taste for Persian Monarchs. Sometimes he could see him reaching out to cut from the pack. Sometimes he could not. The future was wrapped in mist.

'That's a lot of money,' he said.

Ricky was amazed.

'A lot of money? For a going concern right in the heart of London's onion-soup-drinking belt? He's simply giving it away. But he's homesick for New York, and would like to sail to-morrow, if he could. Well, that's the position. He says I can have this going concern for two hundred and fifty, provided I give him the money by the end of the week. And let me tell you, Mr Pott, the potentialities of that bar are stupendous. I've stood there night after night and watched the bottle-party addicts rolling up with their tongues out. It was like a herd of buffaloes stampeding for a waterhole.'

'Then you'd better give him his two hundred and fifty.'

'I would, if I had it. That's exactly the point I was coming to. Can you lend me the money?'

'No.'

'You can have any interest you like.'

'No, sir. Include me out.'

'But you can't say you haven't got it.'

'I have got it, and more. I've got it in cash in my pocket now, on account of the Clothes Stakes I ran at the Drones Club Tuesday.'

'Then why —?'

Mr Pott drained the remains of his tankard, but the noble brew had no mellowing effect. He might have been full of lemonade.

'I'll tell you why. Because if I give it you, you'll go and talk my dear daughter into marrying you. Polly's easily led. She's like her mother. Anything to make people happy. You'd tell her the tale, and she'd act against her better judgement. And then,' said Mr Pott, 'the bitter awakening.'

'What do you mean, the bitter awakening? Polly loves me.'

'What makes you think that?'

'She told me so.'

'That was just being civil. Love you? Coo! What would she want to love you for? If I were a girl, I wouldn't give you one little rose from my hair.'

'You haven't got any hair.'

'There is no occasion to be personal,' said Mr Pott stiffly. 'And hair's not everything, let me tell you. There's been a lot of fellows that found themselves wishing they'd been more like me in that respect. Absalom, for one. And you're wilfully missing the point of my remarks, which is that if I was a girl and had hair and there was a rose in it and you asked me for that rose, I wouldn't give it to you. Because, after all, young G., what are you? Just a poet. Simply a ruddy ink-slinger, that's you. Polly can do better.'

'I'm sorry you dislike me —'

'It's not disliking. It's disapproving of in the capacity of a suitor for my dear daughter's hand. There's nothing fundamentally wrong with you, young G. — I'll admit you've got a sweet left hook — but you aren't an om seerioo. A French term,' explained Mr Pott, 'meaning a fellow that's going to get on in the world and be able to support a sweet girl as a sweet girl ought to be supported. If you were an om seerioo, you wouldn't be wasting your time messing about writing poetry.'

Ricky was telling himself that he must be calm. But calmness was a thing that did not come readily to him in trying circumstances.

'My dear daughter ought to marry a man of substance. This Horace Davenport, now . . .'

'Horace!'

'It's all very well to say "Horace!" in that tone of voice. He's the nephew of a Duke,' said Mr Pott reverently.

'Well, if we're being snobs, so am I the nephew of a Duke.'

'Ah, but your Ma hadn't the stuff, and Horace's Pa had. That's where the difference comes in. The way I got the story, your Ma married beneath her. Too late to regret it now, of course.'

'The thing I regret is that you won't listen to reason.'

'I haven't heard any yet.'

There was a silence. Mr Pott would have liked another tankard of home-brew, but the way things seemed to be shaping, it appeared probable that he would have to pay for it himself.

'Mr Pott,' said Ricky, 'I saved your life once.'

'And on that last awful day when we all have to render account it will be duly chalked up to you on the credit side. Though, as a matter of fact,' said Mr Pott nonchalantly, 'I've no doubt I could have handled those fellows all right myself.'

The muscles inherited from his robust father stood out on Ricky's cheek-bones.

'I hope you will have many more opportunities of doing so,' he said.

Mr Pott seemed wounded.

'That's a nasty thing to say.'

'It was meant to be. Because,' said Ricky, becoming frank, 'if ever there was a pot-bellied little human louse who needed to have the stuffing kicked out of him and his remains jumped on by strong men in hobnailed boots, it is you, Mr Pott. The next time I see a mob in the street setting on you, I shall offer to hold their coats and stand by and cheer.'

Mr Pott rose.

'Ho! If that's the sort of nasty mind you have, I don't wonder she prefers Horace.'

'May I ask where you got the idea that she prefers Horace?'

'I got it by seeing her that night he took her to the Ball. There was a look in her eyes that made me think right away that she was feeling he was her Prince Charming. And this has since been confirmed by a reliable source.'

Ricky laughed.

'Would it interest you to know,' he said, 'that Polly has promised me that she will never see Horace again?'

'It wouldn't interest me in the slightest degree,' retorted Mr Pott. 'Because I happen to know that she's seeing him regular.'

Whether it was excusable in the circumstances for Ricky at this point to tell Mr Pott that he was lying in his teeth, and that only the fact of his being an undersized little squirt whom no decent man would bring himself to touch with a barge pole saved him from having his neck wrung, is open to debate. Mr Pott, who thought not, drew himself up stiffly.

'Young G.,' he said, 'I will wish you a very good afternoon. After that crack, I must decline to hold any association with you. There is such a thing as going too far, and you have gone it. I will take my refreshment elsewhere.'

He went off to the Jolly Cricketers to do so, and for some moments Ricky continued to sit over his tankard. Now that the first spasm of indignation had spent itself, he was feeling more amused than wrathful. The lie had been so clumsy, so easily seen through. He blamed himself for ever having allowed it to annoy him.

If there was one thing certain in an uncertain world, it was that Polly was as straight as a die. How she came to be so with a father like that constituted one of the great mysteries, but there it was. The thought of Polly cheating was inconceivable.

With a glowing heart, Ricky Gilpin rose and walked down the passage that led to the back door of the inn. He felt he wanted air. After having had Mr Pott in it, the bar struck him as a little close.

The garden of the Emsworth Arms runs down to the river, and is a pleasant, scented place on a spring evening. Ricky wished that he could linger there, but he was intending to catch the late afternoon express back to London, and he still had his packing to do. He turned regretfully, and he had just reached the inn, when from somewhere in its interior there came a disembodied voice.

'Hullo,' it was saying. 'Hullo.'

Ricky halted, amazed. There was only one man in the world who said 'Hullo' with just that lilting bleat.

'Hullo . . . Polly?'

Ricky Gilpin's heart seemed to leap straight up into the air twiddling its feet, like a Russian dancer. He had sometimes wondered how fellows in the electric chair must feel when the authorities turned on the juice. Now he knew.

'Hullo? Polly? Polly, old pet, this is Horace. Yes, I know. Never mind all that. I've got to see you immediately. Of course it's important. Matter of life and death. So drop everything like the sweet angel you are, and come along. Meet me at the castle gate, out in the road. I don't want anybody to see us. Eh? What? Yes. All right. I've got my car. I'll be there before you are.'

A red-haired bombshell burst into the lounge of the Emsworth Arms. There, in the corner near the window, stood the telephone, but the speaker had gone. And from outside in the street there came the sound of a car.

Ricky Gilpin leaped to the door. A rakish Bingley was moving off up the High Street, a long, thin, familiar figure at its wheel.

For an instant, he contemplated shouting. Then, perceiving that there was a better way, he ran, sprang and flung himself on to the Bingley's stern.

Horace Davenport, all unconscious that he had taken aboard a stowaway, pressed his foot on the accelerator and the Bingley gathered speed.

Lord Ickenham, much refreshed after his bath, had left his room, and begun to search through Blandings Castle for Polly. Unable to find her, he sought information from Pongo, whom he discovered in the smoking-room staring silently at nothing. The burden of life was weighing on Pongo Twistleton a good deal just now.

'Ah, my boy. Seen Polly anywhere?'

Pongo roused himself from his thoughts.

'Yes, I saw her . . .'

He broke off. His eyes had started from their sockets. He had just observed what it was that the other was holding in his hand.

'My gosh! Money?'

'Yes.'

'How much?'

'Two hundred and fifty pounds.'

'Oh, my golly! Where did you get it?'

'From – you will scarcely credit this – Mustard Pott.'

'What!'

'Yes. Mustard, it will astound you to hear, has just arrived at the castle in his professional capacity, sent for by Bosham to watch our movements. I seem to have dismissed Bosham as a force too lightly. He appears to have seen through my well-meant attempt to convince him that I was not the man who got away with his wallet and to have decided to seek assistance. A dashed deep young man. He took me in completely. What led him to select Mustard from London's myriad sleuths is more than I can tell you. I can only suppose that he must have heard of him from Horace. At any rate, he's here, and he has not been idle. Within half an hour of his arrival, he took this nice round sum off Bosham at Persian Monarchs, and I, after wrestling with him as the angel wrestled with Jacob, have taken it off him.'

Pongo was quivering in every limb.

'But this is stupendous! This is definitely the happy ending, with the maker's name woven into every yard. I had a feeling all along that you would pull it off sooner or later. Good old Uncle Fred! You stand alone. There is none like you, none. Gimme!'

Lord Ickenham perceived that his nephew was labouring under a misapprehension. Regretfully he put him straight.

'Alas, my boy, this is not for you.'

'What do you mean?'

'It is earmarked for Polly. It is the purchase price of that onion soup bar, which will enable her to marry the man she loves. I'm sorry. I can appreciate what a blow this must be for you. All I can say by way of apology is that her need is greater than yours.'

There was the right stuff in Pongo Twistleton. It had seemed to him for an instant that the world was tumbling about him in rending chaos, but already his finer self had begun to take command of things. Yes, he felt – yes, it was better thus. Agony though it was to think that he was not going to get his hooks on the boodle, it was a not unpleasant agony. His great love demanded some such sacrifice.

'I see what you mean,' he said. 'Yes, something in that.'

'Where is she?'

'I think she's gone to Market Blandings.'

'What would she be going to Market Blandings for?'

'Ah, there you have me. But I was on the terrace having a cigarette not long ago and she came out, hatted and booted, and gave the impression, when questioned, that that was where she was heading.'

'Well, go after her and bring the sunlight into her life.'

The idea did not seem immediately attractive to Pongo.

'It's four miles there and back, you know.'

'Well, you're young and strong.'

'Why don't you go?'

'Because Age has its privileges, my boy. My ramble having left me a little drowsy, I propose to snatch a few winks of sleep in my room. I often say there is nothing so pleasant as a nap in front of a crackling fire in a country-house bedroom. Off you go.'

Pongo did not set out with enthusiasm, but he set out, and Lord Ickenham made his way to his room. The fire was bright, the armchair soft, and the thought of his nephew trudging four miles along the high road curiously soothing. It was not long before the stillness was broken by a faint, musical noise like a kettle singing on the hob.

But these good things do not last. A little sleep, a little slumber, a little folding of the hands in sleep, and along comes somebody shaking us by the shoulder.

Lord Ickenham, sitting up, found that the person shaking his shoulder was Horace Davenport.

## Chapter 16

He rose courteously. To say that the sight of this unexpected apparition had left him feeling completely at his ease would be to present the facts incorrectly. For an instant, indeed, his emotions had been practically identical with those of the heroine of a pantomime when the Demon King suddenly pops up out of a trap at her elbow in a cascade of red fire. But his nervous system was under excellent control, and there was nothing in his manner to indicate how deeply he had been stirred.

'Ah, good evening, good evening!' he said. 'Mr Davenport, is it not? Delighted to see you. But what are we doing here? I thought we had decided to go and take a rest cure at Bournemouth. Did something happen to cause us to change our mind?'

'Hoy!' said Horace.

He had raised a protesting hand. His eyes were the eyes of one who has passed through the furnace, and he was vibrating gently, as if he had swallowed a small auxiliary engine.

'I beg your pardon?'

'That "we" stuff. Cut it out. Not in the mood.'

Something seemed to tell Lord Ickenham that this was not the delightfully receptive Horace Davenport of their previous meeting, but he persevered.

'My dear fellow, of course. I'm sorry if it annoyed you. Just one of those professional mannerisms one slips into. Most of my patients seem to find it soothing.'

'They do, do they? You and your bally patients!'

The undisguised bitterness with which the young man spoke these words confirmed Lord Ickenham in his view that there had been a hitch somewhere. However, he continued to do his best.

'I beg your pardon?'

'Don't keep begging my pardon. Though, my gosh,' said Horace shrilly, 'you jolly well ought to. Pulling my leg like that. It may interest you to learn that I know all.'

'Indeed?'

'Yes. You're not Sir Roderick Glossop.'

Lord Ickenham raised his eyebrows.

'That is a very odd statement to make. I confess I do not like the sound of it. It suggests a feverishness. Tell me, do we –'

'Will you stop it! Listen. You're Valerie's Uncle Fred. I've met someone who knows Glossop, and have had him described to me in pitiless detail.'

Lord Ickenham was a man who could accept the inevitable. He might not like it, but he could accept it.

'In that case, as you suggest, it is perhaps hardly worth while to try to keep up the innocent deception. Yes, my dear fellow, you are perfectly right. I am Valerie's Uncle Fred.'

'And it was Pongo Twistleton and Polly Pott that I met in the hall that time. It wasn't a – what's the word? A nice thing that was you three blisters did to me, making me think I was off my rocker. I realize now that there was absolutely nothing wrong with me at all.'

'No doubt you are feeling much relieved.'

'What I'm feeling, if you want to know, is considerably incensed and pretty dashed shirty.'

'Yes, I can appreciate your emotion, and I can only say that I am sorry. It went to my heart to do it, but it was military necessity. You were in the way, and had to be removed by such means as lay to hand. Let me explain what we are all doing, visiting Blandings Castle incognito like this. Believe me, it was no idle whim that brought us here. We are hoping that Polly may succeed in winning the Duke's heart, without his knowing who she is, thus paving the way for her marriage to your cousin Ricky. You know that pumpkin-headed old man's views on class distinctions. If Ricky told him that he wanted to marry a girl of dubious origin – and I defy anyone to think of an origin more dubious than dear old Mustard – he would forbid the banns without hesitation. We are trying to put something over by stealth, and we could not trust your open, honest nature not to give the show away.'

Horace's just wrath gave way momentarily to bewilderment.

'But I thought Ricky and Polly had split up.'

'Far from it. It is true that after that affair at the Ball there was a temporary rift, but Polly's womanly tact smoothed the thing over. He is once more one hundred per cent the devout lover.'

'Then why does he want to murder me?'

'He doesn't.'

'He does, I tell you.'

'You're thinking of someone else.'

'I'm not thinking of someone else. I found him on the back of my car just now, and he distinctly stated that he was going to tear me into little shreds and strew me over the local pasture land.'

'On the back of your car, did you say?'

'Yes. As I climbed down from the front, he climbed down from the back and made a dive at me.'

'I appear not to be abreast of the Stop Press situation,' said Lord Ickenham. 'You had better tell me your story – one, I can see, that promises to be fraught with interest.'

For the first time, Horace brightened. It was plain that some pleasing thought had occurred to him.

'It's going to interest you, all right. Yes, by Jove, you're going to sit up and take notice, believe me. A pretty nasty spot you're in. The curse has come upon me, said the Lady of Shalott. What, what?'

Lord Ickenham found him obscure.

'You speak in riddles, my boy. A little less of the Delphic Oracle. Let your Yea be Yea and your Nay be Nay.'

'All right. If you want the thing in a nutshell, then, Valerie is in full possession of the facts concerning your goings-on, and is coming here to-morrow at the latest.'

Here was something Lord Ickenham had not anticipated. And though it was his habit to present on all occasions an impassive front to the blows of Fate, he started perceptibly, and for an instant his jaunty moustache seemed to droop.

'Valerie? Coming here?'

'I thought that would touch you up.'

'Not at all. I am always glad to see my dear niece, always. You have run into her again, then?'

Horace's manner became more friendly. He was still resentful of the trick that had been played upon him and by no means inclined to accept as an adequate excuse for it the plea of military necessity, but he found it impossible not to admire this iron man.

'I met her at a restaurant last night. I had gone there in pursuance of that idea we discussed of having the binge of a lifetime before tooling off to Bournemouth. You remember agreeing with me that it would be a good thing to go on a binge?'

'Ah, yes. So I did.'

'You also recommended me to steep myself in a beverage called May Queen.'

'That's right. The binge-goer's best friend. Did you like it?'

'Well, yes and no. Peculiar stuff. For a while it makes you feel as if you were sitting on top of the world. But, as you progress, a great sorrow starts to fill you. Quart One – fine. Joy reigning supreme and blue birds singing their little hearts out. The moment you're well into Quart Two, however, the whole situation alters. You find yourself brooding on what a rotten world this is and what a foul time you're having in it. The outlook darkens. Tears spring to the eyes. Everything seems sad and hopeless.'

'This is most interesting. In my day, I never went into the thing as thoroughly as you appear to have done. One-Pint Ickenham, they used to call me.'

'And I had just reached this second stage, when who should come in but Valerie, accompanied by an elderly female who looked as if she might have something to do with breeding Pekingese. They sat down, and the next thing I knew, I had squashed in between them and was telling Valerie how miserable I was.'

'This must have interested her companion.'

'Oh, it did. She seemed absorbed. A decent old bird, at that. I owe everything to her. As soon as she got the hang of the situation, she started advocating my cause in the most sporting fashion. Valerie, I should mention, wasn't frightfully sympathetic at the outset. Her manner was cold and proud, and she kept telling me to take my elbow out of her lap. But this fine old geezer soon altered all that. It seemed that there had been a similar tragedy in her own life, and she told us all about it.'

'You revealed the facts about your broken engagement to this Pekingese-breeder, then?'

'Oh, rather. Right away. There's something about this May Queen of yours that seems to break down one's reserve, if you know what I mean. And when I had given her a full synopsis, she related her story. Something to do with once long ago loving a bloke dearly and quarrelling with him about something and him turning on his heel and going to the Federated Malay States and marrying the widow of a rubber planter, all because she had been too proud to speak the little word that would have fixed everything. And years afterwards there arrived a simple posy of white violets, together with a slip of paper bearing the words: "It might have been."'

'Moving.'

'Very. I cried buckets. She then leaned across me and told Valerie that the quality of mercy was not strained but dropped like something or other on something I didn't catch. I couldn't quite follow it all, but the effects were excellent. I saw Valerie's eye soften, and a tear stole into it. The next moment, we were locked in a close embrace.'

'And then?'

'Well, the long evening wore on, so to speak. The female Pekingese told us more about her Federated Malay Stater, and I went on crying, and Valerie started crying, too, and presently the Peke was also weeping freely, and it was at about this time that the head waiter came up and suggested that we should take our custom elsewhere. So we all went back to my flat and had eggs and bacon. And it was while I was doling out the dishfuls that I suddenly remembered that I was a loony and so had no right to marry a sweet girl. I mentioned this to Valerie, and then the whole story came out.'

'I see.'

'The Peke, it appeared, knew Sir Roderick Glossop well, her cousin Lionel having been treated by him for some form of loopiness, and her description of the man made it clear that you couldn't be him. So it seemed pretty obvious that you must be you.'

'Remorseless reasoning.'

'And when I speculated as to your motives for leading me up the garden path, Valerie snorted a bit and said it was plain that you were up to some kind of hell in this ancient pile and had wanted to get me out of the way. Which you admit to have been the case. She's a most intelligent girl.'

'Most. I have sometimes thought that it would be an admirable thing if she were to choke.'

'And the outcome of the whole affair was that she went down to Ickenham this morning, just to make sure you weren't on the premises – her intention, having ascertained this, being to breeze along here and expose you to one and all. And I saw that what I had got to do was make an early start and get here before she did. Because you see, though all is forgiven and forgotten between us, so to speak, and love has, as it were, come into its own again, there is just one small catch, that she seems a bit curious about Polly.'

'You mean about your relations with her?'

'Yes. She said in rather a sinister way that she supposed Polly was a very pretty girl, and my statement to the effect that she was a plain little thing whom I had taken to the Ball purely out of pity was none too cordially received. Her manner struck me as that of a girl who intended to investigate further.'

'So your desire to have her arrive here and meet Polly and see what she really looks like is slight?'

'Almost nil,' confessed Horace frankly. 'As soon as I could manage it, therefore, I drove here in the car to tell Polly to clear out while there was yet time.'

'Very shrewd.'

'I phoned her from the Emsworth Arms, arranging a meeting at the castle gate. I then hopped into the car and went there. And conceive my astonishment when, alighting from the prow, I observed Ricky alighting from the stern.'

'It must have given you a start.'

'It did. A flying start. I was off like a jack rabbit. And after I had gone about three-quarters of a mile, touching the ground perhaps twice in the process, I found myself outside the castle and stopped and reviewed the situation. And I saw that having missed Polly, the best thing I could do was to get hold of you. I knew which your room was, of course, and I sneaked up with the idea of waiting till you came to dress for dinner. That I should have found you first crack out of the box like this is the one bit of goose I have experienced in the course of a sticky evening.'

'You wish me, I take it, to find Polly and tell her not to be among those present when Valerie arrives?'

'Exactly.'

'She shall be removed. Indeed, I rather think that none of us will be here to welcome the dear girl. I remember telling my nephew Pongo not long ago that the Twistletons do not clear out, but there are exceptions to the rule. If Valerie were in a position to report to GHQ that she had found me at Blandings Castle posing as a brain specialist, the consequences might well be such as would stagger humanity. But if I am gone before she gets here, it seems to me that I am up against nothing that stout denial will not cover. So rest assured, my boy, that I will lose no time in collecting my young associates, and you shall drive us back to London in your car. Unlike the Arabs, who paused to fold their tents before silently stealing away, we will not even stop to pack.'

'But how can I get at the car? I left Ricky standing guard over it.'

'I think I shall be able to adjust your little trouble with Ricky satisfactorily. My first move shall be to go and explain things to him. I would suggest that you remain here till my return. If you prefer to hide in the cupboard in case your uncle happens to look in, by all means do so. Make yourself quite at home.'

The evening was cool and fragrant and a soft wind whispered in the trees, as Lord Ickenham made his way down the drive. Despite the peril that loomed, his mood was serene. He was sorry to be obliged to leave Blandings Castle, which he had found a pleasant spot full of interesting personalities, but he could see that the time had come to move on. And, after all, he reflected, his work was done. Polly had her money, Pongo had been promised his, and the Empress was safe from the Duke's clutching hand. There was really, he felt, nothing to keep him. All he had to do now was to speak a few soothing words to this explosive young poet of Polly's, and an agreeable episode might be considered closed.

He was about half-way to the castle gate when he heard the sound of footsteps. A small figure was coming towards him through the dusk.

'Polly?'

'Hullo.'

It seemed to Lord Ickenham that there was a flat note in the girl's usually musical voice, and as he halted beside her he detected in her bearing a listlessness which struck him as odd.

'What's the matter?'

'Nothing.'

'Don't be evasive, child. The visibility may not be good, but I can see that you are drooping like a tired flower. Your depression is almost Pongoesque. Come on, now, what has happened?'

'Oh, Uncle Fred!'

'Hullo! Here, I say! Dash it, what's all this about?'

It was some moments later that Polly drew away, dabbing at her eyes.

'I'm sorry. I've been making a fool of myself.'

'Nothing of the kind. A good cry is what we all want at times. I shall recommend it to Pongo. I think I can guess what is wrong. I take it that you have been having a talk with your young man. You went to meet Horace at the gate, and found Ricky. And from your manner, I gather that the plug-ugly rather than the poet was uppermost in him.'

'He was awful. Not that you can blame him.'

'Of course not, bless his heart, the little pet.'

'I mean, I can understand how he must have been feeling. I had promised I would never see Horace again, and there I was, sneaking off to him.'

'Don't be so infernally broadminded, child. Why the devil shouldn't you see Horace as often as you like? What right has this sweet-singing baboon to tell you whom you shall see and whom you shan't see? What happened?'

'He raved and yelled at me. He said everything was over.'

'So he did a couple of days ago, after that Ball. But you smoothed him down.'

'I couldn't this time.'

'Did you try?'

'No. I lost my temper, and started being as beastly as he was.'

'Good girl.'

'It was horrible. He hated me.'

'Do you hate him?'

'Of course I don't.'

'You mean that in spite of everything you love him still?'

'Of course I do.'

'Women are amazing. Well, I'll soon fix things. I'm on my way to interview him now.'

'It won't be any use.'

'That's what they said to Columbus. Don't you worry, my dear. I can handle this. I know my potentialities, and sometimes they absolutely stun me. Are there no limits, I ask myself, to the powers of this wonder-man? I am still completely unable to comprehend why you should want the chap, but if you do you must have him.'

He walked on, and coming presently to the gate found the Bingley standing at the roadside. Pacing up and down in its vicinity like a tiger at feeding-time he perceived a sturdy figure.

'Mr Gilpin, I presume?' he said.

## Chapter 17

So many disturbing things had happened to Ricky Gilpin in the course of this April day that it is scarcely to be wondered at that his mood was not sunny. In a world congested with dukes and Potts and Horace Davenports and faithless girls, it is only an exceptionally philosophical man who can preserve his amiability unimpaired, and Ricky had never been that. He scowled darkly. He did not know who this elegant stranger was, but he was prepared to dislike him.

'Who are you?'

'My name is Ickenham.'

'Oh?'

'I see that it is familiar. No doubt Polly has spoken of me?'

'Yes.'

'Then in reciprocal spirit I will now speak of Polly.'

A quiver passed through Ricky Gilpin's solid body.

'No, you won't. I've finished with her.'

'Don't say that.'

'I do say that.'

Lord Ickenham sighed.

'Youth, Youth! How it flings away its happiness like a heedless child,' he said, and pausing for a moment to think what heedless children flung away added, 'blowing bubbles and throwing them idly into the sunlit air. Too bad, too bad. Shall I tell you a little story, Mr Gilpin?'

'No.'

'Years ago' – it would have taken a better man than Ricky to stop Lord Ickenham telling stories – 'I loved a girl.'

'You haven't by any chance seen Horace Davenport, have you?'

'Loved her dearly.'

'If you do, tell him it's no use his skulking away. I intend to wait here for weeks, if necessary.'

'We quarrelled over some trivial matter. Bitter recriminations ensued. And finally she swept out of the room and married a rubber planter.'

'Sooner or later he will have to present himself and be torn into little pieces.'

'And years afterwards there arrived a simple posy of white violets, together with a slip of paper bearing the words: "It might have been." Tragic, eh? If you will allow an old man to advise you, Mr Gilpin – an old man who has suffered – an old man who threw away his happiness just because he was too proud to speak the little word that –'

There was a metallic clang. Ricky Gilpin appeared to have kicked the fender of the car.

'Listen,' he said. 'I may as well tell you at once that you're wasting your time. I know Polly sent you to try to talk me round –'

'Sent me to talk you round? My dear fellow! You little know that proud girl.'

Lord Ickenham paused. Ricky had moved into the golden pool spread by the headlights, and for the first time he was able to see him as more than an indistinct figure in the dusk.

'Tell me,' he said, 'was your father a chap named Billy Gilpin? In some Irish regiment?'

'His name was William, and he was in the Connaught Rangers. Why?'

'I thought so. You're the living spit of him. Well, now I know that, I'm not so surprised that you should have been behaving in this idiotic way. I used to know your father, and I wish I had five pounds for every time I've sat on his head in bars and restaurants in a painstaking effort to make him see reason. Of all the fly-off-the-handle asses that ever went about with a chip on the shoulder, taking offence at the merest trifles –'

'We won't discuss my father. And if you're suggesting that it's the merest trifle, the girl who's supposed to love you going and hobnobbing with Horace Davenport after she had promised –'

'But, my dear boy, don't you understand that it was precisely because she loved you that she did hobnob with Horace? ... Let me explain, and if when I have finished you are not bathed in shame and remorse, you must be dead to all human feeling. In the first place, nothing but her love for you could have dragged her to that Ball at the Albert Hall. You don't suppose a girl enjoys being seen in public with a fellow wearing the costume of a Zulu warrior and tortoiseshell-rimmed spectacles, do you? Polly went to that Ball because she was prepared to endure physical and spiritual agony in order to further your interests. It was her intention to catch Horace in mellow mood and plead with him to advance you the sum which you require for that onion soup bar of yours.'

'What!'

'For weeks she had been sedulously sweetening him by giving him dancing lessons, and that night was to have marked the culmination of the enterprise. She was hoping to be able to come to you and tell you that the weary waiting was over and that you and she could get married and live happy ever after, dishing out onion soup to the blotto survivors of bottle-parties. By your headstrong conduct you ruined her plans that night. A girl can't try to borrow money from a man while he's being taken off to Marlborough Street Police Station. Her instinct tells her that he will not be in the mood. So she had to wait for another opportunity. Learning that Horace was expected here, she came, too. She met him. She got the money –'

'She – what?'

'Certainly. It's in her possession now. She was bringing it to you.'

'But how did she know I was here?'

For perhaps a third of a split second this question had Lord Ickenham in difficulties.

'Woman's intuition,' he suggested.

'But –'

'Well, there it is,' said Lord Ickenham bluffly. 'What does it matter how she knew you were here? Suffice it that she did know, and she came running to you with the money in her hand like a child about to show some cherished treasure. And you – what did you do? You behaved like a cad and a scoundrel. I'm not surprised that she feels she has had a lucky escape.'

'Oh, my gosh! Does she?'

'That is what she was saying when I saw her just now. And I don't blame her. There can be no love without trust, and a pretty exhibition of trustfulness you gave, did you not?'

To Horace Davenport, could he have seen it at this moment,

Ricky Gilpin's face would have come as a revelation. He would scarcely have been able to believe that those incandescent eyes had it in them to blink so sheepishly, or that that iron jaw could have sagged so like a poorly set blancmange. The future Onion Soup King was exhibiting all the symptoms of one who has been struck on the back of the head with a sock full of wet sand.

'I've made a fool of myself,' he said, and his voice was like the earliest pipe of half-awakened birds.

'You have.'

'I've mucked things up properly.'

'I'm glad you realize it.'

'Where is Polly? I must see her.'

'I wouldn't advise it. You don't appear to understand what it means, behaving to a girl of spirit as you have behaved to Polly. She's furious with you. It would be madness to see her. There is only one thing you can do. When are you returning to London?'

'I had meant to catch the evening train.'

'Do so. Polly will be back at her home shortly. As soon as she arrives, go and buy her chocolates – lots of chocolates – and send them round with a grovelling note.'

'I will.'

'You might then plead for an interview. And when I say plead, I mean plead.'

'Of course.'

'If you display a sufficiently humble and contrite spirit, I see no reason for you to despair. She was fond of you once, and it may be that she will grow fond of you again. I will talk to her and do what I can for you.'

'That's awfully kind of you.'

'Not at all. I would like to do a good turn for the son of an old friend. Good evening, Gilpin, my boy, and remember . . . chocolates – humble, remorseful chocolates – and plenty of them.'

It was perhaps fortunate that Pongo Twistleton was not present when his uncle, rejoining Polly, concluded the recital of what had passed between Ricky Gilpin and himself, for there ensued an emotional scene which would have racked him to the foundations of his being.

'Well, there you are,' said Lord Ickenham, at length. 'That is how matters stand, and all you have to do is sit tight and reap the strategic advantages. I'm glad I told him to send you chocolates. I don't suppose a rugged he-man like that would ever dream of giving a girl chocolates in the ordinary course of things. He struck me as a fellow lacking in the softer social graces.'

'But why wouldn't you let him see me?'

'My dear child, it would have undone all the good work I had accomplished. You would have flung yourself into his arms, and he would have gone on thinking he was the boss. As it is, you have got that young man just where you want him. You will accept his chocolates with a cool reserve which will commit you to nothing, and eventually, after he has been running round in circles for some weeks, dashing into his tailors' from time to time for a new suit of sackcloth and ashes and losing pounds in weight through mental anguish, you will forgive him – on the strict understanding that this sort of thing must never occur again. It doesn't do to let that dominant male type of chap think things are too easy.'

Polly frowned. In a world scented with flowers and full of soft music, these sentiments jarred upon her.

'I don't see why it's got to be a sort of fight.'

'Well, it has. Marriage is a battlefield, not a bed of roses. Who said that? It sounds too good to be my own. Not that I don't think of some extraordinarily good things, generally in my bath.'

'I love Ricky.'

'And very nice, too. But the only way of ensuring a happy married life is to get it thoroughly clear at the outset who is going to skipper the team. My own dear wife settled the point during the honeymoon, and ours has been an ideal union.'

Polly halted abruptly.

'It's all nonsense. I'm going to see him.'

'My dear, don't.'

'Yes.'

'You'll regret it.'

'I won't.'

'Think of all the trouble I've taken.'

'I do, and I can't tell you how grateful I am, Uncle Fred. You've been wonderful. You've picked me up out of the mud and changed the whole world for me. But I can't treat Ricky like that. I'd hate myself. I don't care if he does go on thinking he's the boss. So he is, and I like it!'

Lord Ickenham sighed.

'Very well, if that's the way you feel. "His fair large front and eye sublime declared Absolute rule." If that's the sort of thing you want, I suppose it's no use arguing. If you are resolved to chuck away a heaven-sent opportunity of putting this young man in his place, go ahead, my dear, and God bless you. But you can't see him now. He has gone to catch his train. You must wait till to-morrow.'

'But it's such ages. Couldn't I send him a telegram?'

'No,' said Lord Ickenham firmly. 'There are limits. At least preserve a semblance of womanly dignity. Why not get Horace to drive you to London to-night in his car?'

'Would he, do you think? He's had one long drive already to-day.'

'It is his dearest wish to have another, provided you are at his side. Pongo and I can come on in the morning by that eight-twenty-five train of which everybody speaks so highly.'

'But are you leaving, too?'

'We are. Get Horace to tell you all about it. You will find him in my bedroom. If you don't see him, look in the cupboard. I, meanwhile, must be getting in touch with Pongo and communicating the arrangements to him. The news that we are flitting should please him. For some reason, Pongo has not been happy at Blandings Castle. By the way, did you meet him?'

'Yes. As I was coming back after seeing Ricky.'

'Good. I was only wondering if you had got that money all right.'

'He did offer me some money, but I gave it back to him.'

'Gave it back?'

'Yes. I didn't want it.'

'But, my good child, it was the purchase price of the onion soup bar. Your wedding portion!'

'I know. He told me.' Polly laughed amusedly. 'But I had just had that frightful row with Ricky, and we had parted for ever, and I was thinking of drowning myself, so I didn't want a wedding portion. Will you tell him I should like it, after all?'

174

Lord Ickenham groaned softly.

'You would not speak in that airy, casual way, if you knew the circumstances. Informing Pongo that you would like it, after all, is not going to be the pleasant task you seem to think it. I dare say that with the aid of anaesthetic and forceps I shall eventually be able to extract the money from the unhappy young blighter, but there will be a nasty, hacking sound as he coughs up. Still, you may rely on me to protect your interests, no matter what the cost. I will bring the stuff round to the Pott home to-morrow afternoon. And now run along and find Horace. I know he would appreciate an early start.'

'All right. Uncle Fred, you're an angel.'

'Thank you, my dear.'

'If it hadn't been for you –'

Once more Lord Ickenham found his arms full and behaved with a warmth far greater than one of his nephew's austere views would have considered either necessary or suitable. Then he was alone, and Polly a voice in the darkness, singing happily as she went on her way.

It was some ten minutes later that Lord Ickenham, sauntering along the high road in the direction of Market Blandings, heard another voice, also singing happily. He recognized it with a pang. It was not often that Pongo Twistleton cast off his natural gloom in order to carol like a lark, and the thought that it was for him to wipe this unaccustomed melody from the lips of a young man of whom he was very fond was not an agreeable one.

'Pongo?'

'Hullo, Uncle Fred. I say, what a lovely evening!'

'Very.'

'The air! The stars! The scent of growing things!'

'Quite. Er – Pongo, my boy, about that money.'

'The money you gave me to give to Miss Pott? Oh, yes – I was going to tell you about that. I offered it to her, but she would have none of it.'

'Yes – But –'

'She told me that owing to her having parted brass rags with Ricky, she had no need of it.'

'Precisely. But since then –'

'So I trousered it, and toddled along to Market Blandings, and breezed into the post office, and shoved two hundred quid into an envelope addressed to George Budd and fifty into an envelope addressed to Oofy Prosser and sent them off, registered. So all is now well. The relief,' said Pongo, 'is stupendous.'

It was not immediately that Lord Ickenham spoke. For some moments he stood fingering his moustache and gazing at his nephew thoughtfully. He was conscious of a faint resentment against a Providence which was unquestionably making things difficult for a good man.

'This,' he said, 'is a little awkward.'

'Awkward?'

'Yes.'

'How do you mean? It seems to me . . .'

Pongo's voice trailed away. A hideous thought had come to him.

'Oh, my aunt! Don't tell me she's changed her mind and wants the stuff, after all?'

'I fear so.'

'You mean she's made it up with Ricky?'

'Yes.'

'And needs this money to get married on?'

'Exactly.'

'Oh, my sainted bally aunt!'

'Yes,' said Lord Ickenham, 'it is awkward. No getting away from that. I told Ricky the money was actually in her possession, and he went off to catch his train with golden visions of soup-swilling multitudes dancing before his eyes. I told Polly I would bring her the stuff to-morrow, and she went off singing. It is not going to be pleasant to have to reveal the facts. Disappointment will be inevitable.'

'Would it be any good to ring up Budd and Oofy and ask them to give the money back?'

'No.'

'No, I suppose not. Then what?'

Lord Ickenham's face brightened. He had seen that all was not lost. That busy brain was seldom baffled for long.

'I have it! Mustard!'

'Eh?'

'Mustard Pott. He must handle this for us. Obviously, what we must do is unleash Mustard once more. I think he may be a little annoyed when he learns that his former donation, instead of ensuring the happiness of a loved daughter, has gone to ease the financial difficulties of a comparative stranger like yourself, but I have no doubt that a few minutes of my eloquence will persuade him to forget his natural chagrin and have another pop.'

'At Bosham?'

'Not at Bosham. People who play Persian Monarchs with Mustard in the afternoon are seldom in a frame of mind to play again in the evening. Emsworth is the man.'

'Old Emsworth? Oh, I say, dash it!'

Lord Ickenham nodded.

'I know what you mean. You feel that one ought to draw the line at nicking a kindly host, with whose bread and meat we are bursting, and considering the thing as a broad general proposition I agree with you. It will undoubtedly tarnish the Ickenham escutcheon, and I wish it hadn't got to be done. But in a crisis like this one must sink one's finer feelings. I don't believe I told you, did I, that your sister Valerie is expected here shortly?'

'What!'

'So Horace informs me, and you may look on him as a reliable source. This means that we have got to get out of here by tomorrow's eight-twenty-five train without fail, so you will see that we cannot loiter and dally, if we are to secure funds for Polly. It is not a question of asking ourselves "Is it right to take it off Emsworth?" and "Are we ethically justified in skinning this good old man?" but rather "Has he got it?" And he has. Emsworth, therefore, shall give us of his plenty, and I will be going along now and putting the thing in train. I will look in at your room later and report.'

## Chapter 18

It was a sombre, preoccupied Pongo Twistleton who dressed for dinner that night in the small apartment which had been allotted to him on the second floor. As a rule, the process of transforming himself from the chrysalis of daytime to the shimmering butterfly of night was one that gave him pleasure. He liked the soothing shave, the revivifying bath, the soft crackle of the snowy shirt-front and the general feeling that in a few minutes he would be giving the populace an eyeful. But to-night he was moody and distrait. His lips were tight, and his eyes brooded. Even when he tied his tie, he did it without any real animation.

The news that his sister was on her way to join the little circle at Blandings Castle had shaken him a good deal. It had intensified in him the sensation, which he had been experiencing ever since his arrival, of being beset by perils and menaced by bad citizens. A cat in a strange alley, with an eye out for small boys with bricks, would have understood how he felt. And this nervous apprehension would alone have been enough to take his mind off his toilet.

But far more powerful than apprehension as an agent for wrecking his mental peace was remorse. Ever since he had fallen in love at first sight with Polly Pott, he had been dreaming that an occasion might arise which would enable him to make some great sacrifice for her sake. He had pictured himself patting her little hand, as she thanked him brokenly for that astounding act of nobility. He had seen himself gazing down into her eyes with one of those whimsical, twisted, Ronald Colman smiles. He had even gone so far as to knock together a bit of dialogue for the scene – just in case – starting 'There, there, little girl, it was nothing. All I want is your happiness' and getting even more effective as it went on.

And what had actually happened was that, unless her Persian-Monarchs-playing father intervened and saved the situation at the

eleventh hour, he had ruined her life. It takes an unusually well-tied
tie to relieve a mind tottering under a reflection like that, and his,
he found, looking in the mirror, was only so-so. Indeed, it seemed
to him to fall so far short of the ideal that he was just about to scrap
it and start another, when the door opened and Lord Ickenham
came in.

'Well?' cried Pongo eagerly.

Then his heart sank far beyond what a few moments before he
had supposed to have been an all-time low. One glance at his
uncle's face was enough to tell him that this was no exultant bearer
of glad tidings who stood before him.

Lord Ickenham shook his head. There was a gravity in his
manner that struck a nameless chill.

'The United States Marines have failed us, my boy. The garrison
has not been relieved, the water supply is giving out, and the
savages are still howling on the outskirts. In other words, Mustard
has let us down.'

Pongo staggered to a chair. He sat down heavily. And some
rough indication of his frame of mind may be gathered from the
fact that he forgot to pull the knees of his trousers up.

'Wouldn't he take it on?'

'He would, and did. As I had anticipated, there was a certain
huffiness at first, but I soon talked him round and he assented to
the plan, saying in the most sporting spirit that all I had got to do
was to provide Emsworth, and he would do the rest. He pulled out
his pack of cards and fingered it lovingly, like some grand old
warrior testing the keenness of his blade before a battle. And at this
moment Emsworth entered.'

Pongo nodded heavily.

'I see where you're heading. Emsworth wouldn't play?'

'Oh yes, he played. This is a long and intricate story, my boy, and
I think you had better not interrupt too much, or it will be dinner-
time before we can get down to the agenda.'

'What agenda?'

'I have a scheme or plan of action which I propose to place
before you in due course. Meanwhile, let me relate the sequence of
events. As I say, Emsworth entered, and it was plain from his
manner that he was in the grip of some strong emotion. His eyes

goggled, his pince-nez were adrift and he yammered at me silently
for a while, as is his habit when moved. It then came out that his
pig had been stolen. He had gone down to refresh himself with an
after-tea look at it, and it was not there. Its sty was empty, and its
bed had not been slept in.'

'Oh?'

'I should have thought you could have found some more adequate
comment on a great human tragedy than a mere "Oh?",' said Lord
Ickenham reprovingly. 'Youth is very callous. Yes, the pig had
been stolen, and Emsworth's suspicions immediately leaped, of
course, to the Duke. He was considerably taken aback when I
pointed out that the latter could scarcely be the guilty person,
seeing that he had been in his room all the afternoon. He retired
there immediately after lunch, and was not seen again. And he
could not have gone out into the garden through his bedroom
window, because we find that Baxter was sitting on the lawn from
one-thirty onwards. You may recall that Baxter was not with us at
lunch. It appears that he had a slight attack of dyspepsia and
decided to skip the meal. He testifies that Dunstable did not
emerge. The thing, therefore, becomes one of the great historic
mysteries, ranking with the Man in the Iron Mask and the case of
the *Marie Celeste*. One seeks in vain for a solution.'

Pongo, who had been listening to the narrative with growing
impatience, denied this.

'I don't. I don't give a single, solitary damn. Dash all pigs, is the
way I look at it. You didn't come here to talk about pigs, did you?
What happened about Pott and the card game?'

Lord Ickenham apologized.

'I'm sorry. I'm afraid we old fellows have a tendency to ramble
on. I should have remembered that your interest in the fortunes of
Emsworth's pig is only tepid. Well, I suggested to Emsworth that
what he wanted was to take his mind off the thing, and that an
excellent method of doing this would be to play cards. Mustard said
that curiously enough he happened to have a pack handy, and the
next moment they had settled down to the game.'

Lord Ickenham paused, and drew his breath in reverently.

'It was a magnificent exhibition. Persian Monarchs at its best. I
never expect to witness a finer display of pure science than Mustard

gave. He was playing for his daughter's happiness, and the thought seemed to inspire him. Generally, I believe, on these occasions, it is customary to allow the mug to win from time to time as a sort of gesture, but it was clear that Mustard felt that in a crisis like this old-world courtesy would be out of place. Ignoring the traditions, he won every coup, and when they had finished Emsworth got up, thanked him for a pleasant game, said that it was fortunate that they had not been playing for money or he might have lost a considerable sum, and left the room.'

'Oh, my gosh!'

'Yes, it was a little disconcerting. Mustard tells me he was once bitten by a pig, but I doubt if even on that occasion – high spot in his life though it must have been – he can have been more overcome by emotion. For about five minutes after Emsworth's departure, all he could do was to keep saying in a dazed sort of way that this had never happened to him before. One gets new experiences. And then suddenly I saw his face light up, and he seemed to revive like a watered flower. And, looking round, I found that the Duke had come in.'

'Ah!'

Lord Ickenham shook his head.

'It's no good saying "Ah!" my boy. I told you at the beginning that this story hadn't a happy ending.'

'The Duke wouldn't play?'

'You keep saying that people wouldn't play. People always play when Mustard wants them to. He casts a sort of spell. No, the Duke was delighted to play. He said that he had had a boring afternoon, cooped up in his room, and that now he was out for a short breather a game of Persian Monarchs was just what he would enjoy. He said that as a young man he had been very gifted at the pastime. I saw Mustard's eyes glisten. They sat down.'

Lord Ickenham paused. He seemed to be torn between the natural desire of a raconteur to make the most of his material and a humane urge to cut it short and put his nephew out of his suspense. The latter triumphed.

'Dunstable's claim to excellence at the game was proved to the hilt,' he said briefly. 'Mark you, I don't think Mustard was at his best. That supreme effort so short a while before had left him weak and listless. Be that as it may, Dunstable took three hundred pounds off him in ten minutes.'

Pongo was staring.

'Three hundred pounds?'

'That was the sum.'

'In ready money, do you mean?'

'Paid right across the counter.'

'But if he had all that on him, why didn't he give it to Miss Pott?'

'Ah, I see what you mean. Well, Mustard is a peculiar chap in some ways. It is difficult enough to get him to part with his winnings. Not even for a daughter's sake would he give up his working capital. One dimly understands his viewpoint.'

'I don't.'

'Well, there it is.'

'And now what do we do?'

'Eh? Oh, now, of course, we nip into the Duke's room and pinch the stuff.'

That strange nightmare feeling which had grown so familiar to Pongo of late came upon him again. He presumed he had heard aright – his uncle's enunciation had been beautifully clear – but it seemed incredible that he could have done so.

'Pinch it?'

'Pinch it.'

'But you can't pinch money.'

'Dashed bad form, of course, I know. But I shall look upon it as a loan, to be paid back at intervals – irregular intervals – each instalment accompanied by a posy of white violets.'

'But, dash it –'

'I know what you are thinking. To that highly-trained legal mind of yours it is instantly clear that the act will constitute a tort or misdemeanour, if not actual barratry or socage in fief. But it has got to be done. Polly's need is paramount. I remember Mustard saying once, apropos of my affection for Polly, that I seemed to look on her more like a daughter than a what-not, and he was right. I suppose my feelings towards her are roughly those of Emsworth towards his pig, and when I have the chance to ensure her happiness I am not going to allow any far-fetched scruples to stand in my way. I am a mild, law-abiding man, but to make that kid happy I would willingly become one of those fiends with hatchet who seem to spend their time slaying six. So, as I say, we will pinch the stuff.'

'You aren't proposing to lug me into this?'

Lord Ickenham was astounded.

'Lug you? What an extraordinary expression. I had naturally supposed that you would be overjoyed to do your bit.'

'You don't get me mixed up in this sort of game,' said Pongo firmly. 'Dog Races, yes. Crashing the gate at castles, right. Burglary, no.'

'But, my dear boy, when you reflect that but for you Polly would have all the money she needs –'

'Oh, golly!'

Once more, remorse had burst over Pongo like a tidal wave. In the agitation of the moment, he had forgotten this aspect of the affair. He writhed with shame.

'You mustn't overlook that. In a sense, you are morally bound to sit in.'

'That's right.'

'Then you will?'

'Of course. Rather.'

'Good. I knew you would. You shouldn't pull the old man's leg, Pongo. For a minute I thought you were serious. Well, I am relieved, for your co-operation is essential to the success of the little scheme I have roughed out. What sort of voice are you in these days? Ah, but I remember. When we met in the road, you were warbling like a nightingale. I mistook you for Lily Pons. Excellent.'

'Why?'

'Because it will be your task – your simple, easy task – I will attend to all the really testing work – to flit about the lawn outside Dunstable's window, singing the "Bonny Bonny Banks of Loch Lomond".'

'Eh? Why?'

'You do keep saying "Why?" don't you. It is quite simple. Dunstable, for some reason, is keeping closely to his room. Our first move must be to get him out of it. Even a novice to burglary like myself can see that if you are proposing to ransack a man's room for money, it is much pleasanter to do it when he is not there. Your rendering of Loch Lomond will lure him out. We know how readily he responds to that fine old song. I see your role in this affair as a sort of blend of Lorelei and Will-o'-the-Wisp. You get Dunstable out with your siren singing, and you keep him out by flitting ahead of him through the darkness. Meanwhile, I sneak in and do the needful. No flaws in that?'

'Not so long as nobody sees you.'

'You are thinking of Baxter? Quite right. Always think of everything. If Baxter sees us slip away on some mysterious errand, his detective instincts will undoubtedly be roused. But I have the situation well in hand. I shall give Baxter a knock-out drop.'

'A what?'

'Perhaps you are more familiar with it under the name of Mickey Finn.'

'But where on earth are you going to get a knock-out drop?'

'From Mustard. Unless his whole mode of life has changed since I used to know him, he is sure to have one. In the old days, he never moved without them. When he was running that club of his, it was only by a judicious use of knock-out drops that he was able to preserve order and harmony in his little flock.'

'But how do you propose to make him take it?'

'I shall find a way. He would be in his room now, I imagine?'

'I suppose so.'

'Then after paying a brief call on Mustard I will look in on him and enquire after his dyspepsia. You may leave all this side of the thing to me with every confidence. Your duties will not begin till after dinner. Zero hour is at nine-thirty sharp.'

It was plain to Lord Ickenham, directly he thrust his unwanted society on him a few minutes later, that Rupert Baxter was far from being the stern, steely young fellow of their previous encounters. The message, conveyed by Beach the butler to Lady Constance shortly after noon, that Mr Baxter regretted he would be unable to lunch to-day had been no mere ruse on the secretary's part to enable him to secure the solitude and leisure essential to the man who is planning to steal pigs. The effect of his employer's assignment had been to induce a genuine disorder of the digestive organs. There is always a weak spot in the greatest men. With Baxter, as with Napoleon, it was his stomach.

He had felt a little better towards evening, but now the thought that there lay before him the fearful ordeal of removing the Empress from her temporary lodging in the Duke's bathroom to the car which was to convey her to her new home had brought on another and an even severer attack. At the moment of Lord Ickenham's entry, wild cats to the number of about eighteen had just begun to conduct a free-for-all in his interior.

It was not to be expected, therefore, that he should beam upon his visitor. Nor did he. Ceasing for an instant to massage his waistcoat, he glared in a manner which only the dullest person could have failed to recognize as unfriendly.

'Well?' he said, between clenched teeth.

Lord Ickenham, who had not expected cordiality, was in no way disconcerted by his attitude. He proceeded immediately to supply affability enough for two, which was the amount required.

'I just dropped in,' he explained, 'to make enquiries and offer condolences. You will have been thinking me remiss in not coming before, but you know how it is at a country house. Distractions all the time. Well, my dear fellow, how are you? A touch of the collywobbles, I understand. Too bad, too bad. We all missed you at lunch, and there was a great deal of sympathy expressed – by myself, of course, no less than the others.'

'I can do without your sympathy.'

'Can any of us do without sympathy, Baxter, even from the humblest? Mine, moreover, takes a practical and constructive form. I have here,' said Lord Ickenham, producing a white tablet, 'something which I guarantee will make you forget the most absorbing stomach ache. You take it in a little water.'

Baxter regarded the offering suspiciously. His knowledge of impostors told him that they seldom act from purely altruistic motives. Examine an impostor's act of kindness, and you see something with a string attached to it.

And suddenly there came to him, causing him momentarily to forget bodily anguish, an exhilarating thought.

Rupert Baxter had no illusions about his employer. He did not suppose that the gruff exterior of the Duke of Dunstable hid a heart of gold, feeling – correctly – that if the Duke were handed a heart of gold on a plate with watercress round it, he would not know what it was. But he did credit him with an elementary sense of gratitude, and it seemed to him that after he, Baxter, had carried through with success the perilous task of stealing a pig on his behalf, the old hound could scarcely sack him for having attended a fancy-dress Ball without permission. In other words, this man before him, beneath whose iron heel he had been supposing himself to be crushed, no longer had any hold over him and could be defied with impunity.

'I see you have a tumbler there. I place the tablet in it – so. I fill with water – thus. I stir. I mix. And there you are. Drink it down, and let's see what happens.'

Baxter waved away the cup with a sneer.

'You are very kind,' he said, 'but there is no need to beat about the bush. It is obvious that you have come here in the hope of getting round me –'

Lord Ickenham looked pained.

'Yours is a very suspicious nature, Baxter. You would do well to try to overcome this mistrust of your fellow-men.'

'You want something.'

'Merely to see you your old bonny self again.'

'You are trying to conciliate me, and I know why. You have begun to wonder if the hold you suppose yourself to have over me is quite as great as you imagined.'

'Beautifully expressed. I like the way you talk.'

'Let me tell you at once that it is not. You have no hold over me. Since our conversation in the billiard-room, the whole situation has altered. I have been able to perform a great service for my employer, with the result that I am no longer in danger of being dismissed for having gone to that Ball. So I may as well inform you here and now that it is my intention to have you turned out of the house immediately. Ouch!' said Baxter, rather spoiling the effect of a dignified and impressive speech by clutching suddenly at his midriff.

Lord Ickenham eyed him sympathetically.

'My dear fellow, something in your manner tells me you are in pain. You had better drink that mixture.'

'Get out!'

'It will do you all the good in the world.'

'Get out!'

Lord Ickenham sighed.

'Very well, since you wish it,' he said and, turning, collided with Lord Bosham in the doorway.

'Hullo!' said Lord Bosham. 'Hullo-ullo-ullo! Hullo-ullo-ullo-ullo-ullo!'

He spoke with a wealth of meaning in his voice. There was, he felt, something pretty dashed sinister about finding the villain of the piece alone with Baxter in his room like this. An acquaintance with mystery thrillers almost as comprehensive as his brother Freddie's had rendered him familiar with what happened when these chaps got into rooms. On the thin pretext of paying a formal call, they smuggled in cobras and left them there to do their stuff. 'Well, good afternoon,' they said, and bowed themselves out. But the jolly old cobra didn't bow itself out. It stuck around, concealed in the curtain.

'Hullo!' he added, concluding his opening remarks. 'Want anything?'

'Only dinner,' said Lord Ickenham.

'Oh?' said Lord Bosham. 'Well, it'll be ready in a minute. What was that bird after?' he asked tensely, as the door closed.

Baxter did not reply for a moment. He was engaged in beating his breast, like the Wedding Guest.

'I kicked him out before he could tell me,' he said, as the agony abated. 'Ostensibly, his purpose in coming was to bring me something for my indigestion. A tablet. He put it in that glass. What he was really leading up to, of course, was a request that I would refrain from exposing him.'

'But you can't expose him, can you? Wouldn't you lose your job?'

'There is no longer any danger of that.'

'You mean, even if he tells old Dunstable that you were out on a bender that night, you won't get the boot?'

'Precisely.'

'Then now I know where I stand! Now the shackles have fallen from me, and I am in a position to set about these impostors as impostors should be set about. That's really official, is it?'

'Quite. Ouch!'

'Anguish?'

'Oo!'

'If I were you,' said Lord Bosham, 'I'd drink the stuff the blighter gave you. There's no reason why it shouldn't prove efficacious. The fact that a chap is an impostor doesn't necessarily mean that he can't spot a good stomach ache cure when he sees one. Down the hatch with it, my writhing old serpent, with a hey nonny nonny and a hot cha-cha.'

Another twinge caused Baxter to hesitate no longer. He saw that the advice was good. He raised the glass to his lips. He did not drain it with a hey nonny nonny, but he drained it.

It was then too late for him to say 'Hey, nonny nonny,' even if he had wished to.

Down in the hall, like a hound straining at the leash, Beach the butler stood with uplifted stick, waiting for the psychological moment to beat the gong. Lady Constance, as she came downstairs, caught a glimpse of him over the banisters, but she was not accorded leisure to feast her eyes on the spectacle, for along the corridor to her left there came a galloping figure. It was her nephew, Lord Bosham. He reached her, seized her by the wrist and jerked her into an alcove. Accustomed though she was to eccentricity in her nephews, the action momentarily took her breath away.

'Gee-ORGE!' she cried, finding speech.

'Yes, I know, I know. But listen.'

'Are you intoxicated?'

'Of course I'm not. What a dashed silly idea. Much shaken, but sober to the gills. Listen, Aunt Connie. You know those impostors? Impostors A, B, and C? Well, things are getting hot. Impostor A has just laid Baxter out cold with a knock-out drop.'

'What! I don't understand.'

'Well, I can't make it any simpler. That is the bedrock fact. Impostor A has just slipped Baxter a Mickey Finn. And what I'm driving at is, that if these birds are starting to express themselves like this, it means something. It means that tonight's the night. It signifies that whatever dirty work they are contemplating springing on this community will be sprung before to-morrow's sun has risen. Ah!' said Lord Bosham, with animation, as the gong boomed out below. 'Dinner, and not before I was ready for it. Let's go. But mark this, Aunt Connie, and mark it well – the moment we rise from the table, I get my good old gun, and I lurk! I don't know what's up, and you don't know what's up, but that something is up sticks out a mile, and I intend to lurk like a two-year-old. Well, I mean to say, dash it,' said Lord Bosham, with honest heat, 'we can't have this sort of thing, what? If impostors are to be allowed to go chucking their weight about as if they'd bought the place, matters have come to a pretty pass!'

## Chapter 19

At twenty minutes past nine, the Duke of Dunstable, who had dined off a tray in his room, was still there, waiting for his coffee and liqueur. He felt replete, for he was a good trencherman and had done himself well, but he was enjoying none of that sensation of mental peace which should accompany repletion. Each moment that passed found him more worried and fretful. The failure of Rupert Baxter to report for duty was affecting him much as their god's unresponsiveness once affected the priests of Baal. Here it was getting on for goodness knew what hour, and not a sign of him. It would have pained the efficient young secretary, now lying on his bed with both hands pressed to his temples in a well-meant but unsuccessful attempt to keep his head from splitting in half, could he have known the black thoughts his employer was thinking of him.

The opening of the door, followed by the entry of Beach bearing a tray containing coffee and a generous glass of brandy, caused the Duke to brighten for an instant, but the frown returned to his brow as he saw that the butler was not alone. The last thing he wanted at a time like this was a visitor.

'Good evening, my dear fellow. I wonder if you could spare me a moment?'

It was about half-way through dinner that the thought had occurred to Lord Ickenham that there might be an easier and more agreeable method than that which he had planned of obtaining from the Duke the money which he was, as it were, holding in trust for Polly. He had not developed any weak scruples about borrowing it on the lines originally laid down, but the almost complete absence of conversation at the dinner-table had given him time to reflect, and the result of this reflection had been to breed misgivings.

Success in the campaign which he had sketched out would

depend – he had to face it – largely on the effectiveness of his nephew Pongo's performance of the part assigned to him, and he feared lest Pongo, when it came to the pinch, might prove a broken reed. You tell a young man to stand on a lawn and sing the "Bonny Bonny Banks of Loch Lomond", and the first thing you know he has forgotten the tune or gone speechless with stage fright. Far better, it seemed to him, to try what a simple, straightforward appeal to the Duke's better feelings would do – and, if that failed, to have recourse to the equally simple and straightforward Mickey Finn.

That glass of brandy there would make an admirable receptacle for the sedative, and he had taken the precaution, while tapping Mr Pott's store, to help himself to a couple of the magic tablets, one of which still nestled in his waistcoat pocket.

'It's about that money you won from that man – Pott is his name, I believe – this evening,' he went on.

The Duke grunted guardedly.

'I have been talking to him, and he is most distressed about it.'

The Duke grunted again, scornfully this time, and it seemed to Lord Ickenham that an odd sort of echo came from the bathroom. He put it down to some trick of the acoustics.

'Yes, most distressed. It seems that in a sense the money was not his to gamble with.'

'Hey?' The Duke seemed interested. 'What do you mean? Robbed a till or something, did he?'

'No, no. Nothing like that. He is a man of the most scrupulous honesty. But it was a sum which he had been saving up for his daughter's wedding portion. And now it has gone.'

'What do you expect me to do about it?'

'You wouldn't feel inclined to give it back?'

'Give it back?'

'It would be a fine, generous, heart-stirring action.'

'It would be a fine, potty, fatheaded action,' corrected the Duke warmly. 'Give it back, indeed! I never heard of such a thing.'

'He is much distressed.'

'Let him be.'

It began to be borne in upon Lord Ickenham that in planning to appeal to the Duke's better feelings he had omitted to take into his calculations the fact that he might not have any. With a dreamy look in his eye, he took the tablet from his pocket and palmed it thoughtfully.

'It would be a pity if his daughter were not able to get married,' he said.

'Why?' said the Duke, a stout bachelor.

'She is engaged to a fine young poet.'

'Then,' said the Duke, his face beginning to purple – the Dunstables did not easily forget – 'she's jolly well out of it. Don't talk to me about poets! The scum of the earth.'

'So you won't give the money back?'

'No.'

'Reflect,' said Lord Ickenham. 'It is here, in this room – is it not?'

'What's that got to do with it?'

'I was only thinking that there it was – handy – and all you would have to do would be to go to the drawer . . . or cupboard . . .'

He paused expectantly. The Duke maintained a quiet reserve.

'I wish you would reconsider.'

'Well, I won't.'

'The quality of mercy,' said Lord Ickenham, deciding that he could not do better than follow the tested methods of Horace's Pekingese breeder, 'is not strained –'

'The what isn't?'

'The quality of mercy. It droppeth as the gentle rain from heaven upon the place beneath. It is twice blessed –'

'How do you make that out?'

'It blesseth him that gives and him that takes,' explained Lord Ickenham.

'Never heard such rot in my life,' said the Duke. 'I think you're potty. Anyhow, you'll have to go now. I'm expecting my secretary at any moment for an important conference. You haven't seen him anywhere, have you?'

'I had a few words with him before dinner, but I have not seen him since. He is probably amusing himself somewhere.'

'I'll amuse him, when I see him.'

'No doubt he has been unable to tear himself away from the fascinations of the backgammon board or the halma table. Young blood!'

'Young blood be blowed.'

'Ah, that will be he, no doubt.'

'Eh?'

'Someone knocked.'

'I didn't hear anything.'

The Duke went to the door and opened it. Lord Ickenham stretched a hand over the brandy glass and opened it. The Duke came back.

'Nobody there.'

'Ah, then I was mistaken. Well, if you really wish me to go, I will be leaving you. If you don't feel like making the splendid gesture I proposed, there is no more to be said. Good night, my dear fellow,' said Lord Ickenham, and withdrew.

It was perhaps a minute after he had taken his departure that Mr Pott entered the corridor.

Of all the residents of Blandings Castle who had been doing a bit of intensive thinking during dinner – and there were several – Claude Pott was the one who had been thinking hardest. And the result of his thoughts had been to send him hastening to the Duke's room. It was his hope that he would be able to persuade him to play a hand or two of a game called Slippery Joe.

The evening's disaster had left Mr Pott not only out of pocket and humiliated, but full of the liveliest suspicion. How the miracle had been accomplished, he was unable to say, but the more he brooded over the Duke's triumph, the more convinced did he become that he had been cheated and hornswoggled. Honest men, he told himself, did not beat him at Persian Monarchs, and he blamed himself for having selected a game at which it was possible, apparently, for an unscrupulous opponent to put something over. Slippery Joe was open to no such objection. Years of experience had taught him that at Slippery Joe he could always deal himself an unbeatable hand.

He was just about to turn the corner leading to the Garden Suite, hoping for the best, when the Duke came round it, travelling well, and ran into him.

For some moments after Lord Ickenham had left him, the Duke of Dunstable had remained where he sat, frowning peevishly. Then he had risen. Distasteful and even degrading though it might be to go running about after secretaries, there seemed nothing for it but to institute a search for the missing Baxter. He hastened out, and the first thing he knew he was colliding with the frightful feller.

Then he saw that it was not the frightful feller, after all, but another feller, equally frightful – the chap with the wedding-portion daughter, to wit – a man for whom, since listening to Lord Ickenham's remarks, he had come to feel a vivid dislike. He was not fond of many people, but the people of whom he was least fond were those who wanted to get money out of him.

'Gah!' he said, disentangling himself.

Mr Pott smiled an ingratiating smile. It was only a sketchy one, for he had had to assemble it in a hurry, but such as it was he let the Duke have it.

'Hullo, your Grace,' he said.

'Go to hell,' said the Duke and, these brief civilities concluded, stumped off and was lost to sight.

And simultaneously a thought came to Mr Pott like a full-blown rose, flushing his brow.

Until this moment, Mr Pott's only desire had been to recover his lost money through the medium of a game of Slippery Joe. He now saw that there was a simpler and less elaborate way of arriving at the happy ending. Somewhere in the Duke's room there was three hundred pounds morally belonging to himself, and the Duke's room was now unoccupied. To go in and help himself would be to avoid a lot of tedious preliminaries.

Though stout of build, he could move quickly when the occasion called for speed. He bounced along the passage like a rubber ball. Only when he had reached his destination did he find that he need not have hurried. Preoccupied the Duke might have been, but he had not been too preoccupied to remember to lock his door.

The situation was one that might have baffled many men, and for an instant it baffled Mr Pott completely. Then, his native ingenuity asserting itself, he bethought him that the door was not the only means of access to the room. There were french windows, and it was just possible that on a balmy evening like this the Duke might have left them open. Reaching the lawn after a brisk run, rosy and puffing, he discovered that he had not.

This time, Mr Pott accepted defeat. He knew men in London

who would have made short work of those windows. They would have produced a bit of bent wire and opened them as if they had been a sardine tin, laughing lightly the while. But he had no skill in that direction. Rueful but resigned, with some of the feelings of Moses gazing at the Promised Land from the summit of Mount Pisgah, he put an eye to the glass and peered through. There was the dear old room, all ready and waiting, but for practical purposes it might have been a hundred miles away. And presently he saw the door open and the Duke come in.

And he was turning away with a sigh, a beaten man, when from somewhere close at hand a voice in the night began to sing the 'Bonny Bonny Banks of Loch Lomond'. And scarcely had the haunting refrain ceased to annoy the birds roosting in the trees, when the french windows flew open and the Duke of Dunstable, shooting out like a projectile, went whizzing across the lawn, crying 'Hey!' as he did so. To Mr Pott, the thing had been just a song, but to the Duke it seemed to have carried a deeper message.

And such was indeed the case. The interpretation which he had placed upon that sudden burst of melody was that it was Baxter who stood warbling without, and that this was his way of trying to attract his employer's attention. Why Baxter should sing outside his room, instead of walking straight in, was a problem which he found himself at the moment unable to solve. He presumed that the man must have some good reason for a course of conduct which at first glance seemed merely eccentric. Possibly, he reflected, complications had arisen, rendering it necessary for him to communicate with headquarters in this oblique and secret society fashion. He could vaguely recall having read in his boyhood stories in which people in such circumstances had imitated the hoot of the night-owl.

'Hey!' he called, trying to combine the conflicting tasks of shouting and speaking in a cautious undertone. 'Here! Hi! Hey! Where are you, dash it?'

For his efforts to establish contact with the vocalist were being oddly frustrated. Instead of standing still and delivering his report, the other seemed to be receding into the distance. When the 'Bonny Banks' broke out again, it was from somewhere at the farther end of the lawn. With a muffled oath, the Duke galloped in that direction like the man in the poem who followed the Gleam, and

Mr Pott, always an excellent opportunist, slid in through the french windows.

He had scarcely done so, when he heard footsteps. Somebody was approaching across the grass, and approaching so rapidly that there was no time to be lost if an embarrassing encounter was to be avoided. With great presence of mind he dived into the bathroom. And as he closed the door, Lord Ickenham came in.

Lord Ickenham was feeling well pleased. The artistry of his nephew's performance had enchanted him. He had not supposed that the boy had it in him to carry the thing through with such *bravura*. At the best he had hoped for a timid piping, and that full-throated baying, a cross between a bloodhound on the trail and a Scotsman celebrating New Year's Eve, had been as unexpected as it was agreeable. Technical defects there may have been in Pongo's vocalization, but he had certainly brought the Duke out of the room like a cork out of a bottle. Lord Ickenham could not remember ever having seen a duke move quicker.

And he was just settling down to a swift and intensive search for the wedding portion, when his activities were arrested. From behind the bathroom door, freezing him in his tracks, there came the sharp, piercing scream of a human being in distress. The next moment, Mr Pott staggered out, slamming the door behind him.

'Mustard!' cried Lord Ickenham, completely at a loss.

'Coo!' said Mr Pott, and in a lifetime liberally punctuated by that ejaculation he had never said it with stronger emphasis.

Normally, Claude Pott was rather a reserved man. He lived in a world in which if you showed your feelings, you lost money. But there were some things which could break down his poise, and one of these was the discovery that he was closeted in a small bathroom with the largest pig he had ever encountered.

For an instant, after he had entered his hiding-place, the Empress had been just an aroma in the darkness. If Mr Pott had felt that it was a bit stuffy in here, that was all he had felt. Then something cold and moist pressed itself against his dangling hand, and the truth came home to him.

'Mustard, my dear fellow!'

'Cor!' said Mr Pott.

He was shaking in every limb. It is not easy for a man who

weighs nearly two hundred pounds to quiver like an aspen, but he managed to do it. His mind was in a whirl, from which emerged one coherent thought – that he wanted a drink. An imperious desire for a quick restorative swept over him, and suddenly he perceived that there was relief in sight – if only a small relief. That glass of brandy on the table would be of little real use to him. What he really needed was a brimming bucketful. But it would at least be a step in the right direction.

'Mustard! Stop!'

Lord Ickenham's warning cry came too late. The lethal draught had already passed down Mr Pott's throat, and even as he shook his head appreciatively the glass fell to the floor and he followed it. If twenty pigs had bitten Claude Pott simultaneously in twenty different places, he could not have succumbed more completely.

It was with a sympathetic eye and a tut-tut-ing tongue that Lord Ickenham bent over the remains. There was nothing, he knew, to be done. Only Time, the great healer, could make Claude Pott once more the Claude Pott of happier days. He rose, wondering how best to dispose of the body, and as he did so a voice spoke behind him.

'Hullo-ullo-ullo-ullo-ullo!' it said, and in the words there was an unmistakable note of rebuke.

Faithfully and well Lord Bosham had followed out his policy of lurking, as outlined to his Aunt Constance before dinner. He was now standing in the window, his gun comfortably poised.

'What ho, what ho, what ho, what ho, what ho, what, what?' he added, and paused for a reply.

This Lord Ickenham was not able to give. Man of iron nerve though he was, he could be taken aback. The sudden appearance of Horace Davenport earlier in the evening had done it. The equally sudden appearance of Lord Bosham did it again. He found himself at a loss for words, and it was Lord Bosham who eventually resumed the conversation.

'Well, I'm dashed!' he said, still speaking with that strong note of reproof. 'Here's a nice state of things! So you've put it across poor old Pott now, have you? It's a bit thick. We engage detectives at enormous expense, and as fast as we get them in you bowl them over with knock-out drops.'

He paused, struggling with his feelings. It was plain that he could not trust himself to say what he really thought about it all. His eye roamed the room, and lit up as it rested on the door of the cupboard.

'You jolly well get in there,' he said, indicating it with a wave of the gun. 'Into that cupboard with you, quick, and no back chat.'

If Lord Ickenham had had any intention of essaying repartee, he abandoned it. He entered the cupboard, and the key turned in the lock behind him.

Lord Bosham pressed the bell. A stately form appeared in the doorway.

'Oh, Beach.'

'M'lord?'

'Get a flock of footmen and have Mr Pott taken up to his room, will you?'

'Very good, m'lord.'

The butler had betrayed no emotion on beholding what appeared to be a corpse on the floor of the Garden Suite. Nor did the two footmen, Charles and Henry, who subsequently carried out the removal. It was Blandings Castle's pride that its staff was well trained. Mr Pott disappeared feet foremost, like a used gladiator being cleared away from the arena, and Lord Bosham was left to his thoughts.

These might have been expected to be exultant, for he had undoubtedly acted with dash and decision in a testing situation. But they were only partly so. Mingled with a victor's triumph was the chagrin of the conscientious man who sees a task but half done. That he had properly put a stopper on Impostor A was undeniable, but he had hoped also to deal faithfully with Impostor B. He was wondering if the chap was hiding somewhere and, if so, where, when there came to his sensitive ear the sound of a grunt, and he realized that it had proceeded from the bathroom.

'Yoicks!' cried Lord Bosham, and if he had not been a man of action rather than words would have added 'Tally-ho!' He did not pause to ask himself why impostors should grunt. He merely dashed at the bathroom door, flung it open and leaped back, his gun at the ready. There was a moment's pause, and then the Empress sauntered out, a look of mild enquiry on her fine face.

The Empress of Blandings was a pig who took things as they

came. Her motto, like Horace's, was *nil admirari*. But, cool and even aloof though she was as a general rule, she had been a little puzzled by the events of the day. In particular, she had found the bathroom odd. It was the only place she had ever been in where there appeared to be a shortage of food. The best it had to offer was a cake of shaving-soap, and she had been eating this with a thoughtful frown when Mr Pott joined her. As she emerged now, she was still foaming at the mouth a little and it was perhaps this that set the seal on Lord Bosham's astonishment and caused him not only to recoil a yard or two with his eyes popping but also to pull the trigger of his gun.

In the confined space the report sounded like the explosion of an arsenal, and it convinced the Empress, if she had needed to be convinced, that this was no place for a pig of settled habits. Not since she had been a slip of a child had she moved at anything swifter than a dignified walk, but now Jesse Owens could scarcely have got off the mark more briskly. It took her a few moments to get her bearings, but after colliding with the bed, the table and the armchair, in the order named, she succeeded in setting a course for the window and was in the act of disappearing through it when Lord Emsworth burst into the room, followed by Lady Constance.

The firing of guns in bedrooms is always a thing that tends to excite the interest of the owner of a country house, and it was in a spirit of lively curiosity that Lord Emsworth had arrived upon the scene. An 'Eh, what?' was trembling on his lips as he entered. But the sight of those vanishing hindquarters with their flash of curly tail took his mind instantly off such comparative trivialities as indoor artillery practice. With a cry that came straight from the heart, he adjusted his pince-nez and made for the great outdoors. Broken words of endearment could be heard coming from the darkness.

Lady Constance had propped herself against the wall, a shapely hand on her heart. She was panting a little, and her eyes showed a disposition to swivel in their sockets. Long ago she had learned the stern lesson that Blandings Castle was no place for weaklings, but this latest manifestation of what life under its roof could be had proved daunting to even her toughened spirit.

'George!' she whispered feebly.

Lord Bosham was his old buoyant self again.

'Quite all right, Aunt Connie. Just an accident. Sorry you were troubled.'

'What – what has been happening?'

'I thought you would want to know that. Well, it was like this. I came in here, to discover that Impostor A had scuppered our detective with one of those knock-out drops of his. I quelled him with my good old gun, and locked him in the cupboard. I thought I heard Impostor B grunting in the bathroom and flung wide the gates, only to discover that it was the guv'nor's pig. Starting back in natural astonishment, I inadvertently pulled the trigger. All quite simple and in order.'

'I thought the Duke had been murdered.'

'No such luck. By the way, I wonder where he's got to. Ah, here's Beach. He'll tell us. Do you know where the Duke is, Beach?'

'No, m'lord. Pardon me, m'lady.'

'Yes, Beach?'

'A Miss Twistleton has called, m'lady.'

'Miss Twistleton?'

Lord Bosham's memory was good.

'That's the girl who gave Horace the raspberry,' he reminded his aunt.

'I know that,' said Lady Constance, with some impatience. 'What I meant was, what can she be doing here at this hour?'

'I gathered, m'lady, that Miss Twistleton had arrived on the five o'clock train from London.'

'But what can she want?'

'That,' Lord Bosham pointed out, 'we can ascertain by seeing the wench. Where did you park her, Beach?'

'I showed the lady into the drawing-room, m'lord.'

'Then Ho for the drawing-room is what I would suggest. My personal bet is that she supposes Horace to be here and has come to tell him she now regrets those cruel words. Oh, Beach.'

'M'lord?'

'Can you use a gun?'

'As a young lad I was somewhat expert with an air-gun, m'lord.'

'Well, take this. It isn't an air-gun, but the principle's the same. You put it to the shoulder – so – and pull the trigger – thus . . .

Oh, sorry,' said Lord Bosham, as the echoes of the deafening report died away and his aunt and her butler, who had skipped like the high hills, came back to terra firma. 'I forgot that would happen. Silly of me. Now I'll have to reload. There's a miscreant in that cupboard, Beach, a devil of a chap who wants watching like a hawk, and I shall require you to stay here and see that he doesn't get out. At the first sign of any funny business on his part, such as trying to break down the door, whip the weapon to the shoulder and blaze away like billy-o. You follow me, Beach?'

'Yes, m'lord.'

'Then pick up the feet, Aunt Connie,' said Lord Bosham, 'and let's go.'

## Chapter 20

The fruitless pursuit of Loreleis or will-o'-the-wisps through a dark garden, full of things waiting to leap out and crack him over the shins, can never be an agreeable experience to a man of impatient temperament, accustomed to his comforts. It was a puffing and exasperated Duke of Dunstable who limped back to his room a few minutes after Beach had taken up his vigil. His surprise at finding it occupied by a butler – and not merely an ordinary butler, without trimmings, but one who toted a gun – was very marked. Nor did the sight in any way allay his annoyance. There was a silent instant in which he stood brushing from his moustache the insects of the night that had got entangled there and glaring balefully at the intruder. Then he gave tongue.

'Hey? What? What's this? What the devil's all this? What do you mean, you feller, by invading my private apartment with a dashed great cannon? Of all the houses I was ever in, this is certainly the damnedest. I come down here for a nice rest, and before I can so much as relax a muscle, I find my room full of blasted butlers, armed to the teeth. Don't point that thing at me, sir. Put it down, and explain.'

In a difficult situation, Beach preserved the courteous calm which had made him for so many years the finest butler in Shropshire. He found the Duke's manner trying, but he exhibited nothing but a respectful desire to give satisfaction.

'I must apologize for my presence, your Grace,' he said smoothly, 'but I was instructed by Lord Bosham to remain here and act as his deputy during his temporary absence. I am informed by his lordship that he has deposited a miscreant in the cupboard.'

'A what?'

'A miscreant, your Grace. Something, I gather, in the nature of a nocturnal marauder. His lordship gave me to understand that he discovered the man in this room and, having overpowered him, locked him in the cupboard.'

'Hey? Which cupboard?'

The butler indicated the safe deposit in question, and the Duke uttered a stricken cry.

'My God! All in among my spring suits! Let him out at once.'

'His lordship instructed me —'

'Dash his lordship! I'm not going to have smelly miscreants ruining my clothes. What sort of a miscreant?'

'I have no information, your Grace.'

'Probably some foul tramp with the grime of years on him, and the whole outfit will have to go to the cleaner's. Let him out immediately.'

'Very good, your Grace.'

'I'll turn the key and throw the door open, and you stand ready with your gun. Now, then, when I say "Three." One . . . Two . . . Three . . . Good Lord, it's the brain chap!'

Lord Ickenham had not enjoyed his sojourn in the cupboard, which he had found close and uncomfortable, but it had left him his old debonair self.

'Ah, my dear Duke,' he said genially, as he emerged, 'good evening once more. I wonder if I might use your hairbrush? The thatch has become a little disordered.'

The Duke was staring with prawnlike eyes.

'Was that you in there?' he asked. A foolish question, perhaps, but a man's brain is never at its nimblest on these occasions.

Lord Ickenham said it was.

'What on earth were you doing, going into cupboards?'

Lord Ickenham passed the brush lovingly through his grey locks.

'I went in because I was requested to by the man behind the gun. I happened to be strolling on the lawn and saw your windows open, and I thought I might enjoy another chat with you. I had scarcely entered, when Bosham appeared, weapon in hand. I don't know how you feel about these things, my dear fellow, but my view is that when an impetuous young gentleman, fingering the trigger of a gun, tells you to go into a cupboard, it is best to humour him.'

'But why did he tell you to go into the cupboard?'

'Ah, there you take me into deep waters. He gave me no opportunity of enquiring.'

'I mean, you're not a nocturnal marauder.'

'No. The whole thing is very odd.'

'I'm going to get to the bottom of this. Hey, you, go and fetch Lord Bosham.'

'Very good, your Grace.'

'The fact of the matter is,' said the Duke, as the butler left the room like a stately galleon under sail, 'the whole family's potty, as I told you before. I just met Emsworth in the garden. His manner was most peculiar. He called me a pig-stealing pest and a number of other things. I made allowances, of course, for the fact that he's as mad as a hatter, but I shall leave to-morrow and I shan't come here again. They'll miss me, but I can't help that. Did Bosham shoot at you?'

'No.'

'He shot at someone.'

'Yes, I heard a fusillade going on.'

'The feller oughtn't to be at large. Human life isn't safe. Ah, here he is. Here, you!'

Through the door a little procession was entering. It was headed by Lady Constance. Behind her came a tall, handsome girl, in whom Lord Ickenham had no difficulty in recognizing his niece Valerie. The rear was brought up by Lord Bosham. Lady Constance was looking cold and stern, Valerie Twistleton colder and sterner. Lord Bosham looked merely bewildered. He resembled his father and his brother Freddie in not being very strong in the head, and the tale to which he had been listening in the drawing-room had been of a nature not at all suited to the consumption of the weak-minded. A girl claiming to be Miss Twistleton, niece of the Earl of Ickenham, had suddenly blown in from nowhere with the extraordinary story that Impostor A was her uncle, and she had left Lord Bosham with such brain as he possessed in a whirl. He was anxious for further light on a puzzling situation.

'What the devil do you mean . . .' The Duke broke off. He was staring at Lady Constance's companion, whom, owing to the fact that his gaze had been riveted on Lord Bosham, he had not immediately observed. 'Hey, what?' he said. 'Where did you spring from?'

'This is Miss Twistleton, Alaric.'

'Of course she's Miss Twistleton. I know that.'

'Ah!' said Lord Bosham. 'She *is* Miss Twistleton, is she? You identify her?'

'Of course I identify her.'

'My mistake,' said Lord Bosham. 'I thought she might be Impostor D.'

'George, you're an idiot!'

'Right ho, Aunt Connie.'

'Bosham, you're a damned fool!'

'Right ho, Duke.'

'Chump!'

'Right ho, Miss Twistleton. It was just that it occurred to me as a passing thought that Miss Twistleton, though she said she was Miss Twistleton, might not be Miss Twistleton but simply pretending to be Miss Twistleton in order to extricate Impostor A from a nasty spot. But, of course, if you're all solid on the fact of Miss Twistleton really being Miss Twistleton, my theory falls to the ground. Sorry, Miss Twistleton.'

'George, will you please stop drivelling.'

'Right ho, Aunt Connie. Merely mentioning what occurred to me as a passing thought.'

Now that the point of Miss Twistleton's identity – the fact that she was a genuine Miss Twistleton and not a pseudo Miss Twistleton – had been settled, the Duke returned to the grievance which he had started to ventilate a few moments earlier.

'And now perhaps you'll explain, young cloth-headed Bosham, what you mean by shutting your father's guests in cupboards. Do you realize that the man might have messed up my spring suits and died of suffocation?'

Lady Constance intervened.

'We came to let Lord Ickenham out.'

'Let who out?'

'Lord Ickenham.'

'How do you mean, Lord Ickenham?'

'This is Lord Ickenham.'

'Yes,' said Lord Ickenham, 'I am Lord Ickenham. And this,' he went on, bestowing a kindly glance on the glacial Valerie, 'is my favourite niece.'

'I'm your only niece.'

'Perhaps that's the reason,' said Lord Ickenham.

The Duke had now reached an almost Bosham-like condition of mental fog.

'I don't understand all this. If you're Ickenham, why didn't you say you were Ickenham? Why did you tell us you were Glossop?'

'Precisely,' said Lady Constance. 'I am waiting for Lord Ickenham to explain –'

'Me, too,' said Lord Bosham.

'– his extraordinary behaviour.'

'Extraordinary is the word,' assented Lord Bosham. 'As a matter of fact, his behaviour has been extraordinary all along. Most extraordinary. By way of a start, he played the confidence trick on me in London.'

'Just to see whether it could be done, my dear fellow,' explained Lord Ickenham. 'Merely an experiment in the interests of science. I sent your wallet to your home, by the way. You will find it waiting there for you.'

'Oh, really?' said Lord Bosham, somewhat mollified. 'I'm glad to hear that. I value that wallet.'

'A very nice wallet.'

'It is rather, isn't it? My wife gave it me for a birthday present.'

'Indeed? How is your wife?'

'Oh, fine, thanks.'

'Whoso findeth a wife findeth a good thing.'

'I'll tell her that. Rather neat. Your own?'

'Proverbs of Solomon.'

'Oh? Well, I'll pass it along, anyway. It should go well.'

Lady Constance was finding a difficulty in maintaining her patrician calm. This difficulty her nephew's conversation did nothing to diminish.

'Never mind about your wife, George. We are all very fond of Cicely, but we do not want to talk about her now.'

'No, no, of course not. Don't quite know how we got on to the subject. Still, before leaving same, I should just like to mention that she's the best little woman in the world. Right ho, Aunt Connie, carry on. You have the floor.'

There was a frigidity in Lady Constance's manner.

'You have really finished?'

'Oh, rather.'

'You are quite sure?'

'Oh, quite.'

'Then I will ask Lord Ickenham to explain why he came to Blandings Castle pretending to be Sir Roderick Glossop.'

'Yes, let's have a diagram of that.'

'Be quiet, George.'

'Right ho, Aunt Connie.'

Lord Ickenham looked thoughtful.

'Well,' he said, 'it's a long story.'

Valerie Twistleton's eye, as it met her uncle's, was hard and un-friendly.

'Your stories can never be too long,' she said, speaking with a metallic note in her voice. 'And we have the night before us.'

'And why,' asked Lord Bosham, 'did he lay out Baxter and our detective with knock-out drops?'

'Please, George!'

'Yes,' said Lord Ickenham rebukingly, 'we shall never get any-where, if you go wandering off into side issues. It is, as I say, a long story, but if you are sure it won't bore you –'

'Not at all,' said Valerie. 'We shall all be most interested. So will Aunt Jane, when I tell her.'

Lord Ickenham looked concerned.

'My dear child, you mustn't breathe a word to your aunt about meeting me here.'

'Oh, no?'

'Emphatically not. Lady Constance will agree with me, I know, when she has heard what I have to say.'

'Then please say it.'

'Very well. The explanation of the whole thing is absurdly simple. I came here on Emsworth's behalf.'

'I do not understand you.'

'I will make myself plain.'

'I still don't see,' said Lord Bosham, who had been brooding with bent brows, 'why he should have slipped kayo drops in –'

'George!'

'Oh, all right.'

Lord Ickenham regarded the young man for a moment with a reproving eye.

'Emsworth,' he resumed, 'came to me and told me a strange and romantic story –'

'And now,' said Valerie, 'you're telling us one.'

'My dear! It seemed that he had become sentimentally attached to a certain young woman . . . or person . . . or party . . . however you may choose to describe her –'

'What!'

Lord Bosham appeared stunned.

'Why, dash it, he was a hundred last birthday!'

'Your father is a man of about my own age.'

'And mine,' said the Duke.

'I should describe him as being in the prime of life.'

'Exactly,' said the Duke.

'I often say that life begins at sixty.'

'So do I,' said the Duke. 'Frequently.'

'That, at any rate,' proceeded Lord Ickenham, 'was how Emsworth felt. The fever of spring was coursing through his veins, and he told himself that there was life in the old dog yet. I use the expression "old dog" in no derogatory sense. He conceived a deep attachment for this girl, and persuaded me to bring her here as my daughter.'

Lady Constance had now abandoned altogether any attempt at preserving a patrician calm. She uttered a cry which, if it had proceeded from a less aristocratic source, might almost have been called a squeal.

'What! You mean that my brother is infatuated with that child?'

'Where did he meet her?' asked Lord Bosham.

'It was his dearest wish,' said Lord Ickenham, 'to make her his bride.'

'Where did he meet her?' asked Lord Bosham.

'It not infrequently happens that men in the prime of life pass through what might be described as an Indian Summer of the affections, and when this occurs the object of their devotion is generally pretty juvenile.'

'What beats me,' said Lord Bosham, 'is where on earth he could have met her. I didn't know the guv'nor ever stirred from the old home.'

It seemed to Lord Ickenham that this was a line of enquiry which it would be well to check at its source.

'I wish you wouldn't interrupt,' he said, brusquely.

'Yes, dash it, you oaf,' said the Duke, 'stop interrupting.'

'Can't you see, George,' cried Lady Constance despairingly, 'that we are all almost off our heads with worry and anxiety, and you keep interrupting.'

'Very trying,' said Lord Ickenham.

Lord Bosham appeared wounded. He was not an abnormally sensitive young man, but this consensus of hostile feeling seemed to hurt him.

'Well, if a chap can't say a word,' he said, 'perhaps you would prefer that I withdrew.'

'Yes, do.'

'Right ho,' said Lord Bosham. 'Then I will. Anybody who wants me will find me having a hundred up in the billiard-room. Not that I suppose my movements are of the slightest interest.'

He strode away, plainly piqued, and his passing seemed to Lord Ickenham to cause a marked improvement in the atmosphere. He had seldom met a young man with such a gift for asking inconvenient questions. Freed of this heckler, he addressed himself to his explanation with renewed confidence.

'Well, as I say, Emsworth had conceived this infatuation for a girl who, in the prime of life though he was, might have been his granddaughter. And he asked me as an old friend to help him. He anticipated that there would be opposition to the match, and his rather ingenious scheme was that I should come to Blandings Castle posing as the Sir Roderick Glossop who was expected, and should bring the girl with me as my daughter. He was good enough to say that my impressive deportment would make an excellent background for her. His idea – shrewd, however one may deplore it – was that you, Lady Constance, would find yourself so attracted by the girl's personality that the task of revealing the truth to you would become a simple one. He relied on her – I quote his expression – to fascinate you.'

Lady Constance drew a deep, shuddering breath.

'Oh, did he?'

The Duke put a question.

'Who is this frightful girl? An absolute outsider, of course?'

'Yes, her origin is humble. She is the daughter of a retired Silver Ring bookie.'

'My God!'

'Yes. Well, Emsworth came to me and proposed this scheme, and you can picture my dismay as I listened. Argument, I could see, would have been useless. The man was obsessed.'

'You use such lovely language,' said Valerie, who had sniffed.

'Thank you, my dear.'

'Have you ever thought of writing fairy stories?'

'No, I can't say I have.'

'You should.'

The look the Duke cast at the sardonic girl could scarcely have been sourer if she had been Lord Bosham.

'Never mind all that, dash it. First Bosham, now you. Interruptions all the time. Get on, get on, get on. Yes, yes, yes, yes, yes?'

'So,' said Lord Ickenham, 'I did not attempt argument. I agreed to his proposal. The impression I tried to convey – and, I think, succeeded in conveying – was that I approved. I consented to the monstrous suggestion that I should come here under a false name and bring the girl as my daughter. And shall I tell you why?'

'Yes, do,' said Valerie.

'Because a sudden thought had struck me. Was it not possible, I asked myself, that if Emsworth were to see this girl at Blandings Castle – in the surroundings of his own home – with the portraits of his ancestors gazing down at her –'

'Dashed ugly set of mugs,' said the Duke. 'Why they ever wanted to have themselves painted . . . However, never mind that. I see what you're getting at. You thought it might cause him to take another look at the frightful little squirt and realize he was making an ass of himself?'

'Exactly. And that is just what happened. The scales fell from his eyes. His infatuation ceased as suddenly as it had begun. This evening he told her it could never be, and she has left for London.'

'Then, dash it, everything's all right.'

'Thank Heaven!' cried Lady Constance.

Lord Ickenham shook his head gravely.

'I am afraid you are both overlooking something. There are such things as breach of promise cases.'

'What?'

'I fear so. He tells me the girl took the thing badly. She went off muttering threats.'

'Then what is to be done?'

'There is only one thing to be done, Lady Constance. You must make a financial settlement with her.'

'Buy her off,' explained the Duke. 'That's the way to handle it. You can always buy these females off. I recollect, when I was at Oxford ... However, that is neither here nor there. The point is, how much?'

Lord Ickenham considered.

'A girl of that class,' he said, at length, 'would have very limited ideas about money. Three hundred pounds would seem a fortune to her. In fact, I think I might be able to settle with her for two hundred and fifty.'

'Odd,' said the Duke, struck by the coincidence. 'That was the sum my potty nephew was asking me for this afternoon.'

'Curious,' said Lord Ickenham.

'Had some dashed silly story about wanting it so that he could get married.'

'Fancy! Well, then, Lady Constance, if you will give me three hundred pounds – to be on the safe side – I will run up to London to-morrow morning and see what I can do.'

'I will write you a cheque.'

'No, don't do that,' said the Duke. 'What you want on these occasions is to roll the money about in front of them in solid cash. That time at Oxford ... And I happen, strangely enough, to have that exact sum in this very room.'

'Why, so you have,' said Lord Ickenham. 'We were talking about it not long ago, weren't we.'

The Duke unlocked a drawer in the writing-table.

'Here you are,' he said. 'Take it, and see what you can do. Remember, it is imperative to roll it about.'

'And if more is required –' said Lady Constance.

'I doubt if it will be necessary to sweeten the kitty any further. This should be ample. But there is one other thing,' said Lord Ickenham. 'This unfortunate infatuation of Emsworth's must never be allowed to come out.'

'Well, dash it,' said the Duke, staring. 'Of course not. I know, and Connie knows, that Emsworth's as potty as a March hare, but naturally we don't want the world to know it.'

'If people got to hear of this,' said Lady Constance, with a shiver, 'we should be the laughing stock of the county.'

'Exactly,' said Lord Ickenham. 'But there is one danger which does not appear to have occurred to you. It is possible, Valerie, my dear, that you have been thinking of telling your aunt that you met me here.'

Valerie Twistleton smiled a short, sharp smile. Hers was at the same time a loving and a vengeful nature. She loved her Horace, and it was her intention to punish this erring uncle drastically for the alarm and despondency he had caused him. She had been looking forward with bright anticipation to the cosy talk which she would have with Jane, Countess of Ickenham, on the latter's return from the South of France.

'It is,' she said, 'just possible.'

Lord Ickenham's manner was very earnest.

'You mustn't do it, my dear. It would be fatal. You are probably unaware that your aunt expressed a strong wish that I should remain at Ickenham during her absence. If she discovered that I had disobeyed her instructions, I should be compelled, in order to put things right for myself, to tell her the whole story. And my dear wife,' said Lord Ickenham, turning to Lady Constance, 'has just one fault. She is a gossip. With no desire to harm a soul, she would repeat the story. In a week it would be all over England.'

The imperiousness of a hundred fighting ancestors descended upon Lady Constance.

'Miss Twistleton,' she said, in the voice which Lord Emsworth would have recognized as the one which got things done, 'you are not to breathe a word to Lady Ickenham of having met Lord Ickenham here.'

For an instant, it seemed as if Valerie Twistleton was about to essay the mad task of defying this woman. Then, as their eyes met, she seemed to wilt.

'Very well,' she said meekly.

Lord Ickenham's eyes beamed with fond approval. He placed a kindly hand on her shoulder and patted it.

'Thank you, my dear. My favourite niece,' he said.

And he went off to inform Pongo that, owing to having received pennies from heaven, he was in a position not only to solve the tangled affairs of Polly Pott but also to spend nearly three weeks in London with him – with money in his pocket, moreover, to disburse on any little treat that might suggest itself, such as another visit to the Dog Races.

There was a tender expression on his handsome face as he made his way up the stairs. What a pleasure it was, he was feeling, to be able to scatter sweetness and light. Especially in London in the springtime, when, as has been pointed out, he was always at his best.

# UNCLE DYNAMITE

# PART ONE

## *Chapter 1*

On the little branch line which starts at Wockley Junction and conveys passengers to Eggmarsh St John, Ashenden Oakshott, Bishop's Ickenham and other small and somnolent hamlets of the south of England the early afternoon train had just begun its leisurely journey.

It was a train whose patrons, sturdy sons of the soil who did not intend to let a railway company trouser more of their money than they could help, had for the most part purchased third-class tickets. But a first-class compartment had been provided for the rich and thriftless, and today it had two occupants, a large youth of open and ingenuous countenance, much sunburned, and a tall, slim, distinguished-looking man some thirty years his senior with a jaunty grey moustache and a bright and enterprising eye, whose air was that of one who has lived to the full every minute of an enjoyable life and intends to go on doing so till further notice. His hat was on the side of his head, and he bore his cigar like a banner.

For some ten minutes after the train had started, the usual decent silence of the travelling Englishman prevailed in the compartment. Then the young man, who had been casting covert glances at his companion, cleared his throat and said 'Er.'

The elderly gentleman looked up inquiringly. Deepening in colour, for he was of bashful temperament and was already wondering why he had been ass enough to start this, the sunburned youth proceeded.

'I say, excuse me. Aren't you Lord Ickenham?'

'I am.'

'Fine.'

The elderly gentleman seemed puzzled.

'I'm pretty pleased about it myself,' he admitted. 'But why do you rejoice?'

'Well, if you hadn't been –' said the young man, and paused aghast at the thought of what horrors might not have resulted from the wanton addressing of a perfect stranger. 'What I mean is, I used to know you. Years ago. Sort of. I was a pal of your nephew Pongo, and I came over to your place for tennis sometimes. You once tipped me five bob.'

'That's how the money goes.'

'I don't suppose you remember me. Bill Oakshott.'

'Of course I remember you, my dear fellow,' said Lord Ickenham heartily and quite untruthfully. 'I wish I had a tenner for every time I've said to my wife "Whatever became of Bill Oakshott?"'

'No, really? Fine. How is Lady Ickenham?'

'Fine.'

'Fine. She once tipped me half a crown.'

'You will generally find women loosen up less lavishly than me. It's something to do with the bone structure of the head. Yes, my dear wife, I am glad to say, continues in the pink. I've just been seeing her off on the boat at Southampton. She is taking a trip to the West Indies.'

'Jamaica?'

'No, she went of her own free will.'

The human tomato digested this for a moment in silence, seemed on the point of saying 'Fine,' then changed his mind, and inquired after Pongo.

'Pongo,' said Lord Ickenham, 'is in terrific form. He bestrides the world like a Colossus. It would not be too much to say that Moab is his washpot and over what's-its-name has he cast his shoe. He came into the deuce of a lot of money the other day from a deceased godfather in America, and can now face his tailor without a tremor. He is also engaged to be married.'

'Good.'

'Yes,' said Lord Ickenham, rather startled by this evidence of an unexpectedly wide vocabulary. 'Yes, he seems fairly radiant about it. I myself, I must confess, am less enthusiastic. I don't know if you have noticed it, Bill Oakshott, but nothing in this world ever works out one hundred per cent satisfactorily for all parties. Thus, while A. is waving his hat and giving a series of rousing cheers, we see B. frowning dubiously. And the same is true of X. and Z. Take this romance of Pongo's, for instance. I was hoping that he would marry another girl, a particular protégée of mine whom I have watched grow from a child, and a singularly fascinating child, at that, to a young woman of grace, charm and strength of character who in my opinion has everything. Among other advantages which she possesses is sense enough for two, which, it seems to me, is just the amount the wife of Reginald ("Pongo") Twistleton will require. But it was not to be. However, let us look on the bright side. Shall we?'

'Oh, rather.'

'Fine. Well, looking on the bright side, I haven't met this new girl, but she sounds all right. And of course the great thing is to get the young blighter safely married and settled down, thus avoiding the risk of his coming in one day and laying on the mat something with a platinum head and an Oxford accent which he picked up on the pier at Blackpool. You remember what a pushover he always was for the gentle sex.'

'I haven't seen Pongo since we were kids.'

'Even then he was flitting from flower to flower like a willowy butterfly. He was the Don Juan of his dancing class when he wore Little Lord Fauntleroy suits, his heart an open door with "Welcome" on the mat.'

'He'll chuck all that sort of thing now.'

'Let us hope so. But you remember what the fellow said. Can the leopard change his spots, or the Ethiopian his hue? Or is it skin? And talking of Ethiopians,' said Lord Ickenham, allowing himself to become personal, 'has someone been cooking you over a slow fire, or did you sit in the sun without your parasol?'

Bill Oakshott grinned sheepishly.

'I am a bit sunburned, aren't I? I've been in Brazil. I'm on my way home from the boat.'

'You reside in this neighbourhood?'

'At Ashenden Manor.'

'Married?'

'No. I live with my uncle. Or, rather, he lives with me.'

'What is the distinction?'

'Well, what I mean is, Ashenden really belongs to me, but I was only sixteen when my father died, and my uncle came barging over from Cheltenham and took charge. He dug in, and has been there ever since. Running the whole show. You'd think from the way he goes on,' said Bill, stirred to unwonted loquacity by the recollection of his wrongs, 'that he owned the bally place. Well, to give you an instance, he's pinched the best room in the house for his damned collection of African curios.'

'Does he collect African curios? God help him.'

'And that's not all. Who has the star bedroom? Me? No! Uncle Aylmer. Who collars the morning paper? Me? No! Uncle Aylmer. Who gets the brown egg at breakfast?'

'Don't tell me. Let me guess. Uncle Aylmer?'

'Yes. Blast him!'

Lord Ickenham stroked his moustache.

'A certain guarded something in your manner, Bill Oakshott,' he said, 'suggests to me that you do not like having your Uncle Aylmer living at Ashenden Manor. Am I correct?'

'Yes.'

'Then why not bung him out?'

The truculence faded from Bill Oakshott's demeanour, leaving in its place embarrassment. He could have answered the question, but to do so would have involved revealing his great love for his uncle's daughter, Hermione, and agreeable old bird though Lord Ickenham was, he did not feel that he knew him intimately enough.

'Oh, well,' he said, and coyly scraped a shoe like a violin case along the floor of the compartment. 'No, I don't quite see how I could do that.'

'There are complications?'

'Yes. Complications.'

'I understand.'

It was plain to Lord Ickenham that he had stumbled upon a delicate domestic situation, and he tactfully forbore to probe into it. Picking up his *Times*, he turned to the crossword puzzle, and Bill Oakshott sat gazing out of the window at the passing scenery.

But he did not see the familiar fields and spinneys, only the lovely face of his cousin Hermione. It rose before him like some radiant vision, and soon, he reflected, he would be beholding it not merely with the eye of imagination. Yes, at any moment, now that he was back in England again, he was liable to find himself gazing into her beautiful eyes or, if she happened to be standing sideways, staring at her pure, perfect profile.

In which event, what would the procedure be? Would he, as before, just gape and shuffle his feet? Or would he, fortified by three months in bracing Brazil, at last be able to shake off his distressing timidity and bring himself to reveal a silent passion which had been functioning uninterruptedly for some nine years?

He hoped so, but at the same time was compelled to recognize the point as a very moot one.

A tap on the knee interrupted his meditations.

'Next stop, Ashenden Oakshott,' Lord Ickenham reminded him.

'Eh? Oh, yes. That's right, so it is.'

'You had better be girding up your loins.'

'Yes,' said Bill, and rose and hauled down his suitcase from the rack. Then, as the train puffed out of the tunnel, he gave a sudden sharp cry and stood staring. As if unable to believe his eyes, he blinked them twice with great rapidity. But they had not deceived him. He still saw what he thought he had seen.

Under normal conditions there is about the station of Ashenden Oakshott little or nothing to rouse the emotions and purge the soul with pity and terror. Once you have seen the stationmaster's whiskers, which are of a Victorian bushiness and give the impression of having been grown under glass, you have drained it of all it has to offer in the way of thrills, unless you are one of those easily excited persons who can find drama in the spectacle of a small porter wrestling with a series of large milk cans. 'Placid' is the word that springs to the lips.

But today all this was changed, and it was obvious at a glance that Ashenden Oakshott was stepping out. From the penny-in-the-slot machine at the far end to the shed where the porter kept his brooms and buckets the platform was dark with what practically amounted to a sea of humanity. At least forty persons must have been present.

Two, selected for their muscle and endurance, were holding aloft on poles a streamer on which some loving hand, which had not left itself quite enough room, had inscribed the words:

WELCOME HOME, MR WILLᴍ.

and in addition to these the eye noted a Silver Band, some Boy

221

Scouts, a policeman, a clergyman, a mixed assortment of villagers of both sexes, what looked like an Infants' Bible Class (with bouquets) and an impressive personage with a large white moustache, who seemed to be directing the proceedings.

From his post by the window Bill Oakshott continued to stand rigid and open-mouthed, like some character in a fairy story on whom a spell has been cast, and so limpid was his countenance that Lord Ickenham had no difficulty in analysing the situation.

Here, he perceived, was a young man of diffident and retiring disposition, one who shrank from the public eye and quailed at the thought of being conspicuous, and for some reason somebody had organized this stupendous reception for him. That was why he was now looking like a stag at bay.

Publicity was a thing from which Lord Ickenham himself had never been averse. He frankly enjoyed it. If Silver Bands and Boy Scouts had come to welcome him at a station, he would have leaped to meet them with a whoop and a holler, and would have been out taking bows almost before the train had stopped. But it was plain that this young friend of his was differently constituted, and his heart was moved by his distress.

The kindly peer had always been a practical man. He did not, as others might have done, content himself in this crisis with a pitying glance or a silent hand-clasp.

'Nip under the seat,' he advised.

To Bill it seemed like a voice from heaven. It was as if in the hour of deadly peril his guardian angel had suddenly come through with something constructive. He followed the counsel without delay, and presently there was a lurch and a heave and the train resumed its journey.

When he crawled out, dusting his hands, he found his companion regarding him with open admiration.

'As neat a vanishing act as I have ever witnessed,' said Lord Ickenham cordially. 'It was like a performing seal going after a slice of fish. You've done this sort of thing before, Bill Oakshott. No? You amaze me. I would have sworn that you had had years of practice on race trains. Well, you certainly baffled them. I don't think I have ever seen a Silver Band so nonplussed. It was as though a bevy of expectant wolves had overtaken a sleigh and found no Russian peasant aboard, than which I can imagine nothing more sickening. For the wolves, of course.'

Bill Oakshott was still quivering. He gazed gratefully at his benefactor and in broken words thanked him for his inspired counsel.

'Not at all,' said Lord Ickenham. 'My dear fellow, don't mention it. I am like the chap in Damon Runyan's story, who always figured that if he could bring a little joy into any life, no matter how, he was doing a wonderful deed. It all comes under the head of spreading sweetness and light, which is my constant aim.'

'Well, I shall never forget it, never,' said Bill earnestly. 'Do you realize that I should have had to make a speech, besides probably kissing all those ghastly children with the flowers?' He shuddered strongly. 'Did you see them? About a million of them, each with a posy.'

'I did, indeed. And the sight confirmed me in my view that since the days when you used to play tennis at my place you must have become pretty illustrious. I have knocked about the world long enough to know that infants with bouquets don't turn out for every Tom, Dick and Harry. I myself am a hell of a fellow – a first-class Earl who keeps his carriage – but have infants ever offered me bouquets? What have you been doing, Bill Oakshott, to merit this reception – nay, this Durbar?'

'I haven't done a thing.'

'Well, it's all very odd. I suppose it *was* in your honour that the affair was arranged? They would hardly have said "Mr Willm." if they had meant someone else.'

'No, that's true.'

'Have you any suspicions as to the ringleaders?'

'I suppose my uncle was at the bottom of it.'

'Was he the impressive citizen with the moustache, who looked like Clemenceau?'

'Yes. He must have got the thing up.'

'But why?'

'I don't know.'

'Search your memory. Can you think of nothing you have done recently which could have put you in the Silver Band and Boy Scout class?'

'Well, I went on this expedition up the Amazon.'

'Oh, you went on an expedition, did you, and up the Amazon, to boot. I didn't realize that. I assumed that you had merely been connected with the Brazil nut industry or something. That might account for it, of course. And why did you commit this rash act? Wanted to get some girl out of your system, I suppose?'

Bill blushed. It had indeed been the seeming hopelessness of his love for his cousin Hermione that had driven him to try a cure which, as he might have foreseen, had proved quite ineffective.

'Why, yes. Something of the sort.'

'In my day we used to go to the Rocky Mountains and shoot grizzlies. What made you choose Brazil?'

'I happened to see an advertisement in *The Times* about an expedition that was starting off for the Lower Amazon, run by a chap called Major Plank, and I thought it might be a good idea to sign on.'

'I see. Well, I wish I had known of this before. I could have stuck on a lot of dog on the strength of having met you as a boy. But we shall be at Bishop's Ickenham in a minute or two, and the question arises, what do you propose to do? Wait for a train back? Or shall I take you to my place and give you a drink and send you home in the car?'

'Wouldn't that be a nuisance?'

'On the contrary. Nothing could suit my book better. That's settled then. We now come to a matter to which I think we ought to devote some little attention. What story are you going to tell your uncle, to account for your non-appearance at the revels?'

A thoughtful look came into Bill Oakshott's face. He winced slightly, as if a Brazilian alligator had attached itself to the fleshy part of his leg.

'I was rather wondering about that,' he confessed.

'A good, coherent story will undoubtedly be required. He will be feeling chagrined at your failure to materialize, and he looked a dangerous specimen, the sort of man whose bite spells death. What is he? An all-in wrestler? A chap who kills rats with his teeth?'

'He used to be Governor of one of those Crown colonies.'

'Then we must strain every nerve to pacify him. I know these ex-Governors. Tough nuts. You didn't mention his name, by the way.'

'Bostock. Sir Aylmer Bostock.'

'What? Is that who he is? Well, I'll be dashed.'

'You know him?'

'I have not seen him for more than forty years, but at one time I knew him well. We were at school together.'

'Oh, really?'

'Mugsy we used to call him. He was younger than me by some three years, one of those tough, chunky, beetle-browed kids who scowl at their seniors and bully their juniors. I once gave him six of the juiciest with a fives bat in the hope of correcting this latter tendency. Well, the mystery of that civic welcome is now explained. Mugsy is to stand for Parliament shortly, my paper informs me, and no doubt he thought it would give him a leg up. Like me, he hopes to trade on his connexion with a man who has extended the bounds of Civilization.'

'I didn't extend the bounds of Civilization.'

'Nonsense. I'll bet you extended them like elastic. But we are getting away from our discussion of what story you are to tell. How would it be to say that the warmth of the day caused you to drop off into a light slumber, and when you woke up blowed if you weren't at Bishop's Ickenham?'

'Fine.'

'You like it? I don't think it's so bad myself. Simple, which is always good. Impossible to disprove, which is better. And with the added advantage of having a historic precedent; the case, if you remember, of the lady who wanted to go to Birmingham and they were taking her on to Crewe. Yes, I fancy it ought to get by. So that was young Mugsy, was it?' said Lord Ickenham. 'I must say I'm surprised that he should have finished up as anything so comparatively respectable as Governor of a Crown colony. It just shows you never can tell.'

'How long did you say it was since you had met him?'

'Forty-two years come Lammas Eve. Why?'

'I was only wondering why you hadn't run across him. Living so close, I mean.'

'Well, I'll tell you, Bill Oakshott. It is my settled policy to steer pretty clear of the neighbours. You have probably noticed yourself that the British Gawd-help-us seems to flourish particularly luxuriantly in the rural districts. My wife tries to drag me to routs and revels from time to time, but I toss my curls at her and refuse to stir. I often think that the ideal life would be to have plenty of tobacco and be cut by the County. And as regards your uncle, I look back across the years at Mugsy, the boy, and I see nothing that encourages me to fraternize with Mugsy, the man.'

'Something in that.'

'Not an elfin personality, Mugsy's. I'm afraid Pongo doesn't realize what he's up against in taking on such a father-in-law. It's his daughter Hermione that he's gone and got engaged to, and I see a sticky future ahead of the unhappy lad. Ah, here we are,' said Lord Ickenham, as the train slowed down. 'Let's go and get that drink. It's just possible that we may find Pongo at the old shack. He rang me up this morning, saying he was coming to spend the night. He is about to visit Ashenden Manor, to show the old folks what they've got.'

He hopped nimbly on to the platform, prattling gaily, quite unaware that he had to all intents and purposes just struck an estimable young man behind the ear with a sock full of wet sand. The short, quick, gulping grunt, like that of a bulldog kicked in the ribs while eating a mutton chop, which had escaped Bill Oakshott on the cue 'got engaged to', he had mistaken for a hiccup.

## *Chapter 2*

The summer afternoon had mellowed into twilight and Bill Oakshott had long since taken his bruised heart off the premises before Pongo Twistleton fetched up at the home of his ancestors. One of those mysterious breakdowns which affect two-seater cars had delayed him on the road. He arrived just in time to dress for dinner, and the hour of eight found him seated opposite his uncle in the oak-panelled dining-room, restoring his tissues after a trying day.

Lord Ickenham, delighted to see him, was a gay and effervescent host, but during the meal the presence of a hovering butler made conversation of a really intimate nature impossible, and the talk confined itself to matters of general interest. Pongo spoke of New York, whence he had recently returned from a visit connected with the winding up of his godfather's estate, and Lord Ickenham mentioned that Lady Ickenham was on her way to Trinidad to attend the wedding of the daughter of an old friend. Lord Ickenham alluded to his meeting with Pongo's former crony, Bill Oakshott, and Pongo, though confessing that he remembered Bill only imperfectly – 'Beefy stripling with a pink face, unless I'm thinking of someone else' – said that he looked forward to renewing their old friendship when he hit Ashenden Manor.

They also touched on such topics as the weather, dogs, two-seater cars (their treatment in sickness and in health), the foreign policy of the Government, the chances of Jujube for the Goodwood Cup, and what you would do – this subject arising from Pongo's recent literary studies – if you found a dead body in your bath one morning with nothing on but pince-nez and a pair of spats.

It was only when the coffee had been served and the cigars lighted that Lord Ickenham prepared to become more expansive.

'Now we're nice and cosy,' he said contentedly. 'What a relief it always is when the butler pops off. It makes you realize the full meaning of that beautiful line in the hymn book – "Peace, perfect peace, with loved ones far away." Not that I actually love Coggs. A distant affection, rather, tempered with awe. Well, Pongo, I'm extraordinarily glad you blew in. I was wanting a quiet chat with you about your plans and what not.'

'Ah,' said Pongo.

He spoke reservedly. He was a slender, personable young man with lemon-coloured hair and an attractive face, and on this face a close observer would have noted at the moment an austere, wary look, such as might have appeared on that of St Anthony just before the temptations began. He had a strong suspicion that now that they were alone together, it was going to be necessary for him to be very firm with this uncle of his and to maintain an iron front against his insidious wiles.

Watching the head of the family closely during dinner, he had not failed to detect in his eyes, while he was speaking of his wife's voyage to the West Indies, a lurking gleam such as one might discern in the eye of a small boy who has been left alone in the house and knows where the key of the jam cupboard is. He had seen that gleam before, and it had always heralded trouble of a major kind. Noticeable even as early as the soup course, it had become, as its proprietor puffed at his cigar, more marked than ever, and Pongo waited coldly for him to proceed.

'How long are you proposing to inflict yourself on these Bostocks of yours?'

'About a week.'

'And after that?'

'Back to London, I suppose.'

'Good,' said Lord Ickenham heartily. 'That was what I wanted to know. That was what I wished to ascertain. You will return to London. Excellent. I will join you there, and we will have one of our pleasanter and instructive afternoons.'

Pongo stiffened. He did not actually say 'Ha!' but the exclamation was implicit in the keen glance which he shot across the table. His suspicions had been correct. His wife's loving surveillance having been temporarily removed, Frederick Altamont Cornwallis, fifth Earl of Ickenham, was planning to be out and about again.

'You ask me,' a thoughtful Crumpet had once said in the

smoking-room of the Drones Club, 'why it is that at the mention of his Uncle Fred's name Pongo Twistleton blenches to the core and calls for a couple of quick ones. I will tell you. It is because this uncle is pure dynamite. Every time he is in Pongo's midst, with the sap running strongly in his veins, he subjects the unfortunate young egg to some soul-testing experience, luring him out into the open and there, right in the public eye, proceeding to step high, wide and plentiful. For though well stricken in years the old blister becomes on these occasions as young as he feels, which seems to be about twenty-two. I don't know if you happen to know what the word "excesses" means, but those are what he invariably commits, when on the loose. Get Pongo to tell you some time about that day they had together at the dog races.'

It was a critique of which, had he heard it, Lord Ickenham would have been the first to admit the essential justice. From boyhood up his had always been a gay and happy disposition, and in the evening of his life he still retained, together with a juvenile waistline, the bright enthusiasms and the fresh, unspoiled mental outlook of a slightly inebriated undergraduate. He had enjoyed a number of exceedingly agreeable outings in his nephew's society in the course of the last few years, and was pleasantly conscious of having stepped on these occasions as high, wide and plentiful as a man could wish, particularly during that day at the dog races. Though there, he had always maintained, a wiser policeman would have been content with a mere reprimand.

'As you are aware, if you were not asleep while I was talking at dinner,' he said, resuming his remarks, 'your aunt has left me for a few weeks and, as you can well imagine, I am suffering agonies. I feel like one of those fellows in the early nineteenth-century poems who used to go about losing dear gazelles. Still –'

'Now listen,' said Pongo.

'Still, in practically every cloud wrack the knowledgeable eye, if it peers closely enough, can detect some sort of a silver lining, however small, and the horror of my predicament is to a certain extent mitigated by the thought that I now become a mobile force again. Your aunt is the dearest woman in the world, and nobody could be fonder of her than I am, but I sometimes find her presence . . . what is the word I want . . . restrictive. She holds, as you know, peculiar views on the subject of my running around loose in London, as she puts it, and this prevents me fulfilling myself. It is a pity. Living in a rural morgue like Bishop's Ickenham all the time, one gets rusty and out of touch with modern thought. I don't suppose these days I could tell you the name of a single chucker-out in the whole of the West End area, and I used to know them all. That is why —'

'Now listen.'

'That is why the fact of her having packed a toothbrush and popped off to Trinidad, though it blots the sunshine from my life, is not an unrelieved tragedy. Existence may have become for me an arid waste, but let us not forget that I can now be up and doing with a heart for any fate. Notify me when you return to London, and I will be with you with my hair in a braid. Bless my soul, how young I'm feeling these days! It must be the weather.'

Pongo knocked the ash off his cigar and took a sip of brandy. There was a cold, stern look on his face.

'Now listen, Uncle Fred,' he said, and his voice was like music to the ears of the Recording Angel, who felt that this was going to be good. 'All that stuff is out.'

'Out?'

'Right out. You don't get me to the dog races again.'

'I did not specify the dog races. Though they provide an admirable means of studying the soul of the people.'

'Or on any other frightful binge of yours. Get thou behind me, about sums it up. If you come to see me in London, you will get lunch at my flat and afterwards a good book. Nothing more.'

Lord Ickenham sighed, and was silent for a space. He was musing on the curse of wealth. In the old days, when Pongo had been an impecunious young fellow reading for the Bar and attempting at intervals to get into an uncle's ribs for an occasional much-needed fiver, nobody could have been a more sympathetic companion along the primrose path. But coming into money seemed to have changed him completely. The old, old story, felt Lord Ickenham.

'Oh, very well,' he said. 'If that is how you feel —'

'It is,' Pongo assured him. 'Make a note of it on your cuff. And it's no good saying "Ichabod", because I intend to stick to my position with iron resolution. My standing with Hermione is none too secure as it is – she looks askance at my belonging to the Drones – and the faintest breath of scandal would dish me properly. And most unfortunately she knows all about you.'

'My life is an open book.'

'She has heard what a loony you are, and she seems to think it may be hereditary. "I hope you are not like your uncle," she keeps saying, with a sort of brooding look in her eye.'

'You must have misunderstood her. "I hope you *are* like your uncle," she probably said. Or "Do try, darling, to be more like your uncle."'

'Consequently I shall have to watch my step like a ruddy hawk. Let her get the slightest suspicion into her nut that I am not one hundred per cent steady and serious, and bim will go my chances of putting on the spongebag trousers and walking down the aisle with her.'

'Then you would not consider the idea of my coming to Ashenden as your valet, and seeing what innocent fun we could whack out of the deception?'

'My God!'

'Merely a suggestion. And it couldn't be done, anyway. It would involve shaving off my moustache, to which I am greatly attached. When a man has neither chick nor child, he gets very fond of a moustache. So she's that sort of girl, is she?'

'What do you mean, that sort of girl?'

'Noble-minded. High principled. A credit to British woman-hood.'

'Oh, rather. Yes, she's terrific. Must be seen to be believed.'

'I look forward to seeing her.'

'I have a photograph here, if you would care to take a dekko,' said Pongo, producing one of cabinet size from his breast pocket like a conjurer extracting a rabbit from a top hat.

Lord Ickenham took the photograph, and studied it for some moments.

'A striking face.'

'Don't miss the eyes.'

'I've got 'em.'

'The nose, also.'

'I've got that, too. She looks intelligent.'

'And how. Writes novels.'

'Good God!'

A monstrous suspicion had germinated in Pongo's mind.

'Don't you like her?' he asked incredulously.

'Well, I'll tell you,' said Lord Ickenham, feeling his way carefully. 'I can see she's a remarkable girl, but I wouldn't say she was the wife for you.'

'Why not?'

'In my opinion you will be giving away too much weight. Have you studied these features? That chin is a determined chin. Those eyes are flashing eyes.'

'What's the matter with flashing eyes?'

'Dashed unpleasant things to have about the home. To cope with flashing eyes, you have to be a man of steel and ginger. Are you a man of steel and ginger? No. You're like me, a gentle coffee-caddie.'

'A how much?'

'By a coffee-caddie I mean a man – and there is no higher type – whose instinct it is to carry his wife's breakfast up to her room on a tray each morning and bill and coo with her as she wades into it. And what the coffee-caddie needs is not a female novelist with a firm chin and flashing eyes, but a jolly little soul who, when he bills, will herself bill like billy-o, and who will be right there with bells on when he starts to coo. The advice I give to every young man starting out to seek a life partner is to find a girl whom he can tickle. Can you see yourself tickling Hermione Bostock? She would draw herself to her full height and say "Sir!" The ideal wife for you, of course, would have been Sally Painter.'

At the mention of this name, as so often happens when names from the dead past bob up in conversation, Pongo's face became mask-like and a thin coating of ice seemed to form around him. A more sensitive man than Lord Ickenham would have sent for his winter woollies.

'Does Coggs suffer from bunions?' he said distantly. 'I thought he was walking as if he had trouble with his feet.'

'Ever since she came to England,' proceeded Lord Ickenham, refusing to be lured from the subject into realms of speculation, however fascinating, 'I have always hoped that you and Sally would eventually form a merger. And came a day when you appraised me that the thing was on. And then, dammit,' he went on, raising his voice a little in his emotion, 'came another day when you appraised me that it was off. And why, having succeeded in getting engaged to a girl like Sally Painter, you were mad enough to sever relations, is more than I can understand. It was all your fault, I suppose?'

Pongo had intended to maintain a frigid silence until the distasteful subject should have blown over, but this unjust charge shook him out of his proud reserve.

'It wasn't anything of the bally kind. Perhaps you will allow me to place the facts before you.'

'I wish you would. It's about time someone did. I could get nothing out of Sally.'

'You've seen her, then?'

'She came down here with Otis a couple of weeks ago and left one of her busts in my charge. I don't know why. That's it, over there in the corner.'

Pongo gave the bust a brief and uninterested glance.

'And she didn't place the facts before you?'

'She said the engagement was off, which I knew already, but nothing more.'

'Oh? Well,' said Pongo, breathing heavily through the nostrils as he viewed the body of the dead past, 'what happened was this. Just because I wouldn't do something she wanted me to do, she called me a lily-livered poltroon.'

'She probably meant it as a compliment. A lily liver must be very pretty.'

'High words ensued. I said so-and-so, and she said such-and-such. And later that evening ring, letters and all the fixings were returned by district messenger boy.'

'A mere lovers' tiff. I should have thought you would have made it up next day.'

'Well, we jolly well didn't. As a matter of fact, that lily-livered sequence was simply what put the lid on it. We had been getting in each other's hair for some time before that and there was bound to be a smash-up sooner or later.'

'What were the principal subjects of disagreement?'

'For one thing, that damned brother of hers. He makes me sick.'

'Otis isn't everybody's money, I admit. He's a publisher now, Sally tells me. I suppose he will make as big a mess of that as he did of his antique shop. Did you tell her he made you sick?'

'Yes. She got a bit steamed up about it. And then there was more trouble because I wanted her to chuck being a sculptress.'

'Why didn't you like her being a sculptress?'

'I hated her mixing with all that seedy crowd in Chelsea. Bounders with beards,' said Pongo, with an austere shudder. 'I've been in her studio sometimes, and the blighters were crawling out of the woodwork in hundreds, bearded to the eyebrows.'

Lord Ickenham drew thoughtfully at his cigar.

'I was mistaken in saying that you were not a man of steel and ginger. You appear to have thrown your weight about like a sheikh.'

'Well, she threw her weight about with me. She was always trying to boss me.'

'Girls do. Especially American girls. I know, because I married one. It's part of their charm.'

'Well, there's a limit.'

'And with you that was reached – how? You had started to tell me. What was it she wanted you to do?'

'Take some jewellery with me when I went to New York and smuggle it through the customs.'

'Bless her heart, what an enterprising little soul she is. But since when has Sally possessed jewellery?'

'It wasn't for her, it was for one of her rich American pals, a girl named Alice something. This ass of a female had been loading herself up with the stuff in and around Bond Street and didn't like the idea of paying duty on it when she got back to New York, and Sally wanted me to run it through for her.'

'A kindly thought.'

'A fatheaded thought. And so I told her. A nice chump I should have looked, being disembowelled by port officials.'

Lord Ickenham sighed.

'I see. Well, I'm sorry. A wealthy husband like you would have come in very handy for Sally. I'm afraid that girl is on the rocks.'

Pongo's lower jaw dropped a notch. Love might be dead, but he had a feeling heart.

'Oh, I say!'

'I don't believe she gets enough to eat.'

'What rot!'

'It isn't rot. She seemed thin to me, and I didn't like the way she tucked into the lamb and green peas, as if she hadn't had a square meal for weeks. There can't be a fortune in sculpting, if that's the right verb. Who the dickens buys clay busts?'

'Oh, that's all right,' said Pongo, relieved. 'She doesn't depend on her sculpting. She's got a little bit of money an aunt in Kansas City left her.'

'I know. But I'm wondering whether something hasn't gone wrong with that sheet anchor. It's two years since she came to London to join Otis. He may well have wheedled it out of her. A chap like Otis can do a lot in two years.'

'Sally's got too much sense.'

'The most level-headed girls often prove perfect mugs where a loved brother is concerned. At any rate, in answer to a recent communication of mine telling her that I hoped shortly to be in London and would like her to keep an evening free for dinner I got a letter saying she was glad I was coming up, because she wanted to see me on a very urgent matter. She underlined the "very". I didn't like the ring of that statement. It was the sort of thing you used to write to me in the old days, when you were having a passing unpleasantness with your bookie and hoped to float a small loan. Well, I shall be seeing her tomorrow, and I will institute a probe. Poor little Sally, I hope to God she's all right. What an admirable girl she is.'

'Yes.'

'You still feel that, do you?'

'Oh, rather. I'm frightfully fond of Sally. I tried to do her a bit of good just before I left for America. Hermione told me old Bostock wanted a bust of himself, to present to the village club, and I got her to put him on to Sally. I thought she might be glad of the commish.'

'Well, well. An impulsive girl would be touched by a thing like that. Yes, indeed. "The whitest man I know," one can hear her saying. I believe, if you played your cards right, you could still marry her, Pongo.'

'Aren't you overlooking the trifling fact that I happen to be engaged to Hermione?'

'Slide out of it.'

'Ha!'

'It is what your best friends would advise. You are a moody, introspective young man, all too prone to look on the dark side of things. I shall never forget you that day at the dog races. Sombre is the only word to describe your attitude as the cop's fingers closed on your coat collar. You reminded me of Hamlet. What you need is a jolly, lively wife to take you out of yourself, the sort of wife who would set booby traps for the Bishop when he came to spend the night. I don't suppose this Hermione Bostock of yours ever made so much as an apple-pie bed in her life. I'd give her a miss. Send her an affectionate telegram saying you've changed your mind and it's all off. I have a telegraph form in my study.'

A look of intense devoutness came over Pongo's face.

'For your information, Uncle Fred, wild horses wouldn't make me break my engagement.'

'Most unlikely they'll ever try.'

'I worship that girl. There's nothing I wouldn't do for her. Well, to give you a rough idea, I told her I was a teetotaller. And why? Purely because she happened one day to express the hope that I wasn't like so many of these modern young suction pumps, always dropping in at bars and lowering a couple for the tonsils. "Me?" I said. "Good Lord, no. I never touch the stuff." That'll show you.'

'So when you get to Ashenden –'

'– They'll uncork the barley water and bring on the lemonade. I know. I've foreseen that. It'll be agony, but I can take it. For her sake. I worship her, I tell you. If H. Bostock isn't an angel in human shape, then I don't know an angel in human shape when I see one. Until now I have never known what love was.'

'Well, you have had ample opportunity of finding out. I have watched you with the tenderest solicitude through about fifty-seven romances, starting with that freckled child with the missing front tooth at the dancing class, who blacked your eye with a wooden dumb-bell when you kissed her in the cloak-room, and ending with this –'

Lord Ickenham paused, and Pongo eyed him narrowly.

'Well? This what?'

'This gruesome combination of George Eliot, Boadicea and the late Mrs Carrie Nation,' said Lord Ickenham. 'This flashing-eyed governess. This twenty-minute egg with whom no prudent man would allow himself to walk alone down a dark alley.'

It was enough. Pongo rose, a dignified figure.

'Shall we join the ladies?' he said coldly.

'There aren't any,' said Lord Ickenham.

'I don't know why I said that,' said Pongo, annoyed. 'What I meant was, let's stop talking bally rot and go and have a game of billiards.'

## Chapter 3

It was with a light heart and a gay tra-la-la on his lips that Pongo Twistleton set out for Ashenden Manor on the following afternoon, leaving Lord Ickenham, who was not embarking on his metropolitan jaunt till a few hours later, waving benevolently from the front steps.

Nothing so braces a young man in love as the consciousness of having successfully resisted a Tempter who has tried to lure him into a course of action of which the adored object would not approve: and as he recalled the splendid firmness with which he had tied the can to his Uncle Fred's suggestion of a pleasant and instructive afternoon in London, Pongo felt spiritually uplifted.

Pleasant and instructive afternoon, forsooth! Few people have ever come nearer to saying 'Faugh!' than did Pongo as Lord Ickenham's phrase shot through his wincing mind like some loathsome serpent. The crust of the old buster, daring to suggest pleasant and instructive afternoons to a man who had put that sort of thing behind him once and for all. With a shudder of distaste he thrust the whole degrading episode into the hinterland of his consciousness, and turned his thoughts to a more agreeable theme, the coming meeting with Hermione's parents.

This, he was convinced, was going to be a riot from the word Go. He had little data about these two old geezers, of course, but he presumed that they were intelligent old geezers, able to spot a good man when they saw one, and it seemed, accordingly, pretty obvious that a fellow like himself – steady, upright, impervious to avuncular wheedlings and true blue from soup to nuts – would have them eating out of his hand in the first minute. 'My dear, he's *charming*!' they would write to Hermione, and bluff Sir Aylmer, whom he pictured as a sort of modern Cheeryble Brother, would say to Lady Bostock (gentle, sweet-faced, motherly), as they toddled up to bed at the conclusion of a delightful first evening, 'Gad, my dear, nothing much wrong with *that* young chap, what?' – or possibly 'What, what?' He looked forward with bright confidence to grappling them to his soul with hoops of steel.

It was consequently with some annoyance that he found on reaching his destination that there was going to be a slight delay before this desirable state of affairs could be consummated. The first essential preliminary to grappling a householder and his wife to your soul with hoops of steel is that you should be able to get into the house they are holding, and this, he discovered, presented unforeseen difficulties.

Ashenden Manor was one of those solidly built edifices which date from the days when a home was not so much a place for putting on the old slippers and lighting the pipe, as a fortress to be defended against uncouth intruders with battering rams. Its front door was stout and massive, and at the moment tightly closed. Furthermore, the bell appeared to be out of order. He leaned against the button with his full weight for a while, but it soon became clear that this was going to get him nowhere, and the necessity of taking alternative action presented itself.

It was at this point that he observed not far from where he stood an open french window, and it seemed to him that he had found a formula. A bit irregular, perhaps, to start your first visit to a place by strolling in through windows, but a kindly, hearty old boy like Sir Aylmer Bostock would overlook that. Abandoning the front door, accordingly, as a lost cause, he stepped through, and an instant later was experiencing the unpleasant shock which always came to people who found themselves for the first time in the room where the ex-Governor kept the African curios which he had collected during his years of honourable exile. Sir Aylmer Bostock's collection of African curios was probably the most hideous, futile and valueless that even an ex-Governor had ever brought home with him, and many of its items seemed to take Pongo into a different and a dreadful world.

And he had picked up and started to scrutinize the nearest to hand, a peculiar sort of what-not executed in red mud by an artist apparently under the influence of trade gin, and was wondering why even an untutored African should have been chump enough to waste on an effort like this hours which might have been more profitably employed in chasing crocodiles or beaning the neighbours with his knobkerrie, when a voice, having in it many of the qualities of the Last Trump, suddenly split the air.

'REGINALD!'

Starting violently, Pongo dropped the what-not. It crashed to the floor and became a mere *macédoine*. A moment later, a burly figure appeared in the doorway, preceded by a large white moustache.

2

At about the moment when Pongo at Ickenham Hall was springing to the wheel of his Buffy-Porson and pressing a shapely foot on the self-starter, Sir Aylmer Bostock had gone to his wife's bedroom on the first floor of Ashenden Manor to mend a broken slat in the Venetian blind. He was a man who liked to attend to these little domestic chores himself, and he wanted to have it ready when the midday train brought Lady Bostock back from London, where she had been spending a week with her daughter Hermione.

In predicting that this old schoolmate of his would feel chagrined at Bill Oakshott's failure to cooperate in the civic welcome which he had gone to such trouble to arrange for him, Lord Ickenham had shown sound judgement of character. When an ex-Governor, accustomed for years to seeing his official receptions go like clockwork, tastes in a black hour the bitterness of failure and anti-climax, pique is bound to supervene. Fists will be clenched, oaths breathed, lower lips bitten. And this is particularly so if the ex-Governor is one whose mental attitude, even under the most favourable conditions, resembles, as did Sir Aylmer Bostock's, that of a trapped cinnamon bear. As he worked, his brow was dark, his moustache bristling, and from time to time he snorted in a quiet undertone.

He yearned for his wife's company, so that he could pour into her always receptive ear the story of his wrongs, and soon after he had put the finishing touches to the broken slat he got it. A cab drove up to the front door, and presently Lady Bostock appeared, a woman in the late forties who looked like a horse.

'Oh, there you are, dear,' she said brightly. In conversation with her consort she was nearly always obliged to provide brightness enough for both of them. She paused, sniffing. 'What a curious smell there is in here.'

Sir Aylmer frowned. He resented criticism, even of his smells.

'Glue,' he said briefly. 'I've been mending the blind.'

'Oh, how clever of you, darling. Thank you so much,' said Lady Bostock, brighter than ever. 'Well, I suppose you thought I was never coming back. It's lovely to be home again. London was terribly stuffy. I thought Hermione was looking very well. She sent all sorts of messages to you and Reginald. Has he arrived yet?'

On the point of asking who the devil Reginald was, Sir Aylmer remembered that his daughter had recently become betrothed to some young pot of cyanide answering to that name. He replied that Reginald had not yet arrived.

'Hermione said he was coming today.'

'Well, he hasn't.'

'Has he wired?'

'No.'

'I suppose he forgot.'

'Silly fatheaded young poop,' said Sir Aylmer.

Lady Bostock regarded him anxiously. She seemed to sense in his manner an anti-Reginald bias, and she knew his work. He was capable, she was aware, when in anything like shape, of reducing young men who had failed to arouse his enthusiasm to spots of grease in a matter of minutes, and she was intensely desirous that no such disaster should occur on the present occasion. Hermione, seeing her off at Waterloo, had issued definite instructions that her loved one, while at Ashenden Manor, was to enjoy the status of an ewe lamb, and Hermione was a girl whom it did not do to cross. She expected people to carry out her wishes, and those who knew what was good for them invariably did so.

Recalling all the timid young aides-de-camp whom she had seen curling up at the edges like scorched paper beneath his glare during those long and happy years in Lower Barnatoland, she gazed at her husband pleadingly.

'You will be nice to Reginald, dear, won't you?'

'I am always nice.'

'I don't want him to complain to Hermione about his unwelcome. You know what she is like.'

A thoughtful silence fell, as they allowed their minds to dwell on what Hermione was like. Lady Bostock broke it on a note of hope.

'You may become the greatest friends.'

'Bah!'

'Hermione says he is delightful.'

'Probably the usual young pest with brilliantined hair and a giggle,' said Sir Aylmer morosely, refusing to look for the silver lining and try to find the sunny side of life. 'It's bad enough having William around. Add Reginald, and existence will become a hell.'

His words reminded Lady Bostock that there was a topic on which an affectionate aunt ought to have touched earlier.

'William has arrived, then?'

'Yes. Oh, yes, he's arrived.'

'I hope the reception went off well. Such a good idea, I thought, when you told me about it. How surprised he must have been. It's so fortunate that he should have come back in good time for the fête. He is always so useful, looking after the sports. Where is he?'

'I don't know. Dead, I hope . . .'

'Aylmer! What do you mean?'

Sir Aylmer had not snorted since his wife's return and now it was as if all the snorts he might have been snorting had coalesced into one stupendous burst of sound. It was surprising that Pongo, at that moment driving in through the main gates, did not hear it and think one of his tyres had gone.

'I'll tell you what I mean. Do you know what that young hound did? Didn't get out at Ashenden Oakshott. Remained skulking in the train, went on to Bishop's Ickenham and turned up hours later in a car belonging to Lord Ickenham, stewed to the gills.'

One hastens to protest that this was a complete misstatement, attributable solely to prejudice and bitterness of spirit. Considering that he had arrived there reeling beneath the blow of the discovery that the girl he loved was betrothed to another, Bill Oakshott had comported himself at Lord Ickenham's residence with the most exemplary abstemiousness. In a situation where many men would have started lowering the stuff by the pailful, this splendid young fellow had exercised an iron self-control. One fairly quick, followed by another rather slower, and he had been through.

It is true that on encountering his uncle his manner had been such as to give rise to misunderstanding, but something of this kind is bound to happen when a nervous young man meets an incandescent senior, of whom he has always stood in awe, knowing that it is he who has brought him to the boil. In such circumstances the face inevitably becomes suffused and the limbs start twitching, even if the subject is a lifelong abstainer.

So much for this monstrous charge.

Lady Bostock made that clicking noise, like a wet finger touching a hot iron, which women use as a substitute for the masculine 'Well, I'll be damned!'

'A car belonging to Lord Ickenham?'

'Yes.'

'But how did he come to be in a car belonging to Lord Ickenham?'

'They appear to have met on the train.'

'Oh, I see. I was wondering, because we don't know him.'

'I used to, forty years ago. We were at school together. Haven't seen him since, thank God. He's a lunatic.'

'I have always heard that he was very eccentric.' Lady Bostock paused, listening. 'Hark. There's a car driving up. It must be Reginald. You had better go down.'

'I won't go down,' said Sir Aylmer explosively. 'Blast Reginald. Let him cool his heels for a bit. I'm going to finish telling you about William.'

'Yes, dear. Do, dear. He does seem to have behaved most oddly. Had he any explanation?'

'Oh, he had his story all ready, trust him for that. Said he went to sleep and woke up to find himself at Bishop's Ickenham. I didn't swallow a word of it. What happened, obviously, was that on seeing the preparations made for his reception he lost his nerve and remained in the train, the young toad, leaving me to get the Vicar, his wife, a Silver Band, ten Boy Scouts and fourteen members of the Infants' Bible Class back to their homes without any of them starting a riot. And let me tell you it was a very near thing once or twice. Those Bible Class infants were in ugly mood.'

'It must have been dreadfully disappointing for you all.'

'That's not the worst of it. It has probably lost me hundreds of votes.'

'Oh, but, dear, why? It wasn't your fault.'

'What does that matter? People don't reason. The news of a fiasco like that flies all over the county. One man tells another. It gets about that I have been placed in a ridiculous position, and the voters lose confidence in me. And nothing to be done about it. That is the bitter thought. You can't put a fellow of William's age and size across your knee and get at him with the back of a hairbrush . . . COME IN.'

There had been a knock on the door. It was followed by the entry of Jane, the parlourmaid.

'Your ladyship is wanted on the telephone, m'lady,' said Jane, who believed in respect to the titled. 'It's the Vicar, m'lady.'

'Thank you, Jane. I will come at once.'

'And I,' said Sir Aylmer with a weary snort, 'had better go and welcome this blasted Reginald, I suppose.'

'You won't forget about Hermione?'

'No, I won't forget about Hermione,' said Sir Aylmer moodily. He did not waver in his view that his daughter's future husband was bound to be a deleterious slab of damnation like all other young men nowadays, but if Hermione desired it he was prepared to coo to him like a turtle dove; or as nearly like a turtle dove as was within the scope of one whose vocal delivery was always rather reminiscent of a bad-tempered toastmaster.

He made his way to the drawing-room, and finding it empty was for a moment baffled. But ex-Governors are quick-thinking men, trained to deal with emergencies. When an ex-Governor, seeking a Twistleton, arrives in the drawing-room where that Twistleton ought to be and finds no Twistleton there, he does not stand twiddling his thumbs and wondering what to do. He inflates his lungs and shouts.

'REGINALD!' thundered Sir Aylmer.

It seemed to him, as the echoes died away, that he could hear the sound of movements in the collection room across the hall. He went thither, and poked his head in.

It was as he had suspected. Something, presumably of a Twistletonian nature, was standing there. He crossed the threshold, and these two representatives of the older and the younger generation were enabled to see each other steadily and see each other whole.

On both sides the reaction to the scrutiny was unfavourable. Pongo, gazing apprehensively at the rugged face with its top dressing of moustache, was thinking that this Bostock, so far from being the kindly Dickens character of his dreams, was without exception the hardest old gumboil he had ever encountered in a career by no means free from gumboils of varying hardness: while Sir Aylmer, drinking Pongo in from his lemon-coloured hair to his clocked socks and suède shoes, was feeling how right he had been in anticipating that his future son-in-law would be a pot of cyanide and a deleterious young slab of damnation. He could see at a glance that he was both.

However, he had come there grimly resolved to coo like a turtle dove, so he cooed.

'Oh, there you are. Reginald Twistleton?'

'That's right. Twistleton, Reginald.'

'H'ar ye?' roared Sir Aylmer like a lion which has just received an ounce of small shot in the rear quarters while slaking its thirst at a water hole, though, if questioned, he would have insisted that he was still cooing. 'Glad to see yer, Reginald. My wife will be down in a moment. What you doing in here?'

'I was having a look at these – er – objects.'

'My collection of African curios. It's priceless.'

'Really? How priceless!'

'You won't find many collections like that. Took me ten years to get it together. You interested in African curios?'

'Oh, rather. I love 'em.'

The right note had been struck. A sort of writhing movement behind his moustache showed that Sir Aylmer was smiling, and in another moment who knows what beautiful friendship might not have begun to blossom. Unfortunately, however, before the burgeoning process could set in, Sir Aylmer's eyes fell on the remains of the what-not and the smile vanished from his face like breath off a razor blade, to be replaced by a scowl of such malignity that Pongo had the illusion that his interior organs were being scooped out with a spade or trowel.

'Gorbl . . .!' he cried, apparently calling on some tribal god. 'How the . . . What the . . . Did *you* do that?'

'Er, yes,' said Pongo, standing on one leg. 'Frightfully sorry.'

Sir Aylmer, not without some justice, asked what was the use of being sorry, and Pongo, following his reasoning, said Yes, he saw what he meant, supplementing the words with a nervous giggle.

Many people do not like nervous giggles. Sir Aylmer was one of them. On several occasions in the old days he had had to mention this to his aides-de-camp. Not even the thought of his daughter Hermione could restrain him from bestowing on Pongo a second scowl, compared with which its predecessor had been full of loving kindness. He lowered himself to the ground, and, crouched on all fours over the remains like Marius among the ruins of Carthage, began to mutter beneath his breath about young fools and clumsy idiots. Pongo could not catch his remarks in their entirety, but he heard enough to give him the general idea.

He gulped pallidly. A sticky moisture had begun to bedew his brow, as if he had entered the hot room of some Turkish bath of the soul. Governesses in his childhood and schoolmasters in his riper years had sometimes spoken slightingly of his IQ, but he was intelligent enough to realize that on this visit of his, where it was so vital for him to make a smash hit with Hermione's parents, he had got off to a poor start.

It was as Sir Aylmer rose and began to say that the what-not had been the very gem and pearl of his collection and that he wouldn't have parted with it for a hundred pounds, no, not if the intending purchaser had gone on his bended knees to add emphasis to the offer, that there was a whirring sound without, indicating that some solid body was passing down the hall at a high rate of m.p.h. The next moment, Lady Bostock entered, moving tempestuously.

From Lady Bostock's aspect only Sherlock Holmes, perhaps, would have been able to deduce that she had just heard from the Vicar over the telephone that the curate was down with measles, but even Doctor Watson could have seen that her soul had in some way been badly jolted. So moved was she that, though a polished hostess, she paid no attention to Pongo, who was now standing on the other leg.

'Aylmer!'

'Well?'

'Aylmer . . . The Vicar . . .'

'WELL?'

'The Vicar says Mr Brotherhood has got measles. He wants us to go and see him at once.'

'Who the devil's Mr Brotherhood?'

'The curate. You know Mr Brotherhood, the curate. That nice young man with the pimples. He has gone and got measles, and I was relying on him to judge the babies.'

'What babies?'

'The bonny babies. At the fête.'

A word about this fête. It was the high spot of Ashenden Oakshott's social year, when all that was bravest and fairest in the village assembled in the Manor grounds and made various kinds of whoopee. Races were run, country dances danced, bonny babies judged in order of merit in the big tent and tea and buns consumed in almost incredible quantities. Picture a blend of the Derby and a garden party at Buckingham Palace, add Belshazzar's Feast, and you have the Ashenden Oakshott Fête.

One can readily appreciate, therefore, Lady Bostock's concern at the disaster which had occurred. A lady of the manor, with an important fête coming along and the curate in bed with measles, is in the distressing position of an impresario whose star fails him a couple of days before the big production or a general whose crack regiment gets lumbago on the eve of battle.

'It's terrible. Dreadful. I can't think who I can get to take his place.'

Sir Aylmer, who believed in having a thorough understanding about these things at the earliest possible moment, said he was dashed if he was going to do it, and Lady Bostock said No, no, dear, she wouldn't dream of asking him.

'But I must find somebody.' Lady Bostock's eye, rolling in a fine frenzy from heaven to earth, from earth to heaven, picked on Pongo, now back on the leg he had started with, and she stared at him dazedly, like one seeing unpleasant things in a dream. 'Are you Reginald?' she said distractedly.

The emotional scene, following upon his chat with Sir Aylmer about what-nots, had left Pongo in a condition of such mental turmoil that for an instant he was not quite sure. Reginald? Was he Reginald? Was Reginald a likely thing for anyone to be? . . . Why, yes, of course. The woman was perfectly correct.

'Yes, I'm Reginald.'

'How nice to meet you at last,' wailed Lady Bostock like a soul in torment.

It is never easy off-hand to find the ideal reply to such an observation. Discarding 'Yes!' as too complacent and 'What ho!' as too familiar, and not being fortunate enough to think of 'I've been looking forward so much to meeting *you*,' Pongo contented himself with another of his nervous giggles.

A sudden light came into Lady Bostock's haggard eyes.

'Have you ever judged bonny babies, Reginald?'

'Me?' said Pongo, reeling.

Before he could speak further, an angel, in the very effective disguise of Sir Aylmer, intervened to save him from the ghastly peril which had so suddenly risen to confront him.

'You don't want Reginald,' he said, and Pongo, who a moment earlier would have scoffed at the suggestion that it would ever be possible for him to want to leap at his host and kiss him on both cheeks, was conscious of a powerful urge in that direction. 'I'll tell you who gets the job.'

After uttering the words 'I'm dashed if I'm going to do it' and receiving his wife's reassuring reply, Sir Aylmer had fallen into a silence, as if musing or pondering, and it was plain now that the brain work on which he had been engaged had borne fruit. His manner had become animated, and in his eye, which, resting upon Pongo, had been dull and brooding, there was a triumphant gleam.

It was a gleam which might have puzzled an untravelled beholder, but anybody who had ever seen a Corsican feudist suddenly presented with the opportunity of wreaking a sinister vengeance on a family foe would have recognized it immediately. It was that strange, almost unearthly light which comes into the eyes of wronged uncles when they see a chance of getting a bit of their own back from erring nephews.

'I'll tell you who gets the job,' he repeated. 'William.'

'William?'

'William,' said Sir Aylmer, rolling the word round his tongue like vintage port.

Lady Bostock stared.

'But William . . . Surely, dear . . . The very last person . . .'

'William.'

'But he would hate it.'

'William.'

'You know how terribly shy he is.'

'William. I don't want any argument, Emily. It's no good you standing there blinding and sniffing. William judges the bonny babies. I insist. Perhaps now he'll be sorry he skulked in trains and went on toots with old Ickenham.'

Lady Bostock sighed. But a habit of obsequiousness which had started at the altar rails was too strong for her.

'Very well, dear.'

'Good. Tell him when you see him. Meanwhile, you say, the Vicar wants us to go down to the vicarage and confer with him. Right. I'll drive you in the car. Come along.'

He darted through the french windows, followed by Lady Bostock, and after a few moments occupied in mopping his forehead with the handkerchief which so perfectly matched his tie and socks, Pongo followed them.

He felt he needed air. A similar sensation had often come to sensitive native chiefs at the conclusion of an interview with Sir Aylmer Bostock on the subject of unpaid hut taxes.


Sunshine and the pure Hampshire breezes playing about his temples soon did wonders in the way of restoring him to the normal. Presently, feeling almost himself again, he returned to the house, and, as always happened with those who had once seen Sir Aylmer's collection of African curios, there came over him a morbid urge to take another look at these weird exhibits, to ascertain whether they really looked as frightful as they had appeared at first sight. He passed through the french window into the collection room, and a pink policeman, who had been bicycling dreamily up the drive, uttered a sharp 'Ho!' and accelerated his pace, his eyes hard and his jaw protruding belligerently.

The policeman's name was Harold Potter. He represented the awful majesty of the Law in Ashenden Oakshott. His pinkness was due to the warmth of the weather, and he was dreamy because he had been musing on Elsie Bean, the Manor housemaid, to whom he was affianced.

It was in order to enjoy a chat with Elsie Bean that he had come here, and until he turned the corner and was in view of the house his thoughts had been all of love. But at the sight of furtive forms slinking in through french windows Potter, the Romeo, became in a flash Potter, the sleepless guardian of the peace. His substantial feet pressed on the pedals like those of a racing cyclist.

It looked to Harold Potter like a fair cop.

And so it came about that Pongo, his opinion of the intelligence of African natives now even lower than before, was disturbed in his contemplation of their fatuous handiwork by the sound of emotional breathing in his rear. He spun round, to find himself gazing into the steely eyes of a large policeman with a ginger moustache.

'Ho!' he cried, startled.

'Ho!' said Constable Potter, like an echo in the Swiss mountains.

3

It would be idle to pretend that the situation was not one of some embarrassment. It belonged to the type which would have enchanted Lord Ickenham, who enjoyed nothing better than these little variations in the calm monotone of life, but it brought Pongo out from head to foot in a sort of prickly heat.

Unlike most of his lighthearted companions of the Drones Club, who rather made pets of policemen, tipping them when in funds and stealing their helmets on Boat Race night, Pongo had always had a horror of the Force. That sombreness of his on the day at the dog races, for which Lord Ickenham had reproached him, had been occasioned by the fact that a member of that Force, who might have been this one's twin brother, had been attached to his coat collar and advising him to come quietly.

He smiled a weak smile.

'Oh, hullo,' he said.

'Hullo,' replied Constable Potter coldly. 'What's all this?'

'What's all what?'

'What are you doing on these enclosed premises?'

'I've been invited here for a brief visit.'

'Ho!'

It seemed to Pongo that he was not making headway. The

situation, sticky at the outset, appeared to be growing progressively stickier. He was relieved, accordingly, when a third party arrived to break up the *tête-à-tête*.

This was a small, sturdy girl of resolute appearance with blue eyes and a turned-up nose, clad in the uniform of a housemaid. She regarded with interest the picture in still life before her.

'Hullo,' she said. 'Where did you spring from, Harold? And who's this?'

'Chap I've apprehended on enclosed premises,' said Constable Potter briefly.

Pongo, who had been dabbing at his forehead, waved his handkerchief in passionate protest against this too professional view.

'What's all this rot about enclosed premises?' he demanded with spirit. 'I resent the way, officer, you keep chewing the fat about enclosed premises. Why shouldn't I be on enclosed premises, when specially invited? Here, you, what's your name, my dear old housemaid –'

'Miss Bean, my fiancée,' said Constable Potter, frigidly doing the honours.

'Oh really? Heartiest congratulations. Pip-pip, Miss Bean.'

'Toodle-oo.'

'I hope you'll be very, very happy. Well, what I was going to say was that you will be able to bear me out that I'm a guest at this joint. I've just arrived in my car to spend a few days. I'm the celebrated Twistleton, the bird who's engaged to Miss Bostock. You must know all about me. No doubt the place has been ringing with my name.'

'Miss Hermione is engaged to a gentleman named Twistleton.'

'Exactly.'

'And Jane heard them saying at dinner that he was expected here, Harold. I believe this is him.'

'Well spoken, young Bean,' said Pongo with enthusiasm. He had taken an immediate liking to this clear-reasoning girl. 'Of course I'm him. Look,' said Pongo, turning back the pocket of his coat. 'Read this definite statement by one of the most reputable tailors in London. "R. G. Twistleton". There you are, in black and white.'

'It could be somebody else's coat that you'd bought second hand,' argued Constable Potter, fighting in the last ditch.

Pongo gave him a look.

'Don't say such things even in jest, officer. Rather,' he said with a sudden flash of inspiration, 'ring up the Vicar and ask for Sir Aylmer, who is in conference with him on the subject of bonny babies, and put it squarely up to the latter – Sir Aylmer, I mean, not the bonny babies – whether he didn't leave me here only a few moments ago after a pleasant and invigorating chat.'

'You mean you've met Sir Aylmer?'

'Of course I've met Sir Aylmer. We're just like that.'

Constable Potter seemed reluctantly convinced.

'Well, I suppose it's all right, then. I beg your pardon, sir.'

'Quite all right, officer.'

'Then I'll be saying good afternoon, sir. How about a pot of tea in the kitchen, Elsie?'

Elsie Bean elevated her small nose.

'You can go to the kitchen, if you like. Not me. Your sister's there, calling on cook.'

'Ho!' Constable Potter stood for a moment in thought. The conflicting claims of tea and a loved one's society were plainly warring within him. One is sorry to report that the former prevailed. 'Well, I think I'll mooch along and have a cup,' he said, and mooched, as foreshadowed.

Elsie Bean looked after his retreating blue back with a frown.

'You and your sister!' she said.

The note of acerbity in her voice was so manifest that Pongo could not help but be intrigued. Here, he told himself, or he was very much mistaken, was a housemaid with a secret sorrow. He stopped mopping his forehead and cocked an inquiring eye at Elsie Bean.

'Don't you like his sister?'

'No, I don't.'

'Well, if there's any sort of family resemblance, I can fully comprehend,' said Pongo. With Constable Potter's departure Ashenden Manor seemed to him to have become a sweeter, better place. 'Why don't you like his sister? What's the matter with her?'

Elsie Bean was a friendly little soul who, though repeatedly encouraged to do so by her employers, had never succeeded in achieving that demure aloofness which is the hallmark of the well-trained maid. Too often in her dealings with the ruling classes, in circumstances where a distant 'Yes, sir,' or 'No, madam,' would have been more suitable, you would find her becoming expansive and conversational. And on the present occasion she regarded herself as a hostess.

'I'll tell you what's the matter with her. She goes on at him about how he mustn't leave the Force. It's "Don't you do it, Harold," and "Don't you let Elsie talk you into acting against your true interests," all the time. I haven't any patience.'

Pongo concentrated tensely.

'Let me see if I've got this straight,' he said. 'You want him to turn in his boots and truncheon? To cease, in a word, to be a copper?'

'R.'

'But his sister doesn't. Yes, I get the set-up. Why do you want him to turn in his boots and truncheon?' asked Pongo. A man who has been reading for the Bar for some years gets into the way of putting the pertinent question.

Elsie Bean seemed surprised that such a question should have been considered necessary.

'Well, wouldn't you? If you was a girl, would you like to be married to a policeman? Feeling your old man was hated by all. If I went home to Bottleton East and told my family I was going to get spliced to a copper, they'd have a fit. A nice thing for my brother Bert to hear, when he comes out in September.'

Pongo nodded intelligently. Until now, having supposed his companion to be a local product, he had failed to grasp the nub, but her last words made everything clear. He could quite see how a London girl, especially a child of the notoriously rather vivacious quarter of Bottleton East, might shrink from linking her lot with that of a professional tapper on shoulders and grasper of coat collars. In addition to this brother Bert – at the moment, it appeared, unhappily no longer with us – there were no doubt a number of Uncle Herbs and Cousin Georges in her entourage who, were she to commit such a *mésalliance*, would consider, and rightly, that she had inflicted a blot on the Bean escutcheon.

'I see what you mean,' he said. 'But what could he do if he resigned his portfolio? Not easy to find jobs nowadays.'

'I want him to buy a pub. He's got three hundred pounds. He won a football pool last winter.'

'The lucky stiff.'

'But he's scared of that sister of his, and I can't persuade him. "Now, listen, Harold," I keep saying, but he just hums and haws and chews his moustache. Oh, well,' said Elsie philosophically, 'I suppose it'll all come out in the wash. What's that mess on the floor?'

'It's what's left of a sort of gadget I happened to drop.'

'Does he know about it?'

'Oh, yes. The topic came up.'

'I wonder he didn't chew your head off.'

'He did look for a moment as if he were toying with some such idea. Rather a hard nut, what?'

'He's an overbearing dishpot,' said Elsie Bean.

Pongo wandered out into the hall. He had about as much as he required of the collection of African curios for the time being, and he wanted to pace up and down and ponder. He had already formed a reasonably accurate estimate of Sir Aylmer Bostock's character, but it was interesting to find it confirmed by the woman who knew.

An overbearing dishpot? The words had a disagreeable sound. His attitude towards overbearing dishpots resembled that of his companion's circle in Bottleton East towards officers of the Law. He disliked and feared them. It began to look to him as if union with Hermione Bostock, good though it might be in itself, carried with it certain disadvantages which wanted thinking over.

'And Lady Bostock?' he said. 'She flitted only briefly through my life, but she struck me as being slightly less of a man-eater.'

'Yes, she's better than what he is,' agreed Elsie Bean. 'But the one I like is Mr William.'

'Who would he be?'

'Their nephew. Mr Oakshott.'

'Oh, ah, yes. I was forgetting. I know him, or used to. Got a pink face, hasn't he?'

'Well, I'd call it more of a tomato ketchup colour. Owing to the heat of the sun in them parts. He's just come back from Brazil. He was telling me about Brazil this morning,' said Elsie, who had lost no time in buttonholing the returned wanderer and exchanging ideas with him. 'The natives there shoot birds with poisoned darts.'

'Poisoned darts?'

'R. Through blowpipes.'

Pongo was courteous, but he could not let this pass. Though it was some time since he had boned up on his Brazil, memories of 'The Boy Explorers Up the Amazon' still lingered in his mind.

'Not poisoned darts.'

'That's what Mr William told me.'

'He was pulling your leg. They keep those for their wives' relations. Use your intelligence, my dear old housemaid. When a Brazilian native shoots a bird, he does it with a purpose. He intends to employ that bird subsequently in broiled or fricassee form. Obviously, then, if he soaked it with a poisoned dart, he would be defeating his own ends, because no sooner had he bitten into the liver wing than he would kick the bucket in awful agonies. And Brazilian natives, while they may be asses, are not silly asses. If you really want to know how they shoot birds, I will tell you. They fashion a rude sling – thus,' said Pongo, taking out his handkerchief and unfolding it. 'They then look about them for a handy projectile, as it might be this paperweight, and stuff it into the rude sling. This done, they whirl the contraption round their heads and . . . Oh, my God! Where did that one go?'

It had not been his intention to give a practical demonstration. He had planned to stop short of the actual discharge of the projectile, merely indicating its effects verbally. But artistic enthusiasm had carried him too far. A rending crash, and something white in the shadows at the end of the hall was lying in fragments.

'Coo!' said Elsie Bean, awed. 'You aren't half breaking up the home, are you? You'll catch it when His Nibs gets back.'

For the third time since he had entered this house of terror, Pongo's brow grew warm and damp. With that get-together of theirs over the broken what-not still green in his memory, it seemed to him only too sickeningly certain that he would catch it when His Nibs got back.

'What was it?' he quavered, rightly speaking of the object in the past tense.

'It's a sort of sawn-off statue like, that he had presented to him when he give up being Governor of that dog's island out in Africa that he used to be Governor of. A bust, cook says it's called. He thinks the world of it. The other morning he happened to come along while I was giving it a bit of a dusting, and you ought to have heard him go on, just because I kind of rocked it a little. "Be careful, girl! Be careful, girl! Mind what you're doing, my good girl!" Coo!'

Pongo's brow grew damper. A stylist would now have described it as beaded. And simultaneously he found himself chilled to the bone. He was a human replica of one of those peculiar puddings which lure the diner on into supposing that he is biting into a hot *soufflé* and then suddenly turn right around and become ice-cream in the middle.

Matters were even worse, he perceived, than he had feared. This was not one of those minor breakages which get passed off with a light apology on the one side and a jolly laugh on the other. It was as if Sir Aylmer Bostock had had a favourite child on whom he doted and he, Pongo, had socked that child on the occiput and laid it out good and proper. And coming right on top of the what-not misadventure, too! What would be the effect on his temperamental host of this second and possibly even more wrath-provoking outrage?

'Golly!' he moaned, sagging at the knees. 'This is a nice bit of box fruit. Advise me, young Bean. What do I do for the best, do you think?'

It may be that Bottleton East produces an exceptionally quick-witted type of girl, or perhaps all women are like that. At any rate, Elsie Bean, with scarcely a pause for thought, provided the solution hot off the griddle.

'Well, look,' she said. 'It's kind of dark in that corner, so maybe he won't miss his old bust for a bit. He's short-sighted, I know, and he won't wear specs because he thinks they'd make him look silly. Jane heard them talking about it at dinner. If I was you, I'd hop into that car of yours and drive lickerty-split to London and get another bust. And then you drive back and stick it up. Ten to one he won't notice nothing.'

For an instant Pongo's numbed brain was incapable of following her reasoning. Then the mists cleared, and he saw that it was red-hot stuff. This girl had found the way.

Drive lickerty-split to London? No need to do that. He could procure the substitute a dashed sight nearer than London. At Ickenham Hall, to be precise. His mind shot back to last night's dinner-table ... Uncle Fred jerking a thumb at an object in the corner of the room and saying it was a bust which Sally had brought down and left in his charge, and himself – how ironical it seemed now – giving the thing a brief and uninterested glance. It wouldn't be an uninterested glance he would be giving it when he saw it again.

His spirits soared. Ickenham Hall was only a dozen miles away, and he had an owner-driver's touching faith in the ability of his Buffy-Porson to do a dozen miles, if pushed, in about three minutes and a quarter. He could be there and back and have the understudy on its pedestal long before his host had finished conferring with the Vicar.

He beamed upon Elsie Bean.

'That's the set-up. I'll go and get the car.'

'I would.'

'You, meanwhile, might be putting in a bit of earnest brush-and-pan work.'

'Right ho!'

'Fine. Great. Capital. Splendid,' said Pongo, and raced for the stables.

Elsie Bean, her errand of mercy concluded, was standing on the front steps when he drove up. He was conscious, as he saw her, of a twinge of remorse, for it had just come to him that he had churlishly omitted to chuck her so much as a word of thanks for her splendid resourcefulness.

'I say,' he said, 'I forgot to mention it in the swirl and rush of recent events, but I'm most frightfully obliged to you for the very sporting way you've rallied round and saved me from the fate that is worse than death – viz;' explained Pongo, 'getting glared at by that goggle-eyed old Jack the Ripper with the lip fungus.'

Elsie Bean said she was only too pleased, to be sure, and he took her hand in his and pressed it.

'But for you I should have been in the soup and going down for the third time. I owe you more than words can tell.'

He was still pressing her hand, and from that to kissing her in a grateful and brotherly manner was but a short step. He took it, and

Bill Oakshott, coming round the corner after one of the long walks with which he was endeavouring these days to allay the pangs of frustrated love, was able to observe the courteous gesture from start to finish.

Pongo sprang into the car with a lissom bound, waved his hand and drove off, and Bill stared after him, stunned. Pongo belonged to the type of man which changes very little in appearance with the passage of the years, and he recognized him immediately.

Still, to make sure . . .

'Wasn't that Mr Twistleton?' he inquired of Elsie Bean.

'Yes, sir,' said Elsie composedly. She had no inkling of the turmoil in his soul, and would have been astounded to learn that anyone was taking exception to that kiss. In Bottleton East everybody kisses everybody else as a matter of course, like the early Christians. 'He says you were wrong about the natives, Mr William.'

'The what?'

'Those natives in Brazil. They don't shoot birds with poisoned darts, only their wives' relations. They use rude slings.'

With an effort that shook his powerful frame to its foundations Bill Oakshott contrived to keep from saying something ruder about Brazilian natives than any sling fashioned by them. There was no room in his thoughts for Brazilian natives. All the available space was occupied by Pongo.

So this, he was saying to himself, was the man to whom Hermione had entrusted her happiness; a libertine who, once the Don Juan of his dancing class, now went about kissing housemaids on doorsteps. How right, how unerringly right, old Ickenham had been. Can the leopard change his spots, he had speculated. This leopard didn't even seem to want to.

'Gosh!' thought Bill, aghast at the stark horror of the thing.

A minor point presented itself.

'Where's he off to?' he asked, puzzled.

'London, sir.'

'London?'

'Yes, sir.'

'But he's only just arrived.'

'Yes, sir.'

'Did he say why he was going to London?'

Elsie Bean was a good accomplice, cautious, reliable, on the alert against verbal slips.

'No, sir. He just said "Coo! I think I'll go to London," and popped off.'

Bill Oakshott drew a deep breath. It seemed to him that in the years since he had seen him last, his old friend, never very strong in the head, must have become absolutely *non compos*. Do balanced men drive to country houses and immediately upon arrival say 'Coo! I think I'll go to London,' and drive off again? They certainly do not.

His heart, as he filled his pipe, was heavy. Sane libertines, he was thinking, are bad enough, but loony libertines are the limit.

## Chapter 4

It was at a quarter to eight that evening that Lord Ickenham, after a pleasant journey to London in his car and a bath and change at his club, arrived in Budge Street, Chelsea, to pick up Sally Painter and take her to dinner.

Budge Street, Chelsea, in the heart of London's artistic quarter, is, like so many streets in the hearts of artistic quarters, dark, dirty, dingy and depressing. Its residents would appear to be great readers and very fond of fruit, for tattered newspapers can always be found fluttering about its sidewalks and old banana skins, cores of apples, plum stones and squashed strawberries lying in large quantities in its gutters. Its cats are stringy, hard-boiled cats, who look as if they were contemplating, or had just finished perpetrating, a series of murders of the more brutal type.

It was a bit of luck, accordingly, for this dishevelled thoroughfare to be toned up by Lord Ickenham's ornamental presence. With his well-cut clothes and distinguished deportment he lent to the scene a suggestion of the enclosure at Ascot on Cup Day.

And he had not been there long, strolling up and down, when Budge Street had another slice of good fortune. Round the corner from the King's Road there came hurrying a small, alert girl in beige, whose arrival intensified the Ascot note. Nobody, not even Pongo at the very height of that unfortunate discussion about the tint of his liver, had ever attempted to deny that Sally Painter was pretty: and even if she had not been, there was a jauntiness in her carriage which would have gone far to create that illusion.

To Lord Ickenham she seemed like some spirit of the summer day. Watching her as she paused to tickle a passing cat and noting how under the treatment the cat became in an instant a better, more idealistic cat, his heart went out to her.

'Hoy!' he cried paternally, and she came running up, floating into his arms like a columbine.

'I hope I haven't kept you waiting, Uncle Fred. I had to see a man about a bust.'

'Not at all,' said Lord Ickenham. Odd, he was thinking, how everybody seemed to be seeing men about busts to-day. It was only a few hours since Pongo had come charging into his study, clamouring for one. 'Always see men about busts. It is the secret of a happy and successful life.'

Sally linked her arm in his, and gave it a squeeze.

'It's lovely seeing you again, angel.'

'I am always well worth looking at.'

'How wonderful of you to come. And how brave! How did you manage to sneak away?'

'What extraordinary verbs you employ, child.'

'Well, didn't Aunt Jane say she would scalp you with a blunt knife next time you were AWOL?'

'In her playful way she did say something of the sort. Odd, that craving of hers to keep me vegetating in the country. But your honorary Aunt Jane is at the moment on her way to the West Indies. This has eased the situation a good deal. I thought it a good opportunity of broadening my mind.'

'Or playing hookey.'

'That is another way of putting it, of course. Well, let's find a taxi and go and get some dinner. There's one,' said Lord Ickenham, as they turned the corner. 'Hop in. Barribault's,' he said to the driver, and Sally closed her eyes in a sort of ecstasy. A girl who as a rule dined sparingly in Soho, she found enchantment in the mere name of London's premier restaurant.

'Barribault's? We're not dressed.'

'Grill room. Ev. dress not oblig.'

'But do I look smart enough?'

'My dear, you look like Helen of Troy after a good facial.'

Sally leaned back against the cushions.

'Barribault's!' she murmured.

'We Earls step high,' Lord Ickenham assured her. 'The best is none too good for us.'

'It must be great being an Oil.'

'It's terrific. I often lie awake at night, aching with pity for all the poor devils who aren't.'

'Though I suppose you know you're an anachronistic parasite on the body of the State? Or so Otis says. He's just become a Communist.'

'He has, has he? Well, you can tell him from me that if he starts any nonsense of trying to hang me from a lamp-post, I shall speak very sharply to him. Doesn't he like Earls?'

'Not much. He thinks they're blood-suckers.'

'What an ass that boy is, to be sure. Where's the harm in sucking blood? We need it, to keep us rosy. And it isn't as if I hadn't had to work for my little bit of gore. People see me now the dickens of a fellow with five Christian names and a coronet hanging on a peg in the hats and coats cupboard under the stairs, and they forget that I started at the bottom of the ladder. For years I was a younger son, a mere Honourable!'

'Why have you never told me this?'

'I hadn't the heart to. A worm of an Hon. In Debrett, yes, but only in small print.'

'You're making me cry.'

'I can't help that. Do you know how they treat Hons., Sally? Like dogs. They have to go into dinner behind the Vice-Chancellor of the County Palatinate of Lancaster.'

'Well, it's all over now, darling.'

'The only bit of sunshine in their lives is the privilege of being allowed to stand at the bar of the House of Lords during debates. And I couldn't even do that, my time being ear-marked for the cows I was punching in Arizona.'

'I didn't know you had ever punched cows.'

'As a young man, hundreds. I had a beautiful punch in those days, straight and true, like the kick of a mule, and never travelling more than six inches. I also jerked soda, did a bit of newspaper work, which was when I met your father, and had a shot at prospecting in the Mojave Desert. But was I happy? No. Because always at the back of my mind, like some corroding acid, was the thought that I had to go into dinner behind the Vice-Chancellor of the County Palatinate of Lancaster. In the end, by pluck and perseverance, I raised myself from the depths and became what I am to-day. I'd like to see any Vice-Chancellor of the County Palatinate of Lancaster try to squash in ahead of me now.'

'It's like something out of Horatio Alger.'

'Very like. But I'm boring you. I'm afraid we fellows who have made good have a tendency to go rambling on about our early struggles. Tell me of yourself. How are you doing these days, Sally?'

'Well, I still go into dinner behind fashion editresses, but aside from that I'm making out pretty satisfactorily.'

'Trade good?'

'Not so bad.'

The cab drew up at the ornate portal of Barribault's Hotel, and they made their way to the grill room. As they took their seats, Sally was sniffing luxuriously.

'Heaven!' she said.

'Hungry?'

'I'm always hungry.'

Lord Ickenham looked at her a little anxiously.

'You're sure you're not hard up, Sally?'

'Not a bit. Busts are quite brisk. It's odd, when you think how hideous most people are, that so many of them should want to hand their faces down to posterity.'

'You wouldn't deceive me?'

'No, honestly. I'm opulent.'

'Then why did you send me that SOS? What is the very urgent matter you wanted to see me about, with the "very" underlined?'

Sally was silent for a moment, but only because she was eating caviare. It did not often come her way.

'Oh, that? It's about Otis.'

'My God!'

'Well, it is. I'm sorry.'

'Otis again! A thing I've noticed all my life is that the nicest girls always have the ghastliest brothers. It seems to be a law of nature. Well, what's the trouble this time, and what do you want me to do?'

'I'll explain about the trouble later. What I want you to do is to ask Pongo to do something for me.'

'Pongo?'

'I can't very well approach him direct,' said Sally.

There was a sudden flatness in her voice which did not escape Lord Ickenham's quick ear. He leaned across and petted her hand.

'A shame about you and Pongo, Sally.'

'Yes.'

There was a silence. Lord Ickenham stole a glance across the table. Sally was gazing into the middle distance, her eyes, or so it seemed to him, suspiciously bright and with a disposition to moisture which disquieted him. It is rarely that an uncle is able to understand how a nephew of his can possibly cast a fatal spell and, fond as he was of Pongo, Lord Ickenham could not see him as a breaker of hearts. Yet it appeared plain that his loss had left a large gap in this girl's life. Her air was the air of one who was pining for Pongo, and it was a relief when the waiter, arriving with *truite bleue*, broke a tension which had begun to be uncomfortable.

'Tell me about Otis,' he said.

Sally smiled a rather twisted smile.

'You needn't be tactful, Uncle Fred. I don't mind talking about Pongo. At least . . . No, of course I don't. Have you seen him lately?'

'He left me this afternoon. He turned up yesterday and spent the night.'

'How was he looking?'

'Oh, very well.'

'Did he speak about me?'

'Yes. And when I cursed him for being ass enough to part brass rags with you, he told me the inside story.'

'About my wanting him to smuggle Alice Vansittart's jewels into America?'

'Yes.'

'I was a fool to get mad. And it was all so unnecessary, as it turned out.'

'The Vansittart decided on reflection to pay duty?'

'No. But I thought of a much better way of slipping the stuff through. I'm not going to tell even you what it was, but it's a peach of a way. It can't fail. Alice is crazy about it.'

She spoke with a girlish animation which encouraged Lord Ickenham to hope that her heart was, after all, not irretrievably broken. That bright, moist look had gone from her eyes, leaving in its place a gleam not unlike that of which Pongo had so disapproved, when he had seen it in the eyes of his Uncle Fred.

'She is, is she?'

'When I told her, she clapped her hands in glee.'

'You realize, of course, that it is very wrong to deceive the United States Customs authorities?'

'Yes, it makes me miserable. Poor darlings.'

'Still, there it is. So you and Pongo need not have split up at all.'

'No.'

'It was silly of him to take your breaking the engagement so seriously. My dear wife broke ours six times, and each time I came up smiling.'

'I ought to have remembered that Pongo does take things seriously.'

'Yes. A saintly character, but muttonheaded.'

'And now he's gone and got engaged to Hermione, only daughter of Sir Aylmer Bostock and Lady Bostock, of Ashenden Manor, Ashenden Oakshott, Hants. Oh, well. Do you know her, Uncle Fred?'

'No. I've seen her photograph.'

'So have I. It was in the *Tatler*. She's very good-looking.'

'If you admire that type of looks.'

'Pongo seems to.'

'Yes. For the moment you might describe him as being under the ether. But there will be a bitter awakening.'

'You can't know that just from seeing her photograph.'

'Yes, I can. She'll give him the devil.'

'Oh, poor angel.'

There was another silence.

'Well, what is it you want me to ask him to do for you?' said Lord Ickenham. 'I may mention that I'm pretty sure he will do it, whatever it is. He's still damned fond of you, Sally.'

'Oh, no.'

'He is, I tell you. He confessed as much, in so many words.'

A dazzling smile flashed out on Sally's face. The waiter, who was bringing chicken *en casserole*, caught it head-on and nearly dropped the dish.

'Did he?'

'And don't forget that he still retained enough of the old affection to send you a customer in the shape of Sir Aylmer Bostock.'

'Was it Pongo who got me that job? How like him,' said Sally softly. 'I love him for that. Though unfortunately it was through my doing that bust that poor Otis's trouble came about.'

'How did that happen?'

'Well, to begin at the beginning, I did the bust.'

'Quite.'

'And during the process, of course, my sitter and I talked of this and that.'

'Was his conversation entertaining?'

'Not very. He was rather inclined to compare my efforts to their disadvantage with those of a sculptor who did a bust of him when he retired.'

'The one that stands – or stood – in the hall at Ashenden?'

'Yes. However did you know?'

'Wait, my child. I shall shortly be telling you a story of my own. Go on. He conversed with you, but you did not find him very entertaining.'

'No. But he said one thing that gripped my attention, and that was that he had written his Reminiscences and had decided after some thought to pay for their publication. He spoke like a man who had had disappointments. So I said to myself "Ha! A job for Otis."'

'I begin to see. Otis took it on and made a mess of it?'

'Yes. In a negligent moment he slipped in some plates which should have appeared in a book on Modern Art which he was doing. Sir Aylmer didn't like any of them much, but the one he disliked particularly was the nude female with "Myself in the Early Twenties" under it. The first thing I knew about it was when he sent the bust back. Lady Bostock brought it round to my studio with a stiff note. And now he's bringing an action for enormous damages. If it comes off, it will smash Otis's poor little publishing firm. It's all rather unfortunate.'

'Most. But characteristic of Otis.'

'Poor lamb, he's dreamy.'

'Poor fish, he's a nightmare. I suppose you put up money for his publishing firm?'

'A certain amount.'

'Oh, heavens. Well, I'm sorry to say it, my dear, but if what you tell me is correct, any jury will give Bostock Otis's head on a charger.'

'I know. If the thing ever comes into court. That's why I need Pongo's help. I want him to use his influence with Sir Aylmer to get him to withdraw the suit. He might persuade him to settle for some smallish amount which wouldn't ruin Otis.'

'That would be the happy ending, of course. But is Pongo *persona grata* with him?'

'Surely?'

'I wonder. It all depends on how he has come out with that bust. Strange that Otis's future as a publisher, which I don't care a damn about, and your little bit of money, which I do, should depend on Pongo's ability to sneak a clay bust into Ashenden Manor and get away with it. Odd. Bizarre, you might say. Life can be very complicated at times.'

'What do you mean? What bust?'

'That is the story I am about to relate. Have you had enough to eat? Then let's go and have our coffee in the lounge. Yes,' said Lord Ickenham, when they had seated themselves in two of the luxurious armchairs which Barribault's Hotel provides for its patrons, 'very complicated indeed. I told you Pongo came to my place last night.'

'Yes.'

'Today, after lunch, he started out for Ashenden, to fascinate the old folks. I waved him a tender farewell, and thought that that was the last I should see of him for at least a week. I was wrong. He was back again in under two hours. Deeply agitated. More like a cat on hot bricks than anything human.'

'But why?'

'Because, in endeavouring to demonstrate to the Ashenden Manor housemaid how Brazilian natives shoot birds with rude slings, he had happened to break that bust in the hall, of which you were speaking just now.'

'Oh, golly.'

'Hullo! You agitated, too?'

'Of course I'm agitated. Don't you see, Uncle Fred? Sir Aylmer adores that bust. He'll be furious with Pongo –'

'Thus rendering Pongo in no position to plead for Otis? Yes, that seems to follow. But calm yourself. All may yet be well. His motive in coming to me was to borrow another bust to put on the bereaved pedestal, in the hope that the substitution would not be noticed.'

'That was bright.'

'Yes, much too bright for Pongo. It must have been the housemaid who suggested it. He isn't what I would call a quick-witted chap. I remember so well his confusion of mind when they were asking him his name that day at the dog races. He had got as far as "Tw –" when I was fortunately able to lean across and whisper to him that he was Edwin Smith of 11 Nasturtium Road, East Dulwich.'

'And what were you?'

'George Robinson, of number fourteen in the same thoroughfare. Yes, I think we may safely attribute to the housemaid any swift intelligence that was displayed on this occasion. Well, I gave him a bust and he drove off with it. We have no means of knowing as yet, of course, if the simple ruse has proved effective, but I think we may feel reasonably optimistic. He tells me it is darkish in the corner of the hall where the original used to stand, and I don't suppose Mugsy is in the habit of scrutinizing it too carefully. Just a casual glance in passing, and he toddles off to the garden to enjoy the sunshine.'

'Why do you call him Mugsy?'

'We always used to at school.'

'Were you and Sir Aylmer at school together?'

'For years.'

'Then couldn't you plead with him?'

'No, I could not. I was telling his nephew, whom I met in the train yesterday, that I once gave young Mugsy Bostock six with a fives bat, and no doubt the incident still rankles. Pongo is the one who must plead.'

'If everything has gone well.'

'I feel convinced that it has. He says Mugsy is short-sighted and won't wear spectacles, and he described the housemaid as staunch and true and not at all the sort to squeal to the big four.'

'You're a great comfort, Uncle Fred.'

'I try to be, my dear. Sweetness and light, that is my slogan.'

'It was lucky you happened to have a bust handy.'

'Extraordinarily fortunate. For one reason and another Ickenham Hall has never been very well provided with them. Statues, yes. If you came to me with a hurry call for a nude Venus, I could fill the order without any trouble whatsoever. My grandfather specialized in them. "Home isn't home," he used to say, running a thoughtful hand through his whiskers, "without plenty of nude Venuses." The result being that in certain parts of the grounds you have the illusion of having wandered into a Turkish bath on ladies' night. But busts, no. We Ickenhams have somehow never gone in for busts. So if it hadn't been for you providentially leaving one in my care –'

It is not easy to rise in a single bound from a Barribault armchair, but Sally had done so. Her face was pale, and she was staring with wide, horrified eyes.

'Uncle Fred! You didn't give him that one?'

'Yes. Why, what's wrong?'

Sally dropped back into her chair.

'It had Alice's jewels in it,' she said in a toneless whisper.

'What!'

'Yes. I slipped them in at the top of the plaster, and Alice was going to call for the bust next week and take it to America. That was the "way" I was telling you I thought of.'

'Well, dash my wig and buttons!' said Lord Ickenham.

There followed a pregnant silence. Having dashed his wig and buttons, Lord Ickenham, though nobody could have called him an unresourceful man, seemed at a loss. He scratched his chin, he twirled his moustache, he drummed with his fingers on the side of his chair, but without obtaining anything in the nature of an inspiration.

Finally he rose.

'Well, it's no good saying I'm sorry, my dear. Nor is there much to be gained by pointing out that I meant well. What you want is a policy, not remorseful bleatings. I think I'll take a turn up and down outside. The fresh air may assist the flow of thought. And the flow of thought would certainly seem to need all the assistance it can get.'

He went out through the revolving door, his head bowed, his

hands clasped behind his back. When he returned some minutes later, it was with a message of hope. His face had cleared and he was his old bright self again.

'It's all right, my child. This little difficulty can be very simply adjusted. It just needed concentration. You did tell me Mugsy had returned that bust you did of him? You have it at the studio?'

'Yes.'

'Then all is well. We will go down to Ashenden tomorrow in the car, taking it with us, and I will substitute it for the one now in residence.'

'But –'

'Don't say "But."'

'How –?'

'And don't say "How." It's the sort of thing the boys in the back room used to say to Columbus when he told them he was going to discover America, and look how silly he made them feel. I'll find a way. Don't bother your head about the trifling details, leave them to me. You go home and pack a few necessaries and get a good night's rest, while I remain and iron out the one or two points I haven't got quite straight yet. More coffee? No? Then Off you go. Bless my soul,' said Lord Ickenham with boyish relish, as he escorted her to the door, 'what a providential thing that this should have happened. Something on these lines was just what I was needing, to stimulate me and bring back the flush of youth. I feel as I did when Pongo and I started out last spring for Blandings Castle in the roles of Sir Roderick Glossop, the brain specialist, and his nephew Basil. Did he ever tell you about that?'

'No.'

'Odd. I should have thought it would have been one of his dearest memories. You shall have the whole story tomorrow on the journey down. Well, good night, my dear,' said Lord Ickenham, assisting Sally into her taxi. 'Sleep well, and don't worry. You can trust me to look after everything. This is the sort of situation that brings out the best in me. And when you get the best in Frederick Altamont Cornwallis, fifth Earl of good old Ickenham, you've got something.'

# PART TWO

## *Chapter 5*

It was the custom of Lady Bostock, when the weather was fine, to sit in a garden chair on the terrace of Ashenden Manor after luncheon, knitting socks for the deserving poor. A believer, like Lord Ickenham, in spreading sweetness and light, she considered, possibly correctly, that there is nothing that brings the sunshine into grey lives like a sock or two.

On the day following the events which have just been recorded the weather was extremely fine. Soft white clouds floated across a sky of the purest blue, the lake shone like molten silver, and from the adjacent flower-beds came the murmur of bees and the fragrant scent of lavender and mignonette. It was an afternoon to raise the spirits, lighten the heart and set a woman counting her blessings one by one.

Nor did Lady Bostock omit to do this. She recognized these blessings as considerable. It was pleasant to be home again, though she had never really enjoyed life in the country, preferring Cheltenham with its gay society. Mrs Gooch, the cook, had dished up an inspired lunch. And ever since the assignment of judging the bonny babies at the fête had been handed to his nephew William, Sir Aylmer had been in a mood which could almost be called rollicking, a consummation always devoutly to be wished by a wife whose life work it was to keep him in a good temper. She could hear him singing in his study now. Something about his wealth being a burly spear and brand and a right good shield of hides untanned which on his arm he buckled – or, to be absolutely accurate, ber-huckled.

So far, so good. And yet, despite the fineness of the day, the virtuosity of Mrs Gooch and the joviality of her husband, Lady Bostock's heart was heavy. In these days in which we live, when existence has become a thing of infinite complexity and fate, if it slips us a bit of goose with one hand, is pretty sure to give us the sleeve across the windpipe with the other, it is rarely that we find a human being who is unmixedly happy. Always the bitter will be blended with the sweet, and in this *mélange* one can be reasonably certain that it is the former that will predominate.

A severe indictment of our modern civilization, but it can't say it didn't ask for it.

As Lady Bostock sat there, doing two plain, two purl, or whatever it is that women do when knitting socks, a sigh escaped her from time to time. She was thinking of Sally Painter.

Budge Street, Chelsea, brief though her visit there had been, had made a deep impression on this sensitive woman. She had merely driven up in a cab, rung the bell of Sally's studio, handed her parcel to the charwoman and driven swiftly off again, but she had seen enough to recognize Budge Street for the sort of place she had read about in novels, where impoverished artists eke out a miserable existence, supported only by hope. How thankful, she thought, impoverished Miss Painter must have been to get the commission to model that bust of Aylmer, and what anguish must have been hers on having it thrown back on her hands.

She had mentioned this to Sir Aylmer as they were returning from their conference with the Vicar, and had been snubbed with a good deal of brusqueness. And now, though she was too loyal a wife to criticize her husband even in thought, she could not check a fleeting regret that he was always so splendidly firm.

Was there nothing, she asked herself, as she remembered the admirable luncheon which she had recently consumed and pictured Sally gnawing a dry crust and washing it down with a cup of water, was there nothing that she could do? Useless, of course, to make another attempt to persuade Aylmer to change his mind, but suppose she were to send the girl a secret cheque . . .

At this point her musing was interrupted and her despondency increased by the arrival of Bill Oakshott, who came heavily along the terrace smoking a sombre pipe. She eyed him with a sad pity. Ever since she had given him the bad news, the sight of him had made her feel like a soft-hearted Oriental executioner who, acting on orders from the front office, has had to do unpleasant things to an Odalisque with a bow string. It seemed to her sometimes that she would never be able to forget the look of horror and despair which had leaped into his crimson face. Traces of it still lingered on those haggard features.

'Hullo, Aunt Emily,' he said in sepulchral tones. 'Knitting a sock?'

'Yes, dear. A sock.'

'Oh?' said Bill, still speaking like a voice from the tomb. 'A sock? Fine.'

He stood there, staring before him with unseeing eyes, and she touched his hand gently.

'I wouldn't worry about it too much, dear.'

'I don't see how one could,' said Bill. 'How many of these frightful babies will there be?'

'There were forty-three last year.'

'Forty-three!'

'Be brave, William. If Mr Brotherhood could do it, you can.'

The flaw in this reasoning was so obvious that Bill was able to detect it at once.

'Curates are different. They train them specially to judge bonny babies. At the theological colleges. Start them off with ventriloquists' dummies, I shouldn't wonder. Forty-three, did you say? And probably dozens more this time. These blighters breed like rabbits. Gosh, I wish I was back in Brazil.'

'Oh, William.'

'I do. What a country! Nothing but flies and ticks and alligators and snakes and scorpions and tarantulas and a sort of leech that drops on you from trees and sucks your blood. Not a baby to be seen for miles. Listen, Aunt Emily, can't I get someone else to take this ghastly job on?'

'But who?'

'Yes, that's the snag, of course,' said Bill morosely. 'Mugs fatheaded enough to let themselves be talked into judging forty-three bonny babies, all dribbling out of the side of the mouth, must be pretty scarce, pretty scarce. Well, I think I'll be pushing along, Aunt Emily. It seems to help a little if I keep moving.'

He plodded off, listlessly puffing smoke, leaving behind him an aunt with an aching heart. And it was perhaps because Lady Bostock was now so near the nadir of depression that she thought she might as well make a complete job of it. So she began to think of Pongo.

It frequently happens that prospective sons-in-law come as a rather painful shock to their prospective mothers-in-law, and the case of Lady Bostock had provided no exception to the rule. Immediately on seeing Pongo she had found herself completely at a loss to understand why her daughter should have chosen him as a mate. From the very start she had felt herself to be in the presence of one whose soul was not attuned to hers. At moments, indeed, only her perfect breeding had restrained her from beating him over the head with the sock which she was knitting for the deserving poor.

Analysing his repellent personality, she came to the conclusion that while she disliked his nervous giggle, his lemon-coloured hair and the way he had of drooping his lower jaw and letting his eyes get glassy, the thing about him that particularly exasperated her was his extraordinary jumpiness.

Of this she had witnessed a manifestation only an hour or so ago, as they were leaving the dining-room after lunch. As they started to cross the hall, Aylmer had moved in the direction of that bust of his, as if to give it a flick with his handkerchief, as he sometimes did, and Reginald had bounded in his tracks with a soft, animal yelp, recovering his composure only when Aylmer, abandoning the idea of flicking, had moved on again.

A strange young man. Was he half – or even a quarter – witted? Or was his mind, if he had a mind, burdened by some guilty secret?

Speculations like these, indulged in on a warm day after a rather heavy lunch, are apt to induce drowsiness. Her eyelids began to flutter. Somewhere out of sight a lawn-mower was purring hypnotically. The west wind played soothingly on her face.

Lady Bostock slept.

But not for long. Her eyes had scarcely closed when the word 'EMILY', spoken at the extreme limit of a good man's lungs, jerked her from her slumber as if a charge of trinitrotoluol had been exploded beneath her chair.

Sir Aylmer was leaning out of the study window.

'EMILY!'

'Yes, dear? Yes, dear?'

'Come here,' roared Sir Aylmer, like a bo'sun addressing an able-bodied seaman across the deck in the middle of a hurricane. 'Wantcher.'

2

As Lady Bostock made her way to the study, her heart was racing painfully. There had been that in her husband's manner which caused her to fear unnamed disasters, and her first glance at him as she crossed the threshold told her that her apprehensions had been well founded.

His face was purple, and his moustache, always a barometer of the emotions, was dancing about beneath his laboured breath. She had not beheld such activity in it since the night years ago when the youngest and most nervously giggling of the aides-de-camp, twiddling the nut-crackers during the dessert course at dinner at Government House, had snapped the stem of one of his favourite set of wineglasses.

He was not alone. Standing at a respectful distance in one of the corners, as if he knew his place better than to thrust himself forward, was Constable Harold Potter, looking, as policemen do at such moments, as if he had been stuffed by a good taxidermist. She stared from one to the other, bewildered.

'Aylmer! What is it?'

Sir Aylmer Bostock was not a man who beat about bushes. When he had disturbing news to impart, he imparted it.

'Emily,' he said, quivering in every hair, 'there's a damned plot afoot.'

'A what?'

'A PLOT. An infernal outrage against the public weal. You know Potter?'

Lady Bostock knew Potter.

'How do you do, Potter?' she said.

'How do you do, m'lady?' said Constable Potter, coming unstuffed for an instant in order to play his part in the courteous exchanges and then immediately getting stuffed again.

'Potter,' said Sir Aylmer, 'has just come to me with a strange story. Potter!'

'Sir?'

'Tell her ladyship your strange story.'

'Yes, sir.'

'It's about Reginald,' said Sir Aylmer, to whet the interest of the audience. 'Or, rather,' he added, exploding his bombshell, 'the fellow who's posing as Reginald.'

Lady Bostock's eyes were already bulging to almost their maximum extent, but at these words they managed to protrude a little further.

'Posing?'

'Yes.'

'What do you mean?'

'What I say. I can't put it any plainer. The chap who's come here pretending to be Reginald Twistleton is an impostor. He isn't Reginald Twistleton at all. I had my suspicions of him all along. I didn't like his eye. Sly. Shifty. And that sinister giggle of his. What I'd call a criminal type. Potter!'

'Sir?'

'Get on with your strange story.'

'Yes, sir.'

Constable Potter stepped forward, his helmet balanced against his right hip. A glazed look had come into his eyes. It was the look which they always assumed when he was giving evidence in court. His gaze was directed some two feet above Sir Aylmer's head, so that his remarks seemed to be addressed to a bodiless spirit hovering over the scene and taking notes in an invisible notebook.

'On the sixteenth inst. —'

'Yesterday.'

'Yesterday,' proceeded Constable Potter, accepting the emendation. 'On the sixteenth inst., which was yesterday, I was proceeding up the drive of Ashenden Manor on my bicycle, when my attention was drawn to a suspicious figure entering the premises through a window.'

'The window of my collection room.'

'The window of Sir Aylmer Bostock's collection room. I immediately proceeded to follow the man and question him. In reply to my inquiries he made the statement that his name was Twistleton and that he was established as a guest at this residence.'

'Well, so he is,' said Lady Bostock, speaking a little dazedly.

Sir Aylmer waved an imperious hand.

'Wait, wait, wait, wait, WAIT. Mark the sequel.'

He paused, and stood puffing at his moustache. Lady Bostock, who had sunk into a chair, picked up a copy of the parish magazine and began to fan herself with it.

'We're coming to the part where he turns out not to be Twistleton,' said Sir Aylmer, allowing his moustache to subside like an angry sea after a storm. 'Carry on, Potter.'

Constable Potter, who had momentarily removed the glazed look from his eyes, put it back again. Raising his chin, which he had lowered in order to rest the neck muscles, he once more addressed the bodiless spirit.

'Having taken the man's statement, I proceeded to put searching questions to him. These appearing to establish his bona fide, I withdrew, leaving him in the company of Bean, a housemaid, whose evidence had assisted me in establishing the conclusion that his bona fide had been' – Constable Potter paused, searching for the telling verb – 'established,' he said. 'But –'

'Here comes the sequel.'

'But I was not wholly satisfied, and I'll tell you why,' said Constable Potter, suddenly abandoning the official manner and becoming chatty. 'The moment I saw this chap, I had a sort of feeling that his face was kind of familiar, but I couldn't place him. You know how it is. And, what's more, I could have taken my oath that last time we'd met his name hadn't been Twistleton –'

'Or anything like it,' said Sir Aylmer, adroitly snatching the conversational ball from the speaker and proceeding to carry it himself. 'I must start by telling you . . . ARE YOU ASLEEP, EMILY?'

'No, dear. No, dear,' cried Lady Bostock, who had been rash enough to close her eyes for an instant in order to relieve a shooting pain across the forehead.

'I must start by telling you that before Potter came to Ashenden Oakshott he used to be a member of the London police force, and this afternoon, as he was smoking a pipe after his lunch –'

'Cigarette, sir,' interpolated the officer respectfully. He knew the importance of exactitude on these occasions. 'A gasper.'

'– It suddenly flashed on him,' went on Sir Aylmer, having given him a dangerous look, 'that where he had seen this fellow before was at some dog races down Shepherd's Bush way, when he had arrested him, together with an accomplice, and hauled him off in custody.'

'Aylmer!'

'You may well say "Aylmer!" It seems that Potter keeps a scrap album containing newspaper clippings having to do with cases with which he has been connected, and he looked up this scrap album and found that the chap's name, so far from being Twistleton, is Edwin Smith, of 11 Nasturtium Road, East Dulwich. Edwin Smith,' repeated Sir Aylmer, somehow contriving by his intonation to make it seem a name to shudder at. 'Now do you believe me when I say he's an impostor!'

Women, having no moustaches, are handicapped at moments like this. Lady Bostock had begun to pant like a spent horse, but it was not the same thing. She could not hope to rival her husband's impressiveness.

'But what is he doing here?'

'Potter's view is that he is the advance man of a gang of burglars. I think he's right. These fellows always try to simplify matters for themselves by insinuating an accomplice into the house to pave the way for them. When the time is ripe, the bounder opens a window and the other bounders creep in. And if you want to know what this gang is after at Ashenden Manor, it sticks out a mile. My collection of African curios. Where did Potter find this chap? In my collection room. Where did I find him? Again in my collection room. My collection fascinates him. He can't keep away from it. You agree, Potter?'

Constable Potter, though not too well pleased at the way in which he had been degraded from the position of star witness to that of a mere Yes-man, was forced to admit that he agreed.

Lady Bostock was still panting softly.

'But it seems so extraordinary.'

'Why? It's value is enormous.'

'I mean, that he should take such a risk.'

'These fellows are used to taking risks. Eh, Potter?'

'Yes, sir.'

'Doing it all the time, aren't they?'

'Yes, sir.'

'Dangerous devils, what?'

'Yes, sir,' said Constable Potter, now apparently resigned to his demotion.

'But he must have known that Reginald was expected here. How could he tell that he was not going to run into him?'

'My dear Emily, don't be childish. The gang's first step would of course, be to make away with Reginald.'

'Make away with him? How?'

'Good Lord, how do chaps make away with chaps? Don't you ever read detective stories?'

Constable Potter saw his chance, and took it.

'They telephone 'em, m'lady, telling them to come to ruined mills, and then lock 'em up in the cellar. Or they –'

'– Slip drugs in their drinks and carry them off on yachts,' said Sir Aylmer, once more seizing the ball. 'There are a hundred methods. If we looked into it, I expect we should find that the real Reginald is at this moment lying bound and gagged on a pallet bed in Limehouse. Eh, Potter?'

'Yes, sir.'

'Or in the hold of a tramp steamer bound for South America?'

'Yes, sir.'

'I shouldn't wonder if they weren't sticking lighted matches between his toes to make him write them cheques,' said Sir Aylmer dispassionately. 'Well, all right, Potter, that's all. We won't keep you. Would you like a glass of beer?'

'Yes, sir,' said Constable Potter, this time with real enthusiasm.

'Go and get one in the kitchen. And now,' said Sir Aylmer, as the door closed, 'to business.'

'Where are you going?'

'To confront this impostor and kick him out, of course.'

'But, Aylmer.'

'Now what?'

'Suppose there is some mistake.'

'How can there be any mistake?'

'But suppose there *is*. Suppose this young man is really Reginald, and you turn him out of the house, we should never hear the last of it from Hermione.'

3

Something of the gallant fire which was animating him seemed to pass out of Sir Aylmer Bostock. He blinked, like some knight of King Arthur's court, who, galloping to perform a deed of derring-do, has had the misfortune to collide with a tree. Though keeping up a brave front, he, like his wife, had always quailed before Hermione. Native chiefs, accustomed to leap like fawns at a waggle of his moustache, would have marvelled at this weakness in one who had always seemed to them impervious to human emotions, but it existed.

''M, yes,' he said thoughtfully. 'Yes, I see what you mean.'

'She would be furious.'

'That's true.'

'I really don't know what to think myself,' said Lady Bostock distractedly. 'Potter's story did seem very convincing, but it is just possible that he is mistaken in supposing that this man who has come here as Reginald is really Edwin Smith.'

'I'd bet a million on it.'

'Yes, dear, I know. And I must say I have noticed something curiously furtive about the young man, as if he had a guilty secret. But –'

An idea occurred to Sir Aylmer.

'Didn't Hermione give some sort of description of this young poop of hers in that letter she wrote you saying she was engaged?'

'Why, of course. I had forgotten. It's in my desk. I'll go and get it.'

'Well?' said Sir Aylmer a few moments later.

Lady Bostock was skimming through the document.

'She says he is tall and slender, with large, lustrous eyes.'

'There you are! This chap hasn't got lustrous eyes.'

'Wouldn't you say his eyes were lustrous?'

'Certainly not. Like a couple of damned poached eggs. What else?'

'He is very amusing.'

'You see!'

'Oh!'

'What?'

'She says William used to know him as a boy.'

'She does? Then William's evidence will clinch the thing. Where is he? WILLIAM! WILLIAM!! WILLIAM!!!'

It is rarely that this sort of thing does not produce results. Bill Oakshott, who was still on the terrace, smoking his pipe and pondering over his numerous misfortunes, came clattering up the stairs as if pulled at the end of a string.

The fear – or hope – that his uncle was being murdered left him as he entered the room, but not his bewilderment at the summons.

'Hullo?' he said gropingly.

'Oh, there you are,' said Sir Aylmer, who was still bellowing out of the window. 'William, this fellow who calls himself Reginald Twistleton, how about him?'

'How about him?'

'Exactly. How about him?'

'How do you mean, how about him?'

'Good God, boy, can't you understand plain English! I mean How about him?'

Lady Bostock explained.

'We are terribly upset, William. Your uncle thinks that the man who came yesterday is not Reginald, but an impostor pretending to be Reginald.'

'What on earth gives him that idea?'

'Never mind what on earth gives me that idea,' said Sir Aylmer, nettled. 'You knew Reginald Twistleton as a boy?'

'Yes.'

'Good. That's established,' said Sir Aylmer, borrowing from Constable Potter's non-copyright material. 'Now, then, When you saw him yesterday, did you recognize him?'

'Of course.'

'Don't say "Of course" in that airy way. When had you seen him last?'

'About twelve years ago.'

'Then how can you be sure you recognized him?'

'Well, he looked about the same. Grown a bit, of course.'

'Have you discussed boyhood days with him?'

'No.'

'Have you asked him a single question, the response to which would prove that he had known you as a boy?'

'Why, no.'

'There you are, then.'

'But he answers to the name of Pongo.'

Sir Aylmer snorted.

'Of course he answers to the name of Pongo. Do you suppose that an impostor, when addressed as Pongo by somebody claiming to be an old friend of the man he was impersonating, would not have the elementary intelligence to dissemble? Your evidence is completely valueless.'

'Sorry.'

'No good being sorry. Well, I shall have to look into the thing for myself. I shall take the car and go over to Ickenham Hall. The real Reginald is Ickenham's nephew, so the old lunatic will presumably have a photograph of him somewhere on the premises. A glance at that will settle the matter.'

'What a splendid idea, Aylmer!'

'Yes,' said Sir Aylmer, who thought well of it himself. 'Just occurred to me.'

He shot from the room as if propelled from a rude sling in the hands of a Brazilian native, and hurried down the stairs. In the hall he was obliged to check his progress for an instant in order to glare at Pongo, who, like a murderer returning to the scene of his crime, had come thither to gaze at the substitute bust and ask himself for the hundredth time what were its chances of getting by.

'Ha!' said Sir Aylmer.

'Oh, hullo,' said Pongo, smiling weakly.

Sir Aylmer eyed him with that blend of horror and loathing with which honest men eye those who call themselves Twistleton when they are really Edwin Smith of 11, Nasturtium Road, East Dulwich, especially when these latter smile like minor gangsters caught in the act of committing some felony. It seemed to him that if he ever had seen furtive guilt limned on a human face, he had seen it now.

'Ha!' he said again, and went off to get his car.

A few minutes after he had steered it out into the road, tooting fiercely, for he was a noisy driver, another car, coming from the opposite direction, drew up outside the gate.

At its wheel was Lord Ickenham, and beside him Sally.

# *Chapter 6*

Lord Ickenham cast an alert eye up the curving drive, and gave his moustache a carefree twiddle. His air was that of a man who has arrived at some joyous tryst. A restful night and a good lunch had brought his always resilient nature to a fine pitch of buoyancy and optimism. There is an expression in common use which might have been invented to describe the enterprising peer at moments such as this; the expression 'boomps-a-daisy.' You could look askance at his methods, you could shake your head at him in disapproval and click your tongue in reproof, but you could not deny that he was boomps-a-daisy.

'This might be the place, don't you think?' he said.

'It is.'

'You speak confidently.'

'Well, I've been here before. When I was doing the bust.'

'Didn't Mugsy come to the studio?'

'Of course not. Great men like him don't come to the studios of poor working girls.'

Lord Ickenham took her point.

'True,' he said. 'I can't get used to the idea of young Mugsy Bostock being a big pot. To me he remains permanently a pie-faced stripling bending over a chair while I assure him that what is about to occur is going to hurt me more than it does him. A black lie, of course. I enjoyed it. One of the hardest things in life is to realize that people grow up. Nothing, for instance, can convince me that I am not a sprightly young fellow of twenty-five and, as for Pongo, the idea of him being old enough to contemplate marriage fills me with a perpetual astonishment. To me, he still wears sailor suits.'

'He must have looked sweet in a sailor suit.'

'No, he didn't. He looked foul. Like a ballet girl in a nautical musical comedy. But enough of this idle chatter. The time has come,' said Lord Ickenham, 'to discuss strategy and tactics.'

He spoke with the gay lilt in his voice which had so often in the past struck a chill into the heart of his nephew.

'Strategy and tactics,' he repeated. 'Here is the house. We have the bust. All that is needed is to effect an entry into the former, carrying the latter. This, accordingly, I shall now proceed to do. You spoke?'

'No, I only sort of gurgled. I was going to say "How?" but I mustn't, must I, because of Columbus and the boys in the back room.'

Lord Ickenham seemed amazed.

'My dear girl, you are surely not worrying yourself about the simple mechanics of the thing? There are a thousand ways, all child's play to one of my gifts. If I droop my moustache, thus, do I look like a man come to inspect the drains?'

'No.'

'If I turn it up at the ends, so, do I suggest the representative of a journal of rural interest, anxious to obtain Mugsy's views on the mangel-wurzel situation?'

'Not a bit.'

'Then I must try something else. I wonder if Mugsy has a parrot.'

'I know he hasn't. Why?'

'Didn't Pongo ever tell you of our afternoon at The Cedars, Mafeking Road, Mitching Hill?'

'No. What was The Cedars, Mafeking Road, Mitching Hill?'

'A suburban villa, heavily fortified and supposed to be impregnable. But I got in with absurd ease. One moment, I was outside its barred gates, lashed by an April shower; the next, in the sitting-room, toasting my toes at the gas fire. I told the maid I had come from the bird shop to clip the parrot's claws and slipped Pongo in with the statement that he was Mr Walkinshaw, my assistant, who applied the anaesthetic. I'm surprised he never mentioned it. I don't like the way he seems to have kept things from you. An unhealthy spirit. Yes, I think I may say with all due modesty that I am at my best when impersonating officials from bird shops who have called to prune the parrot, and I am sorry to hear you say that Mugsy has not got one. Not that I'm surprised. Only the gentler, kindlier type of man keeps a parrot and makes of it a constant friend. Ah, well, no doubt I shall be able to effect an entry somehow.'

'And what do you do then?'

'That's the easy part. I have the bust under my coat, I engage Mugsy in conversation, and at a selected moment I suddenly say "Look behind you!" He looks behind him, and while his back is turned I switch the busts and come away. So let's go.'

'Wait,' said Sally.

'Is this a time for waiting? The Ickenhams have never waited.'

'Well, they're going to start now. I've a much better plan.'

'Better than mine?' said Lord Ickenham incredulously.

'Better in every way,' said Sally firmly. 'Saner and simpler.'

Lord Ickenham shrugged his shoulders.

'Well, let's hear it. I'll bet I'm not going to like it.'

'You don't have to like it. You are going to stay in the car –'

'Absurd.'

'– While I take that bust to the house.'

'Ridiculous. I knew it was going to be rotten.'

'I shall try, of course, to put the deal through unobserved. But if I am observed, I shall have my story ready, which is more than you would have done.'

'I would have had twenty stories ready, each one better than the last.'

'Each crazier than the last. Mine will be a good one, carrying conviction in every syllable. I shall say I came to see Sir Aylmer –'

'I wish you would call him Mugsy. It's friendlier.'

'I won't call him Mugsy. I shall say I came to see Sir Aylmer, bringing the bust with me, in the hope that I could persuade him to relent and accept it after all.'

'Loathsome.'

'I may even cry a little.'

'Revolting. Where's your pride?'

'The worst that can happen is that he will show me to the door and dismiss me with a cold gesture.'

'And then,' said Lord Ickenham, brightening, 'we will start all over again, this time putting the affair in older and wiser hands than yours. Well, all right. On that understanding I don't mind you trying your way. I don't like it. It's tame. It degrades me to the position of a super supporting a star, and you get all the fun. Still, carry on, if you must. I shall stay here and sulk.'

He lit a cigar, and watched her as she walked up the drive. At the point where it curved out of sight, she turned and waved her hand, and he waved back, filled with a not unmanly emotion. Good old Sally, he was feeling. What a girl!

Lord Ickenham was a man with many friends in the United States where he had spent twenty years of his life, and of all these friends the one of whom he had been fondest was the late George Painter, that amiable and impecunious artist with whom he had shared so many of the joys and sorrows of an agreeably chequered youth. He had loved George, and he loved his daughter Sally.

Sally was just the sort of girl that appealed to him most, the sort America seems to turn out in thousands, gay, grave and adventurous, enjoying life with an almost Ickenhamian relish and resolutely refusing to allow its little difficulties to daunt her spirit.

How admirably, for instance, after the first shock, she had reacted to that unquestionably nasty wallop he had handed her in the lobby of Barribault's Hotel. No tears, no wringing of the hands, no profitless reproaches and recriminations. In the best and deepest sense of the words, a pippin of a girl. And why Pongo had let her go, simply from some finnicky objection to being disembowelled by New York port officials, baffled Lord Ickenham. It was one of the things that make a man who is getting on in years despair of the younger generation.

Time marched on. He looked at his watch. About now, he felt, she would be nearing the front door; about now, doing the quick glide through the hall and the rapid substitution of bust for bust. It would not be long before he saw her again, no doubt threading her way cautiously through the bushes that fringed the drive. He kept a keen eye riveted on those, but when she did appear she was walking in full view, and the first thing that attracted his attention was the fact that her hands were empty. At some point in her progress to and from the house, it would seem, she and her precious burden had parted company.

He could make nothing of this. His eyebrows rose in a silent query. Her face, he saw, was grave. It wore a strained look.

As she reached the car, however, her normal gaiety of disposition seemed to assert itself. She broke into a gurgling laugh, and his eyebrows rose again.

'We are amused?'

'Well, it was funny,' said Sally. 'I can't help laughing, though the absolutely rock-bottom worst has happened, Uncle Fred. We really are up against it now. You'll never guess.'

'I shan't try. Tell me.'

Sally leaned against the side of the car. Her face had become grave once more.

'I must have a cigarette first.'

'Nerves vibrating?'

'I'm shattered.'

She smoked in silence for a moment.

'Ready?'

'Waiting.'

'Very well, then, here it comes. When I got to the house, I found the front door open, which seemed to me about as big a piece of luck as I could want –'

'Always mistrust too much luck at the outset of any enterprise,' said Lord Ickenham judicially. 'It's simply part of Fate's con game. But I mustn't interrupt you. Go on.'

'I looked carefully over both shoulders. Nobody seemed to be about. I listened. I couldn't hear anybody in the hall. Everything was silent. So I sneaked in.'

'Quite.'

'And tiptoed across the hall.'

'You couldn't have done better.'

'And put the bust . . . Shall I call it Bust A., to distinguish it from Bust B.?'

'By all means.'

'You've got them clear? Bust A. was the one I was toting, and Bust B. the one with poor Alice's jewels in it.'

'Exactly.'

Sally drew at her cigarette. Her manner was absent, as if she were reliving an episode which had affected her deeply. She came to herself with something of the air of a sleeper awakening.

'Where was I?'

'Tiptoeing across the hall.'

'Yes, of course. Sorry to be so goofy.'

'Quite all right, my child.'

'I tiptoed across the hall and shifted Bust B. from its stand and put Bust A. in its place and gathered up Bust B. and started to come away . . . fairly quickly. No sense in hanging around, I mean.'

'None whatever. Never outstay your welcome.'

'And just as I got to the door of the room where Sir Aylmer keeps his collection of African curios, out came Lady Bostock from the drawing-room.'

'Dramatic.'

'I'll say it was dramatic. The memory of that moment is going to haunt me for the rest of my life. I don't suppose I shall sleep again for months and months and months.'

'We all sleep too much.'

'She said "Who's that?"'

'And you, I suppose, said "Me," meaning that it was you.'

'I hadn't time to say anything, because she suddenly leaped forward with a sort of pitying cluck –'

'A what?'

'A cluck. Of pity. Like a nice hen. She really is a good sort, Uncle Fred. I had never realized it before. When I was down here, doing the bust, she always seemed stiff and distant. But it was just her manner. She has a heart of gold.'

'A neat phrase, that. I must remember it. In what way did she exhibit this golden heart?'

'Why, by swooping down on me and grabbing the bust and saying in a hoarse whisper that she knew exactly why I had brought it and that she was terribly sorry for me and had begged Sir Aylmer to change his mind, but he wouldn't, so she would keep the bust and send me a cheque secretly and everything would be all right. And then she went into the collection room and locked it up in a cupboard, hurriedly, like a murderer concealing the body. And then she hustled me out. She didn't actually say "Fly!" but it amounted to that. And it all happened so quickly that there wasn't a thing I could do.'

'And there the bust is?'

'Yes. Locked up in a cupboard in Sir Aylmer's collection room with all Alice's jewels in it. Tie that for a disaster, Uncle Fred.'

All through the narrative, Lord Ickenham had been reviving like a watered flower. His air, as it reached its culminating point, was that of one hearing tidings of great joy.

UNCLE DYNAMITE

'Disaster?' he said exuberantly. 'What do you mean, disaster? This is the most admirable thing that could have happened. I now have something I can get my teeth into. It is no longer a question merely of effecting an entry into the house, but of getting myself established there. And if there is one thing I enjoy more than another, it is getting established in other people's houses. It brings the roses to my cheeks and tones up my whole system. Here is the immediate procedure, as I see it. You will drive on to Ickenham, which will serve us as a base, and I will take my suitcase and put up at the local inn and weave my subtle schemes. Expect sensational results shortly.'

'You are really going to establish yourself at the house?'

'I am.'

'And I still mustn't say "How?"'

'You certainly must not. You just leave everything to me, confident that I shall act for the best, as always. But you look grave, my child. I hope not from any lack of faith in my vision and enterprise?'

'I was thinking of Pongo. What will he do, when you suddenly appear?'

'I should imagine he will get the start of his young life and skip like the high hills. And an excellent thing, too. Pongo is a chap who wants taking out of himself.'

The car drove off, and Lord Ickenham hoisted his suitcase and set off for the village. He was just wishing that he had thought of asking Sally to drop him at the inn, for it was a heavy suitcase, when something large and tomato-coloured loomed up before him, and he recognized Bill Oakshott.

2

In Bill Oakshott's demeanour, as he approached, there was the suggestion of a somnambulist who, in addition to having blisters on both feet, is wrestling with an unpleasant nightmare. The scene through which he had recently passed, following so swiftly upon his election as judge of the Bonny Babies contest, had shaken to its foundations a system already weakened by the knowledge that Hermione Bostock loved another, and that other a libertine who

289

kissed housemaids on doorsteps. In response to Lord Ickenham's whoop of welcome he stared dully, like a dying halibut.

'Oh, hullo, Lord Ickenham,' he said.

'Well, well, well!' cried the fifth earl buoyantly. The hour or two which he had spent with this massive youth had left him with a strong appreciation of his sterling worth, and he was delighted to see him again. 'Well, well well, well, well! Bill Oakshott in person. Well met by moonlight, proud Oakshott.'

'Eh?'

'Adaptation of Shakespearian quotation. But let it go. It is not of the slightest importance. And how is every little thing with you, Bill Oakshott? Fine?'

'Well, to be absolutely accurate,' said Bill, 'no.'

Lord Ickenham raised his eyebrows.

'Not fine?'

'No. Bloody awful.'

'My dear chap, you surprise and shock me. I should have thought you would have been so glad to get back from a ghastly country like Brazil that life would have been roses, roses all the way. What's wrong?'

With his affairs in such disorder, Bill was in need of all the sympathy he could get. He decided to withhold nothing from this cordial and well-disposed old buster. It would not have taken much to make him sob on Lord Ickenham's chest.

'Well, to start with,' he said, touching on the most recent of the spiritual brickbats which had assailed his soul, 'my uncle's gone off his onion.'

Lord Ickenham pursed his lips.

'Nuts?'

'Completely nuts.'

'Indeed? That must jar you a good deal. Nothing spoils the quiet home atmosphere more than a goofy uncle on the premises. When did this tragedy occur?'

'Just now.'

'It came on suddenly?'

'Like a flash.'

'What caused it?'

'Pongo.'

Lord Ickenham seemed at a loss.

'You aren't telling me that a single day of Pongo has been enough to set a host sticking straws in his hair? If it had been two weeks . . . What were the symptoms?'

'Well, he gibbered a good bit, and now he's driven over to your place to get a photograph of Pongo.'

'Why?'

'To find out what he looks like.'

'Can't he see what he looks like?'

'He doesn't believe Pongo is Pongo.'

'But doesn't Pongo admit it?'

'He thinks he's an impostor.'

'Why?'

'I don't know. I tell you he's potty. I was out on the terrace and I heard him yelling for me, and I went to the study, and he said Hadn't I known Pongo when he was a kid? And I said Yes. And he said How did I know after all these years that this was the same chap and he was absolutely convinced that Pongo wasn't Pongo, and the only way to settle it was to drive to your place and get a photograph of him.'

Lord Ickenham shook his head.

'A fruitless quest. A man like myself, refined, sensitive, with a love for the rare and the beautiful, does not surround himself with photographs of Pongo. I could do him a nude Venus, if he would like one. Yes, it certainly looks as though you were right, Bill Oakshott, and that Mugsy's brain had come unstuck; the result, no doubt, of some sunstroke in the days when he was the curse of Africa. I'm not surprised that you are worried. The only thing I can suggest is that you give him plenty of aspirins, humour him in conversation and keep him away from razors, dinner knives and other sharp instruments. But apart from this everything is pretty smooth?'

Bill Oakshott laughed one of those hollow, mirthless laughs.

'Is it! If that was all I had to worry me, I should be singing like a lark.'

Lord Ickenham eyed him with concern. In his look, disappointment that he would not be able to hear his young friend singing like a lark was blended with distress at the news that he had further reasons for gloom.

'Don't tell me there is more? What else has happened, my ill-starred youth?'

Bill quivered, and for a moment could not speak.

'I saw Pongo kiss the housemaid,' he said in a low throaty voice.

Lord Ickenham was perplexed.

'But why shouldn't he?'

'Why shouldn't he? Dash it, he's engaged to my cousin Hermione.'

Lord Ickenham's face cleared.

'I see. Ah, yes, I understand. Her happiness is a matter of concern to you, and you do not like to think that she may be linking her lot with that of a Casanova. My dear chap, don't give the matter another thought. He does that sort of thing automatically. Where you or I would light a cigarette and throw off an epigram, Pongo kisses the housemaid. It means nothing. A purely unconscious reflex action.'

'H'm,' said Bill.

'I assure you,' said Lord Ickenham. 'You'll find it in all the case books. They have a scientific name for it. Housemaiditis? No. No, it's gone. But that ends your catalogue of woe? Apart from your uncle's strange seizure and this mannerism of Pongo's, you have nothing on your mind?'

'Haven't I!'

'You have? Is this the head upon which all the sorrows of the world have come? What is the next item?'

'Babies!'

'I beg your pardon?'

'Bonny babies.'

Lord Ickenham groped cautiously for his meaning.

'You are about to become a father?'

'I'm about to become a blasted judge.'

'You speak in riddles, Bill Oakshott. What do you mean, a judge?'

'At the fête.'

'What fête?' said Lord Ickenham. 'You are forgetting that I am a stranger in these parts. Tell me the whole story in your own words.'

He listened with interest while Bill did so, and the latter had no lack of sympathy to complain of when he had finished revealing the facts in connexion with Sir Aylmer Bostock's hideous vengeance.

'Too bad, too bad,' said Lord Ickenham. 'But we might have foreseen something of the sort. As I warned you, these ex-Governors are tough eggs. They strike like lightning. So you are for it?'

'Unless I can find someone else to take on the job.' A sudden thought flushed Bill's brow. 'I say, will you do it?'

Lord Ickenham shook his head.

'Were the conditions right,' he said, 'I would spring to the task, for I can imagine no more delightful experience than judging a gaggle of bonny babies at a rural fête. But the conditions are not right. Mugsy would not accept my nomination. Between him and myself there is, alas, an unfortunate and I fear insurmountable barrier. As I told you on the train it is only the other day that he was curving his person into the posture best adapted for the receipt of six of the juiciest with a fives bat, and I was the motivating force behind the fives bat.'

'But, dash it, he'll have forgotten that.'

'Already?'

'Wasn't it forty years ago?'

'Forty-two. But you grievously underestimate the suppleness of my wrist at the age of eighteen, if you suppose that anyone to whom I administered six with a fives bat would forget it in forty-two years.'

'Well, if he hasn't forgotten it, what does it matter? You'll just have a good laugh together over the whole thing.'

'I disagree with you, Bill Oakshott. Why after your recent experience of his dark malignity you should suppose young Mugsy to be a sort of vat or container for the milk of human kindness, I cannot imagine. You must know perfectly well that in the warped soul of Mugsy Bostock there is no room for sweetness and light. Come now, be honest. Does he not chew broken glass and conduct human sacrifices at the time of the full moon? Of course he does. And yet you cling to this weak pretence that, with the old wounds still throbbing, he will forget and forgive.'

'We could try him.'

'Useless. He would merely scowl darkly and turn me from his door – or your door, didn't you tell me it was? And suppose he did not? Suppose he welcomed me? What then? It would mean starting an association which would last the rest of our lives. He would always be popping over to my place, and I would be expected to pop over here. Wife would meet wife, presents would be exchanged at Christmas, it would be appalling. Even to oblige you, my dear fellow, I could not contemplate such a thing. Did you say "Oh, hell!"?'

'Yes.'

'I thought you did, and it wrung my heart.'

There was a silence. Bill stared moodily at a passing beetle.

'Then I'm sunk.'

'But why? Have you no friends?'

'I've lost touch with them all, being away. The only one I could lay my hands on is Plank.'

'Who is Plank? Ah, yes, I remember. The head of the expedition you went on.'

'That's right. Major Brabazon-Plank.'

'*Brabazon*-Plank? You interest me strangely. I was at school with a fellow named Brabazon-Plank. He still owes me two bob. Is your Brabazon-Plank a pear-shaped chap, rather narrow in the shoulders and very broad in the beam?'

'Yes.'

'Practically all backside?'

'Yes.'

'Then it must be the same fellow. Bimbo we used to call him. Extraordinary what a mine of my old schoolmates you are turning out to be. You don't seem able to mention a name without it proving that of someone with whom in one way or another I used once to pluck the gowans fine. And you think you could contact Bimbo?'

'I have his address in London. We came back on the boat together. But it wouldn't be any use contacting him. If anyone suggested that he should judge bonny babies, he would run like a rabbit. He has a horror of them.'

'Indeed? The well-known baby fixation. See the case books.'

'All the way home on the boat he was moaning that when he got to England he would have to go and see his sisters, and he didn't know how he was going to face it, because all of them were knee-deep in babies which he would be expected to kiss. No, Plank's no good.'

'Then really,' said Lord Ickenham, 'it looks as if you would have to fall back on me.'

Bill, who had been staring dully at the beetle, transferred his gaze to his companion. It was a wide-eyed, gaping gaze, speaking eloquently of a mind imperfectly adjusted to the intellectual pressure of the conversation.

'Eh?'

'I say that you will be compelled, for want of anything better, to avail yourself of my poor services. Invite me to your home, and in return for this hospitality I will judge these bonny babies.'

Bill continued to gape.

'But you said you wouldn't.'

'Surely not?'

'Yes, you did. Just now.'

Lord Ickenham's perplexity vanished.

'Ah, I see where the confusion of thought has arisen,' he said. 'You misunderstood me. I merely meant that, for the reasons which I explained to you, it was impossible for that fine old English aristocrat, Frederick Altamont Cornwallis, Earl of Ickenham, to come barging in on an establishment of which Mugsy Bostock formed a part. What I am proposing now is that I shall throw a modest veil over my glittering identity.'

'Eh?'

'You do keep saying "Eh?" don't you? It is surely quite simple. I am most anxious to visit Ashenden Manor, of which I hear excellent reports, and I suggest that I do so incognito.'

'Under another name, do you mean?'

'Exactly. What a treat it is to deal with an intelligence like yours, Bill Oakshott. Under, as you put it so luminously, another name. As a matter of fact, I never feel comfortable going to stay at houses under my own name. It doesn't seem sporting.'

Bill Oakshott's was not a mind readily receptive of new ideas. As he stared at Lord Ickenham, his resemblance to a fish on a slab was more striking than ever.

'You'll call yourself something else?' he said, for he was a man who liked to approach these things from every angle.

'Precisely.'

'But –'

'I never like that word "But".'

'You couldn't get away with it.'

Lord Ickenham laughed lightly.

'My dear fellow, at The Cedars, Mafeking Road, in the suburb of Mitching Hill last spring I impersonated in a single afternoon and with complete success not only an official from the bird shop, come to clip the claws of the parrot, but Mr Roddis, lessee of The Cedars, and a Mr J. G. Bulstrode, a resident of the same neighbourhood. It has been a lasting grief to me that I was given no opportunity of impersonating the parrot, which I am convinced I should have done on broad, artistic lines. Have no anxiety about my not being able to get away with it. Introduce me into the house, and I will guarantee to do the rest.'

The clearness with which he had expounded his scheme had enabled Bill to grasp it, but he was looking nervous and unhappy, like a man who has grasped the tail of a tiger.

'It's too risky. Suppose my uncle found out.'

'Are you afraid of Mugsy?'

'Yes.'

'More than of the bonny babies?'

Bill quivered. In every limb and feature he betrayed his consciousness of standing at a young man's cross-roads.

'But what's the procedure? You mean you just blow in, calling yourself Jones or Robinson?'

'Not Robinson. I have had occasion in the past to call myself Robinson, but it would not do now. You overlook the fact that the judge of a contest of this importance must be a man who counts. He must have authority and presence. I suggest that I come as Major Brabazon-Plank. It would give me genuine pleasure to impersonate old Bimbo, and I can think of no one more suitable. The whole thing is so plausible. You run into your old chief Plank, who happens to be passing by on a motor tour, and what more natural than that you should insist on him stopping off for a day or two at your home? And, having stopped off, what more natural than that he, learning of this very important and attractive job, a job which will render him the cynosure of all eyes and is in addition right up his street, he being passionately fond of babies, should insist on having it assigned to him? And the crowning beauty of the scheme

UNCLE DYNAMITE

is that I don't see how Mugsy can do anything about it. We've got
him cold. It isn't as if Plank were just an ordinary man. Plank is a
hell of a celebrity, and his wishes have to be deferred to. If you ask
me, Bill Oakshott, if you care to have my unbiased opinion of the
set-up, I think the thing's in the bag.'

Into Bill's fishlike eyes a gleam of enthusiasm had crept. His air
was that of a red-faced young man who has been convinced by the
voice of reason. He still feared the shape of things to come, should
he fall in with his benefactor's suggestion, but he feared still more
the shape of things to come, should he not.

Stamped indelibly on his mental retina was the memory of last
year's fête, when he had watched the Rev. Aubrey Brotherhood
preparing to embark on his duties in the big tent. Intrepid curate
though he was, a man who could dominate the rowdiest Mothers'
Meeting, the Rev. Aubrey had paled visibly at the task confronting
him. Forty-three village matrons, holding in their arms in the hope
of catching the judge's eye forty-three babies of almost the maximum
repulsiveness . . .

'Right!' he cried with sudden resolution. 'Fine. Let's go.'

'Yes, let's,' said Lord Ickenham. 'You can carry the suitcase.'

They walked down the road. Bill, who had begun to think things
over again, was a little silent and thoughtful, but Lord Ickenham
was all gaiety and animation. He talked well and easily of this and
that, and from time to time pointed out objects of interest by the
wayside. They had just reached the Manor gates, when the uproar
of an approaching car caused Bill to turn his head: and, having
turned it, paled beneath his tan and tottered slightly.

'Oh, golly, here comes my uncle. I say, do you think we really
ought –'

'Tush, Bill Oakshott,' said Lord Ickenham, prompt in the hour
of peril to stimulate and encourage. 'This is weakness. Stiffen the
sinews, summon up the blood. Let us stand our ground firmly, and
give him a huge hello.'

3

Sir Aylmer Bostock had spent four minutes at Ickenham Hall, all on
the front door step, and of these four minutes there had not been

one which he had not disliked. Sometimes in our wanderings about the world we meet men of whom it is said that they have passed through the furnace. Of Sir Aylmer it would be more correct to say that he had passed through the frigidaire.

If you call at a country house where you are not known and try to get the butler to let you come in and search the premises for photographs of his employer's nephew, you will generally find this butler chilly in his manner, and Coggs, the major-domo of Ickenham Hall, had been rather chillier than the average. He was a large, stout, moon-faced man with an eye like that of a codfish, and throughout the proceedings he had kept his eye glued on Sir Aylmer's, as if peering into his soul. And anyone who has ever had his soul peered into by a codfish will testify how extremely unpleasant such an ordeal is.

The message in that eye had been only too easy to read. Coggs had not actually accused Sir Aylmer of being after the spoons, but the charge might just as well have been clothed in words. In a voice of ice he had said No, sir, I fear I cannot accede to your request, sir, and had then terminated the interview by backing a step and shutting the door firmly in the visitor's face. And when we say firmly, we mean with a bang which nearly jarred the latter's moustache loose from its foundations.

All this sort of thing is very galling to a proud and arrogant man, accustomed for years to having his lightest word treated as law, and it was consequently in no sunny mood that Sir Aylmer heard Lord Ickenham's huge hello. He was still snorting and muttering to himself, and a native chief who had encountered him in this dangerous mental condition would have called on his protecting ju-ju for quick service and climbed a tree.

Lord Ickenham was made of sterner stuff. He stepped out into the road and gave the huge hello, as planned.

'Hello, there, Mugsy,' he carolled. 'A very happy pip-pip to you, my bright and bounding Bostock.'

It was probably astonishment at being addressed by a name which he supposed that he had lived down years ago, rather than the fact that the speaker was blocking the way, that caused Sir Aylmer to apply the brakes. He brought the car to a halt and leaned forward, glaring through the windscreen. Close scrutiny of Lord

Ickenham afforded no clue to the latter's identity. All that Sir Aylmer was able to say with certainty was that this must be some old schoolfellow of his, and he wished he had the moral courage to drive on and run him over.

It was too late to do this now, for Lord Ickenham had advanced and was standing with a friendly foot on the running board. With an equally friendly hand he slapped Sir Aylmer on the back, and his smile was just as friendly as his hand and foot. Sir Aylmer might not be glad to see this figure from the past, but the figure from the past was plainly glad to see Sir Aylmer.

'Mugsy,' he said with kindly reproach, 'I believe you've forgotten me.'

Sir Aylmer said he had. He contrived to convey in his manner the suggestion that he would willingly do so again.

'Too bad,' said Lord Ickenham. 'Well, to put you out of your suspense, for I see that you are all keyed up, I'm Plank.'

'Plank?'

'Major Brabazon-Plank, Uncle Aylmer,' said Bill, emboldened by the suavity with which his accomplice was conducting these delicate pourparlers. 'Major Plank ran that expedition I went on to Brazil.'

Lord Ickenham was obliged to demur.

'Don't let him mislead you, Mugsy. In a strictly technical sense I suppose you might say I ran that expedition. Officially, no doubt, I was its head. But the real big noise was Bill Oakshott here. He was the life and soul of the party, giving up his water ration to the sick and ailing, conducting himself with cool aplomb among the alligators and encouraging with word and gesture the weaker brethren who got depressed because they couldn't dress for dinner. Chilled Steel Oakshott, we used to call him. You should be proud of such a nephew.'

Sir Aylmer appeared not to have heard these eulogies. He was still wrestling with what might be called the Plank angle of the situation.

'Plank?' he said. 'You can't be Plank.'

'Why not?'

'The Plank who was at school with me?'

'That very Plank.'

'But he was a fellow with an enormous trouser seat.'

'Ah, I see what is on your mind. Yes, yes. As a boy, quite true, I was bountifully endowed with billowy curves in the part you have indicated. But since those days I have been using Slimmo, the sovereign remedy for obesity. The results you see before you. You ought to try it yourself, Mugsy. You've put on weight.'

Sir Aylmer grunted. There was dissatisfaction in his grunt. Plainly, he was unwilling to relinquish his memories of a callipygous Plank.

'Well, I'm damned if I would have recognized you.'

'Nor I you, had not Bill Oakshott given me the office. We've both altered quite a bit. I don't think you had a white moustache at school, did you? And there's no ink on your collar.'

'You're really Plank?'

'None other.'

'And what are you doing here?'

'I'm on a motor tour.'

'Oh, are you?' said Sir Aylmer, brightening. 'Then you'll be wanting to get along. Good-bye, Plank.'

Lord Ickenham smiled a gentle, reassuring smile.

'That sad word will not be required here, Mugsy. Prepare to receive tidings of great joy. I'm coming to stay.'

'What!'

'I had intended to hurry on, but when Bill Oakshott became pressing, I could not refuse. Especially when he told me of this fête which is breaking loose shortly and promised that if I consented to be his guest at Ashenden Manor I might judge the Bonny Babies contest. That decided me. I would go fifty miles to judge bonny babies. Sixty,' said Lord Ickenham. 'Or make it a hundred.'

Sir Aylmer started like a tiger that sees its Indian villager being snatched away from it. His face, already mauve, became an imperial purple.

'You're not going to judge the bonny babies!'

'Yes, I am.'

'No, you're not.'

Lord Ickenham was a genial man, but he could be firm.

'I don't want any lip from you, young Mugsy,' he said sternly. 'Let me give you a word of warning. I see by the papers that you are about to stand for Parliament. Well, don't forget that I could swing the voting against you pretty considerably, if I wanted to, by letting an idealistic electorate in on some of the shady secrets of your boyhood. You won't like it, Mugsy, when questions about your boyhood are thundered at you from the body of the hall while you are outlining your views on the Tariff problem. Do I judge those bonny babies?'

Sir Aylmer sat brooding in silence, his Adam's apple moving up and down as if he were swallowing something hard and jagged. The stoutest man will quail at the prospect of having the veil torn from his past, unless that past is one of exceptional purity. He scowled, but scowling brought no solace. He chewed his moustache, but gained no comfort thereby.

'Very well,' he said at length, speaking as if the words were being pulled out of him with a dentist's forceps. His eye, swivelling round, rested for an instant on Bill's and the young man leaped convulsively. 'Oh, very well.'

'Good,' said Lord Ickenham, his cheery self once more. 'That's settled. And now you shall take me home and show me the model dairy.'

'What model dairy?'

'Haven't you a model dairy? The stables, then.'

'I don't keep horses.'

'Odd. I was always led to believe that hosts at English country houses were divided into two classes: those who, when helpless guests were in their power, showed them the stables and those who showed them the model dairy. There was also, I understood, a minor sub-division which showed them the begonias, but that is a technicality into which we need not go. No model dairy, you say? No horses? Then perhaps I had better be going to the inn, where I have one or two things to do. These seen to, I will present myself at the house and the revels can commence. And as you are doubtless anxious to hurry on and get my room – one with a southern exposure, if possible – swept and garnished, I won't detain you. You coming with me, Bill Oakshott?'

'I think I'll stay here and smoke a pipe.'

'Just as you please. We shall all meet then, at Philippi, and very jolly it will be, too.'

It was with a light and elastic step that Lord Ickenham made his way to the Bull's Head in Ashenden Oakshott's High Street. He was well satisfied with the progress of affairs. Something attempted, something done had, in his opinion, earned the spot of beer to which he had been looking forward for some considerable time, for this spreading of sweetness and light is thirsty work. After putting through a telephone call to his home and speaking to Sally, he sat down to a tankard, and was savouring its amber contents with quiet relish, when the door of the saloon bar burst open with a good deal of violence and Bill Oakshott entered.

That Bill was not at his serenest and most tranquil was indicated at once to Lord Ickenham's experienced eye by his appearance and deportment. His hair was ruffled, as if he had been passing a fevered hand through it, and that glazed look was back in his eyes. He was a young man who, when things went awry, always endeavoured, after the fashion of the modern young man, to preserve the easy repose of manner of a Red Indian at the stake, but it was plain that whatever had occurred to upset him now was of a magnitude which rendered impossible such an exhibition of stoicism.

'Ah, Bill Oakshott,' said Lord Ickenham affably. 'You could not have arrived at a more opportune moment. You find me enjoying a well-earned gargle, like Cæsar in his tent the day he overcame the Nervii. I stress the adjective "well-earned", for I think you will admit that in the recent exchanges I put it across the Nervii properly. Have you ever seen an ex-Governor so baffled? I haven't, and I doubt if anyone has. But you seem disturbed about something, and I would recommend some of this excellent beer. It will strengthen you and help you to look for the silver lining.'

He went to the counter, remained there a while in conversation with the stout blonde behind it, and returned bearing a foaming tankard.

'Nice girl,' he said paternally. 'I've been telling her about Brazil. Quaff that, Bill Oakshott, and having quaffed spill what is on your mind.'

Bill, who had been sitting with his head clasped in his hands, took a deep draught.

'It's about this business of your coming to the house as Plank.'

'Ah yes?'

'You can't go on with it.'

Lord Ickenham raised his eyebrows.

'Can't? A strange word to use to the last of a proud family. Did my ancestors say "Can't" on the stricken fields of the Middle Ages, when told off to go and fight the Paynim? As a matter of fact,' said Lord Ickenham confidentially, 'I believe lots of them did, as you can verify by turning up Richard Cœur de Lion's dispatches, so perhaps it is a pity that I asked the question. Why do you say I can't go on with it?'

'Because you jolly well can't. Shall I tell you what's happened?'

'Do. I'm all agog.'

Bill finished his tankard, and seemed to draw from it strength to continue.

'After you went away,' he said tonelessly, 'Uncle Aylmer drove off in the car, leaving me stuck there with the suitcase.'

'A low trick.'

'I yelled to him to stop and take the damned thing, because it weighed a ton and I didn't want to have to lug it all the way up the drive, but he wouldn't. And I was just starting off with it, when Potter came along on his bike.'

'Who is Potter?'

'The policeman.'

'Ah yes. Pongo spoke of him, I remember. A zealous officer.'

'So I said, "Oh, Potter" and he said "Sir?" and I said "You in a hurry?" and he said "No, sir," and I said "Then I wish you'd take this suitcase up to the house." And he said "Certainly, sir," and hoisted it aboard his bike.'

'I like your dialogue,' said Lord Ickenham critically. 'It's crisp and good. Do you ever write?'

'No.'

'You should. You'd make a packet. But I'm interrupting you.'

'You are a bit.'

'It shall not occur again. You had got to where Potter said "Certainly, sir." Then what?'

'I said "It belongs to Major Brabazon-Plank. He's coming to stay." And Potter said . . . Could I have another beer?'

'Had he already had some beer?'

'I mean, could I have, now? I think it might pull me together.'

Lord Ickenham repeated his trip to the counter.

'You were saying,' he said, having returned with the life-giving fluid, 'that you told Potter that the suitcase belonged to Major Brabazon-Plank. In response to which?'

Bill drank deeply, gasped a little and spoke with a sort of frozen calm.

'In response to which he said, his bally face lighting up joyfully, "Major Brabazon-Plank? Did you say Major Brabazon-Plank? Coo, I know him well. He comes from my old village. Played cricket with him, I have – ah, hundreds of times. If convenient, Mr William, I'll step up and shake him by the hand after I've had my tea." So now what?'

Lord Ickenham remained for a moment in thought.

'You're kidding me, Bill Oakshott. Nobody but a practised writer could have told that story so superbly. Beneath your magic touch Potter seems to live and breathe. You publish your stuff secretly under another name. I believe you're one, if not more, of the Sitwells. But we can go into that later. "So now what?" you say. Yes, I agree that the problem is one that presents certain features of interest, but all problems can be solved with a little earnest thought. How did you articulate when you spoke the words "Brabazon-Plank"? Distinctly?'

'Yes.'

'You didn't mumble?'

'No.'

'So you couldn't say that what you had really said was "Smith" or "Knatchbull-Huguessen"?'

'No.'

Lord Ickenham reflected.

'Well, then, what we must do is tell him that I am your Plank's brother.'

'Do you think you could get away with that?'

'There are no limits to what I can get away with when I am functioning properly. We might go and call upon him now. Where does he live?'

'Just round the corner.'

'Then finish up your beer and let's be off.'

Except for the royal arms over the door and a notice saying

'Police Station,' there was nothing about the residence of Constable Potter to suggest that here was the dreadful headquarters of Law and Justice. Like so many police stations in English villages, it was a cheerful little cottage with a thatched roof and a nice little garden, the latter at the moment occupied by Mr Potter's nephew Basil, aged nine months, who was taking a nap in his perambulator. Lord Ickenham, reaching the garden gate, cocked an inquiring eye at this vehicle.

'Is Potter a married man?'

'No. That's his sister's baby. She lives with him. Her husband's a steward on one of the South American boats. He's away most of the time. Of course, he comes back sometimes.'

'Yes, one guesses that.'

Through an open window there came the sound of a female voice, high and penetrating. It was touching on the subject of socks. How, it was asking, did the invisible person it was addressing contrive to get so many and such large holes in his all the time? The voice itself attributed the phenomenon to carelessness and a wilful lack of consideration for those who had to work their fingers to the bone, darning them. Lord Ickenham consulted Bill with a raised eyebrow.

'Would that be the lady speaking now?'

'Yes.'

'To Potter?'

'I suppose so.'

'She seems to be giving him beans.'

'Yes. He's scared stiff of her, so Elsie tells me.'

'Elsie?'

'The housemaid.'

'Ah, yes, the one Pongo . . . I forget what I was going to say.'

'I know what you were going to say.'

'Well, well, we need not go into that now. Let us saunter in and let our first move be to examine this bonny baby more closely. It will all be practice for the great day.'

# *Chapter 7*

Inside the cottage, in the cosy little kitchen, Constable Potter, guardian of Ashenden Oakshott's peace, at his ease in his shirt sleeves, was enjoying high tea.

The word 'enjoying' is perhaps ill chosen, for he was partaking of the meal under the eye of his sister, Mrs Bella Stubbs, who, if not his best friend, had always been his severest critic. She had already told him not to put his elbows on the table, not to gollop his food like that and not to help himself to butter with his herringy knife, and at the moment when Bill and Lord Ickenham arrived had begun, as has been shown, to touch on the subject of his socks, one of which she held in her hand for purposes of demonstration.

Constable Potter was twenty-eight years old, his sister thirty-three. The simplest of mathematical calculations, therefore, will show that when he was seven she had been twelve, and a strong-willed sister of twelve can establish over a brother of seven a moral ascendancy which lasts a lifetime. In those formative years which mean so much, Harold Potter had been dragged about by the hand, slapped, scolded and told by the future mother of George Basil Percival Stubbs not to do practically everything he wanted to do. She had even – crowning indignity – blown his nose.

These things leave their mark. It was the opinion of Elsie Bean, repeatedly expressed, that her Harold was a cowardy custard; and in the main, one feels, the verdict of history will be that Elsie was right. It is unpleasant to think of an officer of the Law cowering in his chair when a woman puts a finger through a hole in one of his socks and waggles it, but it cannot be disputed that while watching Mrs Stubbs do this Constable Potter had come very near to cowering.

To ease the strain, he bent forward to help himself to butter, being careful this time to use the knife allotted to that purpose, and

the movement enabled him to see through the window the corner
of the garden where George Basil Percival was taking his siesta.

''Ullo,' he said, glad to change the subject. 'There's somebody on
the lawn.'

'Never mind about the lawn. I'm talking about this sock.'

'It's a tall gentleman.'

'Look at it. Like a sieve.'

'A tall gentleman with a grey moustache. He's poking your Basil
in the stomach.'

He had said the one thing calculated to divert his companion's
thoughts from the sock topic. A devoted mother, Mrs Stubbs held
the strongest possible views on the enormity of gentlemen, whether
tall or short, coming into her garden and poking her offspring in
the stomach at a moment when his well-being demanded uninterrupted repose.

'Then go and send him away!'

'Right ho.'

Constable Potter was full to the brim. He had eaten three
kippered herrings, four boiled eggs and half a loaf of bread, and his
impulse would have been to lean back in his chair like a gorged
python and give his gastric juices a chance to fulfil themselves. But,
apart from the fact that his sister Bella's word was law, curiosity
overcame the urge to digest. Scrutinizing Lord Ickenham through
the window, he had a sort of feeling that he had seen him before.
He wanted to get a closer view of this mysterious stranger.

In the garden, when he reached it, Lord Ickenham, wearying of
his attentions to Basil's stomach, had begun to tickle the child
under the chin. Bill, who was not very fond of babies and in any
case preferred them to look less like Edward G. Robinson, had
moved aside as if anxious to disassociate himself from the whole
unpleasant affair, and was thus the first to see the newcomer.

'Oh, hullo, Potter,' he said. 'We thought we'd look in.'

'I was anxious,' said Lord Ickenham, 'to make the acquaintance
of one of whom I had heard so much.'

Constable Potter seemed a little dazed by these civilities.

'Ho!' he said. 'I didn't catch the name, sir.'

'Plank. Brabazon-Plank.'

There was a loud hiccup. It was Constable Potter registering astonishment; and more than astonishment, suspicion. There were few men, in Ashenden Oakshott at any rate, more gifted with the ability to recognize funny business when they were confronted with it, and here, it seemed to Harold Potter, was funny business in excelsis. He fixed on Lord Ickenham the stern and accusing gaze which he would have directed at a dog caught in the act of appearing in public without a collar.

'Brabazon-Plank?'

'Brabazon-Plank.'

'You're not the Major Brabazon-Plank I used to play cricket with at Lower Shagley in Dorsetshire.'

'His brother.'

'I didn't know he had a brother.'

'He kept things from you, did he? Too bad. Yes, I am his elder brother. Bill Oakshott was telling me you knew him.'

'He said you was him.'

'Surely not?'

'Yus, he did.' Constable Potter's gaze grew sterner. He was resolved to probe this thing to the bottom. 'He give me your suitcase to take to the house, and he said "This here belongs to Major Brabazon-Plank."'

Lord Ickenham laughed amusedly.

'Just a slip of the tongue, such as so often occurs. He meant Brabazon-Plank, *major*. As opposed to my brother, who, being younger than me, is, of course, Brabazon-Plank, *minor*. I can understand you being confused,' said Lord Ickenham with a commiserating glance at the officer, into whose face had crept the boiled look of one who finds the conversation becoming abstruse. Three kippers, four eggs and half a loaf of bread, while nourishing the body, take the keen edge off the mental powers. 'And what renders it all the more complex is that as I myself am a mining engineer by profession, anyone who wants to get straight on the Brabazon-Plank situation has got to keep steadily before him the fact that the minor is a major and the major a miner. I have known strong men to break down on realizing this. So you know my minor, the major, do you? Most interesting. It's a small world, I often say. Well, when I say "often," perhaps once a fortnight. Why are you looking like a stuck pig, Bill Oakshott?'

Bill came with a start out of what appeared to be a sort of trance. Pongo, who had had so many opportunities of observing his Uncle Fred in action, could have told him that a trance-like condition was almost always the result of being associated with this good old man when he was going nicely.

'Was I?'

'Yes.'

'Sorry.'

'Don't mention it. Ah, whom have we here?'

Mrs Stubbs had made her appearance, coming towards them with a suggestion in her manner of a lioness hastening to the aid of an imperilled cub. Annoyed by her brother's tardiness in getting rid of these intruders, she had decided to take the matter in hand herself.

'Oh, hullo, Mrs Stubbs,' said Bill. 'We were just giving your baby the once over.'

Lord Ickenham started.

'Your baby? Is this remarkably fine infant yours, madam?'

His bearing was so courteous, his manner so reverent that Mrs Stubbs, who had come in like a lioness, began to envisage the possibility of going out like a lamb.

'Yes, sir,' she said, and went so far as to curtsy. She was not a woman who often curtsied, but there was something about this distinguished-looking elderly gentleman that seemed to call for the tribute. 'It's my little Basil.'

'A sweet name. And a sweet child. A starter I hope?'

'Sir?'

'You have entered him for the Bonny Baby contest at the fête?'

'Oh, yes, sir.'

'Good. Excellent. It would have been madness to hide his light under a bushel. Have you studied this outstanding infant closely, Bill Oakshott? If not, do so now,' said Lord Ickenham, 'for you will never have a better chance of observing a classic yearling. What hocks! What pasterns! And what lungs!' he continued, as George Basil Percival, waking, like Abou ben Adhem, from a deep dream of peace, split the welkin with a sudden howl. 'I always mark heavily for lungs. I should explain, madam, that I am to have the honour of acting as judge at the contest to which I have referred.'

'You are, sir?'

'I am, indeed. Is your husband at home? No? A pity. I would have advised him to pick up a bit of easy money by putting his shirt on this child for the Bonny Baby stakes. Have you a shirt, Mr Potter? Ah, I see you have. Well, slap it on the stable's entry and fear nothing. I have at present, of course, no acquaintance with local form, but I cannot imagine that there will be another competitor of such supreme quality as to nose him out. I see myself at the close of the proceedings raising Basil's hand in the air with the words "The winnah!" Well, Mrs Stubbs,' said Lord Ickenham, with a polished bow in the direction of his hostess and a kindly 'Kitchy-kitchy' to the coming champ, who was staring at him with what a more sensitive man would have considered offensive curiosity, 'we must be pushing along. We have much to do. Good-bye, Mrs Stubbs. Good-bye, baby. Good-bye, off –'

He paused, the word unspoken. Constable Potter had suddenly turned and was making for the cottage at a high rate of speed, and Lord Ickenham stared after him a little blankly.

'Gone without a cry!' he said. 'I suppose he forgot something.'

'His manners,' said Mrs Stubbs tartly. 'The idea!'

'Ah, well,' said Lord Ickenham, always inclined to take the tolerant view, 'what are manners, if the heart be of gold? Good-bye again, Mrs Stubbs. Good-bye, baby. As I say, we must be moving. May I repeat what a privilege it has been to get together with this superb child in what I may term his training quarters and urge you once more, with all the emphasis at my disposal, to put the family shirt on him for the big event. There could be no sounder investment. Good-bye,' said Lord Ickenham, 'good-bye, good-bye,' and took his departure, scattering sweetness and light in all directions.

Out in the road he paused to light a cigar.

'How absurdly simple these things are,' he said, 'when you have someone with elephantiasis of the brain, like myself, directing the operations. A few well-chosen words, and we baffle the constable just as we baffled Mugsy. Odd that he should have left us so abruptly. But perhaps he went in to spray his temples with eau-de-Cologne. I got the impression that he was cracking under the strain a little when I was dishing out the major and minor stuff.'

'How did you come to think of that?'

'Genius,' said Lord Ickenham modestly. 'Pure genius.'

'I wonder if he swallowed it.'

'I think so. I hope so.'

'You laid it on a bit thick about that ruddy baby.'

'Kind words are never wasted, Bill Oakshott. And now for Ashenden Manor, I think, don't you, and the warm English welcome.'

Bill seemed uncertain.

'Do you know, I believe I could do with some more beer.'

'You feel faint?'

'I do, rather.'

'All right, then, you push on to the pub. I must try to find Pongo. Would he be in the house?'

'No, I saw him going out.'

'Then I will scour the countryside for him. It is vital,' said Lord Ickenham, 'that I put him abreast of the position of affairs before he has an opportunity of spilling the beans. We don't want him charging in when I am chatting with Mugsy and calling me "Uncle Fred". Before we settle down to the quiet home evening to which I am looking forward so much, he must be informed that he is losing an uncle but gaining a Brazilian explorer. So for the moment, bung-ho. Where was it I told Mugsy that we should all meet? Ah, yes, at Philippi. See you there, then, when you have drunk your fill.'

2

In times of spiritual disturbance there is nothing like a brisk mystery thriller for taking the mind off its anxieties. Pongo's first move after parting from Sir Aylmer Bostock had been to go to his room and get his copy of *Murder in the Fog*; his second to seek some quiet spot outside the grounds, where there would be no danger of meeting the ex-Governor on his return, and soothe himself with a good read. He found such a spot at the side of the road not far from the Manor gates, and soon became absorbed.

The treatment proved almost immediately effective. That interview with Sir Aylmer in the hall had filled him with numbing fears and rendered him all of a twitter, but now he found his quivering ganglia getting back to mid-season form: and, unlike the heroine of the tale in which he was immersed, who had just got trapped in the underground den of one of those Faceless Fiends who cause so much annoyance, he was feeling quite tranquil, when a shadow fell on the page, a well-remembered voice spoke his name, and he looked up to see his Uncle Fred standing before him.

If there is one occasion more than another when joy might be expected to be unconfined and happiness to reign supreme, it is surely, one would say, when a nephew in the course of a country ramble encounters an uncle who in his time has often dandled him on his knee. At such a moment one would anticipate the quick indrawing of the breath, the raising of the eyes thankfully to heaven and the meeting of hand and hand in a fervent clasp.

It is unpleasant, therefore, to have to record that in Pongo's bosom, as he beheld Lord Ickenham, joy was not the predominating emotion. He could scarcely, indeed, have appeared more disconcerted if the Faceless Fiend from the volume in his hand had popped from its pages to confront him.

'Uncle Fred!' he ejaculated. The burned child fears the fire, and bitter experience had taught Pongo Twistleton to view with concern the presence in his midst of Ickenham's fifth earl. One recalls the words, quoted in a previous chapter, of the thoughtful crumpet. 'Good Lord, Uncle Fred, what on earth are you doing here?'

Lord Ickenham, unlike Sir Aylmer Bostock, was a man who believed in breaking things gently. With a tale to unfold whose lightest word would harrow up his nephew's soul and make his two eyes, like stars, start from their spheres, he decided to hold it in for the time being and to work round gradually and by easy stages to what Pongo would have called the nub. With a gentle smile on his handsome face, he lowered himself to the ground and gave his moustache a twirl.

'Just pottering to and fro, my boy, just pottering to and fro. This road is open for being pottered in at this hour, I believe.'

'But I left you at Ickenham.'

'The parting was agony.'

'You told me you were going to London.'

'So I did.'

'You never said a word about coming here.'

'No, but you know how it is. Things happen. One's plans become modified.'

A passing ant paused to investigate Pongo's wrist. He flung it from him, and the ant, alighting on its head some yards to the sou'-sou'-east, went off to warn other ants to watch out for earth-quakes.

'I might have known it,' he cried passionately. 'You're going to start something.'

'No, no.'

'Then what's up?'

Lord Ickenham considered the question.

'I don't know that I would go so far as to say that anything was actually *up*. The word is too strong. Certain complications have arisen, it is true, but nothing that cannot be adjusted by a couple of cool, calm men of the world who keep their heads. Let me begin at the beginning. I went to London and gave Sally dinner, and in the course of the meal she revealed why it was that she had wanted to see me so urgently. It seemed that her brother Otis is in trouble again. She asked me to tell you all about it and endeavour to enlist your aid.'

As the story of Otis Painter and Sir Aylmer Bostock's Reminiscences unfolded itself, relief poured over Pongo in a healing wave. He blamed himself for having so readily fallen a prey to the agitation which the unexpected appearance of his Uncle Fred was so apt to occasion in him. Up to this point he had been standing. He now sat down with the air of a man who is at his ease. He even laughed, a thing which he was seldom able to do when in conference with his uncle.

'Rather funny,' he said.

'The matter is not without its humorous aspect,' Lord Ickenham agreed. 'But we must not forget that if the action goes through, Sally stands to lose a lot of money.'

'That's true. So she wants me to plead with the old boy and get him to settle the thing out of court. Well, I'll do what I can.'

'You speak doubtfully. Doesn't he love you like a son?'

'I wouldn't say absolutely like a son. You see, I broke one of his African curios.'

'You do break things, don't you? And this has rankled?'

'I fancy it has to some extent. When I met him in the hall just now, he gave me a nasty look and a couple of distinctly unpleasant

"Ha's!" The slant I got was that he had been thinking me over and come to the conclusion that I was a bit of a louse. Still, he may come round.'

'Of course he will. You must persevere.'

'Oh, rather.'

'That's the spirit. Keep after him, exerting all your charm. Remember what it means to Sally.'

'Right ho. And is that really all you wanted to see me about?'

'I think so. Except . . . Now what else was it I wanted to see you about? . . . Ah, yes, I remember. That bust of Sally's. The one you borrowed from my place.'

'Oh, the old busto? Yes, of course. Well, everything went according to plan. I sneaked it in all right. A testing experience, though. If you knew what I went through, beetling across the hall with the thing in my possession, expecting every moment to feel old Bostock's hot breath on the back of my neck!'

'I can readily imagine it. I wonder,' said Lord Ickenham, 'if you know how these busts are made? Sally has been explaining it to me. It is a most interesting process. You first model the clay. Then you slap on it a coat of liquid plaster.'

'Oh, yes?'

'After that you wait a little while until the plaster becomes fairly hard, when you divide it into two neat halves and throw away the clay. You then fill the mould with plaster.'

'Very jolly, if you like that sort of thing,' said Pongo tolerantly. 'How was Sally looking?'

'At first, radiant. Later, somewhat perturbed.'

'About Otis, you mean?'

'About Otis – and other things. But let me finish telling you about the way busts are made. You fill the mould with plaster, leaving a small empty space at the top. This,' said Lord Ickenham, feeling that he had now broken the thing sufficiently gently, 'you utilize as a repository for any jewels that any friend of yours may wish to smuggle into the United States.'

'What!' Pongo shot up in a whirl of arms and legs. Another ant, which climbed on to his wrist in a rather sceptical spirit, took as impressive a toss as its predecessor had done, and might have been observed some moments later rubbing its head and telling a circle of friends that old George had been right when he had spoken of seismic disturbances. 'You don't mean –?'

'Yes. Inadvertently, intending no harm, we appear to have got away with the bust in which Sally had cached her friend Alice Vansittart's bit of stuff. The idea came to her, apparently, shortly after you had refused to help her out. It seems a pity now that you were not more amenable. Of course, as Hamlet very sensibly remarked, there's nothing either good or bad but thinking makes it so; still, a rather sticky situation has unquestionably been precipitated. The Vansittart sails for New York next week.'

'Oh, my gosh!'

'You see the drama of the thing? I thought you would. Well, there it is. You will agree with me, I think, that we are in honour bound to return these trinkets. Can't go snitching a poor girl's little bit of jewellery. Not done. Not cricket.'

Pongo nodded. Nobody could teach him anything about *noblesse oblige*. He shrank from repeating the dreadful performance to which he had forced himself on his arrival at the house, but he quite saw that it had to be done.

'That's right,' he said. 'I'll have to nip over to Ickenham and get another bust. Will Coggs be able to dig me out one?'

'No,' said Lord Ickenham. 'And if he could, it would not be any good. Another complication has occurred, which I must now relate to you. You remember the bust Sally did of Sir Aylmer, the one that was to have been presented to the village club, poor devils. Piqued as the result of this Otis business, he returned it to her, and I brought her down here this afternoon in my car and she crept into the house and substituted it for the one with Miss Vansittart's jewels in it. And just as she was getting away with the latter, Lady Bostock intercepted her, took it away from her and locked it up in a cupboard in the room where the African curios are. And there it now is. So –'

Pongo interrupted, speaking quickly and forcefully. There are limits to what *noblesse* obliges.

'I know what you're going to say,' he cried. 'You want me to sneak down in the middle of the night and break open the cupboard and pinch it. Well, I'm jolly well not going to do it.'

'No, no,' said Lord Ickenham. 'Calm yourself, my dear boy. I would not dream of burdening you with such a responsibility. I will do the pinching.'

'You?'

'In person.'

'But you can't get into the house.'

'I wish people wouldn't tell me I can't do things. It is all going to be perfectly simple. My young friend, Bill Oakshott, has invited me to stay at Ashenden Manor. He wants me to judge the Bonny Babies contest at a fête they are having here shortly. Why his choice fell upon me, one cannot say. I suppose he knew I was good. These things get about.'

Pongo gazed up at the reeling sky and sent his haggard eyes roaming over a countryside that had broken into a sort of Ouled Nail muscle dance. His face was drawn, and his limbs twitched. Lord Ickenham, watching him, received the impression that he did not like the idea of his, Lord Ickenham's, approaching visit to Ashenden Manor.

'You're coming to the house?' he gasped.

'I go into residence this evening. And, by the way,' said Lord Ickenham, 'another small point. I nearly forgot to mention it. My name during my visit will be Brabazon-Plank. Major Brabazon-Plank, the well-known Brazilian explorer. Don't forget it, will you.'

From between Pongo's hands, which he had clasped on either side of his head, as if to prevent it dividing itself into two neat halves like a plaster bust, there proceeded a low moaning sound. Lord Ickenham regarded him sympathetically and, in an endeavour to relieve the situation of some of its tenseness, began to chant in a pleasant baritone an old song hit of his youth. And he was interested some moments later to find that this, starting as a solo, seemed suddenly to have turned into a duet. Glancing over his shoulder, he perceived the reason. Constable Potter was riding up on his bicycle, shouting 'Hoy!'

3

Lord Ickenham was always the soul of courtesy. You had only to shout 'Hoy!' at him from a bicycle to have him drop everything and give you his immediate attention.

'Ah, officer,' he said. 'You crave an audience?'

Constable Potter dismounted, and stood for a space bent over the handle-bars, puffing. His sharp ride, taken at a moment when he was loaded down above the Plimsoll mark with eggs, bread, tea and kippered herrings, had left him short of breath. Lord Ickenham, in his considerate way, begged him to take his time.

Presently the puffing ceased, and Harold Potter spoke.

'Ho!' he said.

'Ho to you,' replied Lord Ickenham civilly. 'Have a cigar?'

With an austere gesture Constable Potter declined the cigar. A conscientious policeman does not accept gifts at the hands of the dregs of the criminal world, and such he now knew this man before him to be.

Ever since that odd episode in the garden, the reader of this record, the chronicler is aware, has been in a fever of impatience to learn what it was that sent this splendid upholder of law and order shooting into his cottage with such curious abruptness. This can now be revealed. The social lapse which had caused Mrs Bella Stubbs to purse her lips and comment acidly on his lack of manners had been occasioned by the fact that he had got the goods on Lord Ickenham. He had remembered where he had seen him before, and he had hurried indoors to consult his scrap album and ascertain his name. Having ascertained his name, he had mounted his bicycle and ridden off to confront and denounce him.

He fixed Lord Ickenham with a gimlet-like eye.

'Brabazon-Plank!' he said.

'Why,' asked Lord Ickenham, 'do you say "Brabazon-Plank" in that strange tone, as if it were some kind of expletive?'

'Ho!'

'Now we're back where we started. This is where we came in.'

Constable Potter decided that the time had come to explode his bombshell. On his face was that hard, keen look which comes into the faces of policemen when they intend to do their duty pitilessly and crush a criminal like a snake beneath the heel. It was the look which Constable Potter's face wore when he was waiting beneath a tree to apprehend a small boy who was up in the branches stealing apples, the merciless expression that turned it to flint when he called at a house to serve a summons on somebody for moving pigs without a permit.

'Brabazon-Plank, eh? You call yourself Brabazon-Plank, do you? Ho! You look to me more like George Robinson of 14 Nasturtium Road, East Dulwich.'

Lord Ickenham stared. He removed the cigar from his mouth and stared again.

'Don't tell me you're the cop who pinched me that day at the dog races!'

'Yus, I am.'

A bubbling cry like that of some strong swimmer in his agony proceeded from Pongo's lips. He glared wildly at the helmeted figure of doom. Lord Ickenham, in sharp contra-distinction, merely beamed, like one of a pair of lovers who have met at journey's end.

'Well, I'll be dashed,' he said cordially. 'What a really remarkable thing. Fancy running into you again like this. I'd never have known you. You've grown a moustache since then, or something. My dear fellow, this is delightful. What are you doing in these parts?'

There was no answering cordiality in Harold Potter's manner as he intensified the gimlet quality of his gaze. He was taut and alert, as became an officer who, after a jog-trot existence of Saturday drunks and failures to abate smoky chimneys, finds himself faced for the first time with crime on a colossal scale.

For that this was the real big stuff he had no doubt whatsoever. All the evidence went, as he himself would have said, to establish it. On the previous afternoon that shambling miscreant, Edwin Smith, had insinuated himself into Ashenden Manor under the alias of Twistleton. This evening along came his sinister associate, George Robinson, under the alias of Brabazon-Plank. And here they were together by the roadside, plotting. If you could not call this the Muster of the Vultures, it would be interesting, Harold Potter felt, to know what set of circumstances did qualify for that description.

'What are *you* doing in these parts, is more like it,' he retorted. 'You and your pal Edwin Smith there.'

'So you've recognized him, too? You have an extraordinary memory for faces. Like the royal family. What are we doing in these parts, you ask? Just paying a country-house visit.'

'Oh, yes?'

'I assure you.'

'You think you are,' corrected Constable Potter. 'But a fat lot of country-house visiting you're going to do.'

Lord Ickenham raised his eyebrows.

'Pongo.'

'Guk?'

'I think the gentleman intends to unmask us.'

'Guk.'

'Do you intend to unmask us, Mr Potter?'

'Yus.'

'I wouldn't.'

'Ho!'

There was infinite kindliness in Lord Ickenham's voice as he went on to explain himself. You could see that he felt the deepest sympathy for Constable Potter.

'No, honestly I wouldn't. Consider what will happen. I shall be ejected –'

'You're right, you'll be ejected!'

'– And my place as judge of the Bonny Babies contest taken by another judge, less prejudiced in favour of your sister's little Basil. The child will finish among the also-rans, and in this event will not your sister make inquiries? And having made them and ascertained that it was through your agency that I was disqualified, will she not have a word or two to say to you on the subject? Think it over, my dear chap, and I fancy you will agree with me that the conditions for unmasking are none too good.'

It sometimes happens to a policeman that he is sharply censured by a bench of magistrates. When this occurs, he feels as if he had been kicked in the stomach by a mule and the world becomes black. The effect of these words on Constable Potter was to give him the illusion that he had been censured by half a dozen benches of magistrates, all speaking at once. His jaw drooped like a lily, and in a low voice, instinct with emotion, he uttered the word 'Coo!'

'You may well say "Coo!"' agreed Lord Ickenham. 'I know Mrs Stubbs only slightly, of course, but she struck me as a woman of high spirit, the last person to mince her words to the man instrumental in robbing her child of the coveted trophy. Potter, I would think twice.'

Constable Potter only needed to think once. For a long instant there was a silence, one of those heavy silences which seem to be made of glue. Then, still without speaking, he mounted his bicycle and rode off.

Lord Ickenham was a fighter who could always be generous to a beaten foe.

'Amazingly fine stuff there is in our policemen,' he said. 'You crush them to earth, and they rise again. You think you've baffled them, and up they pop, their helmets still in the ring. However, this time I fancy the trick has been done. There, in my opinion, pedalled a policeman whose lips are sealed.'

Pongo, always prone to the gloomy view, demurred.

'How do you know? He was heading for the house. He's probably gone off to tell old Bostock the whole story.'

'You say that because you do not know his sister. No, no. Sealed lips, my dear Pongo, sealed lips. You have now nothing whatever to worry about.'

Pongo uttered a mirthless laugh of a quality which would have extorted the admiration of Bill Oakshott, a specialist in that line.

'Nothing to worry about? Ha! With you coming to stay with Hermione's people under a – what's the word –'

'Pseudonym?'

'Pseudonym. And planning to prowl about busting open cupboards!'

'Don't let that trivial matter give you the slightest anxiety, my dear boy. I shall attend to that tonight, and then we can all settle down and enjoy ourselves.'

'Tonight?'

'Yes. I phoned Sally from the inn, and everything is arranged. She will drive over in my car and be waiting in the garden outside the collection room at one ack emma. I shall secure the bust and hand it to her, and she will drive off with it. As simple as that.'

'Simple!'

'What can go wrong?'

'A million things. Suppose you're caught.'

'I am never caught. They know me in the Underworld as The Shadow. I wish I could cure you of this extraordinary tendency of yours always to look on the dark side.'

'Well, what other sides are there?' said Pongo.

4

The dinner hour was approaching. In her room, Lady Bostock had finished dressing and was regarding herself in the mirror, wishing, not for the first time, that she looked less like a horse. It was not that she had anything specific against horses; she just wished she did not look like one.

Footsteps sounded outside the door. Sir Aylmer entered. There was a heavy frown on his face, and it was plain that something had occurred to disturb his always easily disturbed equanimity.

'Emily!'

'Yes, dear?'

'I've just been talking to Potter.'

'Yes, dear?'

'Dam' fool!'

'Why, dear?'

Sir Aylmer picked up a hairbrush, and swished it. There was a wealth of irritation in the movement.

'Do you remember,' he asked, 'the time I played Dick Deadeye in Pinafore at that amateur performance in aid of the Lower Barnatoland Widows and Orphans?'

'Yes, dear. You were splendid.'

'Do you remember the scene where Dick Deadeye goes to the captain to warn him his daughter is going to elope, and won't come out with anything definite?'

'Yes, dear. You were wonderful in that scene.'

'Well, Potter was like that. Mystic.'

'Mystic?'

'It's the only word. Kept hinting that I must be on my guard, but wouldn't say why. I tried to pin him down, but it was no use. It was as if his lips had been sealed. All I could get out of him was that he thought danger threatened us, probably tonight. What are you wriggling like that for?'

Lady Bostock had not wriggled, she had shuddered.

'Danger?' she faltered. 'What did he mean?'

'How the dickens should I know what he meant, when every time he started to say anything he stopped as if somebody had clapped a hand over his mouth? I believe the man's half-witted. But he did go so far as to advise me to be on the alert, and said that he was going to lurk in the garden and watch the house carefully.'

'Aylmer!'

'I wish you wouldn't bellow "Aylmer" like that. You've made me bite my tongue.'

'But, Aylmer –'

'Thinking it over, I have come to the conclusion that he must have found out something further about this impostor who calls himself Twistleton, but why he couldn't say so is more than I can imagine. Well, if this so-called Twistleton is planning to make any sort of move tonight, I shall be ready for him.'

'Ready?'

'Ready.'

'What are you going to do?'

'Never mind,' said Sir Aylmer, rather inconsistently for one who had reproached Constable Potter for being mystic. 'My plans are all perfected. I shall be ready.'

# PART THREE

## *Chapter 8*

The quiet home evening to which Lord Ickenham had so looked forward had drawn to a close. Curfews had tolled the knell of parting day, lowing herds wound slowly o'er the lea. Now slept the crimson petal and the white, and in the silent garden of Ashenden Manor nothing stirred save shy creatures of the night such as owls, mice, rats, gnats, bats and Constable Potter. Down in the village the clock on the church tower, which a quarter of an hour ago had struck twelve, chimed a single chime, informing Pongo, pacing the floor of his bedroom overlooking the terrace, that in just forty-five minutes the balloon was due to go up.

As Pongo paced the floor, from time to time quivering all over like a Brazilian explorer with a touch of malaria, he was still in faultless evening dress, for the idea of going to bed on this night of fear had not even occurred to him. A young man visiting the parents of the girl he loves, and knowing that at one sharp an uncle of the maximum eccentricity will be starting to burgle the house, does not hop between the sheets at eleven-fifteen and sink into a dreamless sleep. He stays up and shudders. Pongo had made one or two attempts to divert his thoughts by reading *Murder in the Fog*, but without success. There are moments when even the most faceless of fiends cannot hope to grip.

In a past the contemplation of which sometimes affected him as if he had bitten into a bad oyster, Pongo Twistleton had frequently been called upon to tremble like an aspen when an unwilling participant in the activities of his Uncle Fred, but seldom had he done it more wholeheartedly than now. He was feeling rather as the heroine of *Murder in the Fog* was wont to do when she got trapped in underground dens, the illusion that his nerves were sticking two inches out of his body and curling at the ends being extraordinarily vivid. And it is probable that mental distress would have unstrung him completely, but for the fact that in addition to suffering agony of the soul he was also in the process of dying of thirst, and this seemed to act on the counter-irritation principle.

The thirst of which he was dying was one of those lively young thirsts which seem to start at the soles of the feet and get worse all the way up. Growing in intensity ever since his arrival at the house, it had reached its peak at eleven o'clock to-night, when Jane, the parlourmaid, had brought the bed-time decanter and syphon into the drawing-room. He was no weakling, but having to sit there watching his host, his uncle and Bill Oakshott getting theirs like so many stags at eve – he himself, in deference to his known prejudice against alcoholic liquor, having been served with barley water – had tested his iron control almost beyond endurance.

For some minutes he continued to pace the floor, cursing the mad impulse which had led him to tell Hermione that he never touched the stuff and sketching out in his mind the series of long, cool ones with which, if he ever got out of here alive, he would correct this thirst of his. And then, as he reached the end of the carpet and was about to turn and pace back again, he stopped abruptly with one foot in the air, looking so like The Soul's Awakening that a seasoned art critic would have been deceived. Two chimes had just sounded from the church tower, and it was as if they had been the voice of a kindly friend whispering in his ear.

'Aren't you,' they seemed to say, 'overlooking the fact that that decanter is still in the drawing-room? One merely throws this out as a suggestion.' And he saw that here was the solution of what had appeared to be an impasse. His guardian angel, for he presumed it was his guardian angel, had pointed out the way. Hats off to the good old guardian angel, was Pongo's attitude.

A minute later he was in the corridor. Three minutes later he was in the drawing-room. Three and a quarter minutes later he was pouring with trembling fingers what promised to be the snifter of a lifetime. And four minutes later, reclining in an armchair with his feet on a small table, he had begun to experience that joy, than which there is none purer, which comes to the unwilling abstainer who has at last succeeded in assembling the materials, when from immediately behind him a voice spoke.

All the voice actually said was 'Coo!' but it was enough. Indeed, in the circumstances, a mere clearing of the throat would have been sufficient. His knotted and combined locks parted, each particular hair standing on end like quills upon the fretful porcupine: his heart broke from its moorings and crashed with a dull thud against his front teeth: and with a wordless cry he shot towards the ceiling.

It was only some moments later, after he had hit the ceiling twice and was starting to descend to terra firma, that the mists cleared from his eyes and he was able to perceive that the intruder was not, as he had supposed, Sir Aylmer Bostock, but Elsie Bean, his old playmate of the rude sling days. She was standing by the door with a hand to her heart, panting a little, as housemaids will when they enter drawing-rooms at twenty minutes to one in the morning and find them occupied by the ruling classes.

The relief was stupendous. Pongo's equanimity returned, and with it a warm gush of the milk of human kindness. To a man who had been anticipating an embarrassing interview with Sir Aylmer Bostock in his dressing-gown Elsie Bean was like something the doctor had ordered. He had no objection whatever to Elsie Bean joining him, quite the reverse. A chat with one of the finest minds in Bottleton East was just what he was in the mood for. He beamed on the girl, and having released his tongue, which had got entangled with his uvula, spoke in a genial and welcoming voice.

'What ho, Bean.'

'What ho, sir.'

'It's you, is it?'

'Yes, sir.'

'You gave me a start.'

'You gave *me* a start, sir.'

'Making two starts in all,' said Pongo, who had taken mathematics at school. 'You must forgive me for seeming a little perturbed for a moment. I thought you were mine host. Thank God you weren't. Do you remember in your inimitable way describing him as an overbearing dishpot? You were right. A dishpot he is, and a dishpot he always will be, and to hell with all dishpots is my view. Well, come along in, young Bean, and tell me your news. How's the Harold situation developing? Any change on the Potter front?'

Elsie Bean's face clouded. She tossed her head, plainly stirred.

'Harold's a mess,' she said, with the frankness which comes

naturally to those reared in the bracing air of Bottleton East. 'He's an obstinate, pig-headed, fat-headed, flat-footed copper. I've no patience.'

'He still refuses to send in his papers?'

'R.'

A pang of pity shot through Pongo. Nothing that he had seen of Constable Potter had tended to build up in his mind the picture of a sort of demon lover for whom women might excusably go wailing through the woods, but he knew that his little friend was deeply attached to this uniformed perisher and his heart bled for her. He was broad-minded enough to be able to appreciate that if you are enamoured of a fat-headed copper and obstacles crop up in the way of your union with him, you mourn just as much as if he were Gregory Peck or Clark Gable.

'He came round to-night after supper, and we talked for an hour and a half, but nothing I could say would move him.'

'No dice, eh? Too bad.'

'It's that sister of his. She won't let him call his soul his own. I don't know what's to come of it, I'm sure.'

A pearly tear appeared at the corner of Elsie Bean's eye, and she sniffed in an overwrought way. Pongo patted her head. It was the least a man of sensibility could do.

'I wouldn't despair,' he said. 'These things seem sticky at the moment, but they generally iron out straight in the end. Give him time, and you'll find he'll be guided by the voice of love.'

Elsie Bean, having sniffed again, became calmer. There was good stuff in this girl.

'What would guide him a lot better,' she said, 'would be being bopped on the nose.'

'Bopped on the nose?'

'R.'

Of the broad, general principle of bopping Constable Potter on the nose Pongo was, of course, a warm adherent. It was a thing that he felt should be done early and often. But he was unable to see how it could pay dividends in the present circumstances.

'I don't quite follow.'

'That would knock some sense into him. Harold's nervous.'

'Nervous?' said Pongo incredulously. He had detected no such basic weakness in the flatty under advisement. A man of iron, he would have said.

'That's why he got himself shifted to the country from London, where he used to be. He found it too hot being a rozzer in London. He had some unpleasant experiences with blokes giving him shiners when he was pinching them, and it shook him. He come here for peace and quiet. So if he found it was too hot being a rozzer here as well, he wouldn't want to be a rozzer anywhere. He'd give his month's notice, and we'd all be happy.'

Pongo saw her point. He could scarcely have done otherwise, for it had been admirably put.

'True,' he said. 'You speak sooth, Bean.'

'If only someone would bop him on the nose, he wouldn't hesitate not for a moment. *You* wouldn't bop him on the nose, would you?'

'No, I would not bop him on the nose.'

'Or squash in his helmet when he wasn't looking?'

Pongo was sorry for the idealistic girl, but he felt it due to himself to discourage this line of thought from the outset.

'A man like Harold is always looking,' he said. 'No, I wish you luck, young Bean, and I shall follow your future career with considerable interest, but don't count on me for anything more than heartfelt sympathy. Still, I fully concur in your view that what you require is an up and coming ally, who will drive home to Harold the risks of the profession, thus causing him to see the light, and I strongly recommend featuring your brother Bert in the part. It's a pity he doesn't come out till September. What's he in for?'

'Resisting of the police in the execution of their duty. He sloshed a slop on the napper with a blunt instrument.'

'There you are, then. The People's Choice. Tails up, my dear old housemaid. Provided, of course, that his sojourn in the coop has not weakened Bert as a force, you should be hearing the warbling of the blue bird by early October at the latest. Meanwhile, switching lightly to another topic, what on earth are you doing here at this time of night?'

'I came to get some whisky.'

All the host in Pongo sprang to life. He blushed for his remissness.

'I'm frightfully sorry,' he said, reaching for the decanter. 'Ought to have offered you a spot ages ago. Can't imagine what I was thinking of.'

'For Harold,' Elsie Bean explained. 'He's lurking in the garden. He chucked a stone at my window, and when I popped my head out he asked me in a hoarse whisper to bring him a drop of something. And I remembered Jane always took the whisky in here last thing before bed. Lurking in the garden!' she proceeded with bitterness. 'What's he lurking in gardens for? Doing some sort of copper's job, I suppose. If he'd give up being a copper, he could stay in bed like other folks. I've no patience.'

She sniffed, and Pongo, fearing another pearly tear, hastened to apply first aid.

'There, there,' he said. 'You mustn't let it get you down. Right will prevail. Have a cigarette?'

'Thanks.'

'Turkish this side, Virginia that,' said Pongo.

He had taken one himself a few moments before, and he proceeded now to light hers from his own. And it was while their faces were in the close juxtaposition necessitated by this process that Bill Oakshott entered the room.

2

Whether one is justified in describing Bill Oakshott and Pongo Twistleton as great minds is perhaps a question open to debate. But they had exhibited to-night the quality which is supposed to be characteristic of great minds, that of thinking alike. Pongo, yearning for a snootful, had suddenly remembered the decanter in the drawing-room, and so had Bill.

Ever since his meeting that afternoon with Lord Ickenham, Bill Oakshott's emotions had been rather similar to those which he would have experienced, had he in the course of a country walk discovered that his coat tails had become attached to the rear end of the Scotch express en route from London to Edinburgh. Like most of those who found themselves associated with the effervescent peer when he was off the chain and starting to go places, he was conscious of a feeling of breathlessness, shot through with a lively apprehension as to what was coming next. This had induced sleeplessness. Sleeplessness had induced thirst. And with thirst had come the recollection of the decanter in the drawing-room.

With Bill, as with Pongo, to think was to act, and only in a minor detail of technique had their procedure differed. Pongo, not knowing whether the bally things creaked or not, had descended the stairs mincingly, like Agag, while Bill, more familiar with the terrain, had taken them three at a time, like a buffalo making for a water hole. He arrived, accordingly, somewhat touched in the wind, and the affectionate scene that met his eyes as he crossed the threshold took away what remained of his breath completely. Elsie Bean, entering the room, had said 'Coo!' Bill for the moment was unable to utter at all. He merely stood and goggled, shocked to the core.

The theory which Lord Ickenham had advanced in extenuation of Pongo's recent kissing of this girl whose nose he was now so nearly touching with his own had not satisfied Bill Oakshott. It might have been, as the kindly peer had said, a mere mannerism, but Bill thought not. The impression he had received on the previous afternoon had been of a licentious clubman operating on all twelve cylinders, and that was the impression he received now. And at the thought that it was in the hands of an all-in Lothario like this that Hermione Bostock had placed her life's happiness his sensitive soul quivered like a jelly. The outlook, to Bill's mind, was bad.

Pongo was the first to break an awkward silence.

'Oh, hullo,' he said.

'Oh, hullo, sir,' said Elsie Bean.

'Oh, hullo,' said Bill.

His manner, as he spoke, was distrait. He was trying to decide whether the fact of Pongo not being, as he had at one time supposed, off his onion improved the general aspect of affairs or merely rendered it darker and sadder. It was plain now that Elsie Bean had been mistaken on the previous day when she had asserted that the other had said 'Coo! I think I'll go to London,' and had driven thither. He had merely, it appeared, taken a short spin somewhere in his Buffy-Porson, which was quite a reasonable thing to do on a fine afternoon. But was this good or bad? Bill had said in his haste that loony libertines are worse than sane ones, but now he was not so sure. It might be a close thing, but were you not entitled to shudder even more strongly at a libertine who was responsible for his actions than at one who was not?

On one point, however, his mind was clear. It was his intention, as soon as they were alone together, to buttonhole this squire of dames and talk to him like an elder brother – as, for instance, one could imagine Brabazon-Plank *major* talking to Brabazon-Plank *minor*.

The opportunity of doing this came earlier than those familiar with Elsie Bean and her regrettable tendency to be a mixer would have anticipated. It is true that all her instincts urged the gregarious little soul to stick around and get the conversation going, but though sometimes failing to see eye to eye with Emily Post she was not without a certain rudimentary regard for the proprieties, and her social sense told her that this would not be the done thing. When a housemaid in curling pins and a kimono finds herself in a drawing-room at one in the morning with her employer and a male guest, she should as soon as possible make a decorous exit. This is in Chapter One of all the etiquette books.

So with a courteous 'Well, good night, all,' she now withdrew. And it was not very long after the door had closed that Pongo, who had become conscious of a feeling of uneasiness, as if he were sitting in a draught, was able to perceive what it was that was causing this. He was being looked at askance.

The rather delicate enterprise of looking askance at an old boyhood friend is one that different men embark on in different ways. Bill's method – for while he was solid on the point that it was about time that a fearless critic came along and pointed out to Pongo some of the aspects in which his behaviour deviated from the ideal, he found it difficult to overcome his natural shyness – was to turn bright vermilion and allow his eyes to protrude like a snail's. He also cleared his throat three times.

Finally he spoke.

'Pongo.'

'Hullo?'

Bill cleared his throat again.

'Pongo.'

'On the spot.'

Bill took a turn up and down the room. It was not easy to think of a good opening sentence, and when you are talking like an elder brother to libertines the opening sentence is extremely important, if not vital. He cleared his throat once more.

'Pongo.'

'Still here, old man.'

Bill cleared his throat for the fifth time, and having replied rather testily in the negative to Pongo's query as to whether he had swallowed a gnat or something, resumed his pacing. This brought his shin into collision with a small chair which was lurking in the shadows, and the sharp agony enabled him to overcome his diffidence.

'Pongo,' he said, and his voice was crisp and firm, 'I haven't mentioned it before, because the subject didn't seem to come up somehow, but when I returned from Brazil the day before yesterday, I was told that you were engaged to my cousin Hermione.'

'That's right.'

'Congratulations.'

'Thanks.'

'I hope you will be very happy.'

'You betcher.'

'And I hope – here's the nub – that you will make *her* happy.'

'Oh, rather.'

'Well, will you? You say you will, but I'm dashed if I see how it's going to be done, if you spend your whole time hobnobbing with housemaids.'

'Eh?'

'You heard.'

'Hobnobbing with housemaids?'

'Hobnobbing with housemaids.'

The charge was one which few men would have been able to hear unmoved. Its effect on Pongo was to make him mix himself another whisky and soda. Grasping this, like King Arthur brandishing his sword Excalibur, he confronted his accuser intrepidly and began a spirited speech for the defence.

It was inaccurate, he pointed out, to say that he spent his whole time hobnobbing with housemaids. Indeed, he doubted if he could just be said to hobnob with them at all. It all depended on what you meant by the expression. To offer a housemaid a cigarette is not hobbing. Nor, when you light it for her, does that constitute nobbing. If you happen – by the merest chance – to be in a drawing-room at one in the morning with a housemaid, you naturally do the civil thing, behaving like a well-bred English gentleman and putting her at her ease.

You chat. You pass the time of day. You offer her a gasper. And when she has got her hooks on it, you light it for her. That, at least, was Pongo's creed, and he believed it would have been the creed of Sir Galahad and the Chevalier Bayard, if he had got the name correctly, neither of whom had to the best of his knowledge ever been called hobnobbers. He concluded by saying that it was a pity that some people, whose identity he did not specify, had minds like sinks and, by the most fortunate of chances remembering a good one at just the right moment, added that to the pure all things were pure.

It was a powerful harangue, and it is not surprising that for an instant Bill Oakshott seemed to falter before it, like some sturdy oak swayed by the storm. But by dint of thinking of the righteousness of his cause and clearing his throat again, he recovered the quiet strength which had marked his manner at the outset.

'All that,' he said coldly, 'would go a lot stronger with me, if I hadn't seen you kissing Elsie Bean yesterday.'

Pongo stared.

'Kissing Elsie Bean?'

'Kissing Elsie Bean.'

'I never kissed Elsie Bean.'

'Yes, you did kiss Elsie Bean. On the front steps.'

Pongo clapped a hand to his forehead.

'Good Lord, yes, so I did. Yes, you're perfectly right. I did, didn't I? It all comes back to me. But only like a brother.'

'Like a brother, my foot.'

'Like a brother,' insisted Pongo, as if he had spent his whole life watching brothers kiss housemaids. 'And if you knew the circumstances –'

Bill raised a hand. He was in no mood to listen to any tale of diseased motives. He drew a step nearer and stared bleakly at

Pongo, as if the latter had been an alligator of the Brazilian swamps whom he was endeavouring to quell with the power of the human eye.

'Twistleton!'

'I wish you wouldn't call me Twistleton.'

'I will call you Twistleton, blast you. And this is what I want to say to you, Twistleton, by way of a friendly warning which you will do well to bear in mind, if you don't want your head pulled off at the roots and your insides ripped from your body —'

'My dear chap!'

'— With my naked hands. Cut it out.'

'Cut what out?'

'You know what. This Don Juan stuff. This butterfly stuff. This way you've got of flitting from flower to flower and sipping. Lay off it, Twistleton. Give it a miss. Curb that impulse. Kiss fewer housemaids. Try to remember that you are engaged to be married to a sweet girl who loves and trusts you.'

'But —'

Pongo, about to speak, paused. Bill had raised his hand again.

The gesture of raising the hand is one which is generally more effective in costume dramas, where it always suffices to quell the fiercest crowd, than in real life: and what made it so potent now was probably the size of the hand. To Pongo's excited imagination it seemed as large as a ham, and he could not overlook the fact that it was in perfect proportion with the rest of his companion's huge body; a body which even the most casual eye would have recognized as being composed mostly of rippling muscle. Taking all this into consideration, he decided to remain silent, and Bill proceeded.

'I suppose you're wondering what business it is of mine?'

'No, no. Any time you're passing —'

'Well, I'll tell you,' said Bill, departing from a lifetime's habit of reticence. 'I've loved Hermione myself for years and years.'

'No, really?'

'Yes. Years and years and years. I've never mentioned it to her.'

'No?'

'No. So she knows nothing about it.'

'Quite. She wouldn't, would she?'

'And loving her like this I feel that it is my job to watch over her like a —'

'Governess?'

'Not governess. Elder brother. To watch over her like an elder brother and protect her and see that no smooth bird comes along and treats her as the plaything of an idle hour.'

This surprised Pongo. The idea of anyone treating Hermione Bostock as the plaything of an idle hour was new to him.

'But –' he began again, and once more Bill raised his hand, bigger and better than ever. In a dreamlike way, Pongo found himself wondering what size he took in gloves.

'As the plaything of an idle hour,' repeated Bill. 'I don't object to her marrying another man –'

'Broad-minded.'

'At least, I do – it's agony – but what I mean is, it's up to her, and if she feels like marrying another man, right ho! So long as it makes her happy. All I want is her happiness.'

'Very creditable.'

'But get this, Twistleton,' continued Bill, and Pongo, meeting his eye, was reminded of that of the headmaster of his private school, with whom some fifteen years previously he had had a painful interview arising from his practice of bringing white mice into the classroom. 'This is what I want to drive into your nut. If I found that that other man was playing fast and loose with her, two-timing her, Twistleton, breaking her gentle heart by going and whooping it up round the corner, I would strangle him like a –'

He paused, snapping his fingers.

'Dog?' said Pongo, to help him out.

'No, not dog, you silly ass. Who the dickens strangles dogs? Like a foul snake.'

Pongo might have argued, had he felt like going into the thing, that the number of people who strangle foul snakes must be very limited, but he did not feel like going into the thing. In a sort of coma he watched his companion look askance at him again, stride to the table, mix himself a medium-strong whisky and soda, drain it and stride to the door. It closed, and he was alone.

And he was just beginning to lose that stunned sensation of having been beaten over the head with something hard and solid which must have come to the policeman whom Elsie Bean's brother Bert had sloshed on the napper with a blunt instrument, when from

across the hall, from the direction of the room where Sir Aylmer
Bostock kept his collection of African curios, there proceeded an
agonized cry, followed by the sound of voices.

Pongo, crouched in his armchair like a hare in its form, his eyes
revolving and his heart going into a sort of adagio dance, was
unable to catch what these voices were saying, but he recognized
them as those of Sir Aylmer and Lord Ickenham. The former
appeared to be speaking heatedly, while the intonation of the latter
was that of a man endeavouring to pour oil on troubled waters.

Presently the door of the collection room slammed, and a few
moments later that of the drawing-room opened, and Lord Ickenham walked in.

## 3

Whatever the nature of the exchanges in which he had been taking
part, they had done nothing to impair Lord Ickenham's calm. His
demeanour, as he entered, was the easy, unembarrassed demeanour
of an English peer who has just remembered that there is a
decanter of whisky in a drawing-room. As always at moments
when lesser men would have been plucking at their ties and
shaking in every limb, this excellent old man preserved the suave
imperturbability of a fish on a cake of ice. It seemed to Pongo,
though it was difficult for him to hear distinctly, for his heart, in
addition to giving its impersonation of Nijinsky, was now making
a noise like a motor-cycle, that the head of the family was humming
lightheartedly.

'Ah, Pongo,' he said, making purposefully for the decanter and
seeming in no way surprised to see his nephew. 'Up and about? One
generally finds you not far from the whisky.' He filled his glass, and
sank gracefully into a chair. 'I always think,' he said, having
refreshed himself with a couple of swallows and a sip, 'that this is
the best hour of the day. The soothing hush, the grateful stimulant,
the pleasant conversation on whatever topic may happen to come
up. Well, my boy, what's new? You seem upset about something.
Nothing wrong, I hope?'

Pongo uttered a curious hissing sound like the death-rattle of a
soda-water syphon. He found the question ironical.

'I don't know what you call wrong. I've just been told that I'm extremely apt to have my insides ripped out.'

'Who told you that?'

'Bill Oakshott.'

'Was he merely reading your future in the tea leaves, or do you mean that he proposed to do the ripping?'

'He proposed to do the ripping with his bare hands.'

'You amaze me. Bill Oakshott? That quiet, lovable young man.'

'Lovable be blowed. He's worse than a Faceless Fiend. He could walk straight into the Chamber of Horrors at Madame Tussaud's, and no questions asked. He also said he would pull my head off at the roots, and strangle me like a foul snake.'

'Difficult to do that, if he had pulled your head off. Assuming, as I think we are entitled to assume, that the neck would come away with the head. But what had you been doing to Bill Oakshott to stir his passions thus?'

'He didn't like my being in here with Elsie Bean.'

'I don't think I remember who Elsie Bean is. One meets so many people.'

'The housemaid.'

'Ah, yes. The one you kiss.'

Pongo raised a tortured face heavenwards, as if he were calling for justice from above.

'I don't kiss her! At least, I may have done once – like a brother – in recognition of a signal service which she had rendered me. The way you and Bill Oakshott talk, you'd think this Bean and I spent twenty-four hours a day playing postman's knock.'

'My dear boy, don't get heated. My attitude is wholly sympathetic. I recollect now that Bill told me he had been a little disturbed by the spectacle of the embrace. He has the interests of your fiancée at heart.'

'He's in love with her.'

'Really?'

'He told me so.'

'Well, well. Poor lad. It must have been a severe jolt for him when I mentioned in the train that she was engaged to you. I feel a gentle pity for Bill Oakshott.'

'I don't. I hope he chokes.'

'The astonishing thing to my mind is that a man like Mugsy can have a daughter who seems to fascinate one and all. One would have expected Mugsy's daughter to be something on the lines of the Gorgon, with snakes instead of hair. Did you happen to hear him just now?'

'Golly, yes. What was all that?'

'Just Mugsy in one of his tantrums.'

'Did he catch you going into the collection room?'

'He was there already. Sleeping among his African curios. All wrong, it seemed to me. Either a man is an African curio, or he is not an African curio. If he is not, he ought not to curl up with them at night.' A cloud came into Lord Ickenham's handsome face, and his voice took on a disapproving note. 'You know, Pongo, there is a kind of low cunning about Mugsy which I do not like to see. Can you conceive the state of mind of a man who would have his bed moved into the collection room and sleep there with a string tied to his big toe and to the handle of the door?'

'He didn't?'

'He certainly did. It's the deceit of the thing that hurts me. Naturally I assumed, when we all wished each other good night and went our separate ways, that Mugsy was off to his bedroom like any decent householder, so I toddled down to the collection room at zero hour without a thought of unpleasantness in my mind. A nice, easy, agreeable job, I was saying to myself. I sauntered to the door, grasped the handle, turned it and gave it a sharp pull.'

'Gosh!'

'I don't know if you have ever, while walking along a dark street, happened to step on an unseen cat? I once had the experience years ago in Waverly Place, New York, and the picture seemed to rise before my eyes just now, when that awful yowl rent the air.'

'What on earth did you say?'

'Well, Mugsy did most of the saying.'

'I mean, how did you explain?'

'Oh, that? That was simple enough. I told him I was walking in my sleep.'

'Did he believe it?'

'I really don't know. The point seemed to me of no interest.'

'Well, this dishes us.'

'Nonsense. That is the pessimist in you speaking. All that has happened is that we have sustained a slight check –'

'Slight!'

'My dear Pongo, there are a thousand ways of getting around a trifling obstacle like this. Mugsy is sleeping in the collection room, is he? Very well, then we simply sit down and think out a good method of eliminating him. A knock-out drop in his bedtime whisky and soda would, of course, be the best method, but I happen to have come here without my knock-out drops. Idiotic of me. It is madness to come to country houses without one's bottle of Mickey Finns. One ought to pack them first thing after one's clean collars. But I'm not worrying about Mugsy. If I can't outsmart an ex-Governor, what was the use of all my early training in the United States of America? The only thing that bothers me a little is the thought of Sally, bless her heart. She is out there in the garden, watching and waiting like Mariana at the moated grange –'

Pongo uttered a stricken cry.

'And so is that blighted Potter out there in the garden, watching and waiting like Mariana at the ruddy moated grange. I'd clean forgotten Elsie Bean told me so. She came in here to get a drink for him.'

Lord Ickenham stroked his chin.

'H'm. I did not know that. He's out in the garden, eh? That may complicate matters a little. I hope –'

He broke off. Shrilling through the quiet night, the front door bell had begun to ring, loudly and continuously, as if someone had placed a large, fat thumb on the button and was keeping it there.

Lord Ickenham looked at Pongo. Pongo looked at Lord Ickenham.

'Potter!' said Lord Ickenham.

'The rotter!' said Pongo.

# Chapter 9

It is a characteristic of England's splendid police force at which many people have pointed with pride, or would have pointed with pride if they had happened to think of it, that its members, thanks to the rigid discipline which has moulded them since they were slips of boys, are always able to bear with philosophic fortitude the hardships and disappointments inseparable from their chosen walk in life. They can, in a word, take it as well as dish it out.

If, for example, they happen to be lurking in the garden of a country house in the small hours, when even a summer night tends to be a bit chilly, and ask their friends to bring them a drop of something to keep the cold out, and after a longish wait it becomes evident that his drop is not going to materialize, they do not wince nor cry aloud. 'Duty, stern daughter of the voice of God,' they say to themselves, and go on lurking.

It had been so with Constable Potter. In their recent Romeo and Juliet scene Elsie Bean had spoken hopefully of whisky in the drawing-room, but he quite realized that obstacles might arise to prevent her connecting with it. And as the minutes went by and she did not appear, he assumed that these obstacles had arisen and with a couple of 'Coo's' and a stifled oath dismissed the whole subject of whisky from his mind.

In surroundings such as those in which he was keeping his vigil a more spiritual man might have felt the urge to try his hand at roughing out a little verse, so much was there that was romantic and inspirational in the garden of Ashenden Manor at this hour. Soft breezes sighed through the trees, bringing with them the scent of stock and tobacco plant. Owls tu-whitted, other owls tu-whooed. Add the silent grandeur of the fine old house and the shimmer of distant water reflecting the twinkling stars above, and you had a set-up well calculated to produce another policeman-poet.

But Harold Potter had never been much of a man for poetry. Even when alone with Elsie Bean in the moonlight he seldom got much further in that direction than a description of the effect which regulation boots had on his corns. What he thought of was beef sandwiches. And he was just sketching out in his mind the beef sandwich supreme which he would eat on returning to his cottage, when in the darkness before him he discerned a dim form. Like himself, it appeared to be lurking.

He pursed his lips disapprovingly. He had taken an instant dislike to this dim form.

It was not the fact that it was dim that offended him. In the garden of Ashenden Manor at one in the morning a form had got to be dim. It had no option. The point, as Constable Potter saw it, was that forms, dim or otherwise, had no business to be in the garden of Ashenden Manor at one in the morning, and he stepped forward, his blood circulating briskly. This might or might not be big stuff, but it had all the appearance of big stuff. 'Intrepid Officer Traps Nocturnal Marauder' seemed to him about the angle from which to look at the thing.

''Ullo,' he boomed. He should have said: 'What's all this?' which is the formula laid down for use on these occasions in 'What Every Young Policeman Ought to Know', but, as so often happens, excitement had made him blow up in his lines. ''Ullo. What are *you* doing here?'

The next moment any doubt which he might have entertained as to the bigness of the stuff was resolved. With a startled squeak the dim figure, which had leaped some six inches into the air on being addressed, broke into hurried flight, and with the deep bay, so like a bloodhound's, of the policeman engaged in the execution of his duty he immediately proceeded to bound after it. 'Night Chase in Darkened Garden', he was feeling as he dropped into his stride.

Into races of a cross-country nature the element of luck always enters largely. One notices this in the Grand National. Had the affair been taking place on a cinder track, few punters would have cared to invest their money on the constable, for he was built for endurance rather than speed and his quarry was showing itself exceptionally nippy on its feet. But in this more difficult going nimbleness was not everything. Some unseen obstacle tripped the dim form. It stumbled, nearly fell. Constable Potter charged up, reached out, seized something. There was a rending sound and he fell back, momentarily deprived of his balance. When he recovered it, he was alone with the owls and the stars. The dim form had disappeared, and he stood there with his hands full of what seemed to be the major part of a woman's dress.

It was at this point that he felt justified, despite the advanced hour, in going to the front door and ringing the bell. And it was not long afterwards that the door opened and he strode masterfully into the hall.

He found himself playing to a gratifyingly full house. He was, indeed, doing absolute capacity. You cannot punch front door bells in the small hours without attracting attention, and Ashenden Manor had turned out en masse to greet him. In addition to such members of his personal circle as Mrs Gooch, the cook, Elsie Bean, his betrothed, Jane, the parlourmaid, and Percy, the boy who cleaned the knives and boots, he noticed Sir Aylmer Bostock, looking like Clemenceau on one of his bad mornings, Lady Bostock, looking like a horse, and their nephew William, looking large and vermilion. There was also present, and a shudder ran through him as he saw them, the scum of the East Dulwich underworld in the person of the scoundrels George Robinson and Edwin Smith. The former was, as ever, debonair; the latter seemed agitated.

Constable Potter fondled his moustache. This was his hour, the high spot in his life when he was going to be fawned on by one and all. Or he thought it was until, just as he was about to speak, Sir Aylmer, who after the incursion of Lord Ickenham had managed to get to sleep again and had woken up cross, exploded like a bomb.

'POTTER!'

'Sir?' said the zealous officer, somewhat taken aback by his manner.

'Was it YOU making that infernal noise?'

'Sir?'

'Ringing the damned bell at this hour! Waking everybody up! Ruining my night's rest! WHAT THE DEVIL DO YOU MEAN BY IT?'

'But, sir, I've caught a marauder.'

'A what?'

'A nocturnal marauder, sir.'

'Then where is he? Don't tell me you let him get away?'

'Well, yes, sir.'

'Ass! Fool! Idiot! Imbecile!' said Sir Aylmer.

Constable Potter was wounded.

'It wasn't my fault, sir. The garments give when I clutched them.'

With the manner of Counsel putting in Exhibit A, he thrust beneath his interlocutor's eyes the flimsy fragment which he was holding, and Sir Aylmer inspected it closely.

'This is a woman's dress,' he said.

'A female's,' corrected Constable Potter, always indefatigable in his quest for exactitude. 'I observed her engaged in suspicious loitering, and when I up and apprehended her she come apart in my hands.'

At this dramatic recital of events which, even if colourlessly related, could scarcely have failed to chill the spine, there proceeded from the group of female members of the staff, huddled together for mutual support, a cry, or as Constable Potter would probably have preferred to put it, an ejaculation, consisting of the monosyllable 'ow!' Weighing the evidence, one would say that the speaker was not Elsie Bean, who would have said 'Coo!' but is more likely to have been Mrs Gooch or Jane the parlourmaid. The interruption had the unfortunate effect of attracting Sir Aylmer's attention to the group, and he started immediately to make his presence felt.

'EMILY!'

'Yes, dear?'

'What are all these women doing here?' Sir Aylmer's reddening eye passed from Mrs Gooch to Jane the parlourmaid, from Jane the parlourmaid to Elsie Bean. 'Good God! The place is full of damned women. Send 'em to bed.'

'Yes, dear.'

'Dishpot!' cried a clear young voice, this time unmistakably that of Miss Bean. She had been looking forward to spending most of the rest of the night in the hall, listening to tales of stirring events and commenting on them in her friendly way, and to get the bum's rush like this in the first five minutes was very bitter to her independent spirit. Not since the evening of her seventh birthday when, excitement having induced an attack of retching and nausea, she had been led out of the Bottleton East Theatre Royal half-way through her first pantomime, had she experienced such a sense of disappointment and frustration.

Sir Aylmer started. These were fighting words.

'Who called me a dishpot?'

'I did,' replied Elsie Bean with quiet fortitude. 'An overbearing dishpot, that's what you are, and I would like to give my month's notice.'

'I would like to give my month's notice,' said Mrs Gooch, struck by the happy thought.

'So would I like to give my month's notice,' said Jane the parlourmaid, falling in with the mob spirit.

Sir Aylmer clutched his dressing-gown. For a moment it seemed as if it were his intention to rend it, like a minor prophet of the Old Testament.

'EMILY!'

'Yes, dear?'

'Are you or are you not going to throw these women out?'

'Yes, dear. At once, dear.'

Briskly, though with a leaden heart, for none knew better than she the difficulty of obtaining domestic help in the country, Lady Bostock shepherded the rebels through the door. Of the wage-earning members of the household only Percy, the knives and boots boy, remained, a pimpled youth with a rather supercilious manner. He had lighted a cigarette, and his whole demeanour showed his satisfaction that the women had gone and that the men could now get together and thresh the thing out in peace.

Sir Aylmer drew a deep breath like a speaker at a public meeting after the hecklers have been ejected.

'Potter.'

'Sir?'

'Tell me your story again.'

The constable told his story again, even better than before, for he had been able to think of some new words, and Sir Aylmer listened frowningly.

'Where was this woman?'

'This Mystery Woman,' corrected Constable Potter. 'In the garden, sir.'

'What part of the garden?'

'Near the window of the room where you keep your thingamajigs, sir.'

'My *what*?'

'Those objects from Africa, sir. Curios is, I believe, the name.'

'Then call them curios.'

'Yes, sir.'

'Not thingamajigs.'

'No, sir.'

'What was she doing?'

'Lying in wait, sir.'

'What for?'

'Don't know, sir.'

Percy flicked the ash off his cigarette.

'If you arst me,' he said, throwing out the suggestion for what it was worth, 'she was expecting the arrival of her accomplice. This is the work of a gang.'

He would have done better to remain in modest obscurity. Compelled by his official status to accept meekly the recriminations of landed proprietors who were also members of the bench of magistrates, Constable Potter could be very terrible when dealing with knives and boots boys, and he had been wanting some form of relief for his feeling ever since Sir Aylmer had called him an ass, a fool, an idiot and an imbecile. To advance and seize Percy by the left ear was with him the work of an instant, to lead him to the door and speed him on his way with a swift kick the work of another. A thud and a yelp, and Percy had ceased to have a seat at the conference table. Constable Potter returned to his place, his air that of a man who has carried out a pleasant task neatly and well.

Percy's head appeared round the door.

'And so would I like to give my month's notice,' he said and withdrew once more.

Lord Ickenham, who had been a genial spectator, spoke for the first time.

'A clean sweep, Mugsy. What, all my pretty chickens at one fell swoop! Too bad. Very difficult these days to get servants in the country.'

Sir Aylmer did not reply. The same thought had come to him

independently, and he was beginning to be a little dubious as to the wisdom of his forthright policy in dealing with domestics. It was Constable Potter who now came before the meeting with a few well-judged words.

'Not but what there ain't a lot in what the lad said,' he observed. He was not fond of Percy, suspecting him of being the hidden hand which had thrown half a brick at him the other day as he cycled up the drive, but he could give credit where credit was due. 'About its being a gang, what I mean. Women don't conduct burglaries on their own hook. They have pals. Established inside the house as like as not,' he added with a significant glance.

It was Pongo who spoke next, as if impelled to utterance by a jab in the trouser seat from a gimlet or bradawl. In saying that Constable Potter's glance was significant, we omitted to state that it was at the last of the Twistletons that it had been directed, nor did we lay anything like sufficient stress on its penetrating qualities. It was silly of us to describe as merely significant something so closely resembling a death ray.

'What are you looking at *me* for?' he asked weakly.

Constable Potter, who could be as epigrammatic as the next man when he wanted to, replied that a cat may look at a king. And he was just smiling at his ready wit, when Sir Aylmer decided that the time for finesse and dissembling was past and that what was required here was direct frontal attack. All the evening he had been irked by the necessity of playing the genial host – or the fairly genial host – to this rat of the underworld, and now not even the thought of possible repercussions from his daughter Hermione could restrain him from speaking out.

'I'll tell you why he's looking at you, my man. Because he happens to be aware that you're a scoundrel and an impostor.'

'Who, me?'

'Yes, you. You thought you had fooled us, didn't you? Well, you hadn't. Potter!'

'Sir?'

'Tell your story about your previous meeting with this fellow.'

'Very good, sir,' said Constable Potter, quickly applying the necessary glaze to his eyes and starting to address the bodiless spirit in mid-air. 'Here's what transpired. On the . . . Coo! I've forgotten when it was, I'd have to look up my scrap album to establish the exact inst., but it was about a year ago, when I was in the C division in the metropolis and they'd put me on duty at the dog races down Shepherd's Bush way. Accused was drawn to my attention along of making himself conspicuous by conduct like as it might have been of a disorderly nature, and I apprehended him. Questioned while in custody, he stated his name was Smith.'

'Not Twistleton?'

'No, sir. Edwin Smith, of 11, Nasturtium Road, East Dulwich.'

'So what have you to say to that?' demanded Sir Aylmer.

Lord Ickenham intervened.

'My dear Mugsy, the whole thing is obviously an absurd misunderstanding. One sees so clearly what must have happened. Scooped in by the police and reluctant to stain the fine old Twistleton escutcheon by revealing his true identity, the boy gave a false name. You've done it yourself a hundred times.'

'I haven't!'

Lord Ickenham shrugged his shoulders.

'Have it your own way, Mugsy. The point is immaterial, and I would be the last man to awaken painful memories. But I can assure you that this really is Reginald Twistleton. Bill Oakshott happened to mention it only this afternoon. He was telling me that you had gone off your onion –'

'He was, was he?'

'– And when I inquired as to the symptoms, he explained that you had got this extraordinary idea that his old friend Reginald Twistleton was not his old friend Reginald Twistleton, whereas that is in reality what his old friend Reginald Twistleton is nothing else but. You will testify, Bill Oakshott, to the hundred per cent Twistletonity of this Reginald?'

'Fine. I mean, oh rather.'

'There you are, then, Mugsy.'

Sir Aylmer blew at his moustache.

'William on his own statement has not seen Reginald Twistleton for more than twelve years. How can he possibly claim to recognize him? Ha! William!'

'Hullo?'

'I see how we can settle this matter. Ask him questions.'

'Questions?'

'About your school days.'

'Pongo and I weren't at school together. I met him in the holidays at Lord Ickenham's place.'

'That alone would seem to be a guarantee of respectability,' said Lord Ickenham. 'A very exclusive house, that, I have always understood. By the way, how did you get on there this afternoon, Mugsy?'

'Never mind,' said Sir Aylmer shortly. 'What was he doing at Lord Ickenham's?'

'He was staying there.'

Sir Aylmer reflected. An inspiration came to him.

'Was there a dog there?'

'Eh?'

'A dog.'

'Oh, you mean a dog. Yes, a –'

'Don't tell him, don't tell him. Ask him.'

Lord Ickenham nodded.

'I see what you mean, Mugsy. Very shrewd. If he was staying at Ickenham Hall, he would remember the resident dog. Boys always remember dogs. Do you remember that dog, prisoner at the bar?'

'Of course I remember the dog. It was a sheep dog.'

'Correct, Bill Oakshott?'

'Absolutely.'

'Called –?'

'Mittens.'

'Accurate, Bill Oakshott?'

'Definitely. Right on the bull's eye. Want any more, Uncle Aylmer?'

'No,' said Sir Aylmer.

'I should hope not,' said Lord Ickenham. 'You've been making an ass of yourself, Mugsy.'

'Oh, have I?' said Sir Aylmer, stung. 'Well, let me tell you that I think the time has come now to ask *you* some questions.'

'Me?'

'Yes. How do I know who you are? You come here claiming to be Plank, and you don't look a bit like Plank, as I remember him –'

'But I explained about the absence of the billowy curves. Slimmo.

347

In the small half-crown or the larger three-and-six-pence bottle. You mix it with your food, and it acts as a gentle, agreeable remedy for hypertrophy of the trouser seat, not habit-forming.'

'I don't believe you are Plank. How do I know that William did not pick up the first stranger he met and talk him into coming and judging the Bonny Baby contest, so that he could get out of it himself?'

'Ridiculous. You have only to look at that pure brow, those candid eyes –'

'There are some damned funny things going on here,' proceeded Sir Aylmer firmly, 'and I intend to get to the bottom –'

'Like Slimmo.'

'This afternoon a man I don't remember from Adam comes and insinuates himself into the house, saying he is an old schoolfellow of mine. Tonight Potter catches a woman prowling in my garden –'

'Not so much prowling, sir, as lurking.'

'SHUT UP!'

'Yes, sir.'

'Potter catches a woman prowling in my garden, obviously trying to establish communication with some man in the house. Who was that man?'

'Ah.'

'It wasn't me.'

'One hopes not, Mugsy.'

'It wasn't William. It wasn't that boy who was in here just now, the one that cleans the knives and boots –'

'How do you know? If I were you, I would watch that boy, watch him closely.'

'It was presumably not Reginald, seeing that Reginald really is Reginald. That leaves you.'

'But, Mugsy, this is absurd. You say this woman was trying to establish communication with some man in the house. Why? What possible evidence have you of that? I see her as some poor, homeless waif who wandered into your garden trying to find shelter for the night in the tool shed or the byre, whatever a byre may be.'

'Poor, homeless waif be damned. And if she was trying to find shelter in the tool shed, why didn't she go there, instead of hanging about –'

'Loitering suspiciously, sir.'

'SHUT UP! Instead of hanging about outside the window of my collection room. She was one of a gang of burglars, that's what she was, and I'm going to find out who the rest of them are. You say you're Plank. Prove it.'

Lord Ickenham beamed.

'My dear Mugsy, why didn't you say so at first? Prove it? Of course I can prove it. But is not the fact that I have been calling you Mugsy from the start in itself a proof?'

'No. You could have found out somewhere that I used to be called that at school.'

'Then let us touch on some of the things which I could not have found out except by actual daily contact with you in those far-off days. Who pinched jam sandwiches at the school shop, Mugsy? Who put the drawing-pin on the French master's chair? Who got six of the best with a fives bat for bullying the juniors? And talking of bullying juniors, do you recollect one term a frail, golden-haired child arriving at the old seminary, a frail, wistful child who looked to you like something sent from heaven? You swooped on that child, Mugsy, as if you had been an Assyrian coming down like a wolf on the fold. You pulled his golden hair. You twisted his slender arm. And just as you had started twisting it, it suddenly uncoiled itself in one of the sweetest left hooks I have ever witnessed and plugged you in the eye. Ten minutes later, after we had helped you to bed, investigation revealed that the child was the previous year's public-school bantam-weight champion, who had been transferred to us from his former place of education because his father thought the air in our part of the world was better for his lungs. On another occasion –'

He paused. A horrible cackling sound, like a turkey with laryngitis, had interrupted the flow of his narrative. It was Constable Potter laughing. He was not a man who laughed easily, and he had not wanted to laugh now. He had, indeed, tried not to laugh. But his sense of the humorous had been too much for him.

'Uck, uck, uck,' he gurgled, and Sir Aylmer turned on him with all the fury of a bantam-weight champion whose arm had been twisted.

'POTTER!'

349

'S-sir?'

'Get out! What the devil are you doing, lounging about in here, when you ought to be finding that woman you were fool enough to let escape?'

The rebuke sobered Constable Potter. He saw that he had been remiss.

'Yes, sir.'

'What do you mean, Yes, sir?'

'I mean No, sir. I mean I'll start instituting a search instanter. It oughtn't to be so hard to find her. She'll be practically in the nood, as the expression is, and that,' said Constable Potter who, when he thought at all, thought clearly, 'will render her conspicuous.'

With a courteous inclination of the head he passed through the door, stern and vigilant, and Sir Aylmer prepared to follow his example.

'I'm off to bed,' he said shortly. 'It must be two o'clock.'

'Past two,' said Lord Ickenham, consulting his watch. 'How time flies when one is agreeably occupied. Then let us all go to bed.'

He linked his arm in that of Pongo, who was breathing stertorously like a fever patient, and together they made their way up the stairs.

2

The bedroom which had been allocated to Lord Ickenham was a spacious apartment on the second floor, looking out over the park. It was thither that he conducted Pongo, bringing him to rest on the chaise-longue which stood beside the window.

'Relax, my boy,' he said, tidying up his nephew's legs, which were showing a tendency to straggle, and gently placing a cushion behind his head. 'You seem a little overwrought. You remind me of an old New York friend of mine named Bream Rockmeteller on the occasion one Fourth of July when somebody touched off a maroon beneath his chair. That same stunned look. Odd. I should have thought that the clearing up of that Edwin Smith misunderstanding would have made you feel as if you had just had a fortnight at Bracing Bognor.'

Pongo sat up, his legs once more shooting out in all directions.

'Come, come,' said Lord Ickenham, rearranging them. 'Are you a man or an octopus? One ought to tie you up with a system of ropes.'

Pongo ignored the rebuke. His eyes were stony.

'Uncle Fred,' he said, speaking in a low, metallic voice, 'I don't know if you know it, but you're Public Scourge Number One. You scatter ruin and desolation on every side like a ruddy sower going forth sowing. Life, liberty and the pursuit of happiness aren't possible when you're around. You're like the Black Death or one of those pestilences of the Middle Ages, taking their toll of thousands.'

His vehemence seemed to occasion Lord Ickenham a mild surprise.

'But, my dear boy, what have I done?'

'All that stuff about my giving a false name at the dog races.'

'Well, I'm dashed. I was looking on that as my day's good deed. But for my timely intervention –'

'I was just going to deny the whole thing, when you butted in.'

Lord Ickenham shook his head.

'You would never have got away with it. Heaven knows that there are few more fervent apostles of the creed of stout denial than myself – I have been practising it for thirty years with your aunt – but it would not have served here. The copper's word would have been accepted, and you would have been branded in Mugsy's eyes as a burglar.'

'Well, look what I'm branded in his eyes as now. A chap who goes on toots and gets pinched at dog races. What's Hermione going to say when he tells her about it? The moment the facts are placed before her, she'll sit down and write me a stinker, calling our engagement off.'

'You think so?'

'I can see her dipping the pen.'

'Well, that'll be good. If I were you, I would give three rousing cheers and let it go at that.'

'I won't give three rousing cheers. I worship the girl. Until now –'

'I know, I know. You have never known what love meant. Quite. Nevertheless, I stick to it that you would be well out of this perilous enterprise of trying to hitch up with a girl who appears to have the austere outlook of the head mistress of a kindergarten and will probably spend most of her married life rapping her husband on the knuckles with a ruler. But we mustn't sit yarning about your amours now. There are graver matters on which we have to rivet our attention.'

'Such as –?'

'My dear Pongo, Sally. Is it nothing to you that she is at this moment roaming Hampshire in her cami-knickers? Where's your chivalry?'

Pongo bowed his head in shame. No appeal to the *preux chevalier* in him was ever wasted. The thought that he had clean forgotten about Sally was a knife in his bosom.

'Oh, golly. Yes, that's right. She'll catch cold.'

'If nothing worse.'

'And may be gathered in by Potter.'

'Exactly.'

'Blast him.'

'Yes, I confess to feeling a little cross with Constable Potter, and in the deepest and truest sense it will be all right with me if he trips over a footprint and breaks his damned neck. In trying to cope with Constable Potter one has the sense of being up against some great natural force. I wouldn't have thought so much zeal could have been packed into a blue uniform and a pair of number eleven boots. Well, see you shortly, Pongo.'

'Where are you going?'

'Out into the great open spaces,' said Lord Ickenham, picking up a flowered dressing-gown. 'God knows where Sally is, but she can't have got far. As Potter said, she will be conspicuous.'

'Shall I come, too?'

'No,' said Lord Ickenham. 'We don't want the thing to look like one of those great race movements. You stay here and think calm, healing thoughts.'

He left the room, walking like one who intends not to let a twig snap beneath his feet, and Pongo leaned back against the cushion and closed his eyes.

'Healing thoughts!' he said to himself bitterly, and laughed one of his mirthless laughs.

But the human mind is capable of strange feats. You never know where you are with it. If questioned at the moment when the door had closed as to the chances of anything in the nature of a healing thought coming into a mind that was more like a maelstrom than a collection of grey cells, Pongo would have offered a hundred to eight against and been surprised if there had been any takers. Yet now, gradually, he discovered that one was beginning to shape itself.

As if painted in flame, the picture of the whisky decanter which he had left standing on the round table in the drawing-room, at least half of its elixir still within it, started to rise before his mental retina, and he sat up, the light of hope dawning in his eyes. He had tested the magic properties of that decanter before, and they had in no way fallen short of his dreams, and now there came upon him the urge to test them again. Reason told him that he would never need one for the tonsils more than in the present pass to which he had been reduced. In fact, added Reason, the first thing any good specialist, seeing him, would recommend – nay, insist on – was a little something in a glass.

Thirty seconds later he had begun his journey to the promised land, and a couple of minutes after that was sitting in his favourite armchair with his feet up, almost calm again.

It was very pleasant in the quiet drawing-room, very pleasant and restorative and soothing. At least, it was for perhaps a quarter of an hour. At the end of that period Sir Aylmer Bostock entered in his dressing-gown. Tossing on his pillow after having had his beauty sleep twice broken, Sir Aylmer had bethought him of the decanter and it had drawn him like a magnet. Experience had taught him that the most stubborn insomnia can often be corrected by means of a couple of quick ones.

His emotions on beholding Pongo established at the fountain-head were sharp and poignant. Although he had been compelled to abandon his view of this young man as a rat of the underworld, he still considered him a rat, and the last thing he desired was a jolly party with him at half-past two in the morning, the glasses clinking and the conversation flowing free. Life, he was thinking, was difficult enough without finding Pongo under one's feet wherever one went. If Sir Aylmer Bostock after two days of his future son-in-law's society had been asked to sketch out a brief description of his ideal world, he would have replied that he was not a fussy man and did not expect perfection but that he did insist on one thing, that it should contain fewer and better Twistletons.

'Ugh!' he said. 'You!'

There are extraordinarily few good answers to the ejaculation 'You!' especially when preceded by the monosyllable 'Ugh!' Pongo could not think of any of them. The other's entry had caused him to repeat that sitting high jump of his, and on descending from the neighbourhood of the ceiling he had found his mind a blank. The best he could achieve was a nervous giggle.

This was unfortunate, for we have made no secret of Sir Aylmer Bostock's views on nervous gigglers. The ex-Governor had never actually fallen on a nervous giggler and torn him limb from limb, but that was simply because he had not wanted to get himself involved in a lot of red tape. But he definitely did not like them. He glared at Pongo, and as he glared observed the glass in the latter's hand, and it was as if someone had whispered in his ear 'What is wrong with this picture?'

'Gar!' he exclaimed, once more calling on one of those tribal gods. 'I thought you told me you were a teetotaller.'

'Eh?'

'Teetotaller.'

'Oh, yes, that's right.'

'How the devil can you be a teetotaller, if you sit swigging whisky all the time?'

'Medicinal.'

'What?'

'I take a drop occasionally for my health,' said Pongo. 'Doctor's orders.'

There are moments in life when, after offering frank and manly explanations of our actions, we are compelled to pause and wonder if they have got by. This was one of them. And it was while Pongo was anxiously scrutinizing his host's face and trying, without much success, to read in its rugged features an expression of childlike trust that Lady Bostock entered the room.

There are critics to whom it will seem one of those strained coincidences which are so inartistic that on this troubled night no fewer than six of the residents of Ashenden Manor should have been seized independently of each other with the idea of going to the drawing-room in order to establish contact with the decanter placed there earlier in the evening by Jane, the parlourmaid, while others will see in the thing that inevitability which was such a feature of the best Greek tragedy. Æschylus once said to Euripides, 'You can't beat inevitability,' and Euripides said he had often thought so, too.

Be that as it may, it was the decanter which had brought Lady Bostock to the spot. Finding a difficulty in getting to sleep after the recent strain upon her nerves, she had thought that a weak whisky and water might prove the specific which she needed.

She, too, was surprised on discovering that she had boon companions.

'Aylmer!' she said. 'You here? And Reginald?' The glass in Pongo's hand attracted her attention, producing reactions identical with those of her husband. 'I thought you were a teetotaller, Reginald.'

Sir Aylmer snorted. A most unpleasant, cynical snort, a sort of nasal 'Oh, yeah.'

'He takes a drop occasionally for his health.'

'Oh, yes?'

'Yes,' said Sir Aylmer. 'Medicinal. Doctor's orders.'

His intonation was so extremely disagreeable, suggesting as it did contempt, disgust and that revolted loathing which temperate men feel when confronted with the world's drink-sodden wrecks, that Pongo, though his sitting high jump had caused him to spill practically all the contents of his glass and he would much have liked to refill it, felt that this was not the moment. Stronger than his desire for one for the road was the passionate wish to be somewhere where Sir Aylmer and Lady Bostock were not.

'Well – er – good night,' he mumbled.

'You're leaving us?' said Sir Aylmer grimly.

'Er – yes. Good night.'

'Good night,' said Sir Aylmer.

'Good night,' said Lady Bostock.

There was an expression of concern on her face as the door closed. She looked like a horse that is worried about the quality of its oats.

'Oh, dear,' she said. 'I do hope Reginald is not a drinker.' A thought occurred to her, and she brightened. 'But, of course, I was forgetting. He isn't Reginald, is he? He's just somebody pretending to be Reginald.'

Sir Aylmer, though reluctant to present himself in the light of one who had been in error, felt obliged to put her abreast of his latest findings.

'Yes, he's Reginald. I've been into that matter, and it now seems pretty well established that he's Reginald all right. Apparently, at those dog races where Potter arrested him, he gave a false name and address.'

'That does not sound very nice.'

'It was not very nice. It wasn't nice at all. It was disgraceful and it throws a blinding light on the true character of Reginald Twistleton. Shows you what sort of a fellow he is. And as to him being a drinker, of course he's a drinker. You can tell it by those shifty eyes and that weak giggle. I knew there was something wrong with the young toad the first time I saw him. Dipsomaniac is written all over him. No doubt he has been absorbing the stuff like a sponge whenever our backs were turned. I don't suppose he has drawn a sober breath since he came here. God help Hermione, married to a chap like that. He'll be seeing pink snakes on the honeymoon. Orange spiders,' said Sir Aylmer, allowing his imagination free rein. 'Gamboge elephants. Purple penguins.'

It is never difficult to touch a mother's heart with this sort of thing. Lady Bostock uttered a stricken neigh.

'Hermione must be warned!'

'Exactly what I was about to suggest myself. You'd better write to her.'

'I'll go and see her.'

'Very well, go and see her.'

'Tomorrow morning!'

'The sooner, the better. Well, if you're going to London in the morning, you'd better go to bed and get some sleep. Can't imagine why you aren't there now.'

'I came down to get a weak whisky. I couldn't sleep.'

'I came to get a strong whisky. I couldn't sleep, either. How the devil can anyone be expected to sleep in a house where fools are incessantly breaking in on you, saying they're somnambulists, and policemen ring door bells all the time? Did you get those women to bed?'

'Yes, dear. They kept giving their notices all the way upstairs.'

'Curse them. Say when, Emily.'

'When. O dear, O dear, O dear.'

'What's the matter now?'

'I was only thinking of Reginald,' said Lady Bostock. 'I wonder if the gold cure would do any good.'

Unaware of the exact nature of what was being said about him by the parents of the girl he loved, but suspecting that his case might have come upon the agenda paper after his withdrawal, Pongo had tottered up the stairs to his room. While not in tip-top form, he found himself enjoying the novel sensation of being separated for a while from members of the human race, a race for which the events of the night had caused him to acquire a rather marked distaste. 'Alone at last,' he was saying to himself, as he opened the door.

A moment later he saw that he had been too optimistic. Seated on the bed was his Uncle Frederick, enjoying a mild cigar, and in the armchair, clad in a flowered dressing-gown, a girl at the sight of whom his heart, already, as we have seen, on several occasions tonight compelled to rival the feverish mobility of a one-armed paperhanger with the hives, executed a leap and a bound surpassing all previous efforts by a wide margin.

'Ah, Pongo,' said Lord Ickenham. 'Come along in. Here's Sally. We climbed up the water pipe.'

3

It was not immediately that Pongo found himself able to speak. Strong emotion often has the effect of tying the vocal cords into a reefer knot, and he was in the grip of not one strong emotion, but two.

As always when confronted with some new manifestation of his uncle's activities, he was filled with a nameless fear, saying to himself, as so often in similar circumstances, 'What will the harvest be?': and in addition to this nameless fear he was experiencing the embarrassment which cannot but come to a young man of sensibility when he encounters unexpectedly a former fiancée from whom he has severed relations in a scene marked on both sides by raised voices and harsh words.

Fortunately women handle these situations more adroitly than the uncouth male. In Sally's demeanour there was no suggestion that she found in this meeting any cause for discomfort. Her eyes, bright and beautiful as he had always remembered them, shone with a friendly light. Her voice, when she spoke, was cordial. And she accompanied her words with a dazzling smile.

'Hullo, Pongo.'

'Hullo, Sally.'

'It's nice to see you again.'

'What ho.'

'You look very well.'

'Oh, rather,' said Pongo.

He spoke absently, for he was distrait. What with going to New York to attend to his financial interests and getting engaged to Hermione Bostock and all the other excitements of what had recently been a full life, he had rather allowed the peculiar properties of Sally's smile to fade from his mind, and getting it between the eyes like this had had a shaking effect, inducing a feeling somewhat similar to that which must have come to Lord Ickenham's friend Bream Rockmeteller in the course of those distant Fourth of July celebrations.

Sally's smile . . .

That smile of Sally's . . .

Yes, he had forgotten just what it could do to your system, suddenly flashing out at you like the lights of a village pub seen through rain and darkness at the end of a ten-mile hike and transporting you into a world of cosiness and joy and laughter. He blinked, and not even his great love for Hermione Bostock could keep him from experiencing a momentary twinge of nostalgia, a swift pang of that self-reproach which comes to a man conscious of having been on a good thing and of having omitted to push it along.

The weakness passed. He thought – hard – of Hermione Bostock, and it did the trick. It was a Reginald Twistleton who was himself again, a strong, firm Reginald Twistleton with not a chink in his armour, who now put the question which he would have put a good deal earlier but for the mental upheaval which we have just been analysing.

'What's all this?' he asked, and Constable Potter himself, addressing a suspicious loiterer, could not have spoken in a colder, more level voice. 'What's the idea, Uncle Fred?'

'The idea?'

'What's Sally doing here?'

'Seeking sanctuary.'

'In my room?'

'Just for the time being, till we can make other arrangements.'

Pongo placed a hand on either side of his head to shore it up. That old, familiar sensation that it was coming unstuck had swept over him.

'Oh, God!'

'Why do you say "Oh, God!" my boy? What seems to you to be the difficulty?'

'How the dickens can she stay in my room?'

'Why not? You will have a shakedown in mine. I can't offer you a bed, but you remember that very comfortable chaise-longue.'

'I don't mean that. I mean, well, dash it, what about people coming in?'

'Where?'

'Here.'

'When?'

'Tomorrow morning.'

'Nobody will come in tomorrow morning except the housemaid. And before nightfall I hope to get the poor child safely away. She tells me she stowed the car in the local garage. I shall take it out and drive over to Ickenham first thing, and bring her back some of my wife's reach-me-downs. She will then be free to go where she lists. A word,' said Lord Ickenham thoughtfully, 'which I have never been able to understand. Why lists? How do lists come into it? However, that is neither here nor there. Getting back to what you were saying, nobody is going to muscle in except the housemaid, and all that is needed, therefore, is to square the housemaid. I wonder if you ever reflected that if only he could square the housemaid, every visitor at a country house would be able to take in paying guests and make a good deal of money.'

'And how are you going to square the housemaid?'

'Odd how when one keeps repeating that it sounds like one of those forgotten sports of the past. Squaring the housemaid. One can picture William the Conqueror being rather good at it. My dear Pongo, have no uneasiness. The housemaid is already squared. Perhaps I had better tell you the story from the beginning. It won't bore you, Sally?'

'Not at all, Uncle Fred.'

'Capital. Well, when I left you, Pongo, I started to make a systematic search of the grounds, exploring every avenue and leaving no stone unturned. I was handicapped by having no bloodhounds, another thing which one ought always to bring with one to a country house, but eventually I located Sally in the potting shed, watering the geraniums with her tears.'

'I wasn't,' said Sally indignantly, and Lord Ickenham rose, kissed the top of her head paternally and returned to the bed.

'I was only making a good story of it, my dear. Actually, your attitude was heroic. I was proud of you. She laughed, Pongo, when she heard my voice. Laughed heartily.'

'I wish I could.'

'Can't you? Not at this happy ending?'

'What do you mean, happy ending?'

'Well, it looks like a happy ending to me. I see Sally as a little storm-tossed boat that has put into harbour after the dickens of a gruelling from the winds and waves, and can now take it easy for a bit. Where was I, Sally?'

'Potting shed.'

'That's right. I found her in the potting shed. I draped her in the dressing-gown, and we crept out into the night. Did you ever hear of Chingachgook?'

'No.'

'A Red Indian of some celebrity in my younger days. I suppose nobody reads Fenimore Cooper now.'

'What about him?'

'I was only going to say that that was what we crept like; softly and silently, as if we were wearing moccasins. And while we were creeping, we heard voices.'

'And did I jump!'

'I, too. I soared up like a rocket. For one of the voices was Constable Potter's. The other was that of the housemaid, Elsie Bean. A rather pleasant feature of life at Ashenden Manor is the way you can always find housemaids sauntering about the grounds at half-past two in the morning. It was she who was doing most of the speaking. She seemed to be reproaching the officer for his professional activities. She was telling him that she had given her month's notice and that before her time expired he must make his decision about resigning from the Force. She said she hadn't any patience, and so alien did she appear to his aims and ideals that I felt that we had found a sympathizer. I was right. Presently, the constable left, his manner that of a man who has had his ears pinned back, and with a slight snort she turned, presumably to re-enter the house. It was at this point that we emerged and contacted her.'

'With a cheery "Hoy!"'

'With, as you say, a cheery "Hoy!" Well, after that everything went with the most delightful smoothness. I think she was a little surprised to see us – indeed, she stated later that that ghastly sound proceeding from the darkness had scared her out of a year's growth – but she soon recovered her poise and showed herself the soul of consideration. It was she who pointed out the water pipe and after I had helped Sally to climb it gave me that preliminary leg-up which a man needs at my time of life, if he is to negotiate water pipes successfully. I don't know when I met a nicer girl, and I don't wonder you –'

'You don't wonder I what?'

'Oh, nothing. So here we are, thanks to her, and she has guaranteed that she will give us all the aid and comfort at her disposal. She said she would look in shortly and confer with us. I suppose she feels that there are one or two details which need discussing.'

Sally clasped her hands.

'My breakfast!'

'That, no doubt, was one of them.'

'I'm starving already.'

'Poor child. In a few minutes I will take you down to the larder and we will knock together a bite of supper which will keep you going till the morning. I could do with a couple of boiled eggs myself. These late hours give one an appetite. Ah, here is Miss Bean. Come in, Miss Bean. I think you know everybody. A cigarette?'

'Thank you, sir.'

'Give the lady a cigarette, Pongo. A chair, Miss Bean? And a footstool for your feet? That's right. And now, Miss Bean, tell us everything that is on your mind. I hope you have come to indicate to us in what way we may make some slight return for all your kindness tonight. Speaking for myself, if a fiver would be any good to you – and when I say a fiver I mean, of course a tenner –'

Elsie Bean tossed her head, setting the curling pins leaping like Sir Aylmer Bostock's moustache.

'I don't want money,' she said, not actually referring to it as dross, but giving the impression that that was what she considered it. 'Thanking you all the same.'

'Not at all.'

'What I want,' said Elsie Bean, once more imparting life to the curling pins, 'is Harold bopped on the nose.'

She spoke with a strange intensity, her face hard and her blue eyes gleaming with a relentless light. That interview with her loved one in the garden seemed to have brought her to a decision. Here, you felt, was a housemaid who had been pushed just so far and could be pushed no further. Nor is the fact surprising. Tempers are quick in Bottleton East, and Constable Potter's way of replying 'Well, I dunno,' to her most impassioned pleadings would have irritated a far less emotional girl.

Lord Ickenham inclined his head courteously.

'Harold?'

'Harold Potter.'

'Ah, yes, our friend the constable. What did you say you wished done to his nose?'

'I want it bopped.'

'Struck, you mean? Socked? Given a biff?'

'R.'

'But why? Not that I want to be inquisitive, of course.'

'I was telling Mr Twistleton. There's only one way to make Harold be sensible and give up being a copper, and that's to dot him a good bop on the nose. Because he's nervous. He don't like being bopped on the nose.'

'Of course, of course. I see just what you mean. Your psychology is unerring. If I were a copper and somebody bopped me on the nose, I would hand in my resignation like a flash. The matter shall be attended to. Pongo –'

Pongo started convulsively.

'Now listen, Uncle Fred. All that's been arranged. This Bean and I have discussed it and are in full agreement that the bird to take the job on is her brother Bert. Bert, I may mention, is a chap who habitually sloshes slops on the napper with blunt instruments, so this will be a picnic to him.'

'But Bert doesn't come out till September.'

Lord Ickenham was shocked.

'Are you suggesting, Pongo, that this poor girl shall wait till September for the fulfilment of her hopes and dreams? It is obvious that time is of the essence and that we must rush to her assistance immediately. I, unfortunately, am a little too old to bop policemen on the nose, much as I should enjoy it, so the task devolves upon you. See to it as soon as possible.'

'But, dash it –'

'And don't say "But, dash it." You remind me of our mutual ancestor, Sir Gervase Twistleton, who got a bad name in the days of the Crusades from curling up in bed and murmuring "Some other time," when they asked him to come and do his bit at the battle of Joppa. I am convinced that this matter could not be placed in better hands than yours, and I would suggest that you and Miss Bean have a talk about ways and means while Sally and I go down to the larder and forage. It might be best if we took the back stairs. Can you direct us to the back stairs, Miss Bean? At the end of the passage? Thank you. I don't suppose we shall have any trouble in finding the larder. Is there a gas range in the kitchen for egg boiling purposes? Excellent. Every convenience. Then come along, Sally. I think I can promise you a blow-out on lavish lines. I have already tested Mugsy's hospitality, and it is princely. I shouldn't wonder if in addition to eggs there might not be a ham and possibly even sausages.'

With a bow of old world courtesy to Elsie Bean, Lord Ickenham escorted Sally from the room, speaking of sausages he had toasted at school on the ends of pens, and Pongo, who had folded his arms in a rather noticeable manner, found on turning to Miss Bean that her set face had relaxed.

'He's a nice old gentleman,' she said.

This seemed to Pongo such a monstrously inaccurate description of one who in his opinion was like a sort of human upas tree, casting its deadly blight on every innocent bystander who came within its sphere of influence, that he uttered a brassy 'Ha!'

'Pardon?'

'I said "Ha!"' said Pongo, and would have gone on to speak further, had there not at this moment occurred an interruption. Knuckles were rapping gently on the door, and through the wood-work there made itself heard a voice.

'Pongo.'

The voice of Bill Oakshott.

4

In the literature and drama which have come down to us through the ages there have been a number of powerful descriptions of men reacting to unpleasant surprises. That of King Claudius watching the unfolding of the play of 'The Mouse Trap' is one of these, and writers of a later date than Shakespeare have treated vividly of the husband who discovers in an inner pocket the letter given to him by his wife to slip in the mail box two weeks previously.

Of all the protagonists in these moving scenes it is perhaps to Macbeth seeing the ghost of Banquo that one may most aptly compare Pongo Twistleton as he heard this voice in the night. He stiffened from the ankles up, his eyes rolling, his hair stirring as if beneath a sudden breeze, his very collar seeming to wilt, and from his ashen lips there came a soft, wordless cry. It was not exactly the Potter–Bean 'Coo!' and not precisely the 'Gar!' of Sir Aylmer Bostock, but a sort of blend or composite of the two. That intelligent Scottish nobleman, Ross, whom very little escaped, said, as he looked at Macbeth, 'His highness is not well,' and he would have said the same if he had been looking at Pongo.

Nor is his emotion hard to understand. When a sensitive young man, animated by a lively consideration for his personal well-being, has been told by a much larger young man of admittedly homicidal tendencies that if he does not abandon his practice of hobnobbing with housemaids in the drawing-room at one-thirty in the morning he, the much larger young man, will scoop out his insides with his bare hands, he shrinks from the prospect of being caught by the other entertaining a housemaid in his bedroom at two forty-five. If Pongo said 'Gar!' or it may have been 'Coo!' and behaved as if an old friend whom he had recently caused to be murdered had dropped in to dinner with dagger wounds all over him, he cannot fairly be blamed. Those hands of Bill Oakshott's seemed to rise before his eyes like dreadful things seen in a nightmare.

But it was only for an instant that he stood inactive. In times of crisis blood will tell, and he had the fortune to belong to a family whose members, having gone through a lot of this sort of thing in their day, had acquired and transmitted to their descendants a certain technique. A good many Twistletons, notably in the eighteenth and early nineteenth centuries, had been constrained by circumstances to think quick on occasions just such as this and, having thought quick, to hide women in cupboards. It was to the cupboard, therefore, acting automatically in accordance with the family tradition, that Pongo now directed Elsie Bean.

'Slide in there!' he hissed. 'And not a sound, not a yip, not a murmur. A human life hangs on your silence.'

He closed the cupboard door, straightened his tie and drawing a deep breath called 'Come in.' And it was while he was smoothing his hair and simultaneously commending his soul to God that Bill Oakshott entered.

'Oh, hullo,' he said.

'Hullo,' said Bill. 'I'm glad you're still up, Pongo. I – er – I wanted a word with you.'

The phrase is one that sometimes has an ominous ring, but it was not menacingly that Bill Oakshott employed it. His voice was soft, even winning, and Pongo was encouraged to see that though looking as large as ever, if not larger, he seemed pacific. Ross, or somebody like that who noticed things, would have said that Bill was embarrassed, and he would have been right.

It often happens that after talking to a boyhood friend like an elder brother a young man of normally kindly disposition, when he has had time to reflect, finds himself wondering if his tone during the interview was not a little brusque. It was so with Bill Oakshott. Musing in solitude and recalling the scene in the drawing-room, it had seemed to him that some of his remarks had taken too anatomical a trend. It was to apologize that he had come to Pongo's bedroom, and he proceeded now to do so.

It would have suited Pongo better if he had put these apologies in writing and submitted them to him in the form of a note, but he accepted them in a generous spirit, though absently, for he was listening to a soft rustling sound which had begun to proceed from the cupboard. It made him feel as if spiders were walking up and down his back. The celebrated Beau Twistleton, in the days of the Regency, had once had a similar experience.

Bill appeared to have heard it, too.

'What's that?' he asked, pausing in his remarks.

'Eh?'

'That sort of scratching noise. In the cupboard.'

Pongo wiped a bead of perspiration from his forehead.

'Mice,' he said.

'Oh, mice. Lots of them about.'

'Yes, quite a good year for mice,' said Pongo. 'Well, good night, Bill, old man.'

But Bill was not yet ready to leave. Like so many large young men, he was sentimental, and this disinclined him to rush these scenes of reconciliation. When he healed rifts with boyhood friends, he liked to assure himself that they were going to stay healed. He sat down on the bed, which creaked beneath his weight.

'Well, I'm glad everything's all right, Pongo. You're sure you're not offended?'

'Not at all, not a-tall.'

'I thought you might have got the impression that I thought you were a foul snake.'

'No, no.'

'I ought never to have suggested such a thing.'

'Not keeping you up, am I, Bill?'

'Not a bit. It was just that when I found you and Elsie Bean in the drawing-room, I thought for a moment —'

'Quite.'

'You know how it is.'

'Oh, rather.'

'You see . . . I'd sock those mice, if I were you.'

'I will – tomorrow – with an iron hand. Regardless of their age and sex.'

'You see, your heads were a bit close together.'

'I was merely lighting her cigarette.'

'Of course, of course. I realize that now. I know that I can trust you.'

'Oh, rather.'

'I know that you love Hermione and will make her happy. You will look on it as a sacred duty.'

'You betcher.'

'Fine,' said Bill, clasping his hands and putting a good deal of soul into his expression. 'That's a bit of goose. I'm devoted to Hermione, Pongo.'

'Yes, you told me.'

'Hermione –'

'How about having a long talk about her in the morning?'

'Not now?'

'Bit late, isn't it?'

'Ay yes, I suppose you want to turn in. I was only going to say that Hermione is the . . . dash it, what are those things?'

'The berries?'

'Lode stars. She is the lode star of my life. I've been crazy about her for years and years and years, and her happiness means everything to me. How wonderful she is, Pongo.'

'Terrific.'

'You don't find many girls like Hermione.'

'Very scarce.'

'So beautiful.'

'Ah.'

'So clever.'

'What ho.'

'You've read her novels, of course?'

Pongo could not repress a guilty start. The question was an awkward one. He was uncomfortably conscious of having devoted to *Murder in the Fog* hours of study which would have been better employed in familiarizing himself with his loved one's output.

'Well, I'll tell you,' he said. 'Up to the moment of going to press, I haven't for one reason and another been able to smack into them to quite the extent I could wish. But she's given me her latest to read while I'm here, and I can see from the first page that it's the bezuzus. Strikes a new note, as you might say.'

'Which one is that?'

'I've forgotten the name, but I know it was called something.'

'How long has it been out?'

'Just published, I understand.'

'Ah, then I haven't seen it. Fine. That's a treat to look forward to. Isn't she amazing, Pongo? Isn't it extraordinary that she can write all those wonderful books –'

'Oh, rather.'

'– And still be a simple, healthy, out-of-doors country girl, never happier than when she is getting up at six in the morning and going for a long walk through the –'

Pongo started.

'Six in the morning?' He spoke in a thin, strained voice, and his jaw had fallen a little. 'She doesn't get up at six in the morning?'

'In the summer always.'

'And in the winter?'

'Seven. I've known her to do a round and a half of golf before breakfast, and if she doesn't play golf it's a long walk through the woods and fields. I tell you, she's marvellous. Well, good night, Pongo, you'll be wanting to go to bed,' said Bill, and heaving himself up took his departure.

It was a pensive Pongo Twistleton who went to the door and listened and then went to the cupboard and extracted Elsie Bean. To say that Bill's words had weakened his great love would perhaps be going too far, for he still thought Hermione Bostock a queen among women and had no intention of replying in the negative when the clergyman said 'Wilt thou, Reginald, take this Hermione to be thy wedded wife?' But the discovery that he was engaged to a girl who habitually got up at six in the morning, and would presumably insist on him getting up at that hour also, had definitely shaken him. His manner as he de-Beaned the cupboard was distrait, and when his guest complained of being in the final stages of suffocation he merely said 'Oh, ah?'

His detachment displeased Elsie Bean. She displayed a captious spirit.

'What did I have to go killing myself in cupboards for? It was only Mr William.'

'Only!' said Pongo, unable to share this easy outlook. 'Do you realize that if he had found you here, he would have pulled my head off at the roots?'

'You don't say?'

'Not to mention scooping out my insides with his bare hands.'

'Coo! What a nut!'

'The word nut understates it. When roused – and finding you on the premises would have roused him like nobody's business – he's a menace to pedestrians and traffic. Gosh!' said Pongo, struck with an idea. 'Why wouldn't he be the man to bop your Harold on the nose?'

'But you're going to do it.'

'In case I can't manage to get around to it, I mean. You know how full one's time is. I believe Bill would be just the chap you want.'

Elsie Bean shook her head.

'No, I asked him.'

'Asked him?'

'R. I met him walking in the garden after I'd helped that nice old gentleman up the water pipe. He said he wouldn't.'

'Why not?'

'He doesn't believe in bopping coppers on the nose.'

It was a prejudice which Pongo shared, but nevertheless he found himself exasperated. One never likes to see a man stifling his natural gifts. The parable of the talents crossed his mind.

'But how on earth do you expect me to do it?' he demanded peevishly. 'The way everybody talks, you'd think it was the simplest thing in the world to walk up to a fifteen-stone policeman and sock him on the beezer. I can't see the procedure. How does one start? One can't just go and do it. It wants leading up to. And even then –'

Elsie seemed to appreciate his difficulty.

'I've been thinking about that,' she said. 'How would it be if you pushed him into the duck pond?'

'What duck pond?'

'The one outside the front gate.'

'But he may not go near the bally duck pond.'

'Yes, he will. He always does, when he's on his beat. He goes and stands there and spits into it.'

Pongo brightened a little. It would be idle to pretend that he found the picture which his companion had conjured up attractive, but it was less repellent than the other.

'Creep up behind him, you mean?'

'R.'

'And give him a hearty shove?'

'R.'

'Yes. Yes, I see what you mean. Well, there is much in what you say, and I will give the matter my attention. It may be that you have found the solution. Meanwhile, go and peer cautiously up and down the passage and see if there's anybody about. If there isn't, pick up your feet and streak along for your dug-out like a flash.'

Before she could reach the door, it had opened to admit Lord Ickenham and Sally. Both looked greatly refreshed, the former in particular wearing the contented expression of a man who has been steeping himself in boiled eggs.

'As good a little meal as I have ever tasted,' he said. 'Really, Mugsy does one extraordinarily well. And now bed, don't you think? The evening is wearing along. You had better be putting a few things together, Pongo.'

Pongo did not reply. He was staring at Sally. Lord Ickenham approached him and drove a kindly finger into his ribs.

'Ouch!'

'Start packing, my boy.'

'Eh? Oh, right, ho!'

'Just a few necessaries. I can lend you a razor and my great sponge, Joyeuse.' Lord Ickenham turned to Elsie Bean. 'You two have settled things, I hope?'

'Yes, sir. Mr Twistleton is going to push Harold into the duck pond.'

'Capital, capital,' said Lord Ickenham heartily. 'An excellent idea. You'll enjoy that, Pongo. Don't forget that in pushing policemen into duck ponds the follow through is everything.'

Pongo, mechanically filling a suitcase, again made no reply. Though he had ceased to stare at Sally, she still occupied his thoughts. The sight of her coming through the door had acted upon him like a powerful electric shock, for her eyes, the eyes of a girl refreshed with tea and eggs, had seemed, if possible, brighter than ever, and once more she had flashed upon him that smile of hers. And this time, though he had immediately thought of Hermione Bostock, it was only to be reminded of her habit of rising at six in the summer and at seven during the winter months.

He closed the suitcase, and stood waiting. Strange thrills were shooting through his streamlined body, and his heart, which had been comparatively inactive recently, was again jumping and bumping. That consciousness of not having pushed a good thing along was now very pronounced.

'Well, good night, Sally,' said Lord Ickenham.

'Good night, Uncle Fred. Good night, Pongo.'

'Eh? Oh, good night.'

'And thanks for the sanctuary.'

'Eh? Oh, not at all.'

'Good night, Miss Bean.'

'Good night, sir.'

'You will be turning in yourself shortly, no doubt? A thousand thanks once more for all your sympathy and kindness. The duck pond, eh?' said Lord Ickenham thoughtfully. 'Yes, admirable, admirable. Come along, Pongo.'

Half-way along the corridor Pongo paused. Lord Ickenham eyed him inquiringly.

'Forgotten something?'

'Eh? Oh, no. I was only thinking about Sally.'

'What about her?'

'She looked dashed pretty in that dressing-gown.'

'Charming. By the way, she tells me she wants a lipstick. See to that tomorrow, will you.'

'Right ho,' said Pongo. 'Lipstick, one. Right.'

He resumed his progress musingly.

# PART FOUR

## *Chapter 10*

---

If you motor to Wockley Junction in the morning, starting from Ashenden Manor reasonably soon after an early-ish breakfast, you can get an express train which deposits you on the arrival platform at Waterloo at twelve-forty-three. The passage of the hours in no way having weakened her determination to visit her child and make plain to her the bleakness of the future awaiting any girl rash enough to put on a white veil and walk down the aisle with her arm linked in that of Reginald Twistleton, Lady Bostock had done this. Bill Oakshott drove her to the junction, and she reached the block of flats where Hermione had her London residence shortly after one, just as Hermione, outside its front door, was about to step into her two-seater.

Privileged to direct a square look at this girl as she stood there in the almost unbelievable splendour of her new hat, her best frock and her carefully selected shoes, gloves and stockings, the dullest eye would have been able to see that she had what it takes. Her father might look like a walrus and her mother like something starting at a hundred to eight in the two-thirty race at Catterick Bridge, but Hermione herself, tall and dark, with large eyes, a perfect profile and an equally perfect figure, was an Oriental potentate's dream of what the harem needed.

Hearing Lady Bostock's bleating cry, she turned and stared, incredulity blended in her gaze with the natural dismay of a daughter who, having said good-bye to her mother on a Monday afternoon after entertaining her for a week at her flat, sees her come hobbling up again on Wednesday morning.

'Mother!' she exclaimed in the rich contralto which for years had been stirring up Bill Oakshott's soul like an egg whisk. 'Whatever . . .'

'Oh, dear,' said Lady Bostock. 'Have you got to go? I came up specially to see you.'

373

'I must. I'm lunching at Barribault's and I'm late already. What did you want to see me about?'

'Oh, dear, oh, dear, oh, dear. Reginald.'

'Reginald?'

'Yes, dear. Your father –'

A smouldering gleam came into Hermione's fine eyes. Those words 'Your father', taken in conjunction with the name of the man to whom she had plighted her troth, had aroused her suspicions. They could only mean, it seemed to her, that in defiance of her explicit instructions Sir Aylmer had not been treating her nominee like an ewe lamb. And she was a girl who when she said ewe lamb meant ewe lamb.

'What has Father been doing to Reginald?' she demanded sternly. 'Has he been barking at him?'

'No, no. Your father never barks. He sometimes raises his voice.'

'Has he been raising his voice, then?'

'Scarcely so that you could notice it. No, what has happened . . . Oh dear, it's such a long story.'

'Then I really can't wait to hear it now. I'm terribly late. And I'm lunching with a publisher.'

'Mr Popgood?'

Hermione laughed a short, dry laugh. In an association which had lasted three years Augustus Popgood, the sponsor of her books, had never offered her so much as a cheese straw. Nor had his partner, Cyril Grooly.

'No,' she said. 'This is a new one. He wrote to me a few days ago, saying that he would like to have me on his list and suggesting luncheon. He seems a most enterprising man, quite different from Popgood and Grooly. He is the head of a firm called Meriday House, a Mr Pointer or Punter or Painter. I couldn't make out the signature on his letter. Good-bye, mother. I'll try to get back about three.'

'I'll wait for you, dear.'

'It's something important, you say?'

'Very, very important.'

'About Reginald?'

'Yes, dear. We find that he –'

'I'm sorry, mother,' said Hermione. 'I must rush.'

She was not without a normal girl's curiosity, but she was also an ambitious young authoress who believed that there is a tide in the affairs of men which taken at the flood leads on to fortune, and there was waiting her at Barribault's Hotel a publisher who, judging from his letter, was evidently a live wire endowed with pep and ginger and all the other qualities which ambitious young authoresses like to see in those responsible for the marketing of their books.

The car moved off. Seated at the wheel, she gave herself up to agreeable thoughts about this pushful Mr Pointer.

Or Punter.

Or possibly Painter.

2

Painter was the name. Not Pointer. Not Punter. Painter. It was Sally's brother Otis who was waiting for Hermione in the lobby of Barribault's Hotel, and at the moment when her two-seater joined the stream of traffic he had sprung from his chair, too nervous to sit any longer, and begun to stride to and fro, his eyes from time to time straying to his wrist watch. The coming luncheon marked a crisis in his affairs.

It was no mere coincidence that Otis Painter, in his capacity of publisher of the book beautiful, should have written to Hermione suggesting a meeting with a view to an agreement. The invitation had been the outcome of some very rapid thinking on his part.

Right from the start it had been plain to Otis Painter that if anything like a happy ending was to be achieved in that matter of the lawsuit which was brooding over him like a thunder cloud, Sir Aylmer Bostock would have to be pleaded with, and he had told Sally to tell Pongo to perform the task. And it was while he was in the grip of that unpleasant sinking feeling which always came to those who placed their affairs in Pongo's hands that he had happened upon the issue of the *Tatler* containing Hermione's photograph.

'Miss Hermione Bostock,' he read, 'daughter of Sir Aylmer and Lady Bostock of Ashenden Manor, Hants. In addition to being prominent in Society, Miss Bostock has written several novels under the pseudonym of Gwynneth Gould.'

*

The words had brought inspiration. His thoughts, as he gazed at the photograph and the caption beneath it, had run roughly as follows. And they seem to us to display an intelligence considerably above the average of what might have been expected in one who had been in his time both an interior decorator and a seller of antiques, besides running a marionette theatre in the Boulevard Raspail.

Q. Who is the best possible person to plead with an old crumb who is threatening to bring a ruinous suit for damages against a shaky young publishing firm?

A. Obviously the crumb's daughter, the apple of his eye to whom he can refuse nothing.

Q. Get hold of the daughter, then, and enlist her in one's cause?

A. Exactly.

Q. But how?

A. Easy. She's an author. Offer her a contract. Her interest will then be identical with those of her publisher, and she will exert her tremendous influence to save him from ruin. Better ask her to lunch.

Q. Right.

A. At Barribault's.

Q. *What?* Have you ever been to Barribault's and seen the prices on the right-hand side?

A. No good spoiling the ship for a ha'porth of tar. You can't swing a deal like this on bottled beer, a mutton chop and two veg.

So now Otis was pacing Barribault's lobby, wondering why his guest did not arrive and what the lunch was going to set him back when she did. A few thoughtful words about acidity might steer her off champagne, but at a place like this even hock was likely to inflict a ghastly gash on the wallet.

Watching Otis Painter walk to and fro with his mouth ajar and his knees clashing like cymbals, for he had the misfortune to suffer from adenoids and to be knock-kneed, a spectator would have been surprised to learn that he was so closely related to Sally. But just as daughters have a way of being easier on the eye than their fathers and mothers, so are sisters frequently more attractive than their brothers. Otis was a stout young man with a pink nose, horn-rimmed spectacles and short side-whiskers, who looked like something from the Anglo-Saxon colony on the east bank of the Seine.

It was, indeed, to the east bank of the Seine that he had migrated immediately after graduating from the college where he had received his education, having sprouted a soul and the side-whiskers simultaneously towards the end of his sophomore year. From the *rive gauche* he had drifted to London, there to try various ventures with a uniform lack of success, and here he was, five years later, the directing executive of Meriday House, formerly Ye Panache Presse, waiting in Barribault's lobby to give lunch to Hermione Bostock.

The hands of his watch were pointing to twenty-seven minutes past one when through the glass of the outer door he saw the gaily apparelled official who stood on the threshold to scoop clients out of their cars and cabs suddenly stiffen himself, touch his hat convulsively and give his moustache a spasmodic twirl, sufficient indication that something pretty sensational was on its way in. And a moment later the door revolved and through it came a figure that made him catch his breath and regret that the pimple on the tip of his nose had not yielded to treatment that morning. There is nothing actually low and degrading about a pimple on the tip of the nose, but there are times when a susceptible young man wishes he did not have one.

He stepped forward devoutly.

'Miss Gould?'

'Oh, how do you do, Mr Pointer?'

'Painter.'

'Punter?'

'Painter.'

'Oh, Painter. I hope I'm not late.'

'No, no. Cocktail?'

'No, thank you. I never drink.'

Otis started. The wallet in his hip pocket seemed to give a joyful leap.

'What, not even at lunch?'

'Only lemonade.'

'Come right in,' said Otis with an enthusiasm which he made no attempt to conceal. 'Come right along in.'

He led the way buoyantly towards the grill room. Lemonade, he happened to know, was half-a-crown.

### 3

It was probably this immediate striking of the right note that made the luncheon such a success. For that it was a success not even the most exacting critic could have disputed. From the first forkful of smoked salmon it went with all the swing of a Babylonian orgy or of one of those conferences between statesmen which are conducted throughout in a spirit of the utmost cordiality.

Too often when a publisher entertains an author at the midday meal a rather sombre note tinges the table talk. The host is apt to sigh a good deal and to choose as the theme of his remarks the hardness of the times, the stagnant condition of the book trade and the growing price of pulp paper. And when his guest tries to cheer him up by suggesting that these disadvantages may be offset by a spirited policy of publicity, he sighs again and says that eulogies of an author's work displayed in the press at the publisher's expense are of little or no value, the only advertising that counts being – how shall he put it – well, what he might perhaps describe as word-of-mouth advertising.

There was nothing of that sort here today. Otis scoffed at the idea that the times were hard. The times, in his opinion, were swell. So was the book trade. Not a trace of stagnation. And as for pulp paper, you might have supposed from the way he spoke that they gave him the stuff.

He then went on to sketch out his policy as regarded advertising.

Otis, said Otis, believed in advertising. When he found an author in whom he had confidence – like you, Miss Gould, if he might say so – the sky was the limit. A column here, a column there. That sort of thing. The cost? He didn't give a darn about the cost. You got it all back on the sales. His motto, he said, coming through smoothly with the only bit of French – except *Oo-la-la* – which had managed to stick from the old left bank days, was *L'audace, l'audace, et toujours l'audace*.

It was a statement of faith well calculated to make any young authoress feel that she was floating on a pink cloud over an ocean of joy, and that was how Hermione felt as she listened. The sensation grew even more acute as her host spoke of commissioning her next three books, sight unseen, and paying royalty on them at the rate of twenty per cent, rising to twenty-five above three thousand. Even when uttered by a man with adenoids the words were like the strains of some grand anthem.

It is possible that the reader of this chronicle, misled by Bill Oakshott's enthusiasm, may have formed an erroneous idea of Hermione Bostock's standing in the world of literature, for her career had been a good deal less triumphant than he had appeared to suggest. She had published three works of fiction through the house of Popgood and Grooly, of which the first two had sold eleven hundred and four and sixteen hundred and eight copies respectively. The last, just out, was reported by Popgood, a gloomy man, to be 'moving slowly'. Grooly, the optimist of the firm, spoke in brighter vein of a possible sale of two thousand.

But even if you strung along with sunny young Grooly you could not say that figures like these were anything but a poor return for a great deal of hard toil, and Hermione attributed them not to any lack of merit in the books themselves, for she knew their merit to be considerable, but to the firm's preference for keeping its money in the old sack chest instead of spending it on advertisements in the papers. She had once taken this matter up with the partners, and Popgood had said that it was no use advertising in the papers, because the only form of advertising that counted was . . . how should he put it?

'Word of mouth?' suggested Grooly.

'Word of mouth!' assented Popgood, looking gratefully at the ingenious phrase-maker.

Little wonder, then, that as Hermione drank in Otis's intoxicating words, soft music seemed to fill the air and even the directing executive of Meriday House became almost beautiful. She listened as if in a dream, and the more he talked the more she liked it. It was only as she was sipping her coffee (two shillings, but unavoidable) that anything crept into his remarks that suggested that all was not for the best in the best of all possible worlds. Quite suddenly, after an eloquent passage surcharged with optimism, he struck a minor chord.

'Yay,' he said, 'that's how I feel. I admire your work and I would like to take hold of your books and push them as they ought to be pushed. But –'

He paused, and Hermione, descending from her pink cloud, looked at him with concern. When a publisher has offered you twenty per cent rising to twenty-five above three thousand and has been talking spaciously of column spreads in all the literate Sunday papers, you do not like to hear him use that word 'but'.

'But –?' she echoed.

Otis removed his horn-rimmed spectacles, polished them and replaced them on his nose which an excellent luncheon had turned from pink to scarlet. He also touched his pimple and polished that, and with a pudgy hand stroked his starboard whisker. The interview had reached its crux, and he wished to reflect before proceeding.

'But . . . Well, the fact is,' he said, 'there's a catch. I'm not so sure I'm going to have the money to do it with. I may go bankrupt before I can start.'

'What!'

'You see, I'm faced with a darned nasty legal action, and my lawyer tells me the damages may be very heavy.'

'But why do you speak as if you were certain to lose?'

'I am, if it ever comes into court. And I don't see how I'm going to stop it coming into court. This man Bostock –'

'Bostock?'

'Sir Aylmer Bostock. He used to be Governor of one of those African colonies, and he wrote his Reminiscences and got me to publish them –'

'But that was Ye Panache Presse.'

'I changed the name to Meriday House. Crisper. Why, say,' said Otis with natural surprise, 'you speak as if you know all about it. You do? Extraordinary how these things get around. Well, if you've heard what happened, I don't have to explain. The point is that this Bostock is showing a very vindictive spirit. And, as I say, if the thing comes into court, I shall be ruined.'

'Ah!' said Hermione.

Lord Ickenham, looking at this girl's photograph, had given it as his opinion that she was a potential eye-flasher. He had been correct. Her eyes were flashing now, and in that simple 'Ah!' there was all the sinister significance of Constable Potter's 'Ho!'

In earlier portions of this chronicle reference was made to the emotions of wolves which overtake sleighs and find no Russian peasant aboard and of tigers deprived of their Indian coolie just as they are sitting down to lunch. More poignant even than these are the feelings of a young authoress who, having just been offered twenty per cent rising to twenty-five above three thousand by a publisher who believes in column spreads in all the literate Sunday papers, learns that her father is planning to rob that publisher of the means to publish.

Hermione rose, grim and resolute.

'Don't worry, Mr Painter. I will see that the suit does not come into court.'

'Eh?'

'I ought to have told you earlier that Gwynneth Gould is merely my pen-name. I am Hermione Bostock. Sir Aylmer's daughter.'

Otis was almost too amazed for words.

'His *daughter*? Well, fancy that. Well, I'll be darned. What an extraordinary thing.'

'I will talk to Father. I will drive down and see him at once.'

'How would it be if you took me along? In case you needed help.'

'I shall not need help.'

'Still, I'd like to be on the spot, to hear the good news as soon as possible.'

'Very well. While I am seeing Father, you can wait at the inn. So if you are ready, Mr Painter, let us be going. My car is outside.'

It was as they were nearing Guildford at sixty miles an hour, for she was a girl who believed that accelerators were made to be stepped on, that a thought which for some time had been groping about the exterior of Hermione's mind, like an inebriated householder fumbling with his latch-key, suddenly succeeded in effecting an entrance, and she gave a gasp.

'Pardon?' said Otis, who also had been gasping. He was finding his companion's driving a novel and terrifying experience.

'Nothing,' said Hermione. 'Just something I happened to remember.'

It was the circumstances of her mother's visit that she had happened to remember, that devoted mother who had now been waiting three hours at her flat to tell her something about Reginald. For an instant she was conscious of a twinge of remorse. Then she told herself that Mother would be all right. She had a comfortable chair and all the illustrated papers.

She pressed her foot on the accelerator, and Otis shut his eyes and commended his soul to God.

# Chapter 11

The afternoon sun, slanting in through the French window of what until the previous night had been Pongo's bedroom, touched Sally's face and woke her from the doze into which she had fallen. She rose and stretched herself, yawning.

The French window opened on a balcony, and she eyed it wistfully. It would have been pleasant on so fine a summer day to go and sit on that balcony. But girls who are known, if only slightly, to the police must be prudent. The best she could do was to stand behind the curtain and from this observation post peer out at the green and golden world beyond.

Soon exhausting the entertainment value of a patch of gravel and part of a rhododendron bush, she was about to return to the chaise-longue, when there appeared on the patch of gravel the tall, distinguished figure of Lord Ickenham, walking jauntily and carrying a small suitcase. He passed from view, and a moment later there was a thud as the suitcase fell on the balcony.

Her heart leaped. An intelligent girl, she realized that this must mean clothes. The fifth earl might have his frivolous moments, but he was not the man to throw suitcases on to balconies in a spirit of mere wantonness. She crawled cautiously on all fours and possessed herself of the rich gift.

Her confidence had not been misplaced. It was clothes, and she hastened to put on what she recognized as a white sports dress and red jacket belonging to Lady Ickenham with all the eagerness of a girl who likes to look nice and for some little time has had to get along with a man's flowered dressing-gown. And it was as she stood examining herself contentedly in the mirror that Lord Ickenham entered.

'So you got them all right?' he said. 'Not a bad shot for a man who has jerked very little since the old soda days. But if you have once jerked soda, you never really lose the knack. I like that red coat. Rather dressy.'

Sally kissed him gratefully.

'You're an angel, Uncle Fred. Nobody saw you, I hope?'

'Not a soul. The enemy's lines were thin and poorly guarded. Your hostess went to London soon after breakfast, and Mugsy is over at a neighbouring village, trying to sell someone a cow, I understand.'

Sally started.

'Then why not do it now? Get the bust, I mean.'

'My dear child, you don't suppose that idea did not occur to me? My first move on learning that the coast was clear was to make a bee-line for the collection room, only to discover that Mugsy had locked the door and gone off with the key. As I was saying to Pongo last night, there is a streak of low cunning in Mugsy's nature which one deplores. Still, don't worry. I'm biding my time. That's the sort of man I'm, as the song says. I shall arrange everything to your full satisfaction quite shortly.'

'Says you.'

'Sally! Don't tell me you're losing confidence in me.'

'Oh, darling Uncle Fred, of course not. Why did I speak those harsh words? Consider them unsaid.'

'They are already expunged from my memory. Yes, you look charming in that coat. Quite a vision. No wonder Pongo loves you.'

'Not any more.'

'More than ever. I was noticing the way his eyes came popping out last night every time they rested on you. Did you ever see a prawn in the mating season? Like that. And one of the last things he said to me was "She looked dashed pretty in that dressing-gown." With a sort of catch in his voice. That means love.'

'If he thought I looked pretty in a dressing-gown made for a man of six feet two, it must mean something.'

'Love, my dear. Love, I tell you. All the old fervour has started gushing up again like a geyser. He worships you. He adores you. He would die for one little rose from your hair. How are conditions at your end?'

'Oh, I haven't changed.'

'You love him still?'

'I'm crazy about him.'

'That's satisfactory. Though odd. I'm very fond of Pongo. In fact, except for my wife and you and my dog, George, I can think of nobody of whom I am fonder. But I can't understand anyone being crazy about him. How do you do it?'

'It's quite easy, bless his precious heart. He's a baa-lamb.'

'You see him from that angle?'

'I always have. A sweet, woolly, baa-lamb that you want to stroke and pet.'

'Well, you may be right. You know more about baa-lambs than I do. But this is official. If I were a girl and he begged me for one little rose from my hair, I wouldn't give it him. He'd have a pretty thin time trying to get roses out of me. Still, the great thing is that you love him, because I have an idea that he will very soon be at liberty to pay his addresses to you. This engagement of his can't last.'

'You certainly do spread sweetness and light, don't you, Uncle Fred?'

'I try to.'

'Tell me more. I could listen for ever. Why do you think the engagement won't last?'

'How can it? What on earth does a girl like Hermione Bostock want to marry Pongo for?'

'Maybe she likes baa-lambs, too.'

'Nonsense. I've only seen her photograph, but I could tell at a glance that what she needs is a large, solid, worshipping husband of the huntin', shootin' and fishin' type, not a metropolitan product like Pongo. Her obvious mate is her cousin, Bill Oakshott, who has been devoted to her for years. But he's too mild in his methods. He doesn't tell his love, but lets concealment like a worm i' the bud feed on his damask cheek. You can't run a business that way. I intend to have a very serious talk with young William Oakshott next time I see him. In fact, I'll go and try to find him now.'

'No, don't go yet. I want to tell you about Pongo.'

'What about him?'

'He's worried to death, the poor pet. My heart aches for him. He was in here not long ago, and he just sat in a chair and groaned.'

'You're sure he wasn't singing?'

'I don't think so. Would he have buried his face in his hands, if he had been singing?'

'No. You're perfectly right. That is the acid test. I have heard Pongo sing on several occasions at our village concert, and it is impossible to mistake the symptoms. He sticks his chin up and throws his head back and lets it go in the direction of the ceiling at an angle of about forty-five. And very unpleasant it is, especially when the song is "Oh, My Dolores, Queen of the Eastern Sea", as too often happens. So he groaned, did he? Why?'

'He doesn't like this idea of pushing the policeman into the duck pond.'

'Doesn't *like* it? Not when he knows it's going to bring happiness and wedding bells to the divine Bean?'

'The impression he gave me was that he wasn't thinking much about the divine Bean and her wedding bells.'

'Looking at the thing principally in the light of how it was going to affect good old Twistleton?' Lord Ickenham sighed. 'Young men are not what they were in my day, Sally. We were all Galahads then. Damsels in distress had merely to press a button, and we would race up with our ears flapping, eager to do their behest. Well, we can't have him backing out. We owe a debt of honour to Miss Bean, and it must be paid. And, dash it, what's he making such heavy weather about? It isn't as if this duck pond were miles away across difficult country.'

A strange look had come into Sally's face, the sort of resolute look you might have surprised on the faces of Joan of Arc or Boadicea.

'Where is it?' she asked. 'He didn't tell me.'

'Outside the front gate. A mere step. And I was speaking to Miss Bean this morning, and she tells me that when Potter arrives there on his beat he always stands beside it for an appreciable space of time, spitting and, one hopes, thinking of her. What simpler and more agreeable task could there be than to saunter up behind a spitting policeman, at a moment when he is wrapped in thought, and push him into a pond? To further the interest of a girl like La Bean, the finest housemaid that ever flicked a duster, I would have pushed twenty policemen into twenty ponds when I was Pongo's age.'

'But Pongo has such a rare, sensitive nature.'

'So had I a rare, sensitive nature. It was the talk of New York. Well, if the thing is to be done today, he ought to be starting. It is at just about this hour, I am informed, that Potter rolls along. Where is he?'

'I don't know. He drifted out.'

'I must find him at once.'

'Just a minute,' said Sally.

The resolute expression on her face had become more noticeable than ever. In addition to looking like Joan of Arc and Boadicea, she could now have been mistaken in a dim light for Jael, the wife of Heber, and Lord Ickenham, pausing on his way to the door, was impressed and vaguely disturbed.

'What's the matter?' he asked. 'You have a strained air. You aren't worrying about Pongo?'

'Yes I am.'

'But I keep assuring you that the task before him is both simple and agreeable.'

'Not for Pongo. He's a baa-lamb. I told you that before.'

'But why should the circumstance of being a baa-lamb unfit a man for pushing policemen into ponds?'

'I don't know. But it does. I've studied this thing of pushing policemen into ponds, Uncle Fred, and I'm convinced that what you need, to get the best results, is a girl whose clothes the policeman tore off on the previous night.'

'Good God, Sally! You don't mean —?'

'Yes, I do. My mind is made up. I'm going to pinch hit for Pongo, and, if it interests you to know it, it is a far, far better thing that I do than I have ever done. Good-bye, Uncle Fred. See you later.'

She disappeared on to the balcony, and a scrabbling sound told Lord Ickenham that she was descending the water pipe. He went out, and was in time to see her vanish into the bushes on the other side of the terrace. For some moments he stood there staring after her, then with a little sigh, the sigh too often extorted from Age by the spectacle of Head-strong Youth doing its stuff, passed thoughtfully from the room. Making his way downstairs, still pensive, he reached the hall.

Bill Oakshott was there, balancing a walking stick on the tip of his nose.

2

That the young squire of Ashenden in essaying this equilibristic feat had not been animated by a mere spirit of frivolity, but was endeavouring rather, as men will in times of mental stress, to divert his thoughts from graver issues, was made clear by a certain touch of the careworn in his manner. It is not easy to look careworn when you are balancing a walking stick on the tip of your nose, but Bill Oakshott contrived to do so.

At the sight of Lord Ickenham he brightened. Ever since he had escorted Lady Bostock to Wockley Junction that morning he had been wanting to see and seek counsel from one on whose judgement he had come to rely, and owing to the fact of having been obliged to fulfil a long-standing luncheon engagement with friends who lived on the Wockley road he had had no opportunity of approaching him earlier.

'Oh, there you are,' he said. 'Fine.'

Lord Ickenham reluctantly put Sally's affairs to one side for the time being. The sight of this massive youth had reminded him that he had a pep talk to deliver.

'The word "fine,"' he replied, 'is happily chosen, for I, too, have been looking forward to this encounter. I want to speak to you, Bill Oakshott.'

'I want to speak to *you*.'

'I have much to say.'

'So have I much to say.'

'Well, if it comes to a duet, I'll bet I can talk louder and quicker than you, and I am willing to back this opinion with notes, cash or lima beans. However, as I am your guest, I suppose courtesy demands that I yield the floor. Proceed.'

Bill marshalled his thoughts.

'Well, it's like this. After breakfast this morning, I drove my aunt to Wockley to catch the express to London. I was feeling a bit tired after being up so late last night, so I didn't talk as we tootled along, just kept an eye on the road and thought of this and that.'

Lord Ickenham interrupted him.

'Skip all this part. I shall be able to read it later, no doubt, in your autobiography, in the chapter headed "Summer Morning Outings With My Aunt". Spring to the point.'

'Well, what I was going to say was that I was keeping an eye on the road and thinking of this and that, when she suddenly said "Dipsomaniac."'

'Why did she call you a dipsomaniac?'

'She didn't. It turned out she was talking about Pongo.'

'Pongo, egad? Was she, indeed?'

'Yes. She said "Dipsomaniac." And I said "Eh?" And she said "He's a dipsomaniac." And I said "Who's a dipsomaniac?" And she said "Reginald Twistleton is a dipsomaniac. Your uncle says he has not been sober since he got here."'

Lord Ickenham drew in his breath with a little hiss of admiration.

'Masterly!' he said. 'Once again, Bill Oakshott, I must pay a marked tribute to your narrative gifts. I never met a man who could tell a story better. Come clean, my boy. You *are* Sinclair Lewis, are you not? Well, I'm convinced you're someone. So your aunt said "Dipsomaniac," and you said "Eh?" and she said . . . and so forth and so on, concluding with this fearless *exposé* of Pongo. Very interesting. Did she mention on what she based the charge?'

'Oh, rather. Apparently she and Uncle Aylmer found him swigging whisky in the drawing-room.'

'I would not attach too much importance to that. Many of our noblest men swig whisky in drawing-rooms. I do myself.'

'But not all night. Well, you might say all night. What I mean is, I found Pongo in the drawing-room, swigging away, at about one o'clock this morning, and my aunt and uncle appear to have found him there, still swigging, at half-past two. That makes one and a half hours. Give him say half an hour before I came in, and you get two hours of solid swigging. And after my aunt and uncle left he must have started swigging again. Because he was unquestionably stinko after breakfast.'

'I decline to believe that anyone could get stinko at breakfast.'

'I didn't say he did get stinko at breakfast. You're missing the point. My theory is that he swigged all night, got stinko round about six a.m. and continued stinko till the incident occurred.'

'To what incident do you allude?'

'It happened just after breakfast. My aunt was waiting for me to bring the car round, and Uncle Aylmer made some unpleasant cracks about the hat she was wearing. So she went up to her room to get another, and as she reached the door she heard someone moving about inside. When she went in, there was nobody to be seen, and then suddenly there came a sneeze from the wardrobe, and there was Pongo, crouching on the floor.'

'She was sure?'

'Sure?'

'It wasn't a shoe or a bit of fluff?'

'No, it was Pongo. She says he smiled weakly and said he had looked in to borrow her lipstick. He must have been as tight as an owl. Because, apart from anything else, a glance at Aunt Emily should have told him she hasn't got a lipstick. And what I've been trying to make up my mind about is, oughtn't Hermione to be warned? Isn't it a bit thick to allow her to breeze gaily into a lifelong union with a chap who's going to spend his married life sitting up all night getting stinko in the drawing-room? I don't see how a wife could possibly be happy under such conditions.'

'She might feel rather at a loose end, might she not? But you are misjudging Pongo in considering him a non-stop swigger. As a general thing he is quite an abstemious young man. Only in exceptional circumstances does he go on anything which a purist would call a bender. At the moment he is under a severe nervous strain.'

'Why?'

'For some reason he always is when we visit a house together. My presence – it is difficult to explain it – seems to do something to him.'

'Then you don't think that Hermione ought to be told?'

'I will have to think it over. But,' said Lord Ickenham, fixing his young friend with a penetrating eye, 'there is something she must be told – without delay, and by you, Bill Oakshott.'

'Eh?'

'And that is that you love her and would make her yours.'

'Eh?'

'Fight against this tendency to keep saying "Eh." You do love her, do you not? You would make her yours, wouldn't you? I have it from an authoritative source that you have been thinking along those lines for years and years.'

Bill had turned a pretty vermilion. He shuffled his feet.

'Why, yes,' he admitted, 'that's right, as a matter of fact. I have. But how can I tell her I would make her mine? She's engaged to Pongo.'

'What of it?'

'You can't go barging in on a girl, telling her you would make her yours, when she's engaged to another chap.'

'Of course you can. How about Young Lochinvar? He did it, and was extremely highly thought of in consequence. You are familiar with the case of Young Lochinvar?'

'Oh, yes. I used to recite the poem as a kid.'

'It must have sounded wonderful,' said Lord Ickenham courteously. 'I myself was best at "It wath the thschooner Hethperuth that thailed the thtormy theas." Well, let me tell you something, my dear chap. You need have no morbid scruples about swinging Hermione Bostock on to your saddle bow, as far as Pongo is concerned. He's in love with somebody else. Do you remember me speaking at our first meeting of a girl I had been hoping he would marry? I don't think I mentioned it then, but he was at one time engaged to her, and all the symptoms point to his wanting to be again. The last time I saw them together, which was quite recently, I received the distinct impression that he would die for one little rose from her hair. So you can go ahead without a qualm. Miss Bostock is in London, I understand. Pop up there and pour your heart out.'

'M'm.'

'Why do you say "M'm"?'

Once again Bill Oakshott shuffled his feet, producing on the parquet floor a sound resembling waves breaking on a stern and rockbound coast.

'It's so difficult.'

'What, to pour out your heart? Nonsense.'

'Well, I've been trying to do it for nine years, but not a ripple. I can't seem to get started.'

Lord Ickenham reflected.

'I think I see where the trouble lies. You have made the mistake of brooding in advance too much, with the result that you have pottered about and accomplished nothing. Swiftness and decision are what is needed. Don't hesitate. Have at her. Sweep her off her feet. Take her by storm.'

'Oh, yes?' said Bill flatly, and Lord Ickenham laid a kindly hand on his shoulder. He knew what was passing in the young man's mind.

'I can understand your feeling a little nervous,' he said. 'When I saw Hermione Bostock's photograph, I was struck at once by something formidable in her face, a touch of that majestic inaccessibility which used to cramp the style of diffident young Greek shepherds in their relations with the more dignified of the goddesses of Mount Olympus. She is what in my day would have been called a proud beauty. And that makes it all the more necessary to take a strong line from the start. Proud beauties have to be dominated.'

'But, dash it, Pongo can't have dominated her.'

'True. But Pongo, so I am informed, is a baa-lamb. Baa-lambs get their results by different methods.'

'You don't think I'm a baa-lamb?'

'I fear not. You're too large, too robust and ruddy of countenance, too obviously a man who does his daily dozen of a morning and likes roly-poly pudding for lunch. Where a Pongo can click by looking fragile and stammering words of endearment, you must be the whirlwind wooer, or nothing. You will have to behave like the heroes of those novels which were so popular at one time, who went about in riding breeches and were not above giving the girl of their choice a couple with a hunting-crop on the spot where it would do most good. Ethel M. Dell. That's the name I was trying to think of. You must comport yourself like the hero of an Ethel M. Dell novel. Buy her works, and study them diligently.'

A firm look came into Bill's face.

'I'm not going to sock her with a hunting-crop.'

'It would help.'

'No. Definitely no.'

'Very well. Cut business with hunting-crop. Then what you must do is stride up to the girl and grab her by the wrist.'

'Oh, gosh!'

'Ignoring her struggles, clasp her to your bosom and shower kisses on her upturned face. You needn't say much. Just "My mate!" or something of that sort. Well, think it over, my dear fellow. But I can assure you that this method will bring home the bacon. It is known as the Ickenham system, and it never fails. And now I fear I must be leaving you. I'm looking for Pongo. You don't happen to know where he is?'

'I saw him half an hour ago walking up and down on the tennis lawn.'

'With bowed head?'

'Yes, I believe his head was bowed, now you mention it.'

'I thought as much. Poor lad, poor lad. Well, I have tidings for him which will bring him up with a jerk. So good-bye for the moment. Oh, by the way,' said Lord Ickenham, reappearing like a benevolent Cheshire cat, 'in grabbing the subject by the wrist, don't behave as if you were handling a delicate piece of china. Grip firmly and waggle her about a bit.'

He disappeared again, and Bill could hear him trolling an old love song of the early nineteen hundreds as he started for the tennis lawn.

## 3

On a shy and diffident young man, accustomed for years just to shuffle his feet and look popeyed when in the presence of the girl he loves, a pep talk along the lines of that delivered by Lord Ickenham has much the same effect as a plunge into icy water on a cold morning. First comes the numbing shock, when everything turns black and the foundations of the soul seem to start reeling. Only later does there follow the glowing reaction.

For some appreciable time after his mentor had taken his departure, Bill stood congealed with horror as he contemplated the picture which the other had limned for him. The thought of showering kisses on Hermione Bostock's upturned face set his spine crawling like something in the Snake House at the Zoo. The idea of grabbing her by the wrist and waggling her about a bit made him feel as he had once felt at his private school after eating six ice-creams in a quarter of an hour because somebody bet him he wouldn't.

And then suddenly, with considerable astonishment, he found that horror had given way to a strange exhilaration. He could now appreciate the solid merits of this Ickenham system, chief among which was the fact that it placed the wooing of Hermione Bostock on the plane of physical action. Physical action was his dish. Give him something to do with his hands, and he knew where he was.

So simple, too. Nothing intricate or elaborate about it. Run over it once more, just to make sure one hadn't forgotten anything.

Stride up and grab?

Easy.

Waggle about?

Pie.

Clasp to bosom and s.k. on upturned f.?

No difficulty there.

Say 'My mate'?

About that he was not so sure. It seemed to him that Lord Ickenham, brilliant as an arranger of stage business, had gone astray as regarded dialogue. Wouldn't a fellow be apt to feel a bit of a chump, saying 'My mate'? Better, surely, just to pant a good deal? Yes, that was the stuff. Stride, grab, waggle, clasp, kiss, pant. Right.

Under the stress of intense thought he had started to walk up and down the hall, his head bent over the fingers on which he was ticking off the various items on the list, and it was as he unconsciously accelerated his pace on getting that inspiration about panting that a bumping sensation and a loud roar of anguish told him that there had been a traffic accident.

Narrowing his gaze, he saw that he had rammed something substantial and white moustached, and narrowing it still further identified this as his uncle. Sir Aylmer Bostock. And he was about to offer suitable apologies, when all thought of injured uncles was wiped from his mind and his heart leaped within him like an adagio dancer trying out a new step. Behind Sir Aylmer, looking more unbelievably beautiful even than he had remembered her, stood Hermione.

Hermione smiled upon him dazzlingly. She was in the sunniest of moods. After dropping Otis at the Bull's Head in the High Street, she had arrived at the front door just in time to see her father driving up, and such was the force of her personality that she had settled that little matter of the proposed legal action of Bostock *v.* Painter in something under two minutes and a quarter. The future of the publishing firm of Meriday House, in so far as concerned civil actions on the part of the late Governor of Lower Barnatoland, was secure.

So she smiled dazzlingly. In an amused, sisterly way she had always been devoted to dear old Bill, and she was glad to see him again.

'Hullo, Bill,' she said.

Bill found speech.

'Oh, hullo, Hermione.'

Sir Aylmer also found speech.

'What the devil are you doing, you great clumsy oaf,' he said, standing on one leg and submitting the other to a system of massage, for the impact had been severe. 'Charging about the place like a damned rhinoceros. Why can't you look where you're going?'

Bill was staring at Hermione. In a dim way he was aware that words were proceeding from this old blighter, but he was unable to concentrate on their import.

'Oh, rather,' he said.

'What do you mean, oh, rather?'

'Yes, isn't it?' said Bill.

To a man who was good at snorting and to whom snorts came easily there was only one answer to this sort of thing. Sir Aylmer snorted, and stumped into the collection room, telling himself that he would go into the matter later on when his nephew seemed more in the mood. Useless to waste good stuff on one who, always deficient in intellect, seemed now to be suffering from some form of mental paralysis.

Hermione continued cordial.

'So you're back, Bill. It's jolly seeing you again. How was Brazil?'

'Oh, fine.'

'Have a good time?'

'Oh, yes, fine, thanks.'

'You're very sunburned. I suppose you had lots of adventures?'

'Oh, rather.'

'Snakes and so on?'

'Oh, yes.'

'Well, you must tell me all about it later. I've got to hurry off now. I have to see a friend of mine at the inn.'

Bill cleared his throat.

'Er – just a second,' he said.

This, he was telling himself, was the moment. Now, if ever, was his opportunity of putting the Ickenham system into practice. Here they were, alone together. A single stride would place him in a position to grab. And he was already panting. More ideal conditions could scarcely have been asked for.

But he found himself unable to move. All through those weary months in Brazil the image of this girl had been constantly before his mental eye, but now that he was seeing her face to face her beauty numbed him, causing trembling of the limbs and that general feeling of debility and run-down-ness which afflicts so many people nowadays and can be corrected only by the use of such specifics as Buck-u-Uppo or Doctor Smythe's Tonic Swamp Juice.

Had he had a bottle – nay, even a tablespoonful – of the tonic swamp juice handy, all might have been well. Lacking it, he merely shuffled his feet and looked popeyed, just as he had been doing for the last nine years.

'Well?' said Hermione.

('Stride, grab, waggle, clasp, kiss, pant,' urged Bill's better self. But his limbs refused to move.)

'Well?'

'Hermione.'

'Yes?'

'Hermione.'

'Well?'

'Oh, nothing,' said Bill.

He found himself alone. From outside came the sound of a car getting into gear and moving off. She had gone.

Nor could he blame her. Reviewing the late scene, recalling that horrible, bleating voice with its hideous resemblance to that of a BBC announcer, he shuddered, marvelling that any being erect upon two legs and bearing the outward semblance of a man could have shown himself so wormlike a poltroon.

Writing in anguish, he thought for a moment of bumping his head against the wall, but on reflection decided against this. No sense in dinting a good wall. Better to go to his room, fling himself on the bed and bury his face in the pillow. He did so.

4

Anxious to get to the Bull's Head and inform Otis as soon as possible of the happy outcome of her interview with her father, Hermione had started up her car and driven off with the minimum of delay. Had she postponed her departure for as long as a minute, she would have observed a wild-eyed young man without a hat making for the house from the direction of the tennis lawn at a feverish canter, his aspect that of a young man who has taken something big. Once before in the course of this chronicle we have heard Reginald Twistleton compared to a cat on hot bricks. It was of a cat on hot bricks that he would have reminded an onlooker now.

Skimming across the terrace, he reached the house and plunged over the threshold. Skimming across the hall, he flew up the stairs. Skimming along the first-floor corridor, he burst into what had formerly been his bedroom, and Sally, who was reclining on the chaise-longue like an Amazon resting after an important battle, rose as he entered. Indeed, she shot up as if a gimlet had suddenly penetrated the cushions and embedded itself in her person. She was a girl of poise, who did not easily lose command of herself, but after pushing policemen into ponds even girls of poise experience a certain tautness of the nerves, and the abrupt opening of the door had given her a momentary impression that here came Constable Potter.

Recognizing her visitor, she became calmer, though still inclined to gasp.

'Oh, Pongo!' she said.

'Oh, Sally!' said Pongo.

To say that the story which Lord Ickenham had related to him on the tennis lawn, before going off to the Bull's Head for a drop of beer and a chat with the boys about Brazil, had stirred Reginald Twistleton would be to indicate but feebly the turmoil which it had created in his bosom. It had caused him to run what is known as the gamut of the emotions, prominent among them gratitude to a girl who could thus risk all on his behalf, shame that his own pusillanimity had rendered her stupendous act of heroism necessary and, above all, a surge of love such as he had never felt before – and he had been falling in love with fair regularity ever since his last summer but one at Eton.

His honourable obligations to Hermione Bostock had passed completely from his mind. He had no other thought than to find Sally and notify her of the trend of his views. Precisely as Bill Oakshott had done, he contemplated a future in which he would stride, grab and waggle, clasp, kiss and pant. With this difference, that whereas Bill, as we have seen, had planned to behave like an osteopath handling a refractory patient, he, Pongo, saw the set-up more in the light of abasing himself at a shrine. The word 'grab' is wrong. So is the word 'waggle'. But 'clasp', 'kiss' and 'pant' may stand.

He was panting now, and he lost no time in proceeding to the other items on the programme which he had sketched out. Bill Oakshott, had he been present, would have received a valuable object lesson on how this sort of thing should be done.

'Oh, Sally!' he said.

'Oh, Pongo!' said Sally.

Time stood still. In the world outside people were going about their various occupations. Constable Potter was in his cottage, changing into a dry uniform. Lord Ickenham, humming a gay stave, was striding along the road to the village. Hermione, half a mile ahead of him, was driving along the same road. Sir Aylmer was messing about with his African curios. Bill Oakshott was burying his face in his pillow. And up in London Lady Bostock, in her daughter's flat, had finished the illustrated papers and fallen into a light doze.

But Pongo and Sally were alone together in a world of their own, enjoying the scent of the violets and roses which sprouted through the bedroom floor and listening to the soft music which an orchestra of exceptional ability, consisting chiefly of harps and violins, was playing near at hand. Of Constable Potter, of Lord Ickenham, of Sir Aylmer Bostock, of Lady Bostock, of Bill Oakshott and of

Hermione they recked nothing; though the time was to come when they, particularly Pongo, would be obliged to reck of the last named quite a good deal.

Presently Pongo, adjusting his arm more comfortably about Sally's waist, for they were now sitting side by side on the chaise-longue, began to speak remorsefully of the past, featuring in his observations the criminal idiocy of the oaf Twistleton, that abysmal sap who had allowed himself to be parted from the only girl on earth whom a discriminating man could possibly wish to marry. He contemplated with unconcealed aversion this mutton-headed Twistleton.

'Gosh, what a chump I was!'

'Not such a chump as me.'

'Much more of a chump than you. No comparison.'

'It was all my fault.'

'No, it wasn't.'

'Yes, it was.'

'It wasn't.'

'It was.'

The dispute threatened to become heated, but just as Pongo was about to say 'It wasn't' again he suddenly paused, and into his sensitive features there crept that look of horror and apprehension which they had worn fourteen hours earlier, on the occasion when Bill Oakshott's knocking had sounded in the silent night.

'What's the matter, precious?' asked Sally solicitously.

Pongo gulped.

'Oh, nothing. At least, nothing much, I just happened to think of Hermione.'

There was a pause. A quick twinge of anxiety and alarm shot through Sally. Much – indeed, her life's happiness – depended on the exact extent to which the Twistletons regarded their word as their bond.

'Oh, Hermione?' she said. 'You don't mean you're too honourable to break off the engagement?'

Pongo gulped again.

'Not too honourable exactly, but . . . You've never met Hermione, have you? Well, it's difficult to explain, but she isn't a frightfully easy girl to break off engagements with. It's a little hard to know how to start.'

'I should just go to her and tell her frankly that you find you have made a mistake.'

'Yes, that's one way.'

'Or you could write her a letter.'

Pongo gave a start, like some strong swimmer in his agony who hears a splash and observes that somebody has thrown him a lifebelt.

'A letter?'

'You might find it less embarrassing.'

'I might,' said Pongo, and, quivering with gratitude to his helpmeet for her timely suggestion, he clasped her to his bosom and showered kisses on her upturned face.

This would probably have gone on for some time, had not Elsie Bean at this moment entered softly with a tray in her hands containing a tea-pot, a cup, some slices of buttered toast and a piece of cake.

'Tea,' said Elsie, and Pongo, soaring ceilingwards, came down and regarded her wrathfully.

'Why the dickens can't you blow your horn?' he demanded with a good deal of heat.

Elsie remained unmoved. The passionate scene which she had interrupted had made little impression upon her. It was the sort of thing that was happening all the time in Bottleton East.

'Tea, toast and a bit-er-cake,' she said. 'Have you pushed Harold into the pond yet, Mr Twistleton?'

Sally took charge of the situation in her competent way.

'Of course he has pushed him into the pond. He said he would, didn't he? You don't suppose Mr Twistleton would fail you?'

'Did he go in with a splash?'

'With a terrific splash. You could hear it for miles.'

'Coo. Well, I'm sure I'm very much obliged to you, Mr Twistleton. Have you seen Miss Hermione?'

Pongo leaped an inch or two.

'She isn't here?'

'Yes, she is. I saw her drive up in her car.'

Pongo remained silent for a space. He was clutching his head.

'I think I'll go and walk up and down on the tennis lawn for a while,' he said. 'This wants brooding over.'

With a brief groan he left the room, once more with that suggestion in his manner of a cat on hot bricks, and Elsie followed him with a critical eye.

'Nice young gentleman, Mr Twistleton,' she said. 'A bit barmy, isn't he?'

'A bit,' agreed Sally. 'I love it.'

5

The Bull's Head was still standing in its old place in the High Street when Hermione drove up, but Otis was no longer on the premises. She was informed that he had stepped out some little time previously, but whither he had stepped was not known. Annoyed, for no girl bringing the good news from Aix to Ghent likes to find Ghent empty when she gets there, Hermione returned to her two-seater and started to drive back along the road by which she had come. It had occurred to her that, now that she was in the Ashenden Manor neighbourhood, she ought to take the opportunity of exchanging a few words with her betrothed. It was the first time since lunch that she had given him a thought.

But her annoyance did not last long, nor did the desire to seek out Pongo. She had just reached the first milestone when something seemed to hit her between the eyes. It felt like a thunderbolt, but actually it was the central idea for the first of that series of three novels at twenty per cent rising to twenty-five above three thousand which Otis Painter would now be in a position to publish. This sort of thing is always happening to authors. They are driving along or walking along or possibly just sitting in a chair, their minds a blank, when all of a sudden – *bing*.

And the first thing an author learns is that it is fatal on these occasions to pigeon-hole the inspiration away at the back of the mind, trusting that memory will produce it when required. Notes must be made immediately. Drawing up her two-seater at the side of the road, Hermione found an old envelope and began to write. She wrote rapidly, breathing tensely through the nose.

At about the same moment Lord Ickenham reached the Bull's Head and turned in at the door of the saloon bar.

## 6

It was with the easy assurance of one confident of his welcome that Lord Ickenham entered the saloon bar, for on his previous visit there he had had an outstanding social success. The stout blonde behind the counter, her uncle the landlord (Jno. Humphreys, licensed to sell ales, wines and spirits) and quite a number of the inn's clients had hung upon his lips. It is not often given to the natives of remote Hampshire hamlets to sit at the feet of a man who knows Brazil like the back of his hand, who has looked his alligator in the eye and made it wilt and who can talk of his adventures fluently and well.

To-day he saw that his audience was to be smaller. Indeed, at the moment only the barmaid was present. He seemed to have struck one of those slack periods which come to all saloon bars. With the best will in the world English villagers cannot be drinking all the time, and this appeared to be one of the times when those of Ashenden Oakshott had decided to allow their gullets a brief respite, no doubt on the *reculer pour mieux sauter* principle.

But your true artist will always give of his best, however thin the house. As Lord Ickenham placed an elbow on the counter and requested the stout blonde to start pouring, there was no suggestion in his manner that he was going to walk through his part. He resumed his saga of life on the Lower Amazon as if he had been addressing a crowded hall, and the barmaid listened with all the impressment which she had shown on the previous day.

'Well, I do call that a pity,' she said, as he paused for an instant to raise his tankard.

'A pity?' said Lord Ickenham, a little hurt, for he had been speaking of the occasion when a puma had only just failed to add him to its bill of fare. 'Ah, I see. You are looking at the incident from the puma's view-point, and your womanly sympathy has been aroused by its failure to get the square meal for which it had been budgeting. Yes, it was tough on the puma. I remember noticing at the time that the animal's eyes were wet with unshed tears.'

'A pity you should have missed that gentleman, I mean. There was a gentleman in here for a quick one not five minutes ago,' explained the barmaid, 'who was telling me he had just come from Brazil. He'd have liked to meet you.'

Lord Ickenham gave her to understand that this was an almost universal aspiration on the part of his fellow men, but privately he was relieved that he had not arrived five minutes earlier. In his present rather delicate circumstances he greatly preferred to avoid gentlemen who had just come from Brazil.

'Too bad,' he said. 'One of the boys, eh? It would have been delightful to have got together and swapped yarns.'

'Why, here he is,' said the barmaid.

The door had opened, revealing an elderly man of square build with a pugnacious, sunburned face. Such was the excellence of the Bull's Head beer that those who went out after having a quick one nearly always came homing back again to have another.

'This is the gentleman I was speaking of. Excuse me, sir,' said the barmaid, addressing the gentleman, who had approached the counter and placed an elbow on it and was now licking his lips in quiet anticipation, 'here's a gentleman you ought to know, you being from Brazil. He knows more about Brazil than you could shake a stick at. Major Plank, the great explorer.'

At this moment a voice from without, recognizable as that of Jno. Humphreys, licensed to sell ales, wines and spirits, made itself heard. It was bellowing 'Myrtle,' and the barmaid, whose parents had inflicted that name on her, vanished with a brief 'Excuse me.' The voice had been urgent, and it was evident that stern experience had taught this niece that her uncle Jno. was a man who did not like to be kept waiting.

'Tell him about the puma, Major Plank,' she said, pausing for an instant in her flight.

Normally, Lord Ickenham would have done this without delay, for he enjoyed telling people about pumas and knew that he was good at it. But one of the things which a man of the world learns early in his career is that there are times when it is best to keep silent on the subject of these fascinating fauna. The gentleman was looking at him fixedly, and in his eye there was no spark of the encouraging light which indicates a willingness to be informed about pumas. There have been some bleak and fishy eyes scattered through this chronicle – those of Coggs, the butler at Ickenham Hall, spring to the mind – but none bleaker and fishier than the gentleman's at this juncture.

'Plank?' he said, speaking raspingly. 'Did I hear her call you Major Plank?'

'That's right,' said Lord Ickenham. 'Major Plank.'

'Are you Major Brabazon-Plank, the explorer?'

'I am.'

'So am I,' said the gentleman, evidently rather impressed by the odd coincidence.

## Chapter 12

When two strong men stand face to face, each claiming to be Major Brabazon-Plank, it is inevitable that there will be a sense of strain, resulting in a momentary silence. There was on this occasion. Lord Ickenham was the first to speak.

'Oh, are you?' he said. 'Then you owe me two bob.'

His companion blinked. The turn the conversation had taken seemed to have surprised him.

'Two bob?'

'If you have nothing but large bills, I can give you change.'

Major Plank's mahogany face took on a richer hue.

'What the devil are you talking about?'

'Two bob.'

'Are you crazy?'

'It is a point on which opinions differ. Some say yes. I maintain no. Two bob,' said Lord Ickenham patiently. 'It is useless for you to pretend that you do not owe me that sum, Bimbo. You took it off me forty-three years ago as we were crossing the cricket field one lovely summer evening. "Barmy," you said, "would you like to lend me two bob?" And I said "No, but I suppose I'll have to," and the money changed hands.'

Major Plank clutched the counter.

'Bimbo? Barmy? Cricket field?' He stared with terrific concentration, and his face suddenly cleared. 'Good God! You're Barmy Twistleton.'

'I was in those days, but I've come on a lot since then, Bimbo. You see before you Frederick Altamont Cornwallis, fifth Earl of Ickenham, and one of the hottest earls that ever donned a coronet. The boy you knew as a wretched Hon. is now a peer of the realm, looked up to like the dickens by one and all. Just mention to anyone that you know Lord Ickenham, and they'll fawn on you and stand you lunch.'

Major Plank took an absent sip from the tankard.

'Barmy Twistleton!' he murmured. It was plain that the encounter had affected him greatly. 'But why did you tell that girl you were me?'

'One has to say something to keep the conversation going.'

'Barmy Twistleton. Well, I'll be damned. After all these years. I wouldn't have recognized you.'

'Exactly what Mugsy Bostock said when we met. You remember Mugsy Bostock? Did you know that he lived in these parts?'

'I knew his nephew, Bill Oakshott, did. I motored down to see him.'

'You aren't on your way to Ashenden Manor?'

'Yes.'

'Turn round and go back, Bimbo,' said Lord Ickenham, patting his shoulder kindly. 'You must not visit Ashenden Manor.'

'Why not?'

'Because I am already in residence there under your name. It would confuse Mugsy and give him a headache if he were confronted with a couple of us. No doubt you will say that you can't have too many Brabazon-Planks about the home, but Mugsy wouldn't look at it that way. He would get bewildered and fret.'

Major Plank took another sip at the tankard, and when Lord Ickenham mentioned that he had paid for its contents and that if his old friend proposed to treat it as a loving cup he would be obliged to charge him a small fee, seemed disinclined to go into the matter. It was the earlier portion of the conversation that was engaging his mind.

'You're staying with Mugsy under my name?'

'Exactly.'

'He thinks you're me?'

'Precisely.'

'Why?' said Major Plank, going right to the core of the problem. 'Why are you staying with Mugsy under my name?'

'It's a long story, Bimbo, and would bore you. But have no uneasiness. Just say to yourself "Would my old crony do this without a motive?" and "Is his motive bound to be a good one?" The answers to these questions are "No" to the first, "Yes" to the second.'

Major Plank relapsed into a sandbagged silence. His was a slow mind, and you could almost hear it creaking as it worked.

'Good God!' he said again.

And then abruptly the full horror of the situation seemed to come home to him. No doubt he had been diving into the past and had brought memories of the boy Twistleton to the surface. It was not for nothing that this man before him had been called 'Barmy' at school. He had applied himself absently to the tankard once more, and his eyes above it suddenly grew round and wrathful.

'What the devil do you mean by staying with people under my name?'

'It's a good name, Bimbo. Got a hyphen and everything.'

'You'll ruin my reputation.'

'On the contrary. The image which I have been building up in the minds of all and sundry is that of what I should describe as a super-Plank or Plank *plus*. You ought to think yourself lucky that a man like me has gone out of his way to shed lustre on your name.'

'Well, I don't. So you had better get back to Mugsy's and start packing, quick. Because as soon as I've had some more of this excellent beer I'm coming up there to expose you.'

'Expose me?' Lord Ickenham's eyebrows rose reproachfully. 'Your old friend?'

'Old friend be damned.'

'A fellow you used to throw inked darts at?'

'Inked darts have nothing to do with the case.'

'And who once lent you two bob?'

'Curse the two bob.'

'You're a hard man, Bimbo.'

'No, I'm not. I've a right to think of my reputation.'

'I have already assured you that it is in safe hands.'

'God knows, what you may not have been up to. If I don't act like lightning, my name will be mud. Listen,' said Major Plank, consulting his watch. 'I shall start exposing you at five sharp. That gives you twenty-three minutes. Better look slippy.'

Lord Ickenham did not look slippy. He stood regarding the friend of his youth with the same gentle commiseration which he had displayed when dealing, in somewhat similar circumstances, with Constable Potter. Essentially kind-hearted, he disliked being compelled to thwart these eager spirits who spoke so hopefully of exposing him. But it had to be done, so with a sigh he embarked on the distasteful task.

'Dismiss all ideas of that sort from your mind, Bimbo. It is hopeless for you to dream of exposing me. Bill Oakshott has told me all about you.'

'What do you mean?'

'You are a man with an Achilles heel, a man with a fatal chink in your armour. You suffer from a strongly marked baby phobia. If anyone points a baby at you, Bill tells me, you run like a rabbit. Well, if you betray my little secret to Mugsy, you will immediately find yourself plunging into a foaming sea of them. A fête is taking place here shortly, and among its numerous features is a contest for bonny babies. And here is the point. In my capacity of Major Brabazon-Plank I have undertaken to act as judge of it. You begin to see the hideous peril confronting you? Eliminate me, and you automatically step into my place.'

'Why?'

'Because, my dear fellow, some variety of Brabazon-Plank has got to judge those bonny babies. This has been officially announced and the whole village is agog. And after my departure you will be the only Brabazon-Plank available. And if you imagine that Mugsy, a determined man, and his wife, a still more determined woman, will let you sneak away, you are living in a fool's paradise. You haven't a hope, Bimbo. You will be for it.'

His pitiless clarity had its effect. Major Plank's tan was so deep that it was impossible to say whether or not he paled beneath it, but he shuddered violently and in his eyes was the look that comes into the eyes of men who peer into frightful abysses.

'Why don't they get the curate to do it?' he cried, plainly struggling with a strong sense of grievance. 'When we had these damned baby competitions at Lower Shagley, it was always the curate who judged them. It's what curates are for.'

'The curate has got measles.'

'Silly ass.'

'An unsympathetic thing to say of a man who is lying on a bed of pain with pink spots all over him, but I can make allowances for your feelings, appreciating how bitter a moment this must be for you, my poor old Bimbo. I suppose there is nothing much more sickening than wanting to expose a fellow and not being able to, and I would love to help you out if I could. But I really don't know what to suggest. You might . . . No, that's no good. Or . . . No, I doubt if that would work, either. I'm afraid you will have to give up the idea. The only poor consolation I can offer you is that it will be all the same in another hundred years. Well, my dear chap, it's been delightful running into you again after all this time, and I wish I could stay and chat, but I fear I must be pushing along. You know how busy we Brabazon-Planks always are. Look me up some time at my residence, which is quite near here, and we will have a long talk about the old school days and Brazil and, of course,' said Lord Ickenham indulgently, 'any other subject you may wish to discuss. If you can raise it by then, bring the two bob with you.'

With another kindly pat on the shoulder he went out, and Major Plank, breathing heavily, reached for the tankard and finished its contents.

2

The plot of Hermione's novel was coming out well. As so often happens when an author gets the central idea for a story and starts to jot it down, all sorts of supplementary ideas had come trooping along, demanding to be jotted down too. It was not many minutes before the envelope proved quite inadequate to contain the golden thoughts which were jostling one another in her brain, and she had just started to use the back of her motor licence when, looking up, she perceived approaching an elderly man of distinguished appearance, who raised his hat with an old-world polish.

'Good afternoon,' he said.

In this lax age in which we live, it not infrequently happens to girls of challenging beauty to find themselves approached by hat-raising strangers of the opposite sex. When Hermione Bostock had this experience, her manner was apt to become a little brusque, so much so that the party of the second part generally tottered off feeling as if he had incurred the displeasure of a wild cat. It is a tribute, therefore, to Lord Ickenham's essential respectability that he gave her pause. Her eyebrows quivered slightly, as if about to rise, but she made no move to shoot the works.

'Miss Bostock, I believe? My name is Brabazon-Plank. I am a guest at your father's house.'

This, of course, made it all quite different. One of the gang. Hermione became cordial.

'Oh, how do you do?'

'How do you do? Could you spare me a moment?'

'Why, of course. How odd that you should have known who I was.'

'Not at all. Yours, if I may say so, are features which, once seen, cannot be forgotten. I have had the privilege of studying a photograph of you.'

'Oh, yes, the one in the *Tatler*.'

'Not the one in the *Tatler*. The one which your cousin, William Oakshott, carries always next to his heart. I should explain,' said Lord Ickenham, 'that I was the leader of the expedition up the Amazon of which Bill Oakshott was so prominent a member, and every time he got a touch of fever he would pull your photograph out and kiss it, murmuring in a faint voice "I love her, I love her, I love her." Very touching, I thought it, and so did all the rest of the personnel of the expedition. It made us feel finer, better men.'

Hermione was staring. Had she been a less beautiful girl, it might have been said that she goggled. This revelation of a passion which she had never so much as suspected had come as a complete surprise. Looking on Bill as a sort of brother, she had always supposed that he looked on her as a sort of sister. It was as if she had lived for years beside some gentle English hill and suddenly discovered one morning that it was a volcano full to the brim of molten lava.

'And don't get the idea,' proceeded Lord Ickenham, 'that he spoke thus only when running a temperature. It was rare for half an hour to pass without him whipping out your photograph and kissing it. So you see he did not forget you while he was away, as so many young men are apt, once they are abroad, to forget the girl to whom they are engaged. His heart was always true. For when he said "I love her, I love her, I love her," it seemed to me that there was only one construction that could be placed on his remarks. He meant that he loved you. And may I be allowed to say,' went on Lord Ickenham with a paternal smile, 'how delighted I am to meet you at last and to see at a glance that you are just the girl for him. This engagement makes me very happy.'

'But –'

'He will be getting a prize. And so, my dear, will you. I know few men whom I respect more than William Oakshott. Of all my circle he is the one I would choose first to be at my side in the event of unpleasantness with an alligator. And while it may be argued, and with perfect justice, that the part which alligators play in the average normal married life is not a large one, it is no bad thing for a girl to have a husband capable of putting them in their place. The man who can prop an alligator's jaws open with a stick and then, avoiding its lashing tail, dispatch it with a meat axe is a man who can be trusted to help fire the cook. So no one will rejoice more heartily than I when the bells ring out in the little village church and you come tripping down the aisle on Bill Oakshott's sinewy arm. This will happen very shortly, I suppose, now that he is back with you once more?'

He paused, beaming benevolently, and Hermione, who had made several attempts to speak, at last found herself able to do so.

'But I am not engaged to Bill.'

'Nonsense. You must be. How about all that "I love her, I love her, I love her" stuff?'

'I am engaged to someone else. If you are staying at the house, you will have met him.'

Lord Ickenham gasped.

'Not the pinhead Twistleton?'

Something of the chill which hat-raising strangers usually induced crept into Hermione's manner.

'His name is Reginald Twistleton,' she said, allowing her eyes to flash for a moment. 'I am sorry you consider him a pinhead.'

'My dear girl, it isn't that I consider him a pinhead. Everyone considers him a pinhead. Walk into any gathering where he is a familiar figure and say to the first man you meet, "Do you know Reginald Twistleton?" and his reply, will be, "Oh, you mean the pinhead?" Good heavens, child, you musn't dream of marrying Reginald Twistleton. Even had you not a Bill Oakshott on your waiting list, it would be madness. How could you be happy with a man who is always getting arrested at dog races?'

'What!'

'Incessantly, you might say. *And* giving a false name and address.'

'You're talking nonsense.'

'My dear, these are well-documented facts. If you don't believe me, creep up behind this young Twistleton and shout "Yoo-hoo, Edwin Smith, 11, Nasturtium Road, East Dulwich!" in his ear and watch him jump. Well, I don't know what you think, but to my mind there is something not very nice in going to dog races at all, for the people you meet there must be very mixed. But if a young man does go to dog races, I maintain that the least he can do is to keep from behaving in so disorderly a manner that he gets scooped in by the constabulary. And if you are going to try to excuse this Twistleton on the ground that he was intoxicated at the time, I can only say that I am unable to share your broad-minded outlook. No doubt he was intoxicated, but I can't see that that makes it any better. You knew, by the way, I suppose, that he is a dipsomaniac?'

'A *what?*'

'So your father tells me.'

'But Reginald is a teetotaller.'

'While your eye is on him, perhaps. But only then. At other times he shifts the stuff like a vacuum cleaner. You should have been here last night. He stole down when everyone was in bed and threw a regular orgy.'

Hermione had been intending to put an end to this conversation by throwing in her clutch and driving off with a stiff word of farewell, but now she saw that she would have to start later. A girl who has been looking on the man of her choice as a pure white soul and suddenly discovers that he is about as pure and white as a stevedore's undervest does not say 'Oh, yes? Well, I must be off.' She sits rigid. She gasps. She waits for more.

'Tell me everything,' she said.

As Lord Ickenham proceeded to do so, the grim expression on Hermione Bostock's lovely face become intensified. If there is one thing a girl of ideals dislikes, it is to learn that she has been nursing a viper in her bosom, and that Reginald Twistleton was a Grade A viper, with all the run-of-the-mill viper's lack of frankness and square shooting, seemed more manifest with every word that was spoken.

'Oh!' she said.

'*Well!*' she said.

'Go on,' she said.

The story wore to its conclusion. Lord Ickenham ceased to speak, and Hermione sat gazing before her with eyes of stone. She was doing something odd with her teeth which may have been that 'grinding' we read about.

'Of course,' said Lord Ickenham, ever charitable, 'he may simply be off his head. I don't know if you know anything of his family history, but he tells me he is the nephew of Lord Ickenham; a fact, surely, that makes one purse the lips dubiously. Do you know Lord Ickenham?'

'Only by reputation.'

'And what a reputation! There is a strong body of opinion which holds that he ought to have been certified years ago. I understand he is always getting flattering offers from Colney Hatch and similar establishments. And insanity so often runs in families. When I first met this young man Twistleton, I received a distinct impression that he was within a short jump of the loony bin, and that curious incident this morning, of which Bill Oakshott was telling me, has strengthened this view.'

Hermione quivered. She had not supposed that there was to be an Act Two.

'Curious incident?'

'It took place shortly after breakfast. Lady Bostock, going to her room, heard movements within, looked in the wardrobe and found Reginald Twistleton in it, crouching on the floor. His explanation was that he had come to borrow her lipstick.'

Hermione gripped her motor licence till the knuckles stood out white under the strain. Act One had stirred her profoundly, but Act Two had topped it.

In speaking of the dislike which high-principled girls have for vipers, we omitted to mention that it becomes still more pronounced when they discover that they use lipstick. That this erstwhile idol of hers should have feet of clay was bad, but that in addition to those feet of clay he should have, at the other end, a mouth that apparently needed touching up from time to time was the pay-off. People still speak of the great market crash of 1929, asking you with a shudder if you remember the way US Steel and Montgomery Ward hit the chutes during the month of October: but in that celebrated devaluation of once gilt-edged shares there was nothing comparable to the swift and dizzy descent at this moment of Twistleton Preferred.

Hermione's teeth came together with a click.

'I shall have a talk with Reginald!'

'I should. I think you owe it to yourself to demand an explanation. One wonders if Reginald Twistleton knows the difference between right and wrong.'

'I'll tell him,' said Hermione.

Lord Ickenham watched her drive off, well content with the way she stepped on the gas. He liked to see her hurrying to the tryst like that. The right spirit, he considered.

He climbed the five-barred gate at the side of the road and lowered himself on to the scented grass beyond it. His eyes fixed on the cloudless sky, he thought how pleasant it was to spread sweetness and light and how fortunate he ought to reckon himself that he had been granted this afternoon such ample opportunity of doing so. If for an instant a pang of pity passed through him as he pictured the meeting between Pongo and this incandescent girl, he suppressed it. Pongo – if he survived – would surely feel nothing but a tender gratitude towards an uncle who had laboured so zealously on his behalf. A drowsiness stole over him, and his eyelids closed in sleep.

Hermione, meanwhile, had reached the house and come to a halt outside its front door with a grinding of brakes and a churning of gravel. And she was about to enter, when from the room to her left she heard her father's voice.

'GET OUT!' it was saying, and a moment later Constable Potter emerged, looking like a policeman who has passed through the furnace. She went to the window.

'Father,' she said, 'do you know where Reginald is?'

'No.'

'I want to see him.'

'Why?' asked Sir Aylmer, as if feeling that such a desire was morbid.

'I intend,' said Hermione, once more grinding her teeth, 'to break off our engagement.'

# UNCLE DYNAMITE

A slender figure pacing the tennis lawn caught her eye. She hastened towards it, little jets of flame shooting from her nostrils.

3

Down at the Bull's Head the girl Myrtle, her conversation with her uncle concluded, had returned to her post in the saloon bar. The gentleman was still at the counter, staring fixedly at the empty tankard, but he was alone.

'Hullo,' she said disappointedly, for she had been hoping to hear more about Brazil, where might is right and the strong man comes into his own. 'Has Major Plank hopped it?'

The gentleman nodded moodily. A shrewder observer than the barmaid would have sensed that the subject of Major Plank was distasteful to him.

'Did he tell you about the puma? No? Well, it was very interesting. It was where he was threading his way through this trackless forest, gathering Brazil nuts, when all of a sudden what should come along but this puma. Pardon?'

The gentleman, who beneath his breath had damned and blasted the puma, did not repeat his observation, but asked for a pint of bitter.

'Would have upset me, I confess,' proceeded the barmaid. 'Yessir, I don't mind saying I'd have been scared stiff. Because pumas jump on the back of your neck and chew you, which you can't say is pleasant. But Major Plank's what I might call intrepid. He had his gun and his trusty native bearer –'

The gentleman repeated his request for bitter in a voice so forceful that it compelled attention. Haughtily, for his tone had offended her, the barmaid pulled the beer handle and delivered the goods, and the gentleman, having drunk deeply, said 'Ha!' The barmaid said nothing. She continued piqued.

But pique is never enough to keep a barmaid silent for long. Presently, having in the meantime polished a few glasses in a marked manner, she resumed the conversation, this time selecting a topic less calculated to inflame the passions.

'Uncle John's in a rare old state.'

'Whose Uncle John?'

415

'My Uncle John. The landlord here. Did you hear him shouting just now?'

The gentleman, mellowed by beer, indicated with an approach to amiability that Jno. Humphrey's agitation had not escaped his notice. Yes, he said, he had heard him shouting just now.

'So I should think. You could have heard him at Land's End. All of a doodah, he is. I must begin by telling you,' said the barmaid, falling easily into her stride, 'that there's a big fête coming on here soon. It's an annual fête, by which I mean that it comes on once a year. And one of the things that happens at this annual fête is a bonny baby competition. Pardon?'

The gentleman said he had not spoken.

'A bonny baby competition,' resumed the barmaid. 'By which I mean a competition for bonny babies. If you've got a bonny baby, I mean to say, you enter it in this bonny baby competition, and if the judge thinks your bonny baby is a bonnier baby than the other bonny babies, it gets the prize. If you see what I mean?'

The gentleman said he saw what she meant.

'Well, Uncle John had entered his little Wilfred and was fully expecting to cop. In fact, he had as much as a hundred bottles of beer on him at eight to one with sportsmen in the village. And now what happens?'

The gentleman said he couldn't imagine.

'Why, Mr Brotherhood, the curate, goes and gets the measles, and the germs spread hither and thither, and now there's so many gone down with it that the Vicar says it isn't safe to have the bonny baby competition, so it's off.'

She paused, well satisfied with the reception of her tale. Her audience might have been hard to grip with anecdotes of Major Plank among the pumas, but he had responded admirably to this simpler narrative of English village life. Though oddly, considering that the story was in its essence a tragic one, the emotion under which he was labouring seemed to be joy. Quite a sunny look had come into his eyes, as if weights had been removed from his mind.

'Off,' said the barmaid. 'By which I mean that it won't take place. So all bets are null and void, as the expression is, and Uncle John won't get his bottles of beer.'

'Too bad,' said the gentleman. 'Can you direct me to Ashenden Manor?'

'Straight along, turning to the right as you leave the door.'

'Thank you,' said the gentleman.

## Chapter 13

That Constable Potter, having returned to his cottage and changed into a dry uniform should then have proceeded without delay to Ashenden Manor to see Sir Aylmer Bostock was only what might have been expected. Sir Aylmer was the chairman of the local bench of magistrates, and he looked upon him as his natural protector. The waters of the pond had scarcely closed over his head before he was saying to himself that here was something to which the big chief's attention would have to be drawn.

He was unaware that in seeking an audience at this particular time he was doing something virtually tantamount to stirring up a bilious tiger with a short stick. No warning voice whispered in his ear 'Have a care, Potter!' adding that as the result of having been compelled to withdraw a suit for damages to which he had been looking forward with bright anticipation for weeks his superior's soul was a bubbling maelstrom of black malignity and that he was far more likely to bite a policeman in the leg than to listen patiently to his tales of woe.

The realization that this was so came, however, almost immediately. He had been speaking for perhaps a minute when Sir Aylmer, interrupting him, put a question.

'Are you tight, you bloodstained Potter?' asked Sir Aylmer, regarding him with a sort of frenzied loathing. When a man has come to his collection room to be alone with his grief, to brood on the shattering of his hopes and to think how sweet life might have been had he had one of those meek, old-fashioned daughters who used to say 'Yes, papa!' the last thing he wants is policemen clumping in with complicated stories. 'What on earth are you talking about? I can't make head nor tail of it.'

Constable Potter was surprised. He was not conscious of having been obscure. It also came as a shock to him to discover that he had

418

misinterpreted the twitching of his audience's limbs and the red glare in that audience's eye. He had been attributing these phenomena to the natural horror of a good man who hears from another good man of outrages committed on his, the second good man's, person and it seemed now that he had been mistaken.

'It's with ref. to this aggravated assault, sir.'

'What aggravated assault?'

'The one I'm telling you about, sir. I was assaulted by the duck pond.'

The suspicion that the speaker had been drinking grew in Sir Aylmer's mind. Even Reginald Twistleton at the height of one of his midnight orgies might have hesitated, he felt, to make a statement like that.

'By the duck pond?' he echoed, his eyes widening.

'Yes, sir.'

'How the devil can you be assaulted by a duck pond?'

Constable Potter saw where the misunderstanding had arisen. The English language is full of these pitfalls.

'When I said "by the duck pond," I didn't mean "by the duck pond," I meant "by the duck pond." That is to say,' proceeded Constable Potter, speaking just in time, '"near" or "adjacent to," in fact "on the edge of." I was the victim of an aggravated assault on the edge of the duck pond, sir. Somebody pushed me in.'

'Pushed you in?'

'Pushed me in, sir. Like as it might have been someone what had a grudge against me.'

'Who was it?'

'A scarlet woman, sir,' said Constable Potter, becoming biblical. 'Well, what I mean to say, she was wearing a red jacket and a kind of red thingummy round her head, like as it might have been a scarf.'

'Was it a scarf?'

'Yes, sir.'

'Then why say "like as it might have been" one? I have had to speak before, from the bench, of the idiotic, asinine way in which you blasted policemen give your evidence. Did you see this woman?'

'Yes and no, sir.'

Sir Aylmer closed his eyes. He seemed to be praying for strength.

'What do you mean, yes and no?'

'I mean to say, sir, that I didn't actually see her, like as it might have been see. I just caught sight of her for a moment as she legged it away, like as it might have been a glimp.'

'Do you mean glimpse?'

'Yes, sir.'

'Then say glimpse. And if you use that expression "like as it might have been" once more, just once more, I'll . . . Could you identify this woman?'

'Establish her identity?' said Constable Potter, gently corrective. 'Yes, sir, if I could apprehend her. But I don't know where she is.'

'Well, I've not got her.'

'No, sir.'

'Then why come bothering me? What do you expect me to do?'

Broadly speaking, Constable Potter expected Sir Aylmer to have the countryside scoured and the ports watched, but before he could say so the latter had touched on another aspect of the affair.

'What were you doing by the duck pond?'

'Spitting and thinking, sir. I generally pause there when on my beat, and I had just paused this afternoon when the outrage occurred. I heard something behind me, like as it might have been a footstep, and the next moment something pushed me in the small of the back, like as if it might have been a hand –'

'GET OUT!' said Sir Aylmer.

Constable Potter withdrew. Crossing the terrace, he made for the bushes on the other side and there, lighting his pipe, stood spitting and thinking. And we make no secret of the fact that his thoughts were bitter thoughts and his expectoration disillusioned.

Just as a boy's best friend is his mother, so is a policeman's prop and stay the chairman of the local bench of magistrates. When skies are dark, it is the thought of the chairman of the local bench of magistrates that brings the sun smiling through, and it is to the chairman of the local bench of magistrates that he feels he can always take his little troubles and be sure of support and sympathy. Who ran to catch me when I fell and would some pretty story tell and kiss the place to make it well? The chairman of the local bench of magistrates. That is the policeman's creed.

Anyone, therefore, who when a boy ever went running to his mother with a tale of wrongs and injuries and instead of condolences received a kick in the pants will be able to appreciate this officer's chagrin as he passed the late scene under mental review. Sir Aylmer's attitude had hurt and disappointed him. If this was how a constable's legitimate complaints were received by those whose duty it was to comfort and console, then Elsie, he felt, was right and the quicker he left the Force, the better.

If you had approached Harold Potter as he stood there in his bush, smoking his pipe and spitting bitterly, and had said, 'Well, Constable Potter, how are you feeling?' he would have replied that he was feeling fed up. And there is little doubt that this black mood would have grown in intensity, had not something happened which abruptly wrenched his thoughts from their contemplation of the policeman's unhappy lot.

Through the branches before him he had a good view of the front of the house, and at this moment there appeared on the balcony of one of the windows on the first floor a female figure in a red jacket, wearing upon its head a red thingummy, like as it might have been a scarf. It came to the balcony rail, looked left and right, then went back into the room.

The spectacle left Harold Potter gaping. A thrill ran through him from the base of the helmet to the soles of his regulation boots. He started to say 'Coo!' but the word froze on his moustache.

Harold Potter was a man who could reason. A mystery woman in a red jacket had pushed him into the duck pond. A mystery woman in a red jacket was in that room on the first floor. It did not take him long to suspect that these two mystery women might be one and the same.

But how to make sure?

It seemed to him that there lay before him the choice between two courses of action. He could go and report to Sir Aylmer, or he could pop along to the potting shed, where there was a light ladder, secure this light ladder, take it to the side of the house, prop it up and climb to that first floor window and peer in. A steady look at close range would establish the identity of the red-jacketed figure.

He did not hesitate long between these alternative plans. Rejecting almost immediately the idea of going and reporting to Sir Aylmer, he knocked out his pipe and started for the potting shed.

UNCLE DYNAMITE

2

Sally, her tea and buttered toast long since consumed, had begun to feel lonely. It was quite a time now since Pongo had left her, and she yearned for his return. Seated on the chaise-longue, she thought what a baa-lamb he was and longed for him to come back so that she could go on stroking his head and telling him how much she loved him.

An odd thing, this love, and one about which it is futile to argue. If individual A. finds in individual B. a glamour which escapes the notice of the general public, the general public has simply got to accept the situation without protest, just as it accepted without protest, though perhaps with a silent sigh of regret, the fact of Mr Brotherhood, the curate, getting measles.

Seeing Sally sitting on the chaise-longue with clasped hands and starry eyes, her heart overflowing with love for Pongo, it would have been useless for a discriminating third party to tap her on the shoulder and try to persuade her that there was nothing in the prospect of a lifelong union with Reginald Twistleton to get starry-eyed about. Fruitless to attempt to sketch for her a picture of Reginald Twistleton as seen by the cooler-headed. She was in love, and she liked it.

The only cloud that darkened her sky was the fear lest a shrewd girl like Hermione Bostock, having secured such a prize, might refuse to relinquish it, but she need have had no anxiety. Hermione was relinquishing the prize at that very moment. When, some twenty minutes after he had left it, Pongo re-entered the room, there was a dazed look on his face as if he had recently been mixed up with typhoons, waterspouts and other Acts of God, but in his eyes shone the light which comes into the eyes of men who have found the blue bird.

Sally was not able to detect this immediately, her vision being obscured by the handkerchief with which he was mopping his forehead, and her first words were reproachful.

'Oh, angel, what a time you've been.'

'Sorry.'

'I went out on to the balcony just now to see if I could see you, but you weren't in sight. I know you had to brood, but need you have brooded so long?'

422

Pongo lowered the handkerchief.

'I wasn't brooding,' he said. 'I was chatting with Hermione.'

Sally gave a jump.

'Then you found her?'

'She found me.'

'And what happened?'

Pongo moved to the mirror and inspected himself in it. He seemed to be looking for grey hairs.

'Well, that I can hardly tell you,' he said. 'The whole thing's a bit of a blur. Have you ever been in a really bad motor smash? Or hit by an atom bomb? No? Then it's hard to explain. Still, the fact that emerges is that the engagement's off.'

'Oh, Pongo!'

'Oh, Sally!'

'Oh, Pongo darling! Then we can live happy ever after.'

Pongo applied the handkerchief to his forehead once more.

'Yes,' he agreed, 'after a brief interval for picking up the pieces and reassembling the faculties. I don't mind telling you the recent scene has left me a bit weak.'

'My poor lamb. I wish I had some smelling salts.'

'So do I. I could use a bucketful.'

'Was it so awful?'

'Quite an ordeal.'

'What did you say to her?'

'I didn't get a chance of saying anything to her, except, "Oh, there you are," right at the start. She bore the burden of the conversash.'

'You don't mean it was she who broke off the engagement?'

'And how! You know, Uncle Fred ought to be in some sort of home.'

'Why?'

'It appears that he met Hermione and spilled the beans with a lavish hand. He told her so many things about me that I wonder she remembered them all. But she did.'

'Such as –?'

'Well, getting pinched at the dog races and going down to the drawing-room last night to get a spot and being caught this morning in Ma Bostock's wardrobe. Things like that.'

'In the wardrobe? What were you doing there?'

'I had gone to her room to get you a lipstick, and –'

'Oh, Pongo! My hero! Did you really do that for me?'

'Not much I wouldn't do for you. Look what you did for me. Pushing Potter into that pond.'

'I think that's what's so splendid about us. Each helps each. It's the foundation of a happy married life. So Uncle Fred told her all that about you? Bless him.'

'Would you put it like that?'

'Well, he saved you from a girl you could never have been happy with.'

'I couldn't be happy with any girl except you. Yes. I suppose he did. I hadn't looked at it in that way.'

'He never minds how much trouble he takes, if he feels that he's spreading sweetness and light.'

'No. There have been complaints about it on all sides, and I still maintain that he ought to be in a padded cell with the board of Lunacy Commissioners sitting on his head. However, I agree that he has smoothed our path. I mean to say, here we are, what?'

'Here we are.'

'All our problems solved. Nothing to worry about any more.'

'Not a thing.'

'Oh, Sally!'

'Oh, Pongo!'

The embrace into which they fell was a close one, close enough, had it taken place in Hollywood, to have caused Eric Johnston to shake his head dubiously and recommend cutting a few hundred feet, but not so close as to deprive Pongo of a view of the window. And Sally, nestling in his arms, was concerned to notice that he had suddenly stiffened, as if he had been turned into a pillar of salt.

'What's the matter?' she asked.

Pongo gave a short gulp. He seemed to find a difficulty in speaking.

'Don't look now,' he said, 'but that blighter Potter has just stepped off a ladder on to the balcony.'

3

It was at about the moment when Constable Potter, having found the light ladder, was starting to lift it and Pongo, in the bedroom on the first floor, had begun his emotional description of the recent conference with Hermione that Major Plank turned his car in at the gates of Ashenden Manor and proceeded up the drive at a high rate of speed.

He had been progressing at a high rate of speed ever since leaving the Bull's Head. He would probably have driven fairly fast in any event, for he was one of those men who do, but what made him so particularly disinclined on the present occasion to loiter and look at the scenery was the fact that the full significance of Lord Ickenham's words in the saloon bar had just come home to him. He had remembered, that is to say, that the man whom he had known as Barmy Twistleton had told him that he was now Lord Ickenham.

There were circles in London where the eccentricities of Lord Ickenham were a favourite topic of conversation, and it was in these circles that Major Plank, when not among the alligators, was accustomed to mix. His old schoolmate's character and habits, therefore, were fully known to him, and he was able to form a vivid picture of what would be the effect on the reputation of anyone whom the other had decided to impersonate.

How long this public menace had been established at Ashenden Manor he did not know, but he felt very strongly that even a single day was too much and that anything like forty-eight hours would have caused a stigma to rest upon the grand old name of Brabazon-Plank which it would take a lifetime to remove.

There is probably no one who moves more slippily than a Brazilian explorer on his way to expose an impostor who has been causing stigmas to rest upon his name, and not even Hermione could have made better speed up the drive than did this fermenting Major. His was a large, flat, solid foot, admirably adapted for treading on accelerators, and he pressed it down with a will.

Arriving at the house, he was in far too great a hurry to ring the front door bell and wait till it was answered. Voices were proceeding from the open French window to his right, presumably that of the drawing-room, and he went thither and walked in. He found himself in the presence of his young subordinate, Bill Oakshott, and a rugged man of an older vintage who was puffing at a white moustache of the soup-strainer class. He had a feeling, looking at them, that they were upset about something.

Nor was he mistaken. Both Bill and his Uncle Aylmer had come to the tea table with their bosoms full of the perilous stuff that weighs upon the heart. The memory of his craven behaviour during that interview with Hermione had not ceased to torture Bill, and Sir Aylmer was still in the grip of the baffled fury which comes to men of imperious nature when their daughters tell them they must not bring actions against publishers, a fury which his conversation with Constable Potter had done nothing to alleviate. To say that William Oakshott and Sir Aylmer Bostock were human powder magazines which it needed but a spark to explode is not only clever, but true.

It is possible, however, that the soothing influence of tea, muffins and cucumber sandwiches might have succeeded in averting disaster, allowing the exchanges to confine themselves to harmless commonplaces, had not Sir Aylmer, too pleased to keep such splendid news to himself, chanced to mention that Hermione had told him that, her romance having sprung an unforeseen leak, he would not have to pass the evening of his life with Reginald Twistleton as his son-in-law. For this led Bill to exclaim 'Oh, gosh!' in an enraptured voice and, pressed to explain his elation, to say that the thought had crossed his mind that if Hermione was back in circulation again, there might be a chance for a chap who had loved her with a growing fervour for years and years and years: and this in its turn led Sir Aylmer to attack him with tooth and claw. There was a smile on his nephew's face which he considered a silly smile, and he addressed himself without delay to the task of wiping it off.

'Gar!' he said, speaking dangerously through a mouthful of muffin, and added that there was no need for Bill to grin all over his beastly face like a damned hyena, because whether free or engaged Hermione would not touch him with a barge pole.

'Why should she?' asked Sir Aylmer. 'You? She looks on you as a –'

'I know,' said Bill, with a return of gloom. 'A brother.'

'Not brother,' corrected Sir Aylmer. 'Sheep.'

A quiver ran through Bill's massive frame. His jaw fell and his eyes widened.

'Sheep?'

'Sheep.'

'*Sheep?*' said Bill.

'Sheep,' said Sir Aylmer firmly. 'A poor, spineless sheep who can't say boo to a goose.'

A more practised debater would have turned this charge to his advantage by challenging the speaker to name three sheep who could say boo to a goose, but Bill merely stood rigid, his fists clenched, his nostrils dilated, his face mantled with the blush of shame and indignation, regretting that ties of blood and his companion's advanced years rendered impossible that slosh in the eye for which the other seemed to him to be asking, nay pleading, with every word.

'Sheep,' said Sir Aylmer, winding up the speech for the prosecution. 'She told me so herself.'

It was on this delicate situation that Major Plank intruded.

'Hullo there,' he said, striding in with the calm assurance of a man accustomed for years to walk uninvited into the huts of native chiefs. 'Hullo, Bill.'

It would be difficult to advance more conclusive proof of the turmoil into which Bill Oakshott's soul had been thrown by his uncle's words than by saying that the unexpected entry of the last man he would have wished to see in the drawing-room of Ashenden Manor did not cause so much as a gleam of horror to come into his eyes. He regarded him dully, his mind still occupied by that sheep sequence. Did Hermione, he was asking himself, really look on him as a sheep? And, arising from that, had she a prejudice against sheep? The evidence went to show that she had none against baa-lambs, but sheep, of course, might be a different matter.

It was left to Sir Aylmer to do the honours.

'Who the hell are you?' he asked, not unthankful that here was another object on which he could work off some of the spleen induced by the chit-chat of daughters and policemen.

Major Plank had had far too much experience of this sort of thing to be abashed by nervous irritability on the part of a host. Many of the householders on whom he had dropped in in his time had said it with spears.

'Who the hell are *you*?' he replied agreeably. 'I'm looking for Mugsy Bostock.'

Sir Aylmer started.

'I am Sir Aylmer Bostock,' he said, and Major Plank stared at him incredulously.

427

'You?' he said. 'Don't be an ass. Mugsy Bostock is younger than me, and you look a million. Have you seen your Uncle Mugsy anywhere, Bill?'

It was at this point that Jane, the parlourmaid, entered bearing strawberries in a bowl, for they did themselves well at tea time at Ashenden Manor – cucumber sandwiches, muffins, strawberries and everything. Sir Aylmer addressed her in the carrying voice which was so characteristic of him.

'JANE!'

A lesser girl would have dropped the bowl. Jane merely shook like an aspen.

'Yes, sir?'

'Tell this son of a . . . this gentleman who I am.'

'Sir Aylmer Bostock, sir.'

'Right,' said Sir Aylmer, like the judge of one of those general knowledge quizzes which are so popular nowadays.

Major Plank said he was dashed.

'It's that ghastly moustache that misled me,' he explained. 'If you go about the place behind a whacking great white moustache, you can't blame people for taking you for a centenarian. Well, nice to see you again, Mugsy, and all that, but, cutting the guff, I came here on business. Plank's my name.'

'Plank!'

'Brabazon-Plank. You may remember me at school. I've just discovered that that raving lunatic, Barmy Twistleton – Lord Ickenham he calls himself now – has been passing himself off as me under your roof, and it's got to stop. I don't know what made him do it, and I don't care, the point is I'll be damned if I'm going to have people thinking that Barmy Twistleton is me. Good God! How would you like it yourself?'

There had been an instant, just after the words, 'Plank's my name,' when Sir Aylmer had given a quick and extraordinarily realistic impersonation of a harpooned whale, shaking from stem to stern as if a barb had entered his flesh. But as the speaker continued, this had given place to a frozen calm, the dangerous calm that heralds the storm.

'I can tell you what made him do it,' he said, allowing his eyes to play upon Bill like flame-throwers. 'He wished to be of assistance to my nephew here. We are holding our annual village fête shortly, and one of its features is a contest for bonny babies. My nephew was to have acted as judge.'

'Barmy told me he was going to be the judge.'

'That was the latest arrangement. My nephew persuaded him to take his place.'

'Very sensible of you, Bill,' said Major Plank cordially. 'Dashed dangerous things, these baby contests. The little beasts are bad enough themselves, but it's the mothers you want to watch out for. Look,' he said, baring his leg and indicating a cicatrice on the calf. 'That's what I got once in Peru for being fool enough to let myself be talked into judging a competition for bonny babies. The mother of one of the Hon. Mentions got after me with a native dagger.'

'The problem then arose,' proceeded Sir Aylmer, still speaking evenly and spacing his words with care, 'of how to introduce Lord Ickenham into my house. He was well aware that I would never allow him to enter my house, if I knew who he was. So he said he was Major Brabazon-Plank, the explorer, and my nephew endorsed this statement. What do you mean,' roared Sir Aylmer, suddenly abandoning the calm, judicial method and becoming a thing of fire and fury, 'what do you mean, you infernal young scallywag, by introducing impostors into my house?'

He would have spoken further, for it was obvious that the greater part of his music was still in him, but at this moment Bill exploded.

A good deal is always required to change a mental attitude which has endured for a number of years. From early boyhood Bill Oakshott had regarded this uncle of his with respectful awe, much as a nervous young prehistoric man might have regarded the leader of his tribe. He had quailed before his wrath, listened obsequiously to his stories, done all that lay in his power to humour him. And had this scene taken place at a time when he was in normal mood, there is little doubt that he would have folded like an accordion and allowed himself to be manhandled without protest.

But Bill was not in normal mood. His soul was seething in rebellion like a cistern struck by a thunderbolt. The interview with Hermione had left him raw and wincing. The information that she regarded him as a sheep had dropped vitriol on the wounds. And now, not once but three times, this white-moustached cuckoo in the nest had alluded to Ashenden Manor as 'my house'. At these emotional moments there is always something, generally trivial in itself, which fulfils the function of the last straw, and with Bill now it was this description of Ashenden Manor.

In the automatic, barely conscious fashion of the English man at tea time he had been continuing to eat and drink throughout his uncle's exposition, and for an instant a muffin prevented him expressing his views. He swallowed it, and was at liberty to proceed.

'"My house?"' he said. 'I like that. Where do you get that "my house" stuff?'

Sir Aylmer said that that was not the point, and was starting to indicate once more what the point was, when he was swept away as if by a tidal wave.

'"My house!"' repeated Bill, choking on the words like one who chokes upon a muffin. 'Of all the crust! Of all the nerve! It's about time, Uncle Aylmer, that we got this thing cleared up about who this ruddy house belongs to. Let's do it now.'

'Yes, let's,' said Major Plank, interested. A man with five sisters and seven aunts, he was well versed in family rows and thought that this one promised to be in the first rank and wanted pushing along. 'Whose house is it?'

'Mine,' thundered Bill. 'Mine. Mine. Mine. Mine. Mine.'

'I see,' said Major Plank, getting his drift. 'Yours. Then where does Mugsy come in?'

'He planted himself here when I was a mere kid, unable to do anything about it. I was only sixteen when my father died, and he barged over from Cheltenham and got into the woodwork.'

'What happened when you came of age?'

'Nothing. He stuck on.'

'You should have booted him out.'

'Of course I should.'

'That was the moment.'

'Yes.'

'Why didn't you?'

'I hadn't the heart.'

'Mistaken kindness.'

'Well, I'm going to do it now. I've had enough of this business of being a . . . what's the word?'

'Fathead?'

'Cipher in the home. I'm sick and tired of being a cipher in the home. You can jolly well clear out, Uncle Aylmer. You understand me? Buzz off. Where you buzz to, I don't care, but buzz. Go back to Cheltenham, if you like. Or Bexhill.'

'Or Bognor Regis,' suggested Major Plank.

'Or Bognor Regis. Go anywhere you like, but you're not going to stay here. Is that clear?'

'Quite clear,' said Major Plank. 'Very well put.'

'Right,' said Bill.

He strode out through the French window, and Major Plank helped himself to a muffin.

'Nice chap, Bill,' he said. 'I like a young fellow who knows his own mind. Extraordinarily good muffins, these, Mugsy. I'll have another.'

4

Emerging through the French window, Bill passed along the terrace, walking rapidly towards the spot where the drive began. His eyes glowed. He was breathing stertorously.

The appetite grows by what it feeds on. So far from soothing him and restoring him to everyday placidity, his throwing off of the shackles had left Bill Oakshott in a mood for fresh encounters. He had tasted blood, and wanted more. It is often so with quiet young men who at long last assert themselves.

He was in the frame of mind when he would have liked to meet Joe Louis and pick a quarrel with him, and as he turned the corner and came into the drive there caught his eye something which seemed to have been sent in direct answer to prayer.

It was not Joe Louis, but it was the next best thing. What he had seen was a stout young man with a pink nose and horn-rimmed spectacles in conversation with Hermione Bostock. And just as he beheld him this young man suddenly folded Hermione in his embrace and started to kiss her.

Bill broke into a gallop, the glow in his eyes intensified, the stertorousness of his breathing still more marked. His general mental attitude was that of the war-horse which said 'Ha!' among the trumpets.

## *Chapter 14*

It is never easy for a high-strung young man whose whole future as a publisher of the book beautiful is being decided at a country house to sit in an inn two miles from that house, waiting patiently for news to be brought to him from the front. With each long minute that goes by his nervousness increases. The limbs twitch, the eyeballs roll, the illusion that there are ants in his pants becomes more and more pronounced, until eventually the urge to be closer to the centre of things grows so imperious that he yields to it.

That was why Otis Painter had been absent from the Bull's Head when Hermione arrived there. He had started to walk to Ashenden Manor. Like Edith of the swan's neck after the Battle of Hastings, he wanted to find out what had been going on.

When we say that Otis had started to walk to Ashenden Manor, it would be more correct to put it that he thought he had; in actual fact, having got his instructions twisted, he had turned to the left instead of to the right on leaving the inn, and it was only after he had proceeded a mile and three quarters through delightful country that he discovered that though he was improving his figure and getting lots of pure air into his lungs, he was diminishing his chances of reaching his destination with every step that he took.

Returning to the Bull's Head, he had borrowed a bicycle from the boy who cleaned the boots, a courteous and obliging lad of the name of Erbut with blacking all over his face, and after a couple of unpleasant spills, for it was many years since he had cycled and the old skill had rather deserted him, had found himself at the top of the drive. There, feeling that this was as far as it was prudent to penetrate into territory where there was a grave risk of meeting Sir Aylmer Bostock, he deposited his machine behind a tree, concealed himself in the bushes and resumed his waiting. And presently Hermione appeared, walking briskly.

As she drew near and he was enabled to get a clear view of her, his heart sank, for he could see that her lips were tightly set, her bosom heaving and her eyes bright and stormy. She looked, in a word, like a daughter who, approaching her father in the matter of withdrawing legal actions against publishers, has come up against something too hot to handle.

Actually, of course, Hermione's appearance was simply the normal appearance of a girl who has just been ticking off a viper. After a dust-up with a viper the female lips always become tightly set, and it is rarely that the bosom does not heave. But Otis did not know this, and it was with a mind filled with the gloomiest forebodings that he stepped from his hiding place. 'Here comes the bad news,' he was saying to himself.

'Well?' he said, uttering the monosyllable loudly and raspingly, as so often happens when the nerves are overstrained.

The briskness of her pace had taken Hermione past him, and it was from behind that he had addressed her. At the sound of a voice suddenly splitting the welkin where no voice should have been she left the ground in an upward direction and came to earth annoyed and ruffled.

'I wish you wouldn't pop out of bushes like that,' she said with a good deal of asperity.

Otis was too agitated to go into the niceties of etiquette and procedure.

'What happened?' he asked.

'I bit my tongue.'

'I mean,' said Otis, clicking his, 'when you saw your father.'

Hermione mastered her emotion. Her tongue was still paining her, but she had remembered that this man was a publisher who believed in column spreads in all the literate Sunday papers.

'Oh, yes,' she said.

The reply dissatisfied Otis. It seemed to him to lack lucidity, and lucidity was what he desired – or, as a literate Sunday paper would put it, desiderated.

'What do you mean, Oh, yes? What did he say?'

Hermione's composure was now restored. She still disapproved of her sponsor's practice of popping out of bushes and speaking like a foghorn down the back of her neck, but was willing to let bygones be bygones.

'It's quite all right, Mr Painter,' she said, smiling kindly upon Otis. 'Father has withdrawn the suit.'

Otis reeled.

'He *has*?'

'Yes.'

'Gee!' said Otis, and it was at this point that he folded Hermione in his embrace and started to kiss her.

The last thing we desire being to cast aspersions on publishers, a most respectable class of men, we hasten to say that behaviour of this kind is very unusual with these fine fellows. Statistics show that the number of authoresses kissed annually by publishers is so small that, if placed end to end, they would reach scarcely any distance. Otis's action was quite exceptional, and Hodder and Stoughton, had they observed it, would have looked askance. So would Jonathan Cape. And we think we speak for Heinemann, Macmillan, Benn, Gollancz and Herbert Jenkins Ltd when we say that they, too, would have been sickened by the spectacle.

In defence of Otis there are several extenuating points to be urged. In the first place, his relief was so intense and his happiness so profound that he had to kiss something. In the second place, Hermione was a very beautiful girl (not that that would have weighed with Faber and Faber) and she had smiled upon him very kindly. And, finally, we cannot judge men who have lived on the left bank of the Seine by the same standards which we apply to those whose home is in London. If Eyre and Spottiswoode had taken a flat in the Rue Jacob, within easy reach of the Boul' Mich', they would have been surprised how quickly they would have forgotten the lessons they had learned at their mother's knee.

It was unfortunate that none of these arguments presented themselves to Bill Oakshott as he turned the corner. In Otis Painter he saw just another libertine, flitting from flower to flower and sipping, and we are already familiar with his prejudice against libertines. His impulse on seeing one, we recall, was to pull his head off at the roots and rip his insides out with his bare hands, and it was with this procedure in mind that he now advanced on the entwined pair. He gripped Otis by the coat collar and tore him from the clinch, and he would almost certainly have started to detach his head, had not Hermione uttered a piercing cry.

'Don't kill him, Bill! He's my publisher.'

And then, as she saw him hesitate, she added:

'He's doing my next three books and giving me twenty per cent rising to twenty-five above three thousand.'

It was enough. Practically berserk though Bill was, he could still reason, and reason told him that publishers of this type must be nursed along rather than disembowelled. Hermione's literary career was as dear to him as to herself, and he knew that he could never forgive himself if he jeopardized it by eviscerating a man capable of planning contracts on these spacious lines. He released Otis, who tottered back against a tree and stood there panting and polishing his spectacles.

Bill, too, was panting. His breath came in loud gasps as he strode up to Hermione and grabbed her by the wrist. There was in his demeanour now no trace of that craven diffidence which had marked it during their previous interview in the hall. Since then William Oakshott, with a victory over a tyrant under his belt, had become a changed man, and the man he had changed into was a sort of composite of James Cagney and Attila the Hun. He felt strong and masterful and in the best possible vein for trying out the Ickenham system. Otis Painter, peering at him through his spectacles, which he had now resumed, was reminded of a Parisian inspecteur who had once arrested him at the Quatz Arts Ball.

Nor was Hermione unimpressed. She was now being waggled about, and she found the process, though physically unpleasant, giving her a thrill of ecstasy.

Like all very beautiful girls, Hermione Bostock had received in her time a great deal of homage from the other sex. For years she had been moving in a world of men who frisked obsequiously about her and curled up like carbon paper if she spoke crossly to them, and she had become surfeited with male worship. Even when accepting Pongo's proposals she had yearned secretly for something rough and tough with a nasty eye and the soul of a second mate of a tramp steamer. And in the last quarter where she would have thought of looking she had found him. She had always been fond of Bill, but in an indulgent, almost contemptuous fashion, regarding him, as she had once mentioned to her father, as a sheep. And now the sheep, casting off its clothing, had revealed itself as one of the wolves and now the worst of them.

Little wonder that Hermione Bostock, as Bill having waggled her about, clasped her to his bosom and showered kisses on her upturned face, felt that here was the man she had been looking for since she first read *The Way of an Eagle*.

'My mate!' said Bill. Then, speaking from between clenched teeth, 'Hermione!'

'Yes, Bill?'

'You're going to marry me.'

'Yes, Bill.'

'That's clearly understood, is it?'

'Yes, Bill.'

'No more fooling about with these Pongos and what not.'

'No, Bill.'

'Right,' said the dominant male. He turned to Otis, who had been looking on at the scene with a sort of nostalgia, for it had reminded him of the old, happy days on the left bank of the Seine. 'So you're going to publish her books, are you?'

'Yes,' said Otis eagerly. He wanted there to be no mistake about this. 'All of them.'

'Giving her twenty per cent rising to twenty-five above three thousand?'

'Yes.'

'Why not a straight twenty-five?' said Bill, and Otis agreed that that would be much better. He had been on the point, he said, of suggesting it himself.

'Fine,' said Bill. 'Well, come along in, both of you, and have some tea.'

Hermione regretfully shook her head.

'I can't, darling. I must be getting back to London. Mother has been waiting for me at my flat since one o'clock, and she may be wondering what has become of me. I shall have to drive like the wind. Can I give you a lift, Mr Painter?'

Otis shuddered.

'I guess I'll go by train.'

'You'll find it slow.'

'I like it slow.'

'Very well. Good-bye, darling.'

'Good-bye,' said Bill. 'I'll be up in London tomorrow.'

'Splendid. Come and see me to the car. I left it outside the house.'

Otis remained, leaning against his tree. He felt a little faint, but very happy. Presently the two-seater, with Hermione bent over the wheel, whizzed round the corner and passed him at a speed which made him close his eyes and say to himself 'There but for the grace of God goes Otis Painter.' When he opened them again, he saw Bill approaching.

'Why not thirty?' said Bill.

'Pardon?'

'Per cent. For her books. Not twenty-five.'

'Oh, ah, yes. Why, sure,' said Otis. 'Thirty might be nicer.'

'You don't want to skimp.'

'That's right. You don't.'

'And publicity. You believe in lots of that, I hope?'

'Oh, sure.'

'Fine. She was always complaining that her last publishers wouldn't push her books.'

'The poor fish. I mean, fishes.'

'Used to stall her off with a lot of rot about all that counted being word of mouth advertising.'

'Crazy saps.'

'You intend to advertise largely?'

'In all the literate Sunday papers.'

'How about the literate weeklies?'

'In those, too. I also thought of sandwich men and posters on the walls.'

Bill had not supposed that he would ever be able to regard this man with affection, but he did so now. He still had him docketed as a libertine, but indulgence must be accorded to libertines whose hearts are in the right place.

'Fine,' he said. 'Posters on the walls? Yes, fine.'

'Of course,' said Otis, 'all that kind of thing costs money.'

'Well spent,' Bill pointed out.

'Sure,' agreed Otis. 'Don't get the idea that I'm weakening. But it begins to look as if I may have to dig up a little more capital from somewhere. There isn't any too much of it in the old sock. You wouldn't feel like putting a thousand pounds into my business, would you?'

'That's an idea. Or two?'

'Or three? Or, say, look why not five? Nice round number.'

'Would you call five a round number?'

'I think so.'

'All right,' said Bill. 'Five, then.'

Otis's eyes closed again, this time in silent ecstasy. He had had his dreams, of course. Somewhere in the world, he had told himself, there must be angels in human shape willing to put money into a shaky publishing firm. But never had he really supposed that he would meet one, and still less that, if he did, such an angel would go as high as five thousand.

Opening his eyes, he found that he was alone. His benefactor had either been snatched back to heaven or had gone round the corner to the terrace. He took his bicycle from behind the tree and flung himself on the saddle like a gay professional rider. And when half-way down the drive he had another of those unfortunate spills, he merely smiled amusedly, as one good-naturedly recognizing that the laugh is on him.

Life looked very good to Otis Painter. In the old left bank days he had been at some pains to cultivate a rather impressive pessimism, but now he was pure optimism from side-whiskers to shoe sole.

If Pippa had happened to pass at that moment, singing of God being in His heaven and all right with the world, he would have shaken her by the hand and told her he knew just how she felt.

2

Bill had not been snatched up to heaven. It was to the terrace that he had made his way on leaving Otis, and he had not been there many minutes when Lord Ickenham appeared, walking jauntily like a man whose forty winks in a field has refreshed him. At the sight of Bill he hurried forward with outstretched hand.

'My dear chap, a thousand congratulations.'

Bill gaped. This seemed to him clairvoyance.

'How on earth did you know?'

Lord Ickenham explained that his young friend's ecstatic expression, rather like that of a cherub or seraph on the point of singing Hosanna, would alone have been enough to tell him.

'But, as a matter of fact,' he said, 'I had the news from an acquaint-ance of mine whom I met bicycling along the road just now. Well, when I say bicycling along the road, he was lying in a ditch with his feet in the air, chuckling softly. He told me everything. It seems that he was a witness of the proceedings, and he speaks highly of your technique. You strode up and grabbed her by the wrist, eh?'

'Yes.'

'Waggled her about a bit?'

'Yes.'

'Then clasped her to your bosom and showered kisses on her upturned face?'

'Yes.'

'With the results that might have been anticipated. I told you the Ickenham system never fails. Brought up against it, the proudest beauty wilts and signs on the dotted line. It saddens you a little now, no doubt, to think of all the years you wasted on timid devotion.'

'It does, rather.'

'Timid devotion gets a lover nowhere. I was chatting with Miss Bean this morning, and she was telling me that she had a good deal of trouble at one time with Constable Potter owing to his devotion being so timid. She says that in the early days of his courtship he used to walk her out and chew his moustache and talk about the situation in China, but no real action. So one evening she said "Come on, my lad, get on with it," and he got on with it. And after that everything went like clockwork.'

'Fine,' said Bill absently. He had been thinking of Hermione. 'Potter?' he went on, his mind returning from its flights. 'That reminds me. You haven't a bit of raw steak on you, have you?'

Lord Ickenham felt in his pockets.

'Sorry, no. I seem to have come out without any. Why? You feel peckish?'

'Elsie Bean was out here a moment ago, saying she was in the market for a bit of raw steak. It's needed for Potter. Apparently someone has been sloshing him in the eye.'

'Indeed? Who?'

'I didn't gather. Her story was confused. I seemed to catch some mention of Pongo, but would Pongo punch policemen in the eye?'

'It seems unlikely.'

'I must have got the name wrong. Still, there it is. Someone has given Potter a shiner, and he's fed to the tonsils. You see, he got pushed into the duck pond this afternoon, and now on top of that comes this biff in the eye, so he feels he's had enough of being a policeman. He's chucking it up and buying a pub, Elsie tells me. She seemed rather braced about it.'

Lord Ickenham drew a deep, slow breath of contentment and satisfaction. He looked pleased with himself, and who shall blame him? A man whose mission in life it is to spread sweetness and light and to bring the young folk together may surely be forgiven a touch of complacency when happy endings start going off like crackers all round him and he sees the young folk coming together in droves.

'Great news, Bill Oakshott,' he said. 'This is . . . what is that neat expression of yours? Ah, yes, "Fine!" . . . This is fine. You're all right. Pongo's all right. And now the divine Bean is all right. It reminds one of the final spasm of a musical comedy.' He paused and regarded his companion with some surprise. 'Are you wearing woolly winter underclothing?' he asked.

'Me? No. Why?'

'You keep wriggling, as though something were irritating the epidermis.'

Bill blushed.

'Well, as a matter of fact,' he confessed, 'I'm finding it awfully difficult to keep still. After what's happened, I mean. You know how it is.'

'I do, indeed. I, too, have lived in Arcady. You would like to go for a long, rapid walk and work off steam? Of course you would. Push off, then.'

'You don't mind me leaving you?'

'Well, one hates to lose you, of course, but better a temporary separation than that you should burst all over the terrace. Au revoir, then, and once more a thousand congratulations.'

Bill disappeared round the corner like a dog let off the chain, gathering momentum with every stride. His pace was so good and his preoccupation so intense that it was not until he was out in the open road a mile away that it suddenly came to him that he had omitted to inform Lord Ickenham of the arrival of Major Plank.

He paused, debated within himself the advisability of going back, decided that it was too late and walked on. And presently Lord Ickenham and Major Plank had faded from his mind and he was thinking again exclusively in terms of wedding bells and honeymoons.

3

As things turned out, it would have been unnecessary for him to retrace his steps, for almost immediately after his departure Major Plank came out of the house, wiping butter from his lips.

'Hullo, Barmy,' he said, sighting Lord Ickenham. 'You're too late for the muffins. I've finished them. And very good they were, too.' He replaced his handkerchief. 'You're surprised to see me here, aren't you? Thought you'd baffled me, eh? Well, what happened was that shortly after you left the pub that well-nourished girl behind the bar told me the bonny baby contest was off. So along I came.'

Lord Ickenham had given a slight start on seeing his old friend, but his voice, when he spoke, was as calm and level as ever.

'Off, is it? Why?'

'Outbreak of measles. Thousands stricken.'

'I see. And have you exposed me?'

'Exposed you is right.'

'Did Mugsy seem interested?'

'Most.'

'One sees how he might well be, of course. You're a ruthless old bird, Bimbo.'

Major Plank bridled.

'Ruthless be blowed. I merely took the necessary steps to protect my reputation. And what do you mean, "old bird"? I'm a year younger than you. My idea of an old bird is Mugsy. I was shocked when I saw how he had aged. He looks like the chap in the Bible, Methuselah, the fellow who lived to a thousand and ate grass.'

'Methuselah didn't eat grass.'

'Yes, he did.'

'He never ate grass in his life. You're thinking of Nebuchadnezzar.'

'Oh, am I? Well, the principle's the same. And now I suppose you'll be sliding off. You'd have done better to start packing when I told you to. Still, you're in luck in one way. You won't run into Mugsy. He's in that room over there, holding a court martial.'

'A what?'

'Court martial. There have been all sorts of stirring goings-on here. Just as I was finishing the muffins, a policeman with a black eye barged into the drawing-room with a tall, thin, light-haired young chap in one hand and a dashed pretty girl in a red jacket in the other, and said that the girl had pushed him into a duck pond and that when he was starting to apprehend her the light-haired young chap had biffed him in the eye. And Mugsy has taken them into that room there and is sitting on the case. I gather he's a magistrate or something and so is entitled to execute summary justice. I'm sorry for that young couple. It looks like a sticky week-end for them.'

Lord Ickenham gave his moustache a thoughtful twirl.

'Leave me, Bimbo,' he said. 'I would be alone.'

'Why?'

'I want to ponder.'

'Oh, ponder? Right ho! I'll go back and have some more strawberries,' said Major Plank.

He returned to the drawing-room, and Lord Ickenham, left alone, lost no time in giving himself up to that survey of ways and means which the other's presence had hindered. For some moments he paced up and down, his hands behind his back and a concentrated look in his eye. The tautness of his features showed that his agile brain was not sparing itself.

And presently it was plain that it had given service. His face cleared. The lips beneath the trim moustache curved in a contented smile.

He crossed the terrace and went into the collection room.

4

Only Sir Aylmer was in the collection room when he entered. He, too, was wearing a contented smile.

For the first time that evening Sir Aylmer was feeling cheerful; as

cheerful as a Colosseum lion which after a trying day when everything has gone wrong has found itself unexpectedly presented with
a couple of Christian martyrs and has been able to deal faithfully
with them. There is nothing which so braces up a chairman of a
bench of magistrates in times of despondency as the infliction of a
sharp sentence on a pair of criminals. It would be too much to say
that he regarded Lord Ickenham amiably, but he did not bite him.

'Ha,' he said. 'It's you, is it?'

Lord Ickenham preserved his suavity.

'Ah, Mugsy,' he said. 'I understand you've met Bimbo Plank.
How did you think he was looking? He thought you had aged.
Where's Sally?'

'Who?'

'Bimbo told me she and my nephew Pongo were in here with
you.'

Sir Aylmer started.

'You know that girl?'

'She is my honorary niece.'

A warm glow pervaded Sir Aylmer's system, as if he had been
taking Doctor Smythe's Tonic Swamp Juice. This was even better
than he had hoped.

'Oh, is she?' he said. 'Then it may interest you to know that I've
just given her thirty days without the option, and your nephew the
same. Potter's locked them up in the scullery while he has his eye
bathed, and in a few minutes he'll be taking them off in custody.'

'A harsh sentence.'

'The only possible sentence. One of the most disgraceful cases
that has ever come before me. She pushed Potter into the duck
pond.'

'Well, what does a policeman expect, if he deliberately goes and
stands on the edge of duck ponds? Girls will be girls.'

'Not while I'm sitting on the bench, they won't.'

'And how about the quality of mercy? It isn't strained, you
know. It droppeth as the gentle rain from heaven upon the place
beneath.'

'Damn the quality of mercy.'

'You'd better not let Shakespeare hear you saying that. Then you
won't reconsider?'

'No, I won't. And now we'll discuss this matter of your coming here under a false name.'

Lord Ickenham nodded.

'Yes, I was hoping you would be able to spare me a minute to tell you about that. But before I begin, I would like to have a witness present.'

Lord Ickenham went to the door and called 'Bimbo', and Major Plank came out of the drawing-room chewing strawberries.

'Could you come here a moment, Bimbo. I need you as a witness. I'm going to tell you a story that will shock you.'

'It isn't the one about the young man of Calcutta, is it? Because I've heard that.'

Lord Ickenham reassured him.

'When I said "shock", I meant that the tale would revolt your moral sense rather than bring the blush of shame to the cheek of modesty. Shall I begin at the beginning?'

'It sounds a good idea.'

'Very well. There was an American girl named Vansittart who came to London and bought a number of trinkets in Bond Street, her plan being to take them back to America and wear them. All straight so far?'

'Quite.'

'What –?' began Sir Aylmer, and Lord Ickenham gave him a stern look.

'Mugsy,' he said, 'if you interrupt, I'll put you over that chair and give you six of the juiciest. I've no doubt Bimbo will be glad to hold you down.'

'Charmed. Quite like old times.'

'Good. Then I will resume. Where were we?'

'This American wench. Bought jewels in Bond Street.'

'Exactly. Well, when she had got them, the thought flashed upon her that on arriving with them in New York, she would have to pay heavy customs duty to the United States Government. She recoiled from this.'

'I don't blame her.'

'So in her innocent, girlish way she decided to smuggle them in.'

'Quite right. Don't pay the bounders a penny, that's what I say. They've got much too much money as it is.'

'Precisely what Miss Vansittart felt. She held that opinion very strongly. But how to work this smuggling project?'

'That's always the snag.'

'She mused a while,' said Lord Ickenham, interrupting Major Plank in what threatened to be rather a long story about how he had once tried to sneak some cigars through at Southampton, 'and was rewarded with an idea. She had a friend, a young sculptress. She went to her, got her to make a clay bust and put the jewels in its head, and was then all set to take them to America in safety and comfort. She reasoned that when the customs authorities saw a clay bust, they would simply yawn and say "Ho hum, a clay bust," and let it through.'

'Very shrewd.'

'So that was that. But . . . this is where you want to hold on to your chair, Bimbo . . . unfortunately this young sculptress was at that time modelling a bust of Mugsy.'

Major Plank was plainly bewildered. He stared at Sir Aylmer, studying his features closely and critically.

'What did Mugsy want a bust of himself for?'

'To present to the village club.'

'Good God.'

'During the sittings,' proceeded Lord Ickenham, 'Mugsy and the young sculptress naturally chatted from time to time, and in the course of these conversations she was rash enough to show him the bust that contained the jewels and to tell him that she was leaving it at my house a few miles from here until Miss Vansittart sailed. And Mugsy . . . I hardly like to tell you this, Bimbo.'

'Go on.'

'Well, you will scarcely credit it, but yesterday Mugsy nipped over to my house, effected an entrance and snitched the bust.'

'The one with the jewels in it?'

'The one with the jewels in it.'

Not even the menace of six of the juiciest could keep Sir Aylmer silent under this charge.

'It's an insane lie!'

Lord Ickenham raised his eyebrows.

'Is there anything to be gained by this bravado, Mugsy? Do you suppose I would bring such an accusation unless I could prove it to the hilt? Yes, Bimbo, he nipped over to my house, was admitted by my butler –'

'I wasn't. He wouldn't let me in.'

'That is your story, is it? It is not the one Coggs tells. He says he admitted you and that you roamed unwatched all over the premises. And, what is more, as you were leaving he noticed a suspicious bulge under your coat. Honestly, Mugsy, I wouldn't bother to persist in this pretence of innocence. It would be manlier if you came clean and threw yourself on the mercy of the court.'

'Much manlier,' agreed Major Plank. 'Whiter altogether.'

'I told you I could prove my accusation, and I will now proceed to do so. You have a nice, large foot, Bimbo. Oblige me by stepping to that cupboard over there and kicking in the door.'

'Right ho!' said Major Plank.

He approached the cupboard and drove at it with his brogue shoe. The niceness and largeness of his foot had not been over-estimated. The fragile door splintered with a rending crash.

'Aha!' he said, peering in.

'You see a clay bust?'

'That's right. Bust, clay, one.'

'Bring it here.'

Sir Aylmer was gaping at the bust like one who gapes at snakes in his path. He sought in vain for an explanation of its presence. His wife could have given him that explanation, but his wife was in London.

'How the devil did that get there?' he gasped.

Lord Ickenham smiled sardonically.

'Really, Mugsy! Good, that, eh, Bimbo?'

'Very good.'

'Break that thing's head.'

'Bust the bust? Right ho!' said Major Plank, and did so. Lord Ickenham stooped and picked from the ruins a chamois leather bag. Before Sir Aylmer's bulging eyes he untied the string and poured forth a glittering stream.

Major Plank's eyes were bulging, too.

'This must have been one of your best hauls,' he said, looking at Sir Aylmer with open admiration.

Lord Ickenham replaced the gems in the bag and put the bag in his pocket.

'Well, there you are,' he said. 'You were asking just now, Mugsy, why I had come here under a false name. It was because I hoped that if I could get into the house I might be able to settle this thing without a scandal. I knew that you were shortly to stand for Parliament and that a scandal would ruin your prospects, and I took the charitable view that you had yielded to a sudden temptation. As far as I am concerned, I am now willing to let the thing drop. I have no wish to be hard on you, now that I have recovered your ill-gotten plunder and can restore it to its owner. We all understand these irresistible temptations. Eh, Bimbo?'

'Oh, quite.'

'We need say no more about the matter?'

'Not a word.'

'You won't tell anyone?'

'Except for a chap or two at the club, not a soul.'

'Then the whole wretched affair can now be forgotten. Of course, this monstrous sentence which you have inflicted on my nephew and Sally Painter must be quashed. You agree to that, Mugsy?' said Lord Ickenham, raising his voice, for he saw that his host was distrait.

Sir Aylmer gave that impersonation of his of a harpooned whale.

'What?' he said feebly.

Lord Ickenham repeated his words, and Sir Aylmer, though evidently finding it difficult to speak, said, 'Yes, certainly.'

'I should think so,' said Lord Ickenham warmly. 'Thirty days without the option for what was a mere girlish – or, in Pongo's case, boyish – freak. It recalls the worst excesses of the Star Chamber. The trouble with you fellows who have been Governors of Crown colonies, Mugsy, is that you get so accustomed to giving our black brothers the run-around that you lose all self-restraint. Then let us go and notify Constable Potter immediately to strike the gyves from the young couple's wrists. We shall find them, I think you said, in the scullery.'

He linked his arm in Sir Aylmer's and led him out. As they started down the hall Major Plank could hear him urging his companion in the kindest way to pull himself together, turn over a new leaf and start life afresh with a genuine determination to go straight in the future. It only needed a little will-power, said Lord

Ickenham, adding that he held it truth with him who sings to one clear harp in divers tones that men may rise on stepping stones of their dead selves to higher things.

For some moments after they had left, Major Plank stood where he was, regarding the African curios with the glazed look of a man whose brain is taking a complete rest. Then gradually there came upon him a sense of something omitted, the feeling which he had so often had in the wilds of Brazil that somewhere there was man's work to be done and that it was for him to do it.

Then he remembered. The strawberries. He went back to the drawing-room to finish them.

# COCKTAIL TIME

## Chapter 1

The train of events, leading up to the publication of the novel *Cocktail Time*, a volume which, priced at twelve shillings and sixpence, was destined to create considerably more than twelve and a half bobsworth of alarm and despondency in one quarter and another, was set in motion in the smoking-room of the Drones Club in the early afternoon of a Friday in July. An Egg and a Bean were digesting their lunch there over a pot of coffee, when they were joined by Pongo Twistleton and a tall, slim, Guards-officer-looking man some thirty years his senior, who walked with a jaunty step and bore his cigar as if it had been a banner with the strange device Excelsior.

'Yo ho,' said the Egg.

'Yo ho,' said the Bean.

'Yo ho,' said Pongo. 'You know my uncle, Lord Ickenham, don't you?'

'Oh, rather,' said the Egg. 'Yo ho, Lord Ickenham.'

'Yo ho,' said the Bean.

'Yo ho,' said Lord Ickenham. 'In fact, I will go further. Yo frightfully ho,' and it was plain to both Bean and Egg that they were in the presence of one who was sitting on top of the world and who, had he been wearing a hat, would have worn it on the side of his head. He looked, they thought, about as bumps-a-daisy as billy-o.

And, indeed, Lord Ickenham was feeling as bumps-a-daisy as he looked. It was a lovely day, all blue skies and ridges of high pressure extending over the greater part of the United Kingdom south of the Shetland Isles: he had just learned that his godson, Johnny Pearce, had at last succeeded in letting that house of his, Hammer Lodge, which had been lying empty for years, and on the strength of this had become engaged to a perfectly charming girl, always pleasant news for an affectionate godfather: and his wife had allowed him to come up to London for the Eton and Harrow match. For the greater part of the year Lady Ickenham kept him firmly down in the country with a watchful eye on him, a policy wholeheartedly applauded by all who knew him, particularly Pongo.

He seated himself, dodged a lump of sugar which a friendly hand had thrown from a neighbouring table, and beamed on his young friends like a Cheshire cat. It was his considered view that joy reigned supreme. If at this moment the poet Browning had come along and suggested to him that the lark was on the wing, the snail on the thorn, God in His heaven and all right with the world, he would have assented with a cheery 'You put it in a nutshell, my dear fellow! How right you are!'

'God bless my soul,' he said, 'it really is extraordinary how fit I'm feeling today. Bright eyes, rosy cheeks, and the sap rising strongly in my veins, as I believe the expression is. It's the London air. It always has that effect on me.'

Pongo started violently, not because another lump of sugar had struck him on the side of the head, for in the smoking-room of the Drones one takes these in one's stride, but because he found the words sinister and ominous. From earliest boyhood the loopiness of this uncle had been an open book to him and, grown to man's estate, he had become more than ever convinced that in failing to add him to their membership list such institutions as Colney Hatch and Hanwell were passing up a good thing, and he quailed when he heard him speak of the London air causing the sap to rise strongly in his veins. It seemed to suggest that his relative was planning to express and fulfil himself again, and when Frederick Altamont Cornwallis Twistleton, fifth Earl of Ickenham, began to express and fulfil himself, strong men – Pongo was one of them – quivered like tuning forks.

'The trouble with Pongo's Uncle Fred,' a thoughtful Crumpet had once observed in this same smoking-room, 'and what, when he is around, makes Pongo blench to the core and call for a couple of quick ones, is that, though well stricken in years, he becomes, on arriving in London, as young as he feels and proceeds to step high, wide and plentiful. It is as though, cooped up in the country all the year round with no way of working it off, he generates, if that's the word I want, a store of loopiness which expends itself with terrific violence on his rare visits to the centre of things. I don't know if you happen to know what the word "excesses" means, but those are what, the moment he sniffs the bracing air of the metropolis, Pongo's Uncle Fred invariably commits. Get Pongo to tell you some time about the day they had together at the dog races.'

Little wonder, then, that as he spoke, the young Twistleton was conscious of a nameless fear. He had been so hoping that it would have been possible to get through today's lunch without the old son of a bachelor perpetrating some major outrage on the public weal. Was this hope to prove an idle one?

It being the opening day of the Eton and Harrow match, the conversation naturally turned to that topic, and the Bean and the Egg, who had received what education they possessed at the Thames-side seminary, were scornful of the opposition's chances. Harrow, they predicted, were in for a sticky week-end and would slink home on the morrow with their ears pinned back.

'Talking of Harrow, by the way,' said the Bean, 'that kid of Barmy Phipps's is with us once more. I saw him in there with Barmy, stoking up on ginger pop and what appeared to be cold steak-and-kidney pie with two veg.'

'You mean Barmy's cousin Egbert from Harrow?'

'That's right. The one who shoots Brazil nuts.'

Lord Ickenham was intrigued. He always welcomed these opportunities to broaden his mind and bring himself abreast of modern thought. The great advantage of lunching at the Drones, he often said, was that you met such interesting people.

'Shoots Brazil nuts, does he? You stir me strangely. In my time I have shot many things – grouse, pheasants, partridges, tigers, gnus and once, when a boy, an aunt by marriage in the seat of her sensible tweed dress with an airgun – but I have never shot a Brazil nut. The fact that, if I understand you aright, this stripling makes a practice of this form of marksmanship shows once again that it takes all sorts to do the world's work. Not sitting Brazil nuts, I trust?'

It was apparent to the Egg that the old gentleman had missed the gist.

'He shoots things *with* Brazil nuts,' he explained.

'Puts them in his catapult and whangs off at people's hats,' said the Bean, clarifying the thing still further. 'Very seldom misses, either. Practically every nut a hat. We think a lot of him here.'

'Why?'

'Well, it's a great gift.'

'Nonsense,' said Lord Ickenham. 'Kindergarten stuff. The sort of thing one learns at one's mother's knee. It is many years since I owned a catapult and was generally referred to in the sporting world as England's answer to Annie Oakley, but if I had one now I would guarantee to go through the hats of London like a dose of salts. Would this child of whom you speak have the murder weapon on his person, do you suppose?'

'Bound to have,' said the Egg.

'Never travels without it,' said the Bean.

'Then present my compliments to him and ask if I might borrow it for a moment. And bring me a Brazil nut.'

A quick shudder shook Pongo from his upper slopes to the extremities of his clocked socks. The fears he had entertained about the shape of things to come had been realized. Even now, if his words meant what they seemed to mean, his uncle was preparing to be off again on one of those effervescent jaunts of his which had done so much to rock civilization and bleach the hair of his nearest and dearest.

He shuddered, accordingly, and in addition to shuddering uttered a sharp quack of anguish such as might have proceeded from some duck which, sauntering in a reverie beside the duck pond, has inadvertently stubbed its toe on a broken soda-water bottle.

'You spoke, Junior?' said Lord Ickenham courteously.

'No, really, Uncle Fred! I mean, dash it, Uncle Fred! I mean really, Uncle Fred, dash it all!'

'I am not sure that I quite follow you, my boy.'

'Are you going to take a pop at someone's hat?'

'It would, I think, be rash not to. One doesn't often get hold of a catapult. And a point we must not overlook is that, toppers being obligatory at the Eton and Harrow match, the spinneys and coverts today will be full of them, and it is of course the top hat rather than the bowler, the gent's Homburg and the fore-and-aft deerstalker as worn by Sherlock Holmes which is one's primary objective. I expect to secure some fine heads. Ah,' said Lord Ickenham, as the Bean returned, 'so this is the instrument. I would have preferred one with a whippier shaft, but we must not grumble. Yes,' he said, moving to the window, 'I think I shall be able to make do. It is not the catapult, it is the man behind it that matters.'

The first lesson your big game hunter learns, when on safari, is to watch and wait, and Lord Ickenham showed no impatience as the minutes went by and the only human souls that came in sight were a couple of shopgirls and a boy in a cloth cap. He was confident that before long something worthy of his Brazil nut would emerge from the Demosthenes Club, which stands across the street from the Drones. He had often lunched there with his wife's half-brother, Sir Raymond Bastable, the eminent barrister, and he knew the place to be full of splendid specimens. In almost no place in London does the tall silk headgear flourish so luxuriantly.

'Stap my vitals,' he said, enlivening the tedium of waiting with pleasant small-talk, 'it's extraordinary how vividly this brings back to me those dear old tiger-shooting days in Bengal. The same tense expectancy, the same breathless feeling that at any moment something hot may steal out from the undergrowth, lashing its top hat. The only difference is that in Sunny Bengal one was up in a tree with a kid tethered to it to act as an added attraction for the monarch of the jungle. Too late now, I suppose, to tether this young cousin of your friend Barmy Phipps to the railings, but if one of you would step out into the street and bleat a little . . . Ha!'

The door of the Demosthenes had swung open, and there had come down the steps a tall, stout, florid man of middle age who wore his high silk hat like the plumed helmet of Henry of Navarre. He stood on the pavement looking about him for a taxi-cab – with a sort of haughty impatience, as though he had thought that, when he wanted a taxi-cab, ten thousand must have sprung from their ranks to serve him.

'Tiger on skyline,' said the Egg.

'Complete with topper,' said the Bean. 'Draw that bead without delay, is my advice.'

'Just waiting till I can see the whites of his eyes,' said Lord Ickenham.

Pongo, whose air now was that of a man who has had it drawn to his attention that there is a ticking bomb attached to his coat-tails, repeated his stricken-duck impersonation, putting this time even more feeling into it. Only the fact that he had brilliantined them while making his toilet that morning kept his knotted and combined locks from parting and each particular hair from standing on end like quills upon the fretful porpentine.

'For heaven's sake, Uncle Fred!'

'My boy?'

'You can't pot that bird's hat!'

'Can't?' Lord Ickenham's eyebrows rose. 'A strange word to hear on the lips of one of our proud family. Did our representative at King Arthur's Round Table say "Can't" when told off by the front office to go and rescue damsels in distress from two-headed giants? When Henry the Fifth at Harfleur cried "Once more unto the breach, dear friends, once more, or close the wall up with our English dead," was he damped by hearing the voice of a Twistleton in the background saying he didn't think he would be able to manage it? No! The Twistleton in question, subsequently to do well at the battle of Agincourt, snapped into it with his hair in a braid and was the life and soul of the party. But it may be that you are dubious concerning my ability. Does the old skill still linger, you are asking yourself? You need have no anxiety. Anything William Tell could do I can do better.'

'But it's old Bastable.'

Lord Ickenham had not failed to observe this, but the discovery did nothing to weaken his resolution. Though fond of Sir Raymond Bastable, he found much to disapprove of in him. He considered the eminent barrister pompous, arrogant and far too pleased with himself.

Nor in forming this diagnosis was he in error. There may have been men in London who thought more highly of Sir Raymond Bastable than did Sir Raymond Bastable, but they would have been hard to find, and the sense of being someone set apart from and superior to the rest of the world inevitably breeds arrogance. Sir Raymond's attitude towards those about him – his nephew Cosmo, his butler Peasemarch, his partners at bridge, the waiters at the Demosthenes and, in particular, his sister, Phoebe Wisdom, who kept house for him and was reduced by him to a blob of tearful jelly almost daily – was always that of an irritable tribal god who intends to stand no nonsense from his worshippers and is prepared, should the smoked offering fall in any way short of the highest standard, to say it with thunderbolts. To have his top hat knocked off with a Brazil nut would, in Lord Ickenham's opinion, make him a better, deeper, more lovable man.

'Yes, there he spouts,' he said.

'He's Aunt Jane's brother.'

'Half-brother is the more correct term. Still, as the wise old saying goes, half a brother is better than no bread.'

'Aunt Jane will skin you alive, if she finds out.'

'She won't find out. That is the thought that sustains me. But I must not waste time chatting with you, my dear Pongo, much as I always enjoy your conversation. I see a taxi-cab approaching, and if I do not give quick service, my quarry will be gone with the wind. From the way his nostrils are quivering as he sniffs the breeze, I am not sure that he has not already scented me.'

Narrowing his gaze, Lord Ickenham released the guided missile, little knowing, as it sped straight and true to its mark, that he was about to enrich English literature and provide another job of work for a number of deserving printers and compositors.

Yet such was indeed the case. The question of how authors come to write their books is generally one not easily answered. Milton, for instance, asked how he got the idea for *Paradise Lost*, would probably have replied with a vague 'Oh, I don't know, you know. These things sort of pop into one's head, don't you know,' leaving the researcher very much where he was before. But with Sir Raymond Bastable's novel *Cocktail Time* we are on firmer ground. It was directly inspired by the accurate catapultmanship of Pongo Twistleton's Uncle Fred.

Had his aim not been so unerring, had he failed, as he might so well have done, to allow for windage, the book would never have been written.

# Chapter 2

Having finished his coffee and accepted the congratulations of friends and well-wishers with a modesty that became him well, the fifth Earl ('Old Sureshot') of Ickenham, accompanied by his nephew Pongo, left the club and hailed a taxi. As the cab rolled off, its destination Lord's cricket ground, Pongo, who had stiffened from head to foot like somebody in the Middle Ages on whom the local wizard had cast a spell, sat staring before him with unseeing eyes.

'What's the matter, my boy?' said Lord Ickenham, regarding him with an uncle's concern. 'You look white and shaken, like a dry martini. Something on your mind or what passes for it?'

Pongo drew a shuddering breath that seemed to come up from the soles of his feet.

'How crazy can you get, Uncle Fred?' he said dully.

Lord Ickenham could not follow him.

'Crazy? I don't understand you. Good heavens,' he said, a bizarre thought occurring to him, 'can it be that you are referring to what took place in the smoking-room just now?'

'Yes, it jolly well can!'

'It struck you as odd that I should have knocked off Raymond Bastable's topper with a Brazil nut?'

'It struck me as about as loopy a proceeding as I ever saw in my puff.'

'My dear boy, that was not loopiness, it was altruism. I was spreading sweetness and light and doing my day's kind act. You don't know Raymond Bastable, do you?'

'Only by sight.'

'He is one of those men of whom one feels instinctively that they *need* a Brazil nut in the topper, for while there is sterling stuff in them, it requires some sudden shock to bring it out. Therapeutic treatment the doctors call it, do they not? I am hoping that the recent nut will have changed his whole mental outlook, causing a revised and improved Raymond Bastable to rise from the ashes of his dead self. Do you know what the trouble is in this world?'

'You ought to. You've started most of it.'

'The trouble in this world,' said Lord Ickenham, ignoring the slur, 'is that so many fellows deteriorate as they grow older. Time, like an ever-rolling stream, bears all their finer qualities away, with the result that the frightfully good chap of twenty-five is changed little by little into the stinker of fifty. Thirty years ago, when he came down from Oxford, where he had been a prominent and popular member of the University rugby football team, Raymond Bastable was as bonhomous a young man as you could have wished to meet. The jovial way he would jump with both feet on the faces of opponents on the football field and the suavity of his deportment when chucked out of the Empire on Boat Race night won all hearts. Beefy, as we used to call him, was a fourteen-stone ray of sunshine in those days. And what is he now? I am still extremely fond of him and always enjoy his society, but I cannot blind myself to the fact that the passing of the years has turned him into what a mutual friend of ours – Elsie Bean, who once held office as housemaid under Sir Aylmer Bostock at Ashenden Manor – would call an overbearing dishpot. It's being at the Bar that's done it, of course.'

'How do you mean?'

'Surely it's obvious. A man can't go on year after year shouting "Chops! Gracious heavens, gentlemen, chops and tomato sauce!" and telling people that their evidence is a tissue of lies and fabrications without getting above himself. His character changes. He becomes a dishpot. What Beefy needs, of course, is a wife.'

'Ah,' said Pongo, who had recently acquired one. 'Now you're talking. If he had someone like Sally –'

'Or like my own dear Jane. You can't beat the holy state, can you? When you get a wife, I often say, you've got something. It was the worst thing that could have happened to Beefy when Barbara Crowe handed him his hat.'

'Who's Barbara Crowe?'

'The one he let get away.'

'I seem to know the name.'

'I have probably mentioned it to you. I've known her for years.

461

She's the widow of a friend of mine who was killed in a motor accident.'

'Isn't she in the movies?'

'Certainly not. She's a junior partner in Edgar Saxby and Sons, the literary agents. Ever heard of them?'

'No.'

'Well, I don't suppose they have ever heard of you, which evens things up. Yes, Beefy was engaged to her at one time, and then I heard that it was all off. Great pity. She's lovely, she's got a wonderful sense of humour, and her golf handicap is well in single figures. Just the wife for Beefy. In addition to improving his putting, always his weak spot, she would have made him human again. But it was not to be. What did you say?'

'I said "Bad show".'

'And you could scarcely have put it more neatly. It's a tragedy. Still, let's look on the bright side. There's always a silver lining. If things are not all that one could wish on the Bastable front, they're fine in the Johnny Pearce sector. How much did I tell you about Johnny at lunch? I can't remember. Did I mention that your Aunt Jane, exercising her subtle arts, had talked Beefy Bastable into taking a five years lease on that Hammer Lodge place of his?'

'Yes, you told me that.'

'And that he's engaged to a delightful girl? Belinda Farringdon, commonly known as Bunny?'

'Yes.'

'Then you're pretty well up in his affairs, and you will probably agree with me that a bright and prosperous future lies before him. Far different from that which, if your young friends at the Drones are to be believed, confronts the athletes of Harrow-on-the-Hill. But here we are at the Mecca of English cricket,' said Lord Ickenham, suspending his remarks as the cab drew up at the entrance of Lord's. 'Golly!'

'Now what?'

'If only,' said Lord Ickenham, surveying the sea of top hats before him, 'I had my catapult with me!'

They entered the ground, and Pongo, cordially invited to remain at his uncle's side, shied like a startled horse and said he would prefer to be pushing along. It was his settled policy, he explained, never again, if he could avoid it, to be associated with the head of the family in a public spot. Look, he argued, what happened that day at the dog races, and Lord Ickenham agreed that the episode to which he alluded had been in some respects an unfortunate one, though he had always maintained, he said, that a wiser magistrate would have been content with a mere reprimand.

A good deal of walking about and hullo-ing is traditionally done at the Eton and Harrow match, and for some little while after parting from his nephew Lord Ickenham proceeded to saunter hither and thither, meeting old acquaintances and exchanging amiable civilities. Many of these old acquaintances had been contemporaries of his at school, and the fact that most of them looked as if they would never see a hundred and four again was a reminder of the passage of time that depressed him, as far as he was capable of being depressed. It was a relief when he observed approaching him someone who, though stout and florid and wearing a top hat with a dent in it, was at least many years from being senile. He greeted him warmly.

'Beefy, my dear fellow!'

'Ah, Frederick.'

Sir Raymond Bastable spoke absently. His thoughts were else-where. He was sufficiently present in spirit to be able to say 'Ah, Frederick,' but his mind was not on his half-brother-in-law. He was thinking of the modern young man. At the moment when Lord Ickenham accosted him, there had just risen before his mental eye a picture of the interior of the Old Bailey, with himself in a wig and silk gown cross-examining with pitiless severity the representative of that sub-species who had knocked his hat off.

When the hat he loved had suddenly parted from its moorings and gone gambolling over the pavement like a lamb in springtime, Sir Raymond Bastable's initial impression that it had been struck by a flying saucer had not lasted long. A clapping of hands and the sound of cheering from across the street drew his attention to the smoking-room window of the Drones Club and he perceived that it framed a sea of happy faces, each split by a six-inch grin. A moment later he had seen lying at his feet a handsome Brazil nut, and all things were made clear to him. What had occurred, it was evident, had been one more exhibition of the brainless hooliganism of the modern young man which all decent people so deplored.

Sir Raymond had never been fond of the modern young man, considering him idiotic, sloppy, disrespectful, inefficient and, generally speaking, a blot on the London scene, and this Brazil-nut sequence put, if one may so express it, the lid on his distaste. It solidified the view he had always held that steps ought to be taken about the modern young man and taken promptly. What steps, he could not at the moment suggest, but if, say, something on the order of the Black Death were shortly to start setting about these young pests and giving them what was coming to them, it would have his full approval. He would hold its coat and cheer it on.

With a powerful effort he removed himself from the Old Bailey.

'So you're here, are you, Frederick?' he said.

'In person,' Lord Ickenham assured him. 'Wonderful, running into you like this. Tell me all your news, my bright and bounding barrister.'

'News?'

'How's everything at home? Phoebe all right?'

'She is quite well.'

'And you?'

'I also am quite well.'

'Splendid. You'll be even better when you're settled in down at Dovetail Hammer. Jane tells me you've taken Johnny Pearce's Hammer Lodge place there.'

'Yes. I shall be moving in shortly. Your godson, isn't he?'

'That's right.'

'I suppose that is why Jane was so insistent on my taking the house.'

'Her motives, I imagine, were mixed. She would, of course, for my sake be anxious to do Johnny a bit of good, but she also had your best interests at heart. She knew Dovetail Hammer was just the place for you. Good fishing, golf within easy reach and excellent fly-swatting to be had in the summer months. You'll be as snug as a bug in a rug there, and you'll find Johnny a pleasant neighbour. He's a capital young fellow.'

'Young?'

'Quite young.'

'Then tell him to keep away from me,' said Sir Raymond tensely. 'If any young man attempts to come near me, I'll set the dog on him.'

Lord Ickenham regarded him with surprise.

'You perplex me, Beefy. Why this bilious attitude towards the younger generation? Doesn't Youth with all its glorious traditions appeal to you?'

'It does not.'

'Why not?'

'Because, if you must know, some young thug knocked off my hat this afternoon.'

'You shock and astound me. With his umbrella?'

'With a Brazil nut.'

'Who was this fiend in human shape?'

'All I know is that he belongs to the Drones Club, which to my lasting regret is situated immediately opposite the Demosthenes. I was standing outside the Demosthenes, waiting for a cab, when something suddenly struck my hat a violent blow, lifting it from my head. I looked down, and saw a Brazil nut. It had obviously been thrown from the room on the ground floor of the Drones Club, for when I looked up the window was full of grinning faces.'

Sir Raymond started. A thought had occurred to him. 'Frederick!'

'Hullo?'

'Frederick!'

'Still here, old man.'

'Frederick, I invited you to lunch with me at the Demosthenes today.'

'And very kind of you it was.'

'You declined because you had a previous engagement to lunch at the Drones Club.'

'Yes. Agony, of course, but I had no option.'

'You did lunch at the Drones Club?'

'Heartily.'

'Did you take your after-luncheon coffee in the smoking-room?'

'I did.'

'Then I put it to you,' said Sir Raymond, pouncing, 'that you must have seen everything that occurred and can identify the individual responsible for the outrage.'

It was plain that Lord Ickenham was impressed by this remorseless reasoning. He stood musing for a space in silence, a frown of concentration on his brow.

'Difficult always to reconstruct a scene,' he said at length, 'but as I close my eyes and think back, I do dimly recall a sort of stir and movement at the window end of the room and a group of young fellows clustered about someone who had . . . yes, by Jove, he had a catapult in his hand.'

'A catapult! Yes, yes, go on.'

'He appeared to be aiming with it at some object across the street, and do you know, Beefy, I am strongly inclined to think that this object may quite possibly have been your hat. To my mind, suspicion seems to point that way.'

'Who was he?'

'He didn't give me his card.'

'But you can describe his appearance.'

'Let me try. I remember a singularly handsome, clean-cut face and on the face a look of ecstasy and exaltation such as Jael, the wife of Heber, must have worn when about to hammer the Brazil nut into the head of Sisera, but . . . no, the mists rise and the vision fades. Too bad.'

'I'd give a hundred pounds to identify the fellow.'

'With a view to instituting reprisals?'

'Exactly.'

'You wouldn't consider just saying "Young blood, young blood" and letting it go at that?'

'I would not.'

'Well, it's for you to decide, of course, but it's rather difficult to see what you can do. You can't write a strong letter to *The Times*.'

'Why not?'

'My dear fellow! It would be fatal. Jane was telling me the other day that you were going to stand for Parliament at . . . where was it? Whitechapel?'

'Bottleton East. Frampton is thinking of retiring, and there will be a by-election there next summer probably. I am expecting the nomination.'

'Well, then, think of the effect of a letter to *The Times* on the electorate. You know what the British voter is like. Let him learn that you have won the Derby or saved a golden-haired child from a burning building, and yours is the name he puts a cross against on his ballot paper, but tell him that somebody has knocked your topper off with a Brazil nut and his confidence in you is shaken. He purses his lips and asks himself if you are the right man to represent him in the mother of Parliaments. I don't defend this attitude, I merely say it exists.'

It was Sir Raymond's turn to muse, and having done so he was forced to admit that there was truth in this. Bottleton East, down Limehouse way, was one of those primitive communities where the native sons, largely recruited from the costermongering and leaning-up-against-the-walls-of-public-houses industries, have a primitive sense of humour and think things funny which are not funny at all. Picturing Bottleton East's probable reaction on learning of the tragedy which had darkened his life, he winced so strongly that his hat fell off and got another dent in it.

'Well,' he said, having picked it up, 'I do not intend to let the matter rest. I shall most certainly do something about it.'

'But what? That is the problem we come up against, is it not? You might . . . no, that wouldn't do. Or . . . no, that wouldn't do, either. I confess I see no daylight. What a pity it is that you're not an author. Then you would be on velvet.'

'I don't understand you. Why?'

'You could have got these views of yours on the younger generation off your chest in a novel. Something on the lines of Evelyn Waugh's *Vile Bodies* — witty, bitter, satirical and calculated to make the younger generation see itself as in a mirror and wish that Brazil nuts had never been invented. But in your case, of course, that is out of the question. You couldn't write a novel if you tried for a hundred years. Well, goodbye, my dear fellow,' said Lord Ickenham, 'I must be moving along. Lot of heavy Hullo-there-how-are-you-old-boy-ages-since-we-met-ing to be done before yonder sun sets. Sorry I could not have been of more help. If anything occurs to me later, I'll let you know.'

He tripped away, and Sir Raymond was conscious of a mounting sense of indignation. He strongly resented that remark about his not being able to write a novel if he tried for a hundred years. Who the devil was Ickenham to say whether he could write a novel or not?

Anything in the nature of a challenge had always been a spur to Sir Raymond Bastable. He was one of those men who take as a personal affront the suggestion that they are not capable of carrying to a successful conclusion any task to which they may see fit to set their hand. Years ago, when a boy at school, he had once eaten seven vanilla ice creams at a sitting because a syndicate of his playmates had betted him he couldn't. It sent him to the sanatorium for three days with frozen gastric juices, but he did it, and the passage of time had in no way diminished this militant spirit.

All through the rest of the day and far into the night he brooded smoulderingly on Lord Ickenham's tactless words, and rose from his bed next morning with his mind made up.

Write a novel?

Of course he could write a novel, and he would. Every man, they say, has one novel in him, and he had the advantage over most commencing authors of being in a state of seething fury. There is nothing like fury for stimulating the pen. Ask Dante. Ask Juvenal.

But though his theme was ready to hand and his rage continued unabated, there were moments, many of them, in the weeks that followed when only the iron Bastable will kept him from giving in and abandoning the project. As early as the middle of Chapter One he had discovered that there is a lot more to this writing business than the casual observer would suppose. Dante could have told him, and so could Juvenal, that it does not come easy. Blood, they would have said, is demanded of the man who sets pen to paper, also sweat and tears.

However, as their fellow poet Swinburne would have reminded them, even the weariest river winds somewhere safe to sea: and came a day when Sir Raymond was able to point at a mass of typescript on his desk, the top sheet of which was inscribed:

COCKTAIL TIME
by
RICHARD BLUNT

and to point at it with pride. His whole soul had gone into *Cocktail Time* – a biting title with its sardonic implication that that was all the younger generation lived for – and he knew it was good. It was an infernal shame, he felt, that circumstances compelled him to hide his identity under a pseudonym.

As, of course, they did. No question about that. It is all very well for your Dantes and your Juvenals to turn out the stuff under their own names, but a man who is hoping for the Conservative nomination at Bottleton East has to be cautious. Literary composition is not entirely barred to those whose ambition it is to carve for themselves a political career, but it has to be the right sort of literary composition – a scholarly Life of Talleyrand, for instance, or a thoughtful study of conditions in the poppet-valve industry. You cannot expect to get far on the road to Downing Street if you come up with something like *Forever Amber*.

And, he was forced to admit as he skimmed through its pages, that there was no gainsaying the fact that in both tone and substance *Cocktail Time* had much in common with Miss Winsor's masterpiece. Sex had crept into it in rather large quantities, for while exposing the modern young man he had not spared the modern young woman. His experiences in the divorce court – notably when appearing for the petitioner in the cases of Bingley versus Bingley, Botts and Frobisher and of Fosdick versus Fosdick, Wills, Milburn, O'Brien, ffrench-ffrench, Hazelgrove-Hazelgrove and others – had given him a low opinion of the modern young woman, and he saw no reason why she, too, should not have her share of the thunderbolts.

Yes, he mused, *Cocktail Time* was unquestionably outspoken in one or two spots, particularly Chapter 13. A Raymond Bastable, revealed as the man behind Chapter 13 and in a somewhat lesser degree Chapters 10, 16, 20, 22 and 24, could never hope to receive the nomination for the impending election at Bottleton East. A prudish Conservative Committee would reject him with a shudder and seek for their candidate elsewhere.

## Chapter 3

Into the early vicissitudes of Sir Raymond's brain-child it is not necessary to go in any great detail, for it had much the same experiences as any other first novel. He sent it from an accommodation address to Pope and Potter, and it came back. He sent it to Simms and Shotter, and it came back; to Melville and Monks, and it came back; to Popgood and Grooly, Bissett and Bassett, Ye Panache Presse and half a dozen other firms, and it came back again. It might have been a boomerang or one of those cats which, transferred from Surbiton to Glasgow, show up in Surbiton three months later a little dusty and footsore but full of the East-West-home's-best spirit. Why it should eventually have found journey's end in the offices of Alfred Tomkins Ltd one cannot say, but it did, and they published it in the spring, with a jacket featuring a young man with a monocle in his right eye doing the rock 'n roll with a young woman in her step-ins.

After that, as is customary on these occasions, nothing much happened. It has been well said that an author who expects results from a first novel is in a position similar to that of a man who drops a rose petal down the Grand Canyon of Arizona and listens for the echo. The book had a rather limited press. The *Peebles Courier* called it not unpromising, the *Basingstoke Journal* thought it not uninteresting, and the *Times Literary Supplement* told its readers that it was published by Alfred Tomkins Ltd and contained 243 pp., but apart from that it received no critical attention. The younger generation at whom it was aimed, if they had known of its existence, would have said in their uncouth way that it had laid an egg.

But Fame was merely crouching for the spring, simply waiting in the wings, as it were, for the cue which would bring it bounding on stage to drape the chaplet about the brow of its favoured son. At two minutes past five one Tuesday afternoon the venerable Bishop of Stortford, entering the room where his daughter Kathleen sat, found her engrossed in what he presumed to be a work of devotion but which proved on closer inspection to be a novel entitled *Cocktail Time*. Peeping over her shoulder, he was able to read a paragraph or two. She had got, it should be mentioned, to the middle of Chapter 13. At 5.5 sharp he was wrenching the volume from her grasp, at 5.6 tottering from the room, at 5.10 in his study scrutinizing Chapter 13 to see if he had really seen what he had thought he had seen.

He had.

At 12.15 on the following Sunday he was in the pulpit of the church of St Jude the Resilient, Eaton Square, delivering a sermon on the text 'He that touches pitch shall be defiled.' (Ecclesiasticus 13,1) which had the fashionable congregation rolling in the aisles and tearing up the pews. The burden of his address was a denunciation of the novel *Cocktail Time* in the course of which he described it as obscene, immoral, shocking, impure, corrupt, shameless, graceless and depraved, and all over the sacred edifice you could see eager men jotting the name down on their shirt cuffs, scarcely able to wait to add it to their library list.

In these days when practically anything from Guildford undertaker bitten in leg by Pekinese to Ronald Plumtree (11) falling off his bicycle in Walthamstow High Street can make the front page of the popular press as a big feature story with headlines of a size formerly reserved for announcing the opening of a world war, it was not to be expected that such an event would pass unnoticed. The popular press did it proud, and there was joy that morning in the offices of Alfred Tomkins Ltd. Just as all American publishers hope that if they are good and lead upright lives, their books will be banned in Boston, so do all English publishers pray that theirs will be denounced from the pulpit by a bishop. Full statistics are not to hand, but it is estimated by competent judges that a good bishop, denouncing from the pulpit with the right organ note in his voice, can add between ten and fifteen thousand to the sales.

Mr Prestwick, the senior partner, read the *Express*, the *Mail* and the *Mirror* in the train coming from his Esher home, and within five minutes of his arrival at the office was on the telephone to Ebenezer

Flapton and Sons, printers of Worcester and London, urging Eben-ezer and the boys to drop everything and start rushing out a large new edition. *Cocktail Time*, which Alfred Tomkins Ltd had been looking on all this while as just another of the stones the builder had refused, was plainly about to become the head stone of the corner.

But there was no corresponding joy in the heart of Sir Raymond Bastable as he paced the lawn of Hammer Lodge. Ever since he had read his morning paper at the breakfast table, his eyes had been glassy, his mind in a ferment.

To anyone who paces the lawn of Hammer Lodge, that desirable residence replete with every modern comfort, a wide choice of scenic beauties is available. He can look to the left and find his eye roving over green pasture land and picturesque woods, or he can look to the right and get an excellent view of the park of Hammer Hall with its lake and noble trees and beyond it the house itself, a lovely legacy from Elizabethan days. He can also, if it is a Monday, Wednesday or Friday, look in front of him and see a jobbing gardener leaning on a spade in a sort of trance in the kitchen garden. There is, in short, no stint.

But Sir Raymond saw none of these attractive sights or, if he did, saw them as through a glass darkly. His whole attention was riveted on the morrow and what it was going to bring forth. In writing *Cocktail Time*, he had had a malevolent hope that he would be starting something, but he had never expected to start anything of these dimensions, and the thought that chilled him to the very spinal marrow was this. Would that pseudonym of his be an adequate safeguard?

If there is one thing the popular press of today is, it is nosy. It tracks down, it ferrets out. Richard Blunt becomes front page news, and it is not long before it is asking itself who is this Richard Blunt? It wants photographs of him smoking a pipe or being kind to the dog and interviews with him telling the world what his favourite breakfast cereal is and what he thinks of the modern girl. It institutes enquiries and discovers that nobody has ever seen the gifted Blunt and that his only address is a sweets-and-tobacco shop in a side street near Waterloo station, and before you know where you are headlines have begun to appear. As it might be:

472

or

or possibly

and from that to exposure is but a step. At this very moment, Sir Raymond felt, a dozen reporters must be sniffing on his trail, and the contemplation of the appalling mess in which he had landed himself made him writhe like an Ouled Nail stomach-dancer.

He was still busily writhing when the voice of Peasemarch, his butler, spoke softly at his side. Albert Peasemarch always spoke softly when addressing Sir Raymond Bastable. He knew what was good for him. It is no pleasure to a butler to be thundered at and asked if he imagines himself to be a barrow boy calling attention to his blood oranges.

'I beg your pardon, Sir Raymond.'

The author of *Cocktail Time* came slowly out of the uneasy dream in which he had been sustaining the role of the stag at bay.

'Eh?'

'It is Madam, sir. I think you should come.'

'Come? What do you mean? Come where?'

'To Madam's room, sir. I am afraid she is not well. I was passing her door a moment ago, and I heard her sobbing. As if her heart would break,' said Peasemarch, who liked to get these things right.

A wave of exasperation and self-pity flooded Sir Raymond's tortured soul. Phoebe, he was thinking, *would* start sobbing at a time like this, when he needed to devote every little grey cell in his brain to the problem of how to elude those infernal reporters. For an instant he was inclined to counter with a firm refusal to go within a mile of Madam's room. He had just been deriving a faint consolation from the thought that, she having breakfasted in bed and he being about to take train and spend the day in London, he would not have to meet her till late tonight, by which time, he hoped, his agitation would be less noticeable. Phoebe, seeing him now, would infallibly ask what was the matter, and when he assured her that nothing was the matter would say 'But what *is* the matter, dear?' and carry on from there.

Then kindlier feelings prevailed, or possibly it was just the curiosity and urge to probe first causes which we all experience when told that someone is crying as if her heart would break. He accompanied Peasemarch back to the house and found his sister sitting up in bed, dabbing at her eyes with a liquid something that looked as if it might have been at one time a pocket handkerchief.

Except that her ears did not stick up and that she went about on two legs instead of four, Phoebe Wisdom was extraordinarily like a white rabbit, a resemblance which was heightened at the moment by the white dressing jacket she was wearing and the fact that much weeping had made her nose and eyes pink. As Sir Raymond closed the door behind him, she uttered a loud gurgling sob which crashed through his disordered nervous system like an expanding bullet, and his manner when he spoke was brusque rather than sympathetic.

'What on earth's the matter?' he demanded.

Another sob shook the stricken woman, and she said something that sounded like 'Cosh him'.

'I beg your pardon?' said Sir Raymond, clenching his hands till the knuckles stood out white under the strain, like the hero of an old-fashioned novel. He was telling himself that he must be calm, calm.

'Cossie!' said his sister, becoming clearer.

'Oh, Cosmo? What about him?'

'He says he's going to shoot himself.'

Sir Raymond was in favour of this. Cosmo Wisdom, the fruit of the unfortunate marriage Phoebe had made twenty-seven years ago, long before he had become influential and important enough to stop her, was a young man he disliked even more than he disliked most young men in these days when the species had deteriorated so lamentably. Algernon Wisdom, Cosmo's father, had at one time sold secondhand cars, at another been vaguely connected with the motion pictures, and had occasionally acted as agent for such commodities as the Magic Pen-Pencil and the Monumento Mouse Trap, but during the greater part of his futile career had been what he euphemistically described as 'between jobs', and Cosmo took after him. He, too, was frequently between jobs. He was one of those young men, with whom almost all families seem to be afflicted, who are in a constant state of having to have something done about them. 'We must do something about poor Cossie,' were words frequently on his mother's lips, and Sir Raymond would say in the unpleasant voice which he used when addressing hostile witnesses that he had no desire to be unduly inquisitive, but would she mind telling him what precisely she meant by the pronoun 'we'.

The most recent attempt on his part to do something about poor Cossie had been to secure him a post in the export and import firm of Boots and Brewer of St Mary Axe, and the letter his sister was reducing to pulp announced, he presumed, that Boots and Brewer had realized that the only way of making a success of importing and exporting was to get rid of him.

'What has he been doing?' he asked.

'What, dear?'

Sir Raymond took a turn about the room. He found it helped a little.

'Why have Boots and Brewer dismissed him? They have, I take it?'

'He doesn't say so. He just says he wants two hundred pounds.'

'He does, does he?'

'And I haven't *got* two hundred pounds.'

'Very fortunate. You won't be tempted to throw it down the drain.'

'What, dear?'

'Letting Cosmo have it would be tantamount to that. Don't give him a penny.'

'He doesn't want a penny, he wants two hundred pounds.'

'Let him want.'

'But he'll shoot himself.'

'Not a hope,' said Sir Raymond, with a wistful little sigh as the bright picture the words had conjured up faded. 'If he tries, he'll be sure to miss. For heaven's sake stop worrying. All that letter means is that he thinks he may get a tenner out of you.'

'He says two hundred pounds.'

'They always say two hundred pounds. It's common form.'

'What, dear?'

'Phoebe, in the name of everything infernal, *must* you put your head on one side like a canary and say "What, dear?" every time I speak to you? It's enough to madden a saint. Well, I can't stand here talking. I shall miss my train. Take an aspirin.'

'What, dear?'

'Take an aspirin. Take two aspirins. Take three,' said Sir Raymond vehemently, and whirled off like a tornado to the car which was waiting to convey him to the station.

# Chapter 4

Of the several appointments he had in London that day the first was lunch with Lord Ickenham at the Demosthenes Club. Arriving there, he found the place its old peaceful self, the smoking-room full of the usual living corpses lying back in armchairs and giving their minds a rest. He eyed them with distaste, resenting this universal calm at a time when he himself was feeling like a character in a Greek tragedy pursued by the Furies. Though he would have said, if you had asked him, that far too much fuss was made about being pursued by Furies. The time to start worrying was when you were pursued by reporters. Curse their notebooks and pencils and damn their soft hats and raincoats. He could see them in his mind's eye, dozens of them, creeping about like leopards and getting nosier every moment.

His guest was late, and to while away the time of waiting he went to the centre table and picked up a paper. One glance at its front page, and he had dropped it as if it had bitten him and was tottering to the nearest chair. It was not often that he indulged in alcoholic stimulant before lunch, but he felt compelled now to order a double dry martini. What he had seen on that front page had made him feel quite faint.

He had just finished it when Lord Ickenham was shown in, all apologies.

'My dear old Beefy, you must be feeling like Mariana at the moated grange. Sorry I'm so late. I started walking here in plenty of time, but I met Barbara in Bond Street.'

'Who?'

'Barbara Crowe.'

'Oh?'

'We got talking. She asked after you.'

'Oh?'

'Affectionately, I thought.'

'Oh?'

Lord Ickenham regarded him disapprovingly.

'It's no good saying "Oh?" in that tone of voice, Beefy, as if you didn't care a damn. You know perfectly well that one word of encouragement from her, and you would be at her side, rolling over on your back with all your paws in the air.'

'Well, really, Frederick!'

'You think I am showing a little too much interest in your private affairs?'

'If you like to put it that way.'

'I'm fond of you, Beefy, stuffed shirt though you have become after a promising youth and young manhood. I wish you well, and want to see you happy.'

'Very good of you. Cocktail?'

'If you'll join me.'

'I have had one.'

'Have another.'

'I think I will. Phoebe upset me this morning. Her son Cosmo appears to have been getting into trouble again. You know him?'

'Just sufficiently well to duck down a side street when I see him coming.'

'He is trying to borrow two hundred pounds.'

'You don't say? Big operator, eh? Will he get it?'

'Not from me.'

'Is Phoebe distressed?'

'Very.'

'And I suppose you yelled at her. That's your great defect, Beefy. You bark and boom and bellow at people. Not at me, for my austere dignity restrains you, but at the world in general. Used you to bellow at Barbara?'

'Shall we change —'

'I'll bet you did, and it was that that made her break off the engagement. But from the way she was speaking of you just now, I got the impression that your stock was still high with her and you've only to stop avoiding her and never seeing her to start things going again. For heaven's sake, what's a broken engagement? Jane broke ours six times. Why don't you look her up and take her out to lunch and make a fuss of her. Show yourself in a good light. Dance before her. Ask her riddles.'

'If you don't mind, Frederick, I really would prefer to change the subject.'

'Do simple conjuring tricks. Sing love songs accompanied on the guitar. And, just to show her you're not such a fool as you look, tell her that you are the author of the best-selling novel, *Cocktail Time*. That'll impress her.'

It is very rarely that the smoking-room of a club in the West End of London suddenly springs into spasmodic life, with its walls, its windows, its chairs, its tables, its members and its waiters pirouetting to and fro as if Arthur Murray had taught them dancing in a hurry, but that was what the smoking-room of the Demosthenes seemed to Sir Raymond Bastable to be doing now. It swayed and shimmied about him like something rehearsed for weeks by a choreographer, and it was through a sort of mist that he stared pallidly at his companion, his eyes wide, his lower jaw drooping, perspiration starting out on his forehead as if he were sitting in the hot room of a Turkish bath.

'What . . . what do you mean?' he gulped.

Lord Ickenham, usually so genial, betrayed a little impatience. His voice, as he spoke, was sharp.

'Now come, Beefy. You aren't going to say you didn't? My dear fellow, to anyone who knows you as I do, it's obvious. At least three scenes in the thing are almost literal transcriptions of stories you've told me yourself. You've used the Brazil nut episode. And apart from the internal evidence we have the statement of Jane.'

'Jane?'

'She came to London one day on a shopping binge and thought it would be the half-sisterly thing to do to look you up and slap you on the back, so she called at your house. You were out, but Peasemarch let her in and parked her in the study. After nosing about awhile, she started, as women will, to tidy your desk, and shoved away at the back of one of the drawers was a brown paper parcel from the publishing house of Simms and Shotter, despatched by them to Richard Blunt at some address which has escaped my memory. She mentioned this to me on her return. So you may as well come clean, Beefy. Denial is useless. You are this Blunt of whom we hear so much, are you not?'

A hollow groan escaped Sir Raymond.

'Yes. I am.'

'Well, I don't see what you're groaning about. With all this publicity you ought to make a packet, and if there's one thing in the world that's right up your street, it's money. You love the stuff.'

'But, Frederick, suppose it comes out? You haven't told anyone?'

'My dear fellow, why would I? I assumed from your having used a pseudonym that you wanted it kept dark.'

'And Jane?'

'Oh, Jane's forgotten all about it ages ago. It just happened to stick in my mind because I remembered saying something to you once about writing a novel. But what does it matter if it comes out?'

'Good heavens, it would mean the end of any hope I have of a political career.'

'Well, why do you want a political career? Have you ever been in the House of Commons and taken a good square look at the inmates? As weird a gaggle of freaks and subhumans as was ever collected in one spot. I wouldn't mix with them for any money you could offer me.'

'Those are not my views. I have set my heart on getting that nomination for Bottleton East, Frederick. And there isn't a chance that they will give it to me, if it's in all the papers that I wrote a book like *Cocktail Time*.'

'Why should it be in all the papers?'

'These reporters. They find things out.'

'Oh? Yes, I see.'

Lord Ickenham was silent for some moments. From the frown of concentration on his forehead he appeared to be exercising that ingenious brain of his.

'Yes,' he said, 'they do find things out. I suppose that's what worried Bacon.'

'Bacon?'

'And made him, according to the Baconians, get hold of Shakespeare and slip him a little something to say he had written the plays. After knocking off a couple of them, he got cold feet. "Come, come, Francis," he said to himself, "this won't do at all. Let it become known that you go in for this sort of thing, and they'll be looking around for another Chancellor of the Exchequer before you can say What-ho. You must find some needy young fellow who for a consideration will consent to take the rap." And he went out and fixed it up with Shakespeare.'

Sir Raymond sat up with a convulsive jerk, spilling his glass. For the first time since breakfast that morning he seemed to see dimly, like the lights of a public-house shining through a London fog, a ray of hope.

'Don't you know any needy young fellows, Beefy? Why, of course you do. One springs immediately to the mind. Your nephew Cosmo.'

'Good God!'

'You say he wants two hundred pounds. Give it him, and tell him he can stick to all the royalties on the book, and the thing's in the bag. You'll find him just as willing and eager to co-operate as Shakespeare was.'

Sir Raymond breathed deeply. The ray of hope had become a blaze. Across the room he could see old Howard Saxby, the Demosthenes Club's leading gargoyle, talking – probably about bird-watching, a pursuit to which he was greatly addicted – to Sir Roderick Glossop, the brain specialist, who was usually ranked as the institution's Number Two gargoyle, and it seemed to him that he had never beheld anything so attractive as the spectacle they presented.

'Frederick,' he said, 'you have solved everything. It's a wonderful idea. I don't know how to thank you . . . Yes?'

A waiter had materialized at his side, one of the waiters who a short while before had been dancing the shimmy with the walls, the tables and the chairs.

'A gentleman to see you, sir.'

As far as was possible in his seated position, Sir Raymond himself did a modified form of the shimmy. A reporter? Already?

'Who is he?' he asked pallidly.

'A Mr Cosmo Wisdom, sir.'

'What!'

'Beefy,' said Lord Ickenham, raising his glass congratulatorily, 'it's all over but the shouting. The hour has produced the man.'

# Chapter 5

It was in uplifted mood and with buoyant step that Sir Raymond a few moments later entered the small smoking-room, which was where visitors at the Demosthenes were deposited. He found his nephew huddled in a chair, nervously sucking the knob of his umbrella, and once again experienced the quick twinge of resentment which always came to him when they met. A social blot who was so constantly having to have something done about him had, in his opinion, no right to be so beautifully dressed. Solomon in all his glory might have had a slight edge on Cosmo Wisdom, but it would have been a near thing. Sir Raymond also objected to his beady eyes and his little black moustache.

'Good morning,' he said.

'Oh – er – hullo,' said Cosmo, standing on one leg.

'You wished to see me?'

'Er – yes,' said Cosmo, standing on the other leg.

'Well, here I am.'

'Quite,' said Cosmo, shifting back to the first leg. He was only too well aware that there he was.

It was as the result of a telephone conversation with his mother that the young man had ventured into the Demosthenes Club this morning. Phoebe, sobbingly regretting her inability to produce more than fifteen shillings and three pence of the two hundred pounds he required, had made a constructive suggestion. 'Why don't you ask your uncle, dear?' she had said, and Cosmo, though he would greatly have preferred to enter the cage of a sleeping tiger and stir it up with a short stick, had seen that this was the only way. A *tête-à-tête* with Sir Raymond Bastable always made him feel as if he were being disembowelled by a clumsy novice who had learned his job through a correspondence school, but when you are up against it for a sum like two hundred pounds it is necessary to sink personal prejudices and go to the man who has got two hundred pounds. Charm of manner, after all, is not everything.

So now, having taken one more refreshing suck at the umbrella knob, he stiffened the sinews, summoned up the blood and said:

'Er – uncle.'

'Yes?'

'Er – uncle, I don't want to bother you, but I wonder if you could . . . if you could manage . . . if you could see your way to letting me have . . .'

'What?'

'Eh?'

Sir Raymond adopted the second of the two manners that got him so disliked by witnesses in court, the heavily sarcastic.

'Let me refresh your memory, my dear Cosmo. After expressing a kindly fear that you might be bothering me – an idle fear, for you are not bothering me in the least – you went on to say "I wonder if you could . . . if you could manage . . . if you could see your way to letting me have . . ." and there you paused, apparently overcome with emotion. Naturally, my curiosity aroused, I ask "What?" meaning by the question, what is it you are hoping that I shall be able to see my way to letting you have? Can it be that your visit has something to do with the letter I found your mother bedewing with her tears this morning?'

'Er – yes.'

'She was somewhat incoherent, but I was able to gather from her that you need two hundred pounds.'

Actually, Cosmo needed two hundred and fifty, but he could not bring himself to name the sum. And anyway, though his bookmaker, to whom he owed two hundred, must be paid immediately, his friend Gordon Carlisle, to whom he was in debt for the remainder, would surely be willing to wait for his money.

'Er – yes. You see –'

Sir Raymond was now enjoying himself thoroughly. He reached for his coat tails as if they had been those of a silk gown and gave a sidelong glance at an invisible jury, indicating to them that they had better listen carefully to this, because it was going to be good.

'With the deepest respect,' he said, 'you are in error. I do not see. I am at a loss. Boots and Brewer pay you a good salary, do they not?'

'I wouldn't call it good.'

Sir Raymond shot another glance at the jury.

'You must pardon me, a rude unlettered man, if by inadvertence I have selected an adjective that fails to meet your critical approval. One is not a Flaubert. I have always considered your emolument – shall we say, adequate.'

'But it isn't. I keep running short. If I don't get two hundred quid today, I don't know what I shall do. I'm half inclined to end it all.'

'So your mother was telling me. An excellent idea, in my opinion, and one that you should consider seriously. But she, I believe, does not see eye to eye with me on that point, so as I have a great fondness for her in spite of her habit of putting her head on one side and saying "What, dear?" I am prepared to save you from making the last supreme sacrifice.'

Cosmo came up from the depths. It was always difficult to understand what his relative was talking about, but there had been something in that last remark that sounded promising.

'You mean –?'

'Two hundred pounds is a lot of money, but it is just possible that I might be able to manage it. What do you want it for?'

'I owe it to a bookie, and he – er – he's making himself rather unpleasant.'

'I can readily imagine it. Bookies are apt to get cross on occasion. Well, I think I can help you out.'

'Oh, uncle!'

'On certain conditions. Let us speak for a while of current literature. Have you read any good books lately, Cosmo? This novel *Cocktail Time*, for instance?'

'The thing there was all that in the *Express* about this morning?'

'Precisely.'

'No, I haven't read it yet, but I'm going to. It sounds hot stuff. Nobody seems to know who wrote it.'

'I wrote it.'

This was so obviously a whimsical jest that Cosmo felt it only civil to smile. He did so, and was asked by his uncle not to grin like a half-witted ape.

'I wrote it, I repeat. I assume that you can understand words of one syllable.'

Cosmo gaped. His hand, as always in moments of surprise and bewilderment, flew to his upper lip.

'That moustache of yours looks like a streak of ink,' said Sir Raymond malevolently. 'Stop fondling it and listen to me. I wrote *Cocktail Time*. Is your weak mind able to grasp that?'

'Oh, rather. Oh, quite. But –'

'But what?'

'Er – why?'

'Never mind why.'

'Well, I'll be damned!'

'And so shall I, if it ever comes out.'

'Is it as bad as all that?'

'It is not bad at all. It is frank and outspoken, but as a work of fiction it is excellent,' said Sir Raymond, pausing to wonder if it was worth while to quote the opinions of the *Peebles Courier* and the *Basingstoke Journal*. He decided that they would be wasted on his present audience. 'It is not, however, the sort of book which a man in my position is expected to write. If those reporters find out that I did write it, my political career will be ruined.'

'It's a bit near the knuckle, you mean?'

'Exactly.'

Cosmo nodded intelligently. The thing was beginning to make sense to him.

'I see.'

'I supposed you would. Now, the thought that immediately flashes into your mind, of course, is that you are in a position on parting from me to hurry off and sell this information to the gutter press for what it will fetch, and I have no doubt that you would leap to the task. But it would be a short-sighted policy. You can do better for yourself than that. Announce that you are the author of *Cocktail Time* –'

'Eh?'

'I want you to give it out that it was you who wrote the book.'

'But I never wrote anything in my life.'

'Yes, you did. You wrote *Cocktail Time*. I think I can make it clear even to an intelligence like yours that our interests in this matter are identical. We both benefit from what I have proposed. I regain my peace of mind, and you get your two hundred pounds.'

'You'll really give it me?'

'I will.'

'Coo!'

'And in addition you may convert to your own use such royalties as may accrue from the book.'

'Coo!' said Cosmo again, and was urged by his uncle to make up his mind whether he was a man or a pigeon.

'These,' said Sir Raymond, 'in light of the publicity it is receiving should be considerable. My contract calls for ten per cent of the published price, and after all this fuss in the papers I should imagine that the thing might sell – well, let us be conservative – say ten thousand copies, which would work out – I am no mathematician, but I suppose it would work out at between six and seven hundred pounds.'

Cosmo blinked as if something had struck him between the eyes.

'Six and seven hundred?'

'Probably more.'

'And I get it?'

'You get it.'

'Coo!' said Cosmo, and this time the ejaculation passed without rebuke.

'I gather,' said Sir Raymond, 'from your manner that you are willing to co-operate. Excellent. Everything can be quite simply arranged. I would suggest a letter to each of the papers which have commented on the affair, hotly contesting the bishop's views, which you consider uncalled for, intemperate and unjust, and revealing yourself as Richard Blunt. If you will come to the writing-room, I will draft out something that will meet the case.'

And having done so, Sir Raymond returned to the smoking-room to tell Lord Ickenham that the thing, as he had predicted it would be, was in the bag.

## Chapter 6

As might have been expected, the announcement, appearing in the papers two days later, that Cosmo Wisdom was the author of the novel *Cocktail Time*, now at the height of its notoriety, did not pass unnoticed. One of the first to notice it was J. P. Boots of Boots and Brewer, and it was the work of an instant for him, on arriving at his office in St Mary Axe, to summon the young man to his presence and inform him that his services, such as they were, would no longer be required. Import and export merchants, whether of St Mary Axe or elsewhere, have the reputation of the firm to think of and cannot afford to retain in their entourage employees capable of writing Chapter 13 of that work. J. P. Boots did not in so many words bid Cosmo go and sin no more, but this was implied in his manner.

It was, however, only this importer and exporter who struck the jarring note. Elsewhere the reactions were uniformly pleasant. Alfred Tomkins Ltd wrote Cosmo an affectionate letter, telling him to come up and see them some time, and an equally affectionate letter came from Howard Saxby of Edgar Saxby and Sons, the literary agents, recommending him to place his affairs in the hands of the Saxby organization (offices in London, New York and Hollywood). This Cosmo, feeling that the situation in which he had been placed was one of those where a fellow needs a friend, decided to do, though wincing a little at the thought of that ten per cent commission.

Two little girls, Ava Rackstraw, aged ten, and Lana Cootes (12) wrote asking for his autograph, saying that he had long been their favourite author and they had read all his books. He was invited to address the Herne Hill Literary Society on 'Some Aspects of the Modern Novel'. Six unpublished authors sent him their unpublished works with a request for a detailed criticism. And Ivor Llewellyn, president of the Superba-Llewellyn motion picture company of Hollywood, about to return to California after a visit to London, told his secretary to go out and buy a copy of the book for him to read on the plane. Mr Llewellyn was always on the look-out for material which, if he could ease it past the Johnston office, would excite the clientele, and *Cocktail Time*, from what everyone was saying about it, seemed likely to be just the sort of thing he wanted.

And, finally, Mrs Gordon Carlisle, breakfasting in the sitting-room of the flat which she shared with her husband, opened her morning paper, looked at page one, started, said something that sounded like 'Cheese!' and lifting her attractive head shouted 'Hey, Oily!'

'Yes, sweetie?'

'Cummere,' said Mrs Carlisle, and there entered from the bedroom a tall, slender, almost excessively gentlemanly man in a flowered dressing-gown, who might have been the son of some noble house or a Latin-American professional dancer.

Actually, he was neither. He was a confidence trick artist whose virtuosity won him considerable respect in the dubious circles in which he moved. American by birth and residence, he had brought his wife to Europe on a pleasure trip. After years of strenuous work he proposed to take a sabbatical, though of course if something really good came up, he was always prepared to get back into harness again. The Carlisles did not spare themselves.

'Yay?' he said, hoping that his loved one had not summoned him to tell him he must wear his thick woollies. She had a way of doing so when the English summer was on the chilly side, and they tickled him. ''Smatter, sweetie?'

'Want to show you somef'n.'

Gertrude ('Sweetie') Carlisle was a strapping young woman with bold hazel eyes and a determined chin. These eyes were now flashing, and the chin protruded. It was plain that what she had read had stirred her.

'Listen, Oily. Didn't you tell me you won fifty pounds from a guy named Cosmo Wisdom the other night?'

Mr Carlisle nodded. It was the sombre nod of a man reluctant to be reminded of a sad experience.

'I did, yes. But he didn't pay me. He turned out to be one of these forty-dollar-a-week city clerks. The woods are full of them over here. They fool you by dressing like dukes, and when it's too late you find they're office boys or something. That's what you get for coming to a strange country. It would never have happened back home.'

'What did you do?'

'I didn't do anything.'

'I'd have busted him one.'

Mr Carlisle could well believe it. Impulsiveness and a sturdy belief in direct action were the leading features of his mate's interesting character. Some time had passed since the incident occurred and the bump had gone down now, but there still remained green in his memory the occasion when a fancied misdemeanour on his part had led her to hit him on the back of the head with a large vase containing gladioli. It had, in his opinion, spoiled the honeymoon.

'Well, too late to do anything now,' he said moodily. 'Just got to write it off as a bad debt.'

'Bad debt nothing. He was playing you for a sucker.'

Mr Carlisle started. His *amour-propre* was wounded.

'A sucker? *Me?*'

'Certainly he was. He was holding out on you. Read this.'

'Read what?'

'This.'

'Which?'

'This stuff in the paper here about him having written this book they're all talking about. He's got oodles of money. It's a best seller.'

Mr Carlisle took the paper, scanned it and said 'Well, I'll be darned!' Gentlemanliness was his aim in life, for he had found it his best professional asset, and he seldom used any stronger expletive.

'Looks like you're right.'

'Sure, I'm right.'

'Unless,' said Oily, struck by a damping thought, 'it's some other Cosmo Wisdom.'

His wife scoffed at the theory. Even in England, she reasoned, there couldn't be two men with a name like that.

'Where does he live, this guy?'

'Down Chelsea way. One of those side streets off the King's Road.'

'Then have a bite of breakfast and go see him.'

'I will.'

'Don't come back without those fifty smackers.'

'I won't.'

'Get tough.'

'You betcher.'

'And wear your thick woollies.'

'Oh, sweetie! Must I?'

'Certainly you must. There's a nasty east wind.'

'But they make me want to scratch.'

'Well, go ahead, then. They can't gaol you for scratching.'

'Oh, hell!' said Oily.

It was not a word he often employed, but it seemed to him that the circumstances justified it.

It was getting on for lunch time when he returned to the little nest, and there was nothing in his face to indicate whether his mission had had a happy ending or the reverse. The better to succeed in his chosen career, Oily Carlisle had trained his features to a uniform impassivity which often caused his wife annoyance. Though recognizing the professional value of a dead pan, she wished that he would not carry it into the life of the home.

'Well?' she said.

'Rustle me up an old-fashioned, will you, sweetie?' said Oily. 'My tongue's hanging out.'

Mrs Carlisle rustled him up an old-fashioned, and having done so said 'Well?' again.

'Did you see him?'

'I saw him.'

'What did he say?'

'Plenty.'

'Did you get the fifty?'

'No. Matter of fact, I lent him another twenty.'

'For heaven's sake!'

'But I got something a darned sight better than fifty pounds.'

'What do you mean?'

'I'll tell you.'

In Oily's demeanour as he took another sip of his cocktail and prepared to speak there was a suggestion of that Ancient Mariner of whom the poet Coleridge wrote. Like him, he knew he had a good story to relate, and he did not intend to hurry it.

'Yes, I saw him, and I said I'd been expecting to hear from him before this, because wasn't there a little matter of a hundred and fifty dollars or so he owed me, and he said Yes, that was right, and I said it would be righter, if he'd come through with it, and he said he hadn't got it.'

'The nerve!'

Oily took in the last drops of his old-fashioned, lit a cigarette and put his feet on the table.

'And he couldn't raise it, he said. Oh, no? I said. How about this book of yours you can't pick up a paper without seeing all that stuff about it? I said. The money must be pouring in like a tidal wave, I said.'

'What did he say to that?'

'Said it wasn't any such thing. These publishers pay up twice a year, he said, and it would be months before he could touch. I said Well, why didn't he get something from them in advance, and he said he'd just been trying to and they'd told him it would be foreign to their policy to anticipate the customary half-yearly statement.'

'Do what?'

'They wouldn't bite. Said he'd have to wait.'

'So what did you say?'

'I said "Too bad".'

A bitter sneer marred the beauty of Gertrude Carlisle's face.

'Got all fierce, didn't you? Scared the pants off him, I shouldn't wonder.'

'I said "Too bad",' proceeded Oily equably, 'and I said "Sweetie will be vexed", I said, and he said "Who's Sweetie?" and I said "Mrs Carlisle". And when Sweetie's vexed, I said, she generally hits people over the head with a bottle. And I told him about you and me and the vase.'

'Oh, honey, we've forgotten all that.'

'I haven't. Forgiven, yes. Forgotten, no. I can remember, just the same as if it had been yesterday, how it feels to get hit on the back of the head with a vase containing gladioli, and I described the symptoms to him. He turned greenish.'

'And then?'

'Then I came away.'

Mrs Carlisle's lips had closed in a tight line, and there was a sombre glow in her fine eyes. Her air was that of a woman thinking in terms of bottles and making a mental note to set aside the next one that became empty.

'What's this guy's address?'

'Why?'

'I thought I'd call around and say Hello.'

'You won't need to. Relax, sweetie. You ain't heard nothing yet. When I told you I came away, I ought to have said I started to come away, because he called me back. Seemed worried, I thought. He was gulping quite a good deal.'

'I'll gulp him!'

'And then he came clean and spilled the whole works. You know what he said? He said he didn't write that book at all.'

'And you believed him?'

'Sure I believed him, after I'd heard the rest of it. He said his uncle wrote it. His uncle's a guy called Sir Raymond Bastable. Big lawyer and going in for politics and knew that if it came out that he had written this *Cocktail Time* thing, he'd be ruined.'

'Why?'

'Seems in England you can't mix writing that sort of book with standing for Parliament, which is what he's set on. So he got our Mr Wisdom to say he'd done it. Well, I needn't tell you what I said to myself when I heard that.'

'Yes, you need. What did you say to yourself?'

'I said "Here's where I touch the big money."'

'I don't get it.'

Oily smiled an indulgent smile.

'Look, sweetie. Use your bean. You're this Bastable character. You write a book, and it's too hot to handle, so you get your nephew to take the rap, and the papers run a big story about it's him that wrote it. All straight so far?'

'Sure, but –'

'Well, what do you do when you get a letter from the nephew

saying he's been thinking it over and his conscience won't let him go on with the ramp, so he's going to tell the world it wasn't him who done it, it was you? Here's what you do – you pay up. You say "How much do you want, to keep this under your hat?" And you get charged as much as the traffic will bear.'

Mrs Carlisle's eyes widened. Her lips parted. She might have known, she was feeling, that she could have trusted her Oily. Gazing at him reverently, she expressed her emotion in a quick 'Gosh!'

'But will he do it?'

'Will who do what?'

'This Wisdom fellow. Will he write the letter?'

'He's done it. I've got it right here in my pocket. I said I'd mail it for him. I explained the idea, and he saw it at once. Very enthusiastic he was. He said his Uncle's got all the money in the world – you know what they pay these big lawyers – and there isn't a chance that he won't cough up prac'lly anything.'

'Protection money.'

'That's right, protection money. So I dictated the letter and brought it away with me. That's when I loaned him that twenty pounds. He said he wanted to celebrate. Now what?' asked Oily, noting that a cloud had passed over the face of the moon of his delight.

'I was only feeling what a pity it is you'll have to split with him. You will, I guess?'

'That's what he guesses, too, but, ask me, he's guessing wrong. I'm taking the letter to this Bastable after lunch – he's living in the country at a place called Dovetail Hammer – and I shall want the money right down on the counter. Well, of course, it's just possible I may decide to give Wisdom his half of it, but I doubt it, sweetie, I doubt it very much indeed.'

'Oily,' said Mrs Carlisle, her eyes shining with a soft light, 'there's no one like you. You're wonderful.'

'I'm pretty good,' agreed Mr Carlisle modestly.

## Chapter 7

The 3.26, Oily decided, having consulted the railway guide, was the train to take to Dovetail Hammer. It would, he pointed out, give them nice time for lunch at the Ritz and Gertie, all enthusiasm, begged him to lead her to it. Too often in her past luncheon had had to be a thing of sandwiches and dill pickles on the home premises, and she was a girl who, like the fifth Earl of Ickenham, enjoyed stepping high, wide and plentiful.

It was at about the moment when they were sipping their coffee and Oily had lighted a seven-and-sixpenny cigar that Lord Ickenham, who had been taking the mid-day meal with his nephew Pongo at the Drones preparatory to going and visiting his godson at Hammer Hall, looked out of the smoking-room window at the Demosthenes across the way and heaved a sigh.

'Boo!' said Pongo.

'I beg your pardon?'

'Just trying to scare you. Said to be good for hiccups.'

'It would take a lot more than that to scare an intrepid man like me. Chilled Steel Ickenham they used to call me in the old regiment. And, anyway, that was not a hiccup, it was a sigh.'

'Why were you sighing?'

'Because I felt a pang. No, sorry, three pangs. What caused one of them was the thought that, going off to stay with Johnny, I shall be deprived for quite a time of your society and those pleasant and instructive afternoons we have so often had together. It would have been delightful to have remained in London, seeing the sights with you.'

'You don't see any ruddy sights with *me*. I know you when you're seeing sights.'

'My second pang – Pang B you might call it – was occasioned by looking across the street at the Demosthenes Club, for it brought

494

my semi-brother-in-law, Beefy Bastable, to my mind. I found myself thinking of something that happened last summer. You have probably forgotten the incident, but about a year ago, seated in this window, I shot his topper off with a Brazil nut.'

'Gosh!'

'Ah, I see you remember. Well, I had hoped that the experience would have proved a turning point in his life, making him a gentler, kinder Beefy, a sweeter, softer Bastable, more patient with and tolerant of his sister Phoebe. I was too sanguine.'

'Isn't he patient with and tolerant of his sister Phoebe?'

'Far from it. My well-meant effort appears to have had no effect whatsoever. According to Peasemarch, his butler, with whom I correspond, his manner towards her is still reminiscent of that of Captain Bligh of the *Bounty* displeased with the behaviour of one of the personnel of the fo'c's'le. Of course, he could make out a case for himself, I suppose. Phoebe, poor lost soul, has a way of putting her head on one side like a canary and saying "What, dear?" when spoken to which must be very annoying to a man accustomed to having one and all hang upon his lightest word. It is when she has done this some six or seven times in the course of a breakfast or luncheon that, according to Peasemarch, he shoots up to the ceiling in a sheet of flame and starts setting about her regardless of her age and sex. Yes, I can see his side of the thing, but it must be very bad for his blood pressure and far from pleasant for all concerned. Peasemarch says it wrings his heart to listen with his ear to the keyhole. You don't know Bert Peasemarch, do you?'

'No.'

'Splendid chap. About as much brain as you could put comfortably into an aspirin bottle, but what are brains if the heart be of gold? I first met him when he was a steward on the Cunard-White Star. Later, he came into some house property and left the sea and settled down in a village near Ickenham. Then, if you remember, war broke out and there was all that bother about the invasion of England, and I joined the Home Guard, and whom should I find standing shoulder to shoulder with me but Bert Peasemarch. We saw it through together, sitting up all night at times, chilled to the bone, but with our upper lips as stiff as our hip joints. Well, two men don't go through all that without becoming buddies. I grew to love Bert like a brother, and he grew to love me like a brother. Two brothers in all. I got him his job with Beefy.'

'I thought you said he came into house property.'

'Quite a bit of it, I understand.'

'Then why did he want to buttle?'

'Ennui, my dear boy, the ennui that always attacks all these fellows who retire in their prime. He missed the brave tang of the old stewarding days. Years of life on the ocean wave had left him ill-fitted to sit on his fat trouser seat and do nothing. Well, a steward is practically a butler, so I advised him to make a career of that. My Coggs down at Ickenham coached him, and when Coggs said the time was ripe, I unloaded him on Beefy.'

'How did he get on with him?'

'I think he found him something of a trial. But that was before Beefy moved to the country. Who knows that living in the country will not improve him out of all knowledge. The quiet rural life does have a wonderful effect on people. Take me. There are times, I admit, when being cooped up at Ickenham makes me feel like a caged skylark, though not of course looking like one, but there is no question that it has been the making of me. I attribute to it the fact that I have become the steady, sensible, perhaps rather stodgy man I am today. I beg your pardon?'

'Eh?'

'I thought you spoke.'

'I said "Ha!" if you call that speaking.'

'Why did you say "Ha!"?'

'Because I felt like saying "Ha!" No objection to me saying "Ha," is there?'

'None whatever. This is Liberty Hall.'

'Thanks. Well, I can't see it.'

'See what?'

'All this about old Bastable becoming a different man. According to you, he still bites pieces out of his sister.'

'Merely because he is always coming up to London and bullying witnesses in court. This makes his progress slower than one could wish. But I am confident that the magic of Dovetail Hammer will eventually work. Give him time. It isn't easy for leopards to change their spots.'

'Do they want to?'

'I couldn't say. I know so few leopards. But I think Beefy will improve. If Barbara Crowe hadn't returned him to store, he would already have become a reformed character. I am convinced that, married to her, he would today be the lovable Beefy of thirty years ago, for she wouldn't have stood that Captain Bligh stuff for a minute. Too bad the union blew a fuse, but how sadly often that happens. When you get to my age, my dear Pongo, you will realize that what's wrong with the world is that there are far too many sundered hearts in it. I've noticed it again and again. It takes so little to set a couple of hearts asunder. That's why I'm worried about Johnny.'

'Isn't he all right?'

'Far from it.'

'Doesn't he like being married?'

'He isn't married. That's the whole trouble. He's been engaged to Bunny Farringdon for more than a year, but not a move on his part to set those wedding bells ringing out in the little village church. She speaks to him of buying two of everything for her trousseau and begs him to let her have the green light, but all she gets is a "Some other time". It gives me a pang.'

'Pang C?'

'Pang, as you say, C. Good heavens,' said Lord Ickenham, looking at his watch. 'Is it as late as that? I must rush. I'm catching the 3.26.'

'But half a second. Tell me more about this. Isn't she getting fed up?'

'Distinctly so. I was having lunch with her yesterday, and the impression I received was that she was becoming as mad as a wet hen. Any day now I expect to see in *The Times* an announcement that the wedding arranged between Jonathan Twistleton Pearce of Hammer Hall, Dovetail Hammer, Berks., and Belinda Farringdon of Plunkett Mews, Onslow Square, South Kensington, will not take place.'

'What do you think's at the bottom of it? Money? Johnny's pretty hard up, of course.'

'Not too well fixed, I agree. The cross he has to bear is that Hammer Hall is one of those betwixt-and-between stately homes of

England, so large that it costs the dickens of a lot to keep up but not large enough to lure the populace into packing sandwiches and hard-boiled eggs and coming in charabancs to inspect it at half-a-crown a head. Still, what with running it as a guest-house and selling an occasional piece of furniture and writing those suspense novels of his, he should be in a position to get married if he wants to. Especially now that he is getting quite a satisfactory rent from Beefy for the Lodge. I don't think money is the trouble.'

Pongo drew thoughtfully at his cigarette. A possible solution of the mystery had occurred to him. Devoted to his Sally, he personally would not have looked at another female – no, not even if she had come leaping at him in the nude out of a pie at a bachelor party, but he was aware that there were other, less admirable men who were inclined to flit like butterflies from flower to flower and to run their lives more on the lines of Don Juan and Casanova. Could it be that his old friend Jonathan Pearce was one of these?

'I don't often get together with Johnny these days,' he said. 'It must be well over a year since I saw him last. How is he as of even date?'

'Quite robust, I believe.'

'I mean in the way of staunchness and steadfastness. It just struck me that the reason he's jibbing at jumping off the dock might be that he's met someone else down at Dovetail Hammer.'

'Do you know Dovetail Hammer?'

'Never been there.'

'I thought you hadn't, or you would not have made a fatuous suggestion like that. It isn't a place where you meet someone else. There's the vicar's daughter, who is engaged to the curate, and the doctor's daughter, betrothed to a chap who's planting coffee in Kenya, and that, except for Phoebe and Johnny's old nurse, Nannie Bruce, exhausts the female population. It's not possible for his heart to have strayed.'

'Well, something must have happened.'

'Unquestionably.'

'You'd better talk to him.'

'I intend to, like a Dutch godfather. We can't have this playing fast and loose with a young girl's affections. Letting the side down, is the way I look at it. And now, young Pongo, stand out of my way, or I'll roll over you like a Juggernaut. If I miss that train, there isn't another till five-forty.'

# Chapter 8

Unless your destination is within comfortable walking distance – the Blue Boar, let us say, or the Beetle and Wedge, both of which are just across the street from the station – the great thing to do on alighting from the train at Dovetail Hammer is to nip out quick and make sure of getting the station cab. (There is only one – Arthur Popworth, proprietor.)

Lord Ickenham, who had been there before and knew the ropes, did this. The afternoon was now warm, and he had no desire to trudge the mile to the Hall carrying a suitcase. He had just bespoken Mr Popworth's services and was about to enter the vehicle, when there emerged from the station a gentlemanly figure crying 'Hey, taxi!' and registering chagrin on perceiving that he had been fore-stalled. Oily Carlisle had lingered on the platform seeking from a porter with no roof to his mouth information as to where Sir Raymond Bastable was to be found.

Lord Ickenham, always the soul of consideration, turned back and beamed with his customary geniality. He did not particularly like Oily's looks, but he was humane.

'If you are going my way, sir,' he said, 'I shall be delighted to give you a lift.'

'Awfully kind of you, sir,' said Oily in the Oxford accent which he had been at some pains to cultivate for professional purposes. 'I want a place called Hammer Hall.'

'My own objective. Are you staying there?'

'No – I'm –'

'I thought you might be. It's a guest-house now.'

'Is that so? No, I'm returning to town. Just run down to see a man on business. Hammer Lodge the porter said the name of his house was, and it's somewhere near the Hall.'

'Just before you get there. I'll drop you.'

'Frightfully kind of you.'

'Not at all, not at all. It all comes under the head of spreading sweetness and light.'

The cab made a noise like an explosion in a boiler factory and began to move. There was a momentary silence in its interior, occupied by Lord Ickenham in wondering what business this dubious character, whose fishiness his practised eye had detected at a glance, could have to conduct with Beefy; by Oily in massaging the small of his back. For a long time now the heavy underclothing on which his loved one had insisted had been irking him.

'Warm day,' said Lord Ickenham at length.

'I'll say,' said Oily. 'And can you beat it?' he went on, having reached the stage of exasperation when a man has to have a confidant, no matter who he be. 'My wife made me wear my thick woollies.'

'You shock me profoundly. Why was that?'

'Said there was a nasty east wind.'

'I hadn't noticed it.'

'Me, neither.'

'You have a sensitive skin?'

'Yes, I have. Very.'

'I suspected that that was the reason why you were behaving like a one-armed paperhanger with the hives. Watching you at work, I was reminded of the young lady of Natchez, whose clothes were all tatters and patches. In alluding to which, she would say, "Well, Ah itch, and wherever Ah itches, Ah scratches." If you wish to undress, pay no attention to me. And Mr Popworth, I know, is a married man and will take the broad view.'

A feeling of irritation, the spiritual equivalent of the one he was feeling in the small of the back, began to grip Oily. He found his companion's manner frivolous and unsympathetic and was conscious of an urge to retaliate in some way, to punish this scoffer for his untimely gaiety, to wipe, in a word, that silly smile off his face. And most fortunately he possessed the means to do so. In his vest pocket there nestled a ring made of what looked like gold, in which was set a large red stone that looked like a ruby. It seemed the moment to produce it.

Oily Carlisle had not always been a man at the top of his

profession, selling stock in non-existent copper mines to the highest in the land and putting through deals that ran into five figures. He had started at the bottom of the ladder as the genial young fellow who had found a ruby ring in the street and was anxious to sell it, the darned thing being of no use to him, and a touch of sentiment led him to carry on his person always this symbol of his beginnings. He regarded it as a sort of charm or luck piece.

Fingering it now, he said:

'Take a look at this.'

Lord Ickenham did so, and felt a pleasurable glow stealing over him. His, in the years before he had succeeded to the title and was an impecunious younger son scratching for a living in New York, Arizona and elsewhere, had been a varied and interesting career, in the course of which he had encountered a considerable number of what are technically known as lumberers, and he had always obtained a great deal of spiritual uplift from their society. To meet once again an optimist who – unless he was sadly wronging this sleek and shiny fellow-traveller – hoped to sell him a ruby ring he had found in the street carried him back to those good old days and would have restored his youth, had his youth needed restoring.

'My word!' he said admiringly. 'That looks valuable. How much did you give for that?'

'Well, I'll tell you,' said Oily. 'It's rather an odd story. You're not a lawyer, by any chance, are you, sir?'

Lord Ickenham said he was not.

'Why I asked was, I was walking along Piccadilly this morning, and saw this lying on the side-walk, and I thought you might be able to tell me if findings are keepings in a case like that.'

'Speaking as a layman, I should say most certainly.'

'You really think so?'

'I do indeed. The advice I always give to young men starting out in life and finding ruby rings in the street is "Grab the money and run for the train." You want to sell it, I suppose?'

'If it's not against the law. I wouldn't want to do anything that wasn't right.'

'Of course not. Naturally. About how much were you thinking of charging?'

Oily, too, had now begun to feel a pleasurable glow. This was pretty elementary stuff, of course, and he knew he ought to have been a little ashamed of himself for stooping to it, but it was giving him something of a nostalgic thrill to be back in the days when he had been a young fellow starting to break into the game.

'That's where I can't seem to make up my mind,' he said. 'If it's genuine, I suppose it's worth a hundred pounds or so, but how's one to tell?'

'Oh, I'm sure it's genuine. Look at that ruby. Very red.'

'That's true.'

'And the gold. Very yellow.'

'That's true, too.'

'I think you would be perfectly justified in asking a hundred pounds for this ring.'

'You do?'

'Fully that.'

'Would you buy it for a hundred pounds?'

'Like a shot.'

'Then —'

'But,' proceeded Lord Ickenham, 'for the fact that as a purchaser of ruby rings from chance-met strangers I am unfortunately situated. Some time ago my wife, who is a woman who believes in a strong, centralized government, decided to take over the family finances and administer them herself, leaving me just that little bit of spending money which a man requires for tobacco, self-respect, golf balls and so on. So I have to watch the pennies. My limit is a shilling. If you would care to settle for that, you have found a customer. Or, as this warm friendship has sprung up between us, shall we say eighteen pence?'

Oily was too much the gentleman to use bad language, but the look he gave his companion was not at all the sort of look he ought to have directed at anyone with whom he had formed a warm friendship.

'You make me sick,' he said, speaking the words from between clenched teeth with no trace of an Oxford accent.

It was in jovial mood that some moments later, having dropped the stowaway outside Hammer Lodge, Lord Ickenham stepped from the station cab at the door of Hammer Hall. He was genuinely grateful to his recent buddy for having given him five minutes of clean, wholesome entertainment, free from all this modern suggestiveness, and he wished him luck if he was planning to sell that ring to Beefy.

The ordinary visitor to the ancestral home of the Pearces, arriving at the front door, stands on the top step and presses the bell, and when nothing happens presses it again, but these formalities are not for godfathers. Lord Ickenham walked right in, noting as he passed through the spacious entrance hall how clean, though shabby, everything was. Nannie Bruce's work, he presumed, with a little assistance, no doubt, from some strong-young-girl-from-the-village.

Externally unchanged in the four hundred years during which it had housed the family of Pearce, internally, like so many country mansions of the post-second-world-war period, Hammer Hall showed unmistakable signs of having seen better days. There were gaps on the walls where tapestries had hung, hiatuses along the floor where chests and tables were missing. A console table which was a particular favourite of his, Lord Ickenham observed, had folded its tents like the Arabs and silently stolen away since his last visit, and he was sorry to see that that hideous imitation walnut cabinet, a survival from Victorian days, had not gone the same way, for it had always offended his educated eye and he had often begged his godson to get rid of it.

He sighed a little, and with a fourth pang added to the three he had mentioned to Pongo made his way to the room down the passage where Johnny Pearce, when not interrupted by Nannie Bruce, wrote those suspense novels which helped, though not very much, to keep Hammer Hall's head above water.

It was apparent that she had interrupted him now, for the first thing Lord Ickenham heard as he opened the door was her voice, speaking coldly and sternly.

'I've no patience, Master Jonathan. Oh, good evening, your lordship.'

Nannie Bruce, a tall, gangling light-heavyweight with a suggestion in her appearance of a private in the Grenadiers dressed up to play the title role in *Charley's Aunt*, was one of those doggedly faithful retainers who adhere to almost all old families like barnacles to the hulls of ships. As what she called a slip of a girl, though it was difficult, seeing her now, to believe that she had ever had a girlish sliphood, she had come to Hammer Hall to act as nurse to the infant Johnny. By the time he went off to his first school and the need for her services might have been supposed to have ceased, the idea of dispensing with them had become an idle dream. She was as much a fixture as the stone lions on the gates or the funny smell in the attic.

'You are in your old room, your lordship,' she said. 'I'll be going and seeing to it. So I'll be glad if you would kindly speak to her, Master Jonathan.'

'She does her best, Nannie.'

'And a poor best it is. She's a gaby, that one. Verily, as a jewel of gold in a swine's snout is a woman which is without discretion. That's what Ecclesiastes wrote in the good book, Master Jonathan,' said Miss Bruce, 'and he was right.'

The door closed behind her, and Johnny Pearce, a personable young man with a pleasant but worried face, sat jabbing moodily with his pen at the sheet of paper on which he had been writing of Inspector Jervis, a fictional character to whom he was greatly addicted. Lord Ickenham eyed him with concern. If vultures were not gnawing at his godson's bosom, he was feeling, he did not know a vulture-gnawed bosom when he saw one. Only the thought that Belinda Farringdon was having similar vulture-trouble and that he had come here to talk to Johnny about it like a Dutch godfather restrained him from condoling and sympathizing.

'What was all that?' he asked.

'The same old thing. Another row with the cook.'

'She has them frequently?'

'All the time.'

'Has the cook given notice?'

'Not yet, but she will. Cooks never stay here more than about five minutes. They can't stand Nannie.'

'She is a bit testing, I suppose, though a useful person to have around if you want to brush up your Ecclesiastes. However, it is not of Nannie and cooks and Ecclesiastes that I wish to speak,' said Lord Ickenham, getting down to it. 'Far more urgent matters are toward. I saw Bunny yesterday.'

'Oh, did you?'

'Gave her lunch. Smoked salmon, *poulet en casserole* and a fruit salad. She toyed with them in the order named. In fact, the word "toyed" overstates it. She pushed her plate away untasted.'

'Good Lord! Isn't she well?'

'Physically, yes, but spiritually considerably below par. It's in the soul that it catches her. She is fretting and chafing because you keep postponing the happy day. Why the devil don't you marry the girl, Johnny?'

'I can't!'

'Of course you can. Better men than you have got married. Myself for one. Nor have I ever regretted it. I'm not saying I enjoyed the actual ceremony. I had the feeling, as I knelt at the altar, that the eyes of everybody in the ringside pews were riveted on the soles of my boots, and it bathed me in confusion. I have a foot as shapely as the next man and my boots were made to order by the best booterers in London, but the illusion that I was wearing a pair of those things people go hunting fish under water in was very strong. That, however, was but a passing *malaise* and the thought that in about another brace of shakes the dearest girl in the world would be mine bucked me up like a week at Bognor Regis. Honestly, Johnny, you ought to nerve yourself and go through it. It only needs will power. You're breaking that pen,' said Lord Ickenham, 'and what is far, far worse, you are breaking the heart of a sweet blue-eyed girl with hair the colour of ripe corn. You should have seen her yesterday. I am a strong man, not easily shaken, but as I watched her recoiling from that *poulet en casserole*, as if it had been something dished up by the Borgias, my eyes were wet with unshed tears. I blush for you, Johnny, and am surprised and hurt that you seem incapable of blushing for yourself. To think that any godson of mine can go about the place giving the woman who has placed her trust in him the sleeve across the windpipe like this makes me realize that godsons are not what they were.'

'You don't understand.'

'Nor does B. Farringdon.'

'I'm in a hell of a jam.'

Johnny Pearce quivered as he spoke, and passed a feverish pen over his brow. The sternness of Lord Ickenham's demeanour softened a little. It had become evident to him that he was the godfather of a toad beneath the harrow, and one has to make allowances for toads so situated.

'Tell me the whole story in your own words, omitting no detail, however slight,' he said. 'Why can't you get married? You haven't got some incurable disease, have you?'

'That's just it. I have.'

'Good heavens! What?'

'Nannie Bruce.'

It seemed to Lord Ickenham that the toad raising a haggard face to his was a toad who spoke in riddles, and he said so.

'What on earth do you mean?'

'Have you ever had a faithful old nurse who stuck to you like a limpet?'

'Never. My personal attendants generally left at the end of the first month, glad to see the last of me. They let me go and presently called the rest of the watch together and thanked God they were rid of a knave. But what have faithful old nurses got to do with it? I don't follow you.'

'It's perfectly simple. Nannie Bruce has been here for twenty-five years – damn it, it's nearer twenty-seven – and she has become the boss of the show. She runs the place. Well, do you suppose that, if I get married, she's going to step meekly down and hand over to my wife? Not a hope.'

'Nonsense.'

'It isn't nonsense. You saw her in action just now. A perfectly good cook melting away like snow on a mountain side, and why? Because Nannie will insist on butting in all the time and criticizing. And it would be the same with Bunny. Nannie would make life impossible for her in a million ways. I'd call her high-spirited, wouldn't you?'

'Nannie?'

'Bunny.'

'Oh, Bunny. Yes, very high-spirited.'

'Well, then. Is she going to enjoy being interfered with and ordered around, told not to do it that way, do it this way, treated as a sort of half-witted underling? And her sniff. You know the way she sniffs.'

'Bunny?'

'Nannie.'

'Oh, Nannie. Yes, she does sniff.'

'And that hissing noise she makes, like a wet thumb drawn across the top of a hot stove. It would drive a young bride potty. And there's another thing,' said Johnny, vigorously plying the pen. 'Do you realize that every single discreditable episode in my past is filed away in Nannie's memory? She could and would tell Bunny things about me which in time would be bound to sap her love. How long could a wife go on looking on her husband as a king among men after hearing an eye-witness's account of his getting jerked before a tribunal and fined three weeks' pocket money for throwing rocks at the kitchen window or a blow-by-blow description of the time he was sick at his birthday party through eating too much almond cake? In about two ticks I should sink to the level of a fifth-rate power. Yes, I know. You're going to say why don't I get rid of her?'

'Exactly,' said Lord Ickenham, who was. It seemed to his alert mind the logical solution.

'How can I? I can't throw her out on her –'

'Please, Johnny! There are gentlemen present.'

'Ear.'

'Oh – ear. Sorry. But couldn't you pension her off?'

'What with?'

'Surely she would not want a fortune. A couple of quid or so a week . . .'

'I know exactly what she wants. Five hundred pounds.'

'In a lump sum?'

'Cash down.'

'It seems unusual. I should have thought a weekly dole . . .'

A sort of frozen calm descended on Johnny Pearce, the calm of despair.

'Let me tell you my story, omitting, as you say, no detail, however slight. I did offer her a weekly dole.'

'And she refused?'

'No, she accepted. That was when I felt justified in proposing to Bunny. I ought to have told you, by the way, that she's engaged to the policeman.'

'Bunny?'

'Nannie.'

'Oh, Nannie. What policeman would that be?'

'The one in the village. There's only one. His name's McMurdo.'

'Short-sighted chap?'

'Not that I know of. Why?'

'I was only thinking that it would be very difficult to be attracted to Nannie Bruce while seeing her steadily and seeing her whole. However, that is neither here nor there. Policemen are paid to take these risks. Proceed with your narrative.'

'Where was I?'

'You had just offered her a weekly sum, and she had accepted it. Which sounds to me like the happy ending, though obviously for some reason it was not. What came unstuck?'

'McMurdo won a football pool last winter. Five hundred pounds.'

'And why was that a disaster?' asked Lord Ickenham, for his godson had made this announcement in a hollow voice and was looking as if his was the head upon which all the ends of the world had come. 'I could do with winning a football pool myself. Wasn't Nannie pleased?'

'No, she wasn't. Her pride was touched, and she said she wasn't going to marry any man who had five hundred quid salted away unless she had the same amount herself. She said her aunt Emily had no money and married a man with a goodish bit of it and he treated her like an orphan child. She had to go to him for everything. If she wanted a new hat, he'd say hadn't he bought her a hat only five or six years ago and get off nasty cracks about women who seemed to think they'd married into the Rothschild family. None of that for her, Nannie said.'

'But, dash it, my dear Johnny, the two cases are entirely different. Musing on Emily, one draws in the breath sharply and drops a silent tear, but Nannie, with a weekly income, wouldn't be in her position at all. She would be able to make whatever kind of splash seemed fit to her. Didn't you point that out to the fatheaded woman?'

'Of course I did, but do you think it's possible to make Nannie see reason, once her mind's made up? Either she had five hundred pounds, or all bets were off. That was final. And that's how matters stand today,' said Johnny.

He dug the pen into Inspector Jervis's latest bit of dialogue once more and resumed.

'I thought I saw a way of straightening things out. It meant taking a chance, but it was no moment for prudence and caution. Did you read that last book of mine, *Inspector Jervis at Bay*?'

'Well, what with one thing and another, trying to catch up with my Proust and Kafka and all that –'

'Don't apologize. The British Isles are stiff with people who didn't read it. You see them on every side. But there were enough who did to enable me to make a hundred and eleven pounds six and threepence out of it.'

'Nice going.'

'So I took the hundred and put it on an outsider in the Derby. Ballymore.'

'My unhappy lad! Beaten by Moke the Second after a photo finish.'

'Yes, if it had had a longer nose, my troubles would have been at an end.'

'And you have no other means of raising that five hundred?'

'Not that I can see.'

'How about the furniture?'

'I've come to the end of the things I'm allowed to sell. All the rest are heirlooms, except the fake walnut cabinet, of course, Great-Uncle Walter's gift to Hammer Hall.'

'That eyesore!'

'I can sell that without getting slapped into gaol. I'm putting it up for auction soon. It might fetch a fiver.'

'From somebody astigmatic.'

'But, as you are about to point out, that would still leave me short four hundred and ninety-five. Oh, hell! Have you ever robbed a bank, Uncle Fred?'

'Not that I can recall. Why?'

'I was just thinking that might be the simplest way out. But, with my luck, if I bust the Bank of England, I'd find they hadn't got five hundred quid in the safe. Still, there's always one consolation.'

'What's that?'

'It'll be all the same in a hundred years. And now, if you don't mind buzzing off and leaving me, I'll be getting back to Inspector Jervis.'

'Yes, it's time that I was moving. The Big Chief said I was on no account to fail to go and pay my respects to Beefy Bastable, and I want to have a chat with my old friend Albert Peasemarch. Lots of thread-picking-up to be done. I shall be back in an hour or so and shall then be wholly at your disposal.'

'Not that there's a damn thing you can do.'

'It is always rash to say that about an Ickenham. We are not easily baffled. I agree that your problem undoubtedly presents certain features of interest, but I am confident that after turning it over in my mind I shall be able to find a formula.'

'You and your formulas!'

'All right, me and my formulas. But wait. That is all I say – wait.'

And with a wave of the hand and a kindly warning to his godson not to take any wooden nickels, Lord Ickenham tilted his hat slightly to one side and set off across the park to Hammer Lodge.

## Chapter 9

There was a thoughtful frown on Lord Ickenham's brow and a pensive look in his eye as he skirted the lake, on the other side of which the grounds of Hammer Lodge lay. A cow was paddling in the shallows, and normally he would have paused to throw a bit of stick at it, but now he hurried on, too preoccupied to do the civil thing.

He was concerned about Johnny. His story would have made it plain to a far less intelligent godfather that the lad was in a spot. He was not on intimate terms with Nannie Bruce, but he was sufficiently acquainted with her personality to recognize the impossibility, once her mind was made up, of persuading her to change it. If Nannie Bruce wanted five hundred pounds cash down, she would get five hundred pounds cash down, or no wedding bells for Officer McMurdo. And as Johnny did not possess five hundred pounds, the situation had all the earmarks of an impasse. It is not too much to say that, though his hat was on the side of his head and his walk as jaunty as ever, Lord Ickenham, as he rang the front door bell of Hammer Lodge and was admitted by his friend Albert Peasemarch, was mourning in spirit.

Butlers came in three sizes – the large, the small and the medium. Albert Peasemarch was one of the smalls. Short and somewhat overweight for his height, he had a round, moonlike face, in which were set, like currants in a suet dumpling, two brown eyes. A captious critic, seeing, as captious critics do, only the dark side, would have commented on the entire absence from these eyes of anything like a gleam of human intelligence: but to anyone non-captious this would have been amply compensated for by their kindliness and honesty. His circle of friends, while passing him over when they wanted someone to explain the Einstein Theory to them, knew that, if they were in trouble, they could rely on his help. True, this help almost invariably made things worse than they had been, for if there was a way of getting everything muddled up, he got it, but his intentions were excellent and his heart in the right place.

His face, usually disciplined to a professional impassivity, melted into a smile of welcome as he recognized the visitor.

'Oh, good evening, m'lord.'

'Hullo, Bert. You're looking very roguish. Is the old folk at home?'

'Sir Raymond is in his study, m'lord, but a gentleman is with him at the moment – a Mr Carlisle.'

'I know the chap you mean. He's probably trying to sell him a ruby ring. Well, then, if the big shot is tied up in conference, we've nice time for a spot of port in your pantry, and very agreeable it will be after a hot and dirty journey. You haven't run short of port?'

'Oh, no, m'lord. If you will step this way, m'lord.'

'California, as you might say, here I come. This,' said Lord Ickenham some moments later, 'is the real stuff. The poet probably had it in mind when he spoke of the port of heaven. "If the Dons sight Devon, I'll quit the port of heaven an' drum them up the Channel as we drummed them long ago." Sir Henry Newbolt. Drake's Drum. Are you familiar with Drake's Drum? But of course you are. What am I thinking of? I've heard you sing it a dozen times round the old camp fire in our Home Guard days.'

'I was always rather partial to Drake's Drum, m'lord.'

'And how you belted the stuffing out of it! It was like hearing a Siberian wolf-hound in full cry after a Siberian wolf. I remember thinking at the time how odd it is that small men nearly always have loud, deep voices. I believe midgets invariably sing bass. Very strange. Nature's law of compensation, no doubt.'

'Very possibly, m'lord.'

Lord Ickenham, who had been about to sip, lowered his glass with a reproachful shake of the head.

'Now listen, Bert. This "M'lord" stuff. I've been meaning to speak to you about it. I'm a Lord, yes, no argument about that, but you don't have to keep rubbing it in all the time. It's no good kidding ourselves. We know what lords are. Anachronistic parasites on the body of the state, is the kindest thing you can say of them. Well, a sensitive man doesn't like to be reminded every half second that he is one of the untouchables, liable at any moment to be strung up on a lamp post or to have his blood flowing in streams down Park Lane. Couldn't you substitute something matier and less wounding to my feelings?'

'I could hardly call your lordship "Ickenham".'

'I was thinking of "Freddie".'

'Oh, no, m'lord.'

'Then how about "old man" or "cully"?'

'Certainly not, m'lord. If your lordship would not object to "Mr I"?'

'The ideal solution. Well, Bert, how are things in the home now? Not much improvement, I gather from your letters. Our mutual friend still a little terse with the flesh and blood, eh?'

'It is not for me to criticize Sir Raymond.'

'Don't come the heavy butler over me, Bert. This meeting is tiled. You may speak freely.'

'Then I must say that I consider that he treats Madam very badly, indeed.'

'Bellows at her?'

'Almost daily, Mr I.'

'They will bring their court manner into private life, these barristers. I was in court once and heard Beefy cross-examining a meek little man who looked like Bill the Lizard in *Alice in Wonderland*. I forget what the actual words were, but the fellow piped up with some perfectly harmless remark, and Beefy fixed him with a glittering eye and thundered "Come, come, sir, don't attempt to browbeat *me*!" And he's still like that in the home, is he?'

'More so now than ever before. Madam is distressed because Mr Cosmo has written this book there is so much talk about. She disapproves of its moral tone. This makes her cry a good deal.'

'And he ticks her off?'

'Most violently. Her tears appear to exasperate him. I sometimes feel I can't bear it any longer.'

'Why don't you hand in your portfolio?'

'And leave her? I couldn't.'

Lord Ickenham looked at him keenly. His host's face, usually, like Oily Carlisle's, an expressionless mask, was working with an odd violence that made him seem much more the Home Guardsman of years ago than the butler of today.

'Hullo!' he said. 'What's this?'

Albert Peasemarch remained for a moment in the process of what is commonly known as struggling for utterance. Finding speech at length, he said in a low, hoarse voice very different from the one he employed when rendering Drake's Drum:

'I love her, Mr I.'

It always took a great deal to surprise Lord Ickenham. Where another man, hearing this cry from the heart, might have leaped in his chair and upset his glass of port, he merely directed at the speaker a look full of sympathy and understanding. His personal feeling that loving Phoebe Wisdom was a thing beyond the scope of the most determined Romeo he concealed. It could apparently, be done.

'My poor old Bert,' he said. 'Tell me all. When did you feel this coming on?'

A dreamy look came into Albert Peasemarch's eye, the look of one who tenderly relives the past.

'It was our rheumatism that first brought us together,' he said, his voice trembling a little.

Lord Ickenham cocked an enquiring eyebrow.

'I'm not sure I quite got that. Rheumatism, did you say?'

'Madam suffers from it in the left shoulder, and I have it in the right leg, and we fell into the habit of discussing it. Every morning Madam would say "And how is your rheumatism, Peasemarch?" and I would tell her, and I would say "How is *your* rheumatism, madam?" and she would tell *me*. And so it went on.'

'I see. Swapping gossip from the lazar house. Yes, I understand. Naturally if you tell a woman day after day about the funny burning feeling in your right leg, and she tells you about the curious shooting sensation in her left shoulder, it forms a bond.'

'And then last winter . . .'

'Yes –?'

A reverent note crept into Albert Peasemarch's voice. 'Last winter I had influenza. Madam nursed me throughout my illness.'

'Smoothed your pillow? Brought you cooling drinks?'

'And read Agatha Christie to me. And something came right over me, Mr I., and I knew that it was love.'

Lord Ickenham was silent for some moments, sipping his port and turning this revelation over in his mind. It still puzzled him that anyone could have had the divine spark touched off in him by Phoebe Wisdom. In a vague way, though he knew her to be more than a decade younger than himself, he had always regarded her as many years his senior. She looked, he considered, about eighty. But presumably she did not look eighty to Albert Peasemarch, and, even if she did, a woman who for years had kept house for Beefy Bastable was surely entitled to look a hundred.

His heart went out to Albert Peasemarch. Dashed unpleasant it must be, he was feeling, for a butler to fall in love with the châtelaine of the establishment. Having to say 'Yes, madam,' 'Very good, madam,' 'The carriage waits, madam' and all that sort of thing, when every fibre of his being was urging him to tell her that she was the tree on which the fruit of his life hung and that for her sake he would pluck the stars from the sky, or whatever it is that butlers say when moved by the fire within. A state of affairs, Lord Ickenham thought, which would give him personally the pip. He resolved to do all that in him lay – and on these occasions there was always quite a lot that in him lay – to push the thing along and bring sweetness and light into these two at present sundered lives.

'Taken any steps about it?' he asked.

'Oh, no, m'lord, I mean Mr I. It wouldn't be proper.'

'This is no time to mess about, being proper,' said Lord Ickenham bluffly. 'Can't get anywhere if you don't take steps.'

'What do you advise, Mr I.?'

'That's more the tone. I don't suppose there's a man alive better equipped to advise you than I am. I'm a specialist at this sort of thing. The couples I've brought together in my time, if placed end to end, not that I suppose one could do it, of course, would reach from Piccadilly Circus to well beyond Hyde Park Corner. You don't know Bill Oakshott, do you? He was one of my clients, my nephew Pongo another. And there was the pink chap down at Mitching Hill, I've forgotten his name, and Polly Pott and Horace Davenport and Elsie Bean the housemaid, oh, and dozens more. With me behind him, the most diffident wooer can get the proudest beauty to sign on the dotted line. In your case, the relationship between you and the adored object being somewhat unusual, one will have to go rather carefully. The Ickenham system, for instance, might seem a little abrupt.'

'The Ickenham system, Mr I.?'

'I call it that. Just giving you the bare outlines, you stride up to the subject, grab her by the wrist, clasp her to your bosom and shower burning kisses on her upturned face. You don't have to say much – just "My mate!" or something of that sort, and, of course, in grabbing by the wrist, don't behave as if you were handling a delicate piece of china. Grip firmly and waggle her about a bit. It seldom fails, and I usually recommend it, but in your case, as I say, it might be better to edge into the thing more gradually. I think that as a starter you should bring her flowers every day, wet with the morning dew. And when I say "bring", I don't mean hand them over as if you were delivering a parcel from the stores. Put them secretly in her room. No message. An anonymous gift from a mystery worshipper. That will pique her curiosity. "Hullo!" she will say to herself. "What's all this in aid of?" and at a suitable moment you reveal that they came from you, and it knocks her base over apex. Wait!' said Lord Ickenham. A thought had come like a full-blown rose, flushing his brow. 'I'm seeing deeper into this thing. Isn't there a language of flowers? I'm sure I've read about it somewhere. I mean, you send a girl nasturtiums or lobelias or whatever it may be, and it signifies "There is one who adores you respectfully from afar" or "Watch out, here comes Albert!" or something. You've heard of that?'

'Oh, yes, indeed. There are books on the subject.'

'Get one, and make of it a constant companion.' Lord Ickenham mused for a moment. 'Is there anything else? Ah, yes. The dog. Has she a dog?'

'A cocker spaniel, Mr I., called Benjy.'

'Conciliate that dog, Bert. Omit no word or act that will lead to a *rapprochement* between yourself and it. The kindly chirrup. The friendly bone. The constant pat on the head or ribs, according to the direction in which your tastes lie. There is no surer way to a woman's heart than to get in solid with her dog.'

He broke off. Through the window of the pantry he had seen a gentlemanly figure pass by.

'The boss's conference has concluded,' he said, rising. 'I'd better go and pass the time of day. You won't forget, Bert? An atmosphere of the utmost cordiality where the dog Benjy is concerned, and the daily gift of flowers.'

'Yes, Mr I.'

'Every morning without fail. It's bound to work. Inevitably the little daily dose will have its effect,' said Lord Ickenham, and went along the passage to the study where, he presumed, Sir Raymond Bastable would still be – gloating, possibly, over the ruby ring he had purchased.

His manner was even more preoccupied than it had been when he ignored the paddling cow. So many problems had presented themselves, coming up one after the other. It was never his habit to grumble and make a fuss when this happened, but he did sometimes, as now, feel that the life work he had set himself of spreading sweetness and light – or, as some preferred to put it, meddling in other people's business – was almost more than any man could be expected to undertake singlehanded. In addition to that of his godson Johnny, he now had Albert Peasemarch's tangled love life to worry about, and to promote a union between a butler and the sister of his employer is in itself a whole-time task, calling for all that one has of resolution and ingenuity. And there was, furthermore, the matter of the reformation of Beefy Bastable, whose attitude towards his sister Phoebe, so like that of a snapping turtle suffering from ulcers, he was determined to correct.

A full programme.

Still, 'Tails up, Ickenham. Remember your triumphs in the past,' he was saying to himself. This was not the first time in his career that the going had been sticky.

He was right about Sir Raymond being in the study, but wrong about the ruby ring. His half-brother-in-law was sitting huddled in a chair with his head between his hands, his air that of a man who, strolling along a country lane thinking of this and that, has caught an unexpected automobile in the small of the back, and his outward appearance mirrored perfectly the emotions within. At about three-fifteen on a November afternoon at Oxford, when the University rugby football team were playing Cardiff, a Welshman with a head constructed apparently of ivory or one of the harder metals had once butted Sir Raymond Bastable in the solar plexus, giving him the illusion that the world had suddenly come to an end and judgement day set in with unusual severity. It had happened a matter of thirty years ago, but the episode had never faded from his memory, and until this evening he had always looked on it as the high spot of his life.

Some five minutes previously, when Oily Carlisle, producing Cosmo Wisdom's letter, had revealed its contents and gone off to give him, as he explained, time to think it over, it had been eclipsed.

## Chapter 10

Lord Ickenham came into the room, concern in every hair of his raised eyebrows. Many men in his place, beholding this poor bit of human wreckage, would have said to themselves 'Oh, my gosh, another toad beneath the harrow' and ducked out quickly to avoid having to listen to the hard luck story which such toads are always so ready to tell, but to the altruistic peer it never occurred to adopt such a course. His was a big heart, and when he saw a toad not only beneath the harrow but apparently suffering from the effects of one of those gas explosions in a London street which slay six, he did not remember an appointment for which he was already late but stuck around and prepared to do whatever lay in his power to alleviate the sufferer's distress.

'Beefy!' he cried. 'My dear old bird, what on earth's the matter? You look like a devastated area.'

It took Sir Raymond some little time to tell him what the matter was, for he had much to say on the subject of the black-hearted villainy of his nephew Cosmo and also a number of pungent remarks to make about Oily Carlisle. As he concluded the recital of their skulduggery, his audience, which he had held spellbound, clicked its tongue. It shocked Lord Ickenham to think that humanity could sink to such depths, and he blamed himself for having allowed this new development to catch him unprepared.

'We should have foreseen this,' he said. 'We should have told ourselves that it was madness to place our confidence in anyone like young Cosmo, a twister compared with whom corkscrews are straight and spiral staircases the shortest line between two points. Seeing that little black moustache of his, we should have refused him the nomination and sought elsewhere for a co-worker. "Never put anything on paper, my boy," my old father used to say to me, "and never trust a man with a small black moustache." And you, my poor Beefy, have done both.'

Sir Raymond's reply was somewhat muffled, for he was having trouble with his vocal cords, but Lord Ickenham understood him to say that it was all his, Lord Ickenham's, fault.

'You suggested him.'

'Surely not? Yes, by Jove, you're right. I was sitting here, you were sitting there, lapping up martinis like a vacuum cleaner, and I said . . . Yes, it all comes back to me. I'm sorry.'

'What's the use of that?'

'Remorse is always useful, Beefy. It stimulates the brain. It has set mine working like a buzz-saw, and already a plan of action is beginning to present itself. You say this fellow went off? Where did he go?'

'How the devil do I know where he went?'

'I ask because I happen to be aware that he has a sensitive skin and is undergoing considerable discomfort because his wife made him put on his winter woollies this morning. I thought he might be in the garden somewhere, stripped to the buff in order to scratch with more authority, in which case his coat would be on the ground or hung from some handy bough, and I could have stolen up, not letting a twig snap beneath my feet, and gone through his pockets. But I doubt if he is the sort of man to be careless with a coat containing important documents. I shall have to try the other plan I spoke of, the one I said was beginning to present itself. Since you last heard from me, I have shaped it out, complete to the last button, and it will, I am convinced, bring home the bacon. You're sure he's coming back?'

'Of course he's coming back, curse him!'

'Through those French windows, no doubt. He would hardly ring the front door bell and have himself announced again. It would confuse Albert Peasemarch and make him fret. All right, Beefy, receive him courteously, ask after his sensitive skin and keep him engaged in conversation till I am with you again.'

'Where are you going?'

'Never mind. When the fields are white with daisies, I'll return,' said Lord Ickenham, and withdrew through the door a minute or so before Oily Carlisle came in through the French windows.

It could scarcely be said that Sir Raymond received Mr Carlisle courteously, unless it is courteous to glare at someone like a basilisk and call him a slimy blackmailer, nor did he enquire after his skin or engage him in conversation. What talk ensued was done by Oily, who was in excellent spirits and plainly feeling that all was for the best in this best of all possible worlds. Cosmo's letter, nestling in his inside coat pocket, made a little crackling sound as he patted it, and it was music to his ears. There was a brisk cheerfulness in his manner as he started talking prices that gashed his companion like a knife.

He had just outlined the tariff and was suggesting that if Sir Raymond would bring out his cheque book and take pen in hand, the whole thing could be cleaned up promptly, neatly and to everybody's satisfaction, when there came to him a sudden doubt as to the world being, as he had supposed, the best of all possible. The door opened, and Albert Peasemarch appeared.

'Inspector Jervis,' he announced, and with an uneasy feeling in his interior, as if he had recently swallowed a heaped tablespoonful of butterflies, Oily recognized, in the tall, slim figure that entered, his fellow-traveller from the station. And noting that his eyes, so genial in the cab, were now hard and his lips, once smiling, tight and set, he quailed visibly. He remembered a palmist at Coney Island once telling him, in return for fifty cents, that a strange man would cross his path and that of this strange man he would do well to beware, but not even the thought that it looked as if he were going to get value for his half dollar was enough to cheer him.

If Lord Ickenham's eyes were hard and his lips set, it was because that was how he saw the role he had undertaken. There were gaps in his knowledge of his godson's literary work, but he had read enough of it to know that when Inspector Jervis found himself in the presence of the criminal classes, he did not beam at them. The eyes hard, the lips set, the voice crisp and official – that was how he envisaged Inspector Jervis.

'Sir Raymond Bastable?' he said. 'Good evening, Sir Raymond, I am from the Yard.'

And looked every inch of it, he was feeling complacently. He was a man who in his time had played many parts, and he took a pride in playing them right. It was his modest boast that there was nothing in existence, except possibly a circus dwarf, owing to his height, or Gina Lollobrigida, owing to her individual shape, which he could not at any moment and without rehearsal depict with complete success. In a single afternoon at The Cedars, Mafeking Road, in the suburb of Mitching Hill, on the occasion when he had befriended the pink chap to whom he had alluded in his talk with Albert Peasemarch, he had portrayed not only an official from the bird shop, come to clip the claws of the resident parrot, but Mr Roddis, owner of The Cedars, and a Mr J. G. Bulstrode, one of the neighbours, and had been disappointed that he was given no opportunity of impersonating the parrot, which he was convinced he would have done on broad, artistic lines.

Oily continued to quail. Not so good, he was saying to himself, not so good. He had never been fond of inspectors, and the time when their society made the smallest appeal to him was when they popped up just as he was concluding an important deal. He did not like the way this one was looking at him and, when he spoke, he liked what he said even less.

'Turn out your pockets,' said Lord Ickenham curtly.

'Eh?'

'And don't say "Eh?" I have been watching this man closely,' said Lord Ickenham, turning to Sir Raymond, whose eyes were bulging like a snail's, 'since I saw him on the station platform in London. His furtive behaviour excited my suspicions. "Picking pockets right and left, that chap," I said to myself. "Helping himself to wallets and what not from all and sundry."'

Oily started, and a hot flush suffused his forehead. His professional pride was piqued. In no section of the community are class distinctions more rigid than among those who make a dishonest living by crime. The burglar looks down on the stick-up man, the stick-up man on the humbler practitioner who steals milk cans. Accuse a high-up confidence artist of petty larceny, and you bring out all the snob in him.

'And when I shared a cab with him to Hammer Hall and discovered on alighting that I was short a cigarette case, a tie pin, a packet of throat pastilles and a fountain pen, I knew that my suspicions had been well founded. Come on, my man, what are we waiting for?'

Oily was still gasping.

'Are you saying I picked pockets? You're crazy. I wouldn't know how.'

'Nonsense. It's perfectly simple. You just dip. It's no use pleading inability. If Peter Piper,' said Lord Ickenham, who on these occasions was always a little inclined to let his tongue run away with him, 'could pick a peck of pickled peppers, I see no reason why you should not be capable of picking a peck of pickled pockets. Has the fellow been left alone in here?' he asked Sir Raymond, who blinked and said he had not.

'Ah? Then he will have had no opportunity of trousering any of your little knick-knacks, even if he still had room for them. But let us see what he has got. It should be worth more than a casual glance.'

'Yes,' said Sir Raymond, at last abreast. He was always rather a slow thinker when not engaged in his profession. 'Turn out your pockets, my man.'

Oily wavered, uncertain what to do for the best. If he had been calmer, it might have struck him that this was a most peculiar inspector, in speech and manner quite unlike the inspectors with whom his professional activities had brought him into contact in his native country, and his suspicions, too, might have been excited. But he was greatly agitated and feeling far from his usual calm self. And perhaps, he was thinking, all English inspectors were like this. He had never met one socially. His acquaintance with Scotland Yard was a purely literary one, the fruit of his reading of the whodunits to which he was greatly addicted.

It was possibly the fact that Sir Raymond was between him and the window that decided him. The Beefy Bastable who had recently celebrated his fifty-second birthday was no longer the lissom athlete of thirty years ago, but he was still an exceedingly tough-looking customer, not lightly to be engaged in physical combat by one who specialized in the persuasive word rather than violence. Drinking in his impressive bulk, Oily reached a decision. Slowly, with a sad sigh as he thought how different it all would have been if his Gertie had been there with her vase of gladioli, he emptied his pockets.

Lord Ickenham appeared surprised at the meagreness of their contents.

'He seems to have cached the swag somewhere, no doubt in a secret spot marked with a cross,' he said. 'But, hullo! What's this? A letter addressed to you, Sir Raymond.'

'You don't say?'

'Written, I should deduce from a superficial glance, by a man with a small black moustache.'

'Well, well.'

'Just what I was going to say myself.'

'Most extraordinary!'

'Very. Will you press a charge against this man for swiping it?'

'I think not.'

'You don't want to see him in a dungeon with dripping walls, getting gnawed to the bone by rats? You string along with the Bard of Avon about the quality of mercy not being strained? Very well. It's up to you, of course. All right, Mr Carlisle, you may go.'

It was at this moment, when everything appeared, as Oily would have put it, to have been cleaned up neatly and to everybody's satisfaction, that the door opened again and Mrs Phoebe Wisdom pottered in, looking so like a white rabbit that the first impulse of any lover of animals would have been to offer her a lettuce.

'Raymond, dear,' she said, 'have you seen my pig?'

For the past half-hour Sir Raymond Bastable had been under a considerable strain, and though relief at the success of his half-brother-in-law's intervention had lessened this, he was still feeling its effects. This sudden introduction of the pig motif seemed to take him into a nightmare world where nothing made sense, and for a moment everything went blank. Swaying a little on his base, he said in a low whisper:

'Your pig?'

'The little gold pig from my charm bracelet. It has dropped off, and I can't find it anywhere. Well, Frederick, how nice to see you after all this time. Peasemarch told me you were here. When did you arrive?'

'I came on the 3.26 train. I'm staying with my godson, Johnny Pearce, at the Hall. You don't look too well, Phoebe. What's the trouble? Not enough yeast?'

'It's this book of Cossie's, Frederick. I can't imagine how he came to write such a book. A bishop denouncing it!'

'Bishops will be bishops.'

'I went up to London yesterday to see him and tell him how upset I was, but he wasn't there.'

'Somewhere else, perhaps?' Lord Ickenham suggested.

Oily had been listening to these exchanges with growing bewilderment. From the first he had thought this Inspector an odd Inspector, but only now was it borne in on him how very odd he was.

'Say, who *is* this guy?' he demanded.

'Hasn't my brother introduced you?' said Phoebe. 'He is my half-sister's husband, Lord Ickenham. *You* haven't seen my pig, have you, Frederick?'

'Phoebe,' said Sir Raymond, 'get out!'

'What, dear?'

'Get out!'

'But I was going to look for my pig.'

'Never mind your pig. Get out!' bellowed Sir Raymond in the voice that had so often brought plaster down from the ceiling of the Old Bailey and caused nervous court officials to swallow their chewing gum.

Phoebe withdrew, sobbing softly and looking like a white rabbit that has had bad news from home, and Oily confronted Lord Ickenham. His face was stern, but there was a song in his heart, as there always is in the hearts of men who see defeat turn into victory.

'So!' he said.

'So what?' said Lord Ickenham.

'I'm afraid you're in a lot of trouble.'

'I am? Why is that?'

'For impersonating an officer. Impersonating an officer is a very serious offence.'

'But, my dear fellow, when did I ever impersonate an officer? Wouldn't dream of doing such a thing.'

'The butler announced you as Inspector Jervis.'

'What the butler said is not evidence. Am I to be blamed because a butler tries to be funny? That was just a little private joke we have together.'

'You said you were from the Yard.'

'I referred to the yard outside the kitchen door. I was smoking a cigarette there.'

'You made me turn out my pockets.'

'*Made* you? I *asked* you to, and you very civilly did.'

'Give me that letter.'

'But it is addressed to Sir Raymond Bastable. It belongs to him.'

'Yes,' boomed Sir Raymond, intervening in the debate, 'it belongs to me, and when you talk of serious offences, you foul excrescence, let me remind you that interfering with the mails is one of them. Give me that letter, Frederick.'

Lord Ickenham, who had been edging to the door, paused with his fingers on the handle.

'No, Beefy,' he said. 'Not yet. You must earn this letter.'

'What!'

'I can speak freely before Mr Carlisle, for I could see from the way he winced that your manner towards your sister Phoebe just now distressed him deeply. I, too, have long been wounded by your manner towards your sister Phoebe, Beefy, considering it to resemble far too closely that of one of the less attractive fauna in the Book of Revelations. Correct this attitude. Turn on that brotherly charm. Coo to her like a cushat dove. Take her up to London for dinner and a theatre from time to time, and when addressing her bear in mind that the voice with the smile wins and that you are not an Oriental potentate dissatisfied with the efficiency of an Ethiopian slave. If I learn from Albert Peasemarch, who will be watching you closely, that there has been a marked and substantial improvement, you shall have this letter. Meanwhile, I am going to keep it and hold it over you like the sword of . . . who was the chap? . . . no, it's gone. Forget my own name next,' said Lord Ickenham, annoyed, and went out, shutting the door behind him.

A moment later, it opened again, and his head appeared.

'Damocles,' he said. 'Sword of Damocles.'

The door closed.

## Chapter 11

On a sunny morning precisely two weeks after Lord Ickenham had adjusted the sword of Damocles over the head of Sir Raymond Bastable, completely spoiling the latter's day and causing him to entertain towards the sweetness-and-light specialist thoughts of a kind that no one ought to have entertained towards a brother-in-law, even a half one, the door of Brixton prison in the suburbs of London was opened by a uniformed gentleman with a large key, and a young man in a form-fitting navy blue suit emerged. Cosmo Wisdom, his debt to Society paid, was in circulation once more. He was thinner and paler than when last seen, and the first act of the beauty-loving authorities had been to remove his moustache. This, however, was not so great a boon to pedestrians and traffic as it might seem, for he was resolved, now that he was in a position to do so, to grow it again.

The Law of Great Britain is a smoothly functioning automatic machine, providing prison sentences to suit all tastes. You put your crime in the slot, and out comes the appropriate penalty – seven years, as it might be, for embezzling trust funds, six months for carving up a business competitor with a razor, and for being drunk and disorderly and while in that condition assaulting the police fourteen days without the option of a fine. Cosmo had drawn the last of these.

When Oily Carlisle in a moment of unwonted generosity had lent Cosmo twenty pounds, the latter, it may be remembered, receiving these pennies from heaven, had expressed his intention of celebrating. He had done so only too heartily. The thought of the good red gold which would soon be gushing like a geyser from the coffers of his Uncle Raymond had given wings to his feet as he started on his way along the primrose path. There was a sound of revelry by night and, one thing leading to another, in what seemed almost no time at all he was kicking Police Constable Styles of the C division, whose manner when he was trying to steal his helmet had offended him, rather severely in the stomach. Whistles blew, colleagues of the injured officer rallied to the spot, and presently stern-faced men were leading Cosmo off to the local hoosegow with gyves upon his wrists.

It was not a case, in the opinion of the magistrate at Bosher Street police court next morning, which could be met by the mere imposition of a fine. Only the jug, the whole jug and nothing but the jug would show the piefaced young son of a what-not where he got off, he said, though he phrased it a little differently, and he seemed chagrined at not being able to dish out more than those fourteen days. The impression he gave was that if he had been a free agent with no book of the rules to hamper him, Cosmo would have been lucky to escape what is known to the Chinese as the Death Of A Thousand Cuts. You could see that he was thinking that they manage these things better in China, and PC Styles, whose stomach was still paining him, thought the same.

The first act of your ex-convict on coming out into the great world after graduating from the Alma Mater is to buy a packet of cigarettes, his second to purchase a morning paper, his third to go and get the substantial lunch of which he has been dreaming ever since he clocked in. During the past two weeks Cosmo, rubbing along on the wholesome but rather meagre prison fare, had given a good deal of thought to the square meal he would have on getting out, and after considering the claims of Barribault's, Mario's, Claridge's and the Savoy, had decided to give his custom to Simpson's in the Strand, being well aware that at no establishment in London are the meals squarer. As he hastened thither, with the picture rising before him of those white-coated carvers wheeling around their massive joints, his mouth watered and a fanatic gleam came into his eyes, as if he had been a python which has just heard the dinner bell. It was one of those warm summer days when most people find their thoughts turning to cold salmon and cucumber salad, but what he wanted was roast beef, smoking hot, with Yorkshire pudding and floury potatoes on the side, followed by something along the lines of roly-poly pudding and Stilton cheese.

The paper he had bought was the *Daily Gazette*, and he glanced at it in the intervals of shovelling nourishing food into himself like a stevedore loading a grain ship. *Cocktail Time*, he noted with a touch of disapproval, had been dislodged from the front page by a big feature story about a twelve-year-old schoolboy who had shaved all his hair off in order to look like Yul Brynner, but it came into its own on page four with a large black headline which read:

FRANK, FORTHRIGHT, FEARLESS
BEGINNING FRIDAY

and beneath this the announcement that *Cocktail Time* was about to appear in the *Daily Gazette* as a serial. 'The sensational novel by Richard Blunt,' said the announcement, adding that this was the pseudonym of Cosmo Wisdom, a prominent young man about town who is, of course, the nephew of the well-known Queen's Counsel, Sir Raymond Bastable.

The roast beef, roly-poly pudding and Stilton cheese had done much to bring Cosmo into a cheerful frame of mind, and the manner in which this manifesto was worded completed the good work. For obviously, if in the eyes of the *Daily Gazette* he was still the author of *Cocktail Time*, it could only mean that his Uncle Raymond, reading that letter, had prudently decided to play for safety and pay the price of secrecy and silence. No doubt, Cosmo felt, there was a communication to that effect waiting at his rooms in Budge Street, Chelsea, and his only regret was that the pangs of hunger had made it impossible for him to go there and read it before making up leeway at Simpson's.

So far, so good. But after he had been gloating happily for some little time over the picture of Uncle Raymond at his desk, pen in hand and writing golden figures in his cheque book, the sunshine was suddenly blotted from his life. It had just occurred to him to speculate on the possible activities of his friend Gordon Carlisle during his enforced absence, and this train of thought was a chilling one. Suppose his friend Gordon Carlisle — shown by his every action to be a man who thought on his feet and did it now — had taken that letter in person to Uncle Raymond, disclosed its contents, got cash down for it and was already on his way back to America, his pockets full of Uncle Raymond's gold. It was fortunate for Cosmo that he had already consumed his roly-poly pudding, for, had he not, it would have turned to ashes in his mouth.

But in envisaging Gordon Carlisle leaning on the rail of an ocean liner, watching porpoises and totting up his ill-gotten gains, he had allowed imagination to mislead him. Oily was not on his way to America. He was at this moment in the process of rising from a table on the opposite side of Chez Simpson, where he had been lunching with his wife Gertie. And though, like Cosmo, he had lunched well, his heart was heavy. There, said those who saw him to each other, went a luncher who had failed to find the blue bird.

Cosmo's inexplicable disappearance had tried Gordon Carlisle sorely. It was holding up everything. Scarcely five minutes after leaving Hammer Lodge his astute brain had grasped what must be done to stabilize the situation, but the scheme he had in mind could not be put into operation without the assistance of Cosmo, and Cosmo had vanished. Every day for the past two weeks Oily had called at Budge Street, hoping for news, and every day he had been sent empty away by a landlady who made no secret of the fact that she was sick of the sight of him. He was in much the same position as a General who, with his strategic plans all polished and ready to be carried out, finds that his army has gone off somewhere, leaving no address.

It is not to be wondered at, therefore, that when, as he made for the door, he heard a voice utter his name and, turning, found himself gazing into the face of the man he had sought so long, his heart leaped up as if he had beheld a rainbow in the sky. Rather more so, in fact, for, unlike the poet Wordsworth, he had never cared much for rainbows.

'Carlisle!' cried Cosmo exuberantly. He was blaming himself for having wronged this man in thought, and remorse lent to his voice something of the warmth which a shepherd exhibits when he sees a lost sheep reporting for duty. 'Sit down, my dear old chap, sit down!'

His dear old chap sat down, but he did so in a reserved and distant manner that showed how deeply he was stirred. Wrath had taken the place of joy in Oily's bosom. Thinking of the strain to which he had been subjected in the last fourteen days, he could not readily forgive. The eye which he fixed on Cosmo was the eye of a man who intends to demand an explanation.

'Mrs Carlisle,' he said curtly, indicating his companion. 'This is the Wisdom guy, sweetie.'

'It is, is it?' said Gertie. Her teeth made a little clicking sound, and as she looked at Cosmo, she, too, seemed to bring a chill into the summer day.

The austerity of their demeanour passed unnoticed by Cosmo. His cordiality and effervescence continued undiminished.

'So here you are!' he said. 'Well?'

Oily had to remember that he was a gentleman before he could trust himself to speak. Words which he had learned in early boyhood were jostling each other in his mind. He turned to his wife.

'He says "Well?"'

'I heard him,' said Gertie grimly.

'"Well?" He sits there and says "Well?" Can you beat it?'

'He's got his nerve,' Gertie agreed. 'He's certainly there with the crust, all right. Listen, you. Where the heck have you been all this time?'

It was an embarrassing question. One likes to have one's little secrets.

'Oh – er – away,' said Cosmo evasively.

The words had the worst effect on his companions. Already cold and austere, they became colder and austerer, and so marked was their displeasure that he was at last forced to realize that he was not among friends. There was a bottle on the table, and a quick shiver ran down his spine as he observed Mrs Carlisle's hand stray absently in its direction. Knowing what a magnetic attraction bottles had for this woman, when cross, he decided that the moment had come to be frank, forthright and fearless.

'As a matter of fact, I've been in prison.'

'What!'

'Yes. I went on a toot and kicked a policeman, and they gave me fourteen days without the option. I got out this morning.'

A magical change came over the Carlisles, Mr and Mrs. An instant before stern and hostile, they looked at him now with the sympathetic eyes of a Mr and Mrs who understood all. The claims of prison are paramount.

'Oh, so that was it!' said Oily. 'I see. I couldn't think what had become of you, but if you were in the cooler . . .'

'How are they over here?' asked Gertie.

'Eh?'

'The coolers.'

'Oh, the coolers. Not too good.'

'Much the same as back home, I guess. Prison's all right for a visit, I always say, but I wouldn't live there if you gave me the place. Well, too bad they pulled you in, but you're here now, so let's not waste any more time. Give him the over-all picture, Oily.'

'Right away, sweetie. Things have gone and got a mite gummed up, Wisdom. You know a guy called Ickenham?'

'Lord Ickenham? Yes. He married my uncle's half-sister. What about him?'

Oily did not believe in breaking things gently.

'He's got that letter.'

Cosmo, as Police Constable Styles had done two weeks previously, made an odd, gurgling sound like water going down a waste pipe.

'My letter?'

'Yay.'

'Old Ickenham has?'

'Yup.'

'But I don't understand.'

'You will.'

Gordon Carlisle's narrative of the happenings at Hammer Lodge was a lengthy one, and long before it had finished Cosmo's jaw had dropped to its fullest extent. He had got the over-all picture, and his spirits were as low as his jaw.

'But what do we do?' he said hoarsely, seeing no ray of light among the clouds.

'Oh, now that I've contacted you, everything's nice and smooth.'

'Nice?'

'Yay.'

'Smooth?'

'Yup.'

'I don't see it,' said Cosmo.

Oily gave a gentlemanly little chuckle.

'Pretty clear, I'd have said. Fairly simple, seems to me. You just write your Uncle another letter, saying you've been thinking it over some more and still feel the same way about letting everybody know that it was him and not you that wrote the book, and you're going to spill the beans in the next couple of days or so. Won't that make him play ball? Of course it will.'

The hearty lunch with which his rather bewildered gastric juices were doing their best to cope had dulled Cosmo's wits a good deal, but they remained bright enough to enable him to grasp the beauty of the scheme.

'Why, of course! It doesn't matter that Ickenham has got the letter, does it?'

'Not a bit.'

'This second one of mine will do the trick.'

'Sure.'

'I'll go home and write it now.'

'No hurry. I see you've got the *Gazette* there. You've read about the serial?'

'Yes. I suppose Saxby sold it to them. I had a letter from a literary agent called Saxby, asking if he could handle the book, and I thought it was a good idea. I told him he could.'

'Well, the first thing you do is go see him and get the money.'

'And the second,' said Gertie, 'is slip Oily his cut. Seventy smackers, if you remember. You owed him fifty, and he loaned you another twenty. Making seventy in all.'

'That's right. It all comes back to me.'

'And now,' said Gertie, speaking with a certain metallic note in her voice, 'it's coming back to Oily. He'll call around at your place in an hour or so and collect it.'

## *Chapter 12*

Old Mr Howard Saxby was seated at his desk in his room at the Edgar Saxby literary agency when Cosmo arrived there. He was knitting a sock. He knitted a good deal, he would tell you if you asked him, to keep himself from smoking, adding that he also smoked a good deal to keep himself from knitting. He was a long, thin old gentleman in his middle seventies with a faraway unseeing look in his eye, not unlike that which a dead halibut on a fishmonger's slab gives the pedestrian as he passes. It was a look which caused many of those who met him to feel like disembodied spirits, so manifest was it that they were making absolutely no impression on his retina. Cosmo, full though he was of roast beef, roly-poly pudding and Stilton cheese, had the momentary illusion as he encountered that blank, vague gaze that he was something diaphanous that had been hurriedly put together with ectoplasm.

'Mr Wisdom,' said the girl who had led him into the presence.

'Ah,' said Howard Saxby, and there was a pause of perhaps three minutes, during which his needles clicked busily. 'Wisdom, did she say?'

'Yes. I wrote *Cocktail Time.*'

'You couldn't have done better,' said Mr Saxby cordially. 'How's your wife, Mr Wisdom?'

Cosmo said he had no wife.

'Surely?'

'I'm a bachelor.'

'Then Wordsworth was wrong. He said you were married to immortal verse. Excuse me a moment,' murmured Mr Saxby, applying himself to the sock again. 'I'm just turning the heel. Do you knit?'

'No.'

'Sleep does. It knits up the ravelled sleave of care.'

In the Demosthenes Club, where he lunched every day, there was considerable speculation as to whether old Saxby was as pronounced an old lunatic as he appeared to be or merely for some whimsical purpose of his own playing a part. The truth probably came midway between these two contending views. As a boy he had always been inclined to let his mind wander – 'needs to concentrate,' his school reports had said – and on entering the family business he had cultivated this tendency because he found it brought results. It disconcerts a publisher, talking terms with an agent, when the agent stares fixedly at him for some moments and then asks him if he plays the harp. He becomes nervous, says fifteen per cent when he meant to say ten, and forgets to mention subsidiary rights altogether.

On Cosmo the Saxby manner acted as an irritant. Though meek in the presence of his Uncle Raymond, he had his pride, and resented being treated as if he were some negligible form of insect life that had strayed out from the woodwork. He coughed sharply, and Mr Saxby's head came up with a startled jerk. It was evident that he had supposed himself alone.

'Goodness, you made me jump!' he said. 'Who are you?'

'My name, as I have already told you, is Wisdom.'

'How did you get in?' asked Mr Saxby with a show of interest.

'I was shown in.'

'And stayed in. I see, Tennyson was right. Knowledge comes, but Wisdom lingers. Take a chair.'

'I have.'

'Take another,' said Mr Saxby hospitably. 'Is there,' he asked, struck by a sudden thought, 'something I can do for you?'

'I came about that serial.'

Mr Saxby frowned. A subject had been brought up on which he held strong views.

'When I was a young man,' he said severely, 'there were no cereals. We ate good wholesome porridge for breakfast and throve on it. Then along came these Americans with their Cute Crispies and Crunchy Whoopsies and so forth, and what's the result? Dyspepsia is rife. England riddled with it.'

'The serial in the paper.'

'Putting the beastly stuff in paper makes no difference,' said Mr Saxby, and returned to his sock.

Cosmo swallowed once or twice. The intellectual pressure of the conversation was making him feel a little light-headed.

'I came,' he said, speaking slowly and carefully, 'about that serial story of mine in the *Daily Gazette*.'

Mr Saxby gave a little cry of triumph.

'I've turned the heel! I beg your pardon? What did you say?'

'I came ... about that serial story of mine ... in the *Daily Gazette*.'

'You want my opinion of it? I would give it gladly, were it not for the fact that I never read serial stories in newspapers. Years ago I promised my mother I wouldn't, and to that promise I have faithfully adhered. Foolishly sentimental, you will say, pointing out that my mother, who has long been in heaven, would never know, but there it is. One has these rules to live by. And now,' said Mr Saxby, putting his sock away in a drawer and rising, 'I fear I must leave you. I have found your conversation very interesting, most interesting, but at this hour I always take a brisk constitutional. It settles my lunch and allows the digestive processes to work smoothly. If more people took brisk constitutionals after meals, there wouldn't be half the deaths there are, if any.'

He left the room, to return a moment later and regard Cosmo with a vague, benevolent eye.

'Do you play leap-frog?' he asked.

Cosmo, speaking rather shortly, said that he did not.

'You should. Neglect no opportunity to play leap-frog. It is the best of all games and will never become professionalized. Well, good-bye, my dear fellow, so glad to have met you. Look in again, and next time bring your wife.'

For some moments after the old gentleman had shuffled out, the dizzy feeling, as of being in some strange nightmare world, which came upon so many people after a *tête-à-tête* with Howard Saxby, had Cosmo strongly in its grip, and he sat motionless, breathing jerkily from between parted lips. Then torpor gave place to indignation. As Roget would have put it in his excellent Thesaurus, he was angry, wroth, irate, ireful, up in arms, flushed with passion and in high dudgeon, and he intended to make his presence felt. He rose, and pressed the bell on Mr Saxby's desk, keeping his thumb on it so forcefully that the girl who answered the summons did so in something of the manner of an athlete completing a four-minute mile, thinking that at last old Mr Saxby must have had the seizure the office force had been anticipating for years.

'I want to see somebody,' said Cosmo.

Wilting beneath his eye, which was blazing like a search-light, the underling panted a little, and said:

'Yes, sir.' Then, for one likes to know these things, 'Who?'

'Anyone, anyone, anyone, anyone!'

'Yes, sir,' said the underling, and withdrew. She went to the second door down the passage, and knocked. Roget would have described her as upset, disconcerted, thrown off her centre and rattled (*colloq.*), and employees of the Edgar Saxby literary agency when thus afflicted always sought out Barbara Crowe, knowing that they could rely on her for sympathy and constructive counsel.

'Come in,' called a musical voice, a voice like a good brand of Burgundy made audible. 'Why, hullo, Marlene, you look agitated. What's the matter?'

'There's a gentleman in old Mr Saxby's room who says he wants to see someone.'

'Can't he see old Mr Saxby?'

'He isn't there, Mrs Crowe.'

'Hell's bells!' said Barbara. She knew old Mr Saxby's habits. 'Left the poor gentleman flat, has he? All right, I'll go and soothe him.'

She spoke confidently, and her confidence was justified, for at the very first sight of her Cosmo's righteous indignation sensibly diminished. A moment before, he would gladly have put the entire personnel of the Edgar Saxby literary agency to the sword, but now he was inclined to make an exception in favour of this member of it. Here, he could see at a glance, was a nice change from the sock-knitting old museum piece whose peculiar methods of conducting a business talk had turned his thoughts in the direction of mayhem.

It is probable that almost anyone, even one of the Jukes family with two heads, would have looked good to Cosmo after old Mr Saxby, but in sealing Barbara Crowe with the stamp of his approval he was perfectly justified. Lord Ickenham, speaking of this woman to Pongo, had used the adjective 'lovely'. While not quite that, she was undeniably attractive. Brown eyes, brown hair, just the right sort of nose and a wide, humorous mouth that smiled readily and was smiling now. Her personality, too, had a distinct appeal of its own. There was about her a kindly briskness which seemed to say 'Yes, yes, you have your troubles, I can see you have, but leave everything to me.' Fierce authors who came into the Saxby offices like lions always went out like lambs after talking with Barbara Crowe.

'Good afternoon,' she said. 'Is there something I can do for you? They tell me you have been in conference with old Mr Saxby. Very rash of you. What made you ask for him?'

'He wrote to me. He said he wanted to handle my novel *Cocktail Time.*'

'*Cocktail Time*? Good heavens! Are you Cosmo Wisdom?'

'Yes.'

'I know your uncle. My name is Mrs Crowe.'

Not moving much in his Uncle Raymond's circle, Cosmo had never seen Barbara Crowe, but he knew all about her from his mother, and looking at her now he was amazed that anyone, having succeeded in becoming engaged to her, could have let her get away. It confirmed the opinion he had always held that his Uncle Raymond, though possibly possessed of a certain rude skill in legal matters, was in every other respect the world's champion fathead.

'How is he?' asked Barbara.

'Uncle Raymond? Well, I don't see very much of him, but somebody who met him two weeks ago said he seemed worried.'

'Worried?'

'A bit on the jumpy side.'

A cloud passed over Barbara's cheerful face. As Lord Ickenham had indicated, she had by no means thrust Sir Raymond Bastable from her thoughts.

'He *will* overwork. He isn't ill?'

'Oh, no. Just . . . nervous,' said Cosmo, finding the *mot juste.*

There was a momentary silence. Then Barbara reminded herself that she was a conscientious literary agent and this young man not merely the nephew of the man whom for all his fatheadedness she still loved but an author, and an author plainly in need of having his hand held.

'But you didn't come here to talk about your uncle, did you? You came to discuss business of some sort. I don't suppose you got far with old Mr Saxby? No, I thought not. Was he knitting?'

Cosmo winced. Her question had touched an exposed nerve.

'Yes,' he said coldly. 'A sock.'

'How was it coming along?'

'I understood him to say that he had turned the heel.'

'Good. Always the testing part. Once past the heel, you're home. But except for learning that the sock was going well, you did not get much satisfaction out of him, I imagine. Not many of our clients do. Old Mr Saxby likes to come here still and potter about, though supposed to have retired at about the time when Gutenberg invented the printing press, but he is not what you would call an active cog in the machine. Our only authors who ever see him now are those who mistakenly ask for Howard Saxby. I suppose you did?'

'Yes. That was the name on the letter I got.'

'It should have been signed H.S., junior. Young Mr Howard Saxby is old Mr Howard Saxby's son. He runs things here, with as much assistance as I am able to give him. He's away today, so I am your only resource. What did you come about?'

'That serial in the *Daily Gazette*.'

'Oh, yes. A cheque for that was sent to you more than a week ago. Didn't you get it?'

'I've – er – been away.'

'Oh, I see. Well, it's waiting for you at your rooms. And we're hoping to have more good news for you at any moment. The movie end.'

It had never occurred to Cosmo that there was a movie end.

'You think the book might sell to the pictures?'

'Our man in Hollywood seems sure it will. He's been sending significant cables almost daily. The last one, which arrived yesterday, said . . . Yes?'

The girl Marlene had entered, bearing a russet envelope. She looked nervously at Cosmo, and sidled out. Barbara Crowe opened the envelope, and uttered an exclamation.

'Well, of all the coincidences!'

'Eh?'

'That you should have been here when this came and just when I was starting to tell you about the movie prospects. It's from our man in Hollywood, and . . . better sit down. Oh, you are sitting down. Well, hold on to your chair. He says he has now had a firm offer for the picture rights of *Cocktail Time* from the Superba-Llewellyn studio. Would it interest you to hear what it is?'

It would, Cosmo intimated, interest him exceedingly.

'A hundred and five thousand dollars,' said Barbara.

## Chapter 13

It was a stunned and dizzy Cosmo Wisdom who some quarter of an hour later tottered from the premises of the Saxby literary agency, hailed a cab and tottered into it. He was feeling very much as his Uncle Raymond had felt on that faraway afternoon at Oxford when he had taken the Welsh forward to his bosom. But whereas Sir Raymond's emotions on that occasion had been of a sombre nature, those of Cosmo, as he drove to Budge Street, Chelsea, can best be described by the adjective ecstatic. It is not easy to drive in a taxi cab of the 1947 vintage and feel that you are floating on a pink cloud high up in the empyrean, but he did it. And this in spite of the fact that his head was still hurting him quite a good deal.

At the moment when Barbara opened the cable from the man in Hollywood, he had been tilting his chair back, and the convulsive spasm which had resulted when she talked figures had caused him to take a nasty toss, bumping his occipital bone with considerable force on the side of old Mr Saxby's desk. But, placed right end up again with a civil 'Upsy-daisy', he had speedily forgotten physical discomfort in the rapture and what Roget would have called oblectation (*rare*) of listening to her subsequent remarks.

For this offer from the Superba-Llewellyn studio was, it appeared, not an end but a beginning. The man in Hollywood, she assured him, would not rest on his laurels with a complacent 'That's that.' He was, like so many men-in-Hollywood, a live wire who, once started, went from strength to strength. There would now, she said, come the bumping-up process – the mentioning to a rival studio that S-L were offering a hundred and five thousand dollars, the extracting from the rival studio of a bid of a hundred and fifty thousand, the trotting back to the Superba-Llewellyn with this information and . . .

'Well, you get the idea,' said Barbara.

Cosmo did indeed get the idea, and nearly injured his occipital bone again when this woman, a ministering angel if ever he saw one, went on to speak of one of the agency's clients whose latest work the man in Hollywood had just bumped up to three hundred and fifty thousand. True, he was feeling as he drove to Budge Street, he could not count on *Cocktail Time* bringing in quite as much as that, but even two hundred thousand would be well worth having. It is evidence of the heady effect which these chats about Hollywood have on authors that he had now begun to look on Superba-Llewellyn's original offer with a sort of amused contempt. Why this parsimony, he was wondering. Money was made to spend. Had no one ever told the Superba-Llewellyn studio that you can't take it with you?

But in every ointment there is a fly, in every good thing a catch of some sort. Elated though he was, Cosmo could not but remember that he had written a letter – in his own personal handwriting and signed with his own name – specifically disclaiming the authorship of *Cocktail Time*, and that this letter was in the possession of Lord Ickenham. For the moment, that blot on the peerage was withholding its contents from the public, but who could say how long he would continue to do so? Somehow, by some means, he must get the fatal paper into his hands and burn it, thus destroying the only evidence that existed that the book was the work of another.

It was not too difficult to sketch out a tentative plan to this end. From Oily, in the course of his narrative at Simpson's, he had learned that Lord Ickenham was staying at Hammer Hall, where paying guests were taken in. His first move must obviously be to become one of these paying guests. A vital document like that letter would presumably be hidden somewhere in the old buster's room, for where else in a country house could anyone hide anything? Once on the spot, he would sooner or later find an opportunity of searching that room. In the stories which were his favourite reading people were always searching rooms, generally with excellent results.

It was with his spirits high again that he entered No. 11 Budge Street. In the hall he encountered his landlady, a Mrs Keating, a gloomy woman whom two weeks of daily visits from Oily had rendered gloomier. Oily often had that effect on people.

'Why, hullo!' she said, plainly surprised at this return to the fold. 'Where you been all this time?'

'Away,' said Cosmo, wondering how often he was going to have to answer this question. 'Staying with friends.'

'You didn't take any luggage.'

'They lent me everything.'

'You're looking thinner.'

Cosmo admitted that he had lost a little weight.

'Tuberculosis, I should say,' said Mrs Keating, brightening a little. 'That's what Keating died of. There's a lot of letters in there for you, and there's been a fellow calling asking for you every day these last two weeks. Carmichael or some such name.'

'Carlisle. I've seen him.'

'Seemed to think I've nothing to do but answer the bell. You be wanting dinner tonight?'

'No, I'm going away again. I just looked in to pack.'

'Odd some folks don't seem able to stay put for two minutes on end. It's this modern restless spirit. Gadding about. I've lived here twenty years and never been further than the King's Road, except to Kensal Green, when Keating was laid to his rest. Wasted away to a shadow, he did, and it wasn't two months before we were wearing our blacks. Tuberculosis it was, same as you've got. Where you going this time?'

'Dovetail Hammer in Berkshire. Forward my letters to Hammer Hall.'

'More work,' said Mrs Keating, and went off to the kitchen to attend to whatever it was on the stove that was making the house smell as if a meal were being prepared for a pack of hounds.

Quite a considerable mail awaited Cosmo in his sitting-room. The table was piled with letters. Most of them had been forwarded from Alfred Tomkins, Ltd, and he read them with enjoyment – an author is always glad to hear from the fans – but the one that pleased him most was the one from the Edgar Saxby literary agency containing that cheque. It was one of those fat, substantial cheques, and he enclosed it in an envelope addressed to his bank. After which, feeling that things were making a good start, he went to his bedroom and began packing. He had filled a large suitcase and was standing on the front steps with it, waiting for a taxi, when Oily arrived – without, he was relieved to see, Sweetie, the bottle addict.

The indications of impending departure which met his eye surprised Oily.

'Where are you going?' he asked.

It was a change from being asked where he had been, but Cosmo made his customary answer.

'Away. Thought I'd have a couple of days at Bournemouth.'

'Why Bournemouth?'

'Why not Bournemouth?' said Cosmo rather cleverly, and Oily appeared to see the justice of this.

'Well, I'm glad I caught you,' he said, having expressed the opinion that his young friend might just as well bury himself alive. Oily was the metropolitan type, never at his ease outside big cities. 'What have you done with the letter?'

Cosmo, rehearsing this scene in the privacy of his bedroom, had decided to be nonchalant. It was nonchalantly that he now replied:

'Oh, the letter? I was going to tell you about that. I've changed my mind. I'm not going to write it.'

'What!'

'No. I think I'll let things stay the way they are. Oh, by the way, I owe you some money, don't I? I wrote a cheque. I've got it somewhere. Yes, here you are. Taxi!' cried Cosmo, waving.

Oily was still standing stunned among the ruins of his hopes and dreams.

'But –'

'It's no good saying "But,"' said Cosmo briskly, 'if you really want to know, I like being the author of *Cocktail Time*. I enjoy getting all these letters from admirers of my work –'

'What do you mean, your work?'

'Well, Uncle Raymond's work. It's the same thing. And being the author of *Cocktail Time* improves my social standing. To give you an instance, I found a note in there from Georgina, Lady Witherspoon, inviting me to one of her Sunday afternoon teas. It isn't everybody by any means whom Georgina, Lady Witherspoon, invites to her Sunday afternoon teas. She runs a sort of salon, and you have to be somebody of importance to get in. I don't feel like throwing away all that just to collect a few hundred pounds or whatever it may be from Uncle Raymond.' Less, probably, he almost said, than the absurd chicken-feed the Superba-Llewellyn people were offering. 'So there you are. Well, good-bye, Carlisle, it's been nice knowing you. I must be off,' said Cosmo, and was, leaving Oily staring blankly after him and asking himself if these things could really be. Even a high-up confidence artist has to expect disappointments and setbacks, of course, from time to time, but he never learns to enjoy them. In the manner of Gordon Carlisle as half an hour later he entered the presence of his wife Gertie there still lingered a suggestion of Napoleon returning from Moscow.

Gertie, having listened frowningly to the tale he had to tell, expressed the opinion that Cosmo was a low-down double-crossing little rat, which was of course quite true.

'There's oompus-boompus going on,' she said.

'Oompus-boompus, sweetie?'

'Yay. Social standing, did he say?'

'That's what he said.'

Gertie emitted what in a less attractive woman would have been a snort.

'Social standing, my left eyeball! When he left us, he was going to see his agent, wasn't he? Well, it's as clear what's happened as if he'd drawn a diagram. The agent told him there's been a movie offer.'

'Gosh!'

'Sure. And a big one, must have been.'

'I never thought of that. You're dead right. It would explain everything.'

'And he isn't going to any Bournemouth – who the hell goes to Bournemouth? – he's going to this Dovetail-what-is-it place to try to snitch that letter off the Ickenham character, because if he can get it and destroy it, there's nothing in the world to prove he didn't write the book. So what we do is go to Dovetail-and-what-have-you and snitch it before he does.'

'I get you. If we swing it, we'll be sitting pretty.'

'In the catbird seat. There we'll be, in the middle, with the Wisdom character bidding for it and the Bastable character bidding for it, and the sky the limit. And it oughtn't to be so hard to find out where the Ickenham character is keeping the thing. We'll go through his room with a fine-tooth comb, and if it isn't there, we'll know he's got it on him. Then all there is to it is beaning him with a blackjack and hunting around in his pockets, see what I mean?'

Oily saw what she meant. She could hardly have been more lucid. He drew an emotional breath, and even the most short-sighted could have seen the lovelight in his eyes.

'What a comfort you are to me, sweetie!' he said.

'I try to be,' said Gertie virtuously. 'I think a wife oughter.'

## *Chapter 14*

It was two days after the vultures had decided to muster at Hammer Hall that a little procession emerged from the front door of Hammer Lodge, the country seat of Sir Raymond Bastable, QC. It was headed by Mrs Phoebe Wisdom, who was followed by the local veterinary surgeon, who was followed by Albert Peasemarch. The veterinary surgeon got into his car, spoke a few parting words of encouragement and good cheer, and drove off. He had been in attendance on Mrs Wisdom's cocker spaniel Benjy, who, as cocker spaniels will, had 'picked up something'. Both Phoebe and Albert, having passed the night at the sick bed, were looking in need of rest and repose, but their morale was high, and they gazed at each other tenderly, like two boys of the old brigade who have been standing shoulder to shoulder.

'I don't know how to thank you, Peasemarch,' said Phoebe.

'It was nothing, madam.'

'Mr Spurrell said that if it had not been for you making the poor angel swallow that mustard and water, the worst would have happened.'

It occurred to Albert Peasemarch as a passing thought that the worst could not have been much worse than what had happened when the invalid reacted to the healing draught. It would, he was convinced, remain for ever photographically lined on the tablets of his memory when a yesterday had faded from its page, just as the eruption of the Old Faithful geyser in Yellowstone Park lingers always in the memory of the tourist who sees it.

'I am glad to have given satisfaction, madam,' he said, remembering a good line taught him by Lord Ickenham's Coggs at the time when he was being coached for the high office he held. And, thinking of Lord Ickenham, he felt how right the clear-seeing peer had been in urging him to spare no effort that would lead to a *rapprochement* between this cocker spaniel and himself. Unless he was greatly mistaken there was a new light in Phoebe's eyes as she gazed at him, the sort of light a knight of King Arthur's Round Table might have observed in the eyes of a damsel in distress, as he dusted his hands after dispatching the dragon which had been causing her annoyance. The vigil of the night had brought them very close together. He found his thoughts turning in the direction of what his mentor had called the Ickenham system. Had the moment come for putting this into operation?

He had the drill, he fancied, pretty clear in his mind. How did it go? Ah, yes. Stride up, grab by wrist, waggle about a bit, say 'My mate!' clasp to bosom and shower burning kisses on upturned face. All quite simple, and yet he hesitated. And, as always happens when a man hesitates, the moment passed. Before he could nerve himself to do something constructive, she had begun to speak of warm milk with a little drop of brandy in it. Mr Spurrell, the veterinary surgeon, had recommended this.

'Will you heat some up in a saucepan, Peasemarch?'

Albert Peasemarch sighed. To put the Ickenham system into operation with any hope of success, a man needs something in the nature of a cue, and cannot hope to give of his best if the saucepan motif is introduced into the conversation. Romeo himself would have been discouraged, if early in the balcony scene Juliet had started talking about saucepans.

'Very good, madam,' he said dully.

'And then you ought to lie down and have a good rest.'

'I was about to suggest the same thing to you, Madam.'

'Yes, I am feeling tired. But I want to speak to Lord Ickenham first.'

'I see his lordship is fishing on the lake, madam. Could I take a message?'

'No, thank you very much, Peasemarch. It's something I must say to him personally.'

'Very good, madam,' said Albert Peasemarch, and went off to heat saucepans with the heavy heart of a man conscious of having missed the bus. Possibly there were ringing in his ears the words of James Graham, first Marquis of Montrose:

He either fears his fate too much
  Or his deserts are small,
That dares not put it to the touch,
  To win or lose at all.

Or, of course, possibly not.

What knitting was to old Mr Saxby, fishing was to Lord Ickenham. He had not yet caught anything, nor was he expecting to, but
sitting in a punt, watching a bobbing float, with the white clouds
drifting across the blue sky above him and a gentle breeze from the
west playing about his temples, helped him to think, and happenings
at Hammer Hall of late had given him much to think about. The
recent muster of the vultures had not escaped his notice, and even
had it done so, the fact that his room had been twice ransacked in
the past two days would have drawn it to his attention. Rooms do
not ransack themselves. There has to be a motivating force behind
the process, and if there are vultures on the premises, one knows
where to look for suspects.

Except for the nuisance of having to tidy up after these vultures,
their arrival had pleased rather than perturbed Lord Ickenham. He
was a man who always liked to have plenty happening around him,
and he found the incursion of Cosmo Wisdom, closely followed by
that of Gordon Carlisle and wife, a pleasant break in what was at
the moment a dull visit. Enjoying the company of his fellows, he
was finding himself distinctly short of it at Hammer Hall. He could
scarcely, after what had occurred, hobnob with Beefy Bastable;
Albert Peasemarch was hard to get hold of; and Johnny Pearce,
racked with anxiety about his Belinda, had been for the last week a
total loss as a companion.

So on the whole, he reflected, it was probably no bad thing to
have a vulture or two about the home. They livened things up.
What puzzled him about this current consignment was the problem
of what had brought them to Hammer Hall and why, being there,
they had ransacked his room. They were apparently searching
eagerly for that letter of young Cosmo's, but he could imagine no
reason for them to consider it of any value. Like Oily, he had seen
immediately that Cosmo could quite easily write another, which

would have precisely the same effect as the first. Eccentric blighters, these vultures, he told himself.

Another thing that perplexed him was that they seemed to be on such distant terms with one another. There was no mistaking the coolness that existed between Mr and Mrs Carlisle on the one side and Cosmo Wisdom on the other. One expects vultures, when they muster, to be a chummy bunch, always exchanging notes and ideas and working together for the good of the show. But every time Gordon Carlisle's eye rested on Cosmo, it rested with distaste, and if Cosmo passed Gordon Carlisle in the hall, he did so without appearing to see him. Very curious.

He was roused from these meditations by hearing his name called, and perceived Phoebe standing on the shore. Reluctantly, for he would have preferred to be alone, he drew in his line and rowed to land. Disembarking and seeing her at close quarters, he was a good deal shocked by her appearance. It reminded him of that of women he had seen at Le Touquet groping their way out into the morning air after an all-night session at the Casino.

'My dear Phoebe,' he exclaimed, 'you appear to be coming apart at the seams somewhat, if you don't mind me being personal. Not your bonny self at all. What's happened?'

'I was up all night with Benjy, Frederick. The poor darling was terribly ill. He picked up something.'

'Good Lord, I'm sorry to hear that. Is he all right now?'

'Yes, thanks to Peasemarch. He was wonderful. But I came to talk about something else, Frederick.'

'Anything you wish, my dear. Had you any particular topic in mind?' said Lord Ickenham, hoping that she had not come to resume yesterday's conversation about her son Cosmo and how thin he looked and how odd it was that, visiting Dovetail Hammer, he should be staying at the Hall and not with his mother at the Lodge. He could hardly explain that Cosmo was at the Hall because he wanted to be on the spot, to ransack people's rooms.

'It's about Raymond, Frederick.'

'Oh, Beefy?' said Lord Ickenham, relieved.

'I'm dreadfully worried about him.'

'Don't tell me he has picked up something?'

'I think he is going off his head.'

'Oh, come!'

'Well, there is insanity in the family, you know. George Winstanley ended his days in an asylum.'

'I'm not so well up on George as I ought to be. Who was he?'

'He was in the Foreign Office. He married my mother's second cousin Alice.'

'And went off his onion?'

'He had to be certified. He thought he was Stalin's nephew.'

'He wasn't, of course?'

'No, but it made it very awkward for everybody. He was always sending secret official papers over to Russia.'

'I see. Well, I doubt if the pottiness of a second cousin by marriage is hereditary,' said Lord Ickenham consolingly. 'I don't think you need have any anxiety about Beefy. What gives you the idea that he has not got all his marbles?'

'His what?'

'Why do you think he is *non compos*?'

'It's the way he's behaving.'

'Tell me all.'

Phoebe brushed away the tears that came so readily to her eyes.

'Well, you know how . . . what shall I say . . . how *impatient* dear Raymond has always been with me. It was the same when we were children. He has always had such a keen brain, and I don't think very quickly, and this seemed to exasperate him. He would say something, and I would say "What?" and he would start shouting. Morning after morning he used to make me cry at breakfast, and that seemed to exasperate him more. Well, quite suddenly one day about two weeks ago he changed completely. He became so sweet and kind and gentle that it took my breath away. I'm sure Peasemarch noticed it, for he was so often in the room when it happened. I mean, things like asking after my rheumatism and would I like a footstool and how nice I looked in that green dress of mine. He was a different man.'

'All to the good, I should have thought.'

'I thought so, too, at first. But as the days went by I began to get uneasy. I knew how overworked he always is, and I thought he must be going to have a nervous breakdown, if not something worse. Frederick,' her voice sank to a whisper, 'he sends me flowers! Every morning. I find them in my room.'

'Very civil. I see no objection to flowers in moderation.'

'But it's so *unnatural*. It alarmed me. I wrote to Sir Roderick Glossop about him. You know him?'

'The loony doctor? I should say so. What I could tell you about old Roddy Glossop!'

'He is a friend of the family, and I thought he would be able to advise me. But I didn't send the letter.'

'I'm glad you didn't,' said Lord Ickenham. His handsome face was grave. 'It would have been a floater of the worst description. There is nothing odd about this change in Beefy's attitude, my dear girl. I can give you the explanation in a word. Peasemarch.'

'Peasemarch?'

'He is behaving like this to conciliate Albert Peasemarch. An observant man, he noticed Albert Peasemarch's silent disapproval of the way he used to carry on, and realized that unless he speedily mended his ways, he would be a butler short, and nobody wants to lose a butler in these hard post-war days. As the fellow said – Ecclesiastes, was it? – I should have to check with Nannie Bruce – whoso findeth a butler findeth a good thing. I know that I would go to even greater lengths to retain the services of my Coggs.'

Phoebe's eyes were round. She looked like a white rabbit that is not abreast of things.

'You mean Peasemarch would have given notice?'

'Exactly. You wouldn't have seen him for dust.'

'But why?'

'Unable to stand the strain of watching you being put through the wringer each morning. No man likes to see a fourteen stone QC hammering the stuffing out of the woman he loves.'

'*Loves?*'

'Surely you must be aware by now that Albert Peasemarch worships the very ground you tread on?'

'But . . . but this is extraordinary!'

'I see nothing remarkable in it. When you don't sit up all night with sick cocker spaniels, you're a very attractive woman, my dear Phoebe.'

'But Peasemarch is a *butler*.'

'Ah, I see what you mean. You are thinking that you have never had a butler in love with you before. One gets new experiences. But

Albert Peasemarch is only a synthetic butler. He is a man of property who took to buttling simply in order to be near you, to be able to exchange notes on your mutual rheumatism, to have you rub his chest with embrocation when he had influenza. Do you remember,' said Lord Ickenham, giving rein to his always rather vivid imagination, 'a day about two years ago when Beefy was standing you and me lunch at the Savoy Grill, and I nodded to a man at the next table?'

'No.'

Lord Ickenham was not surprised.

'That man,' he said, 'was Albert Peasemarch. He came to me later – he is an old friend of mine – and asked who you were. His manner was feverish, and it wasn't long before he was pouring out his soul to me. It was love, my dear Phoebe, love at first sight. How, he asked, could he get to know you? I offered to introduce him to Beefy, but he seemed to think that that wouldn't work. He said what he had seen of Beefy had not given him the impression of a man who would invite him to the home for long week-ends and generally give him the run of the place. I agreed with him. Beefy, when you introduce someone to him, is far too prone to say "Haryer, haryer," and then drop the party of the second part like a hot coal. We needed some mechanism whereby Albert Peasemarch could be constantly in your society, giving you the tender look and occasionally heaving the soft sigh, and to a man of my intelligence the solution was obvious. Who, I asked myself, is the Johnny who is always on the spot, the man who sticketh closer than a brother? The butler, I answered myself. Albert Peasemarch, I said, still addressing myself, must become Beefy's butler. No sooner – or not much sooner – said than done. A few simple lessons from Coggs and there he was, all ready to move in.'

Phoebe was still fluttering. The way the tip of her nose wiggled showed how greatly the story had affected her. She said she had never heard of such a thing, and Lord Ickenham agreed that the set-up was unusual.

'But romantic, don't you think?' he added. 'The sort of policy great lovers through the ages would have pursued, if they had happened to think of it. Hullo,' he said, breaking off. 'I'm afraid I must be leaving you, Phoebe.'

He had seen the station cab drive up to the front door and discharge Johnny Pearce from its interior.

'My godson has returned,' he explained. 'He went up to London to give his fiancée lunch, and I am anxious to learn how everything came out. The course of true love has not been running very smooth of late, I understand. Something of a rift within the lute, I gather, and you know what happens when rifts get into lutes. By and by they make the music mute and ever widening slowly silence all. I shall be glad to receive a reassuring bulletin.'

## Chapter 15

Beside Johnny Pearce, as he stood on the gravel drive, there was lying a battered suitcase. It signified, Lord Ickenham presumed, the advent of another paying guest, and he was delighted that business was booming so briskly. What with himself, this new arrival and the three vultures already in residence, Johnny in his capacity of jovial innkeeper was doing well. Though, now that he was in a position to study him closely, he had doubts as to whether 'jovial' was the right adjective. The young man's face, while not actually haggard, was definitely careworn. He looked like an innkeeper with a good deal on his mind, and when he spoke, his voice was toneless.

'Oh, hullo, Uncle Fred. I've just got back.'

'So I see. And you appear on your travels to have picked up some luggage. Whose suitcase is that?'

'It belongs to a bloke I shared the cab with. I dropped him at the Lodge. He wanted to see Bastable. Saxby he said his name was.'

'Saxby? Was he a fellow in the early forties with a jutting chin and a head like the dome of St Paul's, or a flattened-out septuagenarian who looked as if he had at one time been run over by a steamroller? The latter? Then it must be Saxby senior, the father of the jutting chinner. I've met him at the Demosthenes Club. How did you get on with him?'

'Oh, all right. Odd sort of chap. Why did he ask me if I played the trombone?'

'One has to say something to keep the conversation going. Do you?'

'No.'

'Well, don't let yourself get an inferiority complex about it. Many of our most eminent public men don't play the trombone. Lord Beaverbrook, for one. Yes, that was old Saxby all right. I recognize his peculiar conversational methods. Every time I meet him, he asks me if I have seen Flannery lately. Who on earth Flannery is I have never been able to ascertain. When I reply that I have not, he says "Ah? And how *was* he?" The day old Saxby makes anything remotely resembling sense, they will set the church bells ringing and proclaim a national holiday. I wonder why he was going to see Beefy. Just a social call, I suppose. The question that intrigues one is why is he here at all. Is he staying with you?'

'Yes.'

'Good. Every little bit added to what you've got makes just a little bit more.'

'He may be staying some time. He's a bird-watcher, he tells me.'

'Indeed? I never saw that side of him. Our encounters have always taken place at the Demosthenes, where the birds are few and far between. I believe the committee is very strict about admitting them. Do you watch birds, Johnny?'

'No.'

'Nor I. If I meet one whose looks I like, I give it a nod and a wave of the hand, but I would never dream of prowling about and goggling at our feathered friends in the privacy of their homes. What a curse he must be to them. I can imagine nothing more unpleasant for a chaffinch or a reed-warbler than to get settled down for the evening with a good book and a pipe and then, just as it is saying to itself "This is the life," to look up and see old Saxby peering at it. When you reflect that strong men wilt when they meet that vague, fishy eye of his, you can imagine what its effect must be on a sensitive bird. But pigeon-holing old Saxby for the moment, what happened when you met Bunny? How was she? Gay? Sparkling?'

'Oh, yes.'

'Splendid. I was afraid that, with your relations a bit strained, she might have given you the Farthest North treatment or, as it is sometimes called, the ice-box formula. Cold. Aloof. The long silence and the face turned away to show only the profile. You relieve my mind considerably.'

'I wish someone would relieve mine.'

'Why, what's wrong? You say she was gay and sparkling.'

'Yes, but it wasn't me she was gay and sparkling with.'

Lord Ickenham frowned. His godson seemed to have dropped

again into that habit of his of speaking in riddles, and it annoyed him.

'Don't be cryptic, my boy. Start at the beginning, and let your yea be yea and your nay be nay. You gave her lunch?'

'Yes, and she brought along a blighter called Norbury-Smith.'

Lord Ickenham was shocked and astounded.

'To a lovers' tryst? To what should have been a sacred reunion of two fond hearts after long parting? You amaze me. Did she offer any explanation of what she must have known was a social gaffe?'

'She said he had told her he was at school with me, and she was sure I would like to meet him again.'

'Good God! Smiling brightly as she spoke?'

'Yes, she was smiling quite a lot. Norbury-Smith!' said Johnny bitterly. 'A fellow I thought I'd seen the last of ten years ago. He's a stockbroker now, richer than blazes, and looks like a movie star.'

'Good heavens! Did their relations seem to you cordial?'

'She was all over him. They were prattling away like a couple of honeymooners.'

'Leaving you out of it?'

'I might as well have been painted on the back drop.'

Lord Ickenham drew a sharp breath. His face was grave.

'I don't like this, Johnny.'

'I didn't like it myself.'

'It's the Oh-well-if-you-don't-want-me-there-are-plenty-who-do formula, which too often means that the female of the species, having given the matter considered thought, has decided that she is about ready to call it a day. Do you know what I think, Johnny?'

'What?'

'You'd better marry that girl quick.'

'And bring her here with Nannie Bruce floating about the place like poison gas? We don't have to go into all that again, do we? I wouldn't play such a low trick on her.' Johnny paused, and eyed his companion sourly. 'What,' he asked, 'are you grinning about?'

Lord Ickenham patted his arm in a godfatherly manner.

'If,' he said, 'you allude to the gentle smile which you see on my face – I doubt if somebody like Flaubert, with his passion for the right word, would call it a grin – I will tell you why I smile gently.

I have high hopes that the dark menace of Nannie Bruce will shortly be removed.'

Johnny found himself unable to share this optimistic outlook.

'How can it be removed? I can't raise five hundred pounds.'

'You may not have to. You see that bicycle propped up near the back door,' said Lord Ickenham, pointing. 'Police Constable McMurdo's Arab steed. He's in the kitchen now, getting down to brass tacks with her.'

'It won't do any good.'

'I disagree with you. I anticipate solid results. I must mention that since I got here I have been seeing quite a bit of Officer McMurdo, and he has confided in me as in a sympathetic elder brother. He unloaded a police constable's unspotted heart on me, and I was shocked to learn on what mistaken lines he had been trying to overcome Nannie Bruce's sales-resistance. He had been arguing with her, Johnny, pleading with her, putting his trust in the honeyed word and the voice of reason. As if words, however honeyed, could melt the obstinacy of a woman whose mother, I am convinced, must have been frightened by a deaf adder. Action, Cyril, I told him – his name is Cyril – is what you need, and I urged him with all the vehemence at my disposal to cut the cackle and try the Ickenham system.'

'What's that?'

'It's a little thing I knocked together in my bachelor days. I won't go into the details now, but it has a good many points in common with all-in wrestling and osteopathy. I generally recommend it to diffident wooers, and it always works like magic. Up against it, the proudest beauty – not that that's a very good description of Nannie Bruce – collapses like a dying duck and recognizes the mastery of the dominant male.'

Johnny stared.

'You mean you told McMurdo to . . . *scrag* her?'

'You put it crudely, but yes, something on those lines. And, as I say, I anticipate the best results. At this very moment Nannie Bruce is probably looking up into Officer McMurdo's eyes and meekly murmuring "Yes, Cyril, dear," "Just as you say, Cyril, dear," "How right you are, Cyril, darling," as he imperiously sketches out his plans for hastening on the wedding ceremony. You might go and listen at the kitchen door and see how things are coming along.'

'I might, yes, but what I'm going to do is have a swim in the lake. I'm sweating at every pore.'

'Keep it clean, my boy. No need to stress the purely physical. Well, if you run into McMurdo, tell him I am anxious to receive his report and can be found in the hammock on the back lawn. Is that the evening paper you have there? I might just glance through it.'

'Before going to sleep?'

'The Ickenhams do not sleep. Anything of interest in it?'

'Only that movie thing.'

'To what movie thing do you allude?'

'About this chap Wisdom's book.'

'*Cocktail Time*?'

'Yes. Have you read it?'

'Every word. I thought it was extremely good.'

'It is. It's the sort of thing I should like to write, and I could do it on my head, only the trouble is that, once you start turning out thrillers, they won't take anything else from you. Odd, a fellow like Wisdom being able to do anything as good as that. He doesn't give one the impression of being very bright, do you think?'

'I agree with you. The book seemed to me the product of a much maturer mind. But you were saying something about a movie thing, whatever that is.'

'Oh, yes. Apparently all the studios in Hollywood are bidding frantically for the picture rights. According to the chap who does the movie stuff in that paper, the least Wisdom will get is a hundred and fifty thousand dollars. Oh, well, some people have all the luck,' said Johnny, and went off to take his swim.

The hammock to which Lord Ickenham had alluded was suspended between two trees in a shady nook some distance from the house, and it was in pensive mood that a few minutes later he lowered himself into it. His godson's words had opened up a new line of thought and, as so often happened to Johnny's Inspector Jervis, he saw all. The mystery of why there was this sudden muster of vultures at Hammer Hall had been solved. The motives of these vultures in seeking to secure the letter which was sewn into the lining of the coat he was wearing were crystal clear.

Obviously, with a hundred and fifty thousand dollars coming to the author of *Cocktail Time*, Cosmo Wisdom was not going to look favourably on the idea of writing a second letter to his Uncle Raymond, disclaiming the authorship of the book, and equally obviously he would strain every nerve to secure and destroy the letter he had already written. And the Carlisle duo would naturally strain every nerve to secure it first and start Sir Raymond and nephew bidding against each other for it. No wonder there was that coolness he had noticed between the vulture of the first part and the vultures of the second. With a hundred and fifty thousand dollars at stake, a coolness would have arisen between Damon and Pythias.

It was a mistake on Lord Ickenham's part at this point to close his eyes in order to brood more tensely on the problems this new development had raised, for if you close your eyes in a hammock on a warm summer evening, you are apt to doze off. He had told Johnny that the Ickenhams did not sleep, but there were occasions when they did, and this was one of them. A pleasant drowsiness stole over him. His eyes closed and his breathing took on a gentle whistling note.

It was the abrupt intrusion of a finger between his third and fourth ribs and the sound of a voice that said 'Hey!' that some little while later awakened him. Opening his eyes, he found that Gordon Carlisle was standing on one side of the hammock, his wife Gertie on the other, and he could not fail to notice that in the latter's shapely hand was one of those small but serviceable rubber instruments known as coshes.

She was swinging it negligently, as some dandy of the Regency period might have swung his clouded cane.

# *Chapter 16*

Although there was nothing in the unruffled calm of his manner to show it, Lord Ickenham, as he sat up and prepared to make the party go, was not at his brightest and happiest. He had that self-reproachful feeling of having been remiss which comes to Generals who wake up one morning to discover that they have carelessly allowed themselves to be outflanked. With conditions as they were at Hammer Hall, he should, he told himself, have known better than to loll in hammocks out of sight and earshot of friends and allies. The prudent man, aware that there are vultures in every nook and cranny of the country house he is visiting, watches his step. Failing to watch his, he had placed himself in the sort of position his godson Johnny's Inspector Jervis was always getting into. It was rarely in a Jonathan Pearce novel of suspense that Inspector Jervis did not sooner or later find himself seated on a keg of gunpowder with a lighted fuse attached to it or grappling in a cellar with one of those disagreeable individuals who are generally referred to as Things.

However, though recognizing that this was one of the times that try men's souls, he did his best to ease the strain.

'Well, well, well,' he said heartily, 'so there you are! I must have dropped off for a moment, I think. One is reminded of the experience of the late Abou ben Adhem, who, as you may recall, awoke one night from a deep dream of peace to find an angel at his bedside, writing in a book of gold. Must have given him a nasty start, I have always thought.'

The interest of Oily and his bride in Abou ben Adhem appeared to be slight. Neither showed any disposition to discuss this unusual episode in his life. Mrs Carlisle, in particular, indicated unmistakably that her thoughts were strictly on business.

'Shall I bust him one?' she said.

'Not yet,' said Oily.

'Quite right,' said Lord Ickenham cordially. 'There is, in my opinion, far too much violence in the world today. I deprecate it. Do you read Mickey Spillane?'

This attempt, too, to give the conversation a literary turn proved abortive.

'Gimme,' said Oily. His manner was curt.

'I beg your pardon?'

'You heard. Remember making me turn out my pockets?'

'I don't like the word "making". There was no compulsion.'

'Oh, no? Well, there is now. Let's inspect what you've got in your pockets, Inspector Jervis.'

'Why, of course, my dear fellow, of course,' said Lord Ickenham with a cheerful willingness to oblige which should have lessened the prevailing tension, if not removed it altogether, and in quick succession produced a handkerchief, a cigarette case, a lighter, the notebook in which he jotted down great thoughts when they occurred to him, and a small button which had come off his shirt. Oily regarded the collection with a jaundiced eye, and looked at his wife reproachfully.

'He hasn't got it on him.'

Gertie, with her woman's intuition, was not so easily baffled.

'You poor simp, do you think he'd carry it around in his pocket? It's sewn into his coat or sum'pn.'

This being actually the case, Lord Ickenham was conscious of a passing regret that Gordon Carlisle had not selected a less intelligent mate. Had he led to the altar something more in the nature of a dumb blonde, the situation would have been greatly eased. But he continued to do his best.

'What is it you are looking for?' he asked genially. 'Perhaps I can help you.'

'You know what I'm looking for,' said Oily. 'That letter.'

'Letter? Letter?' Lord Ickenham's face cleared. 'Oh, the *letter*? My dear fellow, why didn't you say so before? You don't suppose I would keep an important document like that on me? It is, of course, lodged at my banker's.'

'Oh, yeah?' said Oily.

'Oh, yeah?' said his wife, and it was abundantly evident that neither had that simple faith which we are assured is so much better than Norman blood. 'Oily!'

'Yes, sweetie?'

'Why *not* let me bust him one?'

It had become borne in on Lord Ickenham more and more that the situation in which his negligence had placed him was one of considerable embarrassment, and he was not finding it easy to think what to do next. Had he been able to rise to his feet, a knowledge of ju-jitsu, acquired in his younger days and, though a little rusty, still efficient, might have served him in good stead, but his chances of being allowed to exhibit this skill were, he realized, slight. Even under the most favourable conditions, a hammock is a difficult thing to get out of with any rapidity, and the conditions here were definitely unfavourable. It was impossible to ignore that cosh. So far, Gordon Carlisle had discouraged his one-tracked-minded wife's wistful yearning to bust him one with it, but were he to give the slightest indication of wishing to leave his little nest, he was convinced that the embargo would be lifted.

Like the youth who slew the Jabberwock, he paused awhile in thought. His problem, he could see, resembled that of his godson Johnny Pearce, in being undoubtedly one that presented certain features of interest, and he was conscious of feeling a little depressed. But it was not long before he was his old debonair self again, his apprehensions removed and the sun smiling through once more. Looking past his two companions, he had seen something that brought the roses back to his cheek and made him feel that, even though he be in a hammock, you cannot keep a good man down.

'I'll tell you –' he began.

Oily, his manner even curter than before, expressed a wish to be handed Lord Ickenham's coat.

'I'll tell you where you of the criminal classes, if you do not mind me so describing you, make your mistake, and a very serious mistake it is, too. You weave your plots and schemes, you spend good money on coshes, you tip-toe with them to people's bedsides, but there is something you omit. You don't allow for the United States Marines.'

'Gimme that coat.'

'Never mind my coat for the moment,' said Lord Ickenham. 'I

want to tell you about the United States Marines. I don't know if you are familiar with the procedure where these fine fellows are concerned. To put it in a word, they arrive. The thing generally works out somewhat after this fashion. A bunch of bad men are beleaguering a bunch of good men in a stockade or an embassy or wherever it may be and seem to be getting along splendidly, and then suddenly the bottom drops out of everything and all is darkness, disillusionment and despair. Looking over their shoulders, they see the United States Marines arriving, and I don't suppose there is anything that makes bad men, when beleaguering someone, sicker. The joy goes out of their lives, the sun disappears behind the clouds, and with a muffled "Oh dear, oh dear, oh dear!" they slink away to their underground dens, feeling like thirty cents. The reason I bring this up,' said Lord Ickenham, hurrying his remarks to a conclusion, for he could see that his audience was becoming restive, 'is that, if you glance behind you, you will notice that the United States Marines are arriving now.'

And with a friendly finger he drew their attention to Police Constable McMurdo, who, dressed in the authority of helmet and blue uniform, was plodding across the lawn towards them, the evening sun gleaming on his substantial official boots.

'I speak as a layman,' he said, 'but I believe the correct thing to do at a moment like this is to say "Cheese it, the cops!" and withdraw with all speed. What a fine, big fellow he is, is he not? Ah, Cyril, were you looking for me?'

'Yes, m'lord. Mr Pearce said I should find you here. But if your lordship is occupied –'

'No, it's quite all right,' said Lord Ickenham, sliding from the hammock. 'We had finished our little talk. I am sure Mr and Mrs Carlisle will excuse me. *Au revoir*, Mr Carlisle. Mrs Carlisle, I kiss your hand. At least, I don't, but you know what I mean. I am wholly at your disposal, Cyril.'

Police Constable McMurdo was a large man with an agreeable, if somewhat stolid and unintellectual face, heavily moustached towards the centre. He had a depressed and dejected look, and the cause of his mental distress was not far to seek, for while one of his cheeks was the normal pink of the rural constable, the other had taken on a bright scarlet hue, seeming to suggest that a woman's hand had recently landed on it like a ton of bricks. In his hot youth, Lord Ickenham, peering into the mirror, had sometimes seen his own cheek looking like that, and he needed no verbal report to tell him what must have happened at the late get-together in the kitchen.

'You bring bad news, I fear,' he said sympathetically, as they made their way to the house. 'The Ickenham system didn't work?'

'No, it didn't.'

Lord Ickenham nodded understandingly.

'It doesn't sometimes. One has to budget for the occasional failure. From the evidence submitted to my notice, I take it that she busted you one.'

'Rrrr!' said Officer McMurdo, with feeling. 'I thought my head had come off!'

'I am not surprised. These nannies pack a wicked punch. How did you leave things?'

'She said if I ever acted that way again, she'd never speak to me as long as she lived.'

'I wouldn't worry too much about that. She didn't break off relations?'

'She nearly broke me.'

'But not her troth. Excellent. I thought she wouldn't. Women try to kid us that they don't like ardour, but they do. I'll bet at this very moment she is pacing the kitchen floor, whispering "What a man!" and wishing you would play a return engagement. You wouldn't consider having another pop? Striking while the iron is hot, as it were?'

'I wouldn't, no.'

'Then we must think of some other way of achieving the happy ending. I will devote my best thought to your problem.'

And also, added Lord Ickenham to himself, to the problem of how to find a safe place to put that letter. The recent conference had left him convinced that the sooner such a place was found, the better. A far duller man than he would have been able to divine from the attitude of the Carlisle family that things were hotting up.

Not that he objected. He liked things to hot up.

# Chapter 17

Old Mr Saxby, looking like something stationed in a corn field to discourage crows, stood on the lawn of Hammer Lodge, raking the countryside with his binoculars. At the moment when he re-enters this chronicle they were focused on the island in the middle of the lake.

The explanation of his presence in Dovetail Hammer, which Lord Ickenham had found mystifying, is a simple one. He was there at a woman's behest. Returning to the office after that brisk constitutional of his, he had been properly ticked off by Barbara Crowe for his uncouth behaviour to Cosmo Wisdom and sternly ordered by her to proceed without delay to Hammer Hall and apologize to him.

'No, a letter will *not* do,' said Barbara severely. 'Especially as you would be sure to forget to post it. You must go to him in person and grovel. Lick his shoes. Kiss the hem of his garment. Cosmo Wisdom has to be conciliated and sucked up to. He's a very important person.'

'He's a squirt.'

'A squirt maybe, but he wrote *Cocktail Time*, on its ten per cent of the proceeds of which the dear old agency expects to be able to afford an extra week at the seaside this year. So none of your larks, young Saxby. I shall want to hear on your return that he has taken you to his bosom.'

There was nothing Mr Saxby, whose view of Cosmo's bosom was a dim one, wanted less than to be taken to it, but he always did what Barbara Crowe told him to, even when it involved getting his hair cut, and he had set out obediently for Dovetail Hammer, consoling himself with the thought that a few days in the country, with plenty of birds to watch, would not be unpleasant. Nice, too, being next door to Bastable. He always enjoyed hobnobbing with Bastable.

Sir Raymond, who did not derive the same uplift from their hobnobbings, received him, when he was ushered into his presence by Albert Peasemarch, with a marked sinking sensation. Learning that his old clubmate was not proposing to make Hammer Lodge his headquarters but would be staying at the Hall, he brightened considerably, took him out on to the lawn to see the view and, finding that he had left his pipe behind, went back to fetch it. He now returned, and found the old gentleman, as has been stated, scrutinizing the island on the lake through his binoculars.

'Watching birds?' he asked, with the heartiness of a man assured that he is not going to have to put Howard Saxby senior up for an indefinite stay.

'Not so much birds,' said Mr Saxby, 'as that chap Scriventhorpe.'

'Chap who?'

'Scriventhorpe. Flannery's friend. I've met him with you at the club. I think you told me he was your son or your brother or something.'

Sir Raymond collected his wits, which, as so often happened when he was conversing with Howard Saxby senior, had been momentarily scattered.

'Do you by any chance mean Ickenham?'

'Didn't I say Ickenham?'

'You said Scriventhorpe.'

'Well, I meant Ickenham. Nice fellow. I don't wonder Flannery's fond of him. He's on that island over there.'

'Oh?' said Sir Raymond without enthusiasm. The only news about his half-brother-in-law that would have brought a sparkle to his eyes would have been that he had fallen out of a boat and was going down for the third time.

'He's tacking to and fro,' proceeded Mr Saxby. 'Now he's crouching down. Seems to be looking for something. No, I see what he's doing. He's not looking for something, he's hiding something. He's got a paper of some kind in his hand, and he seems to be burying it.'

'What!'

'Odd,' said Mr Saxby. 'He jumped up just then and hurried off. Must have gone back to his boat. Yes, here he comes. You can see him rowing away.'

Sir Raymond had never expected that any observation of this clubmate of his would thrill him to the core, but that was what this one had done. He felt as if he had been reclining in an electric chair and some practical joker had turned on the juice.

The problem of what his relative by marriage had done with the fatal letter was one which for two weeks and more had never been out of Sir Raymond Bastable's thoughts. He had mused on it while shaving, while bathing, while breakfasting, while lunching, while taking his afternoon's exercise, while dining, while putting on his pyjamas of a night and while dropping off to sleep. The obvious solution, that Lord Ickenham had hidden it in his bedroom, he rejected. With determined bedroom searchers like Cosmo Wisdom and Mr and Mrs Gordon Carlisle on the premises, such a policy would be madness. He would have thought of some really ingenious place of concealment – a hollow tree, perhaps, or a crevice in some wall. That he would bury the document on an island, like a pirate of the Spanish Main disposing of his treasure, had never occurred to Sir Raymond. Yet to anyone familiar with Frederick Ickenham's boyish outlook on life, how perfectly in character it seemed.

Quivering, he grabbed at his companion's arm, and Mr Saxby quivered, too, for the grip of those fevered fingers had affected him like the bite of a horse. He also said 'Ouch!'

Sir Raymond had no time to waste listening to people saying 'Ouch!' He had seen Lord Ickenham bring his boat to shore, step out of it and disappear in the direction of the house, and he was feeling, as did Brutus, that there is a tide in the affairs of men, which, taken at the flood, leads on to fortune.

'Quick!' he cried.

'When you say "Quick!"' began Mr Saxby, but got no further, for he was being hurried to where the boat lay at a pace that made speech difficult for a man who was getting on in years. He could not remember having whizzed along like this, touching the ground only here and there, since the afternoon sixty-three years ago when, a boy of twelve, he had competed at a village sports meeting in the choirboys' hundred-yard race, open to all those whose voices had not broken by the second Sunday in Epiphany.

It was only natural, therefore, that as Sir Raymond bent to the oars, putting his back into it like a galley slave of the old school, silence should have prevailed in the boat. Mr Saxby was trying to recover his breath, and Sir Raymond was thinking.

The problem that confronted him, the one that so often bothers murderers, was what to do with the body – viz: Mr Saxby's. He had brought the old gentleman along because, having witnessed Lord Ickenham's activities, he would be able to indicate the spot where the treasure lay, but now he was asking himself if this had not been a mistake. There are men – the salt of the earth – who, if they see you searching islands on lakes, preserve a tactful silence and do not ask for explanations, but Mr Saxby, he was convinced, was not one of these. He belonged rather to the more numerous class who want to know what it is all about, and Sir Raymond had no desire for a co-worker of this description. Explanations would be foreign to his policy. By the time they reached their destination he had arrived at the conclusion that the less Mr Saxby saw of what was going on, the better.

'You stay in the boat,' he said, and Mr Saxby thought it a good idea. He was still in the process of trying to recover his breath, and was well content to be spared further exercise for the moment. His stamina was not what it had been in his choirboy days.

'Woof!' he said, meaning that he fully concurred, and Sir Raymond set out into the interior alone.

Alone, that is to say, except for the swan which was at the moment taking it easy in the undergrowth beside the bijou residence where its mate was nesting. It was unexpectedly meeting this swan that had caused Lord Ickenham to revise his intention of burying the letter on the island and take to his boat with all possible speed. The Ickenhams were brave, but they knew when and when not to be among those present.

For some minutes after his companion's departure Mr Saxby, whose breathing apparatus had now returned to normal, gave himself up to thought. But though nothing could be fraught with greater interest than a detailed list of the things he thought about, it is better perhaps to omit such a list and pass on to the moment when he felt restored enough to take up his binoculars again. It was as he scanned the mainland through these that he observed Cosmo Wisdom smoking a cigarette on the gravel outside the front door of the Hall, and the sight reminded him that he was a man with a mission. Long ere this, he felt guiltily, he should have been seeking the young squirt out and kissing the hem of his garment, in accordance with Barbara Crowe's directions.

Though what there was to kiss hems of garments about, he was thinking, as, having completely forgotten Sir Raymond Bastable's existence, he started to row ashore, was more than he could tell you. Young squirt barges in on a fellow while he is knitting his sock and needs every ounce of concentration for the successful turning of the heel. Fellow receives him with the utmost cordiality and civility, though most men, interrupted at such a moment, would have bitten his head off, and they chat pleasantly for a while of this and that. Finally, having threshed out all the matters under discussion, fellow bids squirt a courteous farewell, and goes for his brisk constitutional. Nothing wrong with that, surely? But Barbara Crowe seemed to think there was, and women had to be humoured. As he rowed, he was throwing together in his mind a few graceful expressions of apology which he thought would meet the case.

These, a few minutes later, he delivered with an old-world charm. Their reception was what a dramatic critic would have called adequate. Cosmo did not take him to his bosom, but, the wound to his dignity apparently more or less healed, he offered him a cigarette, and they smoked in reasonable amity for a time, while Mr Saxby, always informative on his favourite subject, spoke at considerable length of birds he had watched. It was mid-way through a description of the peculiar behaviour of a sand martin he had once known in Norfolk – impossible to insert here owing to considerations of space – that he broke off suddenly and said:

'Bless my soul!'

'Now what?' said Cosmo rather sharply. He was finding Mr Saxby on sand martins a little trying.

'Exactly,' said Mr Saxby. 'What? You may well ask. There was something Barbara Crowe told me to tell you, and I've forgotten what it was. Now what could it have been? You don't happen to know, do you?'

At the name Barbara Crowe Cosmo had given a start. For the first time since their conversation had begun he was feeling that this Edwardian relic might be on the verge of saying something worth listening to.

'Was it about the movie end?' he said eagerly.

'The what?'

'Has there been another offer for the film rights of my book?'

Mr Saxby shook his head.

'No, it was nothing like that. Have you written a book?'

'I wrote *Cocktail Time*.'

'Never heard of it,' said Mr Saxby cordially. 'I'll tell you what I'll do. I'll go in and telephone her. She is sure to remember what it was. She has a memory like a steel trap.'

When he returned, he had a slip of paper in his hand, and was beaming.

'You were perfectly right,' he said. 'It *was* connected with what you call the movie end. I wrote it down, so that I should not forget it again. She said . . . Do you know Mrs Crowe?'

'I've met her.'

'Charming woman, though she bullies me unmercifully. Makes me get my hair cut. You don't know what the trouble was between her and your uncle, do you?'

'No.'

'They were engaged.'

'Yes.'

'She broke it off.'

'Yes.'

'Well, who can blame her? I wouldn't want to marry young Bastable myself.'

Cosmo spurned the gravel with an impatient foot.

'What did she *say?*'

'Ah, that we shall never know. What *do* women say on these occasions? Take back your ring and letters, do you think, or something of that sort?'

'About the movie end.'

'Oh, the movie end? Yes, as I told you, I have her very words here.' He peered at the paper. 'She said "Have you apologized?" and I said "Yes, I had apologized," and she said "Did he take you to his bosom?" and I said "No, the young squirt did not take me to his bosom, but he gave me a cigarette," and she said "Well, tell him that Medulla-Oblongata-Glutz have offered a hundred and fifty thousand, and our man in Hollywood has gone back to Superba-Llewellyn to bump them up." Does that convey anything to you?'

Cosmo inhaled deeply.

'Yes,' he said. 'It does.'

And suddenly Mr Saxby, for all his fishy eye and flattened-out-by-a-steamroller appearance, looked almost beautiful to him.

Sir Raymond Bastable, meanwhile, questing hither and thither like a Thurber bloodhound, had begun to regret that he had not availed himself of his shipmate's co-operation. Having no means of knowing whereabouts on this infernal island Mr Saxby had seen Lord Ickenham tacking to and fro and crouching down, he was in the position of one who hunts for pirate gold without the assistance of the yellowing map which says 'E. by N.20,' '16 paces S.' and all that sort of thing, and anyone who has ever hunted for pirate gold will tell you what a handicap this is. The yellowing map is of the essence.

The island was rather densely wooded – or perhaps under-growthed would be a better term – and was rich in spiky shrubs which caught at his ankles and insects which appeared to look on the back of his neck as the ideal rallying ground. 'Let's all go round to the back of Bastable's neck' seemed to be the cry in the insect world. He had become very hot and thirsty, and there was a hissing sound in his ears which he did not like. It suggested to him that his blood pressure was getting out of control. He was always a little nervous about his blood pressure.

It was as he straightened himself after his thirty-second attempt to find one of those spots, so common in fiction, where you can see, if you look closely, that the earth here has been recently disturbed, that he found he had wronged his blood pressure. This hissing sound had proceeded not from it but from the lips of a fine swan which had emerged from a bush behind him and was regarding him with unmistakable menace. There are moments when, meeting a swan, we say to ourselves that we have found a friend. This was not one of them. The chances of any fusion of soul between the bird and himself were, he could see at a glance, of the slightest.

It is always important at times like this to understand the other fellow's point of view, and the swan could certainly have made out a case for itself. With the little woman nesting in the vicinity and wanting to be alone with her eggs, it is not to be wondered at that it found intruders unwelcome. Already it had had to take a strong line with Lord Ickenham, and now, just as it was thinking that the evil had been stamped out, along came another human pest. It was enough to try the patience of any swan, and one feels that the verdict of history will be that in making hissing noises, staring bleakly, spreading its wings to their fullest extent and scrabbling the feet to indicate the impending frontal attack this one was perfectly justified. Swans, as every ornithologist knows, can be pushed only so far.

Sir Raymond, like Lord Ickenham, was not a pusillanimous man. If burglars had broken into Hammer Lodge, he would have sprung to the task of hitting them over the head with his niblick, and he had frequently looked traffic policemen in the eye and made them wilt. But the stoutest-hearted may well quail before an angry swan. It is possible that Sir Raymond, as he now started to withdraw, thought that he was doing so at a dignified walk, but actually he was running like a choirboy intent on winning the hundred yards dash. His one idea was to return as speedily as possible to the boat in which Mr Saxby was awaiting him.

Reaching the waterfront with something of the emotions of Xenophon's Ten Thousand when they won through to the sea, he was disconcerted to find that Mr Saxby was not awaiting him. Nor was there any boat. He saw what the poet Tennyson has described as the shining levels of the lake, but could detect nothing that would enable him to navigate them. And the hissing sound which he had wrongly attributed to his blood pressure was coming nearer all the time. The swan was not one of those swans that abandon a battle half fought. When it set its hand to the plough, it did not readily sheathe the sword. Casting a hasty glance behind him, Sir Raymond could see it arriving like a United States Marine.

It was a time for quick thinking, and he thought quickly. A split second later he was in the water, swimming strongly for the shore.

At the moment when he was making this dash for life, his sister Phoebe was up in her bedroom, trying her hair a new way.

It has so often been the chronicler's melancholy task to introduce this woman into his narrative in a state of agitation and tears that he finds it pleasant now to be able to show her gay and happy. Not even Sherlock Holmes, seeing her as she stood at her mirror, would have been able to deduce that she had been up all night with a sick cocker spaniel. Her eye was bright, her manner bumps-a-daisy. She was humming a light air.

Nor is this to be wondered at. Lord Ickenham's sensational revelation of the fire that burned in the bosom of Albert Peasemarch would alone have been enough to lift her to the heights, and on top of that had come his comforting assurance that her brother Raymond was not, as she had supposed, a candidate for the ministrations of Sir Roderick Glossop. Nothing, except possibly the discovery that the ground on which she treads is worshipped by a butler for whom she has long entertained feelings deeper and warmer than those of ordinary friendship, can raise a woman's spirits more than the knowledge that the brother who is the apple of her eye is, in spite of appearances, in full possession of his marbles. One can understand Phoebe Wisdom humming light airs. A weaker woman would have sung.

The mirror was in the window that looked over the lake and, glancing past it as she turned to examine the new hair-do in profile, she found her eye attracted to something singular that was going on in the water. A seal was there, swimming strongly for the shore, and this surprised her, for she had not supposed that there would be seals in an inland lake.

Nor were there. As she watched the creature emerge at journey's end, she saw that she had formed a wrong impression of its species. It was, as Mr Saxby would have said, not so much a seal as her brother Raymond. He was dressed, as always in the country, in a sports coat, grey flannel trousers and a coloured shirt.

She stared, aghast. Her old fears had swept back over her. Do men who have got all their marbles go swimming in lakes with their clothes on? Very seldom, Phoebe felt, and feared the worst.

# Chapter 18

At the hour of eight forty-five that night Lord Ickenham might have been observed – and was observed by Rupert Morrison, the landlord, licensed to sell ales, wines and spirits, who was polishing glasses behind the counter – sitting in the saloon bar of the village inn, the Beetle and Wedge, with a tankard of home-brew, watching television. Except for an occasional lecture by the vicar on his holiday in the Holy Land, illustrated with lantern slides, there was not a great deal of night life in Dovetail Hammer. The Beetle and Wedge's television set afforded the local pleasure-seekers about their only means of hitting the high spots after sundown.

The statement that Lord Ickenham was watching television is perhaps one calculated to mislead. His eyes, it is true, were directed at the screen, but what was going on there, apparently in a heavy snowstorm, made no impression on his mind. His thoughts were elsewhere. He was reviewing the current crisis in his affairs and turning stones and exploring avenues with a view to deciding how to act for the best.

Although it was his boast that the Ickenhams were not easily baffled, he could not conceal it from himself that the dislocation of his plans by the recent swan had left him in no slight quandary. With a bird as quick on the draw as that doing sentry-go there, burying the letter on the island in the lake was obviously not within the sphere of practical politics, and with two Carlisles and a Cosmo Wisdom prowling and prowling around in the manner popularized by the troops of Midian, any alternative place for its bestowal would have to be a very safe one. It is proof of the knottiness of the problem with which he was wrestling that in a moment of weakness he actually considered doing what he had tried to persuade the sceptical Carlisles that he had done and depositing the document with his bank.

A good deal shocked that he should even for an instant have contemplated a policy so tame and unworthy of an Ickenham, he turned his attention to the television screen. It might, he felt, enable him to come back to the thing with a fresh mind if he gave that mind a temporary rest.

They were doing one of those spy pictures tonight, a repeat performance, and he was interested to observe that by an odd coincidence the hero of it was in precisely the same dilemma as himself. Circumstances had placed this hero – D'Arcy Standish of the Foreign Office – in possession of papers which, if they fell into the hands of an unfriendly power, would make a third world war inevitable, and he was at the moment absolutely dashed if he could think how to hide them from the international spies who were surging around him, all right on their toes and up-and-coming. It was with a sympathetic eye that Lord Ickenham watched D'Arcy running about in circles and behaving generally like a cat on hot bricks. He knew just how the poor chap felt.

And then suddenly he started, violently, as if he had seen a swan entering the saloon bar, and sat up with a jerk, the home-brew trembling in his grasp.

'Egad!' he said.

'M'lord?' said Rupert Morrison.

'Nothing, my dear fellow,' said Lord Ickenham. 'Just Egad.'

As the saloon bar was open for saying Egad in at that hour, Mr Morrison made no further comment. He jerked a thumb at the screen.

'See what he's done?' he said, alluding to D'Arcy Standish. 'He wants to keep those papers safe from all those spies, so he's given 'em to his butler to take care of.'

Lord Ickenham said Yes, he had noticed.

'I call that clever.'

'Very clever.'

'Never occurs to 'em that the butler could have 'em,' proceeded Mr Morrison, who had seen the drama the previous week, 'so they keep after the fellow same as before. Thinking *he's* got 'em. See? But he hasn't. See?'

Lord Ickenham said he saw.

'They burgle his house and trap him in a ruined mill and chase him through the sewers,' Mr Morrison continued, giving the whole plot away, 'and all the time he hasn't got the papers, the butler's got 'em. Made me laugh, that did.'

'I'm not surprised. Have you a telephone here? I wonder if I might use it for a moment,' said Lord Ickenham.

Some minutes later, a fruity voice caressed his ear. Albert Peasemarch's mentor, Coggs, had advised making the telephone-answering voice as fruity as possible in the tradition of the great butlers of the past.

'Sir Raymond Bastable's residence. Sir Raymond's butler speaking.'

'*Not* the Albert Peasemarch there has been so much talk about?'

'Oh, good evening, Mr I. Do you wish to speak to Sir Raymond?'

'No, Bert, I wish to speak to you. I'm at the pub. Can you come here without delay?'

'Certainly, Mr I.'

'Fly like a youthful hart or roe over the hills where spices grow,' said Lord Ickenham, and presently the Beetle and Wedge's picturesque saloon bar was made additionally glamorous by the presence of Albert Peasemarch and his bowler hat. ('Always wear a bowler, chum. It's expected of you' – Coggs.)

'Bert,' said Lord Ickenham, when Rupert Morrison had supplied the ales he was licensed to sell and had withdrawn once more into the background, 'I hated to have to disturb your after-dinner sleep, but I need you in my business. You are probably familiar with the expression "Now is the time for all good men to come to the aid of the party." Well, this is where you do it. Let me start the conversational ball rolling by asking you a question. Do you take an active interest in world politics?'

Albert Peasemarch considered this.

'Not very active, Mr I. What with cleaning the silver and brushing the dog –'

'I know, I know. Your time is so full. Let me put it another way. You realize that there are such things as world politics and that a certain section of the community has the job of looking after them?'

'Oh, yes, Mr I. Diplomats they call them.'

'Diplomats is right. Well – can we be overheard?'

'Not unless someone's listening.'

'I'll whisper.'

'I'm a little deaf in the right ear.'

'Then I'll whisper into your left ear. Well, as I was about to say, the thing to bear in mind is that these diplomats can't get anywhere without papers. No, no,' said Lord Ickenham, as his old friend mentioned that he always read the *Daily Mirror* at breakfast, 'I don't mean that sort of paper, I mean documents. A diplomat without documents is licked from the start. He might just as well turn it up and go back to his crossword puzzle. And you know what I mean when I say documents.'

'Secret documents?'

'Exactly. You follow me like a bloodhound. A diplomat must have secret documents, and he gives these secret documents to trusted underlings to take care of, warning them on no account to let any international spies get their hooks on them. "Watch out for those international spies!" is the cry in what are called the chancelleries.'

This seemed reasonable to Albert Peasemarch.

'You mean if these spies got them, they would start creating?'

'Precisely. Throwing their weight about like nobody's business and making a third world war inevitable.'

'Coo! That would never do, would it?'

'I can imagine nothing more disagreeable. Remember those chilly nights in the Home Guard? I haven't been really warm since. You wouldn't want to go through all that again, would you?'

'I certainly wouldn't.'

'Nor I. Not even for the sake of hearing you sing Drake's Drum round the camp fire. Another beer, Bert?'

'Thank you, Mr I. Though I really shouldn't. I have to watch my figure.'

'If the document now in my possession falls into the hands of the gang that are after it, you won't have any figure to watch. It'll be distributed in little pieces over the countryside.'

To this Albert Peasemarch was prevented from replying immediately by the arrival of Mr Morrison, bringing up supplies. When the cup-bearer had retired and he was able to speak, he did so in the awed voice of a man who is wondering if he can believe his ears.

'What was that, Mr I.? Did you say *you* had a document in your possession?'

'You bet I have, Bert. And it's a pippin.'

'But how –?'

'– did it come into my possession? Very simply. I'm not sure if I ever mentioned to you, when we were comrades of the Home Guard, that I was in the Secret Service. Did I?'

'Not that I can recall, Mr I.'

'Probably slipped my mind. Well, I am, and not long ago the head man sent for me. "Number X 3476," he said – the boys call me Number X 3476 – "you see this document. Top secret, if ever there was one. Guard it day and night," he said, "and don't let those bounders get a smell of it." He was referring, of course, to the international spies.'

Albert Peasemarch drank beer like a man in a trance, if men in trances do drink beer.

'Cor lumme, stone the crows!' he said.

'You may well say "Cor lumme, stone the crows!" In fact, if anything, "Cor lumme, stone the crows" rather understates it.'

Albert Peasemarch drank some more beer, like another man in another trance. His voice, when he spoke, showed how deeply he was intrigued. Like so many of those with whom Lord Ickenham conversed, he was finding new horizons opening before him.

'These spies, Mr I. Are there many of them?'

'More than you could shake a stick at. Professor Moriarty, Doctor Fu Manchu and The Ace of Spades, to name but three. And every one of them the sort of chap who would drop cobras down your chimney or lace your beer with little-known Asiatic poisons as soon as look at you. And the worst of it is that they have got on to it that this document is in my possession, and it is only a question of time before they start chivvying me through the sewers.'

'You won't like that.'

'Exactly the feeling I had. And so, Bert,' said Lord Ickenham, getting down to the *res*, 'I have decided that the only thing to do is to pass the document on to you and let you take care of it.'

Albert Peasemarch was aware of a curious gulping sound. It reminded him of something. Then he knew what it reminded him of, the preliminary gurglings of the dog Benjy before reacting to that dose of mustard and water. It was only after listening to this odd sound for a moment or two that he realized that it was he who was making it.

'You see the devilish cleverness of the idea, Bert. The blighters will be nonplussed. When they chivvy me through the sewers, they'll just be chasing rainbows.'

'But, Mr I.!'

A look compounded of astonishment and incredulity came into Lord Ickenham's face. It was as though he had been a father disappointed in a loved son or an uncle in a loved nephew.

'Bert! Your manner is strange. Don't tell me you are faltering? Don't tell me you are jibbing at taking on this simple assignment? No, no,' said Lord Ickenham, his face clearing. 'I know you better than that. We old Home Guarders don't draw back when we are asked to serve the country we love, do we? This is for England's sake, Bert, and I need scarcely tell you that England expects that every man will do his duty.'

Albert Peasemarch, having gulped again, more like the dog Benjy than ever, raised a point of order.

'But I don't want to be chased through sewers, Mr I.'

'You won't be. I'll attend to the sewer sequence. How on earth are they to know that you have got the thing?'

'You don't think they'll find out?'

'Not a chance. They aren't clairvoyant.'

That a struggle was going on in Albert Peasemarch's soul was plainly to be seen by anyone watching his moonlike face. Lord Ickenham could detect it with the naked eye, and he waited anxiously for the referee's decision. It came after a long pause in four words, spoken in a low, husky voice, similar in its intonation to a voice from the tomb.

'Very well, Mr I.'

'You'll do it? Splendid. Capital. Excellent. I knew you wouldn't fail me. Well, it's no good me giving you the thing now, for the very walls have eyes, so I'll tell you how we'll work it. Where's your bedroom?'

'It's off my pantry.'

'On the ground floor. Couldn't be better. I'll be outside your window at midnight on the dot. I will imitate the cry of the white owl – the white owl, remember, not the brown – and the moment you hear me hooting, you slip out and the document changes hands. It will be in a plain manilla envelope, carefully sealed. Guard it with your life, Bert.'

Albert Peasemarch's manner betrayed a momentary uneasiness.

'How do you mean, my life?'

'Just an expression. Well, that cleans it up, I think, does it not? All you have to do is sit tight and say nothing. And now I ought to be leaving you. We must not be seen together. Hark!' said Lord Ickenham. 'Did you hear a low whistle? No? Then all is well. I thought for a moment those fellows might be lurking outside.'

Albert Peasemarch's uneasiness increased.

'You mean they're *here*, Mr I.? Around these parts?'

'In dozens, my dear fellow, in positive droves. Dovetail Hammer has international spies the way other beauty spots have greenfly and wasps. Still, it all adds to the spice of the thing, does it not?' said Lord Ickenham, and went out, leaving Albert Peasemarch staring with haggard eyes at the bottom of his empty tankard, a prey to the liveliest emotion.

Pongo Twistleton, had he been present, would have understood this emotion. He, too, had often experienced that stunned feeling, as if the solid earth beneath his feet had disintegrated, which was so apt to come to those who associated with the fifth Earl of Ickenham, when that fine old man was going good. And Pongo, in Albert Peasemarch's place, would have pursued precisely the same policy which now suggested itself to the latter.

'Another of the same, please, Mr M.,' he said, and Rupert Morrison once more became the human St Bernard dog.

The results were instantaneous – indeed, magical would scarcely be too strong a word. Until now, the chronicler has merely hinted at the dynamic properties of the Beetle and Wedge home-brew. The time has come to pay it the marked tribute it deserves. It touched the spot. It had everything. It ran like fire through Albert Peasemarch's veins and made a new man of him. The careworn, timorous Albert Peasemarch ceased to be, and in his place there sat an Albert Peasemarch filled to the brim with the spirit of adventure. A man of regular habits, he would normally have shrunk from playing a stellar role in an E. Phillips Oppenheim story, as he appeared to be doing now, but with the home-brew lapping up against his back teeth he liked it. 'Bring on your ruddy spies!' about summed up his attitude.

He had had his tankard refilled for the fourth time and was telling himself militantly that any spies who attempted to get fresh with him would do so at their own risk, when the door of the saloon bar opened and Johnny Pearce and Cosmo Wisdom came in.

It was obvious at a glance that neither was in festive mood. Johnny was thinking hard thoughts about his old school-fellow, Norbury-Smith, whose attitude towards Belinda Farringdon at lunch had seemed to him far too closely modelled on that of a licentious clubman of the old silent films, and Cosmo was brooding on the letter, asking himself how it could be detached from Lord Ickenham's keeping and unable at the moment to see any means of achieving the happy ending. It was with a distrait listlessness that they put in their order for home-brew.

Rupert Morrison delivered the elixir, and looked regretfully at the television set, which was now deep in one of those parlour games designed for the feeble-minded trade. D'Arcy Standish had gone off the air ten minutes ago.

'You've missed the picture, Mr Pearce,' he said.

'Picture? What picture?'

'The spy picture that was on the TV just now. It's where this Foreign Office gentleman has these important papers,' began Mr Morrison, falling easily into his stride, 'and these spies are after them, so he gives them to his butler . . .'

'I saw it last week,' said Johnny. 'It was lousy. Absolute drivel,' he said, leaving no doubt as to how he felt about it. So much of his work had been turned down for television that he had become a stern critic of that medium.

'I do so agree with you, sir,' said Mr Morrison. Actually he had thoroughly enjoyed the picture and would gladly have sat through it a third time, but an innkeeper has to suppress his private feelings and remember that the customer is always right. 'Silly, I thought it. As if any gentleman would give an important paper to a butler to take care of. It just couldn't happen.'

'Oh, couldn't it?' said Albert Peasemarch, rising – a little unsteadily – and regarding the speaker with a glazed but compelling eye.

It is only a man of exceptional self-restraint who is able to keep himself from putting people right when they begin talking ignorantly on subjects on which he happens to be well-informed, especially if he has just had four goes of the Beetle and Wedge homebrew. Knowing that these three were not international spies – in whose presence he would naturally have been more reticent – Albert Peasemarch had no compunction in intervening in the debate and speaking freely.

'Oh, couldn't it?' he said. 'Shows what a fat lot you know about it, Mr M. It may interest you to learn that a most important paper or document has been entrusted to me this very night by a gentleman who shall be nameless, with instructions to guard it with my life. And I'm a butler, aren't I? You should think before you speak, Mr M. I will now,' said Albert Peasemarch, with the air of a kindly uncle unbending at a children's party, 'sing Drake's Drum.'

And having done so, he slapped his bowler hat on his head and took his departure, walking with care, as if along a chalk line.

## Chapter 19

The sun was high in the sky next day when Cosmo, approaching it by a circuitous route, for he had no desire to run into his Uncle Raymond, arrived at the back door of Hammer Lodge and walked in without going through the formality of ringing the bell. He was all eagerness for a word with Albert Peasemarch on a subject very near his heart.

It was the opinion of his late employer, J. P. Boots of Boots and Brewer, export and import merchants, an opinion he had often voiced fearlessly, that Cosmo Wisdom was about as much use to a business organization as a cold in the head, and in holding this view he was substantially correct. But a man may be a total loss at exporting and importing, and still have considerable native shrewdness. Though a broken reed in the eyes of J. P. Boots, Cosmo was quite capable of drawing conclusions and putting two and two together, and on the previous night he had done so. Where Johnny Pearce and Rupert Morrison, listening to Albert Peasemarch, had classified his observations as those of a butler who has had one over the eight, Cosmo had read between the lines of that powerful speech of his. He had divined its inner significance. The nameless gentleman was Lord Ickenham and the paper or document the fatal letter. It stuck out, he considered, a mile. As he hurried to Hammer Lodge, he did not actually say 'Yoicks!' and 'Tally ho!' but that was what he was thinking.

He found Albert Peasemarch in his pantry having his elevenses, two hard-boiled eggs and a bottle of beer. Butlers always like to keep their strength up with a little something in the middle of the morning, and at the moment of Cosmo's entry Albert Peasemarch was finding his in need of all the keeping up it could get. The one defect of the Beetle and Wedge's home-brew is that its stimulus, so powerful over a given period, does not last. Time marches on, and the swashbuckling feeling it induces wears off. Albert Peasemarch, who on the previous night had gone out of the saloon bar like a lion, had come into his pantry this morning like a lamb, and a none too courageous lamb, at that. It is putting it crudely to say that he had cold feet, but the expression unquestionably covers the facts. He was all of a twitter and inclined to start at sudden noises. His reaction to the sudden noise of Cosmo's 'Good morning', spoken in his immediate rear, was to choke on a hard-boiled egg with a wordless cry and soar from his seat in the direction of the ceiling.

His relief on finding that it was not Professor Moriarty or The Ace of Spades who had spoken was extreme.

'Oh, it's you, Mr C.,' he gasped, as his heart, which had crashed against his front teeth, returned slowly to its base.

'Just thought I'd look in for a chat,' said Cosmo. 'Do go on with your egg. Don't mind me.'

It was the beer rather than the egg that appealed to Albert Peasemarch at the moment. He quaffed deeply, and Cosmo proceeded.

'You certainly pulled old Morrison's leg last night with that yarn of yours about the secret document,' he said, chuckling amusedly. 'He believed every word of it. Can you beat it? Never suspected for a moment that you were just kidding him,' said Cosmo, and broke into a jolly laugh. Very droll, he seemed to suggest, it had been, the whole thing.

There was a pause, and during that pause, though it lasted but an instant, Albert Peasemarch decided to tell all. He was in the overwrought state of mind that makes a man yearn for a confidant with whom he can share the burden that has been placed upon him, and surely Mr I. would agree that it was perfectly all right letting Cosmo Wisdom, the child of his half-sister by marriage, in on the ground floor. If Cosmo had still had his little black moustache, he might have hesitated, but, as we have seen, the aesthetic authorities of Brixton prison had lost no time in shaving it off. Gazing into his now unblemished face, Albert Peasemarch could see no possible objection to cleansing his bosom of the perilous stuff which was weighing on his heart. If you cannot confide in the son of the woman you love, in whom can you confide?

'But I wasn't, Mr C.'

'Eh?'

'I wasn't kidding him.'

Cosmo's hand flew to the barren spot where his moustache had been. At times when he was dumbfounded he always twirled it. That he was dumbfounded now was plainly to be seen. He stared incredulously at Albert Peasemarch.

'Now you're pulling *my* leg.'

'No, really, Mr C.'

'You don't mean it's true?'

'Every word of it.'

'Well, I'm blowed!'

'It was like this, Mr C. His lordship sent for me –'

'His lordship?'

'Lord Ickenham, sir.'

'You don't mean he's mixed up in this?'

'It's his document I'm taking care of, the one that was entrusted to him by the head of the Secret Service, of which he is a member.'

'Old Ickenham's in the Secret Service?'

'He is, indeed.'

Cosmo nodded.

'By Jove, yes, so he is. I remember him telling me. One forgets these things. Let's have the whole story from start to finish.'

When Albert Peasemarch had concluded his narrative, Cosmo went through the motion of twirling his lost moustache again.

'I see,' he said slowly. 'So that's how it is. He's left you holding the baby.'

'Yes, sir.'

'It looks to me as if you were in a bit of a spot.'

Albert Peasemarch assented. That, he said, was how it looked to him, too.

'I don't suppose these international spies stick at much.'

'No, sir.'

'If they get on to it that you've got that document, the mildest thing they'll do is shove lighted matches between your toes.' Cosmo mused for a space. 'Look here,' he said, struck with a happy thought. 'Why don't you give it to *me*?'

Albert Peasemarch stared.

'You, sir?'

'It's the only way,' said Cosmo, becoming more and more enthusiastic about the idea. 'Put yourself in the place of these spies. They'll soon find out old Ickenham hasn't got this document, and then they'll start asking themselves what he's done with it, and it won't take them long to realize that he must have handed it on to someone. Then what'll they say? They'll say "To who?"'

'Whom,' murmured Albert Peasemarch mechanically. He was rather a purist. He shuddered a little, for those last words had reminded him of Lord Ickenham imitating the cry of the white owl.

'And they'll pretty soon answer that. They know you and he are friends.'

'Old comrades. Home Guard.'

'Exactly. It'll be obvious to them that he must have given the thing to you.'

Again Albert Peasemarch was reluctantly reminded of his old comrade giving his owl impersonation. He spoke with an increase of animation, for the scheme was beginning to appeal to him.

'I see what you mean, Mr C. They'd never suspect that you had it.'

'Of course they wouldn't. I hardly know old Ickenham. Is it likely he'd give important documents to a fellow who's practically a stranger? Whatever this paper is, it will be as safe with me as if it were in the Bank of England.'

'It's certainly an idea, Mr C.'

'Where is the thing?'

'In my bedroom, sir.'

'The first place spies would look. Go and get it.'

Albert Peasemarch went and got it. But though Cosmo extended a hand invitingly, he did not immediately place the envelope in it. His air was that of a man who lets 'I dare not' wait upon 'I would', as so often happens with cats in adages.

'There's just one thing, Mr C. I must have his lordship's permission.'

'What!'

'Can't make a move like this without consulting his lordship. But it won't take a jiffy to step over to the Hall and get his okay. Five minutes at the outside,' said Albert Peasemarch, reaching for his bowler hat.

It sometimes happens at the Beetle and Wedge that a customer, demanding home-brew and licking his lips at the prospect of getting it, is informed by the voice of doom, speaking in the person of Rupert Morrison, that he has already had enough and cannot be served. On such occasions the customer has the feeling that the great globe itself has faded, leaving not a wrack behind, and that, as in the case of bad men interrupted in their activities by the United States Marines, all is darkness, disillusionment and despair. Such a feeling came to Cosmo Wisdom now. This unforeseen check, just as he had been congratulating himself on having fought the good fight and won it, induced a sudden giddiness and swimming of the head, so that his very vision was affected and he seemed to see two Albert Peasemarches with two round faces reaching for a brace of bowler hats.

Was there, he asked himself desperately, no way out, no means of persuading this man to skip the red tape?

There was. Beside the remains of the two hard-boiled eggs, which in that sudden spasm of spiritual anguish had seemed to him for an instant four hard-boiled eggs, there stood a pepper pot. To snatch this up and project its contents into Albert Peasemarch's face was with Cosmo the work of a moment. Then, leaving the suffering man to his sneezing, he shot out into the great open spaces, where he could be alone, in his pocket the only proof that existed that he was not the author of *Cocktail Time*, for the motion picture rights of which the Superba-Llewellyn studio would, he hoped, shortly be bumped up to an offer of two hundred thousand dollars.

But in assuming that in the great open spaces he would be alone, he was mistaken. Scarcely had he reached them, when a voice that might have been that of an ancient sheep spoke at his elbow.

'Well met by moonlight, proud Wisdom,' it bleated, and spinning on his axis he perceived old Mr Saxby.

'Oh, hullo,' he said, when able to articulate. 'Nice morning, isn't it? The sun and all that. Well, good-bye.'

'Let us not utter that sad word,' said Mr Saxby. 'Are you on your way to the Hall? I will walk with you.'

It was a pity that Cosmo had never taken any great interest in birds, for he was afforded now an admirable opportunity of adding to his information concerning their manners and habits. In considerable detail Mr Saxby spoke of hedge sparrows he had goggled at in their homes and meadow pipits he had surprised while bathing, and, had Cosmo been an ornithologist, he would have found the old gentleman's conversation absorbing. But, like so many of us, he could take meadow pipits or leave them alone, and it was with something of the feeling he had had when released from Brixton prison that at long last he saw the human porous plaster potter off on some business of his own.

It was in the hall of Johnny Pearce's ancestral home that this happened, and at the moment of Mr Saxby's departure he was standing beside one of the comfortable, if shabby, armchairs which were dotted about in it. Into this he now sank. The nervous strain to which he had been subjected, intensified by the society of the late bird *aficionado*, had left him dazed. So much so that it was several minutes before he realized that he ought not to be just sitting here like this, he should be acting. The letter was still in his pocket, undestroyed. He took it out, and removed its manilla wrapping. First and foremost on the agenda paper was the putting of it to the flames – not the tearing of it up and depositing it in the wastepaper basket, for a torn-up letter can be pieced together.

There was a table beside the chair, on it an ashtray and matches. He reached for these, and was in the very act of striking one, when he became aware of a wave of some exotic scent that seemed to proceed from behind him, the sort of scent affected by those mysterious veiled women who are always stealing Naval Treaties from Government officials in Whitehall. Turning sharply, he perceived Mrs Gordon Carlisle, and with considerable emotion noted that she was holding, and in the act of raising, one of those small but serviceable rubber instruments known as coshes. At her side, on his face the contented look of one who feels that his affairs are in excellent hands, stood her husband.

It was almost immediately after this that the roof fell in, and Cosmo knew no more. J. P. Boots, in his sardonic way, would have said that he had not known much even before that.

# *Chapter 20*

═══════════════

'Nice work, sweetie,' said Mr Carlisle, viewing the remains with satisfaction. 'Just behind the ear, that's the spot.'

'Never known it to fail,' said Gertie.

'He isn't dead, is he?'

'Oh, I shouldn't think so.'

'Just as well, maybe. Gimme the letter. And,' added Oily urgently, 'gimme that blackjack.'

'Eh?'

'Someone's coming. We've got to ditch them quick.'

'Slip 'em in your pocket.'

'And have them frisk me and find them there? Talk sense.'

'Yay, I see what you mean.' Gertie's eyes flickered about the hall. 'Look. Dump 'em in that thing over there.'

She alluded to the imitation walnut cabinet, the legacy of Johnny Pearce's Great-Uncle Walter, which had always so jarred on Lord Ickenham, and Oily approved of the suggestion. He darted across the hall, opened and slammed one of the drawers, dusted his hands and returned, just as Johnny appeared.

Johnny was on his way to get a breath of fresh air after a chat with Nannie Bruce about the new cook, concerning whose short-comings, more marked in her opinion even than those of the one who had held office two weeks previously, she had unburdened her mind in a speech containing at least three extracts from Ecclesiastes. He was in a sombre mood, having had his fill of Nannie Bruce, Ecclesiastes and paying guests, and the sight of one of these last apparently asleep in a chair would have left him uninterested, had not Cosmo at this moment slumped to the floor. A man who takes in paying guests can ignore them when they are vertical. When they become horizontal, he has to ask questions.

'What's all this?' he said, an observation which should more properly have been left to Police Constable McMurdo, who was down the passage, talking to Nannie. He had been hanging about outside the door of Johnny's study for some twenty minutes in the hope of finding an opportunity of pleading with her.

Gertie was swift to supply the desired information.

'Seems to me the guy's had some kind of a fit.'

Oily said that that was the way it looked to him, too.

'My husband and I was passing through on our way to our room, when he suddenly keeled over. With a groan.'

'More a gurgle, sweetie.'

'Well, with whatever it was. Could have been a death rattle, of course.'

Johnny frowned darkly. Life these days, he was thinking, was just one damn thing after another. First Nannie with her cooks and Ecclesiastes, then Norbury-Smith, from whom no good woman was safe, and now this groaning, gurgling or possibly death-rattling paying guest. Had even Job, whose troubles have received such wide publicity, ever had anything on this scale to cope with?

He raised his voice in a passionate bellow.

'Nannie!'

Nannie Bruce appeared, followed by Officer McMurdo, whose air was that of a police constable who has not been making much headway.

'Nannie, phone for Doctor Welsh. Tell him to come over right away. Mr Wisdom's had a fit or something. And for heaven's sake don't start yammering about what your biblical friend would have thought of the situation. Get a move on!'

Officer McMurdo looked at him with a wistful admiration. That was telling her, he felt. That was the way to talk to the other sex. Nannie Bruce, who did not hold this view, bridled.

'There is no necessity to shout at me, Master Jonathan, *nor* to make a mock of the holy scriptures. And I disagree with you when you say that Mr Wisdom has had a fit. Look at the way he's lying, with his legs straight out. My Uncle Charlie suffered from fits, and he used to curl up in a ball.' She went to where Cosmo lay, scrutinized him closely and ran an expert finger over his head. 'This man,' she said, 'has been struck with a blunt instrument!'

'What!'

'There's a lump behind his ear as big as a walnut. It's a matter for the police, such,' said Nannie Bruce, eyeing Officer McMurdo coldly, 'as they are. Still, when you say telephone for Doctor Welsh, that's sense. I'll go and do it at once.'

She departed on her errand with the dignity of a woman who does not intend to be ordered about but is willing to oblige, and long before she had disappeared Police Constable McMurdo's notebook was out and his pencil licked and poised.

'Ho!' he said. 'This throws a different light on the matter. I will now proceed to look into it. The great thing here is to ascertain who's responsible for this.'

'Ecclesiastes,' said Johnny bitterly, and Constable McMurdo's pencil leaped like a live thing. As far as was within the power of a man with a face like his, he was looking keen and alert. He eyed Johnny sharply.

'Have you evidence to support that charge, Mr Pearce?'

'No. It was just a suggestion.'

'I should like the address of the suspect Ecclesiastes.'

'I'm afraid I can't help you there.'

'Is he a juvenile delinquent?'

'More elderly than that, I should say.'

The constable pondered.

'I'm beginning to think you're right, sir. As I piece together the jig-saw puzzle, what happened was this. The gentleman was sitting here, dozing as the expression is, and the front door opens and in walks Ecclesiastes. To hit him on the napper with a blunt instrument, him being asleep, would be an easy task.'

Oily intervened in his suavest manner.

'I scarcely see how your theory can be correct, officer. My wife has told you that as we were passing through the hall, we saw Mr Wisdom –'

'Keel over,' said Gertie.

'Exactly. With a gurgle.'

'Or groan.'

'With a groan or gurgle.'

'Like as if somep'n had gone wrong with the works.'

'Precisely. You remember her mentioning it to you.'

'Not to me she didn't mention it.'

'Ah, no, it was to Mr Pearce before you came in. We both received the impression that he had had a fit.'

'Then why isn't he curled up in a ball?'

'There you take me into deep waters, constable.'

'And how do you account for the lump behind his ear, as big as a walnut?'

'That surely is very simply explained. He struck his head against the side of the chair as he was –'

'Keeling over,' said Gertie.

'As he was keeling over. It is far more probable –'

What was far more probable he did not get around to mentioning, for at this moment Cosmo Wisdom stirred, groaned (or gurgled), and sat up. He looked about him with what the poet has called a wild surmise, and said:

'Where am I?'

'Hammer Hall, Dovetail Hammer, Berks., sir,' Officer McMurdo informed him, and would have added the telephone number, if he had remembered it. 'If you'll just lie nice and quiet and relax, the doctor will be here in a moment. You've had some kind of fit or seizure, sir. This gentleman, Mr –'

'Carlisle.'

'This gentleman, Mr Carlisle, was passing through the hall, accompanied by Mrs Carlisle –'

The mention of that name brought memory flooding back to Cosmo. The past ceased to be wrapped in mist. He rose, clutched the chair with one hand, and with the forefinger of the other pointed accusingly.

'She hit me!'

'Sir?'

'That Carlisle woman. She hit me with a cosh. And,' said Cosmo, feeling feverishly through his pockets, 'she and that blasted husband of hers have stolen a very valuable paper from me. Grab them! Don't let them get away.'

Oily's eyebrows rose. He did not smile, of course, for the occasion was a serious one where levity would have been out of place, but his mouth twitched a little.

'Well, really, officer! One makes allowances for a sick man, but . . . well, really!'

Johnny Pearce's attention had been wandering. His thoughts had drifted back to that luncheon. Had he or had he not seen Norbury-Smith squeeze Belinda Farringdon's hand? At a certain point in the meal when Norbury-Smith's foot had collided with his under the table, had that foot's objective been Belinda Farringdon's shoe?

Aware now of raised voices, he came out of his reverie.

'What's the argument?' he enquired.

Constable McMurdo brought him abreast. This gentleman here, he said, had made a statement charging that lady there with having biffed him on the napper with a cosh. It did not, he added, seem plausible to *him*.

'Delicately nurtured female,' he explained.

Johnny could not quite see eye to eye with him in this view. In the stories he wrote you could never rule out females as suspects because they were delicately nurtured. Not once but on several occasions Inspector Jervis had been laid out cold by blondes of just that description. They waited till his back was turned and then let him have it with the butt end of a pistol or a paperweight. He looked at Gertie dubiously.

It was Oily who saw the way of proving his loved one's innocence.

'This is all very absurd,' he said in his gentlemanly way, 'but the thing can be settled, it seems to me, quite simply. If my wife struck Mr Wisdom with a . . . what was the word you used, officer?'

'Cosh, sir.'

'Thank you. I think you must mean what in my native country we call a blackjack. You know what a blackjack is, sweetie?'

'I've heard of 'em.'

'They are used a good deal by the criminal classes. Well, as I was saying, if my wife struck Mr Wisdom with an implement of this description, it is presumably either in her possession or mine. You will probably agree with me that Mrs Carlisle, wearing, as you see, Bermuda shorts and a shirt, would scarcely be able to conceal a weapon of any size on her person, so all that remains is for you to search me, officer. Frisk, is, I believe, the technical expression, is it not, ha, ha. Frisk me, constable, to the bone. You see,' he said, when the arm of the law had apologetically done so. 'Not a thing! So we return to our original conclusion that Mr Wisdom had a fit.'

Police Constable McMurdo scratched his head.

'Why wasn't he curled up in a ball?'

'Ah, there, as I said before, you take me into deep waters. No doubt this gentleman will be able to tell you,' said Oily, as Nannie Bruce returned, ushering in Doctor Welsh with his black bag.

# Chapter 21

The hall emptied soon after Doctor Welsh's arrival, like a theatre when the show is over. The doctor supported Oily's theory that Cosmo must have struck his head on the side of the chair, exercised his healing arts and, assisted by Johnny, helped the injured man to his room. Mr and Mrs Carlisle, confident that the walnut cabinet held their secret well, went up to theirs. When Lord Ickenham came in from the stroll he had been taking in the park, only Officer McMurdo was present. He was standing by the chair, eyeing it with professional intentness. Lord Ickenham greeted him with his customary geniality.

'Ah, Cyril, old friend. A very hearty good morning to you, my merry constable. Or,' he went on, peering more closely, 'are you so dashed merry? I don't believe you are. You seem to me to have a stern, official air, as if you had seen somebody moving pigs without a permit or failing to abate a smoky chimney. Has a crime wave broken out in these parts?'

Officer McMurdo was only too glad to confide in one for whose I.Q. he had a solid respect. What he was registering in his mind as the Wisdom case had left him puzzled.

'That's just what I'd like to ascertain, m'lord. Strange things have been happening at Hammer Hall. I still can't see why he wasn't curled up in a ball.'

'I beg your pardon? That one rather got past me.'

'Mr Wisdom, m'lord. When you have a fit, you curl up in a ball.'

'Oh, do you? Nice to know the etiquette. But what makes you think he had had a fit?'

'That's what the doctor said. He was lying on the floor with his legs straight out.'

'Was he, indeed? Quaint fellows, these doctors. Never know what they'll be up to next.'

'You misunderstand me, m'lord. It wasn't Doctor Welsh that was lying on the floor, it was Mr Wisdom. And Mr Carlisle made a statement that . . . I've got it all in my notebook . . . half a jiffy, yes, here we are . . . made a statement that he and Mrs Carlisle was passing through the hall and observed Mr Wisdom fall out of his chair and knock his head on the side of it, causing a lump behind the ear as big as a walnut. Some sort of a fit, they thought. But mark this, m'lord. On regaining consciousness, Mr Wisdom in his turn issued a statement, accusing Mrs Carlisle of striking him on the napper with a cosh.'

'What!'

'Yes, m'lord. Makes it sort of hard to sift the evidence and arrive at conclusions, don't it? If he'd been curled up in a ball, I'd say there was little credence to be attached to his words, but seeing that his legs was straight out, well, one sort of wonders if there might not be something in it. On the other hand, is it likely that a delicately nurtured female would go biffing –'

He broke off, and his face, which had been like that of a bloodhound on the trail, assumed the expression of a lovelorn sheep. Another delicately nurtured female, in the person of Nannie Bruce, had entered. She gave him a haughty look, and addressed Lord Ickenham.

'Your lordship is wanted on the telephone, m'lord. Sir Raymond Bastable from the Lodge. It's the third time this morning he's rung up, asking for your lordship.'

As Lord Ickenham went down the passage to Johnny's study, where the telephone was, he was conscious of a throbbing about the temples and a dazed feeling usually induced only by the conversation of old Mr Saxby. Officer McMurdo's story had left him bewildered. It was obvious to him, sifting, as the constable would have said, the evidence, that for some reason Mrs Gordon Carlisle had applied that cosh of hers to the skull of Cosmo Wisdom – busted him one, as she would have put it – but why had she done so? Because she disliked the young man? In a spirit of girlish exuberance? Or just because one had to do something to fill in the time before lunch? Better, he felt, to dismiss the problem from his thoughts and not try to fathom her mental processes. These vultures acted according to no known laws.

Arrived in Johnny's sanctum, he took up the receiver, and jumped several inches when a voice suggestive of a lion at feeding time roared in his ear drum.

'Frederick! Where the devil have you been all this while?'

'Just out, Beefy,' said Lord Ickenham mildly. 'Roaming hither and thither and enjoying the lovely sunshine. I hear you've been trying to get me. What's your trouble?'

As far as could be gathered from aural evidence, Sir Raymond appeared to be choking.

'I'll tell you what my trouble is! Do you know what I saw in the paper this morning?'

'I think I can guess. It was in yesterday's evening paper.'

'About *Cocktail Time*? About these people offering a hundred and fifty thousand for the picture rights?'

'Yes. It's a lot of money.'

'A lot of money! I should say it was a lot of money. And all going into that blasted Cosmo's pocket unless you do the decent thing, Frederick.'

'Spread sweetness and light, you mean? It is always my aim, Beefy.'

'Then for God's sake give me that letter of his. It's the only proof there is that I wrote the book. Frederick,' said Sir Raymond, and his voice had taken on a pleading note, 'you can't hold out on me. You must have heard from Phoebe by this time that my behaviour towards her these last two weeks has been ... what's the word?'

'Angelic?'

'Yes, angelic. Ask Peasemarch if I've once so much as raised my voice to her. Ask anybody.'

'No need to institute enquiries, Beefy. It is all over Dovetail Hammer that your attitude where Phoebe is concerned has been that of one brushing flies off a sleeping Venus. Several people have told me that they mistook you in a dim light for the Chevalier Bayard.'

'Well, then?'

'But will this happy state of things last?'

'Of course it will.'

'I have your word for that as a man of honour and an old Oxford rugger blue?'

'Certainly. Wait a minute. Do you see what I've got here?'

'Sorry, Beefy, my vision's limited.'

'A bible, and I'm prepared to swear on it –'

'My dear old man, your word is enough. But aren't you forgetting something? How about your political career?'

'Damn my political career! I don't want a political career, I want a hundred and fifty thousand dollars.'

'All right, Beefy. You can relax. The money's yours. Go and fetch Albert Peasemarch and put him on the phone.'

'Do *what*?'

'So that I can tell him to hand that letter over to you. I had to put it in his charge, for bad men are after it and one never knows if the United States Marines won't sooner or later be caught asleep at the switch. Ring up again when you've got him. I don't want to sit here holding the instrument.'

Lord Ickenham hung up, and went back to the hall, hoping for further conversation with Officer McMurdo. But the constable had vanished, possibly to go about his professional duties but more probably to resume his wooing. The only occupant of the hall was old Mr Saxby, who was sitting in the chair recently vacated by Cosmo. He regarded Lord Ickenham with the eye of a benevolent codfish.

'Ah, Scriventhorpe,' he said. 'Nice to run into you. Have you seen Flannery lately?'

'I'm afraid I haven't.'

'Indeed? And how was he looking? Well, I hope? He suffers a little from sciatica. Is this your first visit to Hammer Hall?'

'No, I often come here. Johnny Pearce is my godson.'

'I used to be somebody's godson once, but many years ago. He has a nice place.'

'Very.'

'And some nice things. But I don't like that imitation walnut cabinet.'

'It's an eyesore, of course. Johnny's getting rid of it.'

'Very sensible of him. You remember what Flannery always says about fake antiques.'

Before Lord Ickenham was able to learn what that mystic man's views were on the subject indicated, Nannie Bruce appeared.

'Sir Raymond Bastable on the telephone, m'lord.'

'Oh, yes. Excuse me.'

'Certainly, certainly. Have you,' Mr Saxby asked Nannie Bruce, as Lord Ickenham left them, 'ever been to Jerusalem?'

'No, sir.'

'Ah. You must tell me all about it some time,' said Mr Saxby.

It is doubtful if even Miss Bruce's Uncle Charlie, at the peak of one of his celebrated fits, could have exhibited a greater agitation than did Sir Raymond Bastable when embarking on this second instalment of his telephone conversation with his half-brother-in-law. His visit to Albert Peasemarch's pantry, where that unfortunate stretcher-case was still sneezing, had left him – we must once more turn to Roget and his Thesaurus for assistance – unhappy, infelicit-ous, woebegone, dejected, heavy-laden, stricken and crushed. It is not easy for a man who is sneezing all the time to tell a story well, but Albert Peasemarch had told his well enough to enable Sir Raymond to grasp its import, and it had affected him like a bomb explosion. This, he said to Lord Ickenham, after he had informed him in a flood of molten words what he thought of his nephew Cosmo, was the end.

'The end,' he repeated, choking on the words. 'The young reptile must have burned the thing by now. Oh, hell and damnation!'

It was probably injudicious of Lord Ickenham to tell him at this moment not to worry, for the kindly advice, judging from the sounds proceeding from the Bastable end of the wire, seemed to have had the worst effects. But there were solid reasons for his doing so. In a flash he had divined the thought behind Mrs Gordon Carlisle's apparently inexplicable behaviour in busting Cosmo Wisdom one with her cosh. In supposing that she had merely been indulging some idle whim, busting just because it seemed a good idea to her at the time, he saw that he had done the woman an injustice. It was from the soundest business motives that she had raised that lump as big as a walnut behind Cosmo's ear.

'Listen,' he said, and started to place the facts before his relative by marriage, hampered a good deal at the outset by the latter's refusal to stop talking.

When he had finished, there was a pause of some moments, occupied by Sir Raymond in making a sort of gargling noise.

'You mean,' he said, becoming articulate, 'that that bounder Carlisle has got the letter?'

'Exactly. So now everything's fine.'

There was another pause. Sir Raymond appeared to be praying for strength.

'Fine?' he said, in a strange, low, husky voice. 'Did you say fine?'

'I did. He will be coming to see you about it shortly, I imagine, so what I want you to do, Beefy, is to step out into the garden and gather some frogs. About half a dozen. To put down the back of his neck,' explained Lord Ickenham. 'You remember what a sensitive skin he has. We grab him and decant the frogs. I shall be vastly surprised if after the third, or possibly fourth, frog has started to do the rock 'n roll on his epidermis, he is not all eagerness to transfer the letter to you. Years ago, when I was a child, a boy named Percy Wilberforce threatened that unless I gave him my all-day sucker, he would put frogs down my back. He got it FOB in three seconds. Even then I was about as intrepid as they come, but I could not face the ordeal. And if an Ickenham weakened like that, is it likely that a Gordon Carlisle will prove more resolute? Off you go, Beefy, and start gathering. Put them in a paper bag,' said Lord Ickenham, and returned to the hall.

He found Mr Saxby pottering about in the vicinity of the walnut cabinet.

'Ah, Scriventhorpe. Back again? I've been having a look at this thing, and it's worse than I thought it was. It's a horrible bit of work. Flannery would hate it. I found something odd in one of the drawers,' said Mr Saxby. 'You don't happen to know what this is?'

Lord Ickenham looked at the object he was holding up, and started.

'It's a cosh.'

'Cosh, did you say?'

'That's right.'

'The word is new to me. What are its uses?'

'Delicately nurtured females bust people one with it.'

'Indeed? Most interesting. I must tell Flannery that when I see him. By the way,' Mr Saxby proceeded, 'I also found this letter addressed to Bastable.'

Lord Ickenham drew a deep breath, the sort of breath a gambler draws who has placed the last of his money on a number at the roulette table and sees it come up.

'May I look at it?' he said, his voice shaking a little. 'Thank you. Yes, you're quite right. It is addressed to Bastable. Perhaps I had better take charge of it. I shall be seeing him soon, and can give it to him. Curious it turning up in that cabinet.'

'A letter of Flannery's once turned up inside the Christmas turkey.'

'Indeed? Strange things happen in this disturbed post-war era, do they not? Rather a lesson to the dear old chap not to eat turkey. Excuse me,' said Lord Ickenham. 'I have to telephone.'

It was Phoebe who answered his ring.

'Oh, hullo, Phoebe,' he said. 'Is Raymond there?'

'He went out into the garden, Frederick. Shall I fetch him?'

'No, don't bother. Just give him a message. Tell him to stop gathering frogs.'

'Stop *what*?'

'Gathering frogs.'

'There must be something wrong with this wire. You sound as if you were telling me to tell Raymond to stop gathering frogs.'

'I am.'

'*Is* he gathering frogs?'

'He told me he was going to.'

'But *why* is he gathering frogs?'

'Ah, who can say? These eccentric barristers, you know. Probably just felt a sudden urge. Good-bye, Phoebe. Where are you at the moment?'

'I'm in Raymond's study.'

'Well, don't forget that Albert Peasemarch worships the very carpet you are standing on,' said Lord Ickenham.

He was humming a gay snatch of melody as he replaced the receiver, for there was no room for doubt in his mind that all things were working together for good. With the letter which had been leaping from vulture to vulture like the chamois of the Alps from crag to crag safely in his coat pocket, he was feeling at the top of his form. Something attempted, something done, had earned a mild cigar, and he was smoking it on the drive and thinking how pleasant it was to be away from Mr Saxby, when he found that he was not. The old gentleman came pottering along, having apparently popped up through a trap.

'Oh, Scriventhorpe.'

'Hullo, Saxby. I was just saying to myself how nice it would be if you were with me.'

'I have been looking for you, Scriventhorpe. I thought it would interest you to hear . . . A water ousel!'

'Worth hearing, are they, these water ousels?'

'There is a water ousel over there. I must go and look at it in a moment. What I started to say was that I thought it would interest you to hear that that beastly walnut cabinet has gone.'

'Has done what?'

'A couple of men came and took it away after you left. I understand it is to be put up for auction.'

Lord Ickenham started. One of those sudden inspirations of his had come to him.

'Put up for auction, eh?'

'So they told me. But I doubt if anyone in his senses would give more than a pound or two for it,' said Mr Saxby, and toddled away, binoculars in hand, to look at his water ousel.

As a rule, men whom old Mr Saxby relieved of his company were conscious of a wave of relief, coupled with a determination not to let him corner them again in a hurry, but Lord Ickenham hardly noticed that he had gone. His whole attention was riveted on a picture which had risen before his mind's eye, the picture of Beefy and Gordon Carlisle bidding furiously against each other for the imitation walnut cabinet, the proceeds of the winning bid to go to Jonathan Twistleton Pearce, that impoverished young man who had to have five hundred pounds in order to marry his Belinda. Knowing Beefy and knowing Gordon Carlisle – their deep purses and their iron resolve to get hold of the fateful letter – he was confident that considerably more than five hundred of the best and brightest would accrue to Jonathan Twistleton Pearce's bank account.

Though there are, of course, drawbacks to everything. In order to achieve this desirable end it would be necessary for him to depart a little from the truth and inform Beefy that the letter was in the cabinet, but he was a man who rather blithely departed from the truth when the occasion called. An altruist whose mission it is to spread sweetness and light is entitled to allow himself a certain licence.

## Chapter 22

The auction sale was to be held in the village hall, a red-brick monstrosity erected in the eighties by the Victorian Pearce who had bought that walnut cabinet, and after lunch on the big day Lord Ickenham, in order to avoid old Mr Saxby, who was showing an increasing disposition to buttonhole him and talk about Flannery, had taken his cigar to his godson's study, feeling that there, if anywhere, a man might be safe. Johnny, his objective a heart-to-heart talk with Belinda Farringdon, had gone up to London in a car borrowed from Mr Morrison of the Beetle and Wedge, looking grim and resolute. It was his intention to take a firm line about this Norbury-Smith nonsense.

It was cool and peaceful in the study, with its french windows opening on the terrace, but on the fifth Earl's face, as he sat there, a frown might have been observed, as though sombre thoughts were troubling him. Nor would anyone who formed this impression have been in error. He was thinking of Beefy Bastable, that luckless toy of Fate who – for one of his wealth and determination could not fail to outbid Oily Carlisle at their coming contest – would shortly be parting with several hundred pounds for an imitation walnut cabinet worth perhaps fifty shillings.

Chatting with Oily while reclining in the hammock, Lord Ickenham, it will be recalled, had laid considerable stress on the spiritual agonies suffered by the dregs of society when they see the United States Marines arriving. Those of Sir Raymond on opening that cabinet and finding no letter in it would, he could not but feel, be even keener. There is a type of man who, however rich he be, has a sturdy distaste for paying out large sums of money for nothing, and it was to this section of humanity that the eminent barrister belonged. Lord Ickenham mourned in spirit for his old friend's distress. Too bad, he felt, that when you started spreading sweetness and light, you so often found that there was not enough to go round and that somebody had to be left out of the distribution.

On the other hand, if nobody was there to bid against Oily, carrying out the manoeuvre known to Barbara Crowe's man-in-Hollywood as bumping him up, the cabinet would be knocked down to that gentlemanly highbinder for about ten shillings, which would not greatly further the interests of a Jonathan Pearce who needed five hundred pounds. The occasion, in a word, was one of those, so common in this imperfect world, where someone has to get the short end of the stick, and only Beefy was available for the role. Lord Ickenham could see clearly enough that it was necessary to sacrifice Beefy for the good of the cause but that did not mean that he had to be happy about it.

To distract himself for a moment from his sad thoughts, he picked up the copy of that morning's *Daily Gazette* which Johnny had left lying on the floor beside his desk, and began to glance through it. It was a paper he had never much admired, and he was not surprised that he found little to intrigue him on pages one, two and three. But on page four the interest quickened. His attention was arrested by one of those large headlines in which this periodical specialized.

FRANK, FORTHRIGHT, FEARLESS

it said, and beneath this:

COCKTAIL TIME
Our Powerful New Serial
by
COSMO WISDOM
Begin It Today

There was also, inset, a photograph of Phoebe's ewe lamb, all shifty eyes and small black moustache, which might have been that of some prominent spiv who had been detained by the police for questioning in connexion with the recent drug-ring raids.

'Cor lumme, stone the crows!' whispered Lord Ickenham, borrowing from Albert Peasemarch's non-copyright material. The scales had fallen from his eyes.

Until this moment it had never occurred to him to regard Cosmo

Wisdom in the light of a potential bidder for the cabinet. He had supposed him to be, if not penniless, certainly several hundred poundsless. It was obvious that he must now revise this view. He knew little of the prices prevailing in the marts of literature, but it was to be presumed that for a serial as frank, forthright and fearless as *Cocktail Time* a paper like the *Gazette*, making more money than it knew what to do with and always on the look-out for a chance of giving it away to someone, would have loosened up on a pretty impressive scale. Cosmo, in other words, so recently a biter of ears for ten bobs to see him through till next Saturday, was plainly in the chips. If on this sunny summer afternoon his hip pocket was not filled to bursting with the right stuff, he, Lord Ickenham, would be dashed.

What, then, could be a happier thought than to substitute the opulent young man for Beefy?

And scarcely had he reached this most satisfactory solution of his problem when, glancing out of the french window, he saw the opulent young man in person. He was pacing the terrace with bent head and leaden feet, like a Volga boatman.

And if anyone might excusably have impersonated a Volga boatman, it was Cosmo Wisdom at this juncture. Behind the left ear of the head he was bending there was a large lump, extremely painful if he made any sudden movement, and this alone would have been enough to lower the *joie de vivre*. But far worse than physical distress was the mental anguish caused by the thought that the letter which meant everything to him was now in the custody of Oily Carlisle. It is scarcely to be wondered at that when he heard a voice call his name and, raising his bent head, saw Lord Ickenham beaming at him from the study window, his manner was not cordial. It was, indeed, rather like that of a timber wolf with its foot in a trap.

'Just come in here for a moment, will you, Cosmo? I want to speak to you.'

'What about?'

'Nothing that can be shouted from the house tops or yelled on terraces. I won't keep you long,' said Lord Ickenham as his young friend stepped through the french windows. 'It's about that letter.'

Cosmo's scowl darkened. He had no wish to talk about that letter.

'It is, is it?' he said unpleasantly. 'Well, you're wasting your time. I haven't got it.'

'I am aware of that. Mr Carlisle has it.'

'Curse him!'

'Certainly, if you wish. I don't like the fellow myself. We must baffle that man, Cosmo, before he can start throwing his weight about. You don't need to peer into any crystal ball to inform yourself of what the future holds in store, if this letter remains in his possession. Not much of that Hollywood largess of yours will be left after he has staked out his claim, for if ever a man believed in sharing the wealth, it is this same Carlisle. He must be foiled and frustrated.'

'A fat lot of good saying that,' said Cosmo, speaking even more unpleasantly than before. 'How the devil can I foil and frustrate him?'

'Listen attentively and I will tell you.'

The effect of Lord Ickenham's brief résumé of the position of affairs on Cosmo was to cause him to start convulsively. And as anything in the nature of a convulsive start makes a man who has recently been struck on the head by a woman's gentle cosh feel as if that head had a red-hot skewer thrust through it, he uttered a yelp of agony, like a Volga boatman stung by a wasp.

'I know, I know,' said Lord Ickenham, nodding sympathetically. 'The after effects of being bust one do linger, don't they? As a young man, in the course of a political argument in a Third Avenue saloon in New York, I was once struck squarely on the topknot by a pewter tankard in the capable hands of a gentleman of the name of Moriarty – no relation of the Professor, I believe – and it was days before I was my old bright self again.'

Cosmo was staring, open-mouthed.

'You mean the letter's in that cabinet?'

'Carlisle certainly put it there.'

'How do you know?'

'I have my ways of getting to know things.'

'And it's up for auction?'

'Precisely.'

'I'll go and bid for it!'

'Exactly what I was about to suggest. You will, of course, have to be prepared to bid high. Carlisle is not going to let the thing go without a struggle. But, what with this serial and everything, I imagine that you are rolling in money these days, and a few hundred pounds here and there mean nothing to you. How is your voice?'

'Eh?'

'Say "Mi-mi". Excellent,' said Lord Ickenham. 'Like a silver bell. The auctioneer will hear your every word. So off you go. Bid till your eyes bubble, my boy, and may heaven speed your efforts.'

And now, he was saying to himself, as Cosmo hurried away and a distant howl told that he had incautiously jerked his head again, to find some simple ruse which would remove Beefy from the centre of things. The village hall must not see Beefy this summer afternoon.

It was seldom that Lord Ickenham sought for inspiration in vain. Why, of course, he was thinking a few moments later. Yes, that would do it. How simple these things always were, if you just sat back and closed your eyes and let the little grey cells take over. It needed but a quick telephone call to Albert Peasemarch, instructing him to lock Beefy up in the wine cellar, and the situation would be stabilized.

He was about to reach for the instrument, glowing as men do when their brains are working well, when it rang its bell at him in the abrupt way telephones have. He took up the receiver.

'Hullo?' he said.

It was Phoebe who replied. As nearly always, she appeared agitated.

## Chapter 23

'Oh, Frederick!' she said, panting like a white rabbit heated in the chase.

'Hullo, Phoebe, my dear,' said Lord Ickenham. 'What's the matter? You seem upset.'

There was a brief pause while she seemed to contemplate the adjective, weighing it as Roget might have done if someone had suggested admitting it into his Thesaurus.

'Well, not upset exactly. But I don't know if I am standing on my head or my heels.'

'Sift the evidence. At which end of you is the ceiling?'

'Oh, don't be silly, Frederick. You know what I mean. Oh dear, I do hope Cossie will approve of this step I'm taking. I mean, it isn't as if I were a young girl. I'm nearly fifty, Frederick. He may think it odd.'

'That you are joining the chorus at the Hippodrome?'

'Whatever are you talking about?'

'Isn't that what you are trying to tell me?'

'Of course it isn't. I'm going to marry again.'

The receiver jumped in Lord Ickenham's right hand, the cigar in his left. This was big stuff. Any popular daily paper would have used it without hesitation as its front page feature story.

'Bert?' he exclaimed. 'Has Bert at last cast off his iron restraint and spoken? Are you going to be Lady Peasemarch?'

'Mrs Peasemarch.'

'For a while, no doubt, yes. But a man of Bert's abilities is bound to get knighted sooner or later. My dear Phoebe, this is news to warm the cockles of the heart. They don't come any truer and stauncher than Bert. You know what Ecclesiastes said about him? He said ... No, sorry, it's gone for the moment, but it was something very flattering. There's only one thing you have to watch out for with Albert Peasemarch, the Drake's Drum side of him. Be careful that he doesn't sing it during the wedding ceremony.'

'What, dear?'

'I was saying that if as you stand at the altar Bert starts singing Drake's Drum, give him a nudge.'

'We are going to be married at a registrar's.'

'Oh, then that's all right. These registrars are good sports. Yours will probably join in the chorus. What does Raymond think of the proposed union?'

'We haven't told him yet. Albert thought it would be better if he finished his month first.'

'Very sensible. It will save Beefy a lot of embarrassment. It's always difficult for a man to be really at his ease with his butler, if he knows the latter is engaged to be married to his sister. A certain constraint when Bert was handing the potatoes would be inevitable. But aren't we skipping some of the early chapters? Tell me how it all happened. Be frank, forthright and fearless.'

'Well –'

'Yes?'

'I was trying to think where to begin. Well, I had gone to Albert's pantry to talk to him about poor little Benjy, who is ever so much better, you will be glad to hear. Albert says his nose is quite cold.'

'I remember it used to get very cold in our Home Guard days.'

'What, dear?'

'You were saying that Albert Peasemarch's nose was cold.'

'No, no, Benjy's.'

'Oh, Benjy's? Well, that's fine, isn't it?'

'And then we got talking, and something Albert said made me think of Raymond. I don't mean I've ever *not* thought of Raymond, but this something Albert said reminded me of what you had said the other day, about him not having got all his marbles.'

'I said he *had* got all his marbles.'

'Oh, did you? I thought you said he hadn't, and it worried me terribly. Thinking of George Winstanley, you know. Because Raymond has been behaving so very oddly this last week or two. I don't mean so much giving me flowers and asking after my rheumatism, but I do think it was strange of him to go swimming in the lake with all his clothes on.'

'Did he do that?'

'I saw him from my window.'

'According to Shakespeare, Julius Caesar used to swim with all his clothes on.'

'But he didn't gather frogs.'

'No, you have a point there. One finds it very difficult to see why Beefy should have wanted to gather frogs. Puzzled me a good deal, that.'

'You must admit that I had enough to worry me.'

'Oh, quite.'

'It seemed to me so dreadfully sad.'

'I don't wonder.'

'And I couldn't help it. I broke down and sobbed. And the next thing I knew, Albert was striding up to me and seizing me by the wrist and pulling me about till I felt quite giddy. And then he said "My mate!" and clasped me to him and –'

'Showered burning kisses on your upturned face?'

'Yes. He told me later that something seemed to snap in him.'

'I believe that often happens. Well, I couldn't be more pleased about this, Phoebe. You have done wisely in linking your lot with Bert's. Instinct told you you were on a good thing, and you very sensibly pushed it along. The ideal husband. Where is Bert, by the way? In his pantry?'

'I think so. He was giving Benjy beef extract.'

'Will you bring him to the phone. I would have speech with him.'

'You want to congratulate him?'

'That, of course. But there is also a little business matter I would like to discuss with him. Just one of those things that crop up from time to time. Oh, Bert,' said Lord Ickenham some moments later, 'I've been hearing the great news. Felicitations by the jugful, my old comrade, and a million wishes for your future happiness. Very interesting to learn that yet another success has to be chalked up to the Ickenham system. It seldom fails, if you remember to waggle with sufficient vigour, as I understand you did. The preliminary waggle is everything. That was probably where Cyril McMurdo went wrong. Well, I suppose you're walking on air and strewing roses from your bowler hat?'

'I do feel extremely grateful for my good fortune, Mr I.'

'I bet you do. There's nothing like getting married. It's the only life, as Brigham Young and King Solomon would tell you, if they were still with us. And now here's something I was wanting to ask you. I wonder if plighting your troth has affected you as plighting mine many years ago affected me. I remember that I was filled with a sort of yeasty benevolence that embraced the whole human race. I wanted to go about doing acts of kindness to everybody I met. Do you feel the same?'

'Oh yes, Mr I. I feel just like that.'

'Splendid! Because there's a little routine job I would like you to do for me. Will your future wife be on the premises during the next hour or so?'

'I shouldn't think so, Mr I. She went off to this sale in the village hall, and wasn't expecting to get back too soon.'

'Excellent. Then there will be no one to hear his cries.'

'Cries, Mr I?'

'The big chief's. I want you to lock him up in the wine cellar, Bert, and I imagine he'll shout a good deal. You know how people do, when you lock them in wine cellars.'

It seemed to be Lord Ickenham's fate these days to extract from those with whom he conversed on the telephone what Mr and Mrs Carlisle called groans or gurgles, though for the sound that now came over the wire a precisian might have preferred the term 'gulp'. Whatever its correct classification, it indicated plainly that his words had made a deep impression on Albert Peasemarch. In the manner in which he spoke there was more than a suggestion of Phoebe Wisdom at her most emotional.

'Do *what* to Sir Raymond, did you say, Mr I.?'

'Lock him in the wine cellar. I wouldn't call him Sir Raymond, though, now that you are linked to him in such sentimental bonds. It's time you were thinking of him as Ray or Beefy. Well, that's all, Bert. Carry on.'

'But, Mr I.!'

Lord Ickenham frowned. Wasted, of course, on a Peasemarch who could not see him.

'You have a rather annoying habit, Bert, when I ask you to do some perfectly simple thing for me, of saying "But, Mr I.",' he said, a little stiffly. 'It's just a mannerism, I know, but I wish you wouldn't. What's on your mind?'

'Well, the question it occurred to me to ask was –'

'Yes?'

'*Why* do you want me to lock Sir Raymond in the wine cellar?'

Lord Ickenham clicked his tongue.

'Never mind why. You know as well as I do that the Secret Service can't give reasons for every move it makes. If I were to tell you why, and it got about through some incautious word of yours, a third world war would be inevitable. And I seem to remember you saying that you were opposed to the idea of a third world war.'

'Oh, I am, Mr I. I wouldn't like it at all. But –'

'That word again!'

'But what I was going to say was How do I go about it?'

'My dear fellow, there are a hundred ways of luring a man into a wine cellar. Tell him you would like his opinion on the last lot of claret. Ask him to come and inspect the ginger ale, because you're afraid the moths have been at it. That part of the thing presents no difficulty. And the locking-in will be equally simple. You just shimmer off while his back is turned and twiddle the key. A child of four could do it. A child of three,' said Lord Ickenham, correcting himself. 'Drake would have done it without missing a drum beat. Snap into it, Bert, and give me a ring when you're through.'

It was some ten minutes later that the telephone bell rang. When Albert Peasemarch spoke, it was in the subdued voice of a nervous novice who had just done his first murder.

'Everything has been attended to, Mr I.'

'He's in storage?'

'Yes, Mr I.'

'Capital! I knew I could rely on you not to bungle it. We of the Home Guard don't bungle. It wasn't so hard, was it?'

'Not hard, no –'

'But it has taken it out of you a little, no doubt,' said Lord Ickenham sympathetically. 'Your pulse is high, your breathing is stertorous and there are floating spots before your eyes. Well, go and lie down and have a nice nap.'

Albert Peasemarch coughed.

'What I was thinking I'd do, Mr I., was take the bus to Reading and catch the train to London, and spend the next week or two there. I would prefer not to encounter Sir Raymond until some little time has elapsed.'

'From what you were able to gather through the closed door, he seemed annoyed, did he?'

'Yes, Mr I.'

'I can't imagine why. I know dozens of men who would think it heaven to be locked in a wine cellar. Still, no doubt you're right. Time, the great healer, and all that sort of thing. Then this is good-bye for the moment, Bert. A thousand thanks. I will see that word of what you have done reaches the proper quarter. And if you're in London long enough, I'll look you up and we'll have a night out together.'

Well pleased, Lord Ickenham replaced the receiver and went on to the terrace. He had been there a few minutes, finishing his cigar and enjoying the peace of the summer afternoon, when a car came by and drew up at the front door. Fearing that this might be the County paying a formal call, he had recoiled a step and was preparing to make a dive for safety, when the occupant of the car alighted, and he saw that it was Barbara Crowe.

## Chapter 24

Lord Ickenham would probably have been deeply offended if he had been told that in any circumstances his mind could run on parallel lines with that of Cosmo Wisdom, a young man whose intelligence he heartily despised, but it is undoubtedly the fact that the sight of Barbara Crowe set him thinking, as Cosmo had done, what a consummate ass Raymond Bastable had been to let this woman go. In her sports dress, with the little green hat that went with it, she was looking more attractive than ever, and nothing could have been more warming to the heart than the smile she gave him as he hailed her.

'Why, Freddie,' she said, 'what on earth are you doing here?'

'I am staying with Johnny Pearce, my godson, while my wife is in Scotland. She wanted me to go with her, but I would have none of it. So, having some foolish prejudice against letting me run loose, as she calls it, in London, she dumped me on Johnny. But what brings you to these parts?'

'I've come to see Cosmo Wisdom about making some appearances on television. And Howard Saxby junior wants me to bring Howard Saxby senior back. He's afraid he'll fall into the lake or something. This place of your godson's is a kind of pub, isn't it?'

'Johnny takes in paying guests, yes.'

'I'd better book a room.'

'Plenty of time. I want to talk to you, Barbara. Let us go and seat ourselves under yonder tree. What I was hoping when I saw you get out of that car,' said Lord Ickenham, having settled her in a deck chair and dropping into one himself, 'was that you had come to see Beefy Bastable.'

Barbara Crowe started.

'Raymond? What do you mean? Is he here?'

'Not actually in Johnny's dosshouse. He lives at the Lodge across the park. We might look in on him later. Not just now, for I know he will be occupied for the next hour or so, but after you have had a wash and brush-up.'

Barbara's cheerful face lost some of its cheerfulness.

'This is a bit awkward.'

'Why?'

'He'll think I'm pursuing him.'

'Of course he will, and a very good thing, too. It will give him the encouragement he sorely needs. He'll say to himself, "Well, dash my buttons, I thought I'd lost her, but if she comes legging it after me like this, things don't look so sticky after all." It will make his day. And from that to restoring relations to their old footing will be but a step. Why,' asked Lord Ickenham, 'do you laugh in that hollow, hacking way?'

'Well, don't you think it's funny?'

'Not in the least. What's funny?'

'The idea you seem to have that Raymond still cares for me.'

'My dear girl, he's potty about you.'

'What nonsense! He's never been near me or phoned me or written to me since . . . it happened.'

'Of course he hasn't. You don't realize what a sensitive plant Beefy is. You see him in court ripping the stuffing out of witnesses, and you say to yourself, "H'm! A tough guy!" little knowing that at heart he is . . . what are those things that shrink? . . . violets, that's the word I was after . . . little knowing that at heart he is a shrinking violet. He's not a coarse-fibred chap like me. Every time my Jane broke our engagement, I hounded her with brutal threats till she mended it again, but Beefy would never do that. Delicacy is his dish. He would assume that when you gave him the old heave-ho, it meant that you didn't want to have any more to do with him, and, though it was agony, he kept away. He should have known that little or no importance is to be attached to these lovers' tiffs. That hacking laugh again! What amuses you?'

'Your calling it a tiff.'

'I believe that is the expression commonly used. If it wasn't a tiff, what was it?'

'A terrific row. A pitched battle, which culminated in my calling him a pompous old stuffed shirt.'

'I wouldn't have thought Beefy would have objected to that. He must know that he is a pompous old stuffed shirt.'

Barbara Crowe blazed into sudden fury.

'He isn't anything of the sort! He's a lamb.'

'A *what*?'

'He's the most wonderful man there ever was.'

'That is your considered opinion?'

'Yes, Frederick Altamont Cornwallis Twistleton, that is my considered opinion.'

Lord Ickenham gave a satisfied nod.

'So, as I suspected, the flame of love still burns! It does, does it not?'

'Yes, it does.'

'One word from him, and you would follow him to the ends of the earth?'

'Yes, I would.'

'Well, he won't be going there, not at the moment, anyway. My dear Barbara, this is extremely gratifying. If that's how things are at your end, we ought to be able to fix this up in no time in a manner agreeable to all parties. I wasn't sure how you felt. I knew, of course, that Beefy loved you. That habit of his, when he thinks he is alone, of burying his face in his hands and muttering "Barbara! Barbara."'

'He always called me "Baby."'

Lord Ickenham started.

'*Beefy* did?'

'Yes.'

'You're sure?'

'Quite sure.'

'Well, you know best. I wouldn't have thought . . . but that is neither here nor there. Then no doubt it was "Baby! Baby!" that he was muttering. It doesn't really matter. The salient point is that he muttered. Well, I must say everything looks pretty smooth now.'

'Does it?'

'Surely? Here, as I see it, are two sundered hearts it will be very simple to bring together.'

'Not so simple as you think.'

'What seems to be the difficulty?'

'The difficulty, my dear Freddie, is that he is determined that Phoebe shall share our little nest, and I'm equally determined that she shan't. That's the real rock we split on.'

'He wanted Phoebe to live with you?'

'Yes. There's a parsimonious streak in Raymond. I suppose it comes from having been so hard up when he was starting at the Bar. He was desperately hard up, you know, before he got going. When I suggested that our married life would run much more smoothly if he gave Phoebe a couple of thousand a year and told her to go off and take a flat in Kensington, or a villa in Bournemouth or whatever she fancied, he said he couldn't possibly afford it. And, as they say, one word led to another. Do you ever lose your temper, Freddie?'

'Very seldom. I'm the equable type.'

'I wish I were. When moved, I spit and scratch. He kept saying things like "We must be practical" and "Women never realize that men are not made of money", and I couldn't take it. That was when I called him a pompous old stuffed shirt. Yes?' said Barbara coldly. 'Why are *you* laughing in that hollow, hacking way?'

'I doubt if those are the right adjectives to describe my little ripple of mirth. They suggest gloom and bitterness and I am anything but gloomy and bitter. I laughed – musically and with an infectious lilt – because it always entertains me to see people creating, as Albert Peasemarch would say, when there is no necessity.'

'No necessity?'

'None whatever.'

'God bless you, Frederick Ickenham. And who is Albert Peasemarch?'

'An intimate friend of mine. To tell you all about him – his career, his adventures by flood and field, his favourite breakfast food and so on – would take too long. What will probably interest you most is the fact that he will very shortly be marrying Phoebe.'

'What!'

'Yes. They fixed it up this afternoon. The expression you are probably groping for,' suggested Lord Ickenham, seeing that his companion was struggling to find speech, 'is "Cor lumme, stone the crows!" – It is the one Bert Peasemarch uses when in the grip of some powerful emotion.'

Barbara found speech.

'He's marrying *Phoebe*?'

'This surprises you?'

'Well, it isn't everybody who would want to marry Phoebe, is it? Who is this humble hero?'

'Beefy's butler. Or perhaps, after what he was saying to me on the telephone just now, I should put an "Ex" before the word.'

'Phoebe's marrying a *butler*?'

'Somebody's got to, or the race of butlers would die out. And Bert will be a notable improvement on the late Algernon Wisdom. You spoke?'

'I said, "Quick, Freddie – your handkerchief!"'

'Cold in the head?'

'Crying. Tears of joy. Oh, Freddie!'

'I thought you might possibly be pleased about it.'

'Pleased! Why, this solves everything.'

'Things have a way of getting solved when an Ickenham takes a hand in them.'

'You mean, you worked it?'

'I think something I said to Phoebe, some casual remark about Albert Peasemarch worshipping the ground she trod on, may have been not without its influence.'

'Freddie, I'm going to kiss you.'

'There is nothing I would enjoy more, but if you will glance over your shoulder, you will see that we are about to have Howard Saxby senior with us. This frequently happens here. Whatever Hammer Hall's shortcomings, there is never any stint of Howard Saxby senior. I have been wondering what has been keeping him away. It is not often that he denies one his society for such a lengthy period. Hullo, Saxby.'

'Ah, Scriventhorpe.'

'Cigarette?'

'No, thank you,' said Mr Saxby, taking needles and a ball of wool from his pocket. 'I would prefer to knit. I'm roughing out a sweater for my little grandson. An ambitious project, but I think something ought to come of it!'

'That's the spirit. Here's Barbara Crowe.'

'So I see. It's an extraordinary thing. I was saying to myself, as I came up, "That woman has quite a look of Barbara Crowe." I understand now why there was such a resemblance. What are you doing here, Barbara?'

'I've come to take you home, young Saxby.'

'I don't want to go home.'

'Howard junior says you must.'

'Then I suppose I'll have to. When did you arrive?'

'About ten minutes ago.'

'I am sorry I was not here to greet you. I have been down at the village hall, watching that sale. You should have been there, Scriventhorpe. That cabinet . . .'

Lord Ickenham sat up alertly.

'How much did it fetch?'

'I wish you would not bark at me like that,' said Mr Saxby a little peevishly. 'You've made me drop a stitch. I was telling you about the sale, was I not? It was replete with interest. You have often accused me, Barbara,' Mr Saxby proceeded, 'of being eccentric, and there may be something in the charge, for others have told me the same. But real eccentricity, eccentricity in the fullest sense of the term, flourishes only in Dovetail Hammer. I must begin by saying – you will forgive me, Scriventhorpe, for going over ground which is already familiar to you – that there was recently on these premises an imitation walnut cabinet which was an offence to the eye and worth at the most a few pounds. It was included in this sale of which I speak, and judge of my astonishment –'

'How much did it fetch?' said Lord Ickenham.

Mr Saxby gave him a cold look.

'And judge of my astonishment when, after several other objects of equal horror had been put up and knocked down for a few shillings, this cabinet was displayed, and I heard a voice say "Fifty pounds".'

'Ha!'

'I wish you wouldn't say "Ha!" in that abrupt way. I've dropped another stitch. It was the voice of that American fellow who is staying at the Hall. Carstairs is, I think, the name.'

'Carlisle.'

'Indeed? Flannery knows a man named Carlisle. You've probably heard him speak of him. A most interesting life he has had,

Flannery says, with curious things constantly happening to him. He was once bitten by a rabbit.'

'You don't say?'

'So Flannery assures me. An angora. It turned on him and sank its teeth in his wrist while he was offering it a carrot.'

'Probably on a diet,' said Lord Ickenham, and Mr Saxby agreed that this might have been so.

'But we must not allow ourselves to get mixed up,' he proceeded. 'It was not that Carlisle, the one who was bitten by a rabbit, who said "Fifty pounds", but this other Carlisle, who is staying at the Hall and has never, to the best of my knowledge, been bitten by a rabbit. He said "Fifty pounds", and I was still gasping with astonishment, when another voice said "A hundred". It was that young fellow who was in my office the other day, Barbara, the squirt, the one you sent me here to apologize to. Though what there was to apologize about . . . However, what is his name? I've forgotten.'

'Cosmo Wisdom.'

'Ah, yes. Connected somehow with the motion picture industry. Well, he said "A hundred pounds"!'

'And to cut a long story short,' said Lord Ickenham.

Mr Saxby never cut long stories short.

'I could scarcely credit my senses. I must emphasize once again that this beastly cabinet would have been dear at five pounds. Sometimes you will see an imitation walnut cabinet that looks reasonably attractive. Some quite good work done in that line, if you know where to find it. But this one had no redeeming features. And yet these two eccentrics persisted in bidding against each other for it, and might have gone on for ever, had not a peculiar interruption occurred. I don't know if either of you are acquainted with Bastable's sister?'

'We know her well,' said Barbara. 'Do get on, young Saxby. Phoebe Wisdom is Freddie's wife's half-sister.'

'Is that so? Who is Freddie?'

'This is Freddie.'

'Oh, really? Did you say Wisdom?'

'Yes.'

'Related in any way to the squirt?'

'His mother.'

'Then I understand everything. She was saving him from himself.'

'Doing what?'

'Preventing him throwing away his money on a cabinet no man of discernment would willingly have been found dead in a ditch with. For as the bidding reached a certain point –'

'What point?' asked Lord Ickenham.

'– this woman, bathed in tears, approached the squirt, accompanied by the village policeman, and after, so I gathered from her manner, pleading with him and trying in vain to use a mother's influence to stop him making a fool of himself signalled to the policeman to lead him away, which he did. So Carstairs got the cabinet.'

'How much for?' said Lord Ickenham.

'Well,' said Mr Saxby, rising, 'I think I will go and take a bath. I got very warm and sticky in that village hall. There was practically no ventilation.'

'Hi!' cried Lord Ickenham.

'You were calling me?' said Mr Saxby, turning.

'How much did Carlisle pay for the cabinet?'

'Oh, didn't I tell you that?' said Mr Saxby. 'I fully intended to. Five hundred pounds.'

He pottered away, and Lord Ickenham expended his breath in a deep sigh of satisfaction. Barbara Crowe shot an enquiring look at him.

'Why are you so interested in this cabinet, Freddie?'

'It belonged to my godson, who was in urgent need of five hundred pounds. Now he's got it.'

'Was it really worth nothing?'

'Practically nothing.'

'Then why did Cosmo Wisdom and that other man bid like that for it?'

'It's a long story.'

'Your stories are never too long.'

'Bless my soul, I remember my niece Valerie saying that to me once. But she spoke with a nasty tinkle in her voice. It was on the occasion when she found me at Blandings Castle, posing – from the best motives – as Sir Roderick Glossop. Did I ever tell you about that?'

'No. And you can save up these reminiscences of your disreputable past for another time. What I want to hear now is about this cabinet. Don't ramble off on to other subjects like old Mr Saxby.'

'I see. You would like it short and crisp. You would wish me, as I was saying to Johnny the other day, to let my Yea be Yea and my Nay be Nay?'

'I would.'

'Then here it comes,' said Lord Ickenham.

It was, as he had predicted, a long story, but it gripped his audience throughout. There was no wandering of attention on Barbara Crowe's part to damp a raconteur's spirits. At each successive twist and turn of the plot her eyes seemed to grow wider. It was some moments after he had finished before she spoke. When she did, it was with a wealth of feeling.

'Cor lumme, stone the crows!' she said.

'I was expecting you to say that,' said Lord Ickenham. 'I must remember, by the way, to ask Albert Peasemarch what the meaning of the expression is. What crows? And why stone them? I have met men who, when moved, have said "Cor chase my Aunt Fanny up a gum tree"!, which seems to me equally cryptic. However, this is not the time to go into all that. I anticipated that you would react impressively to my revelation, for it is of course a sensational tale. Are you feeling faint?'

'Not faint, no, but I think I'm entitled to gasp a bit.'

'Or gurgle. Quite.'

'Fancy Toots writing that book! I wouldn't have thought he had it in him.'

Lord Ickenham clicked his tongue.

'Haven't you been listening? I said the author of *Cocktail Time* was Raymond Bastable.'

'I used to call him Toots.'

'You did?'

'I did.'

'How perfectly foul! And he used to call you Baby?'

'He did.'

'How utterly loathsome! It makes one realize that half the world never knows how the other half lives. Well, you'll soon be calling him that revolting name again. If, that is to say, what I have told you has not killed your love.'

'What do you mean?'

'Lots of people recoil in horror from *Cocktail Time*. The bishop did. So did Phoebe. So, according to Beefy, did about fifty-seven publishers before he finally landed it with the Tomkins people. It doesn't diminish your love for him to know that he is capable of writing a book like that?'

'It does not. If anything was needed to deepen my love for Beefy, as you call him –'

'Better than calling him Toots.'

'– it is the discovery that he has a hundred and fifty thousand dollars coming to him from the movie sale of the first thing he ever wrote. Golly! Think what we'll get for the next one!'

'You feel there will be a next one?'

'Of course there will. I'll see to that. I'm going to make him give up the Bar – I've always hated him being a barrister – and concentrate on his writing. We'll live in the country, where he can breathe decent air and not ruin his lungs by sitting all day in stuffy courts. Have you ever been in the Old Bailey?'

'Once or twice.'

'I believe you can cut the atmosphere there with a spoon. They carve it up in slices and sell it as rat poison. And living in the country, he'll get his golf every day and bring his weight down. He had put on weight terribly the last time I saw him. I suppose he's worse than ever now.'

'He is far from streamlined.'

'I'll adjust that,' said Barbara grimly. 'Do you know when I first saw Raymond? When I was ten. One of my uncles took me to see the Oxford and Cambridge match, and there he was, looking like a Greek god. My uncle introduced me to him after the game, and I got his autograph and fell in love with him there and then. Gosh, he was terrific!'

'You plan to pare him down to the Beefy of thirty years ago?'

'Well, not quite that, perhaps, but some of that too, too solid flesh is certainly going to melt. And now,' said Barbara, rising from her deck chair, 'I think I'll follow our Mr Saxby's excellent example and have a bath. What's the procedure about clocking in here? Do I see your godson and haggle about terms?'

'He's gone to London. You conduct the negotiations with his old nurse. And I'd better come and help you through the ordeal. She's rather formidable.'

If there was a touch of smugness in Lord Ickenham's demeanour as he returned to his deck chair after piloting Barbara Crowe through her interview with Nannie Bruce, it would have been a stern judge who would not have agreed that that smugness was excusable. He had set out for Dovetail Hammer with the intention of spreading sweetness and light among the residents of that inland Garden of Eden, and in not one but several quarters he had spread it like a sower going forth sowing. Thanks to his efforts, Barbara would get her Toots, and Beefy would get his Baby, plus all that lovely cash from the cornucopias of Hollywood. Johnny had got his five hundred pounds, Albert Peasemarch his Phoebe, and it would not be long presumably before Cyril McMurdo got his Nannie Bruce. It was true that both Mr and Mrs Carlisle were at the moment probably feeling a little short of sweetness and light, but, as has already been pointed out, there is seldom enough of that commodity to go round. No doubt in due season they would be able to console themselves with the thought that money is not everything and that disappointments such as they had suffered are sent to us to make us more spiritual.

After perhaps half an hour had elapsed, his meditations were interrupted by the arrival of Johnny Pearce, who approached him on foot, having returned his borrowed car to the Beetle and Wedge. His manner, Lord Ickenham was amused to see, was gloomy. He would soon, as Barbara had put it, adjust that.

'Hullo, Johnny.'

'Hullo, Uncle Fred.'

'Back again?'

'Yes, I'm back.'

'Everything all right?'

'Well, yes and no.'

Lord Ickenham frowned. His objection to his godson's habit of talking in riddles has already been touched on.

'What do you mean, Yes and No? Did you square things with Bunny?'

'Oh, yes. We're getting married next week. At the registrar's.'

'Business is certainly brisk in the registraring industry these days. And I suppose you're asking yourself what the harvest will be when she settles down here with Nannie?'

'Yes, that's what's worrying me.'

'It need worry you no longer, my dear boy. Do you know what happened at that sale this afternoon? You will scarcely credit it, but that cabinet of yours fetched five hundred pounds.'

Johnny collapsed into the deck chair in which Barbara Crowe had sat.

'What!' he gasped. 'You're kidding!'

'Not at all. That was the final bid, five hundred pounds. Going, going, gone, and knocked down to Mr Gordon Carlisle. So all you have to do now is go to Nannie ... Why,' asked Lord Ickenham, breaking off and regarding his godson with amazement, 'aren't you skipping like the high hills? Well, I suppose you could hardly do that, sitting in a deck chair, but why aren't you raising your eyes thankfully to heaven and giving three rousing cheers?'

It was some moments before Johnny was able to speak.

'I'll tell you why I'm not giving three rousing cheers,' he said, and laughed in a way which Lord Ickenham recognized as hollow and hacking. 'That sale was the vicar's jumble sale. I contributed the cabinet to it, glad to get rid of the beastly thing. So not a penny of the five hundred quid comes to me. It will be applied to the renovation and repair of the church heating system, which, I understand,' said Johnny, with another hollow, hacking laugh, 'needs a new boiler.'

## Chapter 25

Mr Saxby, feeling greatly refreshed after his bath, came out into the cool evening air and started to toddle across the park. He had decided not to resume the knitting of his grandson's sweater, which could very well wait till the quiet period after dinner, but to stroll over to Hammer Lodge and tell his friend Bastable about the auction sale. It would, he thought, interest him. For though Bastable had probably never seen that cabinet, whose peculiar foulness was the point of his story, he was convinced that he could describe it sufficiently vividly to make him appreciate the drama of what had occurred.

Nothing happened when he reached the Lodge and rang the front door bell. The butler appeared to be away from his post, down at the Beetle and Wedge perhaps or possibly out having a round of golf. But things like that never deterred Mr Saxby. The door being open, he walked in, and having done so, raised his voice and bleated:

'Bastable! BASTable!'

And from somewhere in the distance there came an answering shout. It seemed to proceed from the depths of the house, as though the shouter were in the cellar. Very strange, Mr Saxby felt. What would Bastable be doing in a cellar? And then the obvious solution presented itself. He was having a look at his wine. The good man loves his wine, and it is only natural that he should go down from time to time to see that all is well with it.

'Bastable,' he said, arriving at the cellar door.

'Who's that?' a muffled voice replied.

'Saxby.'

'Thank God! Let me out!'

'Do what?'

'Let me *out*.'

'But why don't you *come* out?'

'The door's locked.'

'Unlock it.'

'The key's on your side.'

'You're perfectly correct. So it is.'

'Well, turn it, man, turn it.'

Mr Saxby turned it, and there emerged an incandescent figure at the sight of which Albert Peasemarch, had he been present, would have trembled like one stricken with an ague. Lord Ickenham had spoken of men of his acquaintance who would thoroughly have enjoyed being locked up in a wine cellar. Sir Raymond Bastable did not belong to this convivial class. He was, as Gordon Carlisle had put it, when speaking of his wife Gertie, vexed.

'Where's Peasemarch?' he said, glaring about him with reddened eyes.

'Who?'

'Peasemarch.'

'I don't think I know him. Nice fellow?'

Sir Raymond continued to glare to left and right, as if expecting something to materialize out of thin air. As the missing member of his staff did not so materialize, he glared at Mr Saxby.

'How did you get in?'

'I walked in.'

'He didn't let you in?'

'Who didn't?'

Sir Raymond tried another approach.

'Did you see a round little bounder with a face like a suet pudding?'

'Not to my recollection. Who is this round bounder?'

'My butler. Peasemarch. I want to murder him.'

'Oh, really? Why is that?'

'He locked me in that damned cellar.'

'Locked you in the cellar?' bleated Mr Saxby, toiling in the rear as his companion, snorting with visible emotion, led the way to his study. 'Are you sure?'

'Of course I'm sure,' said Sir Raymond, sinking into an armchair and reaching for his pipe. 'I've been there for hours, with nothing to smoke. A-a-a-ah!' he said, puffing out a great cloud.

Tobacco rarely fails to soothe, but you have to give it time. The mixture of Sir Raymond's choice was slow in producing any beneficent effects. As he finished his first pipeful and prepared to light a second, his eyes were still aflame and those emotional snorts continued to proceed from him like minute guns. In a voice which would have been more musical if he had not been shouting all the afternoon, he sketched out the plans he had formed for dealing with Albert Peasemarch, should fate eventually throw them together again.

'I shall strangle him very slowly with my bare hands,' he said, rolling the words round his tongue as if they were vintage port. 'I shall kick his spine up through that beastly bowler hat he wears. I shall twist his head off at the roots. He got me to that cellar saying he wanted me to look at the last lot of claret, and when I went over to look at it, he nipped out, locking the door behind him.'

It was a simple tale, simply told, but it gripped Mr Saxby from the start. He uttered a curious high cry which he had probably picked up from some wild duck of his acquaintance.

'How extremely odd. I have never heard of a butler locking anyone in a wine cellar. I knew one once, many years ago, who kept tropical fish, but that,' said Mr Saxby, who could reason clearly when he gave his mind to it, 'is not, of course, quite the same thing. Do you know what I think, Bastable? Do you know the conviction that recent happenings in Dovetail Hammer have forced on me? It is that there is something in the air here that breeds eccentricity. You see it on all sides. Take the auction sale this afternoon.'

It was agony to Sir Raymond to be reminded of the auction sale, and once again there surged up in him a passionate desire to twist Albert Peasemarch's head off at the roots. But curiosity overcame his reluctance to speak of it.

'What happened?' he asked huskily.

Mr Saxby slid into his narrative with the polished ease of one who even at the Demosthenes, where the species abounds, was regarded as something unusual in the way of club bores. Members who could sit without flinching through Sir Roderick Glossop's stories about his patients or old Mr Lucas-Gore's anecdotes of Henry James, paled beneath their tan when Howard Saxby senior started to tell the tale.

'I must begin by saying,' he began by saying, 'that at Hammer Hall, where, as you know, I am now residing, though my son tells me I must return home, so I shall shortly be leaving, and sorry to go, I assure you, for apart from your delightful society, Bastable, there is a wealth of bird life in these parts which an ornithologist like myself finds richly rewarding –'

'Get on,' said Sir Raymond.

Mr Saxby looked surprised. He had supposed that he was getting on.

'At Hammer Hall, as I was about to say,' he resumed, 'there is – or was – an imitation walnut cabinet, the property of my host Mr Pearce . . . Do you know Mr Pearce?'

'Slightly.'

'Well, this imitation walnut cabinet belonged to him, and it stood in the hall, facing you as you entered through the front door. I stress this, because it was impossible, as you went in and out, not to see the beastly thing, and it had given me some bad moments. I want to impress upon you, Bastable, that this loathsome cabinet was entirely worthless, for that is the core and centre of my story. This afternoon I was relieved to hear that it was being included in the auction sale which was held at the village hall, for words cannot tell you the effect which the sight of that revolting object had on a sensitive eye. It was –'

'I know all about the cabinet,' said Sir Raymond. 'Get on.'

'You do bustle me so, my dear fellow. Men at the club do the same thing, I never know why. Well, this cabinet came up for auction, and judge of my amazement when I heard Carlisle – not the Carlisle who was bitten by an angora rabbit but the one who is staying at the Hall – bid fifty pounds. But more was to come. The next moment, a squirt of the name of Cosmo Wisdom, whom you have probably not met, had bid a hundred. And so it went on. A cabinet, I must again emphasize, of no value whatsoever. Can you wonder that I say that the air of Dovetail Hammer breeds eccentricity? Are you in pain, Bastable?'

Sir Raymond was, and he had been unable to check a groan. The way the story appeared to be heading, it looked to him as though the blow-out or punch of it was going to be that his frightful nephew had won the cabinet, which would be the end of all things.

'Get on,' he said dully.

'How you do keep saying "Get on"! But I think I see what is in your mind. You want to know how it all ended. Well, I always think it spoils a good story to hurry it, but if you must have it in a nutshell, what happened was that just as Carlisle bid five hundred pounds, the squirt's mother with the assistance of the village policeman removed him from the scene, so the distressing cabinet was knocked down to Carlisle at that figure.'

Sir Raymond puffed out a relieved cloud of smoke. Everything was . . . well, not perhaps all right, but much more nearly all right than it might have been. He knew Gordon Carlisle to be a man who had his price. That price would undoubtedly be stiff, but to secure Cosmo's letter he was prepared to pay stiffly. Yes, things, he felt, looked reasonably bright.

'So Carlisle got the cabinet?'

'I told you he did,' said Mr Saxby. 'But when you say "So Carlisle got the cabinet?" as if that were the important thing, it seems to me that you are missing the whole point of my story. It is immaterial which of the two eccentrics made the higher bid, what is so extraordinary is that they were bidding at all in fifties and hundreds for this entirely worthless object. It bears out what I was saying to Barbara Crowe just now –'

Sir Raymond sat up with a jerk. His pipe fell from his mouth in a shower of sparks. Mr Saxby regarded it with a shake of the head.

'That's how fires get started,' he said reprovingly.

'Barbara Crowe?'

'Though Boy Scouts start them, I believe, by rubbing two sticks together. How, I have never been able to understand. Why two sticks, rubbed together, should –'

'Is Barbara Crowe *here*?'

'She was when I went to take my bath. Looking very well, I thought.'

As Sir Raymond picked up his pipe, strange emotions were stirring within him – exultation one of them, tenderness another. There could be only one reason for Barbara's arrival in Dovetail Hammer. She had come to see him, to try to effect a reconciliation. She was, in short, making what is known as the first move, and it touched him deeply that anyone as proud as she could have brought

633

herself to do it. All the old love, so long kept in storage, as if it had been something Albert Peasemarch had locked up in a wine cellar, came popping out as good as new, and in spite of the presence in it of men like Gordon Carlisle and his nephew Cosmo the world seemed to him a very pleasant world indeed.

That strange tenderness grew. He could see now how wrong had been the stand he had taken about Phoebe sharing their home. Of course a bride would not want her home shared by anyone, let alone a woman like his sister Phoebe. Wincing a little, he resolved that, even if it meant paying out the two thousand pounds a year she had mentioned, Barbara must be alone with him in their little nest.

He had just reached this admirable decision, when Lord Ickenham came in through the french windows, and paused, momentarily disconcerted, at the sight of Mr Saxby. He had come to talk to Sir Raymond privately, and there was nothing in Howard Saxby senior's manner to suggest that he did not intend to remain rooted to the spot for hours.

But he had always been a quick thinker. There were ways of removing this adhesive old gentleman, and it took him but an instant to select the one he knew could not fail.

'Oh, there you are, Saxby,' he said. 'I was looking for you. Flannery wants to see you.'

Mr Saxby gave an interested bleat.

'Flannery? Is he here?'

'Just arrived.'

'Why didn't you bring him along?'

'He said he wanted to see you on some private matter.'

'It must be something to do with those Amalgamated Rubber shares.'

Sir Raymond, who had been daydreaming about little nests, came out of his reverie.

'Who's Flannery?'

'He's on the stock exchange. He looks after my investments.'

'They could be in no safer hands,' said Lord Ickenham, with a curious little thrill of satisfaction as he realized that the mists had at last cleared away and he now knew who Flannery was. 'I wouldn't keep him waiting. Beefy,' he went on, as Mr Saxby ambled off, making remarkably good time for a man of his years, 'I come bearing news which will, unless I am greatly mistaken, send you gambolling about the house and grounds like a lamb in springtime. But before going into that,' he said, cocking an interested eyebrow, 'I would like, if I may do so without giving offence, to comment on your personal appearance. Possibly it is my imagination, but you give me the idea of being a bit more dusty than usual. Have you been rolling in something, or do you always have cobwebs in your hair?'

A cloud marred the sunniness of Sir Raymond's mood. This reminder that he was sharing the same planet with Albert Peasemarch caused a purple flush to spread over his face.

'You'd have cobwebs in your hair, if you'd been in a cellar all the afternoon,' he said warmly. 'Do you know where Peasemarch is?'

'I was chatting with him on the phone not long ago, and he told me he was going to London for a week or two, presumably to stay with his sister, who has a house at East Dulwich. I was surprised at his leaving you so suddenly. No unpleasantness, I trust?'

Sir Raymond breathed heavily.

'He locked me in the cellar, if you call that unpleasantness.'

Lord Ickenham seemed staggered, as a man might well be at hearing such sensational words.

'Locked you in the cellar?'

'The wine cellar. If Saxby hadn't come along, I'd be there still. The man's insane.'

'One of the mad Peasemarches, you think? I'm not so sure. I admit that his behaviour was peculiar, but I believe I can understand it. Owing to a singular piece of good fortune which has just befallen him, Albert Peasemarch is a bit above himself this afternoon. Needing an outlet for his high spirits and feeling that he had to do something by way of expressing himself, he chose this unusual course. Where you or I in similar circumstances would have opened a bottle of champagne or gone about giving small boys sixpences, Peasemarch locked you in the cellar. It's just a matter of how these things happen to take you. I suppose he thought you would laugh as heartily as he at the amusing little affair.'

'Well, he was wrong,' said Sir Raymond, still breathing heavily.

'If Peasemarch were here and I could get my hands on him, I would take him apart, limb by limb, and dance on his fragments.'

Lord Ickenham nodded.

'Yes, I can see your side of the thing. Well, when I meet him, I will let him know that you are displeased, and you will certainly get a letter of apology from him, for there is good stuff in Albert Peasemarch and no one is quicker than he to admit it when he knows he has acted mistakenly. But we must not waste precious moments talking of Albert Peasemarch, for there are other and far more important matters that call for our attention. Prepare yourself for a surprise, Beefy. Barbara Crowe is here.'

'It isn't a surprise.'

'You knew?'

'Saxby told me.'

'And what steps do you propose to take?'

'I'm going to tell her I've been a fool.'

'Doesn't she know?'

'And I'm going to marry her, if she'll still have me.'

'Oh, she'll have you, all right. I could tell that by the way, every time I mentioned your name, she buried her face in her hands and murmured "Toots! Toots!"'

'She did?' said Sir Raymond, much moved.

'Brokenly,' Lord Ickenham assured him.

'You know what the trouble was,' said Sir Raymond, removing a cobweb from his left eyebrow. 'She didn't want Phoebe living with us.'

'Very naturally.'

'Yes, I see that now. I'm going to give her two thousand pounds a year and tell her to go off and take a flat somewhere.'

'A sound and generous decision.'

'Or do you think she might settle for fifteen hundred?' said Sir Raymond wistfully.

Lord Ickenham considered the question.

'If I were you, Beefy, I would cross that bridge when you come to it. For all you know, Phoebe may be getting married herself.'

Sir Raymond stared.

'Phoebe?'

'Yes.'

'My sister Phoebe?'

'Stranger things have happened.'

For an instant it seemed that Sir Raymond was about to say 'Name three', but he merely gave a grunt and brushed away another cobweb. Lord Ickenham studied him with a thoughtful eye. He was debating within himself whether or not this was a suitable moment to reveal to the barrister-novelist that he was about to become allied by marriage to the East Dulwich Peasemarches. He decided that it was not. It is only an exceptionally mild and easy-tempered man who can receive with equanimity the news that his sister will shortly be taking for better or for worse a butler who has recently locked him in the wine cellar. Apprised of the impending union, it seemed highly probable to Lord Ickenham that Sir Raymond Bastable would follow in the footsteps of Nannie Bruce's Uncle Charlie and curl up in a ball. He turned to another matter, one to which ever since his momentous talk with Johnny Pearce he had been devoting his powerful mind.

'Well, I'm delighted, my dear fellow, that all is well again between you and Barbara,' he said. 'If there is one thing that braces me up, it is to see two sundered hearts come together, whether it be in Springtime or somewhat later in the year. Oh, blessings on the falling out that all the more endears, as the fellow said. But there's one thing you must budget for, Beefy, when you marry Barbara, and this may come as something of a shock to you. You will have to be prepared to start work on another book.'

'What!'

'Well, of course.'

'But I can't.'

'You'll have to. If you think you can write a novel and sell it for a hundred and fifty thousand dollars and marry a literary agent and not have her make you sit down on your trouser seat and write another, you sadly underestimate the determination and will to win of literary agents. You won't have a moment's peace till you take pen in hand.'

Sir Raymond's lower jaw had fallen to its fullest extent. He stared into the future and was appalled by what he saw.

'But I can't, I tell you! It nearly killed me, writing *Cocktail Time*. You haven't any conception what it means to sweat your way through one of these damned books. I daresay it's all right for fellows who are used to it, but for somebody like myself . . . I'd much rather be torn to pieces with red-hot pincers.'

Lord Ickenham nodded.

'I thought that might possibly be your attitude. But I see a way out of the difficulty. Ever hear of Dumas?'

'Who?'

'Alexandre Dumas. *The Three Musketeers. Count of Monte Cristo.*'

'Oh, Dumas? Yes, of course. Everybody's read Dumas.'

'You're wrong. They just think they have. What they were really getting was the output of his corps of industrious assistants. He was in rather the same position as you. He wanted the money, as much of it as he could gouge out of the reading public, but he strongly objected to having to turn out the stuff. So he assigned the rough spadework – the writing of his books – to others.'

Hope leaped into Sir Raymond's haggard eyes. There flooded over him a relief similar to that which he had experienced when hearing Mr Saxby's voice outside the cellar door. It was as though spiritual United States Marines had arrived.

'You mean I could get someone else to write the infernal thing?'

'Exactly. And who more suitable than my godson, Johnny Pearce?'

'Why, of course! He's an author, isn't he?'

'Been one for years.'

'Would he do it?'

'Nothing would please him more. Like Dumas, he needs the money. Fifty-fifty would be a fair arrangement, I think?'

'Yes, that seems reasonable.'

'And of course he would have to have something down in advance. A refresher you call it at the Bar, don't you? Five hundred pounds suggests itself as a suitable figure. Just step to your desk, Beefy, and write him a cheque for that amount.'

Sir Raymond stared.

'You want me to give him five hundred pounds?'

'In advance of royalties.'

'I'm not going to give him any five hundred pounds.'

'Then I, on my side, am not going to give you that letter of young Cosmo's. I quite forgot to mention, Beefy, that shortly after our Mr Carlisle placed it in the cabinet, I found and removed it. I have it in my pocket now,' said Lord Ickenham, producing it. 'And if,' he added, noting that his companion had begun to stir in his chair and seemed to be gathering himself for a spring, 'you are thinking of rising and busting me one and choking it out of me, let me mention that I have a rudimentary knowledge of ju-jitsu, amply sufficient to enable me to tie you into a lover's knot which it would take you hours and hours to get out of. Five hundred pounds, Beefy, payable to Jonathan Twistleton Pearce.'

There was a silence, during which a man might have uttered the words 'Jonathan Twistleton Pearce' ten or perhaps twelve times, speaking slowly. Then Sir Raymond heaved himself up. His manner was not blithe. Roget, asked to describe it, would have selected some term such as 'resigned' or 'nonresisting' or possibly 'down on his marrowbones (*slang*)', but it was plain, when he spoke, that he had made his decision.

'How do you spell Pearce?' he said. 'P-e-a-r-c-e or P-i-e-r-c-e?'

The shadows were lengthening across the grass as Ickenham started to saunter back through the park to Hammer Hall, the cheque in his pocket which would bring wedding bells to Belinda Farringdon, his godson Johnny, Nannie Bruce and Officer Cyril McMurdo – unless, of course, they were all going to be married at the registrar's, in which event there would be no bells. It was one of those perfect days which come from three to five times in an English summer. The setting sun reddened the waters of the lake, westward the sky was ablaze with green and gold and amethyst and purple, and somewhere a bird, probably an intimate friend of Mr Saxby's, was singing its evensong before knocking off for the night.

Everywhere was peace and gentle stillness, and it made Lord Ickenham think how jolly it would be to be in London.

He had become a little tired of country life. Well enough in its way, of course, but dull ... humdrum ... nothing ever happening. What he needed to tone up his system was a night out in the pleasure-seeking section of the metropolis in the society of some congenial companion.

Not his nephew Pongo. You couldn't dig Pongo out nowadays. Marriage had turned him into a sober citizen out of tune with the hopes and dreams of a man who liked his evenings lively. Ichabod was the word that sprang to the lips when the mind dwelt on Pongo Twistleton, and for a moment, looking back on the days when a telephone call had always been enough to bring his nephew out with, as the expression is, a whoop and a holler, Lord Ickenham was conscious of a slight depression.

Then he was his bright self again. He had remembered that in his little red book in his bedroom at the Hall he had the address of Albert Peasemarch.

What pleasanter than to go to Chatsworth, Mafeking Road, East Dulwich, imitate the cry of the white owl, tell Albert Peasemarch to put on his bowler hat, and, having checked that bowler hat in the cloakroom of some gay restaurant, to plunge with him into London's glittering night life?

Which, he was convinced, would have much to offer to two young fellows up from the country.

# READ MORE IN PENGUIN

In every corner of the world, on every subject under the sun, Penguin represents quality and variety – the very best in publishing today.

For complete information about books available from Penguin – including Puffins, Penguin Classics and Arkana – and how to order them, write to us at the appropriate address below. Please note that for copyright reasons the selection of books varies from country to country.

**In the United Kingdom:** Please write to *Dept. EP, Penguin Books Ltd, Bath Road, Harmondsworth, West Drayton, Middlesex UB7 ODA*

**In the United States:** Please write to *Consumer Sales, Penguin USA, P.O. Box 999, Dept. 17109, Bergenfield, New Jersey 07621-0120.* VISA and MasterCard holders call 1-800-253-6476 to order Penguin titles

**In Canada:** Please write to *Penguin Books Canada Ltd, 10 Alcorn Avenue, Suite 300, Toronto, Ontario M4V 3B2*

**In Australia:** Please write to *Penguin Books Australia Ltd, P.O. Box 257, Ringwood, Victoria 3134*

**In New Zealand:** Please write to *Penguin Books (NZ) Ltd, Private Bag 102902, North Shore Mail Centre, Auckland 10*

**In India:** Please write to *Penguin Books India Pvt Ltd, 706 Eros Apartments, 56 Nehru Place, New Delhi 110 019*

**In the Netherlands:** Please write to *Penguin Books Netherlands bv, Postbus 3507, NL-1001 AH Amsterdam*

**In Germany:** Please write to *Penguin Books Deutschland GmbH, Metzlerstrasse 26, 60594 Frankfurt am Main*

**In Spain:** Please write to *Penguin Books S. A., Bravo Murillo 19, 1° B, 28015 Madrid*

**In Italy:** Please write to *Penguin Italia s.r.l., Via Felice Casati 20, I–20124 Milano*

**In France:** Please write to *Penguin France S. A., 17 rue Lejeune, F–31000 Toulouse*

**In Japan:** Please write to *Penguin Books Japan, Ishikiribashi Building, 2–5–4, Suido, Bunkyo-ku, Tokyo 112*

**In South Africa:** Please write to *Longman Penguin Southern Africa (Pty) Ltd, Private Bag X08, Bertsham 2013*

# PENGUIN AUDIOBOOKS

**A Quality of Writing That Speaks for Itself**

Penguin Books has always led the field in quality publishing. Now you can listen at leisure to your favourite books, read to you by familiar voices from radio, stage and screen. Penguin Audiobooks are produced to an excellent standard, and abridgements are always faithful to the original texts. From thrillers to classic literature, biography to humour, with a wealth of titles in between, Penguin Audiobooks offer you quality, entertainment and the chance to rediscover the pleasure of listening.

You can order Penguin Audiobooks through Penguin Direct by telephoning (0181) 899 4036. The lines are open 24 hours every day. Ask for Penguin Direct, quoting your credit card details.

*A selection of Penguin Audiobooks, published or forthcoming:*

**Sense and Sensibility** by Jane Austen, read by Joanna David

**Cleared for Take-Off** by Dirk Bogarde, read by the author

**A Period of Adjustment** by Dirk Bogarde, read by the author

**A Short Walk from Harrods** by Dirk Bogarde, read by the author

**A Good Man in Africa** by William Boyd, read by Timothy Spall

**The Road to Wellville** by T. Coraghessan Boyle, read by the author

**Jane Eyre** by Charlotte Brontë, read by Juliet Stevenson

**Wuthering Heights** by Emily Brontë, read by Juliet Stevenson

**The Secret Garden** by Frances Hodgson Burnett, read by Helena Bonham Carter

**Oscar and Lucinda** by Peter Carey, read by John Turnbull

**Heart of Darkness** by Joseph Conrad, read by David Threlfall

**The Winter King** by Bernard Cornwell, read by Tim Pigott-Smith

**The Naked Civil Servant** by Quentin Crisp, read by the author

**Great Expectations** by Charles Dickens, read by Hugh Laurie

**Middlemarch** by George Eliot, read by Harriet Walter

**Zlata's Diary** by Zlata Filipovič, read by Dorota Puzio

**To the Hilt** by Dick Francis, read by Martin Jarvis

**The Vulture Fund** by Stephen Frey, read by Colin Stinton

# PENGUIN AUDIOBOOKS

**The Prophet** by Kahlil Gibran, read by Renu Setna

**Virtual Light** by William Gibson, read by Peter Weller

**My Name Escapes Me** by Alec Guinness, read by the author

**Thunderpoint** by Jack Higgins, read by Roger Moore

**The Iliad** by Homer, read by Derek Jacobi

**More Please** by Barry Humphries, read by the author

**Goodbye to Berlin** by Christopher Isherwood, read by Alan Cumming

**One Flew over the Cuckoo's Nest** by Ken Kesey, read by the author

**Nightmares and Dreamscapes** by Stephen King, read by Whoopi Goldberg, Rob Lowe, Stephen King et al.

**Therapy** by David Lodge, read by Warren Clarke

**An Experiment in Love** by Hilary Mantel, read by Billie Whitelaw

**Rebecca** by Daphne du Maurier, read by Joanna David

**Hotel Pastis** by Peter Mayle, read by Tim Pigott-Smith

**How Stella Got Her Groove Back** by Terry McMillan, read by the author

**And when did you last see your father?** by Blake Morrison, read by the author

**Murderers and Other Friends** by John Mortimer, read by the author

**Nineteen Eighty-Four** by George Orwell, read by Timothy West

**Guardian Angel** by Sara Paretsky, read by Jane Kaczmarek

**History: The Home Movie** by Craig Raine, read by the author

**A Peaceful Retirement** by Miss Read, read by June Whitfield

**Frankenstein** by Mary Shelley, read by Richard Pasco

**The Devil's Juggler** by Murray Smith, read by Kenneth Cranham

**Kidnapped** by Robert Louis Stevenson, read by Robbie Coltrane

**Perfume** by Patrick Süskind, read by Sean Barratt

**The Secret History** by Donna Tartt, read by Robert Sean Leonard

**The Pillars of Hercules** by Paul Theroux, read by William Hootkins

**The Brimstone Wedding** by Barbara Vine, read by Jan Francis

# BY THE SAME AUTHOR

## LIFE AT BLANDINGS

*Omnibus editions, also published in separate volumes:*

### Life at Blandings
Something Fresh · Summer Lightning · Heavy Weather

In his inimitable style, P. G. Wodehouse entices us into the demesne of Blandings Castle – an apparent paradise where it is eternal high summer, with jolly house-parties, tea on the lawn and love trysts in the rose garden. But for Clarence, ninth Earl of Emsworth there is always something to disturb this tranquil scene, from avoiding his forceful sister, Lady Constance, to foiling unscrupulous attempts to nobble his beloved pig, the Empress of Blandings. Without at least one imposter on the premises, Blandings Castle is never quite itself.

### Imperial Blandings
Full Moon · Pigs Have Wings · Service with a Smile

Perfect happiness for Lord Emsworth is to listen to the contented night breathing of his medal-winning pig. But so often there is a snake in his Garden of Eden, a crumpled leaf in his bed of roses, a grain of sand in his spiritual spinach. For Blandings is regarded by his sisters as a suitable repository for young women engaged to impecunious suitors. Worse still a bad baronet and a devious Duke attempt some funny business with the ancestral porker. But usually the Hon. Galahad Threepwood or Lord Ickham can bring sweetness and light back into the rose garden and save Lord Emsworth's bacon for him – to *almost* everyone's satisfaction . . .

# BY THE SAME AUTHOR

## THE BLANDINGS BOOKS BY P. G. WODEHOUSE

'For Wodehouse there has been no fall of Man . . . the gardens of Blandings Castle are the original gardens from which we are all exiled' – Evelyn Waugh

The tranquil idyll of life at Blandings is once again shattered by scrapes and skulduggery, mishaps and mix-ups in:

**Galahad at Blandings**

A major mix-up at the Castle, in which Gally introduces yet another impostor to Lord Emsworth's residence, and the Empress of Blandings somehow gets drunk in her sty.

**Heavy Weather**

Forced to seek alternative employment when his editorials for *Tiny Tots* magazine become too adult, Monty Bodkin has been engaged as Lord Emsworth's personal secretary.

*also published*

**Full Moon**
**Pigs Have Wings**
**Something Fresh**
**Sunset at Blandings**
**A Pelican at Blandings**
**Service with a Smile**
**Summer Lightning**
**Uncle Fred in the Springtime**

*and the omnibus editions*

**Lord Emsworth Acts for the Best**
**Imperial Blandings**

# BY THE SAME AUTHOR

**The Adventures of Sally**

Pretty, impecunious Sally never dreamed a fortune could be a disadvantage until she became an heiress. Life in New York became complicated enough, but a trip to England seemed only to make matters worse.

**Bachelors Anonymous**

Their methods were borrowed from Alcoholics Anonymous: whenever a member felt the urge to take a woman out to dinner, he relied on the others to reason with him until the madness passed. But even the most hardened bachelor can occasionally fall by the wayside . . .

**Cocktail Time**

Uncle Fred, off the leash and into the Drones Club, cannot resist firing a well-aimed Brazil nut at the hat of Beefy Bastable. From this incident springs the injured barrister's mistaken exposé of the misdeeds of the younger generation in a novel which causes only trouble for its hapless author.

*also published*

**Big Money    Company for Henry**
**A Damsel in Distress    Do Butlers Burgle Banks?**
**Doctor Sally    French Leave    A Gentleman of Leisure**
**The Girl in Blue    Hot Water    If I Were You**
**The Indiscretions of Archie    Laughing Gas    The Little Nugget**
**The Luck of the Bodkins    Money in the Bank    Money for Nothing**
**Pearls, Girls and Monty Bodkin    Piccadilly Jim**
**Quick Service    Sam the Sudden    The Small Bachelor**
**Spring Fever    Summer Moonshine    Ukridge    Uncle Dynamite**
**Uncle Fred: An Omnibus    Uneasy Money**
**Young Men in Spats**

# BY THE SAME AUTHOR

## THE PSMITH BOOKS

### Leave it to Psmith

Psmith goes to Blandings, where he bemuses Lord Emsworth, embroils Beach, enrages Baxter and enslaves Miss Halliday. But, with his usual aplomb, he brings everything to a satisfactory conclusion, except perhaps for Freddie Threepwood.

### Psmith in the City

Psmith and his friend Mike are sent by their fathers to work in the City – but the ponderous ritual of a mere bank cannot dent Psmith's flippant irresponsibility. A battle of wits develops, and wit has always been Psmith's sharpest weapon . . .

### Psmith, Journalist

The New York magazine *Cosy Moments* did not have a reputation for controversy – until Psmith allowed his literary aspirations to run riot. Soon he and his friend Billy are chased by gangsters, and life is certainly not cosy any more.

*also published:*

**Mike and Psmith**
**Mike at Wrykyn**

*and the omnibus:*

**The World of Psmith**

# BY THE SAME AUTHOR

**SHORT STORIES BY P. G. WODEHOUSE**

**Blandings Castle**

'A collection of short snorts between the solid orgies' was how P. G. Wodehouse regarded these stories, which range from the Blandings of Lord Emsworth to the Hollywood of the Mulliners.

**Eggs, Beans and Crumpet**

Dine out on this feast of stories. They include the antics of Bingo Little, as told in the haven of the Drones Club, further episodes from the life of Ukridge and, of course, the romantic encounters of Mr Mulliner's young relatives.

**Lord Emsworth and Others**

Nine delicious stories which include the disgraceful affair of the crime wave at Blandings, extracts from the unsteady career of Ukridge and more tales from Mr Mulliner and from the Oldest Member at the golf club.

**The Gold Bat and Other School Stories**
**The Pothunters and Other School Stories**

Wodehouse won the first of his many laurels with these school stories where, in the daily round of prefects, fags, dorms and cricket, he creates a gloriously absurd and immortal world which never palls.

*also published:*

**The Man with Two Left Feet**
**The Man Upstairs and Other Stories**